For Angie

Terrence Mercer return.

SCOTLAND YARD.

Terry Mercer sat at his desk in his office scrutinising the case-file spread out before him. His chief inspector Polly Sheppard had specifically asked for him to look into this case. In the last three months, no less than seven young girls ranging from the ages of thirteen to eighteen had gone missing from here in the capitol. Girls were going missing from other areas as well in recent weeks. Twenty-three from other towns and cities, six girls from Birmingham, the rest from other towns and cities in the midlands, Derby, Leicester, Nottingham, and a couple as far north as Manchester. All of these girls had disappeared in the last six months. He knew that girls went missing all the time in Britain, but he also knew that most of them were accounted for eventually, having come here from various parts of the country or indeed Europe to make their fortunes, and then cruelly discovering that London's streets were not paved with gold after all, but instead was populated with certain individuals who would con you out of your last ten pounds, and smile in your face as they done it.

Terry surmised that not even one in a million would fulfil the dream they arrived here with. Many came here completely disillusioned about how young women could prosper in the city if they were prepared to work hard.

Certainly if you arrived with qualifications that could lead you into appropriate brackets of employment, then yes, you could make a good living, but without those qualifications, you should forget about coming anywhere near the place.

Many young women had left London and headed back to their homes, completely devastated, having had a personal education in what life is really like in the city of dreams, and how that same city rejects you if you don't have any money to spend. The ones who returned home broken-hearted were the lucky ones. Other unfortunate girls would be enticed into a world of narcotics, and were very quickly weaned into addiction, Heroin being one of the fastest drugs to become addicted to. In a few short months they would become unrecognisable from the sprightly young women who had arrived with their dreams and ambitions burning brightly in their faces, to pale skinny shapes wearing clothes that now hung off their backs like wet blankets, with eyes sunken and hollow, their gaunt ghostly faces appealing to the passers-by to show them some kindness and throw a coin or two into their tins.

Others, addicted to the drugs, weren't put out onto the streets to earn as much money every faith in him that he would be successful, but he knew, the chances of finding all these girls safe and well were slim, at best. This was going to be difficult, and quite possibly, harrowing…it was that gut feeling of his again, this wasn't going to be a very nice investigation.

---

as possible. In most cases, the girls were given a place to `live,` and therefore a place to `work` from. They were fed with the minimum amount of food to keep them reasonably healthy. Most of the money they earned was confiscated from them. These men, and women, would feed `their` girls the heroin they now craved. The greater their need for a fix, the more trapped they would become, there was no escape. In earlier cases, the girls who were used for these purposes were eastern European, perhaps having arrived here illegally, but the girls who had gone missing lately were all English, or at least British. No doubt some of these girls would have disappeared from the radar quite purposefully, that was always the case, and some of them had good reasons for doing this, but in this instance almost all of the missing girls' parents had been on the phone frantic and desperate for the police to find their loved ones. Some of them had organised search parties in the areas from where they had gone missing. Friends and neighbours had all volunteered to help find them. What was worrying Terry Mercer as he read further into the file, was that none of these girls had been seen since they had gone missing, not one single sighting.

All these girls from Birmingham, Derby, Leicester, Nottingham and Manchester, and not one single sighting of any of them. The odds of this happening were more than a million to one. In most cases, at least one or two of them would have been spotted either by police officers or by CCTV cameras, but in these instances not a single girl had been spotted. Mercer sighed as he weighed up the situation.

There were only two possibilities as far as he was concerned, murdered or abducted. If they had been abducted and kept alive, then he knew only too well what they'd be being used for. And were they all abducted by different people?

Or was there a syndicate working as a team covering all these areas?

He rose to his feet as he looked down onto the table and glanced at the pretty young girls' faces from the missing persons' photographs, all of them smiling up at him. This was going to be challenging to say the least. The first thing he'd have to do would be to visit the grieving parents and find out as much as he possibly could about their `precious daughters`. How he longed to be able to go there and tell them not to worry and that everything would be fine and that he would have the girls back home safe in no time at all. As he gathered all the photographs together he sighed heavily, knowing full well that it would be highly unlikely that he'd ever be able to say that to them. He logged off his computer. Thirty girls, where the hell would he start? The seven missing girls from London had not been from the same areas. They were all from different parts of the city spanning more than thirty miles in diameter. The words needle and haystack came to mind as he weighed up the task before him. Chief inspector Polly Sheppard had

CHAPTER ONE.

BROMLEY. 9:25 A.M.

Sophie Spencer made her way reluctantly down the stairs having just awoken to find she was more than an hour late. Her alarm clock had yet again let her down, either that, or she'd absent-mindedly switched it off...again. Going to school late was bad enough, but being late to meet up with her pals was what was really annoying her the most. She was fifteen years of age and like any other fifteen-year old girl she was unearthly-wise and knew everything there was to know about the world. She cursed inwardly her seventeen-year old brother David, who at this moment in time was still somewhere in his perverted dream-land no doubt, with not a care in the world. Her one and only parent Mandy, was still in her bed as well, having been out until the wee small hours, drinking and partying after she'd finished work, she surmised.
As she reached the bottom of the stairs she shouted up at the top of her voice, to the only family she had in the world, "Lazy fucking bastards!"
As she stumbled into the kitchen barefoot, she let out another curse as she stepped into the cat's bowl of stale food.
"Oh you disgusting...arrgghh!"
It was going to be one of those days, she could tell. Already the first day of the week was turning into a nightmare. When days started like this, they generally just got worse as they progressed. In two days she was going to sit her exams and she just *had* to do well. There was no way she was going to end up like her mother and brother. She was determined to do something with her life, and get out of this `zombie-land shit-hole` where she lived. Six hours a day bar-work was not going to be *her* only achievement in life like it was for her mother, and as for that spoiled bugger David, he was just a waste of space with no ambitions in life whatsoever, other than to take money from his mother's purse and buy cheap carry-out drink for himself and his pals and spend his dole money on dope and scrubbers, and when that ran out, just sit around the house masturbating off to one of the numerous blue movies he watched on the internet in his bedroom.

The reality of the situation was this; Thirty-eight-year old Mandy Spencer loved her two kids like nothing else on earth. She had been deserted by her husband when Sophie was two years old, and since then had struggled continuously to bring her children up the best way she could. For Mandy Spencer, it was a labour of love. These two were all she had left in the world. They were all she had to prove that she'd been here on earth, and indeed had done something worth-while with her life. Their father had taken off somewhere with another woman and had never been seen or heard of again. She had received not one penny from him since he'd departed.

Bringing up kids in this day and age was no easy task, trying to keep them clothed and fed was a major task on its' own, especially when they were both now teenagers. The days when you could buy them clothes that you thought were suitable were long gone. Now it was all bloody designer-gear for both sexes. She worked officially six hours a day at the Golden Moon, here in Bromley, but was allowed to work extra hours when required unofficially, which was very beneficial concerning tax deductions, both for herself and for Sam Conroy her boss. Some weeks she could put more than seventy hours in, and being only taxed on forty-two, it made all the difference to her take home pay. From Mondays to Thursdays, The Golden Moon was closed at eleven thirty at night, but on weekends they were open until one A.M., which meant that by the time she'd cleaned up and cashed in it was nearer two o clock in the morning before she got home. Every week day she made Sophie's packed lunch up for school before she left for work. Her son David was currently unemployed and with no qualifications whatsoever, which meant that whatever employment he would obtain they would be paying him nothing more than the minimum wage. She allowed him to get away with more than the average seventeen-year old boy would get away with, although the Jobcentre Plus were not so kind. If he failed to prove he'd been looking for work and applying for jobs, or if he was late for signing on, then they would stop his benefits immediately, and indefinitely.

This meant that on many occasions she would have to fork out extra money for him. Most mothers would disagree with how she treated him, but it was the guilt she felt for the poor boy growing up without a father figure that she was perhaps too lenient with him, almost to the extent of blaming herself for the absence of his father. But, right or wrong, she was coping with life just fine and her kids were taking no hurt. Sophie was at that age now where everything she said to her had to be questioned, and of course, the inevitable sigh whenever she asked her to do something, but all said and done, Sophie was a good kid. They both were, although there was always the bickering between them, both of them concerned that one was receiving more than the other. In general, a normal family, which for Mandy Spencer, was an amazing achievement considering the predicament she'd been left in thirteen years earlier with a two-year old girl and a four-year-old boy, and not a single penny in the bank owing to the fact that her beloved husband had taken out their last six hundred and twenty quid...and twenty-seven pence, and she, left with no job and a bout of life-threatening depression.

Sophie picked up her bag from the kitchen work-top and headed to the back door to continue this most frustrating day. To make matters worse, it had begun to drizzle and she'd left her brolly at school. Normally in circumstances like these she would have remedied the situation by taking the day off, but because this week, she had the most important exams of her life in front of her, she had no option but to attend, and so was stuck with the situation, there was nothing else for it, but to head out into the hair-ruining bloody weather. There wasn't another bus until ten-thirty, so she'd have to walk. This Monday morning tantrum was nothing new for Sophie, the fact that her mother and brother were still cosy in their beds and she had to get herself up and feed herself and the cat before she headed out for school. It boiled her blood.

Her mum had also requested her not to wear a certain skirt as she felt it was too short to wear to school and gave a false impression to boys, and teachers. Her mother's words echoed in her ears as she headed down the street.

"You're a very attractive young lady Sophie, and a very well developed young woman. Your attire speaks volumes about the kind of person you are, especially at school, so be careful not to wear clothing that suggests that you are something that you're not. I can't complain about the application of your make-up Sophie`, but just be aware of the length of your skirts sweetheart. Boys see girls in ridiculously short skirts, and they think of one thing and one thing only...I'm only saying."

Sophie continued her reluctant walk through the drizzle muttering soliloquys regarding her mother and brother, and then openly cursed as a car whisked past her, splashing her legs with freezing cold water, and soaking the back of her hair, the driver of the car peeping furiously and shouting a sexual obscenity at her. "Is it this short skirt I'm wearing that has attracted the wanker's attention? You fucking prick!!" She shouted after him, her beautiful long brown hair, Sophie's pride and joy, now stuck to the back of her head. "Could this day possibly get any worse?" She thought to herself.

From the minute she'd opened her eyes, it had been nothing but minor disasters. As she continued walking, a black Transit van approached slowing down so that it was level with her and travelled now at the same speed as she was walking. The windows of the van were blacked out and the driver's side window was open only about an inch. Before they got a chance to shout anything rude to her, she stuck out the middle finger of her left hand and raised it up and down several times before entering the little grocer shop where she bought her chewing gum every morning.

"Dream on fuck heads!" she said, as she watched the van pass by the shop.

She closed the shop door and made her way to the counter to purchase her gum. "Good Morning Sophie." Carol Richardson, a thirty-nine year old divorcee and friend of Sophie's mother cheerily greeted the school-girl.

" This is not a good day for me Carol, far from it. I'm soaked to the skin already and I've still got half a bloody mile to walk before I get to school...I've slept in, and there's no chance of that brother of mine waking me up, or my bloody mum, because they're still in their blinking beds snoring their heads off."

"Ah now Sophie, your mum works long hard hours at the pub and fine well you know it, so you can't knock your mum for having a little lie-in, and come on sweetheart, it's not the hardest task in the world to get yourself up for school now is it, especially as Mandy makes up your lunch for you and prepares all your clothes for you. All you have to do is dress yourself and make your breakfast, and talking about dressing yourself, does she know that you're wearing that skirt to school today?" Carol Richardson left the counter and disappeared into a room at the back of the shop. She returned seconds later with a towel and an umbrella. "Here, dry yourself with this Sophie, and you can borrow this brolly. At least you'll stay dry until you get to school, here dry your bloody legs, Mandy will go ballistic if she catches you wearing that, hell Sophie, it barely covers your bottom girl." "Don't Carol, don't become a nag like my mum please, the skirt's not *that* short, don't know what all the fuss is about anyway. And she can't say anything Carol, because when she goes out with you for drinks, she wears skirts on the short side."

"Yes, on the short side Sophie, but not *really* short like that. Listen, I'm not trying to nag you Sophie, but your mum's right you know, you shouldn't flaunt yourself like that, it gives the wrong impression to people."

"You *are* like my mum Carol. Is that why Kaylee doesn't wear skirts to school? Is it because you won't let her?"

"That has nothing at all to do with you young lady what Kaylee and I talk about or how she dresses for school. I know this much though, if I had attempted to wear something like that to school my bloody father would have had a fit, he wouldn't even allow me to stay in my bedroom wearing something that short."

"Yeah well, I haven't got a father so I wouldn't know about that and-."

"Don't you dare attempt to condemn your mother Sophie, if that's what you intend to do next, because she has raised you better than any family I know around here, you *and* your brother. The pair of you want for nothing, and it's all down to your mother's hard work. You are a very lucky girl to have a mum like that, make no mistake about that, anyway, you'd better be getting a move on, you don't want to be later than you already are."

Sophie thanked Carol for the towel and the brolly, and paid for her packet of chewing gum.

"Now you have yourself a good day Sophie, and stop being so bloody bitchy at the rest of the world. Smile Sophie and the whole world will smile with you."

"Yeah smile," said Sophie, brushing her hair as she reached the shop door.
"See you Carol, and thanks again for the brolly."
"You're welcome sweetheart, you have a good day babes." Sophie put up the brolly, happier now that she could keep her hair protected from the sheets of drizzle being driven on to her now by a stiffening breeze. She turned the corner and could see her school in the distance. She would go straight to the showers when she got there and warm herself up, and then blow-dry her hair, then meet up with her friends to catch up with the gossip of the day. As Sophie walked on she had to fight to keep control of the brolly, as the wind picked up and was now tugging away at it from behind her.
The drizzle had now turned to heavy rain and was lashing at her legs.
"Should have put a pair of trousers on…bloody weather." she muttered.
To make Sophie feel even more frustrated, the last quarter of a mile was all up-hill. The road narrowed down here to a very petite two-lane. The pavements either side of the road were narrow as well, allowing only two people to walk side by side. A small sandstone wall was bridged by trees and shrubs giving her some shelter from the now torrential rain. The trees hung so low that she had to unfold the brolly. Up ahead of her, a man wearing luminous-yellow water-proofs brushed the roadside busily with a hard-bristle brush and a two-bin barrow which he moved from the pavement to let Sophie past. She fished out her mobile phone as she passed him to find out whereabouts in the school her friends were hanging out. She was scrutinising the screen on her phone, when suddenly the van screeched to an emergency stop ten metres in front of her. She looked up from her phone. It was the black van from outside the shop.
No-one got out of the van. For some unknown reason she found herself stopping, and just staring at the vehicle.
The man who had been sweeping the roads grabbed her from under the arms and pulled her back so that her feet were trailing on the ground.
Then the back doors of the van burst open and she was bundled inside where another three men who all wore black woollen balaclavas wrestled her to the floor. It had all happened within ten seconds. Sophie felt something soft being tied around her mouth, tightly. The van was moving. The next thing she felt was a prick in her right leg near her buttock. They were injecting her with something.
In less than a minute, she felt herself drifting into unconsciousness.
Try as she might to fight the drug, whatever it was, was useless.
She could feel her grip on her mobile phone weakening.
As the phone fell out of her hand onto the floor of the van, the screen lit up with a message, *"We're in the cafeteria Sophie see you when you get here babes x."*

STRATFORD.

5.15 PM.

Chloe Prowse stepped out onto the high street from her work place, Billingtons Solicitors. It was her eighth week working here as an official employee and she was looking forward to going out with her pals to celebrate her success.

She had worked here for over seven weeks on a probationary period after which she was informed that both Roger and David Billington were pleased to be able to offer her full-time employment. All of her hard work had eventually paid off. She had received her first pay-cheque and was overjoyed at her take home pay. Compared to what she'd been living on this was like winning the lottery. Two of her three pals had had similar luck with their search for employment, and so tonight was going to be a very special night for all concerned, especially as she was going to be eighteen three days from now. At last, she'd be able to take some of the strain off her older sister Susan who had been looking after her for four years now since their parents were tragically killed in a car crash. Because of outstanding debts, there hadn't been much money left after funeral expenses, and so Susan had to keep a roof over their heads and basically just make-do. All of Susan's wages had been used to pay for clothes and food. Now Chloe was in a position to help her sister and share the bills, and allow some of Susan's wages to be kept for herself, instead of every penny going towards her and the upkeep of the house. She was part of the world now, an adult, and most importantly, a worker.

Her life and Susan's would change for the better now. Chloe was very proud of her sister having brought her up on her own since the untimely death of their parents, and although Susan insisted that it was no big deal, she knew how difficult it must have been for her to bring up her little sister and still keep focus on her job, and the responsibilities and stresses that went with that job. Susan Prowse was a psychiatric nurse. But, hopefully now all the stress would be behind Susan, she had done the job of a parent and had raised her to be a very happy young lady. It was Chloe's turn to repay her sister. As she made her way down the `Grove`, she stopped at `Bella's Sauna` where there was an ATM, and withdrew some money. She carried on walking down the Grove until she came to Windmill Lane where her friend Melony lived. From Melony's house they would take a taxi cab over to the town centre where they would rendezvous with the rest of their friends and begin their celebrations. On this particular part of Windmill Lane there was parking on one side of the road only. Up ahead of Chloe, there was a young couple standing arguing quite viciously, cursing and swearing at each other.

Suddenly, the man struck the girl on the side of the face, causing her to stumble and fall to the ground. Chloe was dumbstruck and struggled within herself as to what to do. Should she call the police? Should she try and help the girl? The man seemed to be drunk. It was hard to tell if the girl had been drinking or not. Before Chloe came to any decision, the girl shouted over to her. "Could you help me please. Please, I need to get home. He won't take no for an answer, I've told him we're finished, but he won't leave me, he won't listen, can you help me please?"

Chloe couldn't explain her actions if she tried. She found herself crossing half way over the road. "Hey, just leave her alone. Leave her alone or I'll phone for the police."

"Fuck off bitch this has nothing at all to do with you." The man shouted back at her. "Just fuck off and mind your own business."

The young woman lifted herself up from the pavement and retrieved her handbag, some of its' contents having spilled onto the pavement.

"Why can't you just accept the situation John, we're finished, I don't love you, please just go home, you're drunk and you're going to land yourself in deep trouble if you're not careful, this girl is just about to call the police, please, just go home and I'll talk to you when you're sober." Against all odds, and to Chloe's amazement, the man began to walk away slowly. "You'll talk to me tomorrow Angela will you? Do you promise?"

The woman replied to him, wiping dirt from her jacket. "Yes I promise I will, but please John, just go home and sober up."

"I'm sorry Angela, I'm so sorry, I don't want to lose you, I love you so much babe, please don't finish with me."

"We'll talk when you're sober John," Said the blonde.

Chloe began to walk back over to the pavement she'd left.

"Please, could you help me to find my ring I've dropped it when I fell, could you help me find it please?

"I'll help you find it." The young man said.

"No John, just you get away home, I'll find it, this lady will help me, you just go home please and be careful, don't be getting run over."

The man waved in the air and mumbled something incoherent but staggered off. Chloe approached the young woman who was searching diligently for her lost ring, and now down on her hunkers. "Is it an engagement ring you've lost?" said Chloe as she joined in the search. The young lady pulled back her long blonde hair over her face as she answered Chloe. "It's just a fake diamond dress ring, but he bought me it."

She said, as she pointed to the young man who was now more than twenty metres away. "I wasn't wearing it you see it was in my bag. It must have fallen out when he struck me. He's good at that, striking people when he's upset about something, I'm sick of it, that's why I'm finished with him."

Chloe's back was turned away from the girl as she searched the pavement.

Before she knew anything else, she felt a sharp pain in the back of her head as she slumped forward face down onto the footpath.

Just before she lost consciousness, she heard the girl shouting back at the man who had been arguing with her. "Tell them to bring the van round now, quickly, we'll have to be quick." The woman stepped back as Chloe tried to say something to her, and aimed a kick straight into her ribs. "Hurry up, she repeated, get the fucking van here now!"

Chloe Prowse's limp body lay on the pavement as the Transit van appeared from around the corner. Two men jumped out of the back of the van and bundled Chloe into the vehicle. Ironically, less than one minute later, a police van cruised past where, moments earlier Chloe Prowse had stopped to aid a young woman who looked to be in danger of receiving a beating, and where now, a young blonde haired girl who had Chloe's money and credit card, walked, holding hands with her `boyfriend`, kissing and cuddling as they walked. Sergeant Trent smiled as he drove past. "Young love" he said to his colleague as the two officers continued their rounds, "It's so sweet isn't it Charlie?"

HOUNSLOW. 2am.

WELLINGTON ROAD.

Kirsty Crawford made her way down Wellington Road with her two friends, Sandra and Anya, who were every bit as drunk as she was. Kirsty had been drowning her sorrows because she had just finished with Alan. It wasn't so much that she wanted to be *finished,* but more like being forced into a situation that she had no alternative but to end the relationship, having found out by reliable sources, that Alan had been `dipping his wick` into someone she used to call her friend. It was pride. Pride and hurt, because like any other sixteen-year-old, it seemed like the end of the world for Kirsty. She would never trust another boy as long as she lived. Sandra and Anya had been consoling her all evening as they sat in the pub listening to Kirsty's dilemma. At times it had become quite difficult for Anya to listen to Kirsty's sad story, as she herself had sampled Alan's `wick` for herself and was quite disappointed when he had refused any long term relationship between them. The three young ladies had sat in the same pub all evening and had drunk copious amounts of alcohol bought for them by hopeful young gentlemen who had been attracted by the girls' laughter as they pretended not to give a damn about boys any more, and by older men who for some unknown reason, believed they had more than a fair chance of bedding one of these young ladies and in fact would be able to participate in an affair with them, probably because their wives didn't understand them, or more likely, their wives didn't even exist. No matter, Kirsty felt it was fun letting them buy you drinks. It was amazing what a little flash of leg or a smile could do for a young lady, especially when you didn't have that much money on you. As they made their way down Wellington Road, all of them singing at the top of their voices a rendition of one of their favourite pop songs, a police van stopped. The policeman at the passenger side of the pavement called over to them.
"Keep it down girls, there are people trying to sleep you know. Make your way home quietly please."
"We will officer" cried Kirsty, "We'll be quiet we promise, we've had a few drinks officer." Then Anya shouted out, "She just feenish with her boyfriend, because she sick and tired of him fucking other girls behind her back, and so we've had the drinks, she's my very very best friend, so she is, and she *no* a slut, I don't even leesten to what people say about other peoples like that."
"What the fuck is that all about Anya? Who's been saying I'm a slut? Kirsty shouted out incredulously.

"Keep it down girls" the policeman repeated, "Unless you want to spend the night in the cells."

"Oh you'd like that wouldn't you, you perverted bastard wouldn't you? Cried Sandra, who then proceeded to empty the contents of her stomach onto the pavement losing all control of her balance, and falling onto the ground.

"Oh fack, you've done it now Sandra, he coming over" said Anya, in her beautiful broken English.

The doors of the police van opened and two tall officers came and stood Sandra up onto her feet. "Fuck off, just fuck off and leave me alone, get your fucking hands off my tits, I mean it."

"Right, that's it for you young lady" said one of the officers, as he called in for female assistance. "You're not going home now, you're going to cool off in a cell tonight, and you've got no-one to blame but yourself."

"I'm gonna be sick again, you'd better let go if you know what's good for you…twats."

"Who the fuck said I was a slut Anya, do you know?" cried Kirsty.

Anya sat down on the pavement and lit up a cigarette with great difficulty. Finally, she took a drag and called out to the policemen, "If you taking hurr away, then you taking me as well, she my very best friend in all the world tonight, and that's what she is, has the any one of you pair got the light Meester Polizmen, these fucking thing keep going out, Coorva."

As soon as the policemen released their grip from Sandra, she attempted to make a run for it, but after only a few steps, fell flat on her face, sparking off another bout of profanations. "That was you fuckers pushing me, and I've got witnesses so I have they fucking seen it all, you're both in trouble now…perverts."

"Anya, who the fuck said I was a slut for fuck sakes? Tell me!"

Ten long minutes later, help arrived for the two struggling policemen.

Two female officers came to their assistance, and in no time at all had Sandra and Anya tucked away safely in their van, and had issued Kirsty with a final warning to get herself away home if she knew what was good for her, or she'd be joining her friends down in the cells. The female officers spoke briefly to their colleagues and then returned to their vehicle and drove away.

"Is this yours?" said one of the policemen, holding up a purse.

"It's Sandra's". Replied Kirsty, and what *I'd* like to know is, who said I was a slut, I mean that's not a very good thing to say to me is it?"

The two policemen smiled to each other at Kirsty's grammar.

"Are you going to be able to walk home alright, where do you live?"

"I'm live in Cromwell Road, and it's not even far from here, it's just down there." Kirsty pointed in the general direction she intended walking with her fist.

"Will you be ok to walk home?"

"Yes, I'm fine, and I'm sorry about my friends' officers, it's just that boys are really bad twats really, and so is that fucking Alan, what a bastard...saying *I'm* a fucking sluts, that's all I'd like to know."

It took the policemen a further five minutes to convince themselves that Kirsty Crawford was able-bodied enough to walk herself home. Helping her case was the fact that Cromwell Road was less than a couple of hundred metres from here.

"On you go home now Kirsty, and don't be stopping, you get yourself straight home now, you'll see your friends in the morning, they just need to calm themselves down a bit. Now you take care, and try not to drink so much next time you're out."

Kirsty fumbled in her handbag for her cigarettes and proceeded to light one up with considerably less trouble than her friend had.

The two officers watched her as she made her way towards Cromwell Road. "She'll be fine Joe, one of the policemen said to his colleague. What a bloody mess to get yourself into."

"Yeah, it always looks worse with the girls doesn't it. It just seems to be accepted for the boys to get into that state, but it borders on pathetic to see a young woman in that condition...pitiful."

The two policemen finally drove off convinced that Kirsty would be fine. Kirsty walked on towards Cromwell Road where she would reach the sanctuary of her bedroom and then sleep soundly and forget about Alan and all his bad habits, one of which was screwing every female who came his way. "Fuck *him*" she cried as she relit the cigarette for the third time. "I don't need that fucking twat. He'll regret fucking *me* about. I'll show him, there are plenty of guys interested in me."

Kirsty then proceeded to sit down on the pavement and began to break her heart about losing the love of her life. Even through the alcohol she felt devastated. She loved Alan with `all of her heart`. How could he do this to her?

After five minutes or so, Kirsty lifted herself from the pavement, with the aid of the perimeter wall to a block of flats, and hoisted herself back onto her feet.

As she regained her balance, a van approached her which had been parked across the road just outside of a famous Auto-centre.

The van pulled up along-side Kirsty and came to a stop.

The passenger window was rolled down and a young man said to her in a very polite English accent, "Excuse me love, could you tell me where Cambridge Road is please, we seem to be lost."

Kirsty staggered over to the van smiling. "It's just back there, a couple of hundred metres back you've just missed the turn. My friend lives there, and the police have lifted her, calling *me* a fucking slut indeed."

The young gentleman thanked her as his driver proceeded to drive on and turn the van around so that it was facing the direction of Cambridge Road. As the van drew level with Kirsty again, the driver's door opened and an older man stepped out and approached her, holding a sheet of paper in his hand.

"I wonder could you tell me where this is please?"

Kirsty stood beside the man now looking down onto the piece of paper.

As she did, the man forced a handkerchief over her mouth and nose and squeezed hard so that she couldn't scream. In less than ten seconds Kirsty was unconscious. Two men quickly bundled her into the back of the van, and drove off. Kirsty's cigarette packet and her friend's purse lay on the perimeter wall along with her mobile phone. The screen of Kirsty's phone lit up as her mother texted the message, *"Where the hell are you Kirsty? Your father is frantic."*

A21. BROMLEY.

Terry Mercer drove along Tweedy Road heading for the house where Sophie Spencer lived. He had to make a start somewhere and Sophie's name was the first on the list he possessed. His chief inspector Polly Sheppard had decided that Terry would investigate the missing girls from the London areas. Other detectives were given the task of working with the CID up in the midlands. According to his satellite-navigation, Sophie lived less than five minutes from here. Twenty-five minutes later inspector Mercer rang the doorbell of number six Lexington square, where the Spencer family lived.
The door was opened by Mrs Mandy Spencer, who Terry could tell by the look of the woman's eyes, hadn't had much sleep lately.
"Mister Mercer?"
"Yes, may I come in?" said Mercer, producing his ID.
"Of course, please, come in."
Mandy Spencer opened the door wide and gestured for the detective to enter. She wore dark blue jeans and a pale blue tee-shirt with the words *"Best mum in the world"* bought for her by Sophie for mother's day six months earlier. According to his records, Mandy was thirty-eight years old, and if not for the sleepless nights, would probably look ten years younger than that.
These were very awkward moments for detectives.
When someone who has lost a loved one through illness, it's bad enough, but in a case like this, have lost someone who has just disappeared, all of their hopes are built around you. They depend on you to relieve them from the immense pressure they have been put under. You are the one who can make it better for them. They haven't ever met you before, but you are all they have for hope...they depend on you to bring their lives back to some kind of normality.
Mercer entered the living room where a young man sat on one of the two two-seater sofas. The walls of the living room were adorned by numerous photographs of Sophie and her brother. Even on the sideboard there were photographs of all three Spencers', All smiling happily. The lad reminded him of the seventies pop star Marc Bolan, with his curly-loose permed hair. The lad wore faded Levi jeans and a denim shirt, and looked as though he hadn't shaved for a couple of days. His eyes were almost as red as his mothers'. He rose from the sofa and stretched out his right hand to greet Mercer.
"How do you do sir, my name is David, I'm Sophie's brother."
"How do you do David I am detective Terry Mercer."
Mandy offered him a cup of tea or coffee. He gratefully accepted a coffee.

After twenty minutes Terry had been informed of Sophie's last known activities. As previously arranged, Carol Richardson arrived at the door to inform the detective of her last conversation with Sophie in the shop on the day she disappeared. Three days had elapsed since Sophie's disappearance. Carol looked much the same as Mandy except Carol's hair was blonde whereas Mandy's was mousy brown, both shoulder length. Same build, which was slim and shapely. It was clear to see that both women looked after their bodies and took great pride in their appearances.

"I just don't understand it detective Mercer" she said, sipping her coffee.

"Sophie came in to the shop where I work as usual, she comes in to buy gum most mornings, and we stood and talked for about two or three minutes…maybe five. Sophie informed me she was running late, and was quite annoyed at being soaking wet. Her hair had been stuck to the back of her head. I think someone had splashed her from behind because her legs were soaking wet as well. I gave her a towel to dry herself and a loan of my umbrella."

Mercer leaned forward on the sofa. "What did you and Sophie talk about Carol, can you remember?" Carol seemed to dwell on the question for a while, her face giving a look of confusion, as if she were thinking, "what the hell has that got to do with Sophie disappearing? Eh, we were talking about all kinds of things…in general you know. She was moaning that David and her mum were still in bed while she had to get up and get herself ready for school, oh and feed the cat, you know, all the kind of things that fifteen year-old girls moan about. I had to put her right on those issues and remind her of just how hard her mum works and that it was no big deal to get herself up for school."

"Anything else?" said Mercer, writing something down in his note-book.

Carol just looked at him and shook her head.

"Don't think so…oh, I made a comment about her short skirts and how she should be careful how she dresses herself. Mandy here is always telling her about that, about how it can attract the wrong kind of attention. But you know detective, she's just like any other fifteen-year-old girl, hell they all wear short skirts don't they…I mean, I didn't lecture her or anything, I just gave her some friendly advice. That's about it…then she left the shop and made her way to school, except, as you know, she didn't make it there." Carol's voice had trailed off on her last sentence. "So" said Mercer. "Sophie was wearing a white blouse with her school tie, which is black and red, and a black mini skirt, with black lace-up shoes is that correct Misses Spencer?"

Mandy only nodded, and mumbled the words, "Yes…short."

"She wasn't wearing tights?"

"No Sophie doesn't like them, Mister Mercer, may I say something. My daughter although only fifteen, is very well developed, she could easily pass for a girl nineteen years old or more…when she puts make-up on she never has a problem gaining entry to any of the night clubs or pubs…and that's what's worrying me the most. Sophie thinks I don't know about the night clubs."

Mandy Spencer was almost in tears. It was as if she was betraying her daughter giving this man all these details about her, but she knew, if she was to have any hope of finding her, then the details had to be given. Mandy then completely fell apart and pointed to her son David and said, just as she broke down, "Please find her Mister Mercer, he's missing her ever so much…hell we all are…we all love her so much, every one of us, please find her for us, I don't…I can't live without my baby, she's my…oh my baby I love her so much mister Mercer, please find her."

It had been a very difficult forty minutes for Terry Mercer, but he knew it would be. To see a mother in desperation begging you to bring back her daughter was one of the most harrowing sights to see. How do you give someone like that any hope? What can you say to ease their pain? You can't tell them that everything's going to be alright, because it might not be. Sophie could very well be lying dead in a ditch somewhere, or in someone's basement, or, after three days, could be on the other side of the world for all he knew. In the end, all he could do was tell her the truth, which was, that he would do his very best to find the girl and bring her back home, and that he would be in touch if there was any news whatsoever. Posters would be put around the city on shop windows and cafes, and rewards would be offered to anyone who had any information at all concerning the whereabouts of the girl. Also police protection would be given to anyone who could assist them in their search. Even an appeal to Sophie herself, if she was listening to call her mother and let her know that she was alright, after all, all possibilities had to be covered. This was done by the television companies and local radio networks working along-side the metropolitan police department.

In other words, everything that could be done, had been put into action.

His next port of call was going to be just as harrowing as Lexington Square had been, the same desperation from distraught parents, the same hopelessness in their voices, and the same hope being placed upon *his* shoulders, that *he* can bring them back safely.

UNKNOWN LOCATION.

Sophie Spencer slowly regained consciousness. Her eyes were adjusting to the bright light that shone above her head. Her hands and feet had been bound. She was sitting on a sofa in a living room. The only other piece of furniture in the room was a large dining table. The light above her was being shone by a naked bulb. The walls were of a dull grey colour, like those of freshly plastered walls. She had no idea of how long she'd been unconscious. She struggled with the bindings round her hands but it was useless, they had been bound securely. She could hear voices coming from somewhere near the room she was in, muffled voices, distant and incoherent, male and female voices. The umbrella given to her by Carol Richardson lay on the floor just in front of her. There was no sign of her mobile phone.

There was one window in this room which had been covered by thick black-out curtains which were grey, the same colour as the walls. A giant map lay spread out on the table. Four large brass candle-sticks sat at each of the four corners of the map. A pair of spectacles had been laid down on the map. What the hell was happening? Why had they brought her here? Did they think she was somebody else? What on earth did they want with her? Sophie went through all the details of how her day had started, how she had moaned about her mum and brother lying in their beds, the pervert who had roared at her as he drove past shouting obscenities at her, the black van. Yes, the black van. Suddenly she remembered how the van had skidded to a halt, not far in front of her, and then how she'd felt the arms of someone clutching her from behind. Balaclavas, there were three men in the van wearing balaclavas.

Then she remembered the needle being inserted into her leg…and then…here. Here and now. Where the hell was she? More importantly, why did they abduct her? Of what use could she possibly be to these people, whoever they were. All kinds of scenarios were forming in Sophie's mind. She felt heavy and drowsy. Sleep was beginning to take over her again. She tried to fight it but could feel herself drifting away again with her mother's words echoing in her head. *"You shouldn't dress like that Sophie, with skirts as short as that, it gives a false impression of the kind of person you are. Boys who see girls in ridiculously short skirts think of one thing and one thing only."*

Sophie had no way of knowing how long she had slept, but when she awoke this time, the room was filled with people, now, they were all wearing masks like the men in the van had worn, and those woollen balaclavas. There were six people in here with her now, two females and four males, all of them wearing dark or black jackets and trousers. One of the men had noticed that she had awoken. He rose from the floor where he sat and walked over to her. "Do you need to use the toilet sweetheart?" Although the man had spoken softly to her, his voice was menacing, maleficent. Sophie nodded to the man, afraid even to speak.

Now his voice boomed. "Claire, take the girl to the bathroom, and make sure the window in there is secured, we don't want our little gold mine running out on us." A female approached her and offered her her hand.

"Come on sweetheart, you must be bursting for a pee after all this time, it's a wonder you haven't peed your pants, come on." The last two words were not a suggestion, but rather an order. Come on meant, move now. The woman helped her onto her feet and placed one of her arms around her shoulder, after having removed the bindings from Sophie's feet, and placing her hand around *her* shoulder. Sophie felt awkward and clumsy as she attempted to walk.

"Give us a hand here someone, I can hardly support her."

The other woman came over and supported Sophie from the other side, so that now she was practically being dragged along. The woman who had joined them suddenly placed a hand on her left breast and began to squeeze gently. "There now baby, we'll soon have you sorted out."

Although repulsed, Sophie was powerless to do anything to defend herself.

"Oh I know baby" the woman said, "You probably don't like that being done to you, but you just wait and see…hell that's nothing, a little tit squeeze. Hey you've got a good handful there haven't you, for someone so young. We've had our eye on you for some time now…you and your sexy short skirts, that's what attracted us to you in the first place…yeah, big price for you baby, young girl like you, still developing, you're worth your weight in gold so you are, you'll be a very provocative sex-slave I'll bet, and by God we're going to find out aren't we Claire." The other woman replied. "Indeed we are. You're going to make us a lot of money young lady. You suit your short skirts don't you Sophie…nice legs, very sexy. There are some people coming over tomorrow from Europe…and they'll all be bidding for you. The highest bidder will take you back with them, that'll be nice for you. You'll be able to wear your short skirts all the time Sophie, in fact, they'll encourage it, after all, how you look will determine how much money you'll make for them. Some of their girls will show you how to put make-up on, and attract customers oh you're going to be in for a big change in your life now young lady. Oh, just one more question Sophie…are you a virgin? Because if you are, then you've just gone and made us some more money babes, fifteen-year old virgins are very rare you see, especially around these parts."

The other woman laughed raucously, and then said," yes but you won't be a virgin for very long, of that you can be certain."

They reached the bathroom where one of the women turned and headed back to the living room.

"Don't be leaving her on her own for too long" she said as she turned away.

The woman left with Sophie said "You've got five minutes young lady, and then I'm coming in, so you'd best hurry up, anyway, those men through there will be wanting to take a look at you as soon as they can. Don't worry, they won't do anything to you, they just want to see you standing naked in front of them so as they can take their photographs…it's for the sales you see, they can show their clients that they are telling the truth when describing the ladies they have for sale…well, the girls I should say, but you know what I mean."

All Sophie's questions had now been answered. The information was frightening. She had no idea where she was, or where she was going.

One thing was for sure though, she knew what she was going to be used for, used being the operative word. Now, some other questions came to her mind. Would she ever see her mum and brother again? Would she ever be allowed to go back home?

For Sophie Spencer, the world, or at least the world she was used to living in, had suddenly disappeared, and she had been transported into an unknown realm, a tortuous labyrinth, and here, an apartment in hell perhaps.

WOODFORD. A104.

Chloe Prowse had no idea where on earth she was. As she had regained consciousness she had been able to see a sign on the roadside, like a junction, a road-end, reading Sydney Road. One of her abductors had noticed that she'd regained consciousness and quickly placed a hood over her head. Then she felt her sleeve being pulled up and someone rubbing her left arm vigorously. She felt the needle being injected, and then she felt good again...she felt very good. Her kidnappers were on their way to Loughton to rendezvous with their partners-in-crime, and discuss what would be done with their captured merchandise, and how much they would sell them for. Two of the captors had been watching Chloe for a few weeks now as she went to and fro from her work to her home. Morning and night they'd scrutinised her movements. Everything had to be planned meticulously. When executing a daytime abduction, decoys had to be put into place, just in case someone got suspicious as they drove past.

The road-sweeper was the perfect decoy concerning the abduction of Sophie Spencer. If a vehicle had come along and was suspicious of the obstruction on the road, then the sweeper would look like *he* was causing the obstruction, and therefore make it look like the situation was no more than an innocent minor delay, besides, on really wet days like that motorists were mostly concentrating on their driving, and the conditions were indeed an added bonus to the abductors. They had all done their homework on Chloe Prowse. They knew where she lived. What time she left for work, how long it took her to get there, and what time she returned home. They also knew what time her sister left the house, and where she worked. All that remained to be done was pick a spot where the abduction would take place. Again the decoys worked perfectly, the young couple arguing viciously on the pavement, the fake slap to the face that would send the girl sprawling to the ground. It was easy, it was easy beyond belief to abduct someone. The target themselves were the easiest part, it was the unplanned approaching traffic that could cause the difficulties and problems, or the sudden appearance of someone turning a corner and spotting the crime being committed. Cameras mounted high on trees in certain areas were also a danger, and so extreme surveillance checks had to be carried out. Some people had cameras mounted from the roofs of their garages, or from the eves of their houses. These cameras could span quite a distance and would be easily capable of taking a clear shot of a vehicle's number plate. Weeks, and sometimes months of preparation would be put into place before an abduction would finally be executed. Business was good for the abductors lately.

They were building quite a collection of really good looking young girls.

Their clients from various eastern European countries would pay top-notch prices for pretty English girls, and of course, if proof was produced that they were virgins, then the price automatically rose by another thirty per cent.

Chloe Prowse smiled at the two gentlemen in front of her now relieving her of her clothing and sitting her down on the sofa placing high-heeled shoes on her feet.
A young woman was now applying make-up to her face, the same woman in fact who Chloe had tried to assist when her `boyfriend` had attacked her. The young woman's voice came and went in waves as she spoke to Chloe.
"Fooled you good, didn't we girly huh? Such a goodie-two-shoes you are aren't you? God they're going to pay a fortune for you honey. Nice little sweet baby like you, sit still Chloe. You are top class babe. Untouched by human hands, you're a fucking gold mine really."
The scene was nothing less than pathetic, as Chloe sat smiling and touching the people who were preparing her for her photo-shoot. The blonde girl stood Chloe up onto her feet and began to rub oils all over Chloe's body. Two of the four men joined in and `assisted` the young lady with the application of the lotion, whilst Chloe stood giggling and laughing at the people who planned to sell her off as a sex slave. Chloe was taken to the bathroom by both of the women who proceeded to shave her genitalia. Finally, they brought her back through to the living room and proceeded to take many photographs of the smiling young lady, who to all intents and purposes looked like she was enjoying every minute of the experience, especially when she reached for the blonde girl and began to kiss her full on the mouth. More photos were taken of her wearing short skirts and various skimpy tops, most of them see-through. Finally, she was led into a bedroom, laid down on a single bed, injected again, and then left to sleep.

HOUNSLOW.

Terry Mercer drove along Wellington Road heading for Cromwell Road where Kirsty Crawford lived with her parents, Steven and Pamela. According to the information given to him, Steven Crawford was a self-employed builder and his wife an auxiliary nurse, both of them in their early forties. There were no blemishes on their records. In fact neither of the two had ever been in trouble with the law. Their sixteen-year-old daughter Kirsty had just left school and was about to start part-time work in the local Tesco store until it was time for her to attend university, where she would study Law and Criminology. However, their daughter had mysteriously disappeared after a night out with her two friends Anya Kaplinsky and Sandra Tweedy.
Today Terry was accompanied by a young female detective.
Samantha Reynolds had been informed by Polly Sheppard that she would accompany Mercer until further notice. Samantha was also warned of Mercer's sudden blasphemous outbursts and not to take any offence if he suddenly aimed one of his profanations at her. Very little had been said between the two officers as Mercer had driven through the city and out towards Hounslow. Thirty-two year-old Samantha Reynolds broke the silence. "It's not for me to tell you anything sir, but you shouldn't be smoking in the car...it's illegal as well you know...and it's annoying...sir."
Mercer didn't look at his partner as he drove, but simply replied, "You're right officer Reynolds...it's *not* for you to tell me...open your window, and tell me what number it says on that piece of paper you have in your hands...the number for Cromwell Road, that's what you can tell me."
Officer Reynolds told her superior the number and then said nothing more.
Some people back at HQ had warned her that Mercer was a bit of a loose-cannon and so not to get involved in any kind of argument with him. Staying quiet was the best way to stay in his good books. Five minutes later, Mercer pulled up in front of the house in Cromwell Road. Much to Samantha's surprise he turned to speak to her. "Have you ever done investigations like these before Samantha, by that I mean kidnappings or disappearances?" "No sir, I haven't...not like this."
"Well, the first thing I'm going to tell you is this. These two people, Kirsty's parents, are going to be in a state of anxiety. Their whole world has been torn apart. As far as I know Kirsty is their one and only child. What we mustn't do in here Samantha, is give them false hope. We can't tell them not to worry, or that everything will be alright. So, what we must do is inform them that we will do everything in our powers to locate their daughter and bring her back...if she wants to come back. She's sixteen and is not legally

bound to abide by her parents' wishes. Again, we have to look at all possibilities. She may have disappeared on purpose. Anyway, I'll be doing the talking in here so you just sit and listen. If one of them does ask you a question, then you make sure you answer it carefully, are we all clear on that?"

"Yes sir, clear."

"Good, ok let's go Samantha and get this over with...and what's with the leather coat, are you a kinky bitch or do you fancy yourself as some kind of female inspector Cluseau?"

Reynolds smiled at her superior but said nothing.

"I mean it, tell me, are you a kinky bitch, because if you are-."

"No I am not kinky as you put it, I wear the coat because it keeps me warm."

She smiled again as Mercer rang the doorbell and said, "Oh, I thought you were wearing it to look like a bad bastard...a nasty bitch."

That was another thing her colleagues back at HQ had informed her of, sugar and shit. One minute he'd be laughing and joking with you, the next he was calling you the most incompetent bastard he'd ever come across, you just had to go with it.

A very distraught Mrs Pamela Crawford answered the door and invited the two detectives into her home. Just over an hour later Terry Mercer and Samantha Reynolds returned to their vehicle. Samantha slumped down on the passenger seat and exhaled a massive sigh. As Mercer sat down beside her he said, "I told you kid, it's not easy, it's actually gut-wrenching. You done well Samantha, you done really well...better than I thought actually. To Reynolds' surprise, he tapped her on the shoulders a couple of times. "Well done."

"It's horrible sir, to see and hear a woman in a state like that. She loves her daughter so much and her husband...he loves his little girl."

"Told you Sam, she's all they've got in the world...and what a horrible world it can be. Let's hope we get something to go on Miss Reynolds."

"I will say something though sir that I'm not in total agreement with. Mrs Crawford said that she and her husband were aware of the fact that Kirsty went into pubs with her friends, and quite regularly, I'm not sure I would allow my teenage daughter to go to pubs and-."

Mercer put up his hand.

"In this day and age Samantha, it is better for a parent to be slightly lenient towards their daughters at that tender age rather as forbid them, because once you forbid them, then that's when the trouble starts, and then they *will* rebel against you. Suddenly, you're not their parents, you're their enemy, and then all hell can break loose. They've just been unlucky that's all, and that is to say that Kirsty has been abducted, like I say, we have to look at all the possibilities." Samantha wiped her eyes with a tissue. Cigarette smoke.

"As far as I could make out, they all seemed to have a close-nit relationship. I don't think that Kirsty would leave home voluntarily, and even if she did, I think she'd let them know that she was safe."

Mercer nodded. "Yes" he sighed. "That's why I think she's been abducted Samantha. Of course I'm not going to tell them that." He lit another cigarette and opened his window. "I've heard stories. There seems to be a market for the sale of young British girls. These bastards whoever they are abduct them and then sell them on to the highest bidder. European businessmen come over here and bid for them." He sighed again as he exhaled. "Sell them like fucking cattle, pieces of meat to serve their sordid sexual appetites. We've got a couple of ghosts going round the city asking questions as to where these sales take place. You see, they can't sell them on the internet because that would be too easy for us to catch them. So these ghosts go round making subtle inquiries trying to find out where the sales take place. Once we have a positive lead we'll be onto them, faster than a cat on a mouse, but it's getting that first break. If it were me who was selling the girls, then I wouldn't be using the same place twice. It's my guess Samantha that these animals will be wandering all over the place to make their sales. They may use a hotel room to do their price negotiating, or it could be Jimmy Smith's garden shed, that's just it, we haven't got much of a chance to catch them unless we get a positive lead." Mercer smiled at his young colleague's sense of humour as she replied with a straight face, "Who's Jimmy Smith sir?"

As Terry Mercer started the car and threw out his cigarette end onto the street, he replied, "I sincerely hope Samantha that we find out who he is. Now, what I want you to do when we get back to the office, is to contact our colleagues up in the midlands and find out if they've had any luck with their inquiries. If you're wondering why I'm asking you to do that, it's because I happen to think that it is the same people who are kidnapping the girls here. I don't know why I'm thinking that, but I do. If that is the case Samantha, then I think we'll have a slightly better chance of catching them, and God knows how many people are involved. Not that many I would imagine, because if there is one thing that bastards like these have in common, it's greed, so the fewer people involved in their sick snatch-and-sell caper, then the less money they have to share out."

Samantha Reynolds smiled at her superior as he drove.

Without looking at her he said, "What are you finding funny Samantha?"

"Nothing sir, I just happen to think that you're a very intelligent man. You seem to have a natural ability to sus things out, you know, like how these people work, what makes them tick."

"Samantha, I have been a detective for over fifteen years. If I don't have an insight as to how these recidivists work, then there's not much hope for me, and I hope this is not your way of trying to crawl your way into my good books, because I can tell you right here and now, if-."

"It's not sir, I wouldn't dream of crawling to anyone. I was merely pointing out that you seemed very skilled in these matters that's all, Christ, can I not give you a compliment without you thinking the worst of me…sorry sir, that kind of got away from me there."

"That's alright Samantha" he replied, as he stopped the car and pointed to a baker shop. "You go in there and get me two apple pies, and we'll forget the whole thing." He pulled out his wallet and handed her a twenty-pound note. "Oh, and get yourself something to eat if you wish…it's on me."

Samantha shook her head laughing at her boss. Was it just her, or was Terry Mercer turning out to be quite alright to work with. Only time would reveal the truth about that.

MITCHAM.

Alison Green walked along the B272 heading for Common-side East and where she would then cross over the road and head for Beech Grove, where her grandmother lived. The total journey would be almost a mile in distance from where she lived, but Alison did not grudge the walk, and besides, there was a really dishy boy who lived next door to her gran that she fancied very much. She remembered on her last visit that the boy had been cutting her grans' grass for her, and was stripped to the waist, showing off his lovely body as he majestically `danced` around the garden with the fly-mo. She smiled as she remembered the boy accepting the glass of orange-juice offered to him, and how his hand had touched hers' as he took the beverage, giving her butterflies in her belly. Because the boy lived next door to her gran he was always calling in to see if she wanted anything at the shop, or if there was anything he could do for her. Sometimes he would do a bit of hoovering for her, or some polishing, or he would change a fuse or replace batteries in clocks. Today, Alison was carrying a dozen fresh eggs for her grandmother, free-range of course, and a jam and cream sponge cake, especially baked for her by Alison herself. She had used up all her pocket money and knew there'd be no chance of extra cash from either of her parents and so the cake would be the perfect gift to soften her grans' heart enough to part with some cash. Alison was almost sixteen and felt that her mum and dad treated her like she was six. She knew of girls at her school who had been out with eighteen-year-old boys and had even had sex with them. Both of her parents were away for the day visiting friends and so she had dressed herself just exactly as she wanted to dress herself. Alison had applied make-up to her face and looked older than her sixteen years. Her denim mini skirt hugged her backside, showing off her legs, and her fake leather jacket was open to her midriff. The blouse she wore was `borrowed` from her older sisters' wardrobe, which was also open to her chest. She had no breasts to speak of, but she wasn't worried about that. They would come eventually, in their own time. One of her friends had informed her that if you kept fondling them yourself, they would grow quicker, and so every evening before she went to sleep, she spent fifteen minutes massaging them...so far it hadn't worked. As she walked on her mobile phone buzzed in her handbag. She retrieved it and began to have a conversation with one of her school friends. On this section of the B272, there was only pavement on one side of the road. Up ahead of her, there were two women standing looking at a map in their hands. One of the women was blonde, the other brunette. Both of them looked to be in their twenties. As Alison approached, they both smiled at her and said hello. Alison said she

would call her friend back in a couple of minutes, as one of the women spoke to her.
"Are you from around this area? We seem to be lost."
"Where are you looking for?" said Alison, feeling good with herself at the thought of these young women speaking to her, like she was a friend of theirs'.
The blonde looked at the map and then looked at Alison as she said,
"We're looking for Beech grove. According to this, it doesn't seem to be too far away from here…but we're having no luck whatsoever."
Alison smiled at the women. "Are you joking? That's where I'm going now, my gran lives there it's not that far from here."
"Oh brilliant" the brunette said. "Could you do us a favour? Would you wait here with us until I call my husband, he's in the car trying to find the bloody street. If you're going there, then that would be perfect. You could jump in the car with us and guide us there right to the door, would you do that for us? We'll make it worth your while, we'd be so grateful, honestly, we've been running around here for more than an hour.
My husband's sat-nav has buggered up and so we've been depending on our map reading, which isn't very good as you can tell. Would you do that for us, please honey?"
"Of course I will, and you don't have to make it worth my while, it's worth my while just to be helpful to you, as long as he's not too far away from here, I mean will he be here in less than ten minutes?"
"He won't be long, probably five minutes or less, like I say, we knew we were quite close."
"No problem." said Alison smiling.
One of the women pulled out her mobile phone and pressed digits, the other offered Alison a cigarette, which she accepted, along with a light. The blonde had stepped away slightly from where Alison and the brunette were standing, but as Alison was lighting her cigarette, she thought she heard her saying, yes, we've got her here, please hurry."
Then she had turned around and said, "He's just coming now, he's less than a mile from here. Oh this is brilliant. At last, we can visit our friends, they must be wondering where the hell we are."
Alison thought to herself, "well why didn't you call your friends and explain to them you were lost, surely they would have come and guided you back?" But she said nothing. If Alison had acted upon that thought, then perhaps she'd have saved herself from the course of events that were about to take place.
The two women stood making small talk with Alison and repeatedly thanked her for her help, and praising her for her assistance. In less than five minutes a red Audi Q 5 pulled up by the wayside. A young man called David Weaver who looked about the same age as the women smiled as he pulled the car to a halt. The blonde climbed into the back

seats first. "You get in Alison" said the brunette, as she looked all around her. Finally, she climbed into the back and closed the door behind her. "Here, let me take your parcels from you and put them on the front seat for you, we're really grateful for this Alison, we really are, aren't we guys."

"Oh yes" replied the man, "you've no idea."

The brunette took the bags from Alison's hands and placed them on the front seat. "Here, I've got something for you Alison in my bag, as a reward for you being so fucking gullible you silly girl you, didn't your parents warn you about bastards like us?" Before Alison had fully comprehended what the brunette had said, the blonde grabbed her by the hair of her head and pulled her back so that the brunette could place the handkerchief over her mouth and nose. In seconds Alison Green was unconscious.

SCOTLAND YARD.

BROADWAY VICTORIA.

Terry Mercer sat at his desk awaiting the arrival of his lunch. He had asked Sam Reynolds to nip out and get sandwiches for them. He was also awaiting a return call on his mobile from a colleague who had texted him with the message; *"Think I might have a name for u bud, looking into the matter as we speak. Will be in touch as soon as…"*
If there was one thing that Mercer disliked, it was people who hardly knew him referring to him as bud. He had known inspector Colin Briggs for about two years. He'd seen him going about the place but had never indulged in any long-term conversations with him. They were working colleagues, yes, but nothing more.
"Fucking bud indeed!"
Mercer had replied to his text message and was waiting for a definite lead, a name that he could begin to investigate. He had made inquiries to various snitches throughout the city, and had threatened them with lengthy jail sentences if they withheld any information from him regarding the missing girls, but even with his sincere threats he had come up with nothing. His gut-feelings were telling him that the abductors didn't come from here, or at least not all of them, because he was convinced that whoever was doing this was not working alone. Samantha Reynolds approached him, handing him his sandwich. Today Samantha was wearing her denim jeans and a leather jacket, bomber style, short raven hair with burgundy streaks and pale burgundy lipstick.
"You are Sam, aren't you, you're trying to look like a really bad bastard, you've got this tough-guy fucking sexy-looking thing going on here haven't you, hell I'm frightened to speak to you…fucking hard bitch."
"They didn't have cheese and pickle so I got you cheese and ham, is that alright for you sir?"
Mercer frowned at the choice of cheese and ham although Samantha knew fine well that he liked this.
"Listen Sam, before we go any further, I am well aware of the fact that you know that I'm your superior, so really, there is no need to address me as sir. Just call me Terry, it's a lot easier and it makes me feel better…like there is no divide between us. As far as I'm concerned, we are both equals, ok? Don't have to fucking sir this and sir that, it's just Terry ok? And why do you like to be called Sam? Is it that hard bastard impression thing again? Believe me Samantha you will have many opportunities to impose your hardness onto scoundrels around here. You will be subjected to situations where you'll have to

be hard, you'll need to kick them in the balls from time to time to get answers, and that's when your leather jacket and fucking leather coats should be worn…looking the part girly. In the meantime, you get yourself a chair and have your sandwich along with me, I bet *you* got cheese and pickle ok didn't you? They would find cheese and pickle for you…fucking hard bitch."

He took a bite from his sandwich and with his mouth full he said: "Just as long as you don't start calling me bud, ok? Can't fucking stand that."

It was that sugar and shit again that she'd been warned about. You could never tell if he was about to give you a telling off or if he was going to pay you a compliment. She found that behaving normally worked as well as anything else. "Have you heard anything back from inspector Briggs?" said Samantha, opening up her ploughman's sandwich which contained generous amounts of pickle. Mercer didn't answer her verbally, but just shook his head as he pointed to his phone, which informed Samantha that he was waiting for a return call. Half way through his second sandwich his mobile phone buzzed loudly on his desk. Samantha smiled as Mercer said something incoherent into his mobile. After a few seconds, he picked up a pen and began to write on a piece of torn up cardboard which looked like the inside of a cigarette packet. All he said at the end of the call was, "You're sure, you're absolutely sure Colin, because if I have to fucking go-". He switched off his phone and finished off the rest of his sandwich, looking at his watch. "Let's go Sam, bring your sandwich with you and your drink, did you get me a drink? where the fuck is my drink?"

"It's there right beside you. I wish you wouldn't fly off the handle like that before you even look. Do you think I'd buy myself a drink and not get you one? Christ…sir."

"Come on, we're off to Stratford Samantha, going to visit an Angela Bates."

"Not before I've finished my lunch sir, I've still got a sandwich to finish."

"Listen here missy, when I say we go, then we go, disregarding how far through your lunch you are, don't you forget-."

"It's a syndicate Terry." Mercer was interrupted by Polly Sheppard the chief inspector. "From what I can gather, there is a syndicate abducting these girls. At this point we're unsure if they are operating from here in the city, or up in the midlands, but it's definitely a syndicate." Samantha smiled to herself as Polly Sheppard sat and crossed her legs clad in tight black trousers on the corner of Mercer's desk, the only individual in the whole of Scotland Yard who would be permitted this liberty, and watched as Mercer's eyes took a wander all over them.

"I've been given a name. Colin Briggs who is currently up in the midlands gave me it, a certain Miss Angela Bates. Samantha and I are just about to head over to give her a visit just as soon as she's finished her lunch." Mercer looked at Samantha and then at his watch. "Apparently she lives, or at least operates from Stratford, I'm just waiting for confirmation of her address, and by the time we get confirmation perhaps Samantha will be finished her sandwich.

Sam Reynolds deliberately took a small nibble of her ploughman's lunch and nodded her head. Mercer's phone screen lit up as the address of Angela Bates' appeared.

"Listen Terry" said Polly Sheppard. "Give the girl a chance will you? You always snap at people with that stone-cold sarcasm of yours and you know it doesn't get you anywhere. Sam? You just ignore his sledge-hammer wit because no-one but himself pays him any heed."

It was as though Polly hadn't said a single word.

"Are you finished that bloody sandwich? Could have been over to Stratford and back if I'd been working on my own, look at you nibbling away at that like it was a loaf you were eating...it's a sandwich for fuck sakes, not a horse cock you're taking down there, Christ Samantha it looks like you suffer from Prader-willi."

Polly Sheppard shook her head.

"It's alright Miss Sheppard I'm growing accustomed to his remarks they are fast becoming innocuous, once you get to know him."

"It doesn't matter Samantha, he shouldn't be talking to his colleagues in that manner, he's been warned often enough. Anyway Terry, get over there and see what you can learn from this Angela. When I say syndicate, it could be three, or it could be thirty-three. I honestly fear the worst for these poor girls Terry. Some of them have been missing now for as long as three months. Notice as well Terry, that the girls in question are all very pretty, and very young, the oldest I think is eighteen, all the others are younger than that."

"You think they're selling them off to Europeans Polly?" said Mercer, again glancing at his watch. Polly nodded her head. "Yeah, hence the good looks. The prettier they are, the higher the price, it's bloody fearful Terry. Just think, you could be saying goodbye to your fourteen-year-old daughter as she heads off to school one morning, and you may never see her again, because, if these animals get them over into Europe, then there is little chance of these parents ever getting their kids back." Polly slid back off the table and stood up. She then leaned over Terry's desk on her outstretched arms and looked at the two detectives. "Listen, you two, this is off the record. I'm giving you permission to use any means you wish to obtain the necessary information. Now Terry, I don't want you...I don't want...oh just don't kill them Terry, but if either of you two suspect that they are holding back information from you, then you just...you know what I mean Terry. Listen, it is of the utmost importance that we find out who these people are and put a stop to their bloody games."

Samantha scrunched up the wrapper which had contained her sandwich and threw it into the bin under Mercer's desk, nodding her head to Polly Sheppard, and then looked at her watch. "Ready when you are sir."

Polly smiled at Terry seeing the frustration in his face, then she whispered to the two detectives. "Get these bastards Terry, please get them, and beat the shit right out of them…please. Use those good-for-nothing snitches of yours to find out anything they can, anything, just do anything to get them Terry. Samantha? I didn't think I'd say this so early in your career, but you'll have to learn to be brutal. These people will kill you at the drop of a hat. She pointed to Terry Mercer. "If he says kill them, then you do just that. What do you have by means of firearms?"

"I have a Glock 21, it's light, and very powerful, plus it carries more rounds than the average pistol."

"Good, get another one, and keep it in a safe place where you know you can get it." She pointed at Mercer. "He keeps his spare in his glove compartment. Have you used your gun yet Samantha?"

Mercer jumped in. "By that, she means have you shot anyone yet Samantha?"

Samantha smiled at Terry sarcastically. "Not yet mam, but I've used it on the firing range…I'm quite good."

"Ok Samantha, you might be tested as to how good you really are, do you think you could use it on a human being?"

"Mam, if you're referring to these abductors, then, for a kick-off I do not refer to them as human beings, so yes, I could use it on them without any remorse whatsoever, and with all due respect mam, there are certain people who are not exactly a hundred miles away who I've seriously thought about using it on."

Yet again Polly Sheppard laughed as she replied, "Well, yes Samantha, I have to confess that there have been times when I myself have been seriously tempted, but please, spare him, he's quite a handy…eh…person to have around."

"When you're finished?" said Mercer. "Can we leave now for Stratford? I mean, only if you're finished calling me to the dogs. Whoever the fuck this Angela is, she's had time to take a holiday abroad somewhere in the time we've stood here listening to all this shit. I was hoping we could leave before Sunday if that's ok with you two."

As Polly walked away she said, over her shoulder, "Good luck you pair, enjoy your trip over to Stratford. Let him drive Samantha, it seems to keep his mind occupied and usually his profanations are aimed at other drivers rather than the colleagues who accompany him. Let me know as soon as you've got anything Terry."

"I'll just go to the toilet before we head off sir" said Samantha, smiling at Terry, and taking a drink from her can of cola. Mercer put on his jacket.

"I'll be leaving in five minutes, if you're not sitting beside me in the car by then I'll be away in which case you can report back to Polly, and she'll find something for you to do."

UNKNOWN LOCATION.

Fifteen-year-old Lisa Jenson came to on the huge black leather sofa she had been seated upon. She was dazed and very confused. She knew she'd been sleeping for a long time, but had no idea of exactly how long. The last thing she could remember was a young woman taking her to a bathroom and leaving her there for a few minutes. She was then injected with something and had fallen into a deep sleep. As her vision cleared she took in the surroundings. This place was very luxurious. There were paintings on the walls of ships in stormy waters. Others were of beautiful landscapes. The wallpaper was of a burgundy colour which enhanced the gold frames of all the paintings. The ceilings were very high, about four metres or more. Opposite from where she sat, there was another giant-sized sofa identical to the one she was seated upon. Soft music came from somewhere in the room but she couldn't detect from where exactly. She could smell the aroma of something very pleasant being cooked, like the aromas you would smell as you entered a restaurant. She had been dressed in shorts and a top. Soft comfortable slippers had been placed upon her feet. For the first time in what seemed like an age, she noticed that she wasn't shackled either. Neither her feet nor her hands had been bound. She tried to sit up but found it very difficult to stay upright, dizziness taking over immediately, forcing her to stretch out her hands to support herself and keep from rolling over. She kept trying to stand up but each time she tried she was overcome with dizziness. Her vision swirled if she moved her head too quickly. Whatever drugs they had administered to her were keeping her in a state of semi-consciousness. She was aware of her surroundings but was unable to move. Still the soft music played. Something classical she guessed, sophisticated, soothing. Giving up on trying to stand up she sat back on the giant sofa, and was just about to fall back into slumber when she heard a door being opened from somewhere behind her. Then she heard the door being closed again, and suddenly a woman appeared in front of her. The woman was looking down at her smiling. She had long jet-black hair and was very pretty. Lisa didn't know very much about expensive jewellery but the rings and bracelets she was wearing looked very up-market. She had the face of an angel with beautiful deep-green eyes. Perhaps she was a cat-walk model, her figure and her posture would certainly suggest that. She wore a crimson blouse on top of which she wore a black velvet waistcoat with the buttons opened, deep blue denim jeans which were tight to her legs, and tanned leather boots. The gold chain around her neck sparkled as she got down on her hunkers and placed her manicured hands upon Lisa's thighs. In perfect English, but with a European accent she said, smiling into Lisa's face,

"Ooh my my, very pretty girl Lisa. You are a very pretty girl." She tapped Lisa twice on her right thigh as she rose to her feet again, and walked angelically across the huge living room to a drinks cabinet, where she proceeded to pour a couple of drinks. As she `glided` back over towards Lisa she said, "You do like vodka and coke don't you Lisa?" Lisa's vision was swirling again. As the woman handed her a drink, she briefly saw two hands and two drinks being offered to her, and as she reached out to accept the drink, she seemed momentarily to have two right hands. Now the woman sat down on the sofa beside her. "I know Lisa, you must be very confused as to what has happened to you, but you mustn't worry, everything is going to be alright from now on.
My name is Monica can you say that Lisa? Say my name sweetheart."
Lisa answered the woman somewhat incoherently, "Mon-i-ca."
"Perfect, oh don't worry, the drowsiness will wear off in time. We had to give you sedatives and quite strong ones I don't mind telling you, so that we could get you over here from Great Britain. You're in your new home now Lisa. This is the beginning of your new life. You will want for nothing here, you'll be looked after, in fact you'll be spoiled. Clothes jewellery money, you'll never go without again, I promise you. You and I are going to have lots of fun with lots of men and ladies, won't that be nice? I am going to take you under my wing and I'm going to learn you a whole lot of skilful things that you can do for these men and ladies, and they will pay us lots of money for doing these things with them, won't that be lovely?"
Even through her drowsiness Lisa could feel the fear in her gut. The realisation of what had happened to her smashed her brain like a blacksmith's hammer.
Lisa croaked, through tearful eyes, "Where-am-I?"
"Oh bless my little sweetheart, you're so cute, why I told you Lisa, you're in your new home, to begin your new life, you're in Lithuania my precious child."

STRATFORD.

HUNTINGTON ROAD.

Terry Mercer drove down the narrow road trying to glance at the address given to him by detective Colin Briggs. Samantha Reynolds was reading the case-file held in her hands. She also held her mobile phone in her hands and had already turned on the sat-nav. The torn cigarette packet which had the address written upon it, fell to the floor under Mercer's seat.
"Here it comes" Sam thought to herself, *"Here comes the swearing match, and of course it'll be my fault he's dropped it."*
"Sam, could you try and retrieve that piece of cardboard for me please, bloody thing has fallen off my lap."
"We'll get it later Terry, I've already written the address down on my mobile phone. According to this, we go past the primary school and continue until we come to the road end. Huntington Flats are there at the end of this road, I think I can see them from here."
"Good, what was the number Sam, did you remember to write down the number?" Samantha sighed. "No, I thought I'd just write down the name of the street, and then we could ask someone what number, of course I wrote the bloody number down, what the hell do you take me for?" She told him the number and then put her mobile phone back into the pocket of her leather jacket.
"Listen here, whilst I told you to be less formal with me don't go jumping on your fucking high horse ok? You still be careful how you talk to me, I was only asking you if you'd remembered to write down the bloody number that's all. What do I take you for? I'll tell you something, I've had to work with some fucking dummies in my time, I'm only finding out what calibre you belong to, because if it turns out that you're no good, then you'll be back to typing up fucking shoplifters in one of the trainee offices, so just think on missy…you and your fucking Glock, what the fuck made you pick that for a weapon, it's not much better than a water pistol, nice and light indeed, fuck me!"
"What's wrong with the Glock pistols, they'll still kill somebody if I have to, and it doesn't weigh a bloody ton. Bet I can guess what you use. I know that by your bigoted personality. Bet you carry a great big look at the size of my cock Magnum don't you, like carrying a bloody shopping-trolley around with you in your jacket. I'm right aren't I, that's what you use isn't it?"
"Hey, you never mind what I use, just be grateful I carry something that'll get your arse

out of a fix if needs be…that's all you need to worry about, where the fuck am I supposed to park around here, for fuck sakes!"
Five minutes later they had parked up and were now riding the lift up to the appropriate level.
"You let me do the talking here ok? And pay attention as to how to interview someone who is not quite at this moment in time, a suspect. You have to be subtle how you go about asking questions, making sure that you don't accidently accuse them of the crime, because if you do, then all of a sudden you're dealing with some smart-assed lawyer who will sue the fucking shit right out of you."
"Well thank *you* sir, for that wonderfully worded explanation on how not to interview a would-be suspect, very nicely put sir if you don't mind me saying." Mercer pressed the doorbell. After a few seconds, a sour-faced young man about the age of thirty answered the door, his hair sticking up all over his head.
"What? What do you want?
Mercer cleared his throat. He showed his ID.
"I'm looking for a certain Angela Bates, is she in?" The young man scratched his chin and looked even more frustrated with himself. He sighed heavily. "No, she's not in, she's at work, and her name is no longer Bates. We got married two months ago, her name is now Jennings. If you must speak with her, she's down the high Street in her office, I take it you'd like to speak with her concerning your accounts."
"I beg your pardon, my accounts?"
"Yes your accounts that's what my wife does, she's an accountant, and has been for seven years now. She hasn't got round to changing the name on her shop window, now do you mind if I get back in there and try and get back to sleep, I'm on constant night shift, thank you so bloody much for waking me up three hours early, ringing bloody doorbells at this time of the day, go down the high street and see her, she's not doing anybody's bloody dodgy books from here!" The young man slammed the door on Mercer's face. Even through the closed door Sam could still hear the man ranting. "Bloody clowns."
Mercer looked at his colleague. "*Now* do you see what I mean Sam?"
"About what sir?"
"About bloody idiots, dummies, that fucking clown Briggs has given me the wrong woman. There is obviously another Angela Bates going around here somewhere and that stupid twat has given me the wrong one, either that, or the bastard has deliberately set me up to look like a fool, and if I find out he has, I'll take that fucking Glock of yours and I'll stick it right up his fucking Gypsy arse, I kid you not!"
"I have an idea sir, let's go to the local nick, and see if they have heard of this Angela

Bates. If she has got anything to do with the missing girls, then rest assured she'll be on record somewhere for doing something else."

"Good thinking Sam. You see? You gained points there for using your brains, you know, for not being a dummy. Let's go and see if we can find the right one right after we've been down the street…"

"Down the street sir?"

"Yes, down the street sir, or wherever her shop is. I still want to meet this woman, this Angela Jennings or whatever she calls herself. Just because she's an accountant Sam, doesn't mean that she doesn't kidnap teenage girls, I still want to ask her some questions."

KAUNAS.

LITHUANIA.

The fear in Lisa Jenson's gut was making her feel sick, as this woman called Monica continued to explain to her everything that was going to happen.
"It's always the same whenever we get new girls. Everybody wants to spend time with you. Men and women will pay lots of money to have you, even just for an hour at a time. Of course there are always the big-spenders, they are the kind of customers that we want Lisa. Do you know, some of those men and ladies will pay thousands of Euros to have you overnight, so you must be really nice for them and do everything they ask you to do without question otherwise they start to complain to Mister Saratov, oh, he's the man that you now belong to. He paid a lot of money for you Lisa, so now you must repay him with your body, your good looks, you're a very lucky girl Lisa to have a body like that, and you being so very young. Whoever gets to use you first is going to pay him an awful lot of money, and that is going to keep him in a good mood with you. You keep him happy and he will look after you really well. Now, come on, take a sip of your vodka it'll make you feel better, and don't worry, it's not drugged. There'll be no more of that Lisa. Only nice drugs from now on, drugs that will make you feel nice and relaxed, so that you can have a really good time, it's all part of their sexual fantasies you see, but you mustn't complain Lisa because that is the reason he has purchased you. We belong to him and we are here to do exactly as he tells us. Don't you worry princess you'll be a very skilled young lady in no time at all. You've swallowed sperm before haven't you Lisa? You've probably done that for boyfriends back where you used to come from. It doesn't matter now though princess, all that is behind you now. This is what counts, being here with me and Mister Saratov, and all the other girls, you'll meet them all soon Lisa. Oh I can't wait to get started on you, with your make-up and your clothes, you're going to love it here Lisa, oh Mister Saratov will probably insist that you change your name, he usually does. He will pick a name for you, and then that's who you'll be. All the other girls love it here. Oh there were one or two who were a bit reluctant in the beginning, but after they'd been `persuaded` and had received some money, they soon got their heads round the situation, which is, you have been bought for a price by Mister Saratov and so you now belong to him. One of the girls were really shy in the beginning, she didn't want to do anything with anybody, but once she had received some rewards she soon changed her ways and accepted her situation, just as you will Lisa. She really gets into it now, she is one of the highest paid girls here, she's always in

demand, and she makes Mister Saratov loads of money. Don't worry Lisa I'll show you all kinds of tricks that will make lots of money for him, just you wait and see how much he gives you to buy clothes, appropriate clothes Lisa, appropriate to the kind of work you'll be doing. Remember, the sexier you look the more money you'll make for him, come on now, drink your vodka, and then we'll have lunch with him.
Then I'll introduce you to some of the other girls who live here."
Lisa tried to sit up again offering the glass of vodka and coke to her host.
"I don't want this" she croaked, her throat as dry as sandpaper. "I don't want to be here, I want my mum, I want to go back home, please let me go back home." She began to cry.
Monica smiled at Lisa, but did not accept the glass that she was offering her. "Come on now sweetheart drink your vodka, and before you say anything else, I happen to know that it's your favourite drink. My friends in London told me all about you. They said that you and one or two of your friends like nothing better than to dress up and put make-up on so that you can gain entry to the night clubs. They also told me that you visit the pubs first to mix with all the nice boys, and that you lead them on and allow them to buy you drinks until it's time to go to the night clubs, isn't that right Lisa? That's how we got you. I was in the night club the night they spiked your drink, remember? Do you remember the boy you were kissing in there? Remember how you started to feel unwell? That was the drugs kicking in. Yes, that nice boy explained to the doormen that you'd had too much to drink and that he was taking you home in a taxi, except it wasn't a taxi Lisa, he was a friend of mine, we had it all planned out. I came back over here in an aeroplane, but you travelled back in a ship's cargo-container, and then by car. It took almost four days to get you here, they kept having to give you sedatives to keep you quiet. But, you're here now, and you're here to stay so you may as well get used to the idea. So, come on, drink your vodka, and just think, from now on you can dress just like you've always wanted to and put on as much make-up as you like. You're a woman now, isn't that what you're always telling your mum and your school friends? Well, now you'll get the opportunity to prove just how much of a woman you really are. You are going to be in for the experience of a life-time Lisa. Mister Saratov is going to allow one or two of his friends to watch as you have fun with your first customer so that they can see for themselves what you'll be like. He always likes to watch the new girls' first performances, it's only fair, after all, it's his money that has purchased you. Oh, you're going to love him Lisa, he'll treat you like a princess, he really will."

STRATFORD.

HENSINGHAM FLATS.

Mercer and Reynolds stood on the threshold of number 6b of the flats where the Angela Bates they were *really* looking for lived. A `mistake` had been made by inspector Colin Briggs, who had apologised unreservedly to Terry Mercer. They had rung the bell twice and had received no answer. Loud music could be heard from somewhere inside the building but they couldn't be sure it was coming from 6b. Someone opened the door from two doors along. A pretty, haggard-looking young mother carrying a baby in her arms called out to them. "What the fuck do *you* want? Can't you see they're not home, ringing fucking bells there like fucking Quasimodo, they're not in."
She gently waltzed the baby in her arms attempting to soothe the child by saying "Shoosh now."
Mercer stepped up to the woman producing his ID.
"We're looking for a certain Angela Bates do you know if she lives here?"
The young mother re-lit her roll-up and mumbled, "Huh lives? She's hardly ever in the fucking place. She gets herself away to fuck for days on end, and god knows where she goes. She has two or three different men that come there as well, that's when she is here, goodness knows which one of them fucks her…probably all of them, and she's always got good clothes on, all fashion-like, fancy bloody clothes…never fucking here, and my daughter can't get a house for love nor money, and she's got a kid and no bloody man, it's not right, her with her asthma and everything. Anyway, what's this fucking bitch done? Is she a whore, because I'll tell you something, they're all fucking at it round here, that's how they make their money now, since all those bastards cut all their benefits, fucking bastards that they are, it's made this whole block of flats a whore-house, so it has."
Samantha Reynolds stepped forward. "When was the last time you saw Angela here? Can you remember?"
The baby began to cry again, this time really loud. The woman had to raise her voice to be heard. "Two days ago, I saw her two days ago, but fuck knows when I'll see her again, it could be this afternoon or it could be next fucking Wednesday. Who knows? That's what I'm saying, my daughter can't get a house, and there's that bloody bimbo just comes and goes whenever she pleases, it's not right."
"Could you describe the gentlemen who come here to see her, any of them?"
The woman looked at Sam Reynolds suspiciously and shook her head.

"No, I never get a good look at them. When they come here it's always at night, but I know that one of them speaks with a foreign accent."

"Foreign accent you say, do you know what language specifically he speaks?" "Through the volume of the baby's crying she shouted, "No, he speaks English, but you can tell he's foreign if you know what I mean, he's got that fucking European twang."

Terry Mercer stepped forward. "What's your name?"

"What do you want to know my name for, I've got nothing to do with any of this shit whatever she's been up to, and don't you dare refer to me as the same as these fucking whores, because I'll tell you something-."

"No no no" said Mercer, we wouldn't dream of referring to you as that. No, I want you to do us a favour, and we'll make it worth your while." Terry opened his wallet and produced two twenty pound notes.

"All I want you to do is call this number the next time this Angela woman is home, or any time any of these gentlemen friends of hers' arrive, would you do that for us?"

"You get one thing clear here Mister, I'm no fucking snitch, and I'm not in the habit of helping the likes of you, because you're all as twisted as the criminals you pursue, in fact, you're as much criminals as they are, but I'll do it, because Christmas is coming up and I have to make sure that this wee one gets a good deal, that's the only reason I'm doing this, ok? Don't think that I'm a fucking grass, because I'm not."

"We won't take your help for granted, what's your Christian name?"

"It's Roxanne, you can call me Roxy."

Mercer pulled out a ten pound note and added it to the two twenties.

"Here you are Roxy, you just text me on this number if you don't want to phone me, and let me know the next time anybody comes to this flat, will you do that for us?"

Roxanne took the money and nodded.

"Yeah, I'll let you know."

"Just one more thing Roxy. "said Mercer, "If you get the chance, could you try and get a number plate of the vehicle they arrive in. If you could do that, we'd be very grateful. Again we would make it worth your while. I admire what you're doing here, looking after your daughter's baby, very decent of you."

"What the fuck are you going on about, this isn't my daughter's baby, this is mine, It's my fucking baby, oh, what are you going to say about that?

Something sarcastic no doubt, has that made me drop in your judgemental fucking eyes?"

"Not at all" replied Sam, "there's nothing but respect here Roxy, it's just that you look so young to have a daughter age enough to have children that's all."

"Listen here, I wasn't the first to have a fucking baby at the age of fourteen so don't try and patronise me because it just won't wash." Once again, the baby began to cry. "You'll have to be gone now, she's needing her feed, I'll let you know the next time anybody comes to the whore's house ok?"

"One good turn Roxy" said Terry smiling. "The more you find out for us, the more rewards you will receive, it's been an absolute pleasure talking with you Roxy, you have yourself a lovely day."

"Huh, that's impossible living among these bloody whores and pimps."

The baby began to roar. "I Know I know, fuck sakes, you're going to get fed, fuck, you'll have the nipples chewed right fucking off me the way you're fucking feeding just now...chew me up like a fucking piranha." Roxy re-entered her flat and slammed the door exceptionally hard. As Mercer and Sam Reynolds headed back down the stairs Sam said, "Well, that was an education, think you've met your match there sir, you know, the swearing. Do you see how horrible it sounds when people use continuous profanations?

"Can't say I noticed Officer Reynolds, I do know one thing though, the next time she gives us a tip-off, it's coming out of your pocket."

"The next time? You just gave her fifty quid, and she hasn't even given us any information yet."

"You just wait and see Samantha she'll be all eagle-eyed now if she wasn't before. We'll have our interview with Miss Bates before long, and she'll have no chance of dodging us whilst Roxy lives next door." As they boarded their vehicle Mercer smiled broadly as his colleague's sense of humour once again brightened his mood.

"Do you think it's because baby is so severe on Roxy's nipples that it makes her be so venomous in her vocabulary?"

The smile never left Terry's face.

"You just might have a point there Sam, although the worn nipples thing is probably down to years and years of drunk men chewing on them rather than the poor baby being the cause of the problem, but yes, it could well be the reason she hates everybody and everything in the whole world. You can tell with people like Roxanne what kind of life they've had. The only faces that *that* woman will ever trust will be the ones printed on the bank notes she possesses."

"Yeah well, let's hope she's trustworthy Terry, because you've just given her fifty quid for fuck all...as you would say sir."

KAUNAS.

LITHUANIA.

Lisa Jenson was beginning to come to terms with her predicament. One thing was for sure, there was no way whatsoever out of this situation, at least not at the present moment. She was going to be used by God knows how many perverted men and women and there was absolutely nothing she could do about it. She and her friends had experimented with drugs back home and so she wasn't as frightened as perhaps she would have been at the thought of being given drugs, which, according to Monica, was not perhaps, but imminent. If she was ever going to be able to escape from here then she would have to go along with the situation and look convincingly enough to them, that she had accepted her fate. She would win their confidence and would be cheerful and polite to everyone she came into contact with. No doubt the drugs would help her as these people took advantage of her and used her like a whore for their depraved purposes. Could she do that? She would have to do that. It was the one and only way that she'd ever be given an opportunity to escape this place. She sat now in the living room where she had recovered consciousness on one of the sofas dressed in a beautiful evening dress that came all the way down to her ankles. The dress was Lavender with silver inlays that sparkled under the light of the chandeliers overhead. Whoever had planned her abduction had done their homework on her because the dress fitted her like a glove. The woman called Monica had taken her upstairs to one of the very many bedrooms in the house and had pulled out this dress from a wardrobe. The dress looked like it was brand new and had cellophane draped over it...like it had been pre-bought especially for her. It was obvious that this Monica had been put in charge of her well-being. The sick bitch seemed actually excited about sharing sexual experiences with other people, especially as she was to be added to the menu. Lisa had given one or two of her closest `boyfriends' blow-jobs now and then but had never participated in full sex. That was going to change, and soon, but, she knew it was an absolute necessity if she were to obtain any opportunity of leaving this place, that she applied herself to the *task* in hand. It *would* be a task as well, there was no doubt whatsoever about that. She sat thinking about her mum and dad, and wondered if they would be worrying about her. Her dad had suffered from depression from when he was in the army and also had trouble with one of his legs from a shrapnel wound. Since he'd left the army he had suffered really badly with depression and she knew it was causing friction between her mum and him, to the point of dad accusing her of having an affair.

All that didn't matter now to her. She wasn't going to see them for a long time. As much as she loved them, she would have to put them completely out of her head and forget the fact that they even existed. In the meantime, she was a whore and nothing more than that. A cheap trick to satisfy the sexual depravities of God knows how many men and women. Maybe Monica was right, the drugs would no doubt help her through this. Meanwhile, she would make out to Monica, that she was her best friend in the world, and that she thought the world of her. If she could keep Monica happy, and this Mister Saratov whoever the hell he was, `happy`, then surely it wouldn't be too long before she would have the opportunity to get away from here. Once she had her bearings, she would find out where the nearest police station was, and then she'd report to them just exactly what was going on here. Lisa's thoughts were abruptly brought to a close when the door at the far side of this huge living room was opened. A man in his late sixties entered the room followed closely by Monica, who was now wearing a similar evening dress to that of her own. Monica's was pale blue. The man wore an evening dinner suit which was navy with a cream pin stripe. Already, Lisa put her escape plan into action. She rose from the sofa and curtseyed to the `gentleman`. He seemed overjoyed at this gesture. Monica's face lit up almost as brightly as the chandelier above her.

"Oh my goodness Mister Saratov" she exclaimed. "Isn't my Lisa so beautiful? What a beautiful little lady we have here."

The man, with pure white hair and a red face smiled gleefully at his new piece of meat as he reached out to take hold of Lisa's hand. "Shall we go and have dinner my angel? My name is Michael Saratov. And you're going to love it here."

THE ENGLISH CHANNEL. 2am.

Sophie Spencer Chloe Prowse Kirsty Crawford and Alison Green were all bound, hand and foot, and blind-folded. They hadn't been gagged simply because it was not necessary. They could scream their heads off if they so wished because it would do them no good whatsoever. The crew of this Belgian fishing boat were collaborating with the men who had paid their skipper ten thousand Euros to share between himself and his crew. They were currently sailing in the English Channel but would soon be entering French waters. They would sail along the French coast and then on to Belgium where the girls would disembark in a little port close to Zebrugge. From there, four different cars would take the girls on a very long journey all the way to Lithuania where they would be delivered to a certain Mister Saratov. All four of the girls had been heavily sedated. The `Syndicate` had discussed this before the girls left Great Britain.
To save any problems of sea-sickness the girls would be rendered unconscious, saving everyone involved a lot of trouble. If any of them regained consciousness before they reached their destination it wouldn't be a problem, they would simply be given more sedatives. Two men sat down below smoking cigarettes and drinking tea. It was a journey one of them had experienced many times. They, when they reached Belgium would not disembark The Marianne, but would stay on board for the full duration of the fishing trip, sometimes even lending a hand with the crew, this gesture done no harm whatsoever with the skipper of the boat regarding favours for future trips, although an unknown businessman in Britain paid them handsomely at the end of every trip. The skipper also knew why the two men were on the boat. Everyone has heard tales about wild fishermen who were desperate for female company, having spent four or five days performing hard labour out at sea, and so it was, that the two men, the two armed men were here to make sure that these pretty little things were not interfered with by rampant Belgian seamen. David Weaver and John Buckley sat with their cigarettes and mugs of tea looking at the unconscious girls. "Poor fuckers." said Weaver, a twenty-three-year old recidivist from central London. "They don't know what's in front of them, look at them John, they're no more than little girls." He took a drag of his cigarette. Weaver looked older than his twenty-three years with his shaven head and deep black stubble on a broad weather-beaten face. "Within weeks those fuckers in Lithuania will have them bouncing like bunnies with every Tom Dick and Harry who can afford their price-tag. Fuck they're beautiful girls John, are they not?"
"Yes they are" agreed Buckley, a thirty-eight old ex-soldier. "But it has nothing to do with us Davy boy, and don't you forget it. It is not our concern what they do with them

when we reach our destination, we get paid fucking good money just to ensure their safety across the water and that is as far as I go thinking about them, and talking about money, you need to stop throwing it about the pubs and shouting off to people what you do. Anyway, they're not as innocent as they look kiddo. Oh I've seen them, fourteen-year-old girls all fucking made up with their fancy make-up and hair-do's, fucking skirts up their arses. Yeah, in they prance into the night clubs, and before you know it they've enticed some poor fool into bed with them. The next thing the poor guy knows, he's being charged with having sex with a minor, and then his name is placed on a paedophile list. Some of them do time, and when they do, all the inmates kick fuck out of him because they've been told he's had sex with a child, it's all fucking wrong Davy boy. These little cock-teasing bitches here deserve everything that's coming to them. Here look." Buckley slid over to one of the girls and removed the blanket that had been draped over her. It was Chloe Prowse. "Look how they dress, they deliberately dress provocatively, fucking skirts, look at the legs on this." He pulled back the sheet further. "Look, fucking make-up and fancy jewellery, it's all to attract poor gullible men kiddo, trust me, they fucking know exactly what they're doing, they're all at it. There's a couple of them that come in to the gym that I go to, fucking bending over wearing those tight legging things they wear, and really tight tops with no bras on underneath, no, fuck them Davy, they attracted the wrong people and they've been netted. We didn't abduct them kid, we just escort them safely across the water and prevent any of those Belgian fucks up there from shagging them, and that's it, job done, and don't you ever think anything differently than that." He placed the blanket back over Chloe's legs.
"They are just fuck meat now Davy, and only have themselves to blame. They should have thought about the consequences before they started going around dressed like tarts." Buckley lit up another cigarette and snorted with laughter as he said; "Fuck, they'll get `tarted` just shortly Davy boy."
Weaver looked at Buckley, smiling. "Yeah, I agree with every word you say John, it's just that I can't help thinking about, you know...doesn't matter what they dress like, they're still only kids, and their mothers and fathers, they'll be worried sick, after all, it's not their fault their daughters-."
"Enough! Shut your fucking mouth boy. You better not be going soft kiddo because I'll tell you something right now, you seem to me the kind of cunt who would go blabbing to the filth and grass everybody up."
"No John, I was just-."
"Yeah, you were just. Let me tell you something now, and you'd better listen to me. All I have to do is tell Angela or Claire, or any of the rest of them, that you can't be trusted, and they would slice you up into a thousand pieces and feed you to the pigs. Now I'm

warning you, I don't ever want to hear you talking like that again, do you hear me?" Buckley's stare gave Weaver shivers down his spine. He had heard stories about John Buckley, and what he'd done to two soldiers in his same regiment when they had made a comment about a girl that Buckley had a photograph of. The girl happened to be Buckley's daughter. How he had reacted to those comments was the reason why he was expelled from the army. The full details had never been disclosed but it had been rumoured that he'd stuck his knife into one of the men's testicles and had hammered the other man's teeth with a claw-hammer until every tooth had been smashed to pulp. He continued to lecture Weaver. "The only reason I introduced you to the syndicate in the first place was because your dad always looked out for me, I was merely returning the favour…poor cunt would turn in his grave if he heard you getting all soft with yourself. Now I'll let this go…this time, but if you ever come out with shit like that again, I'll cut your fucking throat myself and throw you overboard, now do I make myself clear? Are we both on the same page now?"

"Yes John…I'm eh…I'm sorry, I just got a bit silly there, sorry."

"Ok, it's forgotten. Look, they're only fuck meat now and they are of no concern to us. There's an old saying David, and it's this, Fly with the crows, and you'll be shot at." He pointed to the girls again. "If they want to dress up like fucking sluts, then they should be prepared to be treated accordingly."

A104. STRATFORD.

Terry Mercer and Sam Reynolds were on their way back to Scotland Yard when Terry's phone buzzed loudly in his jacket pocket. "Sam, could you get my phone out and see what that message is please, I don't like using the phone when I'm driving, it's dangerous, and besides, it's against the law." Samantha smiled as she retrieved the old-fashioned phone from his jacket and then replied; "Oh it's against the law is it? Well, so is smoking in the car when you're driving but that doesn't stop you does it? Of course, poisoning my lungs with your filthy habit doesn't count as breaking the law in your eyes." Mercer did not respond in any way to his colleague's remarks, instead, he glanced at her as she read the message waiting to hear what it was and who it was from. "Well?"

"It says that as soon as you can you have to get yourself over to his place, apparently he has some important information regarding the transportation of the missing girls. Says he's found out from a reliable source how some of the girls are being transported out of the country. He also says bring a handsome payment as well as he could have kept this information to himself. The message was sent by…oh that can't be right, it says here the message was sent by a…Treble Clef. What, or who the hell is Treble-Clef?" Mercer smiled as he skilfully extracted a cigarette from the packet with one hand and then proceeded to light it. Exhaling smoke out of his window he said; "It's a snitch of mine, Geoff, can't remember his surname, a complete waste of a talent. He is an exceptional cello player, absolutely amazing, he used to play with the London Philharmonic orchestra."

"A cellist you mean?"

"Yes a fucking cellist, he's been all over the world and everything, I kid you not he is that good. It's just that he had this habit of taking things that did not belong to him. Things like cars and caravans and money from small town post-offices and the best of it is he's not even good at it. He's done more time than Big Ben, but still he persists. I try my best to keep him out of the slammer because old Geoff is very handy from time to time. The things that man overhears in pubs is unbelievable, how much money are you carrying with you Sam?"

"What?" said Sam incredulously, "Not much, about forty quid or something, but don't think for one minute that I'm giving it to an old man I have never met in my life and-."

"No, that's not enough, I'll have to go to the bank, I gave all my petty cash to Roxanne."

"Yes you did Terry, and she'll be sitting in the pub drinking it now as we speak, or loading up her syringe with a batch of freshly purchased shit, did you notice the holes in

her arms, and the scabs? Whenever she runs out of drink she'll just pick up her phone and tell you that Angela Bates is home, only when we get over there she'll say; "Oh, you weren't fast enough getting here, she's fucking cunting fucking gone, fifty quid please." Terry Mercer actually burst into laughter at Sam's remarks. He laughed heartily as he drove, quite taken aback at his new colleague's sense of humour. She was very skilful at using truths and possibilities, merging them together and delivering an extremely humorous punch-line. Wiping tears from his eyes he continued to drive. Now they were heading to Croydon to see a certain `Treble-Clef.`
God alone knew what Sam would think of this gentleman. Old Geoff had an eye for the ladies. He would say nothing to her regarding Geoff. It would be interesting to say the least how she would react to him.

The humour was short lived. A little while later as they drove towards Croydon on the A236 Samantha said; "Well, if what this Geoff man is telling us is true, then it's official, the girls *are* being transported out of the country. God knows how many have been taken Terry. Unless we can get these European authorities to work with us, or on our behalf then the chances of getting them back are less than slim."
Mercer sighed, nodding his head in agreement. He had a flash-back of Mandy Spencer pleading with him to bring her Sophie back home and another of Pamela and Steven Crawford falling to pieces and begging him to find Kirsty. He sighed again.
"Let's just see what old Geoff can tell us Sam, we'll take it from there, although, as you say, if those girls have already been transported over there into mainland Europe...well." His voice trailed off. To try and brighten the mood Sam said; "Yes but Terry, if we can get enough reliable information we can make sure that they don't take any more girls from this country, we can put a stop to their sickening games."
"Yeah, but try and tell that to Mandy Spencer or Pamela and David Crawford Sam, it would be little conciliation."

PINKERTON ROAD.

CROYDON.

Terry had instructed Samantha to text old Geoff and inform him that they were on their way to visit him and advise him to stay put in his flat until they got there. Treble Clef was waiting for Terry when he and Samantha arrived. Sam was expecting a really old man to answer the door but this man looked to be around fifty or fifty-five perhaps, although his attire would certainly reflect an elderly status. He had thick grey hair, neatly cut, quite a full face, ruddy complexion, probably owing to the copious amounts of whiskey he drank. She could smell whiskey off him now. He stood on his threshold wearing a white vest. The braces that hung over his shoulders protruded from a pair of navy blue trousers with a pale-white pin-stripe running through. He stood maybe five seven, five eight, no more than that, and he spoke with what Sam would describe as "an Original Cockney accent."
Treble-Clef's face lit up as soon as he saw Samantha.
"Cam in cam in I got some twelve bar for you Terry me boy. Is this your new gal then Tel, trainin` er up is ya? Watch im darlin, ar Tel's got` wanderin` ans so e as, al just go and get the `Carlisle to Settle on`."
Samantha looked at Terry as old Geoff headed into his small kitchen.
"He's got some twelve-bar for you Terry? What the hell is that is he talking some kind of code to you?"
"No no, it's just his way of talking, twelve-bar, as in Twelve-bar blues…news Samantha, news." Terry and Sam sat down on the small two-seater sofa. The flat was very tidy and his furniture was well arranged. A classy looking old sideboard played host to numerous music awards that Treble-Clef had accumulated over the years. Over in the far corner of the small living room placed neatly in their stands stood two beautiful cellos. Sam had always associated this instrument with the double bass, however she did know that the cello was played with a bow and that the bass was plucked with fingers.
That was as far as her knowledge extended regarding orchestral stringed instruments.
In less than five minutes all three were seated and drinking tea from bone-china cups.
"What have you got for me Geoff." said Terry glancing at his watch.
The old man put down his cup onto the saucer on the coffee table.
"First of all Terry, pardon me for being so blunt, but what has you got fur me, me old mucka? I got to survive you understand."
Terry pulled out his wallet and peeled out five twenty-pound notes.
"Here, and if your eh, twelve-bar is shit, I'm taking them back, so leave them on the table until you've told me what it is you know."

"Oh it's good Tel but not for the poor `gels` it aint` He took another sip from his cup. "There's a fishing boat that comes over ere all the way from Belgium.  Don't ask me where-about' it docks but it's `rand ere` somewhere. They smuggles the gels onto that boat and it takes em over to Europe, again, don't ask me where. It makes this trip `bat once a mumph.` There's a syndicate of abat six of em kidnaps the gels and sells em to these European fuckas. Sorry for the French darlin`. They inform these businessmen abat the gels and they sells em off. This fishing boat comes and takes em away, and that's all I got Tel."

Terry stared at Treble-Clef and said, "But you wouldn't happen to know the name of the fishing boat would you Treble? You know all that and yet you don't know the name of the boat."

Treble-Clef picked up the twenty-pound notes and thumbed through them. When he realized there was no more money coming his way he said; "Yeah I knows it kid, I'll tell ya Tel, it's called The Marianne."

Terry sipped his tea. "Are you sure that's all you know Treble, because if I find out-."
"Honest Tel, that's all I got, that's the lot, if I gets any more info you know you'll be the first to ere it, I promise ya kid, and thank e kindly for the eh… for the pink Lizzies." (Treble's reference to the twenty-pound notes).

As the two detectives made their way back to HQ Samantha said, "What do you think Terry? Do you think he's telling you the truth? The Marianne? It doesn't sound much like a Belgian name to me for a fishing boat. He's not coming out with a cock and bull story is he Terry?"

Once again Terry Mercer lit up a cigarette. "The glass is always half empty to you isn't it Sam. I happen to know that Geoff is telling the truth, simply because he knows the consequences if he tells me lies…he's only ever lied to me once, and it cost him three months in the slammer…that's how I know he's telling the truth. As soon as we get back we'll look into this fishing boat and where exactly it's registered. I want to know the owner's name and address plus I want to know all the names of the crew and the last time each of them used the toilet, ok? You can get straight on with that when we get back."

Samantha didn't want to ask Terry what he'd be doing while she was busy seeking out this information.

"Well Terry, let's hope this Marianne boat exists because to date you've planted a hundred and fifty quid of your own money and there's no guarantee that it'll bear any fruit. Roxanne will be adjusting her budget even as we speak…she stands to make a lot of money, and I wouldn't mind betting that treble-clef will be heading down to his local

toasting the health of some fictitious Belgian fishermen."
"Oh you wouldn't mind betting would you, well on this occasion I won't take your money from you, because I have every faith in Roxanne and old Treble-clef…you'll see. You have to learn how to trust the right people Sam. That old badger wouldn't lie to me. If he says there's a boat called the Marianne then you can bet your life there is."
"Well, as far as I was led to believe, you can't buy trust.
These people that you're trusting has cost you a small fortune…that's not trust, that's-."
"Hey, that'll do, you just get on with what I've told you to do ok? Your opinion is duly noted…couldn't depend on your succour could I…smart-ass."
"Yes sir" Samantha answered, smiling to herself at how quickly she could ruffle her superior's feathers.
"I'll get onto it as soon as we get back sir."
"Yes you will. What do you know about fucking fishing boats…or Treble-fucking-clef."
She decided to try another angle to keep him calm. "I know sir, you're right I know absolutely nothing when it comes to musical instruments or fishing boats. I'll have to shake this habit of looking at everything suspiciously, trust, as you say sir." Mercer looked at his partner, frowning. "You just get yourself busy finding out about that boat and its' crew, that's all you need to worry about."
"Of course sir, I kind of forgot myself there, it's a bad habit of mine. I always seem to speak my opinion out loud. I'll get onto it as soon as we're back at HQ, oh, and I'll pay for lunch next time, it's not fair you spending all your money on informants all the time."
"I can have you moved as quick as fucking lightning missy, don't push it with your sarcasm smart-ass, I'm warning you…fucking treble-clef."

KAUNAS.

LITHUANIA.

Lisa Jenson sat at the huge dinner table with Monica and the man named Saratov. They'd all had coffee after their meal, and were now sipping glasses of wine.
She tried her best to look as vulnerable and also as humble as she could.
Lisa had never been in a situation as strange as this in her entire life, or as frightening. Here she was, dressed up in the most beautiful evening-dress she had ever seen along with one of the most beautiful women she had ever set eyes upon. Always, at the back of her mind was her plan. It wasn't much of a plan, but then she didn't have much of a choice. Secretly she was petrified about losing her virginity. She had heard so many different stories about what happens when you lose your virginity. Very soon, she feared, she would find out for herself. From what she could gather, this man in front of her had paid someone a lot of money to purchase her. No doubt the people who had abducted her would be the recipients of Saratov's payment.
Who the hell those people were, she had no idea but by what Monica had been saying, when referring to the `other girls` she guessed that she wasn't the first to be abducted. Lisa wondered if the other girls would speak English. If they did, then at least at some point she'd be able to share her story with them. Perhaps they may even join in with her `escape plan`. That was all in the future though, but she knew that it would be some time before she'd even be introduced to them. Right now, was what she had to deal with, and it wasn't going to be easy. Saratov and Monica were talking to each other in a foreign language, occasionally glancing at her and smiling.
Saratov sat at the head of the table with Monica and herself seated on each side, three people sitting at a table that could probably cater for fifty or more.
Monica rose from her seat and came round to sit beside Lisa.
"Did you enjoy your meal Lisa?" She said, as she sat down.
"Yes thank you, it was very nice."
"We're going into one of the lounges just shortly to relax.
Now, you remember what I told you about what the girls do here?"
Lisa looked to the floor despondently. "Yes Miss, I remember."
"Well, Mister Saratov and I have been talking, and we've decided to try something tonight. Instead of getting you to participate immediately, we think it would be better for you if we let you watch one or two of the girls in action. Let you see how much they enjoy what they do. Now, as I told you, most of the girls here

always like to take a little something to help them get into the mood, after all, we are not automatically attracted to everyone we meet, so they snort a little cocaine before they start. Have you ever tried snorting cocaine Lisa?"

"No Miss, I haven't…I've smoked dope, just a little bit…it made me sick."

"Yes, it can do that but you won't be smoking dope tonight Lisa.

Tonight we'll let you try a little cocaine you'll be surprised at how good it will make you feel. It will also relax you, which is most important, because some of Mister Saratov's customers pay him a lot of money, and so they expect to be received by very willing girls. Anyway, you just watch tonight with Mister Saratov and I and you'll soon get into the swing of it. While we're watching Lisa, if at any time you feel like you'd like to join in with any of the girls then you feel free, some of the girls like to please each other as well to entertain their guests, and of course, this always excites the customers."

Lisa was absolutely horrified at Monica's last sentence.

"Now, before we go through to the lounge, we must get you out of your evening dress and into something more…em…appropriate shall we say. By the way, Mister Saratov bought the dress especially for you, do you have something you'd like to say to him Lisa?

`Back to the plan`.

"Lisa once again curtseyed to Mister Saratov.

"Thank you so much sir for buying this beautiful evening gown for me, I am very grateful, thank you."

Saratov rose from his chair, and speaking in his broken accent said,

"My goodness you're welcome, and may I say, it was done with the help of the beautiful lady in front of you. She knew exactly what size to buy and what colour would suit you best. She going to be very helpful to you in the forth-coming months. She will party with you no matter who comes to take you, male or female, or both, Monica will be with you." The man had a kindly face and could pass as anyone's grandfather. He looked charming. He reminded her of a lollipop man who used to help the children to cross the road. His voice too, melodic, he sounded and looked like the nicest old man you could ever wish to meet. How looks can deceive. Her desperate situation was beginning to worsen. Where she was finding her positivity from she had no idea, but positive she was, and would have to remain that way until such times as she could find a way out of this utter nightmare. She also knew that there would be multiple unpleasant experiences to endure before any chance of escape would materialise.

SCOTLAND YARD.

BROADWAY VICTORIA.

It had taken Samantha Reynolds less than twenty minutes to find out all the relevant information about the fishing boat The Marianne. The fact that the boat even existed had proved *her* opinion to be wrong. Terry would be elated. What was strange about the Marianne was the fact that it was indeed a Belgian-based fishing boat, but this boat had been licensed to sail in British waters. The last recorded skipper of the boat was a British man who went by the name of Thomas Mullery. The actual crew members were not obtainable which was perfectly understandable as members would undoubtedly change from time to time. The boat's last official visit to Britain was three weeks previous to the present date. It had docked in Canvey Island. The visit before that, it had docked just North East off Dartford, before that, nothing. There were no further records. Sam entered Terry's office and informed him of the information she had acquired about the Marianne.
"You see that Sam? Now let that be a lesson to you. I knew all along that Treble-clef would be telling us the truth...intuition Sam, you'll have to learn about that."
"Oh intuition Terry? So it has nothing at all to do with the fact that you gave this old dodger a hundred quid. It was all done with intuition, nothing at all to do with money changing hands. All these things you talk about, you know, trust and honesty and ...eh, intuition, none of it concerns money then?"
"What the hell are you implying Sam, come on, spit it out."
"I'm saying that you wouldn't have got any of this information without you paying for it, so, I'm saying that it has nothing at all to do with bloody honesty or trust...or intuition, it has to do with bribery and threats. If you hadn't paid Treble or whatever the hell his name is a hundred pounds, then we'd be no further forward with this case. He knows he's going to get paid by you as soon as he passes on any information to you. If he thought for one minute you wouldn't pay him, he would tell you absolutely nothing and fine well you know it, so please, don't go on about honesty and integrity and trust because none of that exists here does it?" She knew she had yet again overstepped her mark and was just preparing to be bombarded with a lengthy disciplinarian lecture when Terry's phone buzzed on his desk. His face lit up like a Christmas tree.
It was a text message from Roxanne. There was, it had to be said, a certain amount of deciphering that had to be done, but not much. Her exact words were; *That fucking blonde fucker is home if u r interested.*

Samantha laughed. "Yeah, that lady has a way with her words does she not Terry, there's no messing about with Roxanne is there. Now, do you have enough cash on you to deal with your intuition Terry, because I've only got about thirty quid on me."
"I kid you not Samantha" said Mercer putting on his jacket. "You're about this close to getting your arse kicked back onto the beat with the other bobbies, you just keep this sarcasm thing going and see where it lands you."
Samantha took a chance. She stood and wrapped her arms around her superior and said, "You wouldn't do that to me Terry would you, you like me too much to do that to me, and besides, who would you get to run for your cigarettes and sandwiches." She pecked him on the cheek, which actually took Terry a little by surprise, and melted his `anger` "Go and get the car you crazy bitch, and don't be all day doing it."

Less than an hour later they were standing on the threshold of Roxanne Styles' home. "Here goes" said Samantha, "Another lesson in how to use as many swear-words as is humanly possible in one sentence." She smiled at her superior as he simply replied to her, "Be Quiet." Before the door was answered they heard the baby crying loudly from inside. There was a rustle of chains and a lot of clicking noises before finally the door was opened. Roxanne did not disappoint Samantha.
"What the fuck are you doing here? She's home now, did you not get my fucking message? What the fuck is the point of me giving you information if you're not going to trust me, have you been to her door, because I can tell you now she was in half a fucking hour ago. If she's not there now, then that's not my fault...should have got here a lot quicker shouldn't you."
Mercer only smiled at Roxanne. "I know that Roxanne, I am here to pay you respect for the favour. As far as getting here sooner is concerned then I would have been faster if not for this fucker here beside me driving at the same speed as a steam-roller. In future I'll drive myself and then I know that I will arrive at a reasonable time. Here, please accept this with our gratitude Roxanne, and there'll be more."
Roxanne snatched the fifty pounds from Mercer's hand, dressed in her faded jeans and off-white tee-shirt stained with what Samantha hoped was baby food, and grunted something about not being a fucking grass and that she didn't want to be seen at the door while he was knocking on the whore's door.
It was painfully obvious that she wasn't wearing a bra, and she noticed that Terry couldn't help glancing at her ample breasts as he spoke with her.
As if the baby inside knew the situation, it began to scream even louder than before, causing Roxanne to close the door on their faces.
"She's a honey isn't she Terry? You couldn't wish for a nicer woman on God's good

earth, what a breath of fresh air she is."
Mercer and Samantha Reynolds walked the few steps to Angela Bates' door. Much to their surprise the door was answered almost immediately, by a very well-dressed young woman clad in black dress trousers with a pink silk shirt and beautiful black suede boots. Her blonde hair shone. Mercer addressed the woman. "Miss Angela Bates?"
"Yes, I'm Angela Bates, what can I do for you?"
Mercer produced his ID. "No doubt you will have heard on TV or radio that there are a number of girls being abducted from the surrounding areas of London. We were wondering if you have heard anything regarding these incidents?"
"What do you mean by that?" she replied arrogantly.
"Well, we just wondered if you'd seen or heard anything regarding these girls. Did you know any of them personally?"
"No I don't, and may I ask you why you have decided to come to my door, I mean, have you asked any of my neighbours if they've heard anything?
Or is it that you've been given my name by some bull-shit informer lying to you that I am part of these kidnappings. Listen here, I work with children every day, children from the ages of four up to seven year olds. I have been at the Carousel Nursery for coming up to nine years. You have my blessing to check all this out for yourselves. I am second in command at the centre and am looked upon as a trust-worthy guardian for these children. So, why on earth would you be asking me if I knew anything about the abduction of these poor unfortunate girls. I am deeply offended that you come here asking me if I know anything about them. Whoever gave you my name is leading you a merry dance I'm afraid. Now, unless you are here to arrest me or you have unmitigated evidence that I am guilty of something, then I would ask you to leave, and please do not bother me again unless it is for something worth-while, now, if you'll excuse me I have lots to do."
Samantha stepped in and took over the situation, although she'd been told not to, in fact, never to. "Miss Bates, we were given information that a young lady was abducted from here in Stratford recently. We also happen to know about your shop lifting expeditions in recent years as well as the suspended sentence you were given for grievous bodily harm, when you attacked one of the shop-keepers you had been stealing from. So don't stand there as if you have just qualified for citizen of the year because we both know that that will never happen. We have every right to investigate you and will do as many times as we wish both now and in the future, and you have our blessing to check up on our sources of information. My colleague here was merely being polite to you to try and save your face. I on the other hand will be scrutinising every move you make so be warned...you're being watched. Tread very carefully from

now on. Now, you have yourself a nice fucking day sweetie."
Samantha turned away from Angela Bates' door. Before Terry had a chance to say anything to her she stepped back up to Roxanne's door and knocked loudly.
"What the hell are you doing Samantha?"
The door was snatched open.
"What, what the fuck do you want now? I've given you-."
"Shut up Roxanne and listen to me carefully. I have proof that you are running some kind of prostitution game from here. I'm not really interested in what you do, or your daughter for that matter. What I am interested in is, the fact that you willingly take money from my partner here for information which is your dutiful right to give. Now, you just give him his hundred pounds back and we'll turn a blind eye on your whoring, but if you refuse then just wait here for fifteen minutes and then we'll return with a warrant for your arrest, now what in the fucking stinking name of ruddy hell is it going to bloody be Roxanne?"
Terry Mercer was completely gob-smacked. Firstly, about his partners' audaciousness, and secondly where the hell Samantha had the time to gain all this information. He was impressed to say the least. Samantha had answered a lot of questions he'd been asking himself about her, whether or not she was cut out to be a detective.
Did she have the right material to make a first class investigator?
She had just inadvertently answered them all.
Roxanne returned to the door and offered Terry the hundred pounds.
Whether or not he would have taken it they would never know because Samantha gently pushed the money back into Roxanne.
"Take it this time Roxanne, but no more ok?"
"Yeah, understood."
"Good" said Samantha, now you get back in there and deal with that punter you have waiting on your sofa, good business is where you find it…and make sure you look after that baby. I don't want to be coming back here to arrest your arse for negligence ok? Sore nipples or not, you feed that baby Roxanne."
Not a single word was spoken by Reynolds or Mercer as they made their way back to the car. Once seated inside Mercer said; "I knew it, I knew you were a hard bastard right from the first day I set eyes on you. You're a real nasty bitch aren't you Sam."
Samantha turned to look at him. "I am when I think I can see someone being taken a lend of. I've never liked those types of people, people who take advantage of other people's good nature.
" Oh, so you think I've got a good nature then Sam?"
"You ever refer to me as a fucker again, and you'll see what kind of nature I have."

"Listen, how did you get all that information about those two women?"
"I have snitches too you know, I'm not an absolute beginner."
"You and your leather jackets...you *are* a bad bastard bitch I just knew it." said Mercer smiling.

KAUNAS.

LITHUANIA.

Lisa Jensen sat beside Monica in a semi-circle of comfortable soft-chairs in a small lounge. She was in a state of consternation. She knew why she'd been brought in here. It was to introduce her mind to the activities that the young women participated in. It was also, supposedly to put *her* mind at rest. In front of her was a small coffee table with several small clear polythene bags each containing white powder. Monica had dressed her in denim shorts and a vest-top and had applied some make-up to her face. She knew only too well what the white powder was and was now wondering when she'd be invited to snort some of it. All the time in her head she thought about her plan. It was the hardest thing in the world to do, to pretend that you enjoy something when all the time you abhor it. However, she knew that if she was ever going to get the chance to escape she would have to do exactly that.
There were twenty soft chairs in this semi-circle and most of them were now occupied by guests or `customers` of Mister Saratov. There were men and women of all ages seated around the chairs. Monica leaned into her whispering, "Are you ok Lisa? This is going to be fun."
Lisa only smiled, somewhat timidly.
"Ok, now you do just like I show you and you'll feel an awful lot better than you do now I can promise you that." Monica offered Lisa her hand and led her to the table in front of them. "Everyone? This is Lisa. She is a new girl and as far as I know this will be her first time snorting cocaine. Feel free to come and introduce yourselves to her as the night progresses, but remember, she is not on the menu tonight ok? That will have to wait for a few days I'm afraid, but whatever price Mister Saratov puts on her, I'm sure she'll be worth every penny. So, would you all like to say hello to Lisa?"
All of the guests rose to their feet and said hello to the girl who had no idea of why her life had changed for the worst in such a short time. To say this was a nightmare would be an understatement of the highest magnitude. Nervously she got down on her knees with Monica who then handed her a straw. "Now, you just watch what I do Lisa, and then you copy me, ok?"
Lisa nodded reluctantly. Five minutes later, the teenager had snorted two lines of cocaine. She was then led back to her seat and placed back down gently onto her chair. Within seconds, she felt completely at ease. In fact, she felt wonderful. Her head felt numb, almost like she was drunk, but she wasn't drunk, she was in full control of her

feelings, in fact she felt more in control of herself than she had ever felt before. Lisa Jensen was as high as a kite. Monica rose from her seat and headed out of the room. Lisa could only smile as she watched different men and women squeezing and feeling Monica's bottom as she moved past them. Never once did she object to this, and only smiled to the people as she made her way past them. A few moments later she returned with drinks for herself and for Lisa. "Here you are my little princess, an extra-large drink for you and I and there's plenty more where that came from. How are you feeling now Lisa?" she said, smiling broadly at the teen.

"I feel really good thank you. I'm a little dizzy, but I feel really relaxed now."

The tragedy of the situation was the fact that Lisa wasn't telling any lies. Everything around her now seemed so different. Everybody here was friendly. Even through the haze of her high, she kept thinking that someday soon, probably most of the people who were in this room would eventually end up having sex with her. The difference now being, that she didn't fear the situation any more. She took a large drink of the vodka and coke that Monica had brought her.

She really was relaxed. Suddenly the lights dimmed. The coffee table had been removed. In front of them was a huge black sofa that would seat about six people. Two girls appeared from behind a curtain each dressed in swim-suits and high heels. Both of the girls looked beautiful, and none of them looked to be the slightest bit nervous. It was as if they were familiar with the situation.

The girls introduced themselves to the guests and done a fancy little twirl and then sat back down. One of the girls then said to the guests that they would both be available for a party later on in the evening. To give their potential customers an insight as to what they could expect they proclaimed that they would now put on a show to show off their skills. After only a few minutes of gentle petting, the two teenage girls then began to perform full oral sex on each other, much to the guests' delight, who then cheered their approval. Lisa watched in fascination as these two girls exposed themselves to the onlookers.

"No inhibitions here" thought Lisa to herself. The girls had frolicked around with each other for about twenty minutes or so, although frolicked would hardly be the appropriate word. It was full-blown oral sex they were having.

Much to Lisa's surprise, one of the girls stood and invited anyone to join in with them and exclaimed that of course, there would be no charge at this point. Monica placed an arm around Lisa's shoulder.

"Would you like to join in with them Lisa? It would be a start for you."

Lisa declined but then said to her so as not to offend, "I'm enjoying watching them Monica, but I think I'd rather learn with you...on our own in a private room, if that's ok with you."

"I understand sweetheart" Monica replied. "Before you know it Lisa, you'll be making as much money as these girls in front of you. I will personally see to that. You and I are going to be Mister Saratov's top earners. Now, come on, let's go and mingle with the guests, within a few weeks you are going to know them all in a very intimate manner."

Siberiastraat

Antwerp, Flanders

BELGIUM. 3.am.

The rain was torrential as the girls were escorted from the fishing boat The Marianne. All four girls were feeling sluggish and heavy-hearted. One by one different cars pulled up in the cobbled court-yard of the industrial harbour, each vehicle taking one girl with them. Sophie Spencer was the first to be driven away. There was a middle-aged man driving this car and a woman about thirty years old sitting with her in the back seat. The woman had cropped hair like one would imagine a military person would have. The only words she spoke to Sophie were to ask her if she needed to go to the toilet. Sophie had nodded her head but the driver drove off. Two or three minutes later the car came to a halt. Now the woman looked directly at Sophie as she said, "I will only warn you once. If you try in any way to attract attention to us, I will personally see to it that you will be gang-raped and your family back in Britain will die. You will talk to me when I speak to you and only when I speak to you, do you understand what I've just told you, nod your head." Sophie did as she was told.

"We have a very long journey in front of us and so we will spend a night or perhaps two, in motels. Whilst we are staying in these motels you will act like we are friends. You will smile and laugh and you will talk to no-one unless either myself or John here are present." Do you understand?"

"Yes," Croaked a very frightened Sophie Spencer.

"If you obey these things I have told you, then we will have a very pleasant journey. If you do not co-operate with us or if you make a nuisance of yourself, then expect to be dealt with very harshly, do you understand me?"

Sophie nodded her head again. The woman got out of the car and escorted her into the public latrines. She pointed to one of the cubicles and informed her that she would wait right here for her in the cleansing area. The woman then glanced at her watch and informed Sophie to be as quick as possible.

Sophie Spencer had never known fear like this in her entire life. The threats the woman had made to her regarding her family, the reason why she'd been abducted, the strangers who had bound her and drugged her and fondled her and groped her, it was all too much for Sophie and she began to break her heart, sobbing uncontrollably. The woman outside in the foyer calmly spoke through the door to her in a more sympathetic manner than she had been. "Come on now Sophie, it's not going to be all bad girl. You are going to be treated very well if you behave. You're a good girl I know, and I know that this is all a big shock to you, but you'll be fine, you'll see, so come on, stop crying no-one is going to hurt you if you behave yourself. We are going now to a nice bed and breakfast place where you can sleep in a very comfortable bed after a nice breakfast, you don't have anything to worry about."

"I just want to go home cried Sophie, that's all I want, I won't say anything to anyone I promise you, if you'll just let me go home."

"Sophie, you know that that is not going to happen. You'll just have to get used to the idea and once you do, then everything will become a lot easier. I am not your enemy Sophie. I am your friend and companion for this journey. I am being paid to make this journey as comfortable and pleasant as I possibly can for you, and so is John our driver. We are not going to harm you. We are simply here to escort you to your new home. Whether or not you get the chance to return home is a matter for you and your master to discuss, my job is just to escort you there. None of this has anything to do with me Sophie. So, come on, dry your eyes and make the best of the next couple of days that we will spend together."

"My master? I don't have a master, I am not a servant or a slave, I'm just an ordinary school-girl who was minding her own business on her-."

"Now that's enough Sophie, come on, John and I are hungry, and so must you be. We'll get you into something more comfortable for you to wear, I have clothes here for you and toiletries, come on." In the small cubicle Sophie saw a window opened up. It would be large enough for her to crawl through, but where would she go? She didn't even know where she was. All she knew was she wasn't in Great Britain anymore, and anyway, she thought about the woman's threats and decided not to try and escape, undoubtedly, the threat to her family was very real. Eventually, Sophie exited the toilet and joined her `captor`. To her utter surprise, the woman embraced her, patting her gently on her shoulder, and once again repeated, "Everything is going to be fine Sophie, we are going to take good care of you. I had to speak harshly to you because everything I said is true, but now we have got all that out of the way we can be friends. All those other girls who were in the boat with you are being told the very same things. You are all heading to the same destination, but of course, it's a lot safer for us if we escort you all separately, not that there's anyone here looking for you, but you know, it is better to be safe than sorry isn't it." The embrace was held for a further full minute while the woman repeated assurances to the frightened fifteen-year-old. Finally, she pulled away from Sophie and half whispered, "Come on baby, let's get a nice hot bath for you and some breakfast, that will make you feel better huh? It'll be better than travelling in that dirty stinking fishing boat with those foul-mouthed low-lives." In a few moments, they were back in the car and heading off to their first port of call, which, according to the woman, was only a couple of miles from where they were, wherever the hell this was, thought Sophie to herself. And then she remembered what the woman had said as she got into the car. *"Back in Britain."* The realization of the fact that she was no longer in Britain frightened her more than the abduction itself. Right here and now, she loved her mum and her brother more than she had ever loved them before in her life.

BELGRAVIA.

CENTRAL LONDON. 7AM.

John Buckley trusted no-one. Even the people who were paying him large sums of money for escorting the girls across into Europe were warned that if they fucked him about just once, they would regret it for the rest of their lives, if they survived. In the three days that had elapsed since he'd been on the boat with young David Weaver, his mind had given him no rest whatsoever. He had tried to put it out of his head about the weakness in the boy, and the compassion he'd felt for the girls and the girls' parents. David's father had looked after him when he was a kid and had helped him on many an occasion in times of trouble, but that said, sentimentality would not help anyone should any information leak out into the public about the disappearance of these young girls. As it stood now, Buckley was building up a nice little nest-egg for himself with his trips on the Marianne, and he did not want anything interfering with his financial growth. He sat now at a kitchen table in a house in Lyall Street drinking a glass of chilled beer. Across the table from him sat Angela Bates and a young woman called Claire Redgrave. Bates got Buckley's full attention as she casually informed him that the police had been to visit her asking questions about the missing girls. Buckley placed his glass on the table and looked into Bates' face, waiting for her to continue. She continued confidently, informing him that there was nothing at all to worry about and that business would continue as normal. He looked from side to side shaking his head as he addressed the two women.
"Nothing to worry about? Are you for real? The police have been to see you asking questions about the girls and you say there's nothing to worry about? I'll tell you something for nothing right now, if you hadn't just paid me five thousand pounds I'd be round this table and sticking my fist right into your thick fucking heads...nothing to worry about! They're gonna be watching you like a fucking eagle on a rabbit. They'll be following you around like your fucking shadow, how can you be so stupid as to sit there and tell me there's nothing to worry about. They could be outside now in an unmarked car watching this house...Jesus Christ talk about dumb fucking blondes! You're unbelievable you really are!"
"Have you finished?" said Angela Bates calmly.
"Can I say something now? I'm telling you there's nothing to worry about because there isn't. From now on, and until such times that I tell you different, Claire here will be conducting all business concerning further abductions. Of course I know the filth will be

watching me, how stupid do you think I am? I'm going to throw them a red-Herring or two to keep them occupied and out of your way.

You won't see me again after tonight, but I shall be working peripatetically for a while. I'll be up and down from here to the midlands, and don't worry I shan't be participating in any of the abductions. I shall merely be sussing out potential girls and by the way, as far as sticking your fist in my fucking thick head is concerned, I would tread carefully if I were you when it comes to making threats. I could make a phone call tonight, and by tomorrow morning John Buckley would become just someone I used to know, and our main man at the top of the tree wouldn't even question me about it. Your main concern just now is your subordinate. You make sure you can trust him because if I hear any more stories about young boys flashing hundred pound notes about pubs and boasting to all and sundry that he is part of a syndicate, then I will have to immediately terminate our previous agreement."

Buckley lifted his glass, taking a sip of his beer and nodding his head.

He had heard similar stories concerning David Weaver.

The situation regarding David Weaver had now been brought to a close.

A decision had been made.

"You don't have to worry about that anymore." He said to the blonde. "I'll deal with it, and anyway, I don't need anyone else on that boat with me, I can handle it on my own."

Claire Redgrave intervened.

"It doesn't matter what *you* think, John says that you should be accompanied so you'll be accompanied. Find another partner, and this time find someone who you can trust, because we have reason to believe that it was your present partner who put the CID onto Angela's arse, but I'm warning you now, don't you fuck this up in any way. You might be one of those bad-boy soldiers we all hear about, but like Angela says, you can be disposed of, more easily than you think."

Buckley stared at Claire Redgrave across the table inwardly imagining the raven-haired beauty bent over his kitchen top and he drawing the knife straight across her throat as she gargled her last breath. He stood up and took his glass over to the sink, rinsing out the tumbler before placing it neatly in the draining tray. "Listen John" said Angela Bates. "We don't want you leaving here downhearted, all we're saying is, make sure you get someone we can all trust. It's a shame about your young friend David, and we know how his father had helped you out and everything when you were younger, but the lad can't keep his mouth shut. He's boasting to the young easily-impressed girls that he dates how he's involved in top-secret deals and if the wrong ears hear him talking like-."

"I know, I know, I said I'm dealing with it, just give it a rest will you, I'll deal with it!"

Claire Redgrave smiled at him. "Listen John and I don't want you taking this the wrong way, this is not a suggestion that you are weak in any way or form, but we know how close you were to the boy's father, and we'd perfectly understand if you thought you'd have trouble dealing with him. If this in fact is the case, then we can appoint someone else to see to it, so don't think-."

"I'm telling you for the last time, it'll be dealt with…have either of you never made a mistake?"

Angela Bates smiled at him. "You prove to us John that we haven't, and then we'll be happy girls."

CROYDON.

Geoffrey Marsden (Treble-clef) was miles away in his head as he sat with his glass of Johnny Walker and tonic listening to Pierre Fournier playing Dvorak Cello Concerto. He had many favourites but Fournier was right up there simply because he had the pleasure of meeting the man in person one evening long ago in Paris. It was in the late seventies and it was a meeting he would never forget. The cellist had taken the time to share stories with Geoffrey and gave him advice on how to improve his playing. To Geoffrey Marsden, it was like talking to God himself.

As he listened to the soothing music Treble remembered with fondness his days before the drink finally ruined his professional career. There was another life that he belonged to, another realm. He had the tools to make his dreams come true and fulfil every ambition he'd set his heart on, but alas, old Johnny Walker had taken over his life and indeed had taken precedence over all else in his life, his wife included.

A tear rolled down his face as he sipped his beloved beverage, the same beverage in fact that had played a major role in the destruction of all his dreams and achievements, and had led to the eventual expulsion from the London Philharmonic Orchestra. Treble had his earphones on at a very high level setting as he reminisced all the good times. He was just kissing his beautiful wife when Terry Mercer's ginormous hand roughly pulled the earphones from his head, making him jump with fright and making him spill his beloved and cursed Johnny Walker. "Christ and Jesus Tel, what the fuck? You coulda killed me mucca. You shoulda rang the bladdy bell I awmost ad art attack mite.

"Come on Treble you were the one who called us, so we're here. What delightful eh twelve-bar do you have for us today?"

Mercer's abrupt interruption was immediately forgiven as he handed Treble a bottle of Johnny Walker. Samantha Reynolds sat transfixed for the next twenty minutes or so as she listened to Treble informing Terry of what he had overheard in a pub across the city. Even though she tried her best to translate what he was actually saying, she found it impossible to keep up with this banter which was all Greek to her. However, Terry sat writing down details as Treble continued to disclose his information. Eventually, he came to a close and half-heartedly looked to Terry for further payment. Mercer once again pulled out his wallet and peeled out some notes. Treble politely put the notes into his pocket without counting them, which, Sam guessed was a mark of respect to Terry.

"Does ya want some rosy before you go Tel, it won't take me long to make a pot of brew` mucca."

"No, we have to be going Geoff, we've got lots to be getting on with."

"Yes" interrupted Samantha, "He has to go to the bank to get some more money Mister Marsden, maybe some other time though."

Mercer glanced at Samantha, taking note of her sarcasm.

Outside of Treble's flat Terry and Samantha climbed into their car.

Putting on her seatbelt she said, "I only caught bits and bobs of what he was saying Terry. I heard something coherent about a young man named David, am I right?"

"Yeah that's right Sam. According to Treble, there's a young guy going round the pubs flashing off money like he was a millionaire, treating all manner of people to expensive drinks, and buying young ladies jewellery and all sorts. The only thing is, the boy isn't working, he signs on every two weeks and lives with junkies. Of course he's telling anyone who'll listen to him that he works for a syndicate for people in Europe and that he is paid bucket loads of cash for doing whatever it is he's supposed to be doing, he's telling them it's top secret."

"Do you think he has anything to do with the abductions Terry?"

"Well that's what you and I have to find out Sam. If he has anything to do with it, then he'd better hope that none of the other members of his syndicate hears about it, or we'll be dredging him out of the Thames before you can say Sam's paying for lunch."

"Yeah well, I kind of gathered that after watching you empty your wallet into Treble's pocket, once again. Instead of doing that Terry, why don't you try something different, you know, have a different approach, like sticking your big magnum three-fifty-seven under their chins and saying, tell me what you know, or else, that might save you some money."

"Treble's the only one now Sam who'll receive payment for information.

I kind of feel sorry for him. He's had all that success with his cello playing, I mean it's not just any Tom, Dick or Harry that gets in to the London Philharmonic Orchestra you know. He had it all, the money, the fame, recording contracts, everything, and then the bloody demon drink sets in and takes over the show, leaving him rejected from the field of musicians he'd played with for years. Then his wife leaves him, taking every penny she can get. He starts to steal things and then becomes a kleptomaniac, well, of sorts. He loses everything. I sometimes wonder what's worse Sam, having the dream come true and then having it snatched away from you, or not reaching your target and never finding out what it was like to be up there at the top of your game.

He and I have something in common Sam, we've both had everything taken away from us…it's not a nice feeling."

Samantha looked at Terry, unsure of what he meant, or what exactly had happened to him for him to say that. For whatever reason, his kindness towards Treble was undoubtedly eternal. Nothing she would say to him would change that fact. Whatever it was that Terry had lost, she guessed it wasn't anything to do with his work, because whatever else she could say about him, he was good at his job. She had the highest respect for him, even though she would do everything in her power never to disclose that fact to him. But there was something very troublesome eating at Terrence Mercer. She wondered if some day she'd get close enough to him for him to disclose exactly what it was. "So, where do you want to go for lunch Samantha?"

"Don't you think I should be doing the choosing seeing as how it's my money that is going to be paying for it? I've never known a job in my life where it actually costs you hundreds of pounds to *do* the job…it's the weirdest thing I have ever known…still, if you're happy at your work, that's the main thing, but at least leave yourself enough to be able to eat now and again, it's a good job I'm here Terry, although I knew instinctively that I'd be paying for lunch…I used my intuition."

TWICKENHAM.

LINCOLN AVENUE. 3AM.

John Buckley had many friends throughout the Burgh's of London. Many of them were cons, many were recidivists, and some were just plain scared shitless of this man's reputation, which is why, whenever they were approached by him for information, then that information was disclosed to him without a moments' hesitation for fear of the consequences. He had made one or two inquiries the evening before about the whereabouts of a certain master David Weaver. The boy must have known he was under suspicion because he was refusing to answer his mobile. From the moment Buckley had inquired of the lad, it took only thirty-seven minutes before someone approached him at his table and placed a piece of paper down in front of him with an address. Buckley had then rose to his feet and placed a fifty over the bar for the nice lady who'd came up with the answer to the question he was asking, which was, where the fuck is David Weaver? Buckley had then returned to his safe-house and made himself some supper before heading out in his E-TYPE JAG to Twickenham. All thoughts of how David's father had treated him and looked out for him were all but gone.
This was no time for sentiment.
If he had left this, then it would only have been a matter of time before all of the syndicate were exposed. He would never allow that to happen. He couldn't.
His own life would be at risk because he knew that these demon bitches Angela Bates and this Claire woman had their informants too, and their protectors.
He pulled in to Lincoln Avenue at just after three am.
If he was honest with himself he really didn't want to do this, but the lad had done the damage to himself. He'd been warned about shouting his mouth off about how he obtained his money, and about treating every Tom Dick and Harry to copious amounts of alcohol if they would listen to his shit. He hadn't listened to his warning and now he had to be made to shut up. It would only have been a matter of time before the Job Centre was on his ass anyway. Someone would grass him in about the amounts of money he was spending, and him, supposedly struggling on benefits. And then all hell would've broken loose. He would have spilled the beans on everyone and everything that was going on. All said and done, Angela Bates was right, needs be as needs must.
He checked his Glock and attached the silencer with military precision.
He checked the number on the piece of paper in his hand. He had made inquiries about who lived here at this address because he knew that the area was far too good for the

boy to live here. It turned out that David's older sister lived here with her partner and two children. As luck would have it, they were all off on holiday and of course David would have the run of the house. There would be a possibility, in fact a strong possibility that he would have female company with him tonight, probably filling her head with all kinds of stories about what he done for a living. There was no way he was going to kill an innocent victim so he'd have to work something out and get rid of the girl, if indeed he had one here with him. Buckley made his way to the back of the house. A security light suddenly illuminated the whole back yard. It wasn't anything to worry about. The wind was causing several lights to come on throughout the whole area. He pulled out his trusty tool that he carried around with him at all times since his army days. A device similar in looks to an ordinary screw-driver, but to John Buckley, it was the key to so many `secured` properties. It took him less than three minutes to gain entry to the house. He closed the door behind him, placing his `tool` back inside his pocket, he then checked his Glock pistol once more and placed that in his inside jacket pocket. He opened the kitchen door which led into a long hallway conveniently carpeted with thick quality carpets. He could tell that the underlay was of the best quality as well and that was good for him, the thicker the floor covering the less chance of anyone hearing squeaking floorboards. He made his way to the bottom of the stairs. He stood statue-like, thinking he'd heard a noise above him. After about three minutes he convinced himself that all was well. In his experience of house-breaking, he had learned over the years that people were in their deepest sleep between the hours of three am and five am, another plus. As far as he could tell, there were no dogs here, another down-side to breaking and entering. People could boast all they wanted about how good their burglar alarm systems were, but there was nothing like a dog's ears for detecting intruders. As he climbed the stairs one of them creaked making him freeze half way up.

He waited. Nothing. Not a sound. He knew for certain now that there were no dogs in the house. If there had been it would have been barking its' head off by now, or bounding towards him with snarling angry teeth. He continued to climb to the top of the stairs. Carefully he made his way along the landing, listening at each of the three bedroom doors. At the third door he thought he could hear soft snoring sounds…bingo. He slowly pressed down on the handle of the door and pushed, ever so slightly. In seconds, he was standing at the foot of the bed. He crouched down as outside the wind inconveniently lit up the security light momentarily silhouetting the room in daylight. David slept alone. This was going to make the job so much easier. Once more, in the semi darkness, he checked his gun and aimed it directly at the head of David Weaver. Three times he pulled the trigger, and watched the dark stain appear on the pillow. "I'm sorry kid, I really am, but I warned you to stop your blabbering about money, rest in peace kiddo."

It had to be said, that although David Weaver was still "wet behind the ears" as far as this kind of crime was concerned, he was an extremely fast learner. He too had friends around the area although not quite as influential as Buckley's, but none the less, capable enough to be able to warn him that there was a tag on his head, and that that tag was going to be clipped by a certain John Buckley. Weaver had been informed that Buckley was on his way over to do the job on him.

Buckley made his way back down the stairs and into the kitchen, where he proceeded to put the kettle on and make himself a nice cup of coffee. In the basin in the sink he noticed two mugs. One of them had lipstick stains around the edge. He smiled to himself. *"Good lad David, you've had yourself a nice little filly here tonight, that's my boy, you got your end away before I arrived, fucking good on you kid."* Buckley lit up a cigarette and sat down at the kitchen table. There was now no danger whatsoever. The job was done and the owners of the house were off on holiday. He could even stay here for a couple of days if he so wished, but he didn't fancy the smell of the decaying body gradually overpowering the house. No, he'd have his coffee, wash his cup, and then depart from Lincoln Avenue and inform Angela Bates that all was well. After finishing his cigarette, he scrunched up the butt in his hand running it underneath the cold-water tap and then wrapping it in kitchen roll and placing the small bundle into his pocket. Outside the wind had picked up and it was now pouring down, the rain being driven in sheets and making him turn up his collar. His car was less than twenty metres away but in this weather it was far enough away that he'd be soaked before he reached it. As it turned out he didn't get anywhere near his car. As he turned in the darkness from the back door, he began to head for the path that ran by the side of the house. The shed door behind him opened slowly and quietly. The silenced double-barrelled shotgun was aimed at him.
"Hey".
Buckley turned quickly and had almost jumped out of his skin. He then felt pain like nothing he could ever have imagined, in his chest. He tasted copper. When he coughed, blood splattered out onto the path. He felt like his lungs had suddenly collapsed.
He couldn't breathe. He fell to his knees, gasping for breath and holding his hand over his chest. Blood seeped through his fingers. He felt himself urinating uncontrollably.
"You see John, you old-timers think that you know all there is to know.
You continuously depend on your weakening reputations, thinking that you'll always be the king pin. Well John, every dog has his day so they say, and today sure as hell is not

yours. I didn't want to do you in my sister's house, she's got some nice stuff, didn't want your filthy fucking dog blood all over the place. Hey, what did you think of the snoring recording, convincing wasn't it. I bought it at the joke shop. I watched you coming bud."

David Weaver stepped up to the helpless man, grinning all the time.

"Hey John" he whispered as he got down on his hunkers. "Do you know what a simulacrum is? No? Well I'll tell you.

It's when you place things like sheets or any kind of objects under the covers to make it look like there's a body there, a simulacrum...that's what you shot in there bud, just some old rags I found lying about. Oh, I filled the head shape up with tomato sauce. Good enough to fool you though wasn't it huh? Soldier-boy. Anyway, it's been nice knowing you pal, well, most of the time it was, all the other times you were just a wanker."

Weaver raised the sawn-off shot-gun once more, this time aiming it at Buckley's face. See ya pal." He pulled the trigger. Buckley's head exploded all over the back door of his sister's house. No matter, the rain and his brother-in-law's hose would soon see to that. Quickly, he retrieved the tarpaulin from his sister's shed and wrapped it around the body of John Buckley. Next door to David's sister they had at the bottom of their garden, a large concrete bunker-like structure for making compost. Five minutes later, the bunker contained the body of Buckley. The fact that it was now winter would mean that whoever owned this wouldn't be visiting it any time soon with grass cuttings or leaves and so it would be some time before anyone discovered the body and by that time, the body would be well decomposed. All that remained now was to get rid of the nice little Jag that big man had boasted about on so many occasions. By five-fifteen a.m. all traces of John Buckley had been removed, at least for a while. It would only be a matter of time before the bastard stank the place out to the high heavens. The kids would probably smell him if they were out playing in the garden. David Weaver drove out of his sister's Avenue in the bottle-green E-TYPE-JAG, eight hundred pounds richer in cash, and of course Buckley's credit cards of which there were many. Some account inquiries would soon let him know which of the banks contained his savings. If he'd worked this out correctly, he had at least a few days to spend Buckley's cash as he saw fit. He would now sell the JAG to one of his many dodgy car-dealing friends at a remarkably cut-price. Suddenly, he put on the brakes of the car, and about turned back to his sister's place. "Fuck, nearly Johnny boy, nearly." There was the small matter of removing the three bullets that were meant for his head from his sister's pillow-slip. Weaver ended up just throwing out the whole bundle of quilts and covers he'd used, and would give his sister the money to buy some new ones, after all, he had plenty of money now. He would need that money too, because this would mean the end of his fishing boat trips. He'd have to start looking for a different way to earn cash.

As he drove out of Twickenham, he wondered how much he could make if he passed on information about a certain woman named Angela Bates and all of her associates. He was sure the CID would be very interested in his story. He had to do something about her, because when she found out about John Buckley, she'd be putting her hit-men onto him frightened of what he could disclose to the police, and she had every reason to be concerned. Right now, David Weaver held a lot of good cards to his chest, all four aces in fact…or so it would seem.

WINDMILL LANE.

STRATFORD.

Terry and Samantha sat listening intently to an old woman called Sarah Mills. The old lady had called the local police who in turn had contacted Scotland Yard when she told them what she had seen, and of course, the location. They had to be patient as the kindly pensioner explained to them what she had for tea that night and about what time she usually closes her blinds and locked the doors. "I was just putting my tea dishes into the sink when I looked up and saw this black van. It seemed to have stalled or something, at least momentarily, or maybe the driver was allowing whoever was in the back of the van time to close the doors properly, because I saw someone's arm pulling the back door closed. I don't know if it is relevant to the missing girl or not, I mean it could have been a builder's van I suppose, but then, you don't see too many black builders' vans do you.

"No you don't" agreed Samantha. "You wouldn't happen to have seen any passengers or the driver of the van would you Mrs Mills?"

"No, I'm afraid not, it's quite a distance from my window to the bottom of my drive, and my eyes are not what they used to be, and anyway, the windows of the van were blacked out, you wouldn't be able to tell if there was anyone in the front seat or not with the driver." The old woman went on to inform them of what time this had happened, and it did indeed coincide with the time that Chloe Prowse had gone missing. They had then asked Sarah if she had any CCTV cameras or security cameras to which she confessed that she hadn't.

"Oh, but Mister Smith next door has, he may be able to help you."

Thanking the elderly lady for her help, and for the cups of coffee, Mercer and Reynolds left her house. It would be highly unlikely that the gentleman next door would have kept any footage from that particular night, but it would do no harm to try. They were right. The elderly gentleman greeted them rather audaciously. "A black van? Do you know how many bloody cars go past my drive every day? And you're wondering if I've seen a bloody black van, and how long ago was it? I'll tell you what, if you lot would do your jobs properly then these young girls wouldn't be going missing would they. You all just sit there at your bloody fancy desks with your computers and then run around nicking little boys for messing about on a motorbike, that's what you lot do. Why don't you get out there and stop the bloody crimes, the real crimes before they're even committed, that would be more like it."

"Sir, we are doing that, what do you think we're doing now talking to you, we are detectives."

"Huh, detectives my arse, you couldn't detect a fart in a soap shop, you're bloody useless the lot of you."

Mercer and Reynolds walked away from the man shaking their heads. If they had been feeling malicious, they could have given the old badger the shock of his life and arrested him for use of foul language to an officer of the law, but just like the old bastard had said, they had better things to do…more important things to do instead of chasing young boys on motorcycles. They climbed into the car. Before Terry had a chance to say anything Samantha said, "I bet that was them, in the van I mean, it had to be Terry. In their panic or their hurry, they've closed the back doors of the van on the wing so to speak. I'll bet Chloe was in the back of that van. And why has Mrs Mills waited so long to tell us what she saw?"

"It certainly looks like it Sam, and as far as Mrs Mills is concerned, well, we'll never know the answer to that question, they get frightened you know, they don't want to be involved, until they hear on the news that the police would be very grateful for any information, then they pick up the phone. As for that old fucker next door, I bet he watches all those police-camera-action programmes on TV you know, with the helicopters chasing the speeding joyriders across half of Britain, and then, at the end when they catch them, the narrator informs the viewers that the tearaways received six months' probation for their troubles, no wonder he gets the wrong end of the stick."

"Hello? Chloe Prowse? I believe we were discussing if we thought she was in the back of the van?"

"I know Sam, and you know that she probably was. The thing is, we have no number-plate to go on. All we've got is the black van with blacked out windows."

"At least it's something Terry, we might just have their mode of transport. So it's a van they're using, and give me one of those please."

Terry looked at his colleague. "Are you serious? You want a cigarette?"

"Yes please. I gave up about three months ago, and I'm bloody sick of chewing this nicotine bloody chewing gum." Samantha opened her window and disposed of the gum.

"Well I don't want to be held responsible or blamed even for starting you up again. Is this the reason you're such a bloody grumpy bitch sometimes?"

"Are you going to give me one or not, I'm not bloody begging you."

Mercer handed Samantha the pack. "You take as many as you want Sam."

Samantha lit up the cigarette with the lighter he'd handed to her.

She inhaled and then exhaled and sank back into her seat and let out a kind of laugh. Oh that's good…that's very good."

Mercer's phone buzzed in his jacket pocket. It was Treble-clef.
"Back and forwards back and forwards, Christ" exclaimed Mercer.
"What is it?"
"It's Treble, he's-,"
"Oh, don't tell me, he's got some more twelve bar for you hasn't he, well, let's get to the bank then and then to the off-license store for some Johnny Walker."
Mercer sighed. "You enjoy that cigarette Samantha it'll do you the power of good girl. And for your information, Treble has news of a young man who is looking to sell information about some people who are kidnapping young girls…still want to be a sarcastic smart-ass to me eh, hard bitch?"
Samantha just smiled at Terry, she was in seventh heaven.

KAUNAS.

LITHUANIA.

Sophie Spencer Chloe Prowse Kirsty Crawford, Alison Green, and Lisa Jensen all sat upon one of the giant sofas in their new `home`. They had all been here now for over a week with the exception of Lisa Jensen, who had been here for almost three weeks. The girls had all been introduced to cocaine and had been forced as was the case with Alison Green to take it. Now, all five girls were practically addicts, and the fact that they had access to as much of it as they wanted, made their situation all the more pitiful. All of them had now taken part in sexual activities with various customers of Mister Saratov. They were seated here today to be scrutinised by the highest paying customers. These men and women were from various European countries, businessmen and women from all over the continent. Saratov had informed these people that the girls they were about to be introduced to were the closest thing they'd get to virgins. They could pick one or two of the girls to stay with them in their rooms for as long as they wanted, and of course were permitted to have sex with them as often as they wished. The girls would comply with any type of sexual activities without question with the exception of bondage. Saratov sat on the other giant sofa with Monica Carasova, who now sat smiling at all the girls. She had `weaned` them all into addiction and knew now, that nothing much would distress these young girls. All of them sat smiling back at her as she rose to her feet. Standing in really tight denim shorts she addressed the girls. "Now then, you know why you've been brought in here today ladies. Some nice people are coming in here soon, and they will choose one or two of you to join them in their rooms. If you are chosen then you will do exactly what they ask you, anything their hearts desire, which means, no limits to sexual activity, vaginal, oral, or anal, you will comply at all times. If females choose you, then you will perform anything they wish, including the use of vibrators or strap-ons, again, oral, anything, you will do as you are asked. If you satisfy them, and they are impressed with your enthusiasm, then be assured, you will be handsomely rewarded, and I mean handsomely, however, if they come back to me or Mister Saratov complaining that you were reluctant or unwilling, or troublesome, then you can expect punishment, harsh punishment, but, we won't need to talk about that ladies, will we, because we are all going to have lots and lots of fun. I will be popping in and out of each of the rooms throughout their stay to make sure that everything is satisfactory for them, and I will be joining in with some of the sessions to keep you all confident and…em…eager. Now, when these people enter the room, you

will give them time to sit and receive a drink, and then you will all introduce yourselves. If at this stage they place their hands upon anywhere on your anatomy, you will not object, but in fact encourage them to continue. This is why we have dressed you in this manner today. This will be your first opportunity to repay some of the money that Mister Saratov has paid out for you, so don't you be letting him, or yourselves down. You are all sexual objects to be used by high-paying customers so don't let them down either. You all know that you are allowed as much cocaine as you wish so feel free to take what you need into your guest's bedroom with you, because you could be there for some time, as much as a week or longer if the customer decides to stay for an extended break. If you go into this with the correct attitude, then I can assure you, you will have an extraordinary experience, and one that you'll never forget. Now, does anyone have any questions?" None of the girls, although still smiling, said a single word...there was nothing *to* say.
Sophie Spencer and Chloe Prowse were stronger than the rest of the girls. They had been faster than the others to realize the situation they were in and accept it. Already they had discussed their plan to escape. Lisa Jensen as well, was coping better than the other two girls Alison Green and Kirsty Crawford. Although the cocaine was helping them somewhat, they were still struggling. Sophie and Chloe tried their best to help the girls. Lisa was in tune to what Sophie and Chloe were planning, but they all knew there would have to be some very uncomfortable times in front of them before their chance would come. First of all, they had to gain the trust of their captors, and to do that, they would have to participate enthusiastically to say the least. As far as the three girls were concerned, everything was going to plan, they only hoped the others could adjust.

CROYDON.

Geoffrey Marsden was looking nothing less than radiant. Today, he was dressed in an immaculate white shirt and black trousers, worn with a belt this time and minus the hideous braces, a beautiful burgundy and gold necktie and finished off with gold cuff-links. His silver-white hair had been slightly jelled, or `brylcreamed`. His shoes had been shined to a military standard.
"Going somewhere special Treble?" said Mercer, grinning at Samantha, "Or have you just got all done up for to impress this luscious little thing standing here beside me, because if you have, I'll have to inform you that you'll need a lot of money old boy, a lot of money, and you'll need to take her somewhere where they allow leather dress-code, because that's all she wears, she likes the leather Treble...wears nothing else."
Geoffrey explained to Mercer that he was going to a memorial concert. A cellist he used to play along-side in his philharmonic days. They had remained friends even after Geoffrey's expulsion from the orchestra. Today was the first anniversary of his friend's death. Mercer and Reynolds found seats and sat themselves down. All around Treble's living room were music magazines, in particular cellist's magazines. Mercer picked one of them up and flicked through the pages. "Do you ever miss it Treble? Surely you can't spend that amount of time learning an instrument and then just put it down and be done with it, certainly not at the standard that you reached."
"Every day I miss it Tel, every bloody day. Fourteen years it took me to reach the standard I played at. Eight sometimes ten hours a day, for fourteen years...every day I miss it. I miss all the travel, meeting new people, new places, finding out the history of those places."
Treble sighed heavily. "My own stupid fault kiddo, I had it all. Maybe that was my problem. I had too much money, too many friends. I was always being invited to dinners and all manner of functions. Too much time away from home you see, that's when the trouble kicked in. I started having affairs, and when my wife found out, she did too, until at the end, there was nothing left to defend, nothing left to fight for."
Treble rose from his seat and made his way to the small kitchen. By now, he knew how Terry and Samantha liked their coffees. A few moments later he returned with their beverages. Today, Treble *did* look his age Samantha thought to herself as he offered her the coffee-cup.
"Thank you Geoffrey."
"You're welcome sweetheart, `an` don't take any notice `bat` his sarcasm...he `as` `is` trabbles too missy, don't you worry `bat` that." Treble went on to inform the detectives

about a young man he'd met in the pub the previous evening. He'd seen the lad before in several different pubs and had clocked his behaviour, sometimes raucous, in fact often raucous. Last night the boy had been quiet, very quiet. Add to that, the boy had no female company with him, which in itself was a rare thing. He was acting strange, to say the least. The lad had bought Geoffrey a drink, and when he'd returned the compliment he offered the lad some advice. His advice was about how to conduct your behaviour in public bars. And the first item on the agenda was never to flash money around, show off, unless you wanted to land up with your head burst from the neck up and dumped in some alley-way. The young lad had listened intently to him. After a further few rounds of drinks he began to ask him if he knew people he could trust. Trust with really valuable information. Geoffrey said he did, he knew one person he could really trust.

This seemed to impress the lad, the fact that he'd only said one.

"In a nutshell Terry boy, this lad can give you names. There's a syndicate doing these abductions as you know...well, this boy can give you all four names involved in these abductions. He says he doesn't know their addresses but he knows their hangouts. Geoffrey let the information hang in the air for a few seconds.

"He says, he had to kill somebody last night. This man had come to kill him.

He had no alternative. And he says now, there's four people looking out for him to kill *him*. The guy he killed last night was a friend of the syndicate.

Said he was on board the Marianne with him when they took the last lot of girls over to Europe. Said this guy was ex-army, a real bad bastard, that's why he had to kill him."

"Where's the boy now Treble"? Treble shrugged his shoulders.

"Fack knows Tel. `ee's ad to go inta hidin`."

"Well what did you say to him Treble? Did you make some kind of deal with the boy? I mean Samantha and I will have to speak with him, and if he's killed someone, then we really need to speak with him. He isn't in any position to make deals Treble, Christ he's got the whole world looking for him."

Treble nodded his head. "He said you would say that. He says he's got dozens of places he can hang out in. Says he's got places to stay that you'll never find him. There was an awkward silence for a few moments and then Treble said, "He's` wantin` a big pay day Tel, a real big pay day. I told him who you were and that you're the only person in the world that I would trust, and he believed me, but he said you won't ever find them unless he gives you the locations of their hang-outs. Says there's places in and around the city and also places up in the midlands. These four he mentioned are the main team, but there's many more involved, including businessmen and women, influential people, and they're all well-hidden."

Again the silence as Mercer contemplated what Treble had just told him.
"How much is he looking for, this pay day of his, how much?"
There was a half-inch of whiskey left in the Johnny Walker bottle that Terry had given him the day before. Treble picked up the bottle and drank the remaining contents in one. "Half a million `ee wants. `af a million` Tel. It's up to you Tel, if you want to talk to the lad, but if I don't get in touch with him within three days ee says ee won't be seen again around here". Mercer stepped over to where Treble had his cellos and softly plucked one of the strings. With his back to Treble and Sam, he said, "Ok here's the plan. You tell him that I'm prepared to have a chat with him, and we'll see what we can work out from that conversation. I'm not going to agree anything with him until I know he's genuine, honesty and trust works both ways tell him. But I am prepared to listen to what he has to say. Has he given you a contact number for to get in touch with him?"
"Course ee as Tel, but please don't ask me to give you it, eel never be seen again if I give ya is number...ees trusted me Tel."
"Ok Treble, you tell him we'll talk to him preferably as soon as possible, and by the sounds of the predicament he's in, it'll be in his best interest, before these enemies of his catch up with him. Tell him there'll only be Samantha and I, no-one else in the CID will know about this until such times as we've made a deal...or not. Who's the man he's killed? Did he tell you that?"
Treble shook his head. "Na, the boy aint facking stupid Tel, ee aint gonna tell me that now is ee? Now listen, I'll have to be on me way to the memorial Tel. I'll text the lad and tell im what you've said. As soon as ee's got back in touch with me Tel, I'll call ya with his decision. I think the lad's scared Tel."
Mercer turned and looked at his `friend`. "He's got every right to be scared Treble, because if these people are the ones who are abducting the kids, then they'll be very keen to take care of him. There's no half million quid will save his arse unless we get the names off him. As it stands now, he holds the keys to their future, and where they'll spend it, and you tell him from me Treble, if he doesn't agree to meet me and Samantha, then his chances of survival are very slim. There's a good chance that they'll know some of his hiding places. You tell him to arrange this meeting as soon as possible...it's for his own sake, in fact, tell him his life depends on it."
Geoffrey Marsden rose to his feet, checking his collar and tie in the mirror and putting on the jacket that matched his trousers. As he turned to leave he informed Terry of where to put the key when they left.
"Elp yourselves to more tea or coffee Tel, I'll have to fly, see ya soon sweetheart." He said to Samantha as he left his flat.
Terry made more coffee for himself and Sam.

"What do you think Terry? It sounds to me like the boy has landed himself in one hell of a pile of shit, and if we don't get those names from him, well, it doesn't look like he'll be around for long." Terry nodded as he sipped his beverage. "We've got surveillance on Angela Bates and as far as we can make out, she's up in the midlands. She was last spotted in Derby. That doesn't necessarily mean there's anything going on up there, she knows we're watching her, so the last thing that *she'll* be doing is making contact with her companions, and that's to say that she has anything to do with the abductions. We were given her name by detective Briggs, and what I'd like to know is who gave *him* her name. How the hell did he manage to find her name? On top of that Sam, we haven't heard a single thing from him since then. They've been up there for nearly three weeks and we've heard fuck all from them. Three detectives all around the midlands and not one of them have anything to report." Mercer washed his cup as did Samantha hers. She also washed Treble's whiskey glass and his mug, drying them and folding the tea-towel over his cooker and then placing the empty whiskey bottle into the pedal-bin. Mercer couldn't resist. "You'd be good at this home-help Sam, you have a natural instinct, very homely you seem."

"Don't start Terry".

As they made their way back to the car Samantha said something that Terry hadn't given any thought to. "Let's just hope Terry that these people don't hear about this Weaver talking to Geoffrey. If they have people looking around for this lad, then it's quite possible he could have been seen talking to him. The last thing *we* want is for anything to happen to your snitch."

Terry nodded his agreement. He was still thinking about what detective Briggs had been doing up there all this time, and how he had been able to give him this Angela Bates person. To his recollection, Briggs had only been up there about two days when he'd given him the name. He couldn't say how good or bad Briggs was as a detective, but to be able to give him a name as quickly as that had put doubt in his mind. He remembered his old colleague Sam Hargrieves, who had guided him through his early days as a detective, and how he had imprinted into his mind about how important gut-feelings were, and how you would ignore them at your peril. If this Weaver boy refused to have a meeting with himself and Samantha, then they would go up there to the midlands and find out what was going on. Even if the boy *did* agree to a meeting Terry decided that it would be worthwhile for he and Samantha to pay a visit and find out just exactly what Briggs had been doing and why he hadn't been back in touch, because Terry was curious as to why he hadn't, at least asked about the outcome of his meeting with this Angela woman.

"You're miles away Terry" said Samantha, extracting another cigarette from the packet

and lighting up. "Yeah I was Sam. When we get back remind me to ask Polly Sheppard what those guys up in the midlands have been telling her in terms of their progress. Don't ask me why Sam, I smell a rat, there's something not right with what's going on up there."
Samantha handed Mercer the lit cigarette.
"I know Terry, it's that gut feeling of yours again isn't it."
Mercer just glanced at his colleague and nodded. Whatever was happening up in the midlands, Terry Mercer would never ignore his gut-instincts. Many crimes throughout his career had been solved on gut instincts. To receive information like this though about a certain Angela Bates and then not be asked about the outcome of her interview was making him more suspicious than ever before… 'rest in peace Sam Hargrieves`.

SCOTLAND YARD.

BROADWAY VICTORIA.

Polly Sheppard was waiting for Terry and Samantha when they arrived back.
"A body has been discovered Terry over in Twickenham."
She looked at her computer screen and then confirmed the Street.
"Lincoln Avenue. You'd better get yourselves over there. Whoever the man was, he's been shot to ribbons. His body was hidden inside a concrete bunker of some description.
I've been told he's been blasted point-blank in the face with a shotgun, so he's not going to be a very pretty sight."
"Are forensics there now"? Said Terry, pouring himself and Samantha a cup of coffee from Polly's personal coffee maker.
"Yeah, they only discovered the body about an hour ago I don't know how long it's been there."
"Do we have a name?"
"Not yet, I expect forensics will tell you who he is...sorry was."
Mercer decided to say nothing at this point about his conversation with Geoffrey Marsden and about the lad who supposedly had the names of all the main dealers in the syndicate. He had a good idea as did Samantha that the body of the man they were about to overlook was the man that the lad had told old Treble about. Samantha seemed to catch on straightaway to Mercer's thoughts and said nothing. Mercer handed Sam her cup of coffee. "Here, and don't take all day drinking it."
Polly shook her head. "He hasn't improved much has he Samantha, still snapping away at people like they were sub-human, and by the way mister, who said that you can help yourself to my coffee machine?" Mercer stepped forward and looked at Polly's computer screen, and then said to his superior, "You've got the Thames River Police Patrol on the go Polly, well done, you beat me to it." Polly nodded. "If that fishing boat The Marianne comes anywhere near our waters we'll know about it immediately.
And what I was hoping for Terry, is that it *does* come back here, and hopefully whoever these people are will have another bunch of girls ready to board the vessel. This time though, the girls will be saved, and those evil people will be captured. That's the plan Terry, but, as you know, it certainly won't be that easy, it never is." Samantha raised her cup to her lips.
"Thank you for the coffee `mam`" it's lovely."

"You're welcome Samantha, and you're welcome to use my machine any time, even if I'm not in my office, it's just that some people take liberties if you know what I mean." They made small talk for a couple of minutes whilst they drank their coffee, but then Polly sat down on her chair and asked Terry if he had any ideas who this murdered man could be.

He raised his hands. "Could be anybody Polly. We'll soon find out when we get there. Ever seen a dead body Samantha?" said Mercer, smiling at his colleague.

"I'll be looking at one in here if you're not careful, I'll shoot you in the face with my Glock water pistol as you call it."

"Yeah well, make sure you're no more than ten feet away from me or it'll go off-target and you'll miss."

"Huh, couldn't miss a head that size, from fifty feet, your head is the size of Jupiter, in fact I'm sure you suffer from Macrocephaly."

"Come on, let's go, we'd better get off to Twickenham, let's go and see bashed up Billy and who he's been annoying for to end up in this state, come on finish your coffee, and you're driving...do all the bloody driving these days it seems, I thought you were supposed to be a colleague, I'm not your chauffer you know."

As the two detectives left Polly's office she said," Let me know you pair, what you find out, and if there's any connection to the abductions."

Mercer nodded as he closed the door behind him.

Outside in the car Samantha said, "Why didn't you tell her about what Treble told us?"

"There are certain things Sam that are best kept quiet. I tell her that, and she'd have all and sundry over there bothering old Treble and frightening the life out of him, and on top of that, we'd have no chance whatsoever of talking to this kid who thinks he's going to inherit half a million quid...that's why, any more questions? And by the way, what in the name of fuck is Macrocephaly when it's at home?"

"Yes, just one question Jupiter, where do you buy your cigarettes?"

"Let me tell you something Samantha, I have a breaking point you know, concerning tolerance, and you're pushing it lady. I'm a very dangerous man you know, liable to lash out at anyone who crosses that line, so think on missy."

"Yes, I take heed of your warning and must remember to inform all the other female officers within Scotland Yard that you are liable to lash out at them if they annoy you. Heavy-handed then Terry, are we?"

"Start the car bitch and no more of your shit, or I'll take my-."

"Light me up a cigarette sugar would you, I'm busy getting ready to chauffeur you round town, thank you honey."

Mercer was growing fonder all the time of his new colleague. She could match his sarcasm with ease and always had an answer ready at a moment's notice. He noticed as well that she still hadn't answered his question about Macrocephaly. He would look it up when he got home, whenever that would be. He instinctively knew it would be something extremely insulting.

KELVEDON ROAD.

CENTRAL FULHAM.

From the moment John Buckley's murder had been aired David Weaver's problems had multiplied ten-fold. He'd thought that because he'd hidden Buckley's body in a compost container and because of the time of year it was, that there'd be little chance of anyone discovering the corpse, at least for a while. He was wrong. He forgot that people used more than just grass cuttings and leaves to make fertilizer. Scrap food, tea bags, rotting fruit and vegetables including potato peelings, which was what Kathleen Hunter was taking out to the bunker when she discovered the tarpaulin sheet. A minute later her husband was calling the police and trying his best to calm his wife down from the shock she suffered when she'd opened it up.
One of Weaver's problems, and probably his biggest one was that he only knew two of Angela Bates and Claire Redgrave's hit-men. There were more than two, many more. So now he knew that he was in serious trouble. If this detective that old Geoffrey had told him about couldn't or wouldn't help him then there was little chance of his survival. Where he was now he deemed to be reasonably safe, which was, a good hotel in central Fulham. He didn't think there had been anyone following him when he arrived here by taxi the night before and was wearing his hood up until he entered the building. He had accumulated a few thousand pounds from Buckley's bank accounts and credit cards but it was costly if he had to stay full-time in hotels, especially good ones. The truth was, he had bluffed old Geoffrey by telling him to inform the detective that he had many reliable friends who would hide him and that the police would have no chance whatsoever of finding him. In fact, most of his associates would sell their mothers for a tenner. His only hope was that this detective was a man of his word. Weaver knew that the Metropolitan Police were desperate to bring these abductors to book and so this information he held about them was invaluable, but from being in what he thought was a profitable situation to this predicament he was now in, came as quite a shock to him. He had been relying on Buckley's body not being discovered, for at least a few days. That would have given him some time to negotiate with the detective and make some kind of profitable deal. Now, he was facing a life imprisonment term of at least fifteen years, or execution by one of the bitches' hit-men. His fear was fast becoming insurmountable. He was pacing about his room with mobile phone in hand wondering if he should take this chance. Treble-clef had texted him informing him that detective Mercer and his colleague Samantha Reynolds would agree to meet with him

anywhere he chose, and that, at this moment they would not inform any other colleagues in the force. Weaver sighed, finally accepting the fact that he'd dug himself into an enormous shit-hole, he sent Treble-clef the text message to inform inspectors Mercer and Reynolds of his whereabouts. It was done. Now, all he could do was wait. If he'd misjudged the detective's promises' then he could quite easily be sitting in a police cell within the hour. Fifty-seven minutes later there was a knock on his door. Weaver inhaled deeply, and then exhaled as he approached the door.
"Who is it?" he asked cautiously.
"It's Terry Mercer."
Weaver unlocked the door and stepped away.
"David Weaver?" said Mercer as he entered the room, followed by Samantha Reynolds. "Don't worry" Mercer said as he closed the door behind him, "I'm your uncle, and this here is your niece, that's what we told reception so there was no need to show ID. My friend Geoffrey tells me that you have some information that you think the Metropolitan Police would be interested in hearing. He also informs me that you are seeking an extremely large sum of money in return for this information."
Weaver was now sitting upon the bed with his head in his hands. He looked up at the detectives nodding his head slowly.
"Yes sir, I've been very foolish, I thought-. "
"I know" interrupted Mercer, sitting upon one of the chairs. "You thought you'd make yourself a nice little earner here and that you'd collect the half million quid and we'd jail the abductors and everyone would live happily ever after, isn't that what you thought?"
"Something like that sir" said Weaver, admitting defeat.
Sam Reynolds sat down next to Mercer with a note-book and pen in her hands. Mercer continued. "You killed a man David. You killed a man in cold blood, and then you proceeded to hide the corpse in a bunker." Weaver was about to say something but Mercer kept talking. "You then proceeded to steal the victim's car and sell it to a dealer in Chelsea. Now, according to our forensic boys and girls Mister Buckley died between the hours of 3am and 6;30am, almost three days ago, and yet, according to detective Reynolds here, there have been substantial withdrawals from Buckley's accounts since that night, and so, assuming that his middle name isn't Lazarus, then it would seem that someone has access to his credit cards, and so as far as the prosecutors are concerned, they'd be saying that, far from killing this man in self-defence, in fact quite the opposite happened and that the man was murdered in cold blood for nothing more than financial gain. Now with that information disclosed to you, my colleague and I are very curious to say the least as to how you think that you're in any position to demand half a million quid from the MET."

David Weaver rose up slowly from the bed.

"That man came to kill me sir, he'd probably been given orders to.

I know too much about them sir."

"Do you know where any of them live?" said Samantha.

Weaver shook his head. "No I don't mam, but I know when that fishing boat is coming back over to Britain, and as you can probably guess, it won't be anywhere near London. But, what I will say is, the fact that I have killed John Buckley may change the date of the arrival. I also know that they have four more girls in captivity. Usually they wait until they have at least five, five or six. They make a lot of money when they sell them off to the European businessmen, a lot of money." Mercer rose up from his chair and proceeded to fill the kettle.

"Ok, let's recap David. You say you know the main four, you know all four names of the leaders of this syndicate. You also claim to know the date of the Marianne's next arrival, although as you say, that could change since you murdered Buckley. Ok, this is what we'll do. This is what Sam and I propose to you, oh by the way, this is detective Samantha Reynolds my colleague, she's very pretty don't you think? And doesn't she suit the leather coat. If you give us the four names that you know and the place and the time of the fishing boat's arrival, then we will turn a blind eye to your killing John Buckley, because as it stands now David, they don't know who killed John Buckley. The fact that you've confessed to it only helped Samantha and I to save the MET half a million quid. You done a good job David, and in fact, looking at Buckley's criminal record you done the country a favour. So, what this means, is that you walk away from that murder with however much of Buckley's money you have and your life carries on as per usual. Oh but we know that they'll be coming after you David, and so the more names you can give us the less chance there is of one of them sneaking into your room at night, and by the way David, a little advice, when you think there are people out to kill you, then whatever you do, you do not sign in to hotels under your real name like you done in here, you stupid boy. Now then David, what do you think about that for a deal? You can switch off that recorder now Sam."

Weaver was defeated. He was defeated long before the detectives arrived. Mercer poured cups of tea for everyone.

"Do you know where they're hiding these girls David?" said Samantha putting a single tea-spoon full of sugar into her cup.

"They won't let anyone know that information. Only the people directly involved with the abductions know those locations."

Samantha continued. "So where is this boat calling, and when?"

Weaver looked at Mercer.

"Tell her kid, I would tell her if I were you, she is one fucking hard-assed bitch so she is. She'll kick your balls so far up your ass that they'll rattle your tonsils I kid you not, don't let her beauty deceive you. That's why she wears the leather coats and shit, it's to intimidate you, like she's a member of the Schutzstaffel, a nasty piece of work David. She even smokes now, the nasty bitch, sugar and milk David?"
The ghost of a smile appeared on Weaver's face, but no more than that.
"Three days' time, Thursday at just after midnight.
"Where?" said Samantha, sitting back down and taking a sip of her tea.
"Grimsby."
"You're sure about that David", said Mercer lighting up a cigarette.
"You wouldn't fuck us about David would you?"
"No sir, I wouldn't, I'm in enough trouble don't you think without me winding you up."
"Ok David, I'll tell you what we'll do. Do you have anywhere you can stay where you think you'll be safe?"
Weaver sighed. "Not really sir, I can't trust anyone. Some of my associates would grass me in for sure if they were approached."
Mercer looked at Sam and then back at Weaver.
"Ok, we'll find you somewhere safe because if you stay here you'll be dead long before Thursday. Now I'm telling you this right now, when we find you somewhere then you stay there until I tell you anything different, do you understand that?"
"Yes sir, I'll stay put until instructed otherwise."
"Good, because these people will not rest until you are dead. Now if we can't get to them in time, they will come and find you even if you were hiding in the fucking Amazon rain forest. You've really knocked their apple-cart boy, and you have disrupted a very profitable little business they had going for themselves."
"I won't move sir, I promise you."
Samantha stepped over to Weaver and handed him a piece of paper and a pen. "Write down all the names of the people you know who are in this syndicate, and do not leave any names out, do you understand me? Because, if we find later that you've known someone who's name is not on this list then I promise you now, that we will not hesitate to inform our chief inspector of the evidence we now have of John Buckley's murder, are we all clear on that?"
"Yes mam, crystal clear, I'll write down all the names I know. I promise you."
Mercer smiled. "A real bossy bitch isn't she David, she'd have been well suited in the Schutzstaffel."
Samantha's face held no trace of humour whatsoever, she even gave Mercer a glance to remind him that there was a time and a place for humour, and now was not that

time. "Start writing Mister Weaver" she said, and remember what I just told you, because if you fuck this up, you'll wish you really were dealing with the Schutzstaffel and not me."

KAUNAS.

LITHUANIA.

Alison Green and Kirsty Crawford walked hand in hand around the perimeter of the huge house where they were being held. The two girls had been given the day off and were informed by Monica to feel free to wander around the grounds. Their introduction into the adult world had been harsh and sudden, even though Monica had tried to soften their shock. The girls were now grateful for the use of cocaine. Without it their ordeals would have been even worse than they'd been. As they walked, the two girls said very little to each other. It was as though they were taking everything in, their kidnappings, the drugs, and now, the sexual depravities they were forced to endure, in a nut-shell, everything that had happened to them. The hand-holding acted as a comfort to them. Both girls had now started smoking, another source of comfort. Anything, anything at all that would help them get through their days. The clothes they were wearing today, more comfort. Monica had supplied them with a well-stocked wardrobe. Jackets and coats, jeans, thick woollen jumpers and gloves and scarves, as opposed to the skimpy little skirts and tops they were told to wear when `on duty`. The grounds around the house seemed to go on forever. Monica had warned them not to go anywhere near the perimeter fences because they were electrified and would give them an extremely nasty shock if they touched them. They were also told not to go anywhere near the kennels at the back of the house so as not to upset the dogs. Both girls knew why they'd been told this. It was for two good reasons. The first of course was for their own safety, the second was to remind them that any attempt of an escape would be futile. No-one else in the world knew they were here, and so if anything happened to them, they would simply be replaced. The two girls could have been mistaken for being out for an afternoon stroll. No-one would guess what they were being made to do. Neither of the girls exceeded five foot seven and so because they were so petite they were always in demand by the customers who fantasised about school-girl sex. Ironically, some of the girls *were* still school age. Even as they walked now, `customers` could be seen entering and leaving the grounds in their big fancy limo's and large sports cars. They came to a bench and sat down, both of them lighting cigarettes with shaking hands. "Can I ask you something Kirsty?" said Alison inhaling and exhaling the smoke and enjoying the experience.
"Of course."
"How do you cope, you know, when they do those things to you, how do you cope with

it?" Kirsty turned and touched her new friend ever so lightly on the cheek. "I'll tell you Alison. I was studying lots of things before I was due to go to university and one of the subjects I was studying was history, twentieth century history in particular. Of course in that time we had the second-world-war. I had been reading about the Nazis' and their death camps, and what they done to those poor Jewish people.

They were tortured and beaten beyond comprehension. The ones who could work were worked to death. They were starved and left to die. Some of them, thousands in fact, were forced to dig their own graves, men and women all stripped naked and forced to dig huge graves, once completed they were forced onto their knees and then shot in the back of their heads. Others were taken to gas chambers. They were told they were going into shower rooms, those poor women and their babies, all gassed and then their bodies burned in the incinerators. To answer your question Alison, I think about how lucky I am. At the end of our ordeals we can go and have a nice hot shower.

We can have a cup of tea or coffee or have a drink. We can smoke cigarettes and wear nice clothes. They've given us a small library with English-written books we have CD's and DVD's, all these things, that's what I think about Alison, I think about how lucky I am. I'm not sure of my future or even if I have one, all I know is today, that's it, and that's all I need to know. I pray to God with each day that arrives, that somehow the British police will find out about these people and what they are doing to us, but until such times as God answers' my prayers, I think about how lucky I am and hope that He's looking after my mum and dad. Maybe someday Alison they'll let us go back home, who knows, I try not to think about it too much."

"Have you been made to do it with a woman yet Kirsty?"

Kirsty nodded but said nothing.

"How did it make you feel? You know, when they start to kiss you down there, it made me feel weird, really weird…the drugs helped."

Kirsty turned to look at her friend. "Hey, it's our day off, and I for one do not want to talk about what goes on in there. You should feel the same Alison they'll make us do all kinds of disgusting things before they're finished with us, so let's not torture ourselves reliving them. Look all around you, listen to the birds singing, this is normal, this is freedom. Out here is freedom, and today, we are free." Kirsty's voice had broken off on the last of her words. All the emotions and trauma of the past few weeks, the drug taking, the sexual depravities, the humiliation, everything, it all came to a head now and the two girls embraced each other both of them sobbing bitterly, because this was *not* normal, and out here was *not* freedom, but it would be the closest they would come to it until God knows when.

Inside the house in one of the rooms Chloe Prowse was being examined by a female doctor, a woman in her mid-thirties with shoulder-length hair. She was slim in build and had several facial piercings consisting of studs in her nose and mouth, and one noticeably on the end of her tongue. No-one would have guessed that she was in fact a general practitioner by her appearance. Although now a doctor, she'd had experience in all manner of sexual endeavours, including bondage and S and M. Fitting now that she worked among the legalised brothels checking for sexual diseases among the working women. Today however Monica Carosova had called her here to examine Chloe Prowse. The girl had been in one of the rooms with three men. They had paid Saratov huge sums of money for this privilege. The girl had been subjected to a four-hour ordeal with the men and was now in severe pain. She was bleeding from the anus and vagina and suffering spasms of unbearable stomach cramps. Chloe had been lifted onto the gynaecologist's chair because she simply couldn't climb upon it unaided. Tears rolled down her face as the two women examined her, speaking to each other in a foreign language. Now and again the doctor raised her voice pointing to Chloe. She seemed to be blaming Monica for something. Whatever the doctor had done, she'd managed to stop the bleeding from Chloe's rectum. The vaginal bleeding had turned out to be nothing more than mother-nature at work. The two women had then helped Chloe back down from the chair. Monica began to speak to her in a sympathetic tone and in English. "Doctor Vercopte says that you'll be fine Chloe. You will now of course, have the rest of the week off to recover, and in fact I will recommend to Mister Saratov that you refrain from any further activities for at least ten days. It'll give you a chance to recover. The three gentlemen who you were with all spoke very highly of you and have left you a two-hundred Euros tip. I know they can be a bit wild Chloe, I have been with them, but they're really nice people once you get to know them, I'm sure you'll grow to like them."
Monica's last statement informed Chloe that there would be a repeat performance in the future, probably the near future.
"Anyway, you go back to your room Chloe and have a nice little sleep, and when you feel like it, just go down to the kitchens and chef will cook you something to eat. Now here, take this pill now, and I will give you another tonight, don't worry they're only pain-killers, nothing else, on you go, I'll be down to see you as soon as I have finished talking with Doctor Vercopte."
Valarie Vercopte stood shaking her head as she watched the young girl limping out of the room. In her mother tongue of Lietuviu kalba (Lithuanian.) She said to Monica "How on earth can you sleep at nights? Look at the state of that poor wretch, for God's sake she's only a child. Four hours you let those brutes have her. Does Saratov have a

soul or did he sell *that* off at the highest price he could get? Listen, I have worked in lots of brothels Monica and attend the needs of the women who work in them, but these? These are just children, you are stealing their innocence away from them, you're destroying their lives, I don't know-."

"Hey, that's enough Valarie, don't you dare condemn anyone in here, remember, I know your speciality you're as kinky as anyone else. Just because you're a doctor, it doesn't give you the right to condemn people, and don't forget how you got the money to finance your education into university, and I'll tell you something else. Because we are old friends I will not repeat to Mister Saratov what you have just said, but I will warn you here and now, do not speak to anyone outside of these gates about what goes on in here, we know where you live, and you just be careful Valarie, don't you go getting too big for your boots lady. You just come here and do the job you're paid to do, you're well enough paid for it. You don't have any complaints in *that* department do you?"

Valarie Vercopte closed her valise and handed Monica a small jar of tablets. "Make sure the girl finishes the course Monica" she said softly, almost humbly. Monica left the room to go and collect Doctor Vercopte's money, an action that she performed regularly. Valarie stood by the window looking outside and contemplating what Monica had just said. She saw two girls sitting on a bench wrapped up against the cold, smoking cigarettes. From where she stood they looked no older than school-girls…children. What might be their topic of conversation, she wondered, and what *would* they have been talking about if they were still in their own towns at home. Monica's threat still hummed in her ears. Vercopte now knew that she would have to discard any idea she had of helping the girls in here. Her own life was at risk if she continued with this attitude. Michael Saratov had ways of dealing with anyone standing in his way, anyone. She would have to turn a blind eye to what was happening.

One thing she couldn't complain about was the money she was paid by Saratov.

It had just come as such a shock to her, to see that young girl limping out of the room, it was pitiful in fact, but it wasn't her job to judge people on their morals or principals. She would carry on doing her medical checks with the girls and collect her very lucrative payment each time she did. She wasn't sure if Monica would keep quiet to Saratov about what she'd said and so when she returned she praised her and Saratov for the way she was treated whenever she visited, thanking her for her hospitality and apologising for her senseless outburst. "I know you know your business Monica, and from what I can see, you treat the girls very generously. They look like they're well fed, and healthy. It was just, you know, seeing the girl limping out of here, she was in pain." Monica handed the envelope to Valarie nodding. "I know Valarie, I shouldn't have put that kind of trick onto the girl, she wasn't ready for it, but I can assure you she will be rewarded for her uncomfortable experience, although the gentlemen involved said she was very good and quite enthusiastic and willing. I think maybe her body was not yet prepared for what happened, but, she'll heal Valarie."

"Of course" replied the doctor, although in her mind she was thinking, *"she doesn't really have too much of a choice in that department, does she?"*

Valarie then asked if she could share a coffee with her `old friend` before she left. She would have to secure the friendship further to make sure that Monica did not repeat anything to Saratov. She and Monica had been friends for a number of years now, but she was genuinely shocked at the way she'd allowed young girls to be treated like this. In all honesty, they were being raped, and practically round the clock. She never thought Monica would have had anything to do with these acts of paedophilia, because that's what it was. Yes, she herself had funded her university-fees from prostitution, but she'd done it with her own free will. These girls had been kidnapped and forced into these circumstances. Probably the worst nightmare any of them could ever have imagined.

CROYDON.

Geoffrey Marsden sat directly beneath his skylight in his little flat reading the letter that had been sent to him by an old friend of his from his orchestral days. Whilst on tour with the London Philharmonic Orchestra he had formed a friendship with a man named Vladimir Kortov a fellow cellist. He had met Kortov when in Berlin, where Kortov was performing with The Lithuanian National Orchestra. The man could speak fluent English and very soon they forged a friendship, exchanging opinions on their favourite cellists. The friendship had lasted thirty years. Maybe three times a year the old men would send each other a letter, neither of them interested in using the internet. All too often Treble had heard stories on the radio or TV about hackers gaining access to supposedly top-secret information, and so for that reason the two old friends relied upon the old-fashioned method of correspondence, pen and paper. Geoffrey Marsden smiled as he looked up to his skylight which at this moment in time was being pelted with torrential rain. He had been honoured indeed today, beyond belief. He knew that Vladimir was part of the Lithuanian Orchestra committee, but had no idea of how much influence he had. He had been invited to The European Festival of Orchestras as an honoured guest. Inside the envelope there were three tickets for himself and two guests of his choice, all to be accommodated in one of the best hotels. Of all the accolades he'd accumulated throughout the years, this, was by far the highest of them all.

To be acknowledged. To be accepted, and reminded of just how good a cellist he'd been. For anyone who would obtain tickets for the European Festival of Orchestras it would be special enough, but to be invited there as an honorary guest, a special guest, this was beyond comprehension for old Treble-clef. He hadn't been forgotten about as a musician after all. Tears of pride formed in his eyes. He lived here within a community who had not a clue as to how good a musician he was. To be chosen as a performing musician in The London Philharmonic Orchestra was an honour indeed. To be chosen to play with them, you had to be good, very good. But the world had changed, and not for the better. The musical stars of today were so much different compared to what they were yesteryear. Not many people had very much interest in classical music these days. The popularity had waned over the years. No, the stars of today were no more than kids, chosen not for their musical skills but for how good they would look on the cover of a magazine or on a three-minute video. They could pick up a guitar and knock out three or four chords, braying out and screeching about how their `baby done them wrong` and could end up superstars overnight. Half of them couldn't spell guitar, but there they are performing guitar solos in front of thousands of `brainwashed fans` their notes enhanced by guitar effect-pedals and making the instrument scream, and making himself scream even louder. How many of them had taken the time to listen to classical guitarists, real guitarists like Andre Segovia, John Williams, Julian Bream, Xuefei Yang, Craig Ogden or Milos Karadaglic, to name but a few, but no, just a three chord ditty will suffice thank you very much, and as far as classical music is concerned, you can stick that up your arse. Young ladies now as well had jumped on the band-wagon, performing half naked and `strutting their stuff` chewing gum and looking into the camera like she was the most sexually experienced woman on God's good earth, bending over with skirts half way up their backsides and `twerking` rapidly to a bunch of male dancers, and half of *them* wore pink knickers. The whole thing had fucked up. The real meaning and purpose of music had long since disappeared down the toilets of Britain. Meanwhile, a teenager in some far-off quiet room sits down to a piano, or a violin, or a cello, or a guitar and plays a concerto perfectly.

The world will never get to know his or her talent, simply because the world is not interested in real music. Four or five hours a day, every day, since they were six years old up until their present ages, and no-one will ever get to hear or appreciate their talents and these musicians knew that, they know they'll never have the life-style or the money that these pop stars have, so, why do they do it? They do it because they love the music, real music, they feel it, it's in their blood...it's in their souls.

Treble rose to his feet and for no apparent reason found himself saying out loud, "It's about the dedication. Doesn't take much dedication to do that, what did they call it? Rap. Yeah rap. And they rap because they can't blaady sing. Mother-fucking this and mother-fucking that. Yeah, well done boys and girls, swear yer facking eds off and get paid enough dosh to buy yourselves a facking crib. When I was a kid, a crib was somewhere a baby facking slept."

He made his way over to his kettle and popped two slices of bread into the toaster. Today he would indulge in breakfast. He would start his day jentacular. "Yeah dedication" he repeated once again remembering his musical days.

He was thinking how hard it would be for any youngster starting out in the classical music scene today. Like everywhere else corruption and injustices, and it wasn't only in the music scene either.

Talented actors were being refused roles in films because they weren't famous enough, and yet, they gave a man an Oscar for a little over eleven minutes' screen time on a film that lasted two hours or more.

Now old Treble was having a good old-fashioned rant to himself. He felt like he was somebody again.

"Eleven minutes, an ee gets the highest award an acta can get, facking` el, what the fack as `appened to the world. For wearin some kinda facking mouff mask and makin some kinda slevering facking noises, and they give im an Oscar. It carries on like this, they'll be givin some geezer an Oscar for farting through a facking key ole, facking Silence of the facking Lambs indeed."

CENTRAL FULHAM.

David Weaver felt a sense of relief. Now that he had met Terry Mercer and his colleague in person. Relief at the thought of having somewhere safe to stay, and to keep him away from those very dangerous, and by now, very angry women Angela Bates and Claire Redgrave. They had, in all fairness every right to be angry, after all, he'd taken out a highly-valued assistant of theirs. Although at this point it couldn't be proved who had killed John Buckley, they would know instinctively that it was he who had done it, and they would know why. Even if he hadn't murdered Buckley, they'd still be coming after him simply because they wouldn't want him roaming around London with all this information about them floating about in his head. It wouldn't matter now though, Terry Mercer and Samantha Reynolds were coming here at eight o clock tonight, and from then on he would more or less be under police-protection, although not officially. He had no idea where Mercer was taking him, and he couldn't care less, because he knew it would be safer than running around from place to place like he'd been doing before he had spoken to the detective.
He had just been down to reception checking out and explaining to the receptionist that he'd be leaving here tonight just after eight. He stepped out of the elevator on the fourth floor where his room was situated dressed in tee-shirt and jeans. As he walked along the corridor a young lady wearing the hotel uniform came towards him pushing a trolley. They smiled at each other on the passing. He thought he'd seen her before. Then she stopped and spoke to him. "Mister Weaver isn't it?"
"Yes that's right, what can I do for you?"
"No sir nothing, it's just that, I have a steak dinner here which one of the guests ordered, only they've changed their minds and no longer want it. I explained to them that they would still be charged for it on their bill, but they still refused it. I was just wondering sir, if you haven't yet eaten tonight, well you'd be welcome to it, please don't be offended it's just that I hate to see waste."
Weaver jumped at the chance of having a free meal, and thanked the girl by giving her a generous tip. It was the least he could do.
His luck was beginning to change for the better he thought to himself as he headed down the corridor now laden with a rather large aluminium dome-shaped vessel which contained steak and gravy, boiled potatoes and a side-salad. He used his card-key to open his door. Once inside he sat the container down on the coffee table while he retrieved a cold bottle of beer from the small fridge in the corner of his room. Less than two minutes later Mister David Weaver was tucking in to a delicious stake dinner with

side-salad and watching TV. Half way through his meal there was a knock on his door. He instinctively looked at his watch. Mercer said eight o clock, it was now only ten minutes after six. He put down his plate and approached the door cautiously.
"Who is it?"
"It's me sir, room service, I forgot something."
Weaver opened the door. It was the girl who'd gifted him the steak dinner.
She was standing with a bottle of wine in her hands. She handed it to him.
"They paid for this as well sir, I forgot all about it, you may as well have it sir, as I say, it's paid for."
Weaver accepted the wine and thanked the girl again. He then returned to his meal which he devoured in less than five minutes, and washed it down with two large glasses of delicious Aloft Cabernet Sauvignon. Then he proceeded to light up a cigarette, sitting upright on the bed and contemplating where Terry Mercer might take him. He felt that a great burden had been lifted from his shoulders. For the first time in a long while, he actually felt relaxed, but then, just as he was extinguishing the smoked cigarette, a female voice called out to him from his shower-room. "Did you enjoy your meal David?"
Weaver froze on his bed, not because of the female speaking unexpectedly, although Claire Redgraves' voice *did* give him a fright.
Something was happening inside him. His stomach tightened.
He felt sharp pains, stabbing pains, needle-like.
Claire Redgraves stepped out of the shower-room and into his room pulling on a pair of polythene gloves. "You're not exactly a hard man to find are you David, of course, you're new to this game aren't you...oh?"
Weaver began to have convulsions. His stomach began to burn, and then his throat. He couldn't move a muscle, he was paralyzed. Now his stomach felt like it was on fire, the burning ever-intensifying.
"John had big plans for you David. Your father was a good man and he never forgot that."
Weaver's throat seized up completely.
"He would have looked after you, but you had to go and spoil it for yourself didn't you? Going about the bars flashing money about the place like you were a lottery winner, you really are a fucking dummy boy aren't you. Throwing money about and telling all the little scrubbers that you were an important part in a syndicate and how they paid you bucket loads of cash for what you done for them. Highly secret you told them, but there you were blabbing off to any little slut that would listen to your shit. And we did, we did give you lots of money, and you could have made lots more if you'd taken' heed

of John's warnings, but no, you had to be the fucking big man buying all and sundry drinks to listen to your rubbish. Your father would turn in his grave if he knew how fucking stupid you turned out to be, imagine that, twenty-three years of age and you have to be put to death because of your own stupidity, what a shame, I mean, you're a good looking boy. Angela and I have discussed on many occasions the idea of fucking with you. Wouldn't that have been fun?

Weaver coughed, and blood came out of his nostrils and his mouth, along with pieces of flesh. "Oh, that'll be your lungs disintegrating David, your body has consumed vast amounts of poisons. Your insides are practically melting. I thought it would be better than shooting you, shooting you would have been far too quick and easy. This way, you get to suffer a little, while I tell you what a complete waste of fucking time you really are. Angela says we're doing the world a favour, and I must admit I tend to agree. Ok, so I'll just make myself a nice cup of coffee and sit here and watch you eh…pop your clogs as it were, see you in Hell David, and then perhaps we can continue this little conversation." Claire Redgrave pulled a chair up next to Weaver's bed and sat down to enjoy her coffee, watching Weaver coughing and spurting blood and flesh all down his tee-shirt and jeans. A few minutes later, she stubbed out her cigarette and ran it under the cold tap and then placing it into a small polythene bag she put it inside her jacket pocket. She checked one last time for a pulse before opening Weaver's suitcase and retrieving the cash that he had in there. She left Buckley's credit-cards, after all they wouldn't be any good to anyone now. She then left the room and exited the hotel by the fire-door at the back of the premises.

Outside in the car park, the young lady who had posed as the hotel room-service waited for Claire Redgrave, her new boss, in the Audi A4 Saloon, Special-Edition 14T FSI (black) that she had bought for her.

"Well that was easy" said Claire, as she climbed into the vehicle.

The young lady smiled at her. "I thought he'd recognised me. I didn't think he was going to buy it."

"Oh I knew he'd fall for it Beverley, people like Weaver can't refuse anything free offered to them, recognised you from where?"

Beverley explained. "I went home with John Buckley one night. We'd sat in the pub and I ended up getting drunk. I went back to his place, just for a casual fuck, and David interrupted us, he'd come to ask John about something.

To my surprise, John let him in, and Weaver saw me half naked on John's sofa, well, completely naked actually."

Claire burst into laughter. "No wonder he didn't quite recognise you Bev, he wouldn't have been looking at your face girl. Come on, we've to meet Angela tonight and we're

going to have a few drinks. Celebrate your new post as chauffeur. You do as you're asked Beverley, and you'll make a lot of money girl, a lot, but whatever you do, don't be a fucking idiot like that silly bugger back there, because we'll cut your throat Beverley as quick as look at you if you fuck us about, but I'm sure you already know that don't you."
"Yes I do, I would never fuck you about, and I'm sure you know *that*, otherwise you wouldn't have hired me."
Claire Redgrave smiled at her new employee. "Yeah, you're right Bev." As they drove Beverley said, "He gave me a forty quid tip back there, you know for the eh..."
Again Redgrave burst into laughter. "Do you see what I mean about how thick he is, sorry was, he's went and gave you a forty quid tip for giving him the bottle of wine that's going to kill him, but at least he enjoyed a nice meal."

By the time Terry Mercer and Samantha Reynolds arrived at the hotel the forensic team were already there. Mercer took one look at Weaver. "Poisoned?" he said to Andrea Bortelli, head of the forensic team. Clad in her white suit complete with gloves and mouth mask, all of which hid her golden locks and her pretty thirty-two- year-old face, she nodded.
"We've found absolutely nothing. Whoever was in here knew exactly what they were doing. They've worn something over their shoes. If they've consumed any beverage in here they've washed the cup thoroughly. One of the guys found an abandoned dinner trolley in one of the hallways. The management here say it isn't one of theirs. Mister Weaver has recently eaten a meal, but it wasn't that that poisoned him, it was the wine."
Mercer looked at his watch. "What time did you get here?"
"About seven, one of the staff was sent up to his room to inform him that the cleaner was coming to do her service, he was due to leave here at eight."
"I know." said Mercer.
Bortelli continued. "When the girl got no answer she used the hotel key to let herself in, thinking that Weaver had already gone...she found this."
Bortelli pointed to the corpse.
Samantha Reynolds had been wandering around the room.
She continued wandering looking up to the celling and sniffing the air. She turned to Mercer. "It was a woman sir, whoever was in here with him it was a woman, definitely."
"And how might you know that Samantha?" said Mercer.
"I can smell her expensive perfume sir."
Bortelli tutted in frustration, and sighed. "That could have been the domestic's perfume

you're smelling there for goodness sakes, you can't-."

"No mam, the girl who discovered the body was not wearing perfume, she wore deodorant and nothing else." Reynolds even named the particular brand of deodorant the girl was wearing. She then entered the shower room and shouted back through to her superiors, she's been in here sir, she's been in here for quite a while." Mercer tried to bring a little light-heartedness into the discussion, sensing friction between the two women.

"You wouldn't happen to know the name of the brand of perfume would you Samantha?"

Much to his and Andrea Bortelli's surprise she replied, "Yes I do as a matter of fact. She then proceeded to inform them of the specific brand.

"I don't expect *you* to know sir, but Andrea should, it is a very expensive perfume, very expensive indeed. It certainly isn't common. Once you've smelled it, there'd be no mistaking it if you smelled it again somewhere."

Mercer wasn't completely convinced that Samantha wasn't being sarcastic towards him when she said that she didn't expect *him* to know about the expensive perfume.

He looked down to the corpse of David Weaver. "I tried kid, I tried. You should have come to us sooner than you did, bloody shame."

Samantha stepped forward. "Do you think it's been one of those women sir? You know, that Angela or the other one he was on about?"

"Probably Samantha, although at this point, all we can know for certain is the fact that it definitely wasn't fucking Florence Nightingale, that we know for certain." Andrea Bortelli turned away smiling under her mouth-mask at the expense of Samantha Reynolds. Mercer noticed and continued.

"Well, lets' be going Samantha, there's little we can do here until Andrea has finished digging about the mush and shit with her microscope and keen beady little eyes, she is the best in her field Samantha at doing this job, she'll find things among the shit that we never could. Six years at University, learning how to probe in amongst flesh and bones and shit, just to find the clues that'll bring those nasty criminals to book, she does a fantastic job, let's not hold her back any longer. Of course Samantha, I wouldn't expect *you* to know all that. In his own way Mercer was trying to give the women a little clip on the ear and remind them of the importance of their professionalism.

KAUNAS.

LITHUANIA.

Sophie Spencer Kirsty Crawford Alison Green and Lisa Jenson had all gathered in Chloe's room. Although Chloe was the oldest girl among them, she was petite and could easily be mistaken for being four years less than the eighteen she was. None of the girls in fact were very tall. All of them though purposefully chosen for their immaculate figures and their extreme beauty. Every girl in the room had by now experienced sexual depravities of one kind or another. Theirs' indeed was a dire situation. No-one at all as far as they could tell knew where they were. Back home they'd still be making inquiries in and around the areas they came from. If they were ever to get out of this place, it would have to be planned by themselves. All these girls had by now also become regular cocaine-users, for that though, no-one in the world could blame or criticise.
Lisa Jenson and Sophie Spencer had only a few minutes before they were to entertain two women and two men who were currently in the bar having a few drinks with Mister Saratov. They were both dressed, as requested by the clients, in skimpy little tartan mini-skirts with white school-girl socks up to their knees. All of the girls were comforting Chloe after her horrendous experience with the four men which had left her very sore and emotionally scarred. The girls had become accustomed as to what was expected of them in their line of `duty` and had become quite experienced in dealing with their situations. The fact that they didn't have any choice in the matter helped them to come to terms. Lisa Jenson had already formed a plan of sorts in her mind of how to escape from here but it would take some time before she'd be able to execute that plan. In the mean-time, she would have to become a whore and pretend as much or as convincingly as she could, that she enjoyed what she was doing. They were all becoming more and more sexually educated with each day that arrived. They could all apply makeup now as good as any professional, thanks to a certain Miss Monica Carosova who seemed to be over the moon with all the girls' performances thus far. They were all making Mister Saratov lots of money. Lisa began to explain what her plan consisted of. The down-side to this plan was the fact that only one of them would be able to leave here, and so, the girls left here would face the wrath of Saratov and Monica, but the person who escaped would be expected to find the police or authorities as soon as possible and bring them here as fast as they could. She also informed them that the ones left here could quite possibly be beaten or tortured. "They'll always be nice to us while we're making them loads of money, but that would all change if one of us were to escape, and then again,

there'd be no guarantee that my plan will work. When I have a little more time I'll tell you all how we would do it. We can take a vote as to which one of us gets to leave here." There were two soft taps on the door. Monica Carosova entered the room. "Are you ready ladies?" she said, smiling broadly at Lisa Jenson and Sophie Spencer. "Your clients are waiting for you in their room."

As the two girls left the room, Lisa turned and smiled at her friends and then answered Monica enthusiastically, and somewhat devilishly, "Oh I'm ready Monica, more than ready". Much to her friends' amusement, she grabbed Monica's bum as she left, and then tapped it twice, making Monica squeal with mock-delight. Lisa knew exactly what she was doing, she was gaining even more points in Monica's book, and that could never be a bad thing, owing to the fact that, the more she was in favour with her, the easier it would be to escape, or at least, the easier the opportunity of escape would present itself. To Lisa's surprise, Sophie done much the same as she had done, and placed her hand over the area of Monica's genitalia, kissing her full on the mouth. Monica returned the `gesture` to the two girls, by tapping them both on the front of their skirts, but like Saratov, Monica was a business-woman.

"Come on now girls. Now you two play nice today with your clients, you stand to make Mister Saratov a lot of money, and you also stand to make yourselves a huge tip, be nice and treat them good. I have had parties with these people, and they enjoy their sex. So don't you disappoint them, do your stuff girls and I'll see you both later in the bar." Monica followed Lisa and Sophie out of the room, leaving Chloe Alison and Kirsty.

"I wonder what Lisa's plan is" said Alison.

"God knows" said Chloe, but I for one will be listening to it eagerly."

SCOTLAND YARD.

BROADWAY VICTORIA.

Polly Shepard sat in her office with Terry and Samantha.
"I think that Weaver has given us this information ostensibly Terry.
We've checked out the names given to us and none of them seem to be traceable. We were informed by an ex-neighbour of this Claire Redgrave's that she hasn't lived in the address for more than three years. As for the others, well, you know all about Angela Bates, and by the way, she has not been seen since you and Samantha's last visit. As far as the two men are concerned, Charles Deacon and Arthur Ward, well, nobody can trace them anywhere. One of our ghosts is trying to find out anything they can as to their whereabouts but so far, nothing. I don't know if this Buckley has just filled the boy's head with shit, but nothing is materializing with the information he's given us."
Terry sighed heavily. "He told us that he didn't know their addresses so where have they got specific information about where they are or were staying. He said he only knew of their hangouts. He wrote down the names of two or three pubs in and around the boroughs of London, has anyone checked those out?"
Polly nodded, but not enthusiastically. "Nothing Terry. If anyone knows anything about these people, then they are keeping it to themselves, and judging by what they done to young Weaver, who could blame them?"
Mercer fumbled in his jacket pocket for his cigarettes. Placing one in his mouth he said, "If that boy was telling the truth, then they have another four girls ready to be taken over to Europe. I've got a team waiting to pounce tomorrow night at Grimsby, but like the lad said, they could quite easily have changed the date or in fact the harbour. We'll soon find out. I don't think the kid was lying to us Polly, he seemed really grateful for our protection. I think he was sympathetic towards the girls and what was happening to them. Now if this Buckley guy was their main man when shipping the girls overseas then there may well be a change in the time and place where they despatch them." Polly looked at Terry, tapping her pencil against her mouth. "Have we any news as to who owns this boat, The Marianne?"
"The boat is registered within the European fishing Industries. The vessel is legal Polly, but as far as getting an owner's name, well, the Belgian authorities are reluctant to say the least to part with any information. In truth Polly, I don't think they give a fuck."
Samantha spoke, explaining that they had numerous fishing ports around the country being observed in case they had changed the location.

Just about everyone in and around the coastal areas of Britain were on look-out duty to spot the vessel named The Marianne.

Mercer continued. "That boy would have known something, I'm sure of it. If he'd been on that boat, then he'd have known or at least had an idea of where in Europe specifically they are taking them. We've got a couple of numbers from his mobile that we're working on, but whoever killed him took out his SIM card. The bastards would know that he could have given us this information, but because of his own immaturity, he'd sentenced himself to death, Christ he was more wanted than Al Capone."

"Well" said Polly, rather exasperatingly, "all we can do is wait until tomorrow night, and hope that they still intend sailing from Grimsby, and that they have a replacement for this Buckley to supervise the journey."

"If they don't Polly, then there are another four girls going to be taken out of our country and not a bloody thing we can do to save them. I am quite sure there will be people out there who'll have all the details of when they intend to sail, but as we all know, fear is a powerful thing."

"Yes Terry, but so is a reward, a hefty reward. I'm seriously thinking about offering a substantial amount of money, and I mean big. If there is one thing that will challenge anyone's loyalty, it's a life-changing amount of money. If I get permission to go ahead with this, then I'll be putting it in the papers and advertising on the TV and Radio, someone will know, and someone will give in to the temptation of that kind of reward, of course, we will offer them full police protection. Whatever we do Terry, we have to put a stop to all these kidnappings. These poor girls, being ripped out of their lives and taken to God knows where to be used as slaves."

"Well, it's worth a try Polly, said Mercer, rising to his feet. "Although it didn't help young Weaver."

The following morning as Terry and Samantha Reynolds were preparing to leave for Grimsby an officer approached them. A young lady had contacted police at Hounslow, and said she had information which concerned a family member of hers'. An officer had spoken to the girl and had listened to what she had to say. As soon as they heard what it was, she recommended that Terry Mercer and Samantha Reynolds be informed. Mercer looked now at the officer informing him of the message. Sitting at his steering wheel with Samantha beside him he snarled, "Well? Are you going to fucking tell me what was said or am I to just sit here and guess?" The young officer handed a piece of paper to him. "She wants to speak to you sir specifically, or inspector Reynolds, nobody else." Mercer snatched the piece of paper from him and looked at the number.

The recruit attempted to say something further to Mercer, but he'd already began to drive off. After a short discussion with Samantha, Mercer decided to pull in and phone the number given to him. He was just about to switch off his phone when a female voice answered him. "

"Hello"?

Hello"? Replied Mercer. "I believe you wish to speak to me or inspector Reynolds, is that correct?"

"Yes. My name is Leslie Graham."

"Hi Leslie Graham, this is inspector Mercer, how can I be of assistance to you?" There was a short pause and then the girl replied, "It's em…it's about my sister, she's em…she's acting weird and, and she's got money, she's buying expensive clothes and everything. I know she was taking drugs for a while, but now she's, it's strange, she's changed." All this conversation was doing for Terry Mercer, was exacerbating his problems. "Listen Leslie, I really haven't got the time to listen to how your sister is acting strange or what she chooses to buy in terms of her wardrobe, but listen, perhaps one day soon you and I can meet up for a coffee somewhere and we can discuss the latest Paris collections in full, you know, when I'm not hunting kidnappers or murderers, I'll be in touch with you, if you could just-."

"Just fucking listen to me. This is not easy what I'm doing to my sister. She hasn't had a job for over ten months now, but the other day, she pulls up in front of my flat in a brand new fucking Audi. The clothes I'm referring to are not your run of the mill off-the-peg everyday shit. She gave me enough money to pay our rent for another six months in advance. She goes off in her new car and I don't see her again for ages. I'm worried as to how she's obtaining this money, like I say she hasn't had a job for ages, but, hey, if you think I'm wasting your fucking time then I'll just hang up. I just thought that you'd take the time to question her as to how she gets the money, wish I hadn't fucking phoned now, I mean you're always asking the public to assist you in any way they can, and then when somebody does call you, you more or less tell them to fuck off, well fuck you too."

"Hey, slow down Leslie. Listen, is there any way we could meet up this morning. Inspector Reynolds and I could have a little chat with you. I know how much Audi cars cost and I know that it could be a big deal, and we really *do* appreciate you contacting us. Where are you, are you in Hounslow?"

"Yes."

"Tell me where we could meet you and we'll come right over."

A little over an hour later Terry Mercer and Samantha Reynolds sat in a café with the concerned young lady.

"I'm just worried Mister Mercer. My sister is a good kid. She's never been in trouble and she's always had a job. But just lately, this spell of unemployment has been doing her head in. She was spending three hours a day applying for jobs but she hasn't been getting any luck. Anyway, about four months ago, she suddenly comes home loaded with money. She bought me jewellery and clothes, really expensive clothes, you know, as a thank you for not taking any money from her, anyway I couldn't, she didn't have any, but now, she's buying all sorts of things. When I ask her where she gets the money, she just smiles and tells me that she's not doing anything illegal, I mean I even asked her if she was…you know, if she was…em…selling herself. She took offence at that and told me never to ask her anything like that again. She said, I told you I'm not doing anything illegal, and that's all you need to worry about, but I *do* worry. I even asked her if she'd won some money on the lottery but she just said I'm afraid not, and if she did, did I think that she wouldn't tell me. I just don't know, but you want to see this car, I mean its' top-of-the-range stuff, really classy."

Samantha spoke now as she stirred her coffee.

"What's your sister's name Leslie?"

"Her name is Beverley, Beverley Graham."

"Well, I'll tell you what we'll do. We'll arrange for someone to trace her movements for a few days. See who she hangs out with. Don't worry she won't know she's being watched. We'll just take note of her daily routine and try and find out where she's obtaining this money from. Does she still sign on for unemployment benefits?"

"No, not as far as I know, I don't think so, and anyway why would she when she's got all the money she needs." Leslie Graham gave the inspectors her address and thanked them for at least trying to get to the bottom of this. As far as Terry and Samantha were concerned, if the girl wasn't doing anything illegal then there wasn't much else they could do. Mercer smiled at the young lady as he and Samantha rose to their feet.

"I'll keep hold of this number of yours Leslie, if that's ok, and if we hear anything we'll be in touch." He scribbled down his mobile number onto a piece of scrap paper.

"If you hear anything then you let us know ok? Anything at all about what she's doing, and if you want my advice Leslie, don't keep asking her where she's getting anything, take it all in your stride, don't let her see that it bothers you, because if she is doing something illegal, then your questioning could cause her trouble…so, be cool, ok?"

Across the street in the bookmakers, Charles Deacon and Arthur Ward stood gazing out of the window and wondering what on earth Claire's chauffer's sister was talking to the two detectives about.

SCOTLAND YARD.

BROADWAY VICTORIA.

Polly Shepard stood with her mug of tea in her hands contemplating the city. Terry and Samantha could only have been out of her office five minutes when the phone rang on her desk. It was confirmation that another four girls had gone missing. David Weaver had been telling the truth, another four girls, this time from Manchester and the surrounding areas. She stood sipping her tea wondering what on earth had happened to society that these people could snatch young girls off the streets and hold them captive until they decided when to sell them on to foreigners to be their sexual play-things. Most of the girls were still school age, or not much older. The devastating effect this was having on their families played on Polly's mind. She knew the girls were being smuggled into Europe but she didn't know where exactly. It was unlikely that they were being held in France or Belgium even though Weaver had informed them that the fishing boat had docked there. She'd had information given to her that it was Eastern European businessmen who were purchasing the girls but at this point, there was nothing concrete. Poland perhaps or the Ukraine, Lithuania Serbia, they could be anywhere, and unless she had definite proof of the crimes being committed then there was little chance of any of these countries' working with British intelligence. It was a dilemma to say the least. Scotland Yard had decided to bring in M.I.6 into the mix. They were sending two `ghosts` out into Eastern Europe to try and at least find out where the girls were being taken to but the task was mammoth. They would be given three months to try and discover what exactly was happening. The chances of them being successful were slim to no chance at all, because some of these countries were vast, but, all said and done, there was a chance. If they could find out exactly where they were they could start to make progress. Just a country, a pointer, a trigger, then wheels could be put into motion. What kind of people were they, that could take these young girls' freedom, to snatch them away from their families and their futures, their birth-given right to a standard of life, of education, and opportunities, all taken away from them for what? She knew only too well the answer to that question. The question she'd asked herself was in fact rhetorical, and the answer was money. It's what most crime was about, financial gain. Somewhere out there in the capitol, there was a syndicate making trunk loads of money at the expense of these young girls. If only they'd came into contact with David Weaver earlier then perhaps they could have apprehended one or more of the culprits, but the boy had sealed his own fate by flaunting his new-found wealth all over the place and boasting about the syndicate he worked with. Terry had been so close. They'd all but disappeared from the radar. If it hadn't been for the information given to her today, she would have thought that the syndicate had in fact shut down their operations for a while, but no, they hadn't shut down, which meant that every pretty school-girl up and down the country was at risk every time they left their homes.

B272.

Terry and Samantha were on their way to speak with Alison Green's father. The man had called in to request an interview with Mercer regarding information of his daughter's whereabouts. Mercer was told that the man had useful information regarding the location of the missing girls. Neither of the detectives felt optimistic as they pulled up outside of the Green's household. Jillian Green, Alison's mother, opened the door and invited them in. Like so many times before Mercer and Reynolds witnessed for themselves the devastation on the faces of parents grieving and worrying about their children. Jillian Green's face was no exception. Little sleep, loss of appetite, heavy smoking, these were all common factors in the abduction game.

Colin Green had been seated on the sofa when the two detectives entered the room. He rose to his feet and extended his right hand to Mercer and Reynolds.

A few minutes later, having consumed a cup of tea, Colin Green then requested that his remaining daughter Rebecca, and his wife should leave the room. Sam looked at Mercer somewhat surprised at this request, but they both immediately left the room without question. Colin sat back down on the sofa. "How are you getting on with your enquiries? I'm not being sarcastic in any way because I know that little progress has been made. You're only hope realistically is to catch this syndicate and put an end to the kidnappings over here in Britain, and to be quite honest, that's all you can hope for, however, that doesn't help my daughter Mister Mercer, does it, or any of the other girls who have already been taken away from their families. Mercer sighed softly, nodding his head and submitting to the truth. Colin Green smiled almost sympathetically at Mercer. "I know sir that you are doing all that you can, I have no doubts whatsoever about that, and I am extremely grateful for your efforts, but as I say, it's not helping Alison." Mercer looked at the man in front of him. A strong man, a very strong man, his physic suggesting many hours in a gymnasium, either that or extreme hard work on a regular basis. His eyes held no fear, his expression was stone-like. He was a solid confident man, and an ex- military one if he wasn't mistaken.

He wasn't. "Mister Mercer, I am a carpenter to trade. I learned my trade in the forces and I have built up my business in the last eight years through honesty and hard work. I owe my skills to the army, my military days are over, but the skills, the combat skills I learned will be with me for the rest of my life. I have friends who are still in active duty, and we stay in touch. Sometimes-."

Before he finished what he was about to say, Terry Mercer interrupted him.

"You know where your daughter is don't you Colin."

Colin Green lit up a cigarette. As he exhaled the smoke, he said, "I know what country she's in, and the other girls who were taken with her."
Mercer was about to ask the man if he was sure about this but then decided against it. Colin Green was having a hard enough time without him insulting his intelligence.
Green continued. "Before I tell you anything else detective Mercer, I need you and your colleague here to give me your word that you will not repeat to anyone, repeat anyone, what I am about to tell you, can you do that?"
Samantha and Terry knew only too well the dangers of releasing the information. If this information was to do with Green's daughter and the missing girls, and if they approached Polly Sheppard with it, then she could unwittingly put the girls' lives in danger because her superiors would undoubtedly inform the prime minister. Political decisions would be made which could quite easily put the girls' safety in jeopardy. They knew exactly why Green had insisted on their word. In unison the two detectives replied, "We promise."
"They're in Lithuania, my friend is trying even as we speak to find out where.
The girls were picked up in Belgium, again I don't know where exactly, and then they were driven across Europe into Lithuania. Now I didn't have to tell you that remember, so I am counting on your honesty." There was a short silence before Green continued.
"I'm going over there and I'm going to bring my daughter back home along with the rest of those poor girls." Mercer sat nodding his head smiling. "I know Colin that you are a skilled man, and I also know that you will indeed possess all these military skills you talk about, but do you honestly believe that you will be able to march into Lithuania and single-handedly deal with whoever these people are, and disrupt their racket. Even before you get anywhere near those girls, and that's to say you find out their exact location you will be tracked down and shot. Don't you think you're going through enough hard times? Your wife Colin, you can't put her through-."
"My wife already knows what I'm going to do. My other daughter Rebecca doesn't but my wife does, and she knows all the implications if things should go wrong, but I have to try Mister Mercer, I have to get over there, I have to find her, I will find her."
Samantha leaned forward on her chair and softly spoke to Colin Green. "Mister Green, you have to be realistic here. As good as you probably are, you are only one man. One man against God knows how many."
"Wrong detective Reynolds, I am not just one man. I am a hundred men. I am a businessman, I am a lorry driver, I am a chef, I am a gardener, I am anyone I need to be, I will find her."
"Can you speak Lithuanian?" said Reynolds. "We can all dress up to be who we want to be, but if you can't speak the language, and convincingly then you haven't got a hope in

Hell of getting anywhere near your daughter, like Terry said, you don't even know who it is that's holding your daughter, it could quite possibly be someone in high authority, you just don't know, and how on earth are you going to get there? Where will you stay? They'll be asking you why you are there in the first place, I mean when it comes to places to go on holiday Lithuania isn't high up on anyone's list. What you are proposing to do, is preposterous."

Again there was a short silence before Mercer said, "Well, if you intend going ahead with this eh, plan of yours, why did you bother to tell us, because now, all you've done by making me and Sam swear an oath, is to give us something else to worry about, something else that we are completely powerless to do anything about. I fail to see why you informed us at all if we are not to pass on this information to higher authorities. I fail to see your purpose for telling us."

Green stared at Mercer like he was going to shoot him.

"The diplomatic relationships between Britain Poland and Germany are good. If I can find out the exact location of the girls, I will inform you, the Polish and German authorities would work with us, I'd only have to get the girls over the border into Poland, they would assist us from there."

"Us?" said Mercer. "They would assist us? How on earth are you going to get five girls and yourself into Poland? I'm saying five, God knows how many girls are being kept there, Samantha's right, it is preposterous what you're attempting, in fact it's ludicrous. You're off your head Colin, you won't-."

"Hey, you leave all that stuff to me, that's my problem how I get to them not yours. You are detectives, you deal with evidence and cover-ups and deceitfulness, I deal with situations and how to solve or change these situations. No offence but neither of you are capable of dealing with situations like these, I am, and I will find my daughter, you can bet your life on that, and if I die achieving this then you can also be guaranteed that at least ten will die with me. As preposterous as it may sound to you, it's all I've got to work on, and at least it's a positive move. I have a situation that needs to be resolved and I will resolve it. He who dares wins Mister Mercer."

Terry and Samantha left the house feeling despondent. The situation Colin Green was putting himself in was nothing less than suicidal. Analytically speaking it was in fact impossible. His chances of survival Mercer reasoned were the same as that of a lame Gazelle making it across the Serengeti un-noticed. Mercer knew that the man was being driven by the love and affection of his daughter. That was understandable. But he was also being driven by the lack of progress being made here in Britain. After all, it had just been announced on the radio that another four girls had gone missing from

Manchester. Mercer felt frustrated. Perhaps they should have hauled in Angela Bates for intense questioning when they'd had the chance, but he also knew that if they had nothing concrete to charge her with, then she'd have walked right back out as free as a bird, and any further questioning would have been looked upon by some money-grabbing solicitor as harassment. Sam spoke now to him as they made their way to the car. "What do you think Terry? Do you think we should tell Polly about this? If we do nothing, then that man back there is going to die. Maybe if we inform Polly she could contact the chief of police who in turn could contact the foreign minister. Perhaps they could then work something out with the Lithuanian government, because as it stands now I-."

"I know how it stands now Sam!" snapped Mercer. They climbed into their car. To make matters worse, the Greens stood on their threshold with their one remaining daughter waving to them, all smiling softly. Mercer pictured another scene in his head, where Alison Green was standing there with them, perhaps waving off some happy relative. Looking at them now, the picture was incomplete. Colin Green with all good intentions would dive into this suicidal mission of his to be able to stand Alison on that step again and complete the picture. He remembered the SAS's famous motto, He Who Dares Wins. There was another saying though that he was very familiar with.

`Fools Rush-In... where Angels Fear to Tread`.

KAUNAS.

LITHUANIA.

Lisa Jensen looked all around her in one of the hallways of the house. The place was huge, gigantic. In the last few days the British girls had been introduced to some of the other girls here. Today Monica was leading them into a very large lounge. It could have been any lounge in any good hotel. There was a bar at one end of the room complete with bartender and an elderly lady who was collecting glasses from the tables. In the far corner there was an original nineteen fifties juke-box. It was now playing out modern pop music. The lounge was fitted with beautiful aubergine carpet which had gold-coloured flowers etched into its' pattern. The walls were papered with aubergine and white wallpaper. Hanging from the celling were three huge crystal chandeliers all sparkling bright cheerful light. Monica informed them that they could come here on their `days off` and enjoy a few drinks. This room was the only one in the giant house where they were allowed to mix with other girls unless otherwise instructed by Monica or Mister Saratov. Lisa Jensen Alison Green and Sophie Spencer all sat down at a table with Monica. Over on the other side of the room there was a group of girls all dressed like they were going out for the night, complete with beautiful dresses and shoes, make-up and immaculate hair-dos'. They looked a little drunk, all of them smoking cigarettes and drinking some kind of spirits. Bursts of laughter escaped sporadically as they all sat chatting to one another, occasionally glancing over at them. For Lisa Jensen the scene was somewhat confusing. If they had been brought here in the same manner as she had been, then how on earth could they sit and laugh heartily like this? Drink or no drink, surely they would pine for their homes, wherever that was. All of those girls looked European. Polish or German perhaps, no doubt she'd find out soon enough. Half an hour earlier Monica had come in to Lisa's room and told her to get dressed and also to bring some money as they were going for drinks. The statement had given Lisa a spark of hope, thinking they would be leaving the grounds and visiting a local pub or hotel. Opportunity. But no, this is where they would have their drinks. Lisa's heart had sunk as Monica explained to them as they walked that they'd be visiting the `Cosmopolitan` lounge in the house. She also went on to inform them that every four weeks the mobile boutique would arrive here giving them an opportunity to spend their money on clothes and make-up and everything else a girl needs. She asked the girls what they'd like to drink and then headed over to the bar. The handsome young man behind the bar dressed in white shirt and tie and black trousers immediately stopped serving the girls he had been attending to and served Monica.

One of the girls approached Monica and kissed her on the cheek. As Monica left the bar with her four drinks on the tray, the same girl playfully tapped her on her backside. Lisa wondered if the girl was playing the same game as she was, gaining trust and confidence.

"Ok Ladies?" said Monica as she sat down the tray on the table. "I know this is all strange to you just now but I'm quite sure you will all fit in soon enough, all the girls love it here. They can relax and let their hair down and tell each other jokes and share stories with each other. The drinks are really cheap as you will all find out. Everybody is friendly and happy. You're all going to love it here." It was as though she was selling a holiday to them, Lisa thought to herself, as if it were a privilege for them to be here, like they should feel honoured to be allowed to come in here and drink. Like an exclusive elaborate club of some description.

Never mind about apologising to them for stealing them away from their families and friends, for ripping away their futures, for taking them away from their homelands, and for making money from them by using them as whores, no, none of that. "Oh you're going to love it here" was all she'd heard from the minute she'd awoken from the drug induced coma they had administered upon her. There was no remorse whatsoever about what they were doing to them. Rich drunk men and women, paying astronomical amounts of money to use them any way they felt like using them. Some of the girls had been hurt so badly they had bled from their rectums. Others had been physically sick being forced to swallow as the men ejaculated into their mouths.

As far as Lisa Jensen was concerned, these people were just as guilty as her captors, in fact they were even worse. Because of the amounts of money they were spending, they treated the girls as nothing better than sex toys, as though they were not even human. *They* would leave here sexually satisfied and head back out of those gates in their fancy cars back to their `normal` lives, probably with wives and children at home, as if what they had done in here had not even taken place. Masked by alcohol and cocaine, most of the girls in here could cope. They could accept their situation and try and make the best of it. Well not her, not Lisa Jensen. She would find a way of getting herself out of here and she would bring these sick bastards to book. This animal Saratov who had `bought` her from those low-lives`, who were even lower than he, would be brought down. She would make sure of that, or she would die trying. As she looked around, she wondered how many more girls in here felt the same way, or had they accepted what had happened to them, and just intended to make the best of it. Lisa also wondered if they were aware of the fact that most of the `customers` who came here craved the really young girls. Did they ever think of what would happen to them once they got to a certain age? When they became, `less popular`? Not in demand anymore? Surplus to requirements? Did they think that Monica and Saratov were just going to let them leave here and go back to where they'd been taken from? With all this information about what goes on in here with under-age girls?

No sir, that would just not happen, otherwise they'd be lifted and imprisoned before they could say their names. She remembered what Monica had told her when she'd asked if she could go for a walk around the grounds of the house, and she felt a chill now in her spine as she remembered Monica's answer.

"Now whatever you do Lisa, do not go anywhere near those dogs in their kennels at the back of the house, and get them all excited."

SCOTLAND YARD.

BROADWAY VICTORIA.

All the way over to HQ Terry and Samantha had been discussing the situation regarding Colin Green. By law and by the very nature of their investigations they were bound to inform Polly Sheppard. Their biggest worry about doing that was if Polly unwittingly informed the wrong people. There were certain people in office that did not possess the brains they were born with. They could spark off all kinds of scenarios and jeopardise the lives of those girls over there, not to mention the life of Colin Green. If they could unfold this information to Polly and ask her, for the moment at least to keep it to herself, then that would give them some time to work out some kind of plan of action. They would soon find out. They were now riding the elevator up to Polly's office.
"If only we'd had contact with Weaver just a little earlier Terry, who knows what information we could have obtained from him. He was keen to talk to us, very communicative."
"Yeah" agreed Mercer. "He'd dug himself into deep shit and lost his shovel. We were his only hope of staying alive. Anyway, he's gone now, so we'll have to find another source for our information, let's just see how we get on in here first with Polly." Apprehension was building up in Terry, and Sam could see it, even by the way he was looking at her now. She braced herself.
"Is this another leather coat you're wearing? How fucking many leather coats do you own? Half the population of the worlds' animals are being slaughtered just to keep your candy-ass warm, you should think shame on yourself, Christ, and it doesn't even make you look any harder or sexier or whatever the fucking reason is for you wearing them. You're not fucking hard in any way, in fact, you've been put on with me just to get my fags and scones when I need them, you're not fucking hard, as a matter of fact, you're just a girly with a Glock water pistol, so I don't know why you're wearing fucking leather coats all the time!"
"Yes, and this girly has had it to the back teeth with your continuous profanations and senseless banter. You are about ten seconds off me sticking my Glock water pistol up your fucking arse and pulling the trigger, twice."
Polly Sheppard was exiting her office and was just in time to hear Samantha Reynolds inform Mister Terrence Mercer that he was, "Nothing but a moaning frustrating irritable fucking bastard!!"
Polly sighed. "Hello you two" she sighed, reopening her office door. Need I ask how you

are getting on?"

"We need to talk Polly." said Mercer.

"Yes, I can see that. What can I do for you, very little I would imagine, judging by the way you're addressing each-other."

"We have information Polly, and I mean meaningful information. Sam and I have been discussing whether or not to share it with you.

We gave our word you see, we swore we wouldn't tell anyone else, at least for the time being."

"So why are you here Terry if you don't wish to tell me?"

Twenty minutes later, Polly had agreed with the detectives. She wouldn't inform anyone of the girls' whereabouts, with the exception of the two ghosts.

They would be informed and would then be able to investigate where exactly in Lithuania the girls were being held. She also told Terry and Samantha, that if they were so concerned with the safety of Colin Green, she could stop him leaving the country, or at least delay him for a while. Terry looked at Samantha and then surprised her by asking her opinion.

"Ordinarily, I would say yes, stop him, but Colin Green is no ordinary man, he's ex-SAS, and he'll be able to look after himself, plus, no matter what Miss Sheppard does to stop him, he'll know that it was us Terry who broke our word, he's not stupid, and besides, I've just said it, he's ex-SAS. Short of putting him in prison, if he wants to leave the country, then he'll leave the country."

As they left Polly's office she could hear them arguing among themselves again. It reminded Polly of the relationship that Terry used to have with a dear old friend and colleague. It was looking like Terry and Samantha were going to have a similar relationship...chalk and cheese...but it worked, or at least, she hoped it would.

As Terry and Samantha exited the building his mobile phone buzzed in his pocket. Looking at the message he said to Samantha, "Old Treble wants to see us, says he's got some good news."

"Have we *got* time to get to the bank? We visit him, and it costs you half a months' salary to have a coffee."

Mercer didn't reply to Samantha's sarcasm. He handed the car key to her and informed her that she'd be driving everywhere they went from now on and that she'd have to learn to drive at a decent speed and not at the speed of a milk-float. "It's embarrassing when cyclists are overtaking us when we're driving through the city...it looks like you're taking your first driving lesson every time we go out. I mean, do you know that the car has more than three gears Samantha, I'm being serious."

"I wonder what Treble wants to see us about?" said Samantha glancing in her rear-view mirror as she pulled out onto the street. "Whatever it is, it'll be worthwhile you can bet your bottom dollar on that."

"Have you got any money left to bet with Terry? You must hold the record in Scotland Yard for paying out the most money to your snitches. To my knowledge everybody else threatens their snitches into giving them the required information, but not you, you give away twenty pound notes and bottles of Scotch to all and sundry, and fifty pound bonuses to whores who tell you what time their neighbours come home, you've got it sussed haven't you, you've got it all worked out. That's intuition for you, that's using your initiative."

"I hope Treble's still in by the time we get to Croydon, a lot can happen in two hours, Christ, I read the first paragraph of that guy's paper there as we passed him on the pavement."

Samantha had by now a good idea of when and what sparked off Terry's rants, stress, or hunger, and sometimes both. She knew he was concerned about what Colin Green had planned out, and how they were completely powerless to do anything about it. As far as Terry was concerned, and her if she was honest, the man was heading for certain death. Thirty minutes later they pulled up outside of Geoffrey Marsden's flat.

Samantha glanced at her watch. "Well, according to you, I'm an hour and a half early, but he'll be able to fit us in won't he? He'll always find time for you Terry, hell anyone would, you're really quite popular aren't you. When you're finished in here I'm going for something to eat, I'm starving...I'll just make sure I have enough money on me before we leave."

Again, Mercer refused to bite, although he did admire her sarcasm and wit, the girl was talented there was no doubt about that. They entered the flat and Terry called out Treble's name. From the living room they heard the reply that sounded like one continuous word.

"UmineerTel."

Samantha tapped Terry on the shoulder and said, "I think that meant I'm in here."

"That's enough Sam, just leave it out."

They entered the living room to find old `Treble` seated upon his sofa completely drunk. In front of him on a small coffee table there were several plates of untouched sandwiches and a bottle of Johnny Walker which *had* been touched several times, in fact, if it were touched just once more it would be empty.

"Cam in cam in me ole mucka Tel and your giwfriend, cam in buddy boy, I got some facking good twelve-bar for you kid, an befoe ya say anyfing, you're facking welcome kid, cos you're a facking ace, that what you is, facking ace boy, and yer welcome, get yourselves a drink to celebrate, they remembered old facking Treble so they did, we're

going on `oliday pal me and you and yo gel we are."
Terry smiled and looked at Samantha.
"Don't look at me, I'm not a dialectologist. He has spoken so many words there and not one of them coherent. Nobody can say that old Geoffrey speaks laconically can they? He must have spoken a thousand words there in that one sentence."
It took Terry all of fifteen minutes to `translate` what old Treble was attempting to tell him. Eventually, Treble pointed to his credenza and asked Terry to `fetch` the brown envelope over to him. Samantha smiled as Terry rose up from the chair and retrieved the envelope, handing it to his elderly friend. Treble struggled to pull out the letter and the tickets.
"Allow me Treble" he said, taking it from his hands. Slowly but surely, the smile on Terry's face widened as he read on. He stood up and looked at the nicotine-stained ceiling, smiling up at it as though he were smiling to God, like a prayer had been answered. The long and short of it was, that old Treble had been invited over to Lithuania as a special guest at the European Festival of Orchestras and had VIP tickets for himself and two other guests of his choice. Terry was overjoyed that Treble had decided that his two chosen guests would be himself and Samantha. This was going to open all kinds of possibilities for the two detectives. Here was an opportunity for him and Samantha to march straight into Lithuania legally. On top of that, it wasn't going to cost the Metropolitan Police Department a single penny. Add to that, they would be accommodated in a luxurious hotel with all comforts. The only down-side to this was that they would only have three days in which to work. Hopefully, by the time they were due to fly out, the ghosts who were already over there might have found out the girls' exact location. Mercer hadn't felt this exhilarated for a long time.
"Come on Treble, let's get you up and sorted out, here, start eating some of these sandwiches old pal. Have you got any coffee? Where do you keep your coffee?"
Samantha had already rose from her chair and was now in the process of making them all a cup.
"Make his black Sam" said Mercer, sitting Treble straight up and supporting his head on the sofa. "You're a fucking gem Treble, do you know that? I'm going to see to it that you are well rewarded for your gesture, you fucking old diamond that you are."
Samantha brought Treble's coffee through. "Black coffee does not sober anybody up Terry, it's just a myth, really, I thought you'd know that, you know, with all your own personal experiences."
Mercer took the cup from her hands and calmly explained to her why black coffee was given to a drunk person. Smiling, he said "I know perfectly well that it doesn't Sam, but what it does is, it makes the person sick as a dog. Once the person has spewed their

guts up, then there is less chance of them choking in their sleep on their own vomit, you see? On top of that, they start to heal as well, they feel better. The dizziness goes and there is more chance of them being able to walk unsupported, that's why the black coffee, ok? Are you happy now that you've been educated into the purpose of the black coffee?" Mercer and Reynolds stayed with Treble for a full hour almost forcing the cheese and onion sandwiches down his throat. Treble had indeed vomited in the bathroom and was now feeling much better than he had been as he sat now munching away at his `buffet`. Mercer sat opposite the old man on one of the easy-chairs lighting up a cigarette. "You can tell Sam, you can tell real quality when it comes to choosing people you can trust. This old badger here would do anything for me, and not through fear of consequences either, he would just do anything for me. Imagine that Sam, he chooses you and I as his honoured guests, what a fucking gem. Now Sam, we get a chance to actually do something to try and help those poor girls over there, and it's all down to this old fucker here. First-class flights and hotel of his choice, absolutely unbelievable, Christ what an opportunity for us Samantha, and those fuckers in HQ can't piss and moan about anything because it's not costing the miserable bastards anything." Mercer was on a high.

"Thank you Terry, I'm serious, thank you."

"For what? What have you got to thank *me* for, it was old Treble who said you could come, fuck if it were up to me, you wouldn't be going anywhere, let's get that clear ok? It was that old fucker who insisted that you come along, and while we're on the subject, you might want to get your arse over there and give the guy a kiss for such a gesture, at least a big kiss on his cheese and onion Johnny Walker mouth you ungrateful bitch that you are."

Terry Mercer admired his colleague more than he would ever admit openly.

Her wit was second only to his own, (Second only in his opinion.) and her next sentence had him spraying his coffee from his mouth with laughter as she casually replied, rising up to put her empty coffee mug in the sink.

"I might take off my leather coat and suck his whiskey-withered cock for him when he sobers up properly."

SCOTLAND YARD.

BROADWAY VICTORIA.

Polly Sheppard was elated at the news given to her by Terry and Samantha. She informed them that the two ghosts had been informed that the girls were being held somewhere in Lithuania, and that they were making inquiries even as they spoke. It would surely be only a matter of time before they found out their exact location. There was only eight days to go until they were due to fly out there with old Treble. Once there, they would only have three days in which to find the girls. If they stayed any longer than that, then they'd be in trouble, their presence in Lithuania would be illegal. For this reason, Polly explained to the two detectives that they would have to go there as holiday-makers. They were both to take time off so as not to inform the Metropolitan Police of their purpose for going. Then, if they overstayed their time the MET could not be held responsible for their actions. Mercer rose from his seat and proceeded to pour himself another coffee.
"When was the last time you spoke to any of the ghosts Polly?"
"Yesterday, they said they were making intense inquiries to find out the exact location. They are currently in Vilnius, well, one of them is, the other is searching in different areas of the country. Surely they'll hear something soon."
"Let's hope so Polly, we've got about a week before we head out there."
"Listen Terry, this *is* genuine this trip is it? I mean you know what some of these old codgers are like, they make stories up and just-."
"Hey, he's genuine Polly, we've seen the tickets haven't we Sam, the guy was shit-hot Polly. Nobody gives him any praise these days for his skills on the Cello, and here the guy's been given praise and indeed honoured for his services in his work...is he genuine? Fuck Polly, the man was one of the best. He was in the London Philharmonic for goodness sakes...is he genuine, Christ, what a thing to say Polly."
"Could you reach over the desk please Samantha and hit him a crack on the bridge of his nose please with one of those telephones. You've always got to jump up in arms whenever anyone asks you a civil question. I was only saying Terry, the man is an alcoholic, he havers away sometimes about things, you've said it yourself. I didn't want you to get disappointed that's all." Mercer drank his coffee and excused himself.
"Where's he off to Samantha, do you know?"
"Yes, he's off to the bathroom. If he gets up and leaves like that, then that's where he's headed, otherwise he'd be barking orders at me to follow him or telling me to move my

arse into gear." Polly smiled at Sam. "You've got him all weighed up then detective Reynolds."

"Just about Miss Sheppard...just about. He's actually not that bad to work with once you get your head round all the swearing and cursing he does. Actually, he's quite a nice guy. Please don't ever inform him that I said that Miss Sheppard, I beg you."

Again, Polly just smiled at her.

"There is something though, that's eating him up, something really bad I'm guessing. It's as though he's...well...hurting, you know, suffering, emotionally I mean, and it's constant, it's continuous."

Polly leaned across the table and almost whispered. "Oh he's hurting alright Samantha, trust me, and any man who has come through what he's came through...well, you wouldn't wish it upon anyone Sam, let me put it that way. The man has been emotionally tortured beyond belief. One day, if he thinks you're close enough to him, he might let you know what it was that happened to him, and if he ever does, then be prepared to be shocked beyond belief, because if you didn't like him now, then you'd soon change your opinion of him when he's told you what happened, and in fact what still is happening."

"So I was right then Miss Sheppard, I knew it."

Polly sipped *her* coffee. "You have no idea how right you are Samantha, and please, call me Polly, at least when we're in here, oh by the way, don't ever venture to tell him that you know something bad has happened to him, he'd go bloody ballistic, so, if he wants to tell you, he'll tell you in his own time, ok?" Mercer entered the room once again.

"Come on Sam, we're heading back over to Mitcham to see Jillian Green, the poor woman."

"What's happened now Terry, is it her husband? He's not gone and-."

"Yip, he's off, she's just texted me. He's off on his stupid bloody suicide mission. Polly, please contact me straight away if those boys over there find out exactly where the girls are. And why the hell is she bothering to inform me about that, she knew exactly what he intended to do, she accepted it when he told her of his plan. I mean why tell us? We can't bloody do anything to help him, she heard me trying to talk him out of it. It's not as though we can keep an eye on him is it."

"Terry, please, calm yourself down, it's not your fault he's taken off. Go and see what she's saying, she may have some information for you, you know, about where exactly he's going, or maybe a message for you and Sam."

Mercer drained his coffee cup and put on his jacket which had been draped over the chair. Sam was dying to make a comment to him because the jacket was leather. It would have to wait until the appropriate opportunity arose.

Then she would unleash her burning sarcasm upon him.

"Come on" he sighed to Samantha Reynolds, "there's no time to be sitting drinking coffee with Polly all day, move your arse, and let's see if we can get to Mitcham before it's dark."

Polly rose to her feet to fill her own coffee mug. "She can sit here all day drinking coffee with me if I wish her to, and tomorrow if I feel like it. In case you've forgotten, it's me who runs the show around here and don't you ever forget that mister. And the fact that it is now only nine-fifteen a.m. then the daylight comment about Mitcham is your attempt at mocking Sam's driving. Inspector Mercer, I wish you to move your arse now please, and go and visit Jillian Green to see what the poor woman has to say about her husband, and please refrain from these bloody sarcastic inflictions, because I could mock you from here to Holborn and back, so cut it out."

Today Samantha was wearing a soft padded waterproof jacket. She smiled at Polly as she left the room with Mercer and whispered to the chief inspector, "He's got his hard-as-fuck jacket on today. Can't wait to tell him how it doesn't make him look any harder and that he's guilty for half the world's animals being slaughtered just to keep his bloody back warm."

When Terry and Samantha reached Mitcham they were greeted at the door by Jillian Green who seemed quite cheerful, or at least, less stressed than she had been. She invited the detectives into her home and made them comfortable. "He's taken off then Jillian?" said Mercer. Jillian nodded her head. "He's promised to keep me in touch as to his progress. I must admit, I'm not as worried as I initially was, he's going to have help once he gets there."

Mercer fought hard to hold back his sarcasm. Instead, he smiled politely at her and said, "Really, does he know someone who lives in Lithuania then?"

"Yes, well, they don't live there. This person he knows, he used to be in the army with him, he's eh…he's working for the government at the moment.

Mister Mercer, have you ever heard of secret agents who are referred to as ghosts?"

Now it was Mercer's turn to smile. "Indeed I have Jillian, and I have to agree, I feel a little more at ease myself now that I know he has some company, not that I'm doubting for one minute your husband's skills. I take it this ghost is ex S.A.S. as well?"

Jillian nodded her head again. They've stayed in touch since Colin came out of the forces, although Colin never told me what Jim was doing, you know, with this secret kind of work he's doing. It's almost like he's a spy."

"That's correct Jillian, but these guys are the best at what they do.

They are so secret that there is no trace of them on any files.

If he were questioned by any government there'd be no trace of him ever being in the armed forces. In other words, if they land in trouble, they're on their own.

To be a ghost, you have to be at the top of your game. That is why I feel a little more at ease with the situation. Who told you about these ghosts Jillian, because I'm certain that this Jim didn't tell you or your husband what he is."

"Colin already knew. He didn't know that Jim was in Lithuania, that was a bonus for him, but he knew his pal was a ghost."

"You mustn't ever repeat this to anyone else Jillian, do you hear me? Tell no-one about this Jim or what your husband is doing, or it-."

"I know mister Mercer Colin has been through all this stuff with me. Anything at all concerning matters like these I know never to repeat, please don't worry about that."

Jillian rose to make more coffee and shouted through to her guests as she prepared the beverages. "He knows something else Mister Mercer. Jim has found out, or at least he has a good idea where the girls are. There seems to be quite a few girls. Alison is just one of many I'm afraid. But Jim thinks he knows where they are."

"Is it ok if I smoke Jillian?" Mercer called through. Jillian came through with the cups of coffee on a tray.

"Of course it is, I'm going to have one now."

She sat down the tray upon the coffee table and then she said something that made Terry Mercer and Samantha Reynolds jolt with a surge of adrenaline. As she handed the detectives their beverages, she said, "He thinks they're in Kaunas, or near Kaunas. They both know the area as well because they once done a military thing with the Soviet forces, something to do with N.A.T.O. or something like that, but they've both been there, and Jim thinks they're somewhere near there."

Samantha looked at Mercer and grinned. "Good old Treble Clef sure enough Terry, I hope this Jim is right, this is good."

Jillian Green was confused and looked at the detectives with a puzzled expression.

"Oh, sorry Jillian" said Mercer. It's just that a friend of ours has been invited over there to a festival and he has offered to take Samantha and I as his guests.

The festival is in Kaunas.

If this ex colleague of your husband's has knowledge of the girls being held in or around there, then it opens up quite a few avenues of opportunities for Sam and me. I'm not trying to give you false hope Jillian, but this is a very promising situation. We'd have more than just a glimmer of hope...if he can find out for certain the location."

KAUNAS.

Colin Green did not look out of place in the Anna Mesha night club as he sat with a pint of lager awaiting his friend Jim Lawrence. He had been instructed by Jim to come here. He hadn't seen Jim for over four years and wondered if he was still the lively jokester he used to be. He recalled some of the times he and his friend had over the years in their military days. The crowds in here tonight were reminding him of just how wild they used to be. Colin had already been approached three times by three different young ladies to get up and dance, but he'd just smiled and said "Later."
Whether or not they understood him, he was unsure. He glanced at his watch. Jim had said 11-30. It was now 11-28.
From nowhere it seemed Jim Lawrence appeared with a young lady on each of his arms. Was he drunk? What the hell was he playing at? It was hardly the reunion he'd expected.
"How are you my old friend, how's my old mucker?" Colin rose to his feet and shook his friend's hand. "Good to see you Jim, you're looking well pal."
Colin was telling no lies. Although both men were similar ages, Jim looked at least five or six years younger than he did. Obviously this kind of life-style suited him. Whatever he was doing in his life, it was doing him no harm whatsoever.
Jim Lawrence stood just under six feet. His slim build giving the deception that he was taller than that. He was wearing trendy night club gear, a loose blue-checked shirt over cream dress trousers and tanned leather shoes.
He was clean-shaved, as always, in fact in the days when he worked with Jim, his cleanliness could have been categorised as idiosyncratic. He was meticulous with his appearance. Jim said something into one of the girls' ears and sat down beside his friend. The two girls moved away to another table. The music in the club was ear-crunching, even in the lounge where they now sat. Without any hesitation he was right in with the news he had for Colin. "Ok pal, this is what I've got so far. They're being held in a house about six miles from here somewhere in Kaunas County. It's supposedly a huge mansion, owned by a crooked little bastard who goes by the name of Saratov. This little twat has other people working for him, like a madam or a mistress or something. To all intents and purposes Colin, it's a fucking brothel he's running. A high-class brothel, and this little fucker is making a fortune off these girls who have been kidnapped. I'm sorry pal for the graphic description, but that's what's going on bud. From what I can gather there are as many as fifty girls and they all live in this big fuck off house. All the girls are exceptionally beautiful, that's why they were kidnapped, and

he's charging these business-men and women a fortune to use them, sorry Colin, I'm sorry man, but that's what's happening."

Jim could see the hurt in Colin's eyes as he gave his friend the awful truth about what was happening to his daughter. Colin took an extra-large drink of his lager. "Listen, I've got a plan Colin and until we can get some assistance it's the only plan we have. I've taken a job as a chauffeur to this business-man. He owns a string of shops or stores or something. Anyway, he's minted, and I have it on good authority that he likes to indulge in sexual activities...with eh...with, you know, young girls. The fucker speaks a moderate amount of English which is how I was able to get the job. Three or four times a month he visits this place, and get this, his wife is a doctor. It's her that goes to this house and does all the checking up on the girls, you know for cleanliness, sexual cleanliness, sorry pal. Anyway, she doesn't even know that her husband is a regular customer of this fucking place. And as far as I know her husband doesn't know that his wife played this sexual favours game to fund herself into university.

She used to be into bondage and all that kind of shit. And now that she's a doctor, well she'd probably know about what goes on in that Saratov's house...anyway, that's what she does. She's also a sex therapist from what I hear."

The two female `friends" of Jim came back into the lounge carrying trays full of glasses, pints of lager and many miniature glasses of shots. Jim leaned across the table and spoke to his friend. "Listen bud, I know how you must be feeling and this might look to you that I don't give a fuck about your daughter, but you know as well as me Colin, there's precious little we can do until we find out the exact location, but all is not what it seems Colin. This young lady here who has ferried your lager to you is going to show me exactly where this place is. She says she had a friend who was once kept there against her will. She was one of the lucky ones, she got out, but the girl was so afraid of Saratov tracing her, that she emigrated to Germany. I also know Colin that as soon as we do find out where this place is, that you'll be going into your own plan of action. All I'm going to say about that, is do not fuck up anything that I am working on ok? There's another ghost coming here tomorrow, and he'll be booking into a hotel here in the city. He's going to attempt to work with you Colin. Now you are not obligated to work with him, but I tell you pal, I would strongly advise you to."

"Do I know him Jim?"

"No, I only met him two days ago. He's an Irishman, and he's younger than you and I pal, and he's someone you want in your team Colin, trust me pal. I got access to his files. He's spent only five years in the S.A.S. and I can tell you, he's as experienced as any man I've ever come across. He knows about this house as well bud. He'll arrange to meet you somewhere in the city, probably a café or a pub. Work with him Colin, please, because I think the world of you and your wife and I'll feel a lot better knowing that you are in good hands. I probably won't see you again after tonight for at least a while, or until I get something sorted out with how I'm going to approach. First of all, I have to suss the place out so I'll probably visit the house a couple of times. Anyway pal, like I say, nobody can force you to work with him…but."

"When you say you're going to visit the house Jim, I take it you'll be posing as a customer then?"

"Don't worry pal. I'll explain to the girl that I am not an ordinary punter, but unfortunately I won't be able to tell them the real reason why I'm there, unless of course it's your girl Colin, I'll explain then. Do you think she'd remember me? It's been a few years since I've seen her."

"She'll remember you alright Jim, Christ you used to have her rolling about with laughter at your antics, you'll always be her uncle Jimbo. You might not recognise her though, she's a young woman now Jim, she was only eleven or something the last time you saw her…she's fifteen now…she's changed…she's…"

"Hey, come on now pal, we're going to get her back, and the other girls, you have to be positive bud…we'll get her back home. Listen, from what I hear there's only about half a dozen adults there who run this place, it wouldn't be too difficult to storm the place, but like I say, we'll have to find out all the ins and outs of how the place is run. According to my young friend here, there are a lot of influential Lithuanians who visit this place…so, corruption within the law perhaps…caution bud caution." Colin looked at his friend and was grateful indeed for his enthusiasm and encouragement.

"Of course I'll work with him Jim, hell I need all the help that I can get. All I know is that I feel better now that I'm here and not sitting in the bloody house spending sleepless nights with Jillian lying breaking her heart beside me. At least I know that I'm in the same country as my daughter." Jim Lawrence nodded his head. "That's the way to look at it bud, now, before anything else happens at least join me with these two ladies tonight and have a few drinks with me, Christ knows when I'll see you again. I'm going to have to win this guy's confidence that I'm going to be chauffeuring about, so, come on, for old times' Colin, let's have a drink or two."

Colin Green raised his glass not for the first time in his life, to the one and only true friend he had in the world.

The two friends clinked their glasses together as Jim gestured for the girls to come back over and join them. Colin then texted his wife to let her know that he was safe and well and that he was with an old friend. He purposely did not mention who that friend was, knowing that she would know who he was with, and perhaps make it just a little easier for her to get a good nights' sleep.

FINLEY STREET.

HOLBURN. LONDON.6am.

Terry Mercer was on the phone to Geoffrey Marsden. The day had finally arrived to fly out to Lithuania. He was making sure that old Treble was fit and able to fly. The last thing he wanted was for the old codger to be expelled from flying because of the amount of alcohol he'd consumed. Terry had given Samantha his address and was now waiting for her to come and pick him up. From here they would drive over to Treble's flat and pick *him* up. They weren't due to take off until 11-30 but Terry was taking no chances. Even as he spoke to Treble he wandered over to the window phone in hand, looking out for Samantha's arrival. His two beat-up suitcases stood by the living room door. "As soon as Sam gets here we're heading right over to yours Treble, so you have everything ready ok? Don't want to be fucking about looking for passports or shit like that old boy. Have you got your passport there ready Treble, because if you've-."
"Hey, calm down Tel, it's all ear mite I got everything ready that I need, don't you be worrying bat me mucka, has *you* got all the stuff you need, I've fucking flown more times than you've facking farted my ol` pal, I'll be waiting for ya."
"You've not been drinking this morning Treble have you? They won't let you on the plane if you've been-."
"Tel, take it easy, I aint` been drinking boy. I'm gonna have a few on the plane though, they can't stop me doin` that, so don't bloody worry, I'm here waiting and I'm ready, and don't forget anything, see ya` when you get ear` bud".
Terry placed the telephone back onto its' cradle. "Christ...bud."
He finished off his coffee and washed out the cup, placing it upon his draining board in the kitchen. His doorbell rang just as he was drying his hands. Whether it was excitement or apprehension it would be hard to tell, but the doorbell had started him off on one of his rants about the importance of time-keeping. Sam, was at this moment in time, two minutes late. Trundling down his stairs, suitcases in hands he began to lecture her even before he was anywhere near his door. "If I fucking tell you a time, then I expect you to keep that time and be punctual, not fucking arrive two days later for fuck sakes, it's nearly dinner time, the plane took off half an hour ago, Christ Samantha!"
He snatched the door open only to be greeted by a special-delivery girl who asked him his name as she scrutinised the envelope in her hands.
"Oh, yes, I'm Terry Mercer, who's this from?" The young lady replied to him smiling.

"That, I could not tell you sir, we are not permitted to open anyone's mail."
Terry sighed, and signed the document handed to him and then thanked the girl for her service. "You have yourself a good day now sir, sorry to get you out of your bed", she said sarcastically, as she glanced at the cases in the hallway.
"I was expecting someone else miss.. I wasn't in bed, I'm going-."
He stopped himself, realizing that the young post girl had been winding him up.
"Yeah, you have yourself a good day Missy, and don't be getting any fucking flat tyres or anything like that…you little twat."
The post girl trundled down his garden path with her back to him, and with the middle finger of her left hand held high in the air. "And you sir."
He slammed the door and stood in his hallway with the envelope in his hands.
He opened it to find a bundle of Euros and a note from Polly Sheppard.
Thought I'd give you and Samantha a little spending money. Good luck Terry, and please take care of Sam, she's a good one. I wish you both all the best in your quest, because it is a quest. Do what you can Terry to save those girls, but please, be very careful. See you when you get back. Polly." Terry opened out the notes and counted them. There was two thousand Euros in the envelope. The message that Polly had sent him, and indeed the `instructions` to look after Sam had calmed him down considerably. Sam would get here soon. She'd probably been held up in the traffic, there was plenty of time. He lit up a cigarette on his doorstep and stood patiently waiting for his colleague to arrive completely calm again. He even waved to the post-girl as she drove by.
Two minutes later Samantha pulled up outside of his house.
She was bracing herself for a lecture knowing full well that she was ten minutes late, instead, she arrived to find Terry Mercer standing grinning at her and giving her the thumbs up sign as he finished his cigarette. "Good morning Sam, have you got everything you need sweetheart, you've got your passport and everything have you?"
"I'm sorry I'm late Terry, there's been a minor accident half a mile from here. A lorry has spilled it's load onto the road, and so there was a detour."
"There's plenty of time Sam, it's that old bugger I was worrying about, you know, in case he's been drinking. They won't let him on the plane if he has, and he's got the tickets, and the hotel reservations and everything, that's why I want to go now to his place, you know, make sure he doesn't hit the bottle."
"Maybe you should have phoned him Terry, to see if he's out of bed."
Terry's smile broadened. "I already have Sam, he says he's not been drinking and that he's waiting for us." As Terry climbed into the car he noticed how radiant his colleague looked. Her hair had been done and was styled differently than he'd been used to seeing her wearing it. She was wearing a lovely cream top with navy blue dress trousers

and very `trendy` shoes. She looked stunning. "I must say Samantha, you look absolutely beautiful, I mean, well, not beautiful, I didn't mean...em, you look nice, yeah you look really really nice, that's it, and your hair...your hair is nice as well...yeah...nice." Samantha put the car into gear and drove off heading for Treble-clef's place of residence. "Thank you Terry, thank you for letting me know that I look nice, God that must have hurt you to say that."

"Not at all, you do look nice, really.

Not beautiful, but...yeah nice. It'll be a pleasure to sit next to you in the plane, I won't be ashamed of sitting next to you."

She smiled as she drove knowing full well what Terry was telling her, and she took it for the compliment it was meant to be. "I might swap my seat and sit next to old Treble on the plane if you don't mind, because sitting next to him, I *will* look beautiful...don't you agree Terry?"

EUROPA ROYALE HOTEL. KAUNAS.

LITHUANIA.

It was almost midnight on the eve of Colin Green's second night here in Kaunas. Jim had disappeared the night before with one of the girls he'd arrived with, the one who was going to take him to the afore-mentioned house. As he sat on his bed trying his best, unsuccessfully to read a novel he'd brought with him there was a tap on his door. It was so faint that at first he thought he'd imagined it. Then he heard it again. He rose from the bed and opened the bedroom door. A young man who looked to be around twenty-five years of age stood with a hold-all bag over his shoulder. The man looked nothing like a military specialist. He also knew that when Jim said he was worth having around, then he'd be worth having around. Jim never spoke lightly about military professionalism. The young man clad in denims from head to toe looked more like a student than an S.A.S. soldier.
"Hello, are you Mister Colin Green? I believe you've had a conversation with a colleague of mine? You were expecting me?"
Colin invited the man into his room. He surprised him with his opening sentence. "I am really sorry Mister Green to hear about what's going on in this place, you know, concerning your daughter and those other girls being held there, but be assured, I will do everything in my power as is humanly possible to save her. I will undoubtedly need your support and your trust if we are to be successful in our mission. Jim told me you were an excellent soldier, one of the best he'd ever worked with and so I know that you will be of great value to the job in hand, or rather the task in hand that faces us. It's not going to be easy either, but I think you already know that don't you." Colin sat down on one of the chairs in the room and invited his guest to do the same.
"Would you like a drink?" He offered his new friend.
"Just a cup of tea Mister Green if that's ok."
"It's Colin."
"And my name is Alan Hartford, it's a pleasure to meet you Colin, although I wish it could be under better circumstances than these that we were meeting."
Both men sat down with their cups of tea.
"Jim says you know all about this house and what's going on in there. He also informed me that a friend of his was going to show him exactly where it is, it's supposedly in Kaunas County, so surely it can't be far from here."
"Are you an early riser Colin? Because if you are, I am heading out there in a few hours'

time, I have a hired car."
Colin looked at the man. "You know where it is? You know the house?"
"Yes, I know exactly where it is, I haven't been there yet but I have accurate directions, I'll find it. If you decide to come with me Colin, it's going to be very difficult for you to control yourself, you know that don't you. By that I mean, we will be surveying the premises where your daughter is being kept, and it will be very tempting for you to want to storm the place. I'm only saying this to remind you that we cannot do anything on this first visit. I'm only going to survey the place and find out all access points to it. Don't get me wrong Colin, I fully understand how you must be feeling at this moment in time, coming all this way, and then discovering the actual house where your daughter is, it will be extremely tempting. Like I say though, I need you to trust me and any decisions that I make, and if-."
"Hey, let's get one thing straight here Alan. Yes, I will trust you, and you know you have my full support, but if I think for one minute that something is foolish or stupid or too risky then I will be telling you. If I am suddenly presented with an opportunity to save my daughter then I will be taking it, get that straight from the start. Don't forget, I was in the force as well you know, you don't have to talk to me like you're my superior ok? We're in this together, and I am extremely grateful for your assistance, but I am as experienced as you are pal in matters like these." Alan Hartford held up his hands. "My apologies Colin, I wasn't deliberately trying to outrank you, I was merely trying to put your mind at ease, and gain your trust." "You already have my trust. I know that we will have to be extremely careful in everything we do. I know how dangerous this could be, sorry, will be. You have my trust, and my cooperation. What time are you leaving?
"About four o clock."
"Ok, I'll meet you outside the hotel at four, you'd better go and get a couple of hours sleep." Alan Hartford left the hotel room and disappeared to wherever he was staying. That was the thing with these ghosts, you never ever get to know their comings and goings. They appear and disappear before your eyes and you're left none the wiser. Colin was indeed grateful for Alan's assistance. He was going to make an almost impossible job at least attemptable. If Jim was right and he had never known him to be otherwise, then there was hope indeed for Alison and the other girls. Colin had also been informed by Jim Lawrence that detectives Terry Mercer and his colleague Samantha Reynolds were coming over here to a music festival of some description. Colin smiled to himself as he imagined Terry Mercer sitting somewhere listening intently to musicians. He just didn't look like that kind of guy. Again, he was grateful for Terry's assistance because he knew the man was desperate to help him. How he had managed to get himself and his colleague over here was a mystery, but if he was

honest, he was glad that he had. Alan Hartford would no doubt put him to good use…or Mercer would put Alan to good use.

HEATHROW AIRPORT.

LONDON.

Samantha was pleasantly surprised at how Treble was conducting his behaviour. She had imagined him kind of half drunk and blabbering on to Terry about how good it was to be friends, and how important it was to be loyal to those friends. Instead, he sat now at his preferred seat at the window reading a magazine about the history of chamber music. He reminded her of a child engrossed in their favourite comic, smiling away to himself as he read. Terry as well had surprised her. He was studying a map of Lithuania on his lap, particularly the areas surrounding Kaunas. He sat with his white shirt and his brand new jeans. This experience would indeed be unique. She would be in his company for the next two or three hours or so and would not hear one single profanation from his mouth, or so she thought. Terry caught her glancing at him.
"Everything ok Sam?"
"Yes, fine Terry. Treble seems happy enough doesn't he?"
"He's as happy as a hog in shit, leave him while he's quiet. Huh, just wait till the stewardess comes with the trolley, he'll be making good use of the drinks offered, mind you, he's done himself proud by staying off the drink all last night and today, he deserves one or two." Samantha could tell that Terry was in deep thought about Kaunas. He was hoping to receive some information about the exact location of the girls, information that could save them. He was calm just now, and he was trying his best to hide his apprehension, but it wouldn't take much to spark him off on one of his rants.
All Treble would have to do would be to do or say something wrong in Terry's eyes and that would be that, however, hope springs eternal.
He leaned over his seat to whisper something into her ear.
Samantha thought he was going to say something concerning old Treble again.
"I hope he has plenty of company when we get over there, you know, some of his old friends otherwise we're going to look awfully ungrateful not spending any time with him, especially as how we are supposed to be here as his guests."
"I'm sure he'll have lots of people to meet with", said Samantha, fishing out one of her fashion magazines from her hand bag. "Old friends I suppose from his playing days. I must say, looking at him now you wouldn't think he was a first class musician would you?"
"Yeah I know" said Terry smiling, "he looks more like a first class fuck-up doesn't he,

and what are you doing? Reading that shit, we're not here on holiday, you know that don't you, we're not on vacation, reading fucking magazines and shit." "Terry? Don't start. I know we're not on holiday, but we're not there yet so calm yourself down, there's nothing we can do to help those girls sitting up here thousands of feet in the air. Just you read your map and study it. When we get to Vilnius we'll have to arrange transport over to Kaunas. I think I read that it's only fifty-seven miles from Vilnius to Kaunas. As soon as we get there Terry then we'll set about our plans. Until then, be quiet so I can read my magazine in peace please. Old Treble there is showing you up with his perfect behaviour, if you keep ranting on about shit, I'll have no choice but to move and sit beside him, now give it a rest will you?"

Samantha was genuinely surprised when Terry responded to her by saying, "Yeah, you're right Sam, I'm sorry about that, it's just that I'm looking forward to trying to at least do something to help those poor girls...sorry."

In front of Terry on the middle seat of three, a young boy was looking at him from his perched position. The child held some kind of soldier toy in his hand and was aiming the gun from the soldier directly at him, making some pretend shooting sounds from his mouth and spraying Terry with saliva.

"Is that your hero there is it? Said Terry, enthusiastically to the five-year-old.

The boys' mouth stopped spraying momentarily as he answered Terry with a venomous "Shut up stinky idiot man!" The smile broadened on Terry's face as he stared at the child. Treble then spoke for the first time since the plane had taken off.

"Hey Tell, did you know that?"-

"Hey, just read your magazine Treble, we're not interested in how much it costs for a new cello, just sit there and behave yourself, you'll get a drink soon enough, here she comes now with the trolley, Jesus Christ Treble!"

The stress was beginning to get to Terry. More than anything, he did not want to admit to Samantha that he had a fear of flying. He tried to concentrate on the situation regarding the girls. It was of the utmost importance that they found out where exactly they were being held. Three days was not long, certainly not long enough if they didn't know where to look. On top of that, they would be expected to attend at least one of the shows with old Treble after all, if not for his kindness they wouldn't even be here.

Sam sat glancing side-ways past her magazine at Terry. The signs were starting to show. His fingers were locking together and then releasing, his fists were clenching like he was on a white-knuckle ride at the fare. Before he `tore` into old Treble again with venomous sarcasm she stepped in to save the day.

"What would you like to drink Terry, my treat, we may as well have a little tipple before we get on with business in hand."

"I'm not wanting alcoholic drinks, cup of tea will do me, you can sit there and get rat-arsed if you like, I intend to stay sober...I'll have a drink when those poor girls are safely out of their hell-hole and-."
Sam interrupted him hissing her words quietly into his ear. "Just shut up Terry, honestly, you're getting worse. Look I know how desperate those girls' situation is, but we can't do anything until such times as we find their location, and that is no-one's fault, I'm sure Polly will be in touch soon enough regarding that. You're snapping away there at old Treble for no good reason, just calm yourself down will you, have a bloody drink for Christ's sake, hell even that little boy could sense your ill-naturedness, now get a bloody drink, we'll be landing in an hour, surely you can do without a cigarette until then. I'm sick to the back teeth of your bloody snapping and growling at people for nothing. Everything that goes wrong or whenever a problem arises is all everybody else's fault isn't it, it's never your fault, now sit there and shut your bloody mouth!"
Terry did not reply, but rose to his feet and headed for the bathroom.
It wasn't Samantha's intention, but she had just inadvertently pollardised him right in front of Treble-clef...and a smiling five-year-old boy.

KAUNAS COUNTY.

LITHUANIA.

Alan Hartford lay flat on the ground along with Colin Green in the midst of a forest somewhere in Kaunas County. Alan was looking through his trusty night-vision binoculars at a huge house about half a mile from where they lay. He handed his field glasses to Colin. "There it is Colin, Jim was spot on with his directions. Look to the left of the house, do you see the two girls walking?"
"Yes. What the hell are they doing out walking at this time of the morning, it's not even six o clock."
Alan looked at Colin and was about to give a reason why the girls could be out walking so early, but then thought about what they'd probably just been forced to do and so he kept the answer to himself. Alan took the binoculars back and peered through them again. "It would be easy enough to infiltrate the house, it's what might be waiting for us once we got inside. This man won't be running something like this and not have protection. He'll have security of some kind in there, he'd be mad not to. He'll be well protected don't you worry about that, there's too much at risk. Jim said he'd be here soon with his new boss, but wasn't sure if he'd be permitted entry or not. If he wasn't then he said he'd be in touch with me and that we'd have to hatch an alternative plan. We'll need to find out about the lay-out of the house and just how many girls are being kept there. Once we have a plan, he says he has connections in Poland who would smuggle the girls over there where they could be taken care of. He's very hesitant for some reason about contacting the Lithuanian police…he must know something I don't. Plus, we have no idea of just how many girls are in there. By the way Jim was talking he said he thought that there'd probably be quite a number of them. We'll just have to wait and see what he says."
Dawn was just beginning to break as the two men made their way back to the hired car. As they walked Alan said, "Watch your feet, bloody dog shit everywhere, and that's not a good sign."
Colin agreed nodding his head and looking back in the direction they'd just came.
"Yeah, escape from there would be just about impossible. Even if they did make it this far, the dogs would catch them before they reached the road."
Neither man spoke again as they walked the few hundred metres back to the car. The woods were dense. It would be practically impossible to run if you were being chased. Apart from the closeness of the trees there were thick bushes to negotiate, wild ferns in

abundance, just the thing to trip you up if you were attempting to run, and finally the dogs. Whoever this Saratov was, he had dogs somewhere back at that house, probably way out of sight from his mansion of iniquity. Colin was in deep thought. He'd just seen the house where he knew his daughter was being held, and here he was, unable to help her, unable to reach her. What he would give now just to hold her in his arms.
He would get her though. It may take time but he would get her.
He would use all his military professionalism and his own wits, but he would save Alison, if it was the last thing he ever did.
They reached the car and both men sighed heavily as they were seated.
"It's not going to be easy Alan, but then nothing worth-while ever is.
I haven't got a clue how to go about it but somehow...somehow I'll get her back home to her mum and sister."
Alan lit his cigarette and nodded to his new friend. "You bet your life we will.
But Colin, be optimistic, at least we know where she is, that's a start my friend, that's a bonus compared to what we had this time last week.
That's progress my friend."
As Alan drove back to Kaunas Colin Green agreed inwardly with what his friend had just said. This time last week he was on the other side of Europe without a clue where his daughter was. Now, as Alan had just said, he knew exactly where she was, and yes, he was right, it was progress, bloody good progress. He wondered if Terry Mercer could assist in any way once he'd informed him of his daughter's whereabouts. He knew Mercer was on his way over, but that was all he knew. It would be unlikely that the British Metropolitan police had anything to do with Mercer's arrival. Rarely had he witnessed such dedication from an officer of the law. The man was constantly racking his brains to bring the kidnappers to justice. It was as though he had suffered a loss himself of a child or loved-one. He seemed more determined than anyone to catch these evil people and bring them to book. You could see the steel in his eyes...hatred even, for these sub-humans.
Hartford dropped Colin Green off at the hotel in Kaunas and said he'd be in touch. He didn't question Hartford's instructions and respected the man's judgement.
He surmised that he and Jim Lawrence would be in constant contact.
He got the feeling that Jim and Alan would be planning something, something that wouldn't include him. He would just have to wait and see, and like he'd promised both men, trust them. Even when he'd been surveying the house with Hartford, he got the feeling that there was something else going on in the man's head, a separate plan. Colin wasn't exactly worried about it, nor offended, after all, they worked to their own schedules and arrangements, and they answered to no-one...they were ghosts. He

believed that Hartford had invited him along to survey the house for another reason. If anything was to go wrong with their plan, then at least he would know the location of the place where the girls were being held. Whatever they had planned, it probably wouldn't involve him he surmised. As Colin entered the hotel, he was collared by a pretty young Lithuanian girl, who was one of the hotel's receptionists and who fortunately spoke some English, all-be-it broken English. As soon as she saw him enter the hotel she waved him over to the desk.

"Meester Green? Man here looking for you with woman, he say he friend."
The girl looked at a piece of paper on her desk. "Meester Mercer, he say can he speak to you, he staying here, he in room feefty-two."
Colin thanked the girl and made his way to the elevator.
So Mercer was here. He had to admit that he felt a little better now that he knew the detective was here. How on earth he'd managed to *get* here was a mystery.
It hardly mattered now, he was here and that was the main thing. The fact that Mercer and his colleague had both thought that what he was doing was suicidal perhaps made him more determined to get over here and assist in some way. To his way of thinking, he would be here to protect him, as much as he could. Half an hour later he was sitting in Mercer's room with detective Samantha Reynolds. He had informed both detectives that he'd found the location and that it was about only a twenty-minute drive from the city. He also described the immediate area surrounding the house and that there seemed to be only one entrance for vehicles. He hadn't had a chance to survey the back of the premises. Colin had given Mercer the name of the other ghost and informed him that it was he who had taken him to see the place, and to show him the location.
"Would you be able to find it, you know, if it were just us three going there, you could find it alright?" Green looked at Mercer as though he was offended. "I'm sorry Colin, I didn't mean to..."
"Listen Terry, slim Jim and Alan, they seem to have some kind of plan in their heads that they are working to. Hartford has asked me to stay put until he contacts me again. He pleaded with me not to do anything until instructed to by either him or Jim Lawrence. He also informed me, or rather hinted to me, that they did not trust the Lithuanian police force, certainly not the Kaunas police force. He hinted to corruption or something." Mercer studied the ex S.A.S man's face. "Ok Colin, but what if we were to go to that house, you know, just to take another look. We won't do anything, I'd just like to see the place, would you be up for taking us there? Like I say, we won't attempt anything."
"Sure, I'll take us there, but we'll have to be careful. The first thing we'll have to do is buy ourselves a pair of binoculars because we won't get anywhere near the place.

Where Alan and I were, we were about half a mile off it I would say, and still I felt uneasy, as though even there, *we* were being surveyed. It is situated in the midst of a massive woodland, and its' well off the main roads. If you didn't know where this place was, it would be extremely hard to locate."

It was arranged that Terry Mercer, Samantha Reynolds and Colin Green would all take a little trip later that afternoon to the house. Colin would hire a car.

In the meantime, they would return to their rooms until the time came for them to leave. Although Terry and Samantha were here purely as holiday-makers the less they were seen in public the better, and besides poor old Treble was in his room having behaved exceptionally well on the journey here. Terry would treat him to a couple of drinks.

KAUNAS.

LITHUANIA. THE MANSION.

Sophie Spencer, Chloe Prowse, Kirsty Crawford, Alison Green and Lisa Jenson all stood in a line dressed in their skimpy attire. One or two of Saratov's `dignitaries` walked along scrutinising each of the girls, sometimes groping their breasts or feeling their legs or their backsides, turning them around and studying them from all angles. Even through the effect of the cocaine they'd all just snorted Sophie Spencer felt irritated and deeply offended. Today, she couldn't play the `game`. She actually felt like attacking these animals in front of her. Being probed and poked like they were all just pieces of meat made her fury rise inside her. One of the men reached down and stroked her between her legs. Sophie snapped.
"Hey, listen to me you cheap fucking bastard that you are, you touch me there again and I will cut your fucking balls off and ram them down your throat, you piece of shit that you are, who the fuck do you think you are that you can treat us like this? We don't belong to you, you fucking rat!"
Monica Carosova moved in as quick as lightning and pulled Sophie gently to one side. "Come with me Sophie, we need to have a little talk." The rest of the girls were left to be poked and prodded and spun around until their inspectors decided which of them they would like to spend their money on. Sophie was led into a lounge and sat down on a chair where she was told not to move until she returned. When Monica did return she was accompanied by Mister Saratov and two men dressed in suits. Two huge men, like bouncers, or as Sophie would have described them, thugs.
Saratov sat down on a chair opposite Sophie and lit up a cigar.
He looked at Sophie smiling. The smile looked maleficent.
After he had taken a couple of draws from his cigar he leaned forward on his chair.
"Monica has informed me of your outburst. Luckily for you, none of those customers can speak English, so no offence was taken on their behalf. However, your behaviour is not going to go unpunished young lady. You must learn that you are here to please whoever enters these premises, and you are there at their beck and call, do you understand me? I thought that all this had been explained to you at the beginning. Forget any life you had in the past. This is your life now. This is all you have. You behave according to the rules in here and you will be well looked after, and you are well looked after, you *and* your British friends, but today's behaviour is unacceptable and you are going to learn one way or another that you are no more than a sex slave, that's why you

were chosen. Now Monica has treated all you girls with nothing but kindness but here you are cursing and swearing at my customers like you were something special, when in fact you are nothing, you are worthless. Outside of here you are helpless.

This place is now your only life-line. Without myself or Monica here you would starve. Now, for your outburst, you shall be punished. Let's see if a little solitary confinement will help you with your attitude. I told you as I'm sure Monica has, that you are here for one reason and one reason only, and that reason is to give yourself freely to anyone who is willing to pay money for your sexual favours.

Sophie still could not contain herself. She'd had enough of this Saratov's coercion. "And just who the hell do you think that you are? You have paid money to people who have kidnapped us and drugged us. You've paid money to have us smuggled over here and to be used by your so-called customers, but we were never yours to buy. You call me a slut and a nobody while here you are making money from unwilling under-aged teenagers who have been torn ruthlessly away from their homes and families. It is *you* Mister Saratov who is the nothing, the nobody. You should think shame on yourself for what you are doing here, and I hope the authorities catch up with"-

"Enough, take her out of my sight!"

The two giant men lifted Sophie from the chair and escorted her back to her room where they then locked the door and left her to contemplate what was coming to her. As she sat there she made a decision. No matter what the risks, she was going to attempt to break out of here and make a run for it. The only way anyone would come and rescue them was for the authorities to be informed of what was happening here. Someone had to be brave enough to get out of here and notify the police. Only then would help arrive. If nobody attempted to escape, then they may as well just accept this tortuous life as normal, Heaven or Hell. Less than half an hour later, the two `thugs` returned and lifted her from her bed. There was no point in struggling. Without a single word being spoken to her, they led her right out of the house and around the back of the building. She hadn't been this way before when she'd been out here walking with some of the other girls. She had spotted the tall wooden gate on several occasions but hadn't ventured to go through it. One of the men then produced a key and unlocked it. The padlock and chain seemed heavy-duty and oversized for the job. The gate was opened and she was led down concrete steps, each of them about a foot deep. There were lots of them, more than thirty. The surrounding trees robbed the steps of daylight as she was led down to the bottom of the giant stairway. Now, in front of her was a huge wrought-iron door with another heavy chain wrapped around a giant padlock. The same man who'd opened the gate now produced another key and unlocked the door. She was gently pushed into a small bunker-like compartment. Before Sophie had a chance to say anything the door was slammed behind her, and she was left in total darkness. The floor was smooth concrete. The walls were brick. She attempted to search in the darkness for a light switch but there didn't seem to be any. She remembered Monica telling her about some girls who had been difficult and stubborn at the beginning of their stay, and how they had to be punished for their disobedience. So this was it. This is what belies the fate of those who step out of line here. She carefully trailed her hand along the walls trying at least to get some idea of the dimensions of the `room`. As far as she could tell it measured about ten feet by eight. One single room. No other doors, no bathroom, no wash-hand basin, nothing. Sophie leaned against the wall and slid down onto her hunkers, her head between her knees. How long would they keep her in here? Would they bring her any food? How would she manage to do the toilet? The floor was damp and very cold. It wouldn't take long to break anyone subjected to this. She wasn't in any way afraid of the darkness, but there was one phobia she suffered from, and if she was not mistaken she'd just heard high-pitched squeals coming from somewhere close. Upon inspection, there were several bricks missing at the bottom of the walls. She could feel on her hands colder air. Now it seemed that the squeals were getting louder...rats.

EUROPA ROYALE HOTEL.

KAUNAS.

Terry and Samantha were over the moon. They had just been texted by Polly Sheppard who had confirmed to them that they'd be allowed to stay in Lithuania for a further two weeks. Everything had been taken care of and was all above board. The hotel management here in Kaunas had also been informed of the change of plan and had been paid in full for the extra time that Terrence Mercer and Samantha Reynolds would be staying with them. All that remained for them to do was to go down to the manager's office here in the hotel, and sign the ledger for extended accommodation. This was a bonus indeed for the detectives. As well as making their enquiries they could actually attend one or two of Treble's concerts, which would also make Treble look good, the fact that his guests were here not just for a free holiday but actually show an interest in classical music. They had been with Colin Green to see for themselves' this `house` where the girls were being held. It was indeed an extremely difficult place to find. Even Colin had made a wrong turn and had to turn back and drive a half mile back to a cut in the road, there were dozens of cut-offs from the main road and very little in the way of land-marks. Every road looked the same as the next. Millions of Birch trees along with firs and oaks were all that was to be seen for as far as the eye could see. Then, when Colin had stopped the car, they could see in the distance, this beautiful huge mansion, built with light grey stone. Other than its' shape, it could have been a castle. Colin Green had shared his binoculars with the two detectives as they'd surveyed this `prison`. No-one would have guessed in a thousand years that it was being used for the illicit purposes that it was. The ex S.A.S. man informed them that he would be surveying the area more intensely himself and that he would keep them informed of anything that was important. He also promised them that he would not be venturing to do any heroics on his own and that he was merely looking to gain an advantage by surveying the area unaccompanied. He would wait, as instructed by the ghosts until he was required to assist, after all it was those two who were in charge of all operations. "They told me they'd be in touch very soon, and so, until then, I am merely familiarising myself with the surrounding areas. There may be other routes to the house but I doubt it very much, the woods look like they're way too thick behind the house for any road to exist, but, we'll soon find out. In the meantime, you two just enjoy the city, enjoy your break. I can personally recommend a night club, it's called Anna Mesha, you two would enjoy it."

The fact that Colin Green was smiling when he said the name of the club immediately put Mercer on the defence.

"Hmm, yeah, think we'll give it a miss Mister Green if it's all the same to you."

He pointed to Samantha. "I'm in charge of her you know, she's my responsibility, can't let her loose in a room with a bunch of dangerous boys filled to the brim with testosterone coming out of their ears, God she'd have them in a frenzy with her leather trousers or skirts or whatever else she's brought over here with her that's made out of leather, Christ everything she wears is leather…she's got a fetish I'm sure of it."

Samantha completely ignored Mercer's sarcasm although she knew what he was doing. He was trying his best to be light-hearted and jovial in an attempt to take Colin's mind off his daughter, even if it was only temporarily. Colin had driven them back to the hotel and dropped them off in the car park.

"As soon as I hear anything Terry, I'll be in touch I promise. Let me know if either of them gets in touch with you, see you later."

That evening Terry and Samantha accompanied Geoffrey Marsden to the Baltic Wind Chamber Music Hall. Treble was overjoyed at the attention he was given by lots of old friends and from the highest dignitaries in the Lithuanian Orchestras. Mercer smiled as the old man shook hands with countless people, some of which actually bowed to him.

"Christ almighty Terry" said Samantha, "How bloody good *was* this old bugger?"

" I told you Sam, he must have impressed a few people in his time with his music, look at them."

Treble looked nothing less than sensational in his brand new jet black tuxedos. No-one would ever guess the problems this man had concerning his alcohol consumption. He looked like a million dollars. Terry was genuinely filled with joy as he watched his old `friend` soaking up the attention. He was also thrilled at the fact that Treble was taking great delight in introducing his two friends. He smiled as he watched gentlemen bowing as they kissed Samantha's hand upon   introduction, and smiling at Terry as if to say, "You lucky man that you are, taking this to bed with you." Mercer had no idea whatsoever what they were saying to him as they shook hands, he simply watched Treble who just told him to smile and nod at them. He took a step back and gazed in complete admiration at his colleague. Samantha had bought herself a beautiful crimson evening dress that came down to her feet. She had placed a red rose in her hair and some kind of `sparkly thing` that resembled a Tamara.

At that very moment, he actually felt butterflies in his stomach. He hadn't really paid much attention to her as they left the hotel in the taxi, but looking at her here and now, he was absolutely engulfed in her beauty. He remembered his wife Kathy wearing a similar dress on their tenth wedding anniversary…this feeling here tonight matched the one he'd felt all those years ago.

Samantha caught him looking at her. "What's wrong Terry, you don't look well."

Whether or not his brain had anything planned in reference to an answer, he would never know, because all that came out of his mouth was, "I'm so sorry Sam, for giving you such a hard time, I'm just…I'm so sorry, please forgive me for being an idiot."

"Don't be silly Terry, you can't help being an idiot, it's what you'll always be…it can't be helped, come on, let's have a little drink and leave Treble to enjoy his night, come on back to our seats."

"Seriously Samantha, I'm sorry, and you are too nice to be a detective, you should have been something else instead of this."

"God almighty, and you've only had two drinks Terry, I thought it was Treble who had the drink problem, come on…silly."

Perhaps Terry had been caught up in the moment, but it was the first time he'd actually saw Samantha for the woman she was. Whatever the reason, he had a very different opinion of her now and not just because of her beauty. She was an excellent detective and he was glad she was permitted to come over here with him. They were going to be a team. They were a team. The only trouble with that was every other time he'd mentioned the words team or partnership his colleagues had ended up dead…he considered himself something of a Jonah. The last thing he wanted was anything to happen to this woman. Yes, he was guilty of swearing and cursing and snapping at her, but she seemed now to be immune to his insults. No offence seemed to be taken. She was also tough, he knew that, and she certainly wouldn't let anyone walk over her, himself included, but seeing her dressed like this, she looked vulnerable and in need of protection, she deserved to be protected. He would never forgive himself if anything happened to Samantha Reynolds.

KAUNAS COUNTY.

LITHUANIA.

Viktor Kulbertinov sat comfortably in the back of his Rolls Royce scrutinising some documents on his lap and sipping a glass of chilled Aloft Cabernet Sauvignon.
His chauffer Jim Lawrence was busy scanning his sat-nav as he drove although he knew the route to the Saratov house off by heart now. He had visited the area on numerous occasions. Kulbertinov, a forty-two-year old businessman had inherited a number of grocery stores from his father and had expanded his business over the years. He also owned a night club and a couple of diners and a house almost as big as the one he was now going to visit. Jim Lawrence glanced in the rear-view mirror at the man who was now his `employer`.
Viktor certainly knew how to dress. He sat now studying his documents in an immaculate navy-blue Armani suit and white shirt with a multi-coloured necktie.
Lawrence's first task in hand would be to gain the man's confidence.
Once he'd done that, he could begin to work out some plans concerning the rescue of the girls. He decided to test the depths of his working relationship with the businessman.
"Pardon me sir, would you like me to wait in the car whilst you conduct your business with Mister Saratov, or do you wish me to come in with you?"
Kulbertinov did not even look up from his document and did not offer an answer.
"Ok" Thought Lawrence to himself, "Speak only when spoken to, I get it."
Finally, Kulbertinov looked up from his papers, looking around the area as they drove. "I don't know how long I will be in here Mister Lawrence these meetings vary in length. I could be two hours or I could be four, but I wish to inform you of something before I go in here. First of all James, can I rely on your trust, by that I mean can I depend on you to say nothing to anyone about what goes on in this house, can I rely on your confidentiality?"
"Of course sir, it is no business of mine whatever you are here for, I was merely asking sir about the time of your business to try and enhance myself. To try and win favour, to em, improve if I might make my job secure, yes security, that's why sir."
"Look Mister Lawrence, let me make one thing clear to you now. Unless you do something drastic to displease me or my wife, then your employment with me is as secure as it possibly could be, have no fear of that.
What I need you to be is...able to keep secrets James, can you keep secrets?"

"Yes sir, without a shadow of doubt I can."

"Good, well then, perhaps now I can explain the reason I am visiting these friends of mine. You see, there are certain ladies in here who will do, how shall I say it, favours for people, sexual favours. It is no secret that there are prostitutes in abundance wherever you travel, but in here, the prostitutes are particularly young, very young in fact. They come from all over Europe. I pay my friend money and I can have as many of these young girls in my room with me for as long as I wish, of course the prices vary depending upon how many girls you wish to have. This is not your run-of-the-mill brothel James, these girls are young and fresh, and there is no chance whatsoever of contracting any sexual diseases, which puts my mind at rest with regards to Valerie my wife. Now then James, what she *doesn't* know is that I am a regular customer here. My wife is the doctor who comes here once a month to check out the girls and administer medication when required. Now, are you comfortable with what I have just told you, now that you know the purpose of my visit?"

Jim Lawrence's stomach was churning. He felt physically sick. He had a vision of Colin's girl being sexually abused by animals like the one sitting behind him.

Jim was remembering the girl as he had last seen her when she was about eleven or twelve. He forced himself to smile at the bastard he dearly would love to shoot in the balls right here and now.

"Of course sir, and I have forgotten completely what you just told me. Would you like me to wait for you in the car sir, or do you wish me to head back into town and then come back and collect you?"

"It's entirely up to you James, but, there is a bar in here if you wish to wait for me, although you know you'll not be able to consume alcoholic drinks don't you."

"Of course not sir, but yes, if it's all the same to you, I could wait in the bar, and then sir, if you felt like leaving early, well then I would already be there, you wouldn't have to wait for me returning."

"Ok then James, that's it settled then. Has my wife given you any instructions with regards to her plans today, I know she doesn't come here on certain days, and of course, this is one of those days.

"No sir, she hasn't informed me of anything regarding her travels today."

"May I ask you something James?"

"Of course sir." Jim Lawrence was almost caught out with the question that followed.

"No, I was just wondering how on earth you've managed to drive all the way here without once asking me for directions, it's not the easiest place in the world to find and yet here we are almost-."

"Pardon me sir, but when you informed me last night where we were going today, I took the liberty of going on to Google maps and finding out the location of Mister Saratov, again sir, it's just my way of trying to be efficient, I've got it here on the sat-nav sir."

Viktor Kulbertinov smiled as they drove on. "Efficient indeed Mister Lawrence, well done, I admire your, how do you say, keenness."

"Thank you sir."

Nothing more was said as they drove on.

When they reached the house they had to wait outside of the gate.

The drive was only large enough for one vehicle at a time to leave or enter.

As they waited, a young woman drove out of the drive in her bright red brand new Maserati and `rolled` down her window to speak with Kulbertinov.

The woman looked like she was in her early thirties. Her jewellery suggested bucket loads of cash, Gold earrings and necklace, well-manicured nails highlighted by bright red nail-polish. Her hair was shoulder-length and cut short to perfection.

"Minted." Thought Lawrence to himself.

"Try Alison Viktor, the English girl, she's a bit special, I've Just had a couple of hours with her, she's worth the money for sure."

Again, Jim Lawrence felt sick. Was she referring to his pal's daughter Alison?

And this woman was English, or at least she spoke immaculate English.

He didn't detect any foreign accent. The window of the Maserati slid silently back up and she drove off, smiling at the monster behind him and blowing him a kiss.

"As you can gather James, there are certain women who use these facilities as well…it takes all kinds Mister Lawrence."

"It certainly does, everyone to their own sir."

"Exactly James, now, park around the back of the house please.

When we get inside I'll show you where the bar is. The people in here are very friendly, they'll make you feel at home, or at least, at ease, you will be looked after James."

James Lawrence held the door open for his `boss` to enter. Elaborate was not the word for this. Everywhere he looked in the giant hallway there were crystal chandeliers, and expensive oil-paintings. The carpets caressed his feet as he `glided` into the foyer. A young lady approached him and his employer, or at least headed in their direction. She walked straight past Jim and greeted Kulbertinov with a smile and a kiss on the cheek.

"So nice to see you again Mister Kulbertinov, it's always nice to see you.

Are you staying for a while today sir? We have some new ones for you, some English girls, very nice, very young Mister Kulbertinov, I think you'll like."

The girl could have been a waitress, dressed in white blouse and black knee-length skirt. Her hair tied back underneath a colourful hair-band. She looked briefly at Jim but only briefly. The look she gave informed him that he was of the same value as dog shit. He didn't matter. Kulbertinov slipped off his jacket and handed it to the girl who draped it over her forearm. "Now then Katrina, I want you to show my driver where the bar is, and I want him looked after, make sure he gets anything he desires, apart from alcohol of course, we wouldn't want to be picked up by the police because of a drunk chauffeur now would we? Get him a menu and serve him whatever he wants, you take good care of him, his name is James, and he'll be with me whenever I come here so, get used to him being around, he is a nice man."

Katrina smiled at Kulbertinov. "Of course sir, I'll just show him now where the bar is, there's a couple of spare rooms if he fancies watching television."

"Well, you can sort that out with him Katrina, now where is Monica or Mister Saratov, please inform them that I am here for business. James? You go with Katrina now, she'll take care of you, I'll see you later."

"As you wish sir," Replied Lawrence who's adrenaline was flowing with the bonus of being able to survey the premises without suspicion. He couldn't have planned this any better himself if he tried. He would take full advantage as well of the hospitality offered to him. He would react the same way as any other employee would react when offered these perks by their boss. Added to this bonus was the knowledge that he'd be returning here quite frequently according to Kulbertinov. Surely he'd be able to locate where exactly the girls' rooms were. It wouldn't take him long to befriend the `waitress` and get information out of her. Perhaps she was one of the girls on offer although he doubted that very much. You wouldn't put a girl out as a `receptionist` and then offer her to customers for sex. But she obviously knew what went on in the general run of the place. She knew there were English girls on offer therefore she must be in contact with this Saratov. Kulbertinov walked away and Katrina immediately held out her arm to Lawrence gesturing him to follow her. All of a sudden he wasn't dog shit any more.

"This way sir, I'll show you where the bar is. Would you like to see the menu for lunch? You are to have anything you wish to eat, Mister Kulbertinov is lovely man, he's very generous and is kind."

"He is indeed." Jim replied. "He seems to be very popular around here. He tells me he's here quite often."

The girl stopped in her tracks and looked straight into Lawrence's face, smiling. Almost whispering she said, "Mister Kulbertinov is one of our best customers." She then placed her pointing finger over her mouth suggesting for him to tell no-one else.

They entered the barroom. Again, this room was adorned with elaborate furnishings and fittings. "I leave you here sir I have to go back to desk, very busy you see. If you have any problem, you just come and see me. You no pay for anything in here, barman

knows, and he tell chef if you want to eat dinner or anything ok? I see you later."
And with that, Katrina was gone. Lawrence surmised to himself that the girl would be probably as close as you could get to being innocent. Yes, she knew exactly what went on in here but he was unsure if she would know how the girls were obtained.
She would be introduced to them believing that they were all here of their own free wills, after all, once they'd been groomed into the job they would certainly come over that way. Perhaps not today, but someday soon, he'd be able to take a little tour of the place, an internal tour and try and discover just how many girls were here. He approached the bar where a young gentleman greeted him with a smile.
"Yes sir, what can I get you?" Lawrence ordered a fresh orange-juice and a packet of salted peanuts. "Take a seat sir, and I'll bring your order over to you."
Before he moved away from the bar, he noticed above the barman's head a gallery of girls' faces on photographs, all smiling cheerfully as though the snaps had been taken whilst they were on the holiday of their lives.
And then he spotted her.
Alison Green's face seemed to smile at him specifically.
He half expected the photograph to come to life, and for the girl to shout out,
"Hi uncle Jimbo, are you going to stay for tea today?"
If Colin had felt helpless the other day as Alan had informed him, then today, *he* felt utterly useless. Colin could see the house where they kept his little girl, but here *he* was, *in* the actual house where they had her, and still not able to come to the girl's rescue…but now, it was just a matter of time. He would learn a lot from his two or three hours in here today. He would observe, and he would listen to every word of English that was spoken. The barman came over to his table carrying a tray with one glass of orange-juice and a bag of nuts. He placed a napkin on the table and then the glass and the nuts. "Excuse me." Said Lawrence, could you show me where the bathroom is please?"
The barman answered him cheerfully.
"Certainly sir, follow me."
He led Jim Lawrence down a long corridor which was luxuriously carpeted, as was the rest of the house, if house was the correct term for this place. They made a couple of turns before they finally reached the toilets, which was convenient for him. Now he had a perfect excuse if he was caught wandering around. He could say he got lost searching for the latrines.

EUROPA HOTEL.

KUANAS.

Terry had been out for a walk around the immediate area of the hotel. He was familiarising himself with the locations of cafes and `tobacconists`. He had also visited a couple of bars and had consumed a couple of beers on his travels. He was trying to give Samantha a little breathing space. These last few weeks he'd been a bit severe with her and constantly criticising her. She'd done well to persevere with his short-tempered ways. Always he found himself snapping at her, and down-talking any point of view she put forward. The sun shone brightly on this crisp winter day as he sat down on a public bench to contemplate his behaviour and the people who passed him by all hurrying as though they had a limited time to reach their next destination, scurrying and running around like busy ants.

Here he was, in the middle of Lithuania with not a clue on how he would go about trying to save those poor girls. It was alright for Alan Hartford and Jim Lawrence telling him to keep calm and do nothing until they contacted him but he was desperate to get those girls out of there. These men were trained for situations such as these and like Colin Green had informed him, *he* wasn't. Polly had done her best by extending their stay here but right now he felt absolutely useless.

What the hell was the point of him and Samantha being here?

Somehow he'd figured it out differently. He thought he'd be more involved, but thus far, all he and Samantha had succeeded in doing was to observe the house where the girls were being kept.

He drew hard on his cigarette as he sat more or less staring into space.

Before he done anything else, the first thing he'd have to do would be to improve the manner in which he spoke to Sam, she was every bit as good as anyone else he'd ever worked with. He admired the way she brushed off his sarcastic remarks and returned them with even more venomous ones aimed at where it hurts. She instinctively seemed to know his weak points. Nobody in this world was ever going to walk over Miss Samantha Reynolds that was for sure. She never questioned anything he done or told her to do, and so, starting from when he arrived back at the hotel he was going to change his attitude towards her, and he was going to listen genuinely to anything she had to offer. Truth be known, she was every bit as qualified as a detective as he was. He was going to have to dispose of this bitterness that *so* consumed his personality, after all, there were plenty of other people in the world who had been dished out shit

deals, he wasn't unique in any way and so as soon as he came to terms with that fact the better it would be for everyone concerned, namely Samantha Reynolds.
"Poor old treble clef as well, bloody snapping at the poor bugger like he was a dog, if it hadn't been for *him* they wouldn't even *be* here." He drew on his cigarette again glancing up at the sky. Terry Mercer was going to have to change his ways. He rose up from the bench extinguishing his cigarette and discarding the stub in a litter bin. He and Samantha were going to have to have a chat.   As far as he could tell they were going to be of no use whatsoever here.   The three S.A.S men had enough experience and expertise to handle this situation.
For want of putting it bluntly, he and Samantha were surplus to requirements.
They would do as Jim Lawrence had told them, and just sit tight for the duration of their remaining time here until such times as they were required, and if they weren't, then they'd accompany treble to some more of his concerts and show the man some gratitude for him inviting them here as his `special` guests. Terry found himself grunting as he rose from the bench and began the short walk back to the hotel.
Five minutes later he entered the hotel room to find Samantha sitting on the bed looking lugubrious. Beside her, her mobile phone and a scrap of paper, a telephone number scribbled upon it.
"Have I come in at a bad time Samantha?" he said, as he made his way to the coffee percolator. Samantha shook her head but gave him no verbal answer.
"Is there anything I can help you with Sam?" he said soothingly, because he knew that whatever was bothering her, it would not be a trivial matter. Again she shook her head, this time rising to her feet. "No Terry, nothing you can do. I'm sorry, but I'll have to go home, Polly has booked me a flight for later this afternoon."
He mistakenly thought that this is what was bothering her. Without thinking he began to rant. "What the fucking hell has she done that for? She knows how important you are over here with me, and I can't-."
"My mother has died Terry, I have to go back home."
"Oh shit I'm sorry Sam. I thought…oh Christ I'm sorry."
He poured two cups of coffee and handed one to her.
"Has she been ill Samantha? I mean, was it sudden or…"
Samantha sipped her coffee.
"Haven't got a clue Terry if she was ill or not, I haven't spoken to her for more than fourteen years. We fell out, and I never went back.
She's never attempted to contact me nor me her.
I was crying because I remembered how happy I was when I was a kid. I have a brother, older than me. He emigrated to America years ago and so I lost him.

A couple years later, my dad died, and that was it for me, that's' when my life stopped being...happy. About four years later my mother met this guy and moved him in. After a few months the bastard raped me. He raped me several times.
When I told my mother what kind of man she had accepted into her home she just laughed, accusing me of being jealous of her happiness and for making stories up and that it wasn't just `Alan`, it would be any man she took a liking to because they weren't my real daddy, or something like that, words to that effect. Anyway, that was that. I packed my bags and moved out. When I told her I was doing this, she just replied,"
"Oh well, you suit yourself, but don't think for one minute when things start to go wrong for you, and they will, that you'll be waltzing back in here, because you won't. You walk out that door then you walk out for good, understood? You jealous little madam that you are!"
Terry sat down on the bed beside his colleague.
He could have told her that he'd had parent trouble as well in the form of his father mocking him when he suggested joining the police force and that he intended to become a detective, and how his father had openly mocked him, between his bouts of whiskey-drinking, exclaiming to him that," *You couldn't detect a whore in a brothel...fucking Nancy boy."* If only the bastard was still alive, so that he could crack him on the jaw for every time he'd witnessed him striking his mother.
He sighed and tapped Samantha on the knee a couple of times.
"Must have shattered you Sam. I can't imagine what that must be like, for your mother not to believe you. But, never mind babe, it was her loss...look how you've turned out, your dad would be proud of you, and if there is a heaven up there, then you can bet your bottom dollar that he is smiling down on you even as we speak, especially as you have me looking out for your ass."
Samantha smiled and thanked him for trying to cheer her up, or at least in his own little way, trying to lighten the moment. She rose up from the bed once more and began to pack her case and bags. He observed Samantha as she packed her clothes, neatly folding every garment and placing them into her bags.
"I just want you to know something Sam, and I'm not just saying this in light of what has just happened with your mum. I've been doing some soul-searching lately and I have fallen short, very short on how I should have been treating you as a colleague. Sometimes I think that what happened to me in my past has actually poisoned my personality, I snap at people whenever something goes wrong always blaming others for the situation."
Samantha turned to look at him. "Is there something that I can help *you* with Terry? I am your colleague and would like to think, your friend, so you can tell me anything you

want you know, it doesn't go any further. I think I knew that there was or is something that is tearing you to pieces and it comes out in your conversations, I mean your profanations are bordering on Tourette's, it's every second word Terry. Is it the stress from this job that makes you swear so much, the pressure? If you need to talk to someone about it Terry, then I'm here to help you...if I can. If I can't help then I can at least listen to your problem...if you have one...I think you have." Samantha continued to pack her clothes. "Would you like another coffee Sam?"

"No thanks Terry, I'm fine. Oh, Jim Lawrence was in touch, he sent me a text letting us know that there had been a little bit of progress made in connection with contacting the girls., just said he would be in touch soon."

Terry had to check himself from heading into one of his rants. The fact that Lawrence had contacted Samantha and not him almost tipped his scales, after all *he* was Samantha's superior, so why the hell was he contacting *her*?

Sam still had her back to him as she packed.

He fished out his mobile from his jacket pocket, and low and behold, there was the text message from Jim Lawrence. He sighed in frustration at his own short-tempered sledge-hammer attitude. He almost ripped into Samantha accusing her of trying to pull rank over him, but there it was, the man had contacted him obviously before he'd contacted Samantha. Still he couldn't resist the temptation, just to make sure. "What time did he text us Sam?"

A minute later it was confirmed that Lawrence had texted Terry two minutes before he'd texted Sam. Mercer was calm again.

"Has anybody else been in touch Sam? Colin or Alan?"

"Terry, I think they'd get in touch with you first, don't you think? I mean you are the head detective here not me, they won't contact me before they speak to you now will they, don't be so bloody stupid."

Mercer smiled to himself as he continued watching Sam packing.

"There are none of us detectives here Sam, officially, we're supposed to be here on holiday, so, it's not a question of who is in charge. How long are you going to be back in Britain? I mean, you'll be coming back over here won't you?"

"I doubt that very much Terry, they could take over a week sorting out funeral plans you know, I honestly don't know how long it'll take. But, I shall be keeping an eye out for our friend Angela Bates if she shows her face back at her flat, I might give your friend Roxanne a visit as well, get an update about Angela if she's been anywhere near the place, and I can assure you Terry it won't cost me a penny."

"Yeah, it might be worth having a little chat with our bad-tempered termagant Samantha...if she's not too busy...raucous Roxanne."

SARATOV'S MANSION.

KAUNAS.

Jim Lawrence had been enjoying a glass of fruit-juice in the bar as he waited yet again for his boss Mister Kulbertinov to `attend` his business here in the mansion of shame. He wandered around the empty lounge glancing out of the various windows which overlooked the car park. The barman had disappeared somewhere.
As he stood by one of the windows something caught his eye.
He saw two men who seemed to be escorting a young woman somewhere.
The girl walked in front of the men and so he couldn't see her face.
They were heading around the side of the house. From the angle of the window where he stood he couldn't see where they were taking her. He decided to exit the building and see where they were heading. As he left the house he glanced at his watch to remind him of how long Kulbertinov had been occupied. As he rounded the gable-end of the house he was just in time to see the two men's heads disappearing down a set of steps. There was a tall wooden gate that led to the steps. The gate had been left open. Lawrence moved into the cover of the trees that surrounded the house.
A few moments later, the two men reappeared and locked the gate.
They continued walking towards the back of the house. He wondered how many more men were here working for Saratov. In all the time he'd spent surveying the place he'd only seen three different men and a couple of women come and go at the back of the premises. Other than that, the only people who came here were `customers`.
Where had they taken the girl?
Was there another building down there?
He decided to find out. Kulbertinov had only been occupied for about twenty minutes and so he'd have at least another hour or so before there was any danger of him reappearing. Lawrence strolled casually back round to the front of the house and into the car park. From the boot of Kulbertinov's Rolls Royce Jim Lawrence searched inside a canvas bag full of all sorts of gadgets and tools. Before he joined the army he had been a compulsive thief, and an expert in lock picking. He boasted at one time when he was seventeen, that there hadn't been a car built that he could not gain entry to. He'd learned his trade from an old recidivist who had taken him under his wing. He showed Jim how to beat any locking system that used a key, with a piece of wire. Thus far, he had never failed. He gently closed the trunk of the car and glanced around to see if anyone was watching him. Satisfied that no-one was he headed back round towards the

tall gate. Instead of picking the gate lock he simply scaled the gate and climbed down the concrete steps. He found the large wrought-iron door at the bottom.
Instinctively, he listened at the door for activity.
Nothing.
There was no other entry point, other than this door. Trees and shrubs grew all over and around the bunker. From any other angle you would never be able to detect that there was anything here. If they'd brought the girl down here, then she must be inside.
It took Jim Lawrence a total of three minutes and twelve seconds to master the padlock. He pushed the door open gently and jumped with fright as a flurry or rats ran past his feet, some of them climbing the concrete steps, others swiftly returning from where they'd came. If the girl was in here, then she'd been left for half an hour or so. As he pushed the door to its' widest point he saw her. She was standing in the corner with her hands covering her ears and shaking her head. She was distressed, to the extreme.
The girl turned round to face him shielding her eyes from the sudden daylight exclaiming that she was deeply sorry for her outburst, and that she promised to behave from now on. Jim approached the girl cautiously so as not to panic her further.
"Why have they put you in here"? He said softly, taking her by the hand.
The girl wrapped her hands around his neck and cuddled him, shivering convulsively, sobbing into his shoulders and repeating to him that she'd behave herself.
"Please, please, get me away from the rats, please."
All he could do was console her by patting her on the shoulder and telling her that it was going to be alright. But now he had a decision to make. Does he try to explain to her that help is on the way and leave her here until such times as he could return with reinforcements to help all the girls, or does he take a chance and smuggle her into the boot of his `boss's` car and take her into the city where she could then contact the authorities and inform them of what was going on here. Surely not all the police-force would be corrupt, and therefore save all the girls, after all, it didn't matter *who* came to the girls' rescue, as long as someone did. She felt stone cold in his arms, she was dressed only in a skimpy mini-dress, her body shook with fear of the rats and the low temperature in this bunker.
It took him the best part of three minutes to finally calm the girl down long enough for him to explain to her that he had nothing to do with the people who ran the mansion.
He now had a dilemma. His boss may be as long as another two hours before he returned and so if he hid the girl in the boot of the car, she would have a considerable length of time to remain there before he'd be able to release her. To add risk to this option was the fact that those two men could return here to extract the girl before Kulbertinov was finished. If that happened, then he was in big trouble. He would have

to take the chance. There was no way this girl could stand in here any longer. He gently took her by the shoulders and began to speak to her reassuringly.

"What's your name sweetheart?"

"Sophie, my name is Sophie Spencer. They kidnapped me and brought me here along with other British girls, and they make us have sex with people, they make us do all kinds of things and they charge them money for using us and we-."

"Hey, it's ok, calm down Sophie. I am here to help you. Now, can you listen to me carefully while I tell you our plan? Can you do that for me?"

The girl nodded her head as she deliberately kept her vision on the ceiling so as not to see the rats scurrying around the floor at her feet.

"Ok Sophie, I am going to try and get you out of here, but you must do exactly as I tell you, will you do that for me?"

Again the girl nodded her head eagerly.

"Ok, I am going to take you from here back up the steps to the car park. I want you to hide in the trees until I come round with the car. You will then climb into the boot of the car and I will close the trunk. Now then Sophie, the thing is you could be in there for quite a while before I am able to release you. Do you think you can do that? Remember, it could be a long while until I get the chance to release you. I will then give you further instructions as to what we'll do next. We'll take it from there, now do you think you'll be able to do that?" The girl nodded enthusiastically, smiling nervously at Lawrence.

"You won't forget about me in the boot will you?"

"I promise you Sophie I will not forget you. You are the reason that I am here, but you must trust me, like I say, the man I am working for is in there with one of your friends, I have no idea how long he'll be in there, but I will let you out of the boot as soon as it's safe. I'll bring you some water and a couple of sandwiches out to the car when I come over for you. I'm going to hide you in the bushes when I get you out of here. As soon as I can, I'll come over with the car and get you into the trunk, ok?" For the third time the girl nodded her head. "Yes, ok, I'll wait until you tell me to move I'll hide, but please, get me away from these rats."

Jim Lawrence led Sophie by the hand to the foot of the steps. He closed the heavy door of the bunker behind them and relocked the padlock.

Now he was on borrowed time. He was in the hands of the Gods.

"Wait here Sophie until I come and give you the signal. You can sit half way up the steps but whatever you do, do not show your face above the top, they may and probably will have cameras on the gate. So, I'll be as quick as I can alright?"

Sophie sat half way up the steps with her head between her knees.

Lawrence tapped her on the shoulder a couple of times to reassure her.

Quickly and efficiently he scaled the gate and casually strolled towards the front of the car park, and then round the gable end and back into the front of the building.

He returned to the bar lounge where the young barman had re-appeared to continue his duties. He stood now polishing glasses with a tea-towel and smiling at Jim.

"Everything ok sir?" He said to Lawrence.

"Yes, fine, I was just strolling round the house, you know, the car park and the surrounding areas...it's very nice, lovely gardens.

The young gentleman looked at him as he continued cleaning the tumbler, a tall young man, very slim, almost to the point of being skinny, complete with wire-rimmed spectacles.

"Yes sir, very nice indeed."

The lad looked distinctively eastern European. Lawrence tried to put the wheels into motion.

"I wonder if you could help me, do you think you could order me a round of sandwiches please from the chef, see I was told to order anything I-."

"Certainly sir, I will tell chef now. What kind would you like?"

"Oh, just ham and salad will do thank you, and maybe a piece of cake, would that be alright?"

"Of course sir, I'll just go and order them for you now, I won't be very long sir. Would you like me to wait for chef to make them up and I will bring them right here to you, would that be suitable?"

Lawrence smiled at the boy and told him that that would be perfect.

"I'm just going to bring the car round the front in case my boss arrives. I like to be efficient you see. So, if I am not here when you return then you know that I won't be long, and thank you very much indeed for your help, I appreciate it very much."

"Not at all sir, I'll be as quick as I can sir."

"Yeah, and so will I" said Lawrence to himself. Once again Jim Lawrence walked casually across the car park to where the Rolls Royce was parked. He climbed in and fired the ignition. Slowly he drove across to the other side of the parking area. If anyone came out now they would be wondering what on earth he was doing. He stopped the car just in front of where the tall wooden gate was situated so that the car would obscure anyone's vision from within the house. Casually, he opened the boot of the car and walked round. As quick as lightning, he scaled the wooden gate. Sophie was crouched down shivering. "Come on kid, let's get you into the car, are you ok Sophie?"

She nodded her head. "Now remember what I told you. You might be in here for some considerable time but don't you worry, I promise you I won't forget you're in there, you have to trust me Sophie, do you trust me?"

"Yes I trust you. What's your name, I don't know your name?"
"My name is Jim, now, come on babes, let's get you into the car. Once you're in the boot Sophie, try your best not to make a noise, even if you're panicking, please don't make a sound. If we get caught, I shudder to think what they'll do to us, are you ready?"
"Yes."
Lawrence lifted the girl with ease so that she could climb over the wooden gate and down into the bushes. He was over the gate in seconds. Quickly he helped her into the boot of the car and gently closed the trunk informing Sophie that he'd see her soon, or as soon as possible. Just at that point a man appeared at the front door of the mansion.
"Hey!"
Lawrence looked over towards the front door. The young barman stood waving at him.
"Come and get your sandwiches sir, they're ready."
He waved back over to the young man and climbed into the car, slowly driving across the car park and bringing the vehicle to a stop just to the side of the front doors. He'd done it. Now it was just a matter of time as to how long Kulbertinov would take to finish his `business`.
The chef had been kind as well. He was handed three double sandwiches by the young barman.
"Oh, there's too much here for me I only wanted a round, thank you so much. Perhaps I could put a couple of these into the car for later, would that be alright sir?"
The barman smiled, "Of course sir, they're your sandwiches, you do with them what you please." He re-entered the building to continue his duties.
Lawrence took the double sandwich outside and cautiously opened the boot, placing the paper bag inside, together with a bottle of water. "Sshh" he said as he closed the boot again and returned to the lounge where he proceeded to eat his sandwich. As he sat making small talk with the `over-helpful` barman, he began to send text messages to Alan Hartford and to inform him of the situation, and that he would most definitely need his assistance before long. He had no idea whatsoever where Alan was at this point of time but he knew the man would be there for him when the time came, so he would keep Alan informed of his locations until such times as he felt it safe to make a move. For some unknown reason the two S.A.S men had both agreed that they did not trust the Lithuanian police department, at least not around these parts and so they would have to work out something with regards to Sophie's safety. When they'd finally discover that she'd escaped from the bunker then all hell would break loose for those girls still in there. Perhaps Alan had something worked out. He said that Colin had friends in Poland who would help them, but that would remain to be seen. There was also detective Mercer, but then, there was very little he could do in a situation like this.

This was new territory for Lawrence.

Under normal circumstances a plan would be laid out, and each part of that plan would be executed to perfection, but these were anything but normal circumstances, in fact, it was down-right dangerous. The safety of those other girls would undoubtedly be put into jeopardy. But, on the bright side or rather the positive side, he had one of the girls out of there. All they needed to do now would be to inform the authorities of what was happening inside that house, but only if they thought that they could be trusted. That was the trouble though, both he and Alan were in total agreement that for some unknown reason they weren't about to trust the local police. That gut feeling, and when both men had it, then it wasn't even up for discussion. Going to the police here in Kaunas was not going to be an option. They would just *have* to come up with something else.

EUROPA HOTEL.

KAUNAS.

Samantha Reynolds was gone and on her way back to London. Terry Mercer was now talking on the phone to Polly Sheppard. He was frustrated because it seemed he hadn't been included in anything that the S.A.S men were doing. He was poorly informed of what was happening, if anything, and was practically being ignored. "You've got me booked in here Polly for another seven days but if you think for one minute that I'm just going to sit here doing nothing then you're up a gum tree. I haven't even heard from Colin Green, he's not in his room. I don't know if he's working on something with those two S.A.S fuckers because no-one is telling me anything. I haven't even got Samantha here to talk to. If I haven't heard anything from those twats by tonight, then I'm out of here Polly, I'm getting the first flight out in the morning back to London, I've had enough of these fucking know-alls telling me to sit quiet and be patient. I thought that because I was here in Lithuania that I'd have at least an opportunity to help those poor girls, but because I'm doing what I've been told, I can't get anywhere near them. Christ Polly, I'd be just as well in fucking Benidorm. A month ago we had no idea where on earth those girls were, and here I am now, practically within touching distance from them and yet I can't even do a bloody thing to help them, fucking sit tight and do nothing until I tell you indeed. I've had it Polly, if they've not contacted me by tonight then that's it."
Polly could be heard sighing heavily, as though she was at the end of her tether. Her voice when she spoke was calm though. "Terry, I know how frustrating this is for you. I know how you always have to be active and running around, I know all that, but listen you have to trust these men. They don't act impulsively Terry, they plan everything they do, and if that fails, then they have a plan B. And if that fails, they have a plan C, that's why they are the best. They won't just storm the place and put people's lives at risk, they do things discretely and deliberately. If they are not getting in touch with you just now then they must be coping fine and well, but just because they're not in constant contact with you doesn't mean for one minute that they won't have to rely on you. For all you know they could be depending on you. Please Terry just hold out until your time is officially up, I had to move mountains to get you that extension. Now, if you're doing nothing else, go and spend some time with old Geoffrey at his concerts, as long as you're there if those ghosts need you and by the way Terry, I'm not even supposed to be talking to you about them, in fact, you really shouldn't be told of their existence, so

please, just do as they asked you Terry, and be on stand-by for them because as I say, for all we know they might have to rely on you, and if you're not there-" "Alright, alright Polly, point taken, I'll do as I'm fucking told once again. Maybe someday soon I'll be able to make a decision of my own and work on my own merit God forbid, Christ."
"Terry, I'll talk to you soon, please, just wait until you hear from them, they will be in touch they know how eager you are to help those girls, so just be there for them if they need you. If it turns out that they can do this without you, then fair enough Terry, as long as the girls are released then that's all that matters, but I strongly believe that they'll need you before this draws to a close."
"Well the least they could do would be to keep in touch Polly, let me know how things are progressing, but no, not a bloody word, and Colin, God knows where he is, I haven't heard from him for a couple of days, he's not answering his phone and there's no answer at his room, I've been three times, I only hope he's with those other two, they could let me know Polly, surely that's not too much to ask for."
Polly had no option but to agree with Terry, they should have been keeping in touch with him, but then, these ghosts were *so* used to working under the radar as it were, that they very seldom felt it necessary to contact anyone, at least until their mission had been completed and after all, if anything happened to them, if they landed in trouble, they were on their own, there would be no help coming to them, so she supposed that secrecy was their policy. The less people knew what they were doing the better, add to that, Terry was here officially on holiday. They wouldn't want him caught snooping around the grounds of Saratov's mansion when he was supposed to be here listening to classical music. She managed to calm Terry down sufficiently enough for him to give his word that he'd stay put until he was contacted, and that on its' own was no mean fete.

KAUNAS.

It was late afternoon and darkness was falling as Jim Lawrence drove in the car he'd hired with a certain Miss Sophie Spencer who was laying on the floor at the foot of the back seats. She'd been instructed to do so by Jim just in case anyone was watching him. As he drove he continuously asked Sophie questions about the running of the mansion, in particular how many staff ran the place, and how many of them were male. Did she ever see anyone armed? The fact that he had Sophie with him had inconvenienced Alan Hartford's plan, but, all said and done it was only a minor inconvenience. Lawrence was now driving to the Polish border with Sophie. Colin Green had already been instructed by Hartford to head across the border into Poland. Colin Green was in fact waiting for Jim Lawrence with some Polish friends he'd met years earlier whilst being stationed there. These friends of his were all ex-military as well. One of them lived in a very small village near the Lithuanian border called Olkiny a village in the administrative district of Gmina Wizajny in the county of Suwalki. Less than two hundred people lived here, but in one of the cottages there were two women and three men eagerly waiting for a phone call from Lawrence informing them that he was approaching the Polish border. Colin had explained to his friends what was going on in the mansion in Kaunas and how the girls had been abducted in England and then smuggled over here to be used as sex slaves. Jakub Nowak and his girlfriend Lena Kowalski had lived here since they'd both retired from the forces and truth be known were waiting for an opportunity like this. They missed the excitement of being in the military. Very soon, they would venture into something extremely dangerous. From here they would drive over to Kaunas and attempt to snatch the girls to safety by driving them back over here in numerous hired vehicles back to Poland, where they could receive help. Lena, a thirty-two-year-old ex-army sergeant lived for moments like these, as did her boyfriend Jakub who had also been a sergeant. Their friends, Amelia Wisniewski, Antoni Dabrowski and Kacper Kaminski had all been in the forces together. They had all befriended Colin Green when they'd met through a military exorcise some years earlier. They all admired and respected the British S.A.S. Colin Green sat nervously drinking his cup of tea awaiting the call from Jim Lawrence. Lawrence had informed Colin Green that he had one of the girls with him in the car, and could he make arrangements for one of his friends to guide the girl safely through Poland and board her on to a flight back to London. False papers would be needed to do this. Failing that, get her to the British Embassy. Lena had friends who could help to see to that, but it would take a couple of days.
The girl would be safe enough here until it had been arranged. Colin Green jumped

from his seat as his mobile phone buzzed loudly on the table. It was Jim Lawrence. "Colin, I'm about a mile from the border, can someone come and meet me to collect the girl."
"Just keep driving Jim, we'll be looking out for you, don't worry we'll pick the girl up." Lawrence explained where exactly he was and as soon as he did Lena Kowalski was up off her chair and heading to her pick-up truck with Kacper Kaminski. Fifteen minutes later, Jim Lawrence was sharing a mug of tea with his new friends and making plans for their manoeuvres concerning their ascending the mansion in Kaunas. All of the Poles spoke moderate English so there would be no problems concerning communication. Sophie Spencer sat at the table red-eyed and frightened. Confused as to what was happening. Amelia Wisniewski consoled her and tried to re-assure her that she was safe now and that no matter what else happened, she wouldn't be going back to that horrible man. It was very difficult for the fifteen-year-old to believe anything anyone said to her. She'd heard nothing but nice pleasant voices from European people telling her that everything would be alright but despite all the nice words very horrible things had happened to her and her friends. All she wanted to do was to call her mother and her brother David, just to be able to hear their voices and to let them know that she was alright, at least for the time-being. Colin Green approached her and knelt by her side. "Hi Sophie, my name is Colin. I know what you've been through and we are all here to help you."
Sophie interrupted him. "Everybody tells me they're here to help me, but still..."
"I know Sophie, I know, but we are different. Sophie, my daughter is in there, Alison Green, did you see her there Sophie?" Sophie looked at Colin.
"Yes, I know her, I mean I know her now, I didn't before this happened, she's nice, she's a nice girl."
"Yes, and that is why we are here Sophie. We are going to try and get all the girls out of there, we know what's been going on and we intend to put a stop to all this. We *are* different to all the others Sophie, you can trust us, believe me, I want my daughter out of there."
Jim Lawrence approached Colin and informed him that he'd already asked Sophie all the important questions. He also took him aside to tell him that, according to Sophie, through all the cocaine the girls were taking it had left them all almost in a state of numbness, as though they were phlegmatic. Colin sighed heavily and Jim knew exactly why. No wonder the man was anxious. He tapped him on the shoulder a couple of times. "Soon pal, very soon we'll have her out of there, and all the other girls. Our next move is to get back over to Kaunas and wait for Alan's signal. Then we infiltrate the building and deal with whatever we have to deal with. There are other European girls in

there as well as British girls, God knows how many, but if we can get them to the Polish border then they'll be able to make arrangements. The main thing is, to free them and bring their ordeals to an end. After that, we can contact the authorities to inform them of what has been going on there and get that bastard Saratov into jail and all his subordinates."

EUROPA HOTEL.

KAUNAS.

Alan Hartford was talking to Terry Mercer on his mobile, and was informing him of what their plan was. He had also informed Mercer that he'd obtained a people-carrier for him to drive. The plan was that Mercer would wait for a signal from either Hartford or Lawrence when to pull into the car park at the mansion. Terry was to take all of the British girls with him in his carrier and head to the Polish border. The two S.A.S men would meet up with him in a village called Olkiny. From there, the girls would be transported to safety and then flown back over to Great Britain. After they had all rendezvoused at Olkiny, the British girls would be driven (By Terry) to Bialystok and then on to Warsaw where they would then be flown back over to Britain.

Terry Mercer felt elated. At last, he would be involved in something concerning the girls and getting them to safety. Hartford would arrive at the Europa hotel in fifteen minutes to deliver the people-carrier, complete with a full tank of diesel. Then he was to wait until either Hartford or Lawrence contacted him with a time to leave.

He wished that Samantha could be here to play her part in this operation.

Against all the odds it seemed that the girls were going to be freed after all, if of course, everything went to plan. He would certainly play *his* role and would follow their instructions to the letter. Twenty minutes later, Alan Hartford pulled up outside the Europa hotel in a Toyota Proace Verso, falcon grey. Hartford climbed into the passenger seat and let Terry drive out to the mansion. On the way he explained everything to him in great detail, although in Terry's opinion there wasn't much to take in.

Wait at the appointed place until informed when to move, and then move.

"These S.A.S fuckers have got to dramatize everything they do."

But then he knew how important timing was to them and how it was crucial for everyone to know exactly what they were to do, otherwise... pandemonium, disaster.

Hartford set the sat-nav for Olkiny when they reached their destination.

He explained to Terry how to get from the mansion out onto the main road.

The sat-nav would guide him there.

"You're going to be something of a hero Terry when we get back to Britain, everybody will be congratulating you when you bring-."

"Hey, no offence pal, but don't count your chickens. I'm not sure that that old bastard doesn't have some kind of protection system in place. For all we know, he could have a dozen armed people in there all willing to die for him.

All the congratulations will wait until we get to Britain, and anyway it's not me who is the hero, it's you guys, all I'll be doing is driving them to those places you told me, and I hope to fuck your sat-nav is spot on, otherwise I'll be fucked and so will those poor girls."

"Terry, trust me bud, it'll be fine, Jim has done some internal investigations and he assures me that there are only three or four guys to worry about. Up until we show up, Saratov has had no reason to pay for high security after all it's his own private mansion. Only the people who are rich enough to spend astronomical amounts of money know about this place. These people are the Lithuanian aristocratic cream of the big spenders."

"I still don't take anything for granted Alan, I'll just be glad when we get those girls over the border and into Poland."

Alan Hartford glanced at his watch and just as he did Jim Lawrence pulled up in his hired vehicle in front of theirs.

"Ok Terry, that's us ready. As soon as the coast is clear we'll call you to drive into the car park of the mansion. Just drive right up to the front door and don't whatever you do get out, we will escort the girls into your vehicle. Then that's it, you just drive until you get to Olkiny." Mercer nodded, lighting up a cigarette. "Ok, be careful you guys."

Hartford smiled at Mercer. "I didn't know you cared Terry."

"Ok then" said Terry, "Let's see how good you guys really are, we hear enough fucking stories about your bravery, let's just see…hurry up."

Hartford climbed into the car smiling and the two S.A.S men disappeared around the bend. Terry Mercer sat smoking his cigarette contemplating the situation. He hoped above all else that they would be successful in their mission. They had done well to find out what they had in such a short time here, and they certainly weren't wasting any time in getting the girls out. Whoever these Polish friends of theirs were they must trust them unconditionally. They themselves were taking a chance sneaking into another country and collaborating with these S.A.S men. Mercer's mind wandered back over to Britain as he thought about the agony that the parents' of these girls would be going through. No-one would have been in touch with them he supposed for the simple reason that there was nothing to report. He remembered the parents desperate and breaking down with the stress of losing their daughters this way. How many more had been kidnapped since he had been over here? Samantha was going to keep an eye out for any of those women who were apparently the leaders of these kidnapping gangs. Even if they were apprehended though, someone else would take over their operations. The need for money, or indeed the greed for money would continue to drive human beings into doing very despicable acts. Morality or principles had no place in the minds

of these individuals. They would sell their own mothers if the price was right. Britain had changed in many ways over the last few years. Gone was that friendship between neighbours, the way it was when he grew up. People used to have time for each other in those days. They would be helpful in so many ways. Now, no-one hardly knows who their neighbours are let alone be friendly. Mercer sighed as he waited for the phone call, sad at what had happened to his Britain. Once, it was the envy of the world. It used to mean something if you were British, or if something was `Made in Britain`.
"There's nothing great about it now, selling their own nationals for money to Eastern-Europeans as though they were cuts of meat, never thinking or caring about the amount of devastation they were causing, as long as they had their money for their drugs or their drink or their fancy life-styles.
Huh, morality died a long time ago in Britain."
Maybe someday they would bring back Capital punishment and at least the guilty parties would be eliminated from society, instead of them walking free after two or three years in the slammer. He wondered now if the S.A.S men intended to eliminate Saratov and his collaborators. He certainly hoped so. What kind of a man could do that to someone else's kids, selling them to businessmen to use as sexual toys. And what kind of people could enjoy doing these despicable things to teenage girls, some of them not even out of school. The world to Terry Mercer was rotten to the core. He had witnessed victims left in a room castrated because they couldn't pay back the money to these loan-sharks. He'd seen babies left to starve to death while their mothers' were out whoring for drug-money. Women poisoned by Aconite, a poison also known as Wolfsbane. The poison was extracted from the plant Monkshood. If you even touched the plant without wearing gloves you could die. He had witnessed women who'd had the leaves of the plant stuffed down their throats, and dying by means of asphyxiation, before the poison even kicked in, all because they hadn't made enough money for their pimps or they had made a couple of quid more than they'd declared to them.
And all these things had happened in Britain.
All these murders had taken place on the streets of the towns and cities of Great Britain. Just as he was drifting into a state of depression his phone buzzed.
"Come now Terry, quick as you like."
He slipped into first gear and began the short drive to the Mansion.
Reaching the car park he drove up to the front doors as instructed and waited with the engine still running. He hoped that everything had gone to plan for them. Mercer wasn't convinced that it would be plain sailing. Surely this evil little man would have some kind of security. With all the money he was raking in it would be in his best interest to have some kind of protection if something went wrong.

Or was he so disillusioned that he thought he wouldn't ever need protection. Word would get around about places like these. Surely the locals would have heard about the comings and goings of this place. And stories would be told, rumours concerning the teenage girls who lived here. He was abruptly brought out of his thoughts as the two main front doors burst open. Four teenage girls emerged and made their way towards the van, followed closely by Jim Lawrence. He opened the side doors of the people carrier and helped the girls into the vehicle.

"Be back in a minute Terry." He managed before he returned to the house. Mercer looked in his rear-view mirror and noticed two of the girls were marked on their faces. One of them had a black eye. The girls were all hysterical, one of them crying another holding her hands over her ears as though she couldn't stand the din. Suddenly, from inside the house Mercer heard a gun going off, then another shot, and a third. Now he *did* feel apprehension. He reassuringly felt his gun in his jacket pocket. "Calm down girls" he heard himself saying. "Everything will be alright, don't worry." He hoped with all his heart he was telling them the truth. Alan Hartford appeared at the door. Another two girls came down the steps. Hartford escorted them to the vehicle and helped them in. His words were authoritative. "Ok Terry, that's you bud, on you go, we'll see you at Olkiny. Just follow the sat-nav pal, see you soon Tel."

"Is everything alright Alan?"

"Don't worry about a thing Terry, just get on your way bud Jim and I will see to everything else, move!"

Terry glanced at the sat-nav screen as he exited the car park. He wondered what had gone on in the mansion. There had obviously been some kind of trouble. Three gun shots. He just hoped that Jim Lawrence hadn't been on the wrong end of one of those shots, but by the way Alan Hartford had been talking everything seemed to be ok.

"Keep calm girls, we're on our way ladies, stay calm, you're safe now."

Again, his statement was more of a prayer than a fact. He hoped above all hope that he wouldn't be stopped by anyone employed by the Lithuanian Police department or the Lithuanian military. He'd heard stories about migrants who used an `unknown` route through Lithuania into EU. Chechen smugglers were alleged to have used it.

The last thing he needed would be to be confronted as a tourist in a Lithuanian hired vehicle with a group of scantily clad teenage girls. All hell *would* break loose then. He chased the thought from his head, and concentrated on his sat-nav, praying that it wouldn't be too long until he reached the Polish border. Once over there, their troubles were over. After a few minutes the girls had all calmed themselves down. They were all now huddled together one or two of them smoking cigarettes all of them believing for the first time, that they were actually going to be freed from their sexual hell. Terry drove on scrutinising the sat-nav and meticulously following the route. Finally, after what seemed like four hours, when in fact it had been three quarters of an hour, Terry Mercer was greeted by Amelia Wisniewski and Antoni Dabrowski outside of a small cottage in the village of Olkiny. He had made it. He was now in Poland. Now he only hoped that everything else had gone to plan for the S.A.S men who had informed him that they would meet him here. Amelia Wisniewski was a petite young woman with what Terry would call, a boys' haircut, light brown. She approached the vehicle, and opened the sliding side door inviting the girls to climb out. In her beautiful broken English she exclaimed to them, "Have lovely surprise for you all, come and see in house, she waiting for you." As the girls climbed out of the Toyota Proace, they squealed with excitement as Sophie Spencer came out of the cottage waving, happy to be reunited with her `friends`.

Mercer watched in fascination as the girls all greeted Sophie hugging and laughing. He wondered when the last time would have been when they laughed genuinely. Mercer approached Amelia. "Could we have the girls inside Amelia, I'm nervous about standing out here."

Some other people came out of their cottages curious as to what the commotion was all about making Terry even more anxious.

He didn't like them all congregated out here in the open, about half a dozen of them. Amelia smiled at Mercer.

"Of course Mister Mercer, you are very brave man, you are very good man.
I take the girls inside and you feel better ok? Alan and Jim will be here soon and make you feel better, you nervous ok?"

"Yes I'm nervous, I am very nervous, please could we get them inside these people are giving us some very weird looks, I don't want them phoning the police."

Amelia waved down the road to one or two of the curious pensioners, who then waved back to her, smiling. "Everything is going to be ok Mister Mercer, come on girls let's go and get the tea and making the coffee."

Terry smiled at the girls' English, but admired the fact that so many foreign people took the time to learn another language. He had always meant to learn a language but had never got round to it. Antoni Dabrowski approached Terry now smiling. "Are you ok Mister Mercer? You've done very well but you seem frightened, please don't be, you are ok now and the girls, you are now in Poland. We will get the girls to the Polish authorities and they will arrange flights back to Britain, they'll all be back home in about two days from now, maybe even sooner than that. Come and get a cup of tea and a bite to eat, your friends will be here soon. Colin Green is already in Warsaw, he will soon be reunited with his daughter." He then tapped Terry a couple of times on the shoulder and laughed, "It's ok, it's ok, I told you. You're in Poland now, the girls are safe." Terry thanked the giant young man who must have stood six foot six and weighed about three hundred pounds. The two taps on his shoulder made his body vibrate and actually put him momentarily off-balance. The giant teen spoke again to Terry as they walked over to the cottage. "When Jim and Alan get here they will decide whether to travel today or tomorrow morning. The girls will be taken to Bialystok, and then from there they will be taken to Warsaw, and then home. And then Mister Mercer, they can carry on their lives as normal."

Mercer smiled at the young man but in his head he thought, *"Yeah, they'll be back home kid, but as far as anything ever being normal again is concerned, I don't think that'll be happening any time soon. How could anything ever be normal again after what these young girls had been through."*

When Terry entered the cottage, Amelia had all the girls seated around a large table which took up most of the space in this very small living room. To these girls though it would seem like a castle. Terry stood beside Antoni smiling at the girls as they chattered now as though they were in a cafe at home. Now all he wanted was for Alan and Jim to phone him and tell him they were on their way, or a text message, anything to put his mind at ease, because even though he was now in Poland, he was here without official permission. The cottage was stone-floored and had a very low ceiling. The place was smoky enough without him adding to it, and besides he wanted back outside to the fresh air and also, if Jim or Alan called him he wanted to talk to them about travel arrangements for the girls. All said and done, he just wanted them to call him and tell him they were on their way. It was in Terrence Mercer's nature to be nervous. As he lit his cigarette outside his phone buzzed in his pocket. It was Alan informing him that he would be there in about five minutes, everything had gone to plan. When Terry had asked him about the three shots in the mansion and what exactly had happened, he was just told that everything went to plan and that there was nothing at all for him to worry about. "I'll explain when I see you Terry." The phone went dead. Now he was happy. Now he could relax...at least for the time being. When he re-entered the cottage Amelia was busy taking the girls measurements. They had been told to leave by the S.A.S men in what clothes they were wearing. Amelia would see to it that they all had appropriate clothes to travel in. If the plan hadn't changed they would be staying overnight in a hotel in Bialystok before heading off to Warsaw where they would catch their flight home. Jakub and Lena were on the phone now to Amelia. Terry was quite taken aback at the effort these people were making for their friends. When the three S.A.S men had said they had Polish friends who were willing to help them, he didn't for one minute think they would go to this much trouble. He was impressed beyond belief at their kindness. Amelia switched off her phone and approached him.

"Is all sorted out now Terry. The girls they soon get different clothes. Lena be here in an hour or nearly."

Again Terry couldn't help himself from smiling at the kind-hearted girl in front of him and her beautiful melodic broken English tones. Alan had informed him that all of these people were ex-military. He wondered what Amelia would be like in arm to arm combat. She would surprise anyone with her fighting skills he surmised. He imagined her informing her enemy of what she was going to do to them.

"Probably fights like a fucking Honey Badger." *"Ok I be smashing your jaw now into the pieces."*

Much to Mercer's relief, he heard a vehicle pulling up outside the cottage.

Jim Lawrence climbed out of the B.M.W and approached him.

"Well done Terry, you got them here ok. Did you have any problems?"

"None whatsoever, Alan set the sat-nav for me and I merely followed the route, it was you guys I was worried about, where is Alan?"

Jim walked round to the back of the car and opened the boot. Alan Hartford climbed out stretching his arms. He smiled at Terry.

"Well done pal, good job."

After a lengthy discussion it was decided that Jim Lawrence would drive the girls to Bialystok. He would take Lena's Sherpa van. Alan would then drive the B.M.W back to Kaunas. Terry would take the Toyota. Terry's flight home had been arranged for the following morning. Geoffrey Marsden would be on that same flight. The two S.A.S men had been in touch with Polly Sheppard and all the arrangements had been made. Colin Green was waiting in a hotel in Warsaw. He would accompany the girls on their flight. Terry thanked the Polish people for all of their help and informed them that if they were ever over in London they were welcome to free accommodation for the duration of their visit. All the girls thanked Terry for bringing them here and all embraced him individually. Terry said he would see them soon. He would come and visit them in their homes. Alan Hartford came outside with him and set the sat-nav for Kaunas.

"Just the same Terry, follow the route and you'll be fine bud. I'm not leaving for another half hour or so but when you get to the hotel just park up, and I'll do the rest when I get there. Lawrence came out as well and thanked Terry for his participation. All three men shook hands, and with that, Terry was back on his way to Kaunas. There was a lot of questions he wanted to ask. They still hadn't told him about the three shots fired in the mansion. He didn't know if anyone had been killed and what bothered him most was the fact that they were extremely reluctant to talk about it.

"Everything went to plan Terry, there's nothing for you to worry about pal."

As he drove he thought to himself that maybe it was better if he didn't know what happened. Now all he was worrying about was if he was going to make it back to Kaunas as easily as he had got here. It all seemed to be too good to be true.

He remembered what his old colleague used to say to him in situations like these, Sam Hargrieves. "If it seems too good to be true Terry boy, then it probably is." However, less than an hour later he was pulling up in front of the Europa hotel in Kaunas. He parked the Toyota up and walked into the hotel. The pretty young receptionist approached him immediately. Terry gave the car key to the girl informing her that someone would come to collect it from reception.

"Meester Mercer, may I have word with you in private please, is important." Mercer followed the girl into a small room.

"Meester Mercer, has anyone been in touch with you on phone, because we got telephone message from Britain, girl called Polly, she say you have to come home tomorrow, bereavement Meester Mercer...someone die...someone die in your family, you have to go back home tomorrow please."

He nodded to the girl, relieved that that was what it was about.

"Yes, I know miss. I have to be at the airport tomorrow morning early, I've been told. Thank you so much for speaking to me in private, you are very kind." "Meester Mercer, we are so sorry for this. You been enjoying your stay with us I hope?"

"Indeed I have, and I shall be back soon to have another holiday, you are very lovely people here in Lithuania, you are all very helpful indeed."

The girl smiled at him, grateful for the compliment.

"So sorry for this what happens Meester Mercer."

He placed fifty Euros down on the counter. "This is for you miss, thank you for all your help I am very grateful to you." The young lady thanked him and informed him that if he needed anything at all between now and tomorrow morning he was just to ask for Karina. Mercer returned to his room exhausted. Not just because of the nervous drive but the relief from all the stress he'd felt every minute of those journeys. He lay back on his bed and fell asleep remembering the desperate words from a desperate mother, Mandy Spencer. *"Bring her back to us Mister Mercer, we love her and miss her, we all miss her, please bring her back to me."*

He awoke early the following morning having slept for more than ten hours.
He felt refreshed rejuvenated and ready to face the day ahead. Against all the odds and doubts and fears he'd had, the girls were free, and all being well would be flying back

home this morning. He stood shaving at the bathroom mirror and found himself daydreaming about Samantha Reynolds. He hoped that everything had gone well for her at her mother's funeral. If there was ever an event where families kicked off and decided to sort out their differences, it was weddings and funerals. His phone buzzed on one of the bathroom shelves. It was Colin Green. *"Just boarding the aeroplane Tel in Warsaw, got all the girls here safely. Everyone is well and looking forward to seeing you back in London. Thank you for all your support bud. We'll have a beer me and you when I see you, take care."* Terry tried to reply to the text but was informed that the person had switched their phone off. This was it then. All that remained to be done was to contact treble clef and remind him not to be late for the airport, but even as he was thinking this, his phone rang. "Hi Tel, I'll be at the airport in half an hour. Sorry I haven't been staying at the hotel but I've met some old friends and have been staying at their place. I hope ya `hasn't` been too worried mite bout me."

Terry let out a little school-boy snigger. Truth be known he hadn't even given old treble a second thought. He had been so wrapped up in spending time with Samantha, and of course trying to find out what had been happening with the girls. Only now did he feel any guilt. "That's ok treble, don't worry pal, have you got your ticket and your passport ready?"

"Yeah I got it ere mite, don't warry Tel."

"Ok Treble, I'll see you at the airport pal." Mercer smiled into his mirror.

"God bless him." He'd invited Samantha and him over for the music festival and they'd spent a grand total of five and a half hours in his company at the concerts. Having said that, old Geoffrey was neither up nor down about it, he was just pleased to be among like-minded people who loved and appreciated music. He'd been in his element, in fact he'd all but admitted that he hadn't given Samantha and him any thought. Fifteen minutes later he was all packed and was waiting for the taxi he'd ordered to pick him up at the front door of the hotel. As he stood waiting, the young receptionist called Karina had come out and wished him well for the future and hoped that everything worked out for him and his family. Terry almost felt guilty having to pretend to the girl that there really had been a bereavement in his family, but all said and done, he wasn't causing any harm to anyone. Just as the young lady re-entered the hotel, his taxi pulled up in front of him.

Just over six hours later Terry Mercer and Geoffrey Marsden stepped off the plane at Heathrow. As soon as he was off the plain his phone buzzed, a text message from Polly Sheppard.

"The girls are all safely back here in Britain Terry, and are now being transported by taxi to their homes. Call in tomorrow morning to see me I expect you'll be tired after your recent excursions."

Terry was anything but tired. His long lie-in had charged his batteries and he felt now that he could carry on for another twenty-four hours before he'd need any sleep.

"Come on Treble, I'll pay the taxi to get you home pal, and by the way, I'm going to see to it that you are rewarded for your generosity old mucker, It was really appreciated what you done."

"It's alright Tel, I only invited the two of you because I `fought` that you `ad` a thing for the young `Samamfa`, I was giving you the chance to sort it `at` mite. Did `ya` get any luck?" Mercer smiled at the pensioner.

"Yes and no Treble, yes and no mate. Tell you what Treble, do you fancy a little aperitif before we go home? The drinks are on me my old pal."

"That'd be just great Tel, thank ye kindly. I got one or two friends coming over Tel in abat three weeks, they're gonna stay for a week or so, it'll be great having company that I can talk to `abat` music, you missed a lot of good stuff Tel back there. It's so good `ta` see young musicians with so much enthusiasm…there's still `ope` for classical music Tel."

A couple of hours later Terry was back home having dropped off Treble at his flat. There were no messages on his machine, and more importantly there had been no messages on his mobile. He had thought that he might have heard from Samantha by now. Surely the funeral would be over by now. Maybe he was being silly, but he actually thought that she'd have been in touch letting him know how the funeral had gone. He poured himself a vodka and coke and sat down on his favourite easy chair. He gave himself a talking to. "It's got nothing to do with you how the funeral went, and anyway, she is far too young for you, get a grip of yourself would you?" At that point his phone buzzed.

"Hi Terry, Colin Green here, remember the conversation we had at my house a few weeks ago? I told you I'd get her back home safely didn't I?"

Terry remembered only too well, and he also remembered he and Samantha informing Colin of how absurd his idea was, almost to the point of mockery. The man had done it though, he had his daughter back home and Terry had never been so pleased to be proved wrong. The way everything had turned out, all the arrangements, everything had gone to plan. "Those S.A.S guys really did know no fear…in fact they were nothing less than absolutely fucking crazy." He sat back in his chair and put his earphones on to listen to one of his favourite tracks of all time, and some of his colleagues would agree that the title well suited him. It was Pink Floyd's *"Shine on you crazy diamond."*

PART TWO.

Scotland Yard.

Broadway Victoria. 9.am.

Terry Mercer tapped on the door of his chief inspector's office. Polly Sheppard answered.
"Just a minute."
He sat down on one of the chairs outside in the corridor. After a few minutes Polly's door opened and two female junior officers stepped out into the hallway.
Polly held the door for Terry to enter.
"Coffee Terry? She said, smiling broadly. "Well, everything turned out ok in the end. All the girls are safely home and you and Samantha had a little break thanks to your mister Marsden. How did the funeral go Terry, I know she wasn't very keen on leaving Lithuania prematurely, I think she was enjoying her time over there."
Terry shrugged his shoulders. "I don't know Polly I haven't spoken to her since she's been back here in London. Has she not been in touch with you?"
"She only texted me to tell me she was going to make some enquiries after the funeral was over and done with. Something about that Angela woman, of course that was before the girls were rescued. Has she not sent you any text messages Terry?"
Terry shook his head. "No nothing. I tried to text her this morning but her phone was switched off."
Polly looked at Terry. "That's strange her phone was switched off when I tried yesterday. I think the funeral was about four days ago Terry."
"Try her land line now Polly, surely she would let us know if she was taking more time off."
"Surely." said Polly as she tapped out the digits for Samantha's land line.
After allowing the phone to ring for a full minute Polly shook her head.
"No, no answer Terry."
"I'm going round Polly. I'm going round to her house. No-one has heard from her in three days or more, no, something's wrong, definitely. She would have been in touch if she needed more time off, I'm going round to her house. I'll keep sending messages to her mobile just in case, but I think she's not answering for the simple reason that she can't."
Terry rose from his seat having not even had a sip from his coffee mug.

"I'll be in touch as soon as Polly."
"Now Terry, don't be getting all worked up, there could be a perfectly simple reason why she isn't answering her phone, don't be getting yourself into a state of consternation."
Mercer ignored Polly's statement. "She was going to visit Angela did you say?"
"Yes Terry, but that was before the girls were rescued, calm yourself down, come and finish your coffee."
Again Terry completely ignored what was said to him. "I'll be in touch Polly as soon as I've got any news." And with that Terry was out of the office and heading briskly to the car-park. On his way to the car he recalled a couple of times that he and Samantha had tried to catch this Angela Bates woman at home but were unsuccessful.
He and Samantha were in agreement that they suspected that this woman had something to do with the kidnappings, her and a woman named Claire Redgrave. If this was the case, then he wondered how much contact they would have with the people they sold the girls to. If they were in regular contact, then they would surely have been informed about what had happened in Kaunas. Now his mind was racing. First of all, he would go to Samantha's house and if she wasn't home then he'd be off to this Angela Bates' house. If he got no joy there, he would be knocking on Roxanne's door. She wouldn't miss a thing if there had been any activity in her vicinity. One thing he knew for sure, Samantha would never deliberately ignore phone calls from her colleagues. As he descended the elevator he thought to himself that this was fate's way of paying him back for everything going so smoothly in Lithuania. Nothing but nothing ran smoothly in Terry Mercer's life. "Yeah" he said to himself as he climbed into his car, "back to the status quo bud."

The car seemed empty without Samantha sitting beside him. Already he'd grown accustomed to the sarcastic banter between them, it was part of their day…and he would have to admit, she was bloody good at it. Terry was now on his way to Mitcham to fulfil a promise he'd made to Alison Green and her father. Samantha was still not at home. He decided to give it another day before he started to panic about her well-being. All kinds of things could have happened at her mother's funeral. Perhaps there were financial matters to resolve. He still couldn't believe how events had turned out over in Lithuania, of course the fact that Colin had Polish friends helped them immensely. They were a dream come true owing to the fact that they had safety alternatives lined up in case anything went wrong. And they were wholeheartedly committed into doing whatever they could to help. One way or another they were determined to get those girls over the border into Poland.

He smiled as he drove remembering the giant sized youth Antoni Dabrowsky who tried to reassure him that everyone was safe.
Also the petite Lena as well with her beautiful broken English.
Still smiling he thought about how many people she'd surprised with her fighting skills.
"Probably fights like a frenzied Grizzly."
A little over half an hour later he pulled up in front of the Green's residence in Mitcham. He hardly made it to the gate when the front door opened and Jillian Green came rushing outside followed by Alison and her sister Rebecca. All three embraced him at their front gate. Jillian stepped back and smiled at him in complete adoration. "You done it Mister Mercer, you got her home safely." Another cuddle.
"I beg your pardon Jillian, it was that husband of yours' who done it, along with two of his military buddies, that's who done it, all I done was to drive a vehicle from A to B, it's hardly heroic stuff, it's Colin who deserves the praise here."
Now he was being ushered into the house where he was greeted by a smiling Colin Green. "Good to see you again Terry, especially under circumstances like these, I'm a sucker for happy endings."
"Me too" Mercer replied. Terry was made to sit down on the sofa while Jillian and her two daughters ferried sandwiches and biscuits from the kitchen. For over an hour all the Green family made conversation with Terry who noticed, that not once did Alison mention anything at all about her ordeal, and he knew only too well why that was. She would have to tell someone but it certainly wouldn't be anyone in this room.
He hoped that Colin had sorted the girl out with a psychiatrist or a psychologist.
Eventually Terry explained that he'd have to make himself scarce.
Colin came to the front door with him. Once outside he almost whispered to Terry, "We have to talk pal."
"About what Colin?"
"You know what about Terry. We have to put a stop to this once and for all." Terry met his eyes and saw the steel there.
"Nobody's ever going to do that to my daughter again or anyone else's daughter. If you help me Terry, I can eliminate these bastards one by one and no-one needs to know a thing about it."
"Colin, listen, I know how you feel, but this is different, we'd never get away with it. I'm in total agreement with you, but we can't bud, we can't just take them out without hell breaking loose, we're in Britain now Colin, it's so much different than-"
"Don't give me that shit Terry, I know perfectly well where we are, and that's just it, if we don't eliminate these fuckers it'll no longer be the Britain we know. We can't just let these people take our children off the streets and sell them off like cattle to the highest

bidder, we have to do something Terry. What if that was *your* kid they took, would you still be so uncertain about how to deal with them, and just supposing we do catch them, you know as well as me what the British justice system is like, a few years in jail? big deal. They'll be back out and carrying on with their meat sales as usual. Well, I'm not having it. If you won't help me then I'll do it myself."

He pointed back into his house as he said, "I'll tell you something now Terry, I never want my wife or my daughters to be put through anything like that again. Have you any idea how much this has affected Jillian? You can see how much this has aged her. And my daughter, I have to make plans for her to see a councillor and a psychiatrist...this could take years for her to recover from, if she ever does. No, this stops now Terry. Now I know that your hands are tied to an extent, but mine aren't. If you don't help me it'll take me longer to accomplish what I'm setting out to do...but I'll fucking do it Terry, I swear on my kids' lives I'm going to do it. I am so sick and tired of everybody walking over this country like it's some fucking free-for-all lawless joke. I'm going to give them justice. They won't be walking away from me laughing, like the fuckers do in our courts."

As terry reached the car he said, "Have you spoken to Alan or Jim about how you feel?"

"I can't speak to them, they're away Terry, ghosts remember? We won't be seeing them again, they could be in Timbuctoo for all we know. I turned to speak to one of them at the airport not long after they'd landed, and they were gone.

When I tried to text them, my phone couldn't send the message...ghosts.

Listen, I know your hands are tied Terry, but you can find out things, names addresses phone numbers. You just get me the information, and I will deal with the rest, no-one will know anything about it I'll make sure of that. No blame or accusations will be pointed to you I guarantee it." Again Colin pointed back at his house.

"Imagine if it happened again Terry. Imagine how you'd feel, it would kill my wife...I'm not going to let that happen Pal. You take care bud, and think about what I've said."

Terry nodded to his new friend, knowing full well that the man had a point.

What if it *did* happen again? Just before he drove off he waved at the Green family all standing together on their threshold. He also remembered on one occasion when he'd been here with Samantha and one of their family were missing. The picture was complete again now. They were all standing waving happily and radiant. He waved back to them as he pulled away with that horrible possibility still vibrating in his brain.

"Imagine if it happened again Terry. Imagine how you'd feel. It would kill my wife."

BROMLEY.

Terry's next port of call was to visit the Spencer family. Again he remembered the state of anxiety that Mandy Spencer was in just a few short weeks ago. Once again he was greeted with cheerful smiles and embraces as Mandy Spencer opened the front door. Sophie Spencer offered him a special whispered thank you, and a special embrace that lasted longer than the others.
"Thank you so much Terry for being part of the rescue, I don't know how much longer I would have been able to stand it...thank you."
Terry smiled at the young lady and told her it was his pleasure to be of assistance and that it was the other men who done all the dangerous work, and their Polish friends, they deserved all the praise.
"Mister Mercer, you drove us to the Polish border and indeed over the border. You didn't know what could have happened on that journey but you were still prepared to do it, that, as far as I am concerned was a very brave thing to do indeed, and no matter who organised what, it was you as far as all the girls are concerned who drove us to our freedom." Mandy's friend Carol Richardson was here as well with her daughter Kaylee. He remembered Carol telling him what she and Sophie had been discussing on the morning of her disappearance. As far as he could recall she was advising Sophie on the shortness of her skirts and the dangers of wrong signals given out to eager young men. He smiled to himself as Kaylee sat now on the sofa with a skirt so short that you'd be hard pushed to prove she was even wearing one. He clocked young David glancing at the girls' legs from time to time.
And Kaylee knew it.
Mandy looked at least ten years younger than when he'd last visited her. She was radiant. Her hair shone like gold in the sunlight coming through the living room window. She wore make-up today and was very smartly dressed in a knee-length skirt and blouse with dress shoes. A complete contrast to how she had looked when she'd been ravaged by stress. Sophie and her mum went into the kitchen to make more coffee for everyone. Sophie wore jeans now and a long-sleeved shirt. Carol leaned forward on the sofa and whispered to Terry. "Sophie's had to go and have tests taken at the doctors. She's been examined as well at the hospital and they've recommended her to see a psychiatrist."
"Well that's Misses Spencer and Sophie's business" he replied politely.
"She'll receive counselling and as much help as she needs, the girl's had one hell of an experience, all those girls have. We have to admire their resilience."

Mandy and Sophie returned with buttered scones and coffees and all manner of types of biscuits. Terry made his excuses and rose to his feet.

"I'll have to be going now" he explained, but I'll visit you from time to time Sophie if that's ok with your mum. If you have any problems, then please get in touch with the authorities straight away."

Terry was referring to Sophie specifically in case she was struggling to cope after her ordeal. Sophie's brother David followed Terry to the hallway and stretched out his hand to the detective.

"I want to thank you personally sir for all your help, you know, getting my sister over the Polish border and everything. My mum and I are very grateful to you."

Terry put his hand on the boy's shoulder.

"I was only too pleased to be of assistance to the people who really helped them son, I done very little, but I am as pleased as you are that she's home safe and well, you're welcome kid. You take care of them and I'll come back and visit you soon."

As Terry stood on the threshold Sophie appeared and asked her brother if she could have a word with Terry in private. Terry stood by his car with Sophie standing beside him. "Mister Mercer, I have to tell you something. Those people back in Lithuania." Sophie looked at the pavement for a couple of seconds before she continued. "They allowed very bad things to happen to us, very bad...very disgusting things Mister Mercer, and I-."

"Sophie, I know sweetheart, I know what they'd have done to you. Carol tells me that you are to see a psychiatrist, these people are amazing Sophie, you know, how they can help you, they'll be able to-."

"You must be joking, forget? I will never forget what they have done to me.
Mister Green has been round to see us and he was telling my mum what he intends to do, I overheard them, and my mum was in total agreement with him. What I want to know Mister Mercer is, are you going to help him? Do you know what they done to his daughter? They made her swallow sperm from a tumbler while those disgusting men and women continued violating her...in both orifices. Can you imagine what that'd be like Mister Mercer? And these animals over here are still kidnapping girls nearly every day. Mister Green is already making plans about how to capture them. He wants to torture them first before he kills them. And if I can help him in any way, then I'll be the first to inflict pain onto them...and I will laugh Mister Mercer, I will fucking laugh at them while they writhe in their agony!"

Terry Mercer was completely overwhelmed at the ferocity of the girls' anger. "Listen Sophie, Mister Green has no right to be having a conversation with your mother about such matters, and he will land himself in serious trouble if he's not careful. Now I understand your appetite for revenge, you wouldn't be normal if you didn't have anger and rage about what has happened to you, but that doesn't mean that-."

"Hey, don't. Don't you dare tell me that you understand, you weren't there, you weren't having stinking fat giant men drooling over you, sweating profusely as they ejaculated into your mouth with foul disgusting-tasting sperm.

Fat middle-aged sweat monsters using your body for their play things, don't you dare tell me you understand my anger. Mister Green understands my anger, because his daughter informed him of every degrading act that was inflicted upon her…and there were many. No, I want to see these bastards die. They don't deserve to live, and Mister Green is going to see to it." Sophie turned to head back into the house. She stood on the step smiling at Terry along with her mum and Carol Richardson waving, along with Kaylee who's skirt was even shorter than Terry had predicted, a perfect target for the monsters who were searching diligently for innocent girls like her, so much for learning a lesson. Terry climbed into his car laboriously, hoping above all hope that Samantha would get in touch with him soon…very soon. Without a doubt there was going to be trouble. The last thing he needed was Colin Green taking matters into his own hands, and according to Sophie, he was all but boasting about it.

THE MANSION.

LITHUANIA.

Saratov sat at a table with Monica Carosova contemplating his plan. He and Monica had been tied and bound on the day the S.A.S men had stormed the building, catching everyone off guard and snatching the British girls from right under their noses. He had spent a whole lot of money obtaining them and had gone to a lot of trouble paying for them to be brought over here. He was furious at two of his henchmen who had done little or nothing to stop them. Only the third one had attempted to stop proceedings and it had cost him his life. He had fired a shot at one of the infiltrators and had missed. The S.A.S man had swivelled round as he fell to the ground and fired off two rapid-fire shots into his head. Only a handful of girls remained here with him, the rest had taken their opportunity to escape amidst all the confusion. Now, he would have to start over again and it would cost him a lot of money to restock.
Monica smoked her cigarette and seemed calm about the whole affair. She had also put a quite considerable amount of money into the `business`. She seemed quite relaxed. Not so Michael Saratov. He was raging inside with a burning need for vengeance.
"How dare these strangers just march into Lithuania and indeed into his home and disrupt everything." On top of all this, he'd been informed about a detective who had been over here with a friend supposedly to listen to classical music, but was in fact part of the plan hatched by the S.A.S men. The woman he had arrived here with was also a detective, and quite obviously involved in proceedings. They too would be put in their place. He knew there would be very little chance of them returning here and so he'd have to work out a plan. One way or another they would be punished for the humiliation he'd suffered. Monica spoke across the table as she stubbed out her cigarette. "I've been in touch with Angela in London. I told her what had happened."
"What did she say?" He said with a disinterested tone. Monica looked at Saratov and casually said, "She's offered to help us. We've just to let her know what we want."
Saratov rose to his feet. He walked slowly over to the window and looked out onto the grounds of his property. Finally he said, "Tell her I'm coming over to Britain. I want to talk to her. I want to find out if she can locate these detectives' addresses. I'm going to scrutinise these people." He sighed as he poured himself and Monica another drink.
"They can come over here and break into my home? Well I'm going to show them that I can do the very same to them. He's probably on his high-horse just now, him and those two military men, soaking up all the praise for returning their innocent little girls back

home safe and sound. No, in second thoughts, say nothing to this Angela, don't inform her that I'm coming over. The less people who know I'm coming the better for us. I want you to come with me Monica, are you ok with that?"

"Of course Michael, we have to restart that's all, it's a minor inconvenience, apart from our financial loss of course, but we will soon be stocked up again with fresh young girls. It will take us no more than a month maybe six weeks, and this time we will not be so generous with our payments, it will not cost half as much this time, trust me I'll see to it. There are plenty of unemployed people on Britain's streets who would be more than willing to kidnap girls for a fraction of the price we were paying...London is full of opportunists."

Michael Saratov and Monica Carosova had overlooked one or two issues.
Because they'd been untroubled in all the time they'd been running their `business` perhaps they thought that they were immune to investigations. As they both sat now in one of the upper lounges the mansion was being raided by the Lithuanian S.I.S. (Secret Investigation Service.) One or two of the European girls who'd escaped had reported to the authorities just what had been taking place in Saratov's mansion. The girls who had remained here were being bundled into vans outside of the house. The first Saratov knew that there was anyone in his house was when the door was burst open and three armed men entered his lounge, announcing to the unsuspecting pair that they were both under arrest for illicit profiteering with underage girls. He was also being charged with organising kidnappings and tax evasion. The two were hand-cuffed and taken outside where they were placed into two different vehicles. There would be little chance of them having a private conversation now. They would be made to give statements. Saratov knew that he was in big trouble now. He would have to call on a few favours from various friends to pull him out of this hole. If he couldn't contact any of them, then he and Monica stood to be serving very long prison sentences. If he was angry before about the intrusion of his house by the British military, then now, he was positively livid. He would get out of this somehow, and then they would pay for their interference. This wasn't about kidnapping young girls any more, this was about killing the people who had caused him so much grief, and he would pay very generously to have the executions arranged. He would have a list printed out, and he knew who was going to be heading that list. There would be little chance of locating the S.A.S men, but it wouldn't be very difficult to find the two detectives who'd accompanied them. First things first though. He would have to get himself and Monica out of jail before he done anything. It wouldn't be too difficult owing to the fact that he had film-footage of the Lithuanian Chief of Police frolicking around one of the rooms in here with three naked

young girls giggling and laughing and snorting cocaine and each of them taking turns sucking his tiny penis. If he valued his position then surely he would pull strings to see to it that he and Monica were released, either that, or Lena Smertsov, his wife, may have something to say about her husband snorting cocaine with underage girls and having them arouse him orally while they slapped his fat naked ass.

The stern-faced driver of the car looked into the rear-view mirror and asked Saratov if he was sitting comfortably, and then informed him that he was going to be jailed for a very long time. "You've got a lot to answer for Michael, you're a nasty piece of work by all accounts." He smiled sarcastically as he said, "You're going to learn what it's like to be violated my friend. See how *you* like giving head to nasty bastards...it'll be a lot of fun for them, they don't take too kindly to people who kidnap children and force them to have sex...you're going to learn old man about violation."

Saratov merely smiled back at him and replied, "Perhaps."

Scotland Yard.

Broadway Victoria.

Polly Sheppard looked troubled as Terry entered her office, and before he'd even asked her he knew why. He had tried to contact Samantha three different times already today and had received no joy. "Sit down Terry. I'm worried now if I wasn't before, it's been far too long."

"I'm going to her house today Polly, and if I get no joy then I'm breaking in. Something is seriously wrong, she wouldn't ignore our calls and besides, she said she didn't get on with her mother, so it's not as if she's suffering from emotional breakdowns or anything, and even if she was she'd be letting us know what was going on. We should have been reacting quicker than this Polly, Christ the mind boggles...I've got a horrible feeling about this."

"I must admit Terry, I'm getting quite worried myself, and there was me telling you not to get all worked up. What the hell could have happened to her Terry?"

Terry sat down to drink his coffee. He shook his head in reaction to Polly's question, rubbing his chin vigorously as he always did when he was agitated.

"I dread to think Polly honestly, and if anything *has* happened to her, well, we've left it a bit late to do anything, she could be anywhere."

"Terry, in the meantime I want you to work with someone else until we-"

"No Polly, please, don't put me on with anyone else just now, I'll make better progress on my own. Samantha Reynolds is my partner and I need to find out what has happened to her. If the worst comes to the worst Polly, then I'll work with someone else but please, let me deal with this myself. If I need assistance I promise you I will ask for someone, I give you my word, and I will keep you informed of proceedings right from the start. I will stay in constant contact with you, I promise you."

Polly sighed, not with exasperation but with worry more than anything else. She knew he was right, they should have been making enquiries a lot earlier than this. She nodded her head. "Ok Terry, but you keep in touch with me, you promised. I need to be able to contact you at the drop of a hat, do you understand? I don't want to be having to ask Tom Dick and Harry where you are, alright?"

"I give you my word Polly. The first thing I'm going to do is head over to Stratford to speak with a certain Roxanne Styles, she'll be able to tell me if there's been anyone over there visiting this Angela Bates. Samantha said she was going over there to try and have an interview with her. If she's been there, then Roxanne will have seen her and spoken to her."

Polly nodded her head in agreement. "Yes, she told me she was going over there as well. Ok Terry, good luck with that, and remember, you stay in touch."

Terry rose up from his chair and rinsed out his cup, something that Samantha had instilled in him. She glanced at his worried face.

"What do you *really* think has happened to her Terry, you must have an idea."

"I shudder to think that I'm right Polly, but I actually think she's been kidnapped, I hope to God that I'm wrong, but there's no other explanation is there…the only other alternative is…she's dead, I'll be in touch, and remember Polly, if by some miracle she contacts you, then you let me know straight away and-"

"Get out." Polly replied in response to the stupid statement.

He smiled to himself as he exited the office.

All the way over to Stratford he went over in his mind all the possibilities of why she was not responding. In conclusion, he admitted to himself there remained only one possibility, she'd been abducted. He would learn from Roxanne if she'd made it to the flats to try and catch this Angela at home, at least from there he could perhaps have something to go on. As it stood now, it was nothing but a complete mystery.

HENSINGHAM APARTMENTS

STRATFORD.

As predicted there was no answer at Angela Bates' apartment. Mercer stood outside of Roxanne Styles' door awaiting an answer. He could hear activity inside and smiled to himself as he counted out the seconds it would take Roxanne to put her knickers back on and then curse the door even before she reached it for this untimely intrusion on her precious privacy. He was not disappointed. The door was opened and Roxanne stood with a man's shirt fastened to her midriff, the sleeves trailing more than six inches over her wrists. Whoever the shirt belonged to needed to be informed that it had seen better days, it was more a pale grey than the white it was supposed to be.
"What? What the fuck is it now? I'm getting sick of answering questions. What do you want, I'm busy, fuck!"
A man's voice called out to her from inside the flat.
"Who the hell is it Roxanne, tell them to fuck off just now, we're not finished, hurry up." Mercer remained calm and remembered what Samantha had found out about his informant, and so he tried his luck into bluffing her. "I'm afraid I'm going to have to take you in Roxanne unless you can help me, and speak to me in a more civilised manner than this, now, what's it to be? Do you want to help me or do we take a journey down to the nearest police station, the choice is yours'."
She replied softly to him. "Just a minute, I'll have to get rid of this, I won't be a minute." She closed the door gently. Obviously his bluff had worked. He could hear her voice through the very cheaply assembled door. "Get yourself up and away to fuck out of here, and I'm only giving you a tenner back, you've been with me for nearly half an hour, come on move your fat stinking arse up off my fucking sofa you pathetic bastard, and don't you fucking dare ask me who's at my fucking door you piece of shit, now fucking move yourself or you'll be getting no fucking refund, shite bag that you are, this shirt is fucking stinking!" Roxanne opened the door a little and peered out speaking softly again. "I won't be a minute mister Mercer." Terry took a few steps down the hall to save Roxanne's customer any embarrassment and to give her some time to get dressed. Five minutes later, the chubby middle-aged man had left her apartment complete with dated shirt and Roxanne once again appeared at her door this time dressed in denim jeans and a blouse that fitted her considerably better than the shirt had. "Do you want to come in Mister Mercer?" There's no baby now they've taken the baby off me, they said it was for the best, and they said I wasn't fit to look after a child,

huh, what do they know?"

Mercer stepped into a very untidy kitchen. Clothes were strewn across the floor ready for the next wash. Wallpaper hung off the walls in areas. A single naked light bulb of very low wattage attempted to brighten the room.

A washing machine was spinning furiously vibrating the floor beneath his feet. He wondered how it would sound to the people who lived below her.

Roxanne would put the washing machine on any time she wished. He imagined it wouldn't matter a jot what time of day it was. He was led through to the living room where again clothes lay here and there all around the place. Towels and tights hung over the one radiator in this very small room. He was invited to sit down on the one piece of furniture which was a battered old sofa. He moved several garments of clothing from one of the cushions and sat down. "Do you want a cup of coffee mister Mercer? If you do you'll have to take it without milk, that fat bastard that was here has just finished the last of it."

Mercer declined.

"Where's your side-kick today, has she left you on your own?"

She sat down next to the detective.

"That's why I'm here Roxanne. When was the last time you saw detective Reynolds?"

Roxanne lit up a cigarette and exhaled. "Three days ago. She was at that bitches' house along the hall, but surprise surprise, she wasn't in, or at least she wasn't answering her door anyway."

"What time was this Roxanne?"

Again Roxanne pulled hard on her cigarette and pulled a face as though he'd asked her the square route of fifteen thousand. "It would be about maybe half past ten, eleven o clock maybe, somewhere about there, it was certainly before midnight because that's when I see my eh...you know, I work through the night. The fuckers are drunk then, it's easier to get money from them when they're drunk, half of the bastards are married you see."

"You're sure it was three days ago?"

"Positive, absolutely positive, yeah three days."

"And she hasn't been back here since then?" Roxanne shook her head.

"*She* has though, you know that Angela woman, she's been here quite a few times. There's been a lot of activity in that flat this week. But she hasn't been back for a couple of days now, whatever the fuck she's up to. And why are you asking about your detective friend, has she gone missing or something?"

"Have you still got my number Roxanne?"

"Of course I have, and before you say, I'll be in contact with you should anyone arrive at that flat. I can see that you're keen as mustard to talk to her."

"When you say activity Roxanne, what do you mean by that, has there been gentlemen friends' of Angela arriving here again?"

Roxanne nodded. "Yes, quite a few of them actually, and new ones, ones I've never seen before. Couldn't tell you if these guys were foreign or not, they all arrive at night, and they're not here for long, twenty minutes, half an hour and then the fuckers are gone."

Mercer rose to his feet. "You know the procedure Roxanne, as soon as she arrives, you let me know, and anyway you should have been informing me when she'd been appearing here...you didn't call me did you?"

"How the fuck can I inform you when you're not in the country? I was told you were away abroad somewhere, I'm sure you'd have been over the moon if I'd interrupted your holiday."

"Well, I'm back now, so, any time, any time at all that she appears then you let me know ok?"

"I will." She reassured him. As Terry Mercer exited the flats he felt a sense of dread rising up within him. By the looks of it Samantha had done exactly what she said she was going to do, and that was to attempt to visit Angela Bates. Something had happened, something bad. Now Colin Green's words were literally reverberating round his brain. *"Imagine if it were to happen again Terry, imagine how you'd feel."* He climbed into his car and began the journey back to Scotland Yard. The first thing he'd have to do would be to put surveillance onto these flats. He'd be a fool to rely on a second-grade whore to supply him with accurate information. Roxanne couldn't give a fuck about anybody but herself. But it was necessary to remain friendly with her, she may after all come up with some important information. As he made his way back to his car he began to think about Roxanne's attitude. Here was a woman who by the looks of things had no morals whatsoever. She didn't even flinch when she informed him of the authorities confiscating her baby. They may as well have taken her old fridge away. What chance do kids have in life when they are unfortunate enough to have a mother with that attitude and being a slave to heroin. There would be little chance of Roxanne ever taking a Sunday-school class. But still he had this element of sympathy for her. Underneath those hard lines on her face was a very beautiful woman. Perhaps it was fate, or just sheer bad luck, maybe long ago she'd fallen into the wrong kind of company. Whatever the reason he couldn't help feeling sorry for her. Maybe it was fate, after all we can't all of us live happy care-free lives. Poor Roxanne just happened to pull the short straw. Fate is cruel.

WALWORTH.

ROYAL ROAD APARTMENTS.

As soon as he arrived back at Scotland Yard he was greeted by Polly Sheppard and a young man he hadn't seen before. Polly had sent for a forensic to assist him in the search of Samantha's apartment. The guy also just happened to have been a locksmith before joining the police force. Terry now stood in the landing outside of Samantha's door having yet again received no answer. The young man who didn't look to be any more than twenty-five looked up at Terry from his hunkered position and smiled. Armed only with a small piece of wire he said, "This won't take very long Terry, couple of minutes and we'll be in pal."

There was that petty hate thing again that Terry despised, people calling him bud or pal when they didn't even know him. Terry stood with one hand leaning on the wall and the other on his hip looking like he was bored with the whole thing.

He certainly showed no interest in what the man was doing, as though anyone could pick a lock and that it was no big deal. He waited a few seconds before sighing and looking at his watch giving the impression that he should have had the door opened by now.

"I thought you said-".

CLICK.

"That's us Terry, we're in now mate." Terry pulled out the polythene shoe-covers and gloves and placed them over his shoes. He put on the gloves with difficulty. "They have to make everything so fucking tight these days don't they, as if we're all fucking size zero."

Forensic officer Cameron Lee had been pre-warned about Terry's searing temper fits and his raucous blasphemies, especially when he was feeling apprehensions in certain situations, like this situation here today. Lee had been informed that it was Mercer's partner who'd gone missing and so to expect random outbursts of profanations, and quite possibly aimed specifically at him, and for no apparent reason. He was finally advised not to counter-react to the cursing as they would eventually wane into nothing but incoherent mumbo-jumbo. "What's your name kid, can't keep calling each other buddy or pal or mate because we're none of those things are we. So, what's your name?" "Cameron...Cameron Lee."

"Ok Cameron, my name is Terry Mercer, and not bud or pal or fucking buddy...ok?"

"Ok Terry no bother pal, sorry."

"Ok, you start in here and I'll start in the bedroom."

After fifteen minutes or so, the forensic officer came into Samantha's bedroom. Mercer's eyes followed the forensic. Without saying anything to Terry Mercer he opened the wardrobe door and began inspecting the clothes hanging up in there.

"Have you finished in the living room?"

Sarcasm.

Cameron continued searching through the garments sliding each coat-hanger along as he checked them, as though Terry hadn't spoken.

"Hey! What the fuck is it you're looking for? Don't you think that I'm capable of doing a fucking search?"

"Terry, calm down, I'll tell you what I'm looking for, and why, just be patient would you?"

Polly's words immediately came flooding back to him from earlier that morning; *And whatever you do Cameron, do not tell him to calm down, if you do, then may God himself help you."*

"Ok Terry, in the living room Samantha has been sitting on the armchair, and-"

"Fuck, you don't say, fancy that Cameron, Samantha's been sitting here in her own flat on her own easy-chair, fuck what are the chances?"

"If you'd let me finish Terry. On the sofa two people have been sitting there recently. Two men to be precise, do you know of any men-friends that she has?" Terry found himself hurting from the question, as if stabbed in the heart at the possibility of Samantha having men-friends. "How the fuck do I know who she sees, she's my partner not my fucking wife, what a bastard question to ask anyone." Terry made his way through to the kitchen where he intended to open the window and smoke a cigarette. As he got there he shouted through to his `colleague`. "You needn't bother searching any more, here's three cups in the sink they will tell you everything you need to know."

A little over an hour later, Cameron and Terry were back in the labs where Terry was informed that there had been two men sitting in Samantha's flat with her. The fact that three mugs had been placed into the sink gave the impression that they were there as guests of Samantha's. There had been no forced entry and there were no signs of struggles in the apartment. Cameron Lee had given the D.N.A samples to the C.S.I department who had informed him that there was no criminal match to the samples given. Lee turned to Terry Mercer.

"You say there had been a bereavement in her family Terry?"

"Yes, her mother, although she told me she hadn't set eyes on her for a lot of years...she wasn't what you could say the best mother in the world according to Samantha...there was no love lost, or indeed given...it's just what Samantha had said, I don't-"

"So you don't think that these men could have been relatives of hers then?"

"She has one brother, he lives in the states but she hasn't seen him for years."

"And didn't she ever mention to you anything about gentlemen guests coming to see her at all?"

Terry Mercer felt a surge of temper running through him. How dare this little prick talk to him in this manner, a fucking trainee no less.

"For your sake sonny, I'm getting to fuck out of here. You're asking me questions here like I was a fucking recidivist, just keep out of my way ok? I'll make my own enquiries. You just get your full team over there to her flat and do a thorough investigation, and make sure you fetch your superior with you, you're talking there like you're a fucking expert in everything, you little pretentious shit that you are, who the fuck do you think you're talking to?!"

"Terry, I wasn't trying to-"

"Just shut the fuck up, I've had it with pricks like you. You just learn your fucking job kid and then come back and ask me questions, and don't be going over there licking Polly's arse telling her that I've been reluctant to work with you because I gave you the chance to work with me. All you've done is open a fucking door and then speak nothing but shit, I'm out of here…Pal!"

HOUSES OF PARLEMENT.

WESTMINSTER.

Polly Sheppard along with various dignitaries from New Scotland Yard had come to have a meeting with MP's about televising a warning to all parents in and around London who had teenage daughters. Having given the PM all the details of the recent abductions it was deemed necessary to issue a warning to all concerned. Parents would be warned about the danger their daughters could face if they walked to school unaccompanied, or if their journey took them through any secluded areas. Also it was recommended that parents had a discussion with them about their attire. All of the girls who had been recently kidnapped had all been wearing short or very short skirts. It was the girls' figures that was attracting the kidnappers, and of course, their ages. Any girl between the ages of thirteen to eighteen were potential bate. The prime minister together with a handful of MP's sat listening to Polly Sheppard as she explained in great detail all the events of the previous kidnappings, and emphasising just how lucky they were to have the girls back home. "We may not be so lucky next time" she exclaimed. To cut the risk of abduction considerably she advised that each girl went to school accompanied by at least one other person, be that a school friend or a parent, or any trustworthy adult. This would make the abductions almost impossible and eradicate the possibility of anything happening to them, simple procedures that could save them from a harrowing experience. The PM was in full support of everything Polly was suggesting and promised that he'd put a plan into action immediately and that warnings would be televised as soon as possible. These warnings would go out nightly for about a month. The warnings would be broadcast during peak-time viewing. He shook hands with Polly and thanked her personally for her concern for the teenage girls and hoped that parents and children alike would take notice of the dangers that faced them if they chose to ignore the warnings. Polly was more than pleased with the prime minister's commitment to the project. It was all they could do to attempt to put an end to the abductions, although she was almost certain they would continue.

SCOTLAND YARD.

BROADWAY VICTORIA.

Terry Mercer stood in Polly's office sipping coffee awaiting her return from the houses of parliament. He was also waiting to hear from the forensic team who were searching Samantha's apartment. As yet, there was not a single clue as to her whereabouts. He stood by the window gazing over the Victoria embankment at nothing in particular. The London Eye spun ever so slowly on the opposite side of the river Thames, each of its' pods filled with excited tourists from all over the world. Barges floated silently up and down stream ferrying yet more tourists. His mobile phone buzzed in his jacket pocket. It was Jim Lawrence.
"Terry? Listen, I can't stay on this phone for long. I just thought you should know, the man I worked for over in Lithuania, Kulbertinov, well he's over there in London. Haven't got a clue why he'd be there, just thought you should know Terry."
"Do you know how long he's been here Jim?"
"Couldn't say pal, I just found out today. I know one thing though he wouldn't be very happy with me when he found out that I'd duped him. He may even be over there looking for me Terry, but, anyway, I just thought you should know. I've e-mailed some photographs of him to Polly's computer, just keep an eye out Tel."
"How long do you think he's-".
The phone was dead, and as usual when Terry tried to call him back, the signal or the line was dead as well. Now his brain was in gear. All sorts of scenarios were forming in his head. It was looking more and more likely that Samantha had indeed been kidnapped. The trouble was, they had no idea when she'd been abducted. He shuddered to think of the implications. Had they taken her for revenge? They would not be happy now that most of the girls had been rescued. And this Saratov was he over here as well? Surely if they *had* abducted Samantha, they would be boasting about it, or demanding money or something, they would be in touch surely, they would wallow in their achievement. Terry had never met this Kulbertinov but Jim had explained how he'd tricked him and became his chauffer. The man was wealthy, as were the rest of Saratov's customers. If he remembered correctly, he owned shops and night clubs. So why was he here in London? Perhaps he *was* searching for Jim Lawrence. He would be furious at being humiliated. There wouldn't be too many people who'd be able to trick him. These successful businessmen are sharp and are usually on the ball when it comes to taking on staff in terms of being trustworthy. Jim must have put on a believable

performance. Polly entered her office.

"Hi Terry, have you had any luck locating Samantha?"

Terry shook his head. "I've just had Jim Lawrence on the phone. There's a guy over in Lithuania, a kind of businessman come wide boy. He used to go to the mansion where the girls were being kept...and of course he used the services there. He's a friend of this Saratov. Jim tricked him into being hired as his chauffer, that was how he got to survey the place, anyway, this Kulbertinov is over here and somehow I think it has something to do with the disappearance of Samantha, I could be wrong Polly and I sincerely hope I am."

"Do you think they've got Samantha?"

Mercer sighed heavily as he extracted a cigarette from his packet. "I don't know what to think Polly. If she was ok she'd have been in touch with us. If she's been abducted, then you have to start thinking about *who* would be wanting to abduct her and for what purpose. As far as I can see Polly, there's only one option, and it's those bastards from Lithuania. Forensics are over in her apartment now, although my hopes are not high for them finding anything worthwhile. That clown you sent with me is there now with a proper team, obnoxious little twat, asking me questions about if I knew of any men friends she has or her comings and goings. I was a detective before he was old enough to pour the milk onto his own cornflakes...little shit."

"What about your snitches Terry, do you think *they'll* know anything?"

"I'm going over now Polly to old Treble's place, see if he's heard anything, poor bugger, taking us over to Lithuania for the music festival and we hardly spent any time at all with him, some guests we turned out to be. I'll make it up to him. I'll get him a couple of bottles of Johnny Walker."

PINKERTON ROAD.

CROYDEN.

Terry drove down Dingwall Road on his way out to Treble's apartment.
He felt terrible. He hadn't been to see old Geoffrey since he'd arrived back from Europe with the girls. All said and done, if it hadn't been for old Treble it would have made the job harder for the three S.A.S men.
The fact that he was there staying in Lithuania as a guest of Trebles' in a hotel and available to drive the car for them made their job a little easier, and it also made him feel that he'd played a part in rescuing the unfortunate teens. And it was all down to Treble. He glanced at the two bottles of whiskey he'd purchased for his old snitch hoping that they would compensate for his absence at the music festival…he was fairly sure they would. Ten minutes later he pulled up outside the Pinkerton Road apartments and found a parking spot. At four thirty in the afternoon the daylight was all but gone. The hall was dimly lit and looked anything but inviting to a visitor with graffiti scrolled across walls in coloured paint along with swastikas painted around each of the corners of the hallway in glorious red and black. Broken glass lay scattered all around the floor. Prams with missing wheels, shopping trolleys with traffic cones wedged into them sat along the hallways. When he entered the block three teenage girls sat on the concrete steps along with two teenage boys. There'd be little chance of these teenage girls being abducted. All of them were wearing jeans and trainers that had seen better days. Nose piercings and tattoos were the order of the day for these young ladies and by the looks of the holes in their arms heroin would be their preferred nightcap. The boys were dressed similarly complete with tattoos revealing skulls and various skeletal masks of death. One of them sat whittling a piece of wood with a knife that looked as large as a butchers'. None of them it appeared had any intention of moving out of the way for him. He stood and scrutinised the youths before finally saying, "Would you like to let me past please?"
One of the boys looked up at him and replied, "Would you like to fuck off please?"
Mercer reacted by holding out his I.D card. "Would you like to go to fucking jail please?"
The teens scattered with lightning speed all heading off in different directions. He began to ascend the stairs suddenly feeling apprehensive. Why was he feeling like this? He retrieved the key from the plant pot that stood in the corner of the hallway outside of Treble's door. He did not need the key, Treble was home. Terry entered the inadequately illuminated room to find the pensioner sitting on his sofa with

headphones on. Instead of the usual glass of whiskey on the coffee table there was a mug of tea. Terry switched on the living room lights making Treble open his eyes and remove his headset. Terry sat the two bottles of whiskey down upon the table and greeted his old `friend`. He made his apologies to Geoffrey and explained why he and Samantha were unable to attend the concerts as often as they'd have liked. Geoffrey rose from the sofa to make fresh tea for himself and his guest. As he did Terry wondered if Treble had heard anything. The fact that he hadn't even asked where Samantha was gave him a clue that perhaps he *had* heard something. A few moments later Treble sat down the two mugs of tea on the table and then re-seated himself on the sofa. With a sigh he said to Terry, "I've heard some things Terry me boy, and they aint good."

Terry sat down opposite Treble lighting up a cigarette.

"Come on buddy, let's hear it, what have you heard?"

"They know Tel, that `Lifuanian` man who's `ouse` you took the girls from, well ee's over ere Tel, and he aint alone. Ee's got `evies` wiv im. He's been asking questions `abat` you an `Samanfa` asking people if they knew you. Ee's `talkin` bat revenge `mite`. That was a couple days ago Tel, he aint been seen since, and that's all I got."

"You know Samantha is missing Treble?"

Treble nodded his head as he sipped his tea. "Yeah I heard Terry. Do ya think they've got her?"

"Nothing sure yet, but it's looking that way my friend. Where were these Lithuanians when they were asking questions do you know?"

"Yeah, they `wus rand` in the den. The den was Trebles' nickname for his local bar.

"But they aint been back Tel, they aint come back there, I've got a couple of guys who'll let me know if they do, cos I thought I should inform you, especially as they seem to be looking for you. God I hope yer gal's alright Terry boy. If it *is* them who's got `er` then you got a serious problem, God forbid if they take her back over to Lifuania."

"I shudder to think Treble if that is the case, but, in the meantime, they are taking a chance coming here as well, because now *they* are wanted by the British authorities for the abduction of teenage girls and for holding them against their will to be used for sexual gratification, they are in big trouble if we find them, whether they have taken Samantha or not, there'll be no diplomatic immunity for these bastards."

"Well if I `eer anyfing` at all `mite`, you'll be the first to know, I promise you that Tel, `an` don't worry about the concerts, I knew all along why you `wus` there. You did good Terry to get those poor gals out of there, the trouble is, these `Lifuanians` will be out to bloody re-stock their `broffel`.

Terry stepped into the kitchen and rinsed out his mug, placing it back onto the Celloshaped mug tree. "You've been tidying up Treble, good to see buddy, you've got it looking really nice in here now."

"Well, I got friends coming over Tel from `Lifuania`, cellists like, good people, so I got to make an effort Tel, can't `ave em` staying in `bladdy squalla`. I've gone an bought brand new bed sheets an `everyfing`."

"Good on you Treble, now you remember to let me know if you hear anything at all ok? Especially if you find out where these bastards are staying."

As soon as Terry had spoken the words, Roxanne Styles' words came back into his head regarding activity in her neighbouring flat. *"Yes, quite a few of them, and ones I haven't seen before."*

"Thanks for the whiskey Tel, but I'm trying to give it up. I'll give it to a couple of my guests when they arrive, if that's alright with you. I've got to change my ways Tel…been drinking too much, it's already messed up my marriage and my career Tel…enough is enough."

"You're doing well Treble, keep up the good work, and you know what they say…cleanliness is next to Godliness, however Treble, because of your past, I doubt very much that you'll ever become a saint, see you pal."

UNKNOWN LOCATION.

Samantha Reynolds slowly regained consciousness. She had no idea of how long she'd been knocked out. She had lost all trace of day or time because she'd been drugged so many times. Needles had been inserted into her arms on so many occasions. She could not tell if she'd been here one day or ten days. She was seated upon a small wooden kitchen chair in a small bedroom, but *where* this bedroom was, was anyone's guess. She was so sluggish that she could not move from the chair. Her head was finally clearing allowing her to at least focus on why she had been abducted. Her mother's funeral had been a quiet affair and had not taken long at all. There were less than ten mourners at the service if mourners was the correct word. Her brother had not attended. She'd arrived back at her apartment shortly after four in the afternoon more than ready for a cup of coffee. As she sat down on her favourite chair, two men, one of them brandishing a pistol suddenly appeared from her bedroom and made themselves comfortable on her sofa. It was at that point that the young woman entered the living room also appearing from the bedroom.

"These two gentlemen in front of you are friends of mine. You know me miss Reynolds don't you, always nosing around my apartment with that horrible man Mercer, oh, by the way, did the two of you enjoy your little holiday in Lithuania? Very handy that wasn't it, being invited by the old drunken bastard Marsden. You did a bit of meddling around over there as well didn't you, you and Mister fucking Mercer."

Angela Bates pulled out a Glock pistol from her handbag and aimed it straight at Samantha's head.

"These gentlemen are going to tie you up now and if you as much as blink while they're doing it, I will take great pleasure in blowing your fucking head off. They are going to ask you some simple questions and you had better give the correct answers I can assure you. Between yourself and Mercer you have disrupted a very profitable little business. As soon as I heard you were over there in Lithuania I knew what you'd be up to. It's a good job those S.A.S bastards have made themselves scarce as well, saves us having to deal with them. One of the men began to bind Samantha's hands to the chair wrapping masking tape around and around her wrists and legs. As her vision cleared she focussed on the smaller man seated on her sofa. He spoke to the man who was securing her to the chair in a foreign language. She did not recognise the language but surmised by the soviet-sounding words that it must be Lithuanian. The tall man had finished securing her and re-seated himself. Angela Bates spoke again, kneeling down on her hunkers directly in front of her, and placing her hands upon her knees, her soft voice sounded

maleficent. "We're going to learn you and your side-kick a lesson in how not to interfere in other people's business. Samantha could not help herself.
"Oh you mean kidnapping people's children and selling them off to European scum like this in front of me, to be used as sex slaves is that what you mean by business?"
The blonde woman unleashed a back-handed swipe across her face cutting open her bottom lip with the rough edge of one of her diamond rings.
"You're not here to talk or pass opinion bitch, you are here to listen and answer when spoken to, and by the way, a lot of good your rescuing done, we've already taken another four girls off the streets of London and they are at this moment in time being prepared for departure, so you see it was just a complete waste of time what Mercer and his super-heroes done. You won't stop us lady, let me make that clear to you, in fact all you've done is made us all the more determined to carry on with our kidnappings. As a special treat to you though, we've decided that the girls should be tried out before we take them over there, so you will personally witness the girls being…eh…tried out. We might even give you a try out. Do you think you could handle three or four well-endowed men at once, it'd be fun to see you try. I wonder what your Mister Mercer would think about that if we should proceed. Do you know he hasn't got a clue where on God's earth you are, and either do you for that matter." She stood looking at Samantha, grinning.
"Yes, you and Mercer caused us a whole lot of trouble. Two men have now died because of you bastards, two of our men, well, like I say, you are going to learn a lesson for interfering where you shouldn't…sometimes it pays us to turn a blind eye Samantha, you should know that."
She couldn't be certain but by what this bitch had said, it sounded very much like she was still in the country.
"Being prepared for departure" would surely suggest that they were still in Britain. The blonde wasn't exactly the sharpest tool in the box, pretty as she was. The smaller man seated on the sofa leaned forward still sitting and smiled at her. He looked to be in his sixties. He had a ruddy complexion with silver hair pulled over to one side of his head. His face looked kindly, but she guessed that somehow he would be anything but that. He too had a sinister look in his eyes when you looked close enough at him.
The smile remained on his face as he spoke in his broken English.
"Mees Reyno` we have special `peoples` help us to get `girlz yes yes, special, very good `peoples`. They with you, they part of you, they detective, no-one know you see. We will never be caught, he never be suspected. He tell us where we get the `girlz` and we get. He work em…what is word Viktor?"
The other man spoke. "Peripatetically". He spoke the word slowly emphasising each

syllable.

"Yes, that's `eet`, peripatetically, so strange these English word. You will never find out who he be who help us, never. We could keel you now but we using you for the `traps`, we `got` Mercer in the `traps`. Soon he come looking for you, and then BANG!! And we `be keel` him.

And, `mees Reyno`, we have `peoples` looking for these S.A.S hero men.

I know lots of peoples `mees Reyno`, and these peoples know where they find them, and they `keel` them too, very soon `Mees Reyno`...very soon."

There was a few seconds of silence before he continued. "So, you see, I need to get the `girlz`, they make me a lot of money and anyway, they like the sex. They get used to it, and then they like it, and they happy, they make the money too, and they like to make the money. They like it miss `Reyno` they do."

Samantha took a chance with her life. "I'm afraid you are all very disillusioned, you see, you are all being hunted, you are all wanted for kidnapping and for all of your illegal activities in *my* country, and I'm also vexed to tell you that you will not be going on trial. You will all be shot dead, and you can take that as a solemn promise. It won't take them long to locate you, you'll see, and-"

Angela Bates unleashed yet another savage blow to Samantha's face, this time with her fist. "Next time you speak out of turn, I'll shoot you in the head."   Painful as it was Samantha knew she'd got to them. She could see the seeds of doubt etched in the two men's faces, especially the older one. He looked worried now, or at least agitated. He rose up from the sofa and approached Samantha. Having regained his composure, he said," You may think that these friends of you will find us, but you are very mistaken `mees Reyno`, I tell you just five minutes ago...they no coming, not here. They never find here. One of your `detective` he very clever and I pay him a lot of the money.

He know all your moves and he know where to hide us, your friends will never find you here. So, I warn you to keep the `Eenglish focking` mouth shut if you know what `is the good` for you ok? If you make any more fancy talking to Angela, she keel you, I make that the promise to *you*."

The two men left the room leaving Angela alone with Samantha.

"Because of all your interference Miss Reynolds, a number of people are going to die, including your Terry Mercer. These men you have spoken with have lots and lots of contacts in London...mercenaries to be precise, and they will kill at the drop of a hat. They care nothing about rank or status I assure you, and they are right at this moment in time queuing up to take Mercer out. They use those fancy long-range rifles you see. They could be nearly half a mile away from him as they pull the trigger, and they will Samantha, trust me, they will, because mister Saratov there has put a contract out on him." Angela sighed mockingly at Samantha. "I'm afraid you have spoken to Terry for the last time. I hope you had a good day with him, because it'll be your last. He's going down...we promise *you* that Samantha."

Samantha was left on her own again. The amount of information the blonde had given her was unbelievable. She now knew that the small man was Saratov and the other, judging by his Christian name of Viktor was this Kulbertinov, the man that Jim Lawrence was chauffer to. And who was this detective he said was helping them? No wonder they were proving difficult to catch. If only she could find a way of getting out of here they could wrap this case up in no time at all...but there was little chance of that happening. She only hoped that Terry was wise to the fact that the Lithuanians were here, because if he didn't know, he would die.

HENSINGHAM APARTMENTS.

STRATFORD.

Roxanne had texted Terry informing him that there were three men at Angela Bates' flat. It had taken Terry the best part of twenty-five minutes to arrive here, and of course, by the time he had arrived, surprise surprise, they were gone. Much to his frustration he asked her if she'd got a look at the men, a description. Roxanne had done better than that, she had taken several photographs of the men with her phone which she had concealed in her duster (A scrunched up mini skirt.) as she `pretended to clean her door. She knew she was taking a chance doing this, but she also knew that Mercer would be extremely grateful to say the least, and that in all probability he would boost her finances considerably, especially if the female detective was not accompanying him. She was right. Terry sat down on Roxanne's sofa and smiled as he studied the images. "Well done Roxanne. These are going to be very useful. Now, you just send those photos to my phone and I'll be on my way. Obviously, the men did not spot you taking these photographs…you took a chance there Roxanne, and I am grateful. Did any of them look at you?"

"Only one of the fuckers, he just glanced at me, but I think it was because my tits were drooping down a bit, it's this fucking vest, it's as loose as fuck, fuckers nearly pop out when I bend over you see."

Mercer grinned at Roxanne's description of her loosely-fitting vest-top.

His phone lit up. The photographs were there. Now he had something to go on. He would locate these men and they would be separately `interviewed`.

"Thank you Roxanne, you have helped considerably, these photos are invaluable."

Much to Roxanne's delight he pulled out his wallet and pulled out some notes. Roxanne flushed. He then proceeded to hand her four five pound notes. Although she thanked him she had a look upon her face as though he'd placed some dog dirt there. As he got to the door he thanked her again, and told her to keep contacting him when she witnessed any activity at Angela's flat. Grudgingly she said she would, still looking at the five pound notes in her hand. At this point Mercer burst out laughing and returned to Roxanne. "Give me those back you silly girl. Do you think I'd only give you that for what you've done for me, come here silly."

Mercer then returned to his wallet this time pulling out five twenty pound notes. Here, I'll swap you for those."

He gave Roxanne a cuddle and kissed her on the cheek. Then he spoke to her in her own kind of language.

"You're an absolute gem Roxanne did you fucking know that babe?"

As he pulled away from her, he accidently brushed against her ample breasts making enough contact with them to know that this lady does not bother with braziers.

She smiled at his embarrassment.

"Don't blush mister Mercer, these fuckers get felt about a hundred times a week, that's what attracts them to me, cause it aint `me` fucking face, I don't care."

Terry left Roxanne's apartment feeling considerably happier than when he'd first arrived here. She had done well this time, these photos were indeed invaluable. As he walked along the hallway she shouted after him. She caught up with him and whispered. "I'm just saying mister Mercer, if you ever get lonely, you'd be welcome to come here for a little comfort if you know what I mean, I mean I don't know if you and that woman detective have got anything going on there, I'm just saying…I'll be here if you need to…you know."

"Thank you for the offer Roxanne" he replied as he continued to walk, smiling to himself at the very thought of it. As he reached his car he came to the conclusion that there'd be a better chance of Christ walking through Soho than him taking up Roxanne's offer to bed her.

CHISLEHURST.

ROYAL PARADE. 1am.

Sandra Knox rose up from her bed and dried her eyes. Her boyfriend Trevor Smith had once again let her down. Despite all the warnings Sandra had received from her friends about Trevor's attitude concerning serious relationships she had gone ahead and started dating him. At first everything had been going really well, so much so that Sandra began to think that her friends had perhaps been a trifle jealous of her boyfriend and that perhaps they had been rejected by Trevor some- time in the past. He was, it had to be said an extremely attractive young man. But alas, it was only a matter of time before she came to realize that Trevor looked upon their relationship as nothing more than a dalliance. She would have to admit that she had approached him somewhat lasciviously and had offered herself far too easily. Perhaps this was the reason he hadn't taken their relationship as seriously as she hoped he would, that she was too easily available. Tonight however, one of her friends had sent her a photograph of Trevor sitting on a bench somewhere on the outskirts of town with a girl, and by the looks of the photo he seemed to be trying his best to lose sight of his tongue by burying it as far down the girl's throat as he could. His right hand was cupped around the girl's head. She couldn't tell what his left hand was doing because it was submerged underneath the girl's skirt somewhere. Although this was the first time she'd received irrefutable evidence of his infidelity it hadn't been the first time she'd been informed of his blatant unfaithfulness. So, good looking or not, as from three hours ago the relationship between Sandra Knox and Trevor Smith was well and truly over. She'd had enough of his hedonistic ways. The boy would be better suited to dating whores. Perhaps they would have better luck in taming his sexual audaciousness. Sandra made her way to the bathroom where she applied skin moisturiser to her face. She was due to begin university soon anyway and so perhaps it was maybe just as well she'd found him out now before she even left town. She returned to her bedroom where she proceeded to send him a text message informing him that she never wanted to see him again as long as she lived and that she hoped he would contract some horrible sexual disease that might learn him a lesson in how to treat girls with a little respect instead of going through life treating them like they were nothing more than sexual objects, there for his pleasing only. Even though she pressed send on her phone it was still hurting. If only Trevor could control himself he would indeed be a good catch for any girl. She sighed heavily, knowing that *that* was purely wishful thinking. The boy was nothing but a pure male chauvinist bastard with only one thing on his mind. She lay back down on her bed and attempted to sleep but it was useless. Her mind was spinning in turmoil at the thought of what Trevor would be doing right now with his `new` love. Her bedroom door opened and a moment later she was pounced upon by Floppy, her little terrier. The dog happily lapped at her brow and all over her face making her laugh. "Come on Floppy lie down." The animal was far too excited to settle and seemed eager to be out and running around. Perhaps he needed to pee. She knew she did. Sandra rose from her bed once more and slipped on a pair of jeans and trainers and then made her way to the bathroom. Inevitably Floppy followed her nudging the door open. "Come on Floppy, it's a good job John's over at his friend's house and mum and dad's not back home or else everybody would be getting a bird's-eye view wouldn't they? You silly dog." Sandra's fifteen-year-old brother was having a sleep-over at one of his heavy-metal head-banging idiot friends of his. Her mum and dad would not be home until the wee small hours because they always went back to one of their friend's houses after their nights out. She decided she would take Floppy out for a walk and try and burn off this new lease of life he'd suddenly sprang. She returned to her bedroom and put on a vest-top and a thin jacket and then made her way down to the kitchen to retrieve Floppy's lead. As soon as she picked up the chain the dog went frantic, bouncing up and down and running from one end of the kitchen to the other. The little dog refused to stand still long enough for her to attach the leash. "Right, we're not going anywhere then if you don't stand still, I'll go myself for a walk." As though the dog could understand her he approached and managed (with an effort.) to stand still long enough for Sandra to attach the lead. At 1:28 am Sandra Knox and Floppy left their house in Royal Parade to go for their medicinal walk, one of them to work off his excessive energy, the other, to try and forget about an immature hedonistic bastard who's hobby seemed to be to screw with as many different girls as he possibly could.

As she walked she passed a group of little shops including the restaurant where she and Trevor had sat only days before enjoying a lovely Italian meal and she thinking that maybe everybody had got Trevor all wrong and that he was not that nasty little two-timer they all said he was.

As she passed the `Ristorante Italiano` one of her friends came out hand in hand with her boyfriend. She waved over to Sandra, smiling and looking rather smug with herself with a hint of mockery in her smile Sandra thought. The Germans had a word for it. Schadenfreude. Taking pleasure in someone else's misfortune.

"Hiya babes, are you alright? Sorry to hear about what Trevor's been doing...but we told you didn't we"?

Sandra only waved over but kept on walking, aided by Floppy who was tugging hard on his lead.

"Fuck you Mandy". She thought to herself. Mandy was one of those girls who actually enjoyed other people's downfalls. She seemed to gloat in other people's misery, and how she knew about Trevor only hours after he'd been discovered didn't take much working out. One of her other `friends` had obviously put something on face book or twitter. "So much for friends looking out for each other", she muttered to herself. Sandra walked on crossing the road over to Kenmal Road where Floppy would have an absolute abundance of trees to relieve himself. The usually busy road was quite deserted tonight compared to what it was like during the day but still she couldn't trust Floppy off the lead. Knowing her luck, he would run across the road and a car or lorry would appear from nowhere at all and kill him. Floppy at this moment in time was the only true friend she could actually rely upon. She smiled down at her little companion as he pulled and tugged to sniff trees and grass and just about everything he came across. He was five years old now which was quite old for a dog. Her mum and dad had bought him for her eleventh birthday. How different the world had seemed then when she was that age. She was a young woman now and had, thanks to Trevor Smith experienced her first real heart-ache. Things would be a lot better once she'd got settled into uni though. She would meet other boys there, mature boys who would respect girls and treat them as equals rather than the selfish bastard that she'd just split up with who genuinely thought that girls were put on this earth to satisfy his sexual needs. Sandra sighed as she walked, enjoying the peace and quiet of the night. Nights like these were beautiful. You could walk and walk and think about all the things that were bothering or worrying you and in most cases you always found an answer, or a remedy to a problem. Sometimes there was a lot to be said for solitude.

A police car cruised beside her on the opposite side of the road.

The driver's window went down. "Are you ok miss?" The officer called from the vehicle.

"Yes, I'm fine thank you."

"Are you going far?"

"No, in fact I'm just about to turn around and head back home, just needed to get some fresh air."

The young officer smiled at her. "Where do you live?"

Sandra looked at him as though he'd asked her a personal question, but then realized he was only concerned about her. "I live in Royal Parade, it's not far from here, I'm just going back now."

"Well, you take care miss. It's not a good idea to be walking around on your own at this time of the morning, would you like us to give you a lift back home?"

For the first time Sandra noticed the police woman seated beside him.

"No thank you, I'll be fine, but thank you anyway."

"Well, you take care miss, be safe."

The window was rolled back up and the car moved off ahead of her disappearing into the night. Without realizing how far she'd walked she found herself about a mile from home. "Come on Floppy let's be getting you back home, perhaps you'll sleep now when we get back."

Floppy was now walking at heel his excess energy taken care of. Sandra smiled down at her faithful little friend who kept looking up at her, eager now it seemed to be back in his basket.

Suddenly, from nowhere a car came past her and skidded into the side of the road, coming to a halt half on the pavement about fifty feet in front of her.

The passenger door opened and a frantic young woman emerged calling out to Sandra for help. "Please, could you help us, I think my husband is having a heart attack, help me please."

Sandra ran up to the woman and looked inside the car. A man sat slumped over the steering wheel, panting and sputtering.

"Help me get this seat belt off him, I think it's restricting his breathing, can you reach over and unfasten it for me please."

Without thinking Sandra handed the dog lead to the woman and reached across the passenger seat to unhook the belt. As she did the man suddenly sat up and pulled Sandra back by the head in a vice-like head lock.

"Tie the fucking dog up quick and get in Angela, quick, we need to get to fuck out of here."

Angela Bates climbed into the back of the car and closed the door.

She then produced a syringe and inserted the needle into Sandra's left arm.

In only a few seconds Sandra Knox was unconscious. From start to finish, the incident had taken a total of thirty-nine seconds.

The car pulled away at speed, leaving a rather confused little Floppy tied to a tree, wondering what on earth was happening.

UNKNOWN LOCATION.

Samantha sat in complete silence. Not a sound could be heard from any other part of the house, if indeed it was a house where they were holding her.
She could be anywhere. When Angela Bates had left her here she could hear her footsteps walking upon uncovered floorboards. The footsteps becoming less and less audible as she walked, and judging by the sounds it was very spacious.
They could be in an abandoned mansion, but it would be useless to guess.
She continued listening to the silence and it seemed to her, that the silence was listening to her. Angela had blindfolded her before she left for whatever reason.
It seemed pretty pointless and meaningless considering she'd been rendered unconscious before they'd brought her here, adding to that she'd been secured to the chair she was sitting upon and so it wasn't as if she could go anywhere. Perhaps she was in a basement, but there was not even the faintest sound of distant traffic, no voices, nothing. Her mind drifted to thoughts of Terry and in particular, his well-being. These people were out to get him. From what Polly had told her, Terry was merely the get-away driver for the girls but this lot were treating him as though the whole plan had been devised by him. They were holding him solely responsible for the girls' escape. All she could do was sit here and hope that eventually they would move her somewhere else, something, anything to give her an opportunity to free herself from here, wherever the hell here was.
Suddenly, the silence was broken. She could hear the sound of a car engine.
Car doors being closed, footsteps on gravel, voices. The sounds were coming from above her head. So she was being held in a basement. Then she heard footsteps on bare floorboards, also overhead. She heard a door being opened and then more voices. She recognised Angela Bates' voice. The footsteps became louder. They were coming down stairs. The door of the room where she was being held suddenly burst open. She heard the sound of a chair being scraped across the floor, and then a soft thump, then masking tape being wrapped around. Then there was silence again. Whoever had come in here with Angela were still here, no-one had left the room, but still the silence. And then she jumped with fright as Angela Bates' voice boomed right in her ear. "We've brought another little scrubber in here for you, you know, just to keep you company. She won't be talking to you for a while though she's been given a nice little sedative to keep her hysterics at bay.
Do you see what I mean now miss Reynolds, I told you we'd have mister Saratov's mansion furnished with new little scrubbers in no time, that's five we've got now, he'll

be back to full business in no time at all. This one's a little beauty as well, a bonus no less, out walking her little doggie on her own in the early hours of the morning...silly girl. Mister Saratov is playing with the idea of just shooting you now and getting you out of the way, but I think that Viktor is convincing him, or at least trying to, that it'd be better for us if we keep you alive, and that way Mister Terrence Mercer would walk straight into our hands and saving Mister Saratov a lot of money...but we'll see."

This time Samantha felt it would be better to say nothing in reply. She was in the hands of the gods. One thing was for sure, the freeing of the girls in Lithuania was merely a minor inconvenience. They were re-stocking at lightning speed it would seem, unless of course Angela was bluffing, but she doubted that very much. She had to face facts, and the fact was that she was being held here, and God knows where, and no-one but no-one on God's good earth had the slightest clue where she was. There was a contract on Terry Mercer and so, unless a minor miracle was to take place, both she and Terry had not long to live. The most frustrating thing about all of this was that it was one of their own who were supplying these sick people with all the information they needed, and allowing them to smuggle these girls out of the country. And the bastard or bastards who were doing it would not lose a single minute's sleep.

Nothing more was said to Samantha. She heard the footsteps leaving the room. The door was slammed shut and then their footsteps could be heard once more ascending the stairs. She could hear the faint sound of the girl's breathing in the darkness. Another one, another careless teen walking around in the wee small hours unaccompanied. Another reason for the prime minister's TV warnings and advice. Samantha heard the footsteps on the gravel again and car doors closing.

Then the sound of the gravel crunching under the wheels of the car as it pulled away. It would be some time before the girl in here awoke from her stupor, and of course the inevitable panic when she *did* awake. She would wonder what the hell had happened to her, and she would have no idea whatsoever of the ordeal she was about to be put through. These people were ruthless and merciless. These young girls were nothing more than a quick way to make money. Starting with Angela Bates, money would be made from them, first by the kidnapping of the girls, then, after they were transferred over to Lithuania they would in turn make the money back paid to the kidnappers by being forced to whore themselves to these wealthy sick-minded people who got their kicks by having sex with young girls. Perhaps a real woman would put them to shame by revealing just how inadequate they really were, and so, having sex with inexperienced youths perhaps gave them an element of superiority. Samantha sat in the silence once again contemplating the situation, and the situation was nothing less than dire. It wasn't as if there was anyone out there who could be badgered into confessing what

they knew, because no-one knew anything about these disappearances.
The kidnappings were lightning fast and there were never any witnesses who could give descriptions. As for her own abduction, they had timed that to perfection. She had been placed on bereavement leave and so there would be no suspicions as to her absence. Terry and Polly would automatically think she was taking extended leave.
It was hopeless to say the least. All that remained now was how long they were going to keep her alive. If someone out there managed to dispose of Terry, then her execution would be instant. As it was, it was imminent.

SCOTLAND YARD.

BROADWAY VICTORIA.

Polly Shepard was looking stressed, a familiar sight these days. She had just received news of a girl gone missing in Chislehurst. She had been out walking her dog. Whoever had snatched her had left the animal tied up to a tree.
The dog's name tag had an address. Someone had come across the dog whilst out walking with their own pet. Terry Mercer looked grimly at the document before him. He sighed heavily as he asked Polly what time they found the animal.
"Six o clock this morning Terry, but the girl could have been taken much earlier than that...if she has been abducted. Her parents are being interviewed as we speak."
"What age is the girl? Dare I ask."
"Sixteen, almost seventeen. No arguments with her parents, no reasons for her to run away. She has a happy relationship with them and her younger brother.
She's due to start university shortly studying law and English literature.
All said and done Terry, she seems to be a happy contented teenager."
"Any history of drugs? Shoplifting? Anything?"
"Nothing Terry, just a happy young girl with her whole life in front of her."
"I'll have to go over there and have a chat with her parents, poor buggers.
Christ Polly, this seems to be never ending. We rescue some of them and they're back over here continuing to snatch up more. On top of that, Treble informs me that the Lithuanians are here. They've been asking questions about me, and I'm all but certain its' they who have taken Samantha. If it is, then we have serious problems." He pulled out his phone and showed Polly the photographs taken by Roxanne of the men who visited Angela Bates' flat.
"I'm going over to see Colin Green, he'll know if any of these three men were at the mansion in Lithuania. The silly bugger seems to think that he's going to take this lot down himself, he was asking me to find out names for him."
Polly looked at him. "The way things are turning out Terry, it might not be a bad idea to let him loose, I'm joking of course."
"Anyway I'm off to see him, if for no other reason than to warn him not to take matters into his own hands. I think what happened to his daughter has fucked up his head Polly, I mean really. And that girl Sophie Spencer, she's on about joining him in his bid to exact revenge, Christ that's all we'd need, a teenage girl and an ex SAS soldier wreaking havoc about the place. I think he sees himself as some kind of do-gooder vigilante or

something. But you know, he said something to me that made me think. He said, imagine if it happened again Terry, imagine how you'd feel. Well, it is happening again and I feel so bloody useless not having a single clue where to start to find these bastards and truth be known Polly, right now I don't give one flying fuck where I get my next lead from, I'll be in touch." "Terry? You be bloody careful out there, I mean it. If these people are asking about you then it would seem they are seeking some kind of vengeance of their own. Maybe that's why they've taken Samantha, and by the way, who, or what in Gods' name is Treble?" Terry smiled at his superior as he reached the door. "Right now Polly, Treble is my one and only life-line. If there is anything to hear worth hearing, then he'll be the one to hear it. I would dearly love it if he happened to find out where the hell Samantha was. See you later."

Polly sat scrutinising the case-file in front of her. Another girl, another innocent girl snatched from her everyday life into a frightening world of drugs and forced sex. Another two parents left in a state of shock and horror, wondering what on earth had happened to their baby, and here *they* were, the metropolitan police force unable to keep their own children safe in their own country. What the hell was happening to us that these low-lives could come across here and take them without as much as a challenge? Maybe Colin Green had the right idea after all, this lot only knew one rule, and that was the rule of the wild. Live or die. Maybe she could come to some kind of deal with him that would give him the authority to take out any of these evil people. Be a ghost, be a ghost here in Britain, and fight fire with fire. As time was passing, it was becoming more and more of a possibility. And who could be better than an ex SAS man to do the job. Ruthless, when needed to be, and clinical. It would certainly give those bastards something to think about…consequences.

MITCHAM.

Mercer had driven all the way over from Chislehurst to Mitcham to see Colin Green. Brian and Louise Knox had all but brought a tear to his eye with their grief. Once again he had to go through the procedure of letting them know that everything that could be done, would be done in a bid to find their daughter. And once again he had come away from their premises utterly devastated by the hopelessness in their pleas. His own partner as well, what on earth had they done with Samantha? He arrived at Colin Green's house only to be informed by his wife that she hadn't seen him in two days. Colin had texted her to let her know that he was ok and that she had nothing to worry about, and that, all being well, he'd be back home tomorrow. He was invited in for a chat but he declined the offer. He asked after Alison and how she was coping with everything but then politely made his way back to his car. He would send Colin a text message and ask him what was happening. He hoped he hadn't set off on a vigilante quest. He climbed back into his car and drove off towards Caesars Walk and then on to the A239. Today he was feeling more stressed than ever. His eyes were feeling heavy and he was struggling to concentrate on his driving. He needed to sleep.

He decided to head back to Holborn and have a couple of hours on the sofa, after all, he was on this case twenty-four seven, and if he didn't, then it was only a matter time until he had an accident. He sent Polly a text message informing her of his intentions who in turn informed him that twenty-four seven surveillance had been put on to Hensingham apartments in Stratford. Surely soon, one of them would reappear there and then they could start getting some worthwhile information. Then, quite suddenly a blast of adrenalin shot through his body almost like an electrical shock, chasing all tiredness away, at least momentarily. It was a text message from Samantha. He pulled in to the side of the road to read it. The message read; *See you soon sweetheart. They're going to kill us together. Isn't that so nice of them Terry?* As he studied the message it became clear what they were doing. They were actually informing him that they were going to kidnap him. There was no if's or but's, they were going to do it. And they were going to execute them together. At least, according to their text message, Samantha at this point was still alive. It wasn't much hope, but it was hope. And how did they think they were going to kidnap him? Did they think that he wasn't capable of defending himself? That he would just capitulate to them without a struggle?

He sat by the roadside smoking his cigarette and contemplating the message, and its' implications. Even through all this negativity he still felt slightly exhilarated in the fact that he was now ninety per cent certain that his partner was still alive. Although he didn't feel like it he would have to keep his word and inform Polly about the message. He would ask her to tell no-one else about it, no-one at all. He would also inform her that he was now heading back to Holborn to have a couple of hours sleep and from there he was going to visit old Treble to see if he'd heard anything else about these foreign men who'd been asking about him though his hopes weren't high, there was no message from Treble on his phone and if there had been further sightings of these men, he'd have been in touch by now. First things first though. He would have his medicinal sleep to recharge his batteries and then he'd head over to Croydon to see Treble clef. Perhaps these Lithuanians were planning to kidnap him from his own house in Holborn. He wondered if they'd have the audacity to attempt such a thing, although, having said that, it wouldn't be the first time he'd been abducted from his own home. This time however, he had some lovely surprises for the would-be kidnappers should they attempt it.

PINKERTON ROAD.

CROYDON. 10pm.

Geoffrey Marsden was feeling proud of himself at this moment in time, for two reasons. One, he had news for Terry concerning these Lithuanian gentlemen who'd been asking about him, and two, because he was now almost in full control of his drinking. To leave the pub at this time of the evening would have been unheard of less than a year ago, but he'd been quietly attempting to ease himself off the drink, or at least the desperate need for it. Recently he'd gone two days at home without a drink of whiskey, allowing himself a couple of glasses of beer instead, a major achievement for him. Since he'd been at the European festival and had contact with fellow musicians he seemed to have an urge to take control of his life again. It seemed so long since he had that privilege. Respectability perhaps, or maybe it was the fact that just for once, people had actually listened and was interested in what he was saying. He'd already made changes in his flat, preparing for his guests to come over to see him. A complete transformation as to what it had been like only weeks before. Respectability, that was it. He was getting his self-respect back, something he'd thought was gone forever. He drained the last of his beer and thanked the barmaid for her services. She asked him if she couldn't tempt him into having another before he went home. Treble smiled at the young girl informing her that the days were long gone for him to be tempted by *anything* that she could offer...that part of his life was well and truly gone forever.
"See you tomorrow Geoffrey" she said as he left the premises.
He didn't have far to walk to his flat and he enjoyed the short walk back home. Once there he proceeded to put the kettle on and make himself a nice cup of tea before he retired for the night. Two of his guests were arriving from Lithuania in a couple of weeks' time and so tomorrow he would continue to clean and tidy his apartment. First things first though, he would have to inform Terry that there was a woman and a man in the pub earlier today asking the whereabouts of a certain Terry Mercer, wondering if anyone knew where he lived. These people however were not Lithuanian, they were both English. He popped himself a couple of slices of bread into the toaster and kicked off his shoes which he then put into his hallway, neatly beside his other footwear. Less than five minutes later, he was sitting enjoying his cup of tea and his buttered toast listening to one of his favourite concertos. Life for Geoffrey Marsden was taking a turn for the better. As he sat listening to his music, he recalled something his father had once told him; *"God helps those who help themselves."* And so it would seem. Because

the more effort he'd put in to tidying his home and with trying to control his drinking, the more, good things were happening for him.

He now had regular correspondence with people who shared his interests, people sending him invitations to musical events here in London, something that hadn't happened for years. He presumed it was his friends in Lithuania who had seen to that. He rose up from his sofa to turn off his stereo. As he bent down to unplug the device he felt something cold on his neck, really cold.

"You just sit yourself back down there old man on that sofa. You and me need to talk." A young blonde woman about thirty years of age sat herself down on an easy-chair opposite Geoffrey. The same girl he had seen earlier in the day. She placed the giant pistol in her right hand beside her on the arm of the chair.

"Now then Mister drunken-good-for-nothing-Marsden, I need you to give me some information, and I think you know who I want to know about. Depending upon the accuracy of your answers will determine how long you live. In my opinion you are nothing but a waste of fucking space, however you may gain some of my respect if you give me the information I require."

Geoffrey Marsden sat petrified looking at the young woman. He could tell that she would kill him without a second thought.

He began to stammer; "I really don't think that I can-"

"Shut your mouth, you piece of shit, you don't talk unless I ask you a question, have we got that clear Geoffrey?"

The old man nodded his head. With shaking hands, he reached for his cigarettes on his coffee table and proceeded to light one up. The woman rose up from the chair, taking the pistol with her. She began slowly wandering around the room and keeping her eyes on him at all times. She stopped at the cellos. She tapped one of them with the gun gently on the top of the instrument.

"Do you like playing these violin things do you?"

The ignorance of the girl made something stir inside him. She didn't even know what the instrument was.

"It would be a shame indeed if anything were to happen to these wouldn't it Geoffrey? They must be special to you or you wouldn't have them sitting up on these fucking stand things now would you? I'm asking you a question old man. Are these things special to you? Are they worth money? You can talk."

Old Geoffrey smiled as he looked at his beloved instruments. "Yes and no miss. Yes, they are very special to me, and no, they aren't worth much money at all. They are simply little pieces of my past that reminds me that I wasn't always a good for nothing piece of shit all my life…"

"So you know what you are, well, there's a start. Acknowledging the fact that you're worthless shit is a good start, we can build on that, and you can start building by giving me the address of that nosey bastard detective Mercer, now, where does he live? Talk to me!" Geoffrey took a drag of his cigarette and exhaled the smoke up to the ceiling. "Being honest miss, I haven't got a clue. I'm a snitch for him, yes, but surely you would know he's not going to give the likes of me his home address, I can give you his phone number or his mobile number, but I'm afraid I haven't got a clue as to where he resides." The blonde sat back down on the chair clasping her hands together as if to pray and crossing her legs. She could have been a therapist. Geoffrey observed the blonde's attire. Black, everything black, like her life he supposed. Black jacket and black top, boots the same, black jeans. The only colourful things about her was her hair and the diamond necklace she wore around her neck, and the bright red nail varnish on the tips of her fingers. She tapped the hand gun a couple of times while she contemplated his answer, and then returned to the praying stance. "Tell you what old-timer. Here's a good idea, why don't you send him a text message now explaining to him that you have some worthwhile information for him, information that requires his urgent attention. How would that do, do you think you could do that for me, I mean, are you sober enough to perform that act? Or do I have to do it for you, you drunken old bastard that you are. You can answer me shit-pile."

At this point, Geoffrey knew he didn't have long to live. This bitch was not going to let him live no matter what information he gave her. To his advantage, he'd only had two beers tonight. He had also been eating more healthily as well which had gained him some strength. He'd been feeling a lot stronger these days, and less breathless owing to the fact that he'd cut down the number of cigarettes he'd been smoking. He was now wondering when to pounce upon the bitch and overcome her. She looked strong. Far stronger than him in fact, but, if he done this right and took her by surprise, all he would have to do would be to grab the hand gun and everything would be sorted, one way or another. What Treble didn't know was that there were another two men accompanying the blonde who were waiting outside.

It would be the last thing she expected, but if he got his timing wrong, it would be the last thing he would ever do. As he leaned forward to stub out his cigarette he glanced to see where her hands were. The gun sat on the arm of the chair and she sat once more with her hands clasped together and her legs crossed.

It was now or never.

FINLEY STREET.

HOLBURN.

Terry awoke to the sound of Roy Wood singing Blackberry Way on his radio alarm clock. He knew he'd have to set the alarm or else he may have slept forever. Even now as he sat up on his bed, his body was craving him to lie back down and continue to sleep. The two hours would have to suffice for now. He checked his mobile. There were two messages, one from Polly Shepard and one from Treble-clef. He gave Polly precedence over Treble...just this once. As he made himself a cup of coffee he phoned Polly.
"Terry? Where are you?"
"I'm at home, I'm just heading out, why? I told you I was having a couple of hours."
"Terry what's the address of that snitch of yours, is it Pinkerton Road?"
"Yes, why? What's wrong?"
"You'd better get round there Terry, forensics are there already, oh Christ Terry."
Mercer did not want to hear any more. He put on his jacket and ran out to his car. Forty minutes later he pulled up outside of Treble's apartment.
Red and blue lights flashed furiously in the night from police cars and an ambulance. Two uniforms guarded the entrance, both officers looking down to the ground as Terry walked past them. He walked because there was no point in running. There was no hope for Treble, the fact that Polly had said the forensics were already here gave him all the information he needed. The two policemen at the door were actually cringing as Terry made his way past them, in fear of some kind of back-lash they would receive from him. His bad-tempered reputation preceded him. He climbed the concrete steps that led up to Treble's apartment laboriously, his legs feeling like they were going to give way any minute. As he reached the top of the stairs he was greeted by a grim faced Andrea Bortelli the chief forensic officer. "There's no need for you to go in Terry. You don't want to see this pal, really. He's dead, that's all you need to know fella`." Andrea even attempted to stop him entering by taking hold of him softly by the shoulders but it was to no avail. "Terry, don't torture yourself, please." Terry entered the living room. The sight that greeted him made him utter an indescribable sound as he put his hand up to his mouth. It was a sound of hopelessness and grief. Less than fifteen feet in front of him the body of Geoffrey Marsden hung upside-down from his ceiling, his body, but not his head. His head had been placed, or rather wedged on top of one of his cellos facing him, on the machine-head-stock, a note pinned through one of his eye sockets. Treble's other cello lay in pieces all around his living room, along with broken trophies

and medals he had accumulated over the years. Honours and ribbons and sashes and all manner of awards lay strewn across the blood-stained floor.

Mercer could feel nothing at this moment in time, nothing at all, neither anger nor pain or the need for revenge, or sadness, absolutely nothing. Numb.

He stood motionless as he took in this scene from Hell.

A pool of blood lay on the floor underneath Treble's body which covered almost half of the living room space, and still growing in size.

Andrea Bortelli came from behind him and gently coaxed him outside into the hallway again. She had already lit the cigarette before she handed it to him.

"Come on Terry, let's smoke our cigarette away from all that shit in there." Without another word, she wrapped her arms around the man like she was his mother, tapping him continuously on the shoulder. Finally, he pulled away from Andrea, rubbing his face like he did whenever he was agitated, or distressed. He took a drag of his cigarette and asked her what was written on the note. Andrea just shook her head at first as if trying to discard the subject as meaningless, but Terry looked at her raising his eyebrows and waiting for the answer. She sighed, smiling. "The usual Terry, they say they're coming for you next, and that there is no escaping your fate."

He walked away from the forensic and climbed the steps up to the living room once again. Upon closer inspection he spotted the bruises on Treble's hands and arms. Three of the knuckles on his left hand were broken. They had obviously tortured the poor man before killing him. On his right arm there were several cigarette burns. Once again Terry Mercer stood motionless staring at the corpse of his old `pal`. They had become friends over the years. There was a kind of trust between them. Anything Treble told him was usually accurate. The poor old bugger had been trying to change his ways of late, weaning himself off the whiskey, tidying his house, dressing himself properly. Taking pride in himself had been his main focus for months now. Since he'd been to Lithuania and met all those nice people there he'd become a different man, certainly making efforts to improve his life-style. His musician friends had sparked something off in him that woke him up to believing in himself again. Respectability, he was getting respect. People were listening to what he had to say. Terry remembered being quite surprised at how many people approached him when they were in Lithuania, influential people from the world of classical music. Treble had obviously impressed a lot of people on his journeys, and he could see that the old man's face lit up as each of these people introduced themselves to him, looking actually honoured to be in his company. He wondered now just what his old buddy had endured in the last minutes of his life. Judging by the broken bones and the cigarette burns it would appear that they'd been trying to extract information from him. Now he wondered if Treble had given in to them, hell, no-one would blame him, but if he did, did they now know where he lived? They had obviously found out where Samantha lived, and judging by the text message, they were holding her somewhere. The message read that he and Samantha were going to die together, so they would attempt to at least abduct him. He would have surveillance put on in Finley Street, twenty-four-hour surveillance.

He drove back to HQ and informed Polly of the `mess` in Pinkerton Road, and of course, the content of the note they had left, and where exactly they had left it. Polly had already put surveillance on Finlay Street, in fact she had sent two cars there so that front and back could be observed at all times. No-one was getting into Terry's house without her knowing about it. "You look exhausted Terry if you don't mind me saying, in fact, I don't think you've been quite yourself since you come back from Lithuania. Are you eating properly? I know you're not sleeping healthily, any fool can see that. All this shit is not helping matters either is it?" As to form Terry completely took her by surprise. "You've had your hair done Polly, it's lovely, really nice, you suit that colour, oh and you've got those highlights running through, yeah, really lovely, you look amazing, well, not amazing, you know, nice...yeah, you look...nice."
Polly's phone rang on her desk. She picked it up. The light-hearted humour didn't last for long. Terry watched as Polly's face changed expression.
Whatever it was, it wasn't good. Nothing was good these days, and now, an old friend who he'd formed a friendship with had been taken away, tortured and killed for no other reason than the fact that he'd known Terry Mercer...and just when he'd finally built up the courage to give life another try, and that opportunity had come his way through the love of his beloved cello. "So long Geoffrey Marsden."

HENSINGHAM APARTMENTS.

STRATFORD.

Roxanne Styles had had a very busy lucrative night. Satisfied not from any sexual gratification from her `punters` but from the amount of money she had extracted from their wallets. Since seven o clock the previous evening until now, two am, she had accumulated no less than eight hundred pounds, and two IOU's adding to another one hundred and fifty pounds. All said and done, it had been easy money, with minimal effort. Two of her punters had lasted only a little over three minutes. They could say what they liked about diamonds but as far as any working girl was concerned, it was premature ejaculation that was every girl's best friend in this game. "Easy fucking money honey…come again why don't you." She sipped her glass of white wine from the side of her bath where she was now soaking away the `vigour's` of the day. The bottle of chilled wine sat on the floor beside her bath in an old biscuit tin half filled with cold water. As she refilled her glass she suddenly froze. Had she heard her front door handle being tried? She sat listening intently for a few moments. She dried her hands and reached down for her cigarettes, another favourite past-time of hers', smoking a cigarette with her wine in the bath-tub. To Roxanne it was the closest she would ever get to luxury. She had in one night made enough money to cover the months' rent. Everything she made now for the rest of the month was hers'. She exhaled smoke up to towards the ceiling. If only every night could be as easy as this. Still, she couldn't complain, there were plenty around here who were not as fortunate as her, struggling to feed and clothe their children. The authorities had taken that burden away from her when they decided that she wasn't fit to be a mother. She would try and do everything possible to get her little girl back. People thought that she didn't care about her daughter but she did. It was just that she had this addiction problem with heroin, and while she was a registered addict there was no chance whatsoever of her retrieving her child. She refilled her glass and took another drag of her cigarette. Again she froze. This time the sound came from her living room. A thump, like someone had banged into something accidently, a fumble. But there was definitely someone in her house, there was no doubt about it. But her front door was locked. She always locked the door no matter what time of day she had a bath. More noises now from the living room. Whoever was in here were making no secret of the fact. She sprang out of the bathtub and put on her dressing gown which had been hanging on the back of her bathroom door. All she had to defend herself with was the half-finished bottle of wine.

Before she opened her bathroom door she shouted out loud; "Who's there?"
For a few seconds she heard nothing, and then a man's voice called out in broken English. "Hurry up slut, we haven't got all night, breeng yor cheap-trash Eenglish arse out here whore, we need to be talk to you."
Roxanne retaliated in the only way she knew how.
"You'd better get to fuck out of my house or you'll be very sorry.
I'll smash this fucking wine bottle right into your fucking eyes, now get to fuck out of here, or I promise you, you will regret it, fuck off!!"
Silence.
She opened her bathroom door again and peered into her hallway.
Whoever was here had switched off her lights. The fact that her bathroom light was the only one switched on now in the whole house, made her hallway look foreboding, eerie. Again she tried to bluff her unwanted guest.
"What the fuck do you want?" She switched on her hall light.
The living room door was ajar. She could only see to the far end of the room.
She approached her living room and gently opened the door, wine bottle in hand.
Under normal circumstances she wouldn't even attempt to re-enter her living room in a situation like this but all the money she had made from the night before was in her top drawer of her sideboard. She wasn't giving that up without a fight. "I'm fucking warning you for the last time, you'd better get to fuck out of-."
A hand grabbed her seemingly from nowhere around her neck. She was thrown down onto her sofa. A very tall, very strong man sat down there beside her.
He held her in a head lock. "Behave and seet steel beach, or I break the facking neck ok? We need to be ask you some question."
Roxanne was powerless to do anything. The bottle she had wielded had been wrenched away from her without effort. Another man sat on the one and only `easy chair`. He cleared his throat before speaking. "Now then, facking Eenglish slut. We know you be talk to the Mercer. What we need to know is, where does he leeve? If you be tell us lies, we snap your facking spine ok? Now where he leeve?"
Roxanne looked at the silhouette of the stranger on her chair and answered honestly.
"I don't know where he lives. He comes here and asks me things and then he leaves here. He's not going to tell me where he lives now is he, use your head. I'm just a whore like you say, he's not going to tell a whore where he lives is he? Christ."
"He come here quite often. We see him plenty times, and sometimes with other beetch, you facking know this."
"Of course I know this, I've just told you that. But he doesn't fucking tell me where he lives, he's a detective, I'm a whore, work it out for yourselves, now do you mind getting

to fuck out of my house!"

The man who was holding her on the sofa rose to his feet and stared at her.

He stood at least six feet tall and was built like a heavyweight boxer.

He had a shaved head and dark stubble around his chin, giving him a menacing sinister look. The heavy leather coat he wore added to his maleficence.

He looked at his friend. "I don't facking believe these beetch, she facking basta liar. I think she need to wake up to thee danger she in, she facking liar whore and she know where basta Mercer leeve."

The man on the easy chair said as he lit up a cigarette; "Help her to see the danger Lukas, help her see how much trabble she in here…we serious girl."

"I know you're serious, fuck I guessed that much, but I don't-."

The man who had held her unleashed a vicious punch which landed square on Roxanne's jaw, snapping her jawbone as it did. Roxanne was now semi-conscious lying on the floor.

"Peek her up Lukas, maybe hit the other side now, break the other side of the whore jaw…help her see they danger she in."

The man held Roxanne's swollen face in his hands.

"Where thees Mercer leeve bitch" he said softly.

"Tell me and I stop thees…no more of the pain, you can help."

Even if Roxanne had anything to say, she couldn't talk if she tried. He swung back with his enormous fist and landed an even harder punch on the other side of the helpless girl's face. Roxanne was now in a world of silence and blackness. At this moment in time, Roxanne Styles didn't even exist.

The man lifted her limp body off the floor and laid her down on her sofa.

Then he bent down and retrieved three teeth from the floor and placed them upon the coffee table.

"She don't know where he leeve, she would tell if she know."

The man on the chair rose to his feet and straightened his coat.

"Well, we wait. Make tea Lukas and we wait until she stir. She know samtheeng about heem, she mast know. If she won't write it down we start on her legs and we torture the truth out…she facking know samtheeng."

The beast who'd beat on Roxanne bent over checking her radial artery in her wrist to check for a pulse. "She steel ok, but maybe another whack and she die boss, she just got faint pulse now even, she no take another punch."

"Move her on the side Lukas in case she choke from the bleeding teeth." Roxanne Styles lay on the sofa, blood pouring from her mouth. Her whole face was swollen to almost twice it's normal size. Her eyes were hidden under two puffed out orbs that protruded from each side of her temple.

She was barely alive. Both sides of her jaw completely snapped.

Although unconscious her hands were trembling and jerking violently, her body in complete shock. Roxanne had never had much luck in her life, born into a world of drug addiction and alcoholism, a violent mother and an even more violent father. She'd had to wear second hand clothes most of her life. Her clothes had been acquired from various charity shops or from her mothers' `friends` who passed on anything they thought would be useful to her, boys' jeans or shirts, it didn't matter to Roxanne's mother. The girl had never known what it was like to live in an environment where she was loved or even wanted. Was it any wonder she had turned out the way she had, selling herself for a price, and even *that* was negotiable. She'd had to fend for herself practically since she was able to talk. Growing up with absolutely no qualifications whatsoever she turned to the only thing she knew. She learned to survive using her wits and her body. She lay now in a coma-like state oblivious to anything else in the world. Only a minor miracle could save her life now, and heaven would know, she was owed a few.

The `man` named Lukas was in the kitchen making tea when Colin Green appeared from behind him and wrapped the cheese-wire around his throat.

A young lady named Sophie Spencer produced a knife from the back of her jeans and thrust it deep into the man's stomach. A ring of red spilled around the man's neck and flowed down his body. Sophie pulled out the knife from his stomach and then thrust the knife even deeper this time further down his belly. This time the man fell to his knees, gargling from his mouth and half-heartedly attempting to remove the knife.

"Sshh now" she whispered menacingly, "You just die like the dog you are...you are a very fucking lucky pig you know dying like this, you deserve to hang by the balls you Russian bastard."

Colin Green then entered the living room. He was brandishing a Magnum pistol which looked even bigger than it actually was due to the fact that Colin had attached a silencer to the end of it. Aiming it at the man's head who was seated upon the sofa he said, "I dare you to reach for the gun in your pocket, I fucking dare you. Before the man could react verbally or physically, Colin shot him in the left knee. He then proceeded to shoot out his other knee.

"Who are you working for?" he said to the Lithuanian who was now in complete agony and unable to stand. He groaned in hopeless agony, and crying with the excruciating pain.

"If I have to repeat the question then it'll cost you and arm, now, answer me. I'll give you to the count of five, one, two."

He raised the gun and aimed it at the man's shoulder.
"Three".
"Veektor Kulbertinov, please, please, don't shoot, I begging you."
Before Colin Green had infiltrated the flat he'd scanned the immediate area. There was an empty flat about four doors down from Roxanne's.
"Come in here Sophie, here take this gun. If he as much as farts, then shoot him in the throat, I won't be a minute. The ex SAS man returned to the kitchen and dragged the semi-dead Lithuanian along the short distance to the unoccupied flat.
He had already taken care of the locks.
He dragged the man through to the bathroom and laid him down into the putrid bathtub. "Whoever has been in here must have used the tub to gut fish by the stench of it. Just perfect for you my friend."
There was no way he could take any chances with this man. Although he looked at death's door just now, he would have to make absolutely sure. He produced a knife from his jacket and drew it along both of the man's wrists, twice on each wrist. There now partner, you won't be belting any more innocent little women any more...fucking hard man."
When he returned to Roxanne's flat he found Sophie having a conversation of sorts with the `gorilla`. "I'm saying Colin, this fucker was a customer at the mansion, I'm sure of it. He says he wasn't but I could almost swear he was there, and more than once if I'm not mistaken.
"Doesn't matter Sophie, shoot the bastard now, shoot him in the head.
We have to get him into the empty flat and then get an ambulance for this poor wretch, Christ he's messed her up bad. Shoot him in the head Sophie, if you can do it, if not I'll do it, there's no time angel, we have to help this girl."
Without a moment's hesitation Sophie Spencer raised the gun and held it in both hands firing a shot into the centre of the man's brow. She then fired a second shot into his mouth. Foam rose up into the air above Roxanne's sofa, fluttering back down onto the corpse's head. After they had disposed of the corpse, they called for an ambulance for Roxanne Styles. To the paramedics it would just look like someone had attacked the woman and ransacked the flat. An old dirty-looking antimacassar would hide the bullet holes for now. There would be no search for further bodies. Although whoever would be allocated the flat down the hall would get an unbelievable shock, finding the two Lithuanians in the stinking bath tub, behind the rancid shower curtain.
"There's money in here" said Sophie who had had a quick scan of the drawers. "Take it Sophie, and keep it for her, because sure as hell, someone will help themselves to it if we don't. Not all coppers are good guys Sophie."

She looked at Colin, nodding. "I fucking know that Mister Green. I learned that in Lithuania."

As Colin Green and Sophie Spencer made their way out of the area, an ambulance could be heard approaching fast. Whether or not it was fast enough would remain to be seen. Roxanne Styles was beginning to haemorrhage.

Colin and Sophie had only driven a few hundred metres when Sophie exclaimed, "Stop the car, quickly, stop the car!" Sophie only just managed to reach the pavement before emptying the contents of her stomach. Down on her hunkers she spewed for more than two minutes. Finally, pale as a sheet, she climbed back into the car. "Sorry about that Colin, I've never killed anyone before, it was the shock-."

"I know what it was Sophie, and I shouldn't have encouraged you to do it."

"You didn't encourage me, and you know it. I didn't feel any pity for that bastard I stabbed, and neither did I feel any remorse for shooting the other pig, so even if you weren't letting me come along with you I would still be doing this.

They fucked me up well and truly in Lithuania, and the law over here doesn't seem to be in any hurry to do anything about it, fuck they're back over here abducting more girls. Well, if I hear about where they are I will do my utmost to find and kill them. They are ruthless and relentless and unmerciful, fine, I will be too, they will suffer before they die. You didn't see what we had to endure over there Colin, I don't know if your daughter has disclosed any details to you, but I can tell you now, it changed my opinion on human beings, I can tell you that, and it's changed my opinion on the politics of this country...fine, I'll deal with it in my own way."

Nothing more was said as Colin drove on into the night. Sophie wasn't Sophie any more, and Colin Green was beginning to feel like he'd maybe made a mistake.

She would return back home without her mother having any suspicion as to what she'd been doing. Colin Green had taken great pains to clean up behind them in both flats, and leaving it difficult to say the least for the forensics to be able to pin anything on them. As far as Mandy Spencer was concerned, Sophie was out dating a young boy she'd met recently. Sophie had never lied to her mother before, but then, there had been a lot of things that Sophie Spencer had done recently that she hadn't done before, and it was this that had now changed the person she'd been into this revenge hell-bent ferocious teenager who would kill at the drop of a hat.

From the young sprightly girl who'd been heading off to school that day with not a care in the world, other than the annoying weather, she had transformed into a cold callous human being, with not a care about the value of a human soul.

There was no right or wrongs now in Sophie's mind, only justice...and revenge.

The people who had used and abused her body for weeks on end in Lithuania, had inadvertently poisoned her mind. Violence now was her only true friend. Violence made amends for wrong-doings. Using it was the only reliable guarantee that she had, to make sure that that would never again happen to her. The British justice system was inadequate. In fact, the British Justice system was shit.

St MARY'S ROYAL INFIRMARY.

STRATFORD.

Terry Mercer and Polly Shepard stood looking over the bed of Roxanne Styles. The only reason they knew it was Roxanne was because the name-tag on the bar of her bed told them so, along with the medical chart hanging beside it containing all the information of her numerous serious injuries. Wires and tubes protruded from several parts of her body. An intravenous drip stood like a robot beside her bed, tentacles hanging down connecting to Roxanne's arm giving the woman the nutrition she required. Her bloated face reminded Mercer of a giant balloon with some of the air taken out of it. Almost all of her face was purple and black. Even from where he stood he could see that several of her teeth had been extracted. One side of her head had been shaved. He stood with his hands in his pockets just staring at the mess in front of him that used to be a pretty woman. Another machine beeped and buzzed quietly monitoring her pulse.
Roxanne had just had major surgery. She'd had a blood-clot very close to the brain.
A six-hour operation had been performed by two major neurosurgeons.
Neither of them were confident that Roxanne would recover.
One of the surgeons had spoken with Mercer trying to explain the extent of some of Roxanne's injuries, additional to the blood clot.
"Miss Styles has suffered multiple fractures on both the Mandible and Maxilla bones, on both sides of her face.
There was blood-clotting in her Maxillary Sinus which caused the blood clot near her brain.
She also has damage to her Colum and spine.
She has sustained extensive inner ear injury as well.
Damage in her Cochlea and Labyrinth near the nerves of her ear is also noticeable. How bad, we cannot say at the moment. If she survives, it's quite possible that she could lose the hearing in her left ear, as I say, if, she survives. We've managed to pin both her Mandible and Maxilla together again but she'll be fed by drip for the near future, if she em...if she can manage to...pull through. We've done all we can detective Mercer it's just a matter of how strong she is, or how much of a will she has to live. She's suffered quite a beating I don't mind telling you."
Terry hadn't really taken in half of what the surgeon had said to him, but he knew without question that Roxanne Styles was literally fighting for her life.
Polly excused herself and set off to find the latrines but Terry could see that his superior

was visibly shaken at the sight of poor Roxanne. He pulled up a chair and sat it down beside Roxanne's bed. Ever so gently he touched her arm and tapped it smiling at the unconscious woman. In his mind he prayed for her. There certainly wouldn't be anyone else coming to talk to her, other than her daughter perhaps.

Outwardly, he whispered to her.

"You can do this girl, this is no problem to you. You're made of hardy stuff lady. It'll take more than this to beat Roxanne Styles. I need you to get better, so that I can look after you and watch out for you. You can fight Roxanne, better than any of the rest of us. You won't give up little angel. I'm coming to your house for tea and cigarettes sweetheart, and a chat. I have to go soon, but I'll be back to see you.

I'll be back every day to see you my brave angel. Now you fight Roxanne, do you hear me? We are friends now, and I don't have many of those left, so I'm counting on you to get better, I'll see you tomorrow princess ok?"

Terry rubbed her arm ever so gently and kissed her on her forehead and then rose to his feet, wiping a tear from his eye.

He turned to look just before he exited the room.

She lay motionless on the hospital bed, machines beeping quietly and green and red lights flashing off and on...keeping her stable, he supposed.

He wondered if this was going to be the last time that he would see Roxanne Styles `alive`.

UNKNOWN LOCATION.

Sandra Knox suddenly released an ear-splitting scream as she regained consciousness from the sedatives, making Samantha jump with fright and waking her out of a dazed sleep. "Hello? Can you hear me"? She said to the petrified girl.
"Where am I? What do you want from me? Why am I bound to this chair?" Samantha had to calm the girl down. At least attempt to. "I'm tied up as well, are you blindfolded?"
"Yes, and my hands and legs are tied as well, why have they kidnapped us? What have we done? I'm so cold."
"I know, so am I. What's your name?"
"My name is Sandra Knox, what have they done with my dog? Where's Floppy?" Samantha tried to calm her again. "I don't know what they've done with your dog Sandra. Listen, I am a detective. These people have abducted me. I'm not sure how long it will be, but my colleagues will come looking for us. I have no idea where we are but I'm sure they'll come and get us. What we have to do Sandra is remain as calm as possible sweetheart. I know it's hard, but if we stay calm then we'll hear what they talk about when they come back here, perhaps they'll give us a clue as to where we are...but we have to stay calm ok Sandra?" She could hear the girl crying.
It was understandable, snatched from her everyday life into a nightmare of hellish proportions. It would be hard indeed for any girl to stay calm. The reality was very different though, Sandra knew. It was alright telling the girl to remain calm but she knew what ordeals would face the teenager if help did not arrive, and anyway, arrive from where? No-one knew where they were.
"I'm sure they'll be here soon Sandra to get us out of here. At least we have each other to talk to. I've been here alone for quite a while now, it's good to be able to talk to someone."
"I need to pee." The girl said, her voice quivering.
"I know, so do I Sandra. Maybe our captors will return and allow us to use the bathroom, just try to not think about it. If they come back Sandra, do not say a thing unless they ask you a question, ok? Don't speak unless they speak to you first. These people can be quite violent when they're riled. They're not going to kill you, I can guarantee that sweetheart. If you behave they'll be ok with you I'm sure. As for me, I don't know what they plan to do with me. They know I'm a detective...they don't like me very much." Suddenly, they could hear the sound of car tyres on the gravel up above them. Car doors opened and closed and now footsteps could be heard walking

upon the bare floorboards. Another door opened in the house, and then numerous footsteps could be heard descending the stairs. The door burst open. High-heeled footsteps walked across the floor. Claire Redgrave removed the blindfold from Sandra Knox's face.

"Oh, you're awake slut, that's nice. Oh Angela was right, you are a pretty one aren't you, you'll be worth a few quid."

Through fear more than anything else, Sandra forgot what Samantha had told her. "Who are you? What do you want with me? And why are you calling me a slut, I haven't-"

Claire Redgrave unleashed a hard slap on to the right side of Sandra's face making her scream pitifully. This would be the first time in Sandra Knox's life that an adult had actually struck her. Her voice now came out as a whisper.

"Why? Why are you hurting me?"

Another hard slap, this time on the opposite side of her face.

"I'm learning you little scrubber to talk only when spoken to, are you starting to grasp the situation slut?"

Samantha shouted out loud, "Don't talk Sandra, don't say another word sweetheart, they're just scum babes, they're just cowardly scum."

High-heeled steps could be heard as Clair Redgrave stepped over to Samantha's chair. With her fist Redgrave smacked Samantha square on the chin, sending her reeling over the back of the chair and cracking her head on the floor.

"Pick her up David."

Sandra watched one of the two men who accompanied this woman pick Samantha up from the floor, still attached to the chair, and place her back where she had been. Redgrave stood back and unleashed an even harder punch onto Samantha's face, this time bursting open her nose, and again she fell to the floor attached to the chair.

"Pick her up David."

"Leave her alone!"

Sandra cried in desperation, "Just leave her alone, why are you doing this?"

This time the other man stepped over to Sandra's chair and produced a pocket knife. He then proceeded to cut the girl's clothes, starting with her top.

The girl screamed in fear.

"Leave her be just now John. Go back up there and make us all a nice cup of tea, we need to have a chat in here. We need to explain to Sandra why exactly she is here, and why we had to kill this fucking bitch here right in front of her, oh, and fetch my bag from the car please, I left my cigarettes in there, and don't be all fucking day John about it.

And you!"

She looked at Samantha.

"Your fucking time is up bitch. We no longer need to keep you alive. You are now surplus to requirements bitch. I'm having this cup of tea and then I'm going to put a bullet in your head. We now know where bastard Mercer lives, we found out easily enough. Your `colleague` mister Briggs informed us of his address. He really is so helpful. It was he who informed us of your address, wasn't that nice of him."

Blood streamed down Samantha's face from her nose onto her blouse.

Again, Samantha decided not to say anything in reply to the bitch who she would dearly love to face in a one on one situation, but that was never going to happen. They were going to kill her and that was that. There was nothing she could do to save the teenager sitting close to her either, and by the sound of things, there were many more going to be joining her in Lithuania. On top of everything else they were talking about raping her in front of the girl and then make her watch as they shot her. Claire Redgrave stepped forward again. Samantha could feel her breath on her face. She flinched as she suddenly felt cold steel on her burning ear. Redgrave cut away the masking tape and tore it roughly from Samantha's eyes.

"Now, you open your mouth one more time to me and I promise you I'll pluck both of your eyes right out of their sockets."

She held a long pointed knife in front of Samantha's face.

Samantha winced at the sudden exposure to light having been blind-folded for so many hours.

"You might as well see what happens to you when my friends rape you, you interfering bitch. It'll be the last bit of fun you'll have before you fuck off to the sweet by and by. And Sandra here can tell her friends over in Lithuania just how much of a slut you really were."

The innocent petrified teen shouted out, "You've got the wrong person, I don't know anyone in Lithuania, *I* don't have any friends in Lithuania."

John Buckley had exited the house to retrieve Claire's cigarettes from the car whilst the kettle was boiling. As he approached the vehicle he could see the car in the distance turning into the drive and heading towards them. It was not a vehicle he recognised. What was he to do? Should he run inside and inform Claire of the approaching car, and by doing so, perhaps make a complete fool of himself in the process if it turned out to be friends of theirs, or did he stay put and hide until he found out for sure. He decided to hide in the bushes until he knew for certain. The red BMW 3 series pulled in to the car park just short of Claire Redgrave's white Mercedes-Benz C class. Buckley lay flat on

the ground, peering through the tall grass at these intruders. He knew one of them. There was no mistaking Terry Mercer. Buckley mumbled to himself. "How the fuck has he found out about *this* house?" He was the cause of all this trouble and inconveniences to their lucrative `game`. He was accompanied by another two men, probably detectives as well. He watched as the three men entered the house. Another predicament.
Does he follow straight away or does he wait to find out the outcome.
They would take Claire and David by surprise there was no doubt about that. Being the coward that he was, he remained where he was until the confrontation had come to an end…he wasn't that keen on Claire Redgrave anyway.

Back in the basement of the mansion Claire Redgrave was explaining in great detail to Sandra Knox the reason she had been abducted, and what exactly was going to happen to her. "You see Sandra, we deliver cute little girls like yourself to our friends in Lithuania and they pay us handsomely for finding you. You are going to be a very busy little whore, working your cute-ass off for your employer. You will sleep with loads and loads of men and women and you will make your employer a happy man. In other words Sandra, you will whore yourself for your keep. Oh I hear the girls really enjoy their new life-style once they get used to it. Most of them turn out to be really grateful little scrubbers, and you will too once you get your head round it. From what I hear, some of the girls get massive tips from their customers for enthusiastic performances…you'll even be on first name terms with lots of them. Everything you've ever known in your life, well, just forget about it now, your mum and dad as well, they're all in your past. Your new job and your new life is to be a busy little whore, so, that's why we abducted you, oh and don't worry about your little dog, we left him tied to a tree. Some kind soul would stop and give him a home or return him to your parents, they'll be happy now they've got their little dog back home with them. As for you, they'll be adjusting to life without you even as we speak."
"Will they now?" said Terry Mercer pointing his trusty Magnum at Claire Redgrave's head.
"You fucking move really slowly across to Samantha there and you untie her.
If you as much as breathe on her, I will blow your head clean off your disgusting fucking shoulders. And you!" He pointed to David Wilton, another of Redgrave's associates.
"You untie this girl here as well, and remember, one silly move and your head comes off as well, now move…slowly. Face me and my colleagues as you do it. In fact, both of you, relieve yourselves of your firearms first before you do anything else, slowly."
Mercer stepped forward towards Redgrave. She pulled out her handgun from her

denim jacket and briefly looked at it. "It's up to you bitch, if you think you're fast enough, you try if you want."

Redgrave placed the gun on the floor.

David Wilton done the same with his.

They both stood awaiting further instructions.

"What the fuck are you waiting for, get them untied you fucking rats, I've told you what to do and how to do it."

As soon as Samantha was untied she rose up to her feet. She was cramped from sitting so long in that one position, her nose still bleeding. After a few moments she walked over to Terry Mercer and took the Magnum from his hand.

"Step aside Terry, look away Sandra.

On your fucking knees bitch!" she said to Redgrave. "On your fucking knees now, and beg me for your life."

Redgrave looked at her, sneering, thinking she'd be safe within the `law`.

"Never in a million years will I ever beg to you for anything you filthy cunt!"

"Fine, have it your way" said Samantha Reynolds smiling.

Once again she warned Sandra Knox to look away.

Without further hesitation she shot Redgrave in the head.

The corpse fell to the floor in a crumpled heap.

Terry Mercer was genuinely shocked.

Wilton immediately fell to his knees. "She made us do it, it was her, she was the one who made us kidnap the girls, her and Angela Bates. I'll tell you anything you want to know, just don't shoot me, please, I'm begging you."

Outside in the car park John Buckley heard the gun going off. It had started.

He waited to hear more gun shots. He heard nothing more, no shouting or screaming, nothing, and no-one coming out either. He was confused.

He positioned himself closer to the house hoping to hear or see something that would give him encouragement. Nothing happened. No-one appeared.

Finally, with his gun in his hand, he decided to creep into the house and try and hear what was going on down in the basement.

As he reached the end of the hallway, he heard voices coming from below.

Then he heard David Wilton's voice begging for his life and...crying. Hard man Wilton, crying? "The situation must be dire." He would sneak back out and escape in the Mercedes before any of this lot down here could follow him.

First he would relieve their car tyres of some of the air in them to further his chances of escape. Should there be any repercussions from Angela he would explain that he was coming for help and that he sensed his friends were in trouble. He reversed back in the

Mercedes and began to drive towards the safety of the road. He had only driven a few yards when he felt the gun on his neck.

"Just pull up nice and slow pal, nice and easy, and after you stop the car you make sure you keep your hands on that fucking steering wheel, your life depends on it." Buckley pulled the car up to a halt and switched off the engine. Both of his hands were firmly on the steering wheel.

"Just answer my questions ok? Said Colin Green as he dug the pistol into Buckley's neck. "Are you carrying any weapons?"

Buckley nodded his head.

"Ok, place your hands upon your head and keep them there until further notice. Open your door first, then climb out…with your hands on your head, and then get down on your knees, do you understand what I've just said to you?"

Buckley nodded again.

"Ok, proceed, and remember, your life depends on your obedience."

Buckley climbed out of the car and done as he was told.

"Sophie? Relieve him of his gun sweetheart."

From the back of the car Sophie Spencer climbed out and searched the man thoroughly. He was only carrying one weapon. With his hands on his head John Buckley knelt obediently on the gravel car-park wondering what they were going to do with him. Colin Green stepped forward into his view.

"Right, back to the questions my friend. Now, this quiz has certain rules, and very strict ones. If for any reason Sophie or I think that you're telling lies, then you will receive harsh punishment. By that I mean that you could quite easily lose a limb. A hand or a foot or something, but the quiz will continue believe me until we have obtained the information we require, are we quite clear on the rules of the quiz bud?"

Buckley nodded his head again.

"Ok then, Sophie here has a list. Each time she ticks off the required answers the better your chance of survival, are you ready?"

Buckley said nothing.

Five minutes later, Sophie and Colin Green had Angela Bates' address of her `safe-house` along with the name of the hotel where Kulbertinov and Saratov were staying. They also had the name of the fishing boat which was due to sail off to Europe the following morning, and where that boat was docked.

"One final question my friend. How many of your scum friends are in there with my friends?"

Buckley held up two fingers.

"You're quite sure about that are you? I don't want to have to execute you because of

your absent-minded mathematics."
Buckley croaked. "There are only two, Claire Redgrave and David Wilton, that's all that's here."
"Over to you Sophie." said Green, smiling at Buckley.
Sophie approached the prisoner and got down on her hunkers in front of him.
"Hi" she said quietly. "My name is Sophie Spencer. The name won't mean anything to you, but you were probably partly at least responsible for my kidnapping. Now, it's my turn to ask you some questions, only this time it's a lose lose situation for you. Do you know what a bullwhip is?"
Buckley looked up at the girl with great fear.
"Do you!?"
"Yes." He managed.
"Ok then, this is what's going to happen. This quiz is called truth or bear."
She walked over to the BMW and opened the back door. She pulled out a bullwhip from the back seat and walked back over to the now petrified John Buckley. She got down on her hunkers again and spread out the whip in front of him. In a maleficent whisper she said, "This is all yours...pal."
Colin Green leaned on the car and rolled himself a cigarette.
He shouted over to John Buckley. "I've been teaching her how to use it John. She's really good...a fast learner you see, aren't we all John."
"First question John." said Sophie. "Now then, were you involved with the kidnapping of any of the girls in and around the boroughs of London, yes or no?" Buckley's head went down. "Three seconds to answer one...two."
"Yes, yes I was involved."
"That's good, at least you're honest about how much of a fucking loser you are. Now, what do you want, do you want the gun? Or the whip?
If I use the gun, I won't be killing you mind, I'll just be shooting your hand off or your foot, and then we'll continue. If you choose the whip, then it's just three hard lashes on your bare back...and then we'll continue with the questioning, so, what's it to be pal?"
John Buckley looked up at the girl and pleaded with her not to use the whip.
He promised to give them all the information he could regarding the kidnappings, and anything else he could help them with concerning Angela Bates.
"It's not as easy as that John." said Colin Green. "You see, my daughter was one of the innocent girls you lot abducted and sent to their fate in Lithuania.
You were in no fucking hurry to help the authorities then were you?
You were quite happy working for your whore Angela Bates and co whilst you raked in a share of the profits you made from that old Lithuanian bastard.

My daughter was forced to have sex with numerous hideous-looking fuckers like yourself. No, you need to learn a lesson sonny boy. You need to be degraded and hurt and humiliated beyond belief.

Sophie here suffered the same fate as my daughter, and possibly worse. And you think you can just sit and beg forgiveness and everything will be forgotten, is that what you think? Sophie has been mentally scarred for life. Her life, like that of my daughters' will never be the same again thanks to you and your scum friends, well, your day is done pal. Your goose is cooked."

Colin Green stepped over to Buckley and lifted him by his arms and walked him over to the Mercedes.

"Take your shirt off John."

"Please, I beg you please don't do this to –"

"Too late John." said Colin Green, smiling. "Way too late buddy, you left all those girls to their fate and you didn't give a fuck about them now did you? Be honest, it never entered your head to help them in any way, and why should you?

You were making loads of money from them weren't you?

The more girls you kidnapped, the more money you made. But you see John, fate is a funny thing isn't it pal. One minute you could be sailing on lovely calm waters, your life as sweet as it could possibly be, the next, as in this moment here, you could be placed in a corner of some immensity in hell as Sophie here will verify to you just shortly, come on, shirt off John, it's payback time buddy, time to pay your debts."

Buckley reluctantly removed his shirt and threw it to the ground.

"Don't throw it away John." said Sophie, "you'll need it to wipe the blood from your back. I'll warn you now, this is going to be bloody painful, honestly, I mean, really painful, so brace yourself." She stepped over to the bushes and retrieved a small stick.

"Here, bite on this John, I've seen it in the movies, it must help with pain thing." She jammed the stick into his mouth. "Fucking bite on this!"

Without saying anything else, Colin Green pushed John Buckley over the bonnet of the car face down. Sophie rolled the whip in the air and flicked with her wrist, making a loud cracking sound in the air.

"Hear that John? The next one will be on your back, are you ready?"

"Oh please, I'm begging you, don't do this."

Sophie stood enough distance from herself and the `animal` in front of her.

She remembered her first encounter with a greasy fat Lithuanian businessman as he took her from behind, and as she begged to him not to proceed.

"That's what I said John, the first time I was raped. Didn't fucking do me any good though."

She drew back with her right arm and unleashed an ear-splitting crack on the man's back, making him roar with the pain as the leather ripped into his skin.
Buckley fell to the ground.
"Come on John, we've only just started." said Colin Green, picking him back up and throwing his body back over the car.
Sophie stood back again and stretched the whip out to its' full length.
Then she unleashed an even harder blow to his back, catching him on the back of the head as well as his back. Again the man fell to the ground screaming.
"Up we get John." said Green. "Come on, one more and then you'll get a couple of minutes reprieve pal…before she continues, you're getting bloody good with that Sophie, but after your next shot, I'm going to show you how to get the full use of the weapon, so that you can administer really hard meaningful swipes."

Fifteen minutes later, and after John Buckley had received fifteen lashes from the skin-ripping weapon, he was dragged down the stairs of the mansion by the legs, his face bumping down each of the steps. They dropped the limp body of John Buckley onto the floor as they entered the room.
"It's a good job me and Sophie were here Terry, or you were all goners boy.
This piece of shit was on his way to inform Angela Bates of the activities going on here. They would have been here with God knows how many rats…you wouldn't have stood a chance."
Terry Mercer looked at Colin Green, smiling. "Yeah, thanks Colin, but we would have managed."
Colin handed Terry a piece of paper. Mercer looked at it briefly.
"Yes I know Colin. Polly put surveillance on to Briggs, found out everything we needed, but hey, good work my friend."
He took one look at the back of the man on the floor, "Somebody's handiwork?"
"Yeah, it was Sophie mostly, I had a couple of cracks at him, but it was mainly Sophie's handiwork. He'll think twice now before he kidnaps any more girls…he was crying before Sophie had even started with the whip, but boy, when she started…"
Terry had numerous things to talk to Colin about, but here and now was not the right time. He couldn't allow him to go on with this vigilante-type revenge, although Mercer and Samantha were very grateful for Colin's presence, and Sophie's.
Samantha was busy going through Claire Redgrave's belongings in her jacket, finding only a couple of pieces of paper with telephone numbers written upon them. Sophie stepped forward, handing Samantha Redgrave's hand bag.
"This was in the Mercedes outside." she said, glancing at the corpse on the floor.

Samantha thanked her and stood up approaching Terry Mercer.

"How the hell did you find us Terry? I didn't hold much hope of you finding me, none in fact. As far as you were concerned it must have looked like I'd just disappeared."

"It was all thanks to Polly Samantha, Polly and Colin here…and Sophie."

"Terry, it's bloody Colin Briggs, that's who's been giving them all the information, this piece of shit on the floor here informed me. Very proud she was of the fact that it was one of our own who was helping them all along. How the hell did Polly find out, or even get suspicious?"

Mercer shrugged his shoulders.

"Don't know Samantha, but I'm sure as hell pleased that she did."

Samantha then approached Sandra Knox who was being consoled by the two detectives who'd accompanied Terry.

"Are you ok Sandra? It's all good now sweetheart. As soon as we get back home we'll inform your parents that you are safe and well."

The teenager stared at Samantha with fear in her eyes having just witnessed her shooting a woman in the head. How could she talk to her like this now, so pleasantly?

"We are very lucky Sandra, me and you. This could have turned out so much worse. We'll have you home very soon I promise. Go and get her some tea."

She instructed the detectives who looked at her disdainfully, but then led the girl past the unconscious body of John Buckley up to the kitchen. Samantha could see that the girl was reluctant to get to her feet. Then she saw why. Poor Sandra had wet herself with fear through all of these proceedings.

Mercer approached and blew out a sigh of relief.

"I'm so relieved Samantha that you're safe and well, I honestly thought I'd lost you…thought they would take you over to Lithuania and…you know, and that would be the last we would see of you."

"Where the hell am I Terry? I have no idea how many times they sedated me, I've lost all track of time."

"We're in an old mansion just outside of High Wycombe Samantha, it's in Buckinghamshire, that's where we are."

"I bloody know High Wycombe is in Buckinghamshire wise ass, oh it doesn't take you long does it, to get back to your sarcasm."

She pointed to John Buckley lying on the floor.

"What the hell are we going to do with him?" Samantha was referring to the hideous mess that used to be the skin of the mans' back, and how they would explain it to their superiors.

Before Mercer had a chance to reply Colin Green stepped forward with a Glock pistol and shot the man in the back of the head." There, that's how you'll explain it Samantha, he went for his gun." He then turned and shot David Wilton in the head. "Both of them went for their guns."

"Jess Christ Colin! Hey, just cut it out! You can't keep killing people like this!"

He grabbed the gun from Green and pulled him to one side.

"Sit down here, and you listen to me! It's over Colin, it's fucking over, do you hear me? If you as much as pull someone's hair I'll take you in and prosecute you.

I know what they done, I know what you and your wife and family have been through, but hey, no more. This fucking stops now. You're encouraging that school girl to bloody kill at will. Do you know the damage that *you* are doing?"

He sighed deeply. "Listen Colin, I am grateful for all your help my friend, and we probably couldn't have done any of this without your help, I appreciate that, but this is not a free-for-all Colin, you're not in the army any more. I'll cover this up today with that on the floor, but after today Colin, it has to stop. It's done.

Now, do we have a deal?"

The ex SAS man nodded his head in silence, as though in defeat.

"Ok Terry, it's a deal, but let me tell you something. If anyone ever approaches any of my family or friends and threatens their lives or well-being in any way, I swear I'll do the time, because I will without a shadow of a doubt blow them straight to hell. No-one is ever going to put my family through this ever again."

He pointed to the body of John Buckley. "You see that there Terry? That is the start of total disorder in our country, fucking running around spending money and living the high-life from their profits selling their own people down the drain for some deranged old bastard who can hardly speak a word of our language. You saw his fucking mansion in Lithuania Terry. You saw how he lives. Fancy cars and houses and the best of everything, all bought from the profits of these innocent school girls who's lives had not even begun, thinking himself untouchable and impenetrable. Well, he may be able to hide from you, but he won't be successful hiding from me I can guarantee you that. I'll stop just now Terry, but as soon as it starts again, and believe me it will, I'll be back out there searching for the culprits, and I will deal with them in a way that the law can't, that way I guarantee you they will never reoffend. And you're asking *me* if I know the damage *I'm* causing? Sophie feels justified Terry, that three of the bastards who completely ripped her life apart are dead. She got to inflict a bit of pain onto one of the bastards who made her worst nightmare come true. That's not damage Terry. That's not deranged…that's called revenge Terry, that's what it's called, and there's nothing wrong with that, there's nothing wrong with revenge. She knows as well as you do what would have become of them if they were put on trial. They would each receive some meaningless sentence that would be reduced with remission after a couple of years, and they would go out there and do exactly the fucking same thing again. Someone else's kid heading off to school with their whole lives in front of them, snatched away never to be seen again. Tell me you disagree Terry with anything I have just said. Tell me if there was at any point in that statement that I told a lie."

Samantha stepped forward. "Colin, leave Terry out of this, he's doing his job. You're talking there like it's almost his fault that these low-lives walk away. We do our jobs Colin, and we do them well. Our job is to withhold the law. Sometimes we are not in total agreement with the law, but we still uphold it. As far as your defending your family is concerned, no-one could blame you for having that attitude, many people would hold the same view as yourself, but I'm going to tell you something now, and I speak to you now as a friend. If, at any time in the future, you feel it necessary to kill someone, then all I can say is you'd better cover your tracks very carefully, because if we find out it's you who has committed the murder, then we will not hesitate to put you on trial, and you can find out for yourself just how meaningless the sentences in this country really are."

"Yeah? and what about you Samantha? Did I not just witness you killing a woman in cold blood? Or do the rules only apply to people outside of the law. You shot her in the fucking head and you done the right thing and fine well you know it. You've done the country a favour. She's beat you up a bit by the looks of things, and as soon as the opportunity arose, you took the chance to inflict revenge on her. Well done I say, she won't cause anyone else any misery...end of.

You and Terry here have tried your best to help me through all this, right from the word go, but I have to say, your help would be to no avail if you rely upon the law of this land. All those fucking slime-balls out there will have been taking note of proceedings in all these kidnapping stories they've seen on their news programmes in the last few months, and they'll be trying to cash in on the abduction game.

You'll see, this won't stop now I can guarantee it, so you better be prepared for wild goose-chases you'll be sent on. What you've just experienced in the last few months is just the beginning."

Colin Green sat down on a chair next to the corpse of Claire Redgrave, and rolled a cigarette.

"I know you guys have rules to go by, and yes, I shouldn't have done that there, not in front of you anyway, but the bastard deserves what he got and I just know that you two agree with me, I just know it."

Even Colin Green looked shocked as Sophie Spencer stood and spat over the corpse of John Buckley and proclaimed, "I should have whipped him a whole fucking lot more

Colin, I should have lashed the skin of his face as well before you killed him. He's right mister Mercer, they are taking the piss out of the law. All those things me and my friends went through? They laugh and joke about it as they share out the money they make from selling us. Colin is right to do what he does. His daughter was there with me. Unless you've been raped mister Mercer, you don't know how anyone feels. I want to rip the skin off every one of those bastards who interfered with me and my friends. I want to hear them scream for mercy…just like I did."

SCOTLAND YARD.

BROADWAY VICTORIA.

Everything had been brought to a close. Kulbertinov and Saratov had both been unsuccessful in their attempt to be tried in Lithuania. Extradition was not an option for them. They would be tried and sentenced here in Britain, and they would serve the full sentence in this country. Colin Briggs, one of Scotland Yard's own was also being held in custody until his trial came up. Another detective from Manchester was also being held in custody having been part of the corruption with Briggs. Money had been paid into these men's bank accounts on a regular basis from an undisclosed source. Large amounts of money. When Colin Briggs' house was searched, a list of names and addresses were found in a valise belonging to him. Dozens of photographs of young school girls were found there also. Crude hand-made maps and routes were discovered along with certain times written beside some of them. He had obviously been observing the girls, watching when and where they were in certain secluded areas on a regular basis. As far as Terry Mercer was concerned, Briggs was as guilty as the men who had actually had sex with these girls. If he had his way, he would hang him.
Instead, he would have to let the course of justice run its' predictable paths which would inevitably be disappointing as far as the sentencing was concerned.
He understood perfectly Colin Green's point of view.
Terry and Samantha sat before Polly Shepard each sipping their cups of coffee. Both detectives had been praising and thanking their superior for the role she played in apprehending the criminals. They had to ask her just what it was that had made her put surveillance on Briggs and therefore discover his involvement with the kidnappings. Polly had answered them smiling.
"I knew you'd ask me that, and I can't deny the fact, that yet again Terry, it was you. You see I do listen to what you say when you're not spitting out profanations all the time. You sat in here one day, months ago and said something to me about detective Briggs. Seeing that he'd been posted up in the north in Manchester, you actually said to me, and Samantha in fact, that you were curious as to how he could give you a name and address for someone around here, when he was up there. On top of that Terry, he'd only been on the case for a couple of days or so when he gave you that name. Well, I kept that in mind. Recently I was going through names of detectives who were on this case and I just happened to look at his file.
I then received information from one of our officers informing me that he'd been seen

with two women and a couple of men quite a few times, in bars and restaurants in *this* area when he should have been up north. That's what sparked it off Terry. The rest as they say, is history."

Mercer rose to wash out his cup at the sink.

"Where are you going Terry on your week off, anywhere nice?" said Polly finishing off her coffee. As he dried his cup he turned to look at her.

"I'm going up to Wolverhampton, I'm going to visit a couple of people I know there…used to know anyway." As soon as Terry had said Wolverhampton Polly knew exactly where he was heading. She also knew that these trips up there done him no good whatsoever because they were just reminders of how cruel and ruthless people in the world could be. His wife and son had lived in a state of vegetation now for almost three years, but now and then Terry would take the time to go and visit them, even though they hadn't a clue who he was. He used to tell her that he went to visit them to soothe his soul but every time he returned, he would come back all bleak and moody and snapping at everyone who spoke to him. To Polly, it wasn't soul-soothing, it was gut-wrenching, even soul-destroying. But Terry Mercer would make the visit two or three times a year.

"What about you Samantha? What have you got planned for your week off?" "Nothing Polly, nothing at all, I think I'm just grateful that I'm alive and well, and I know Terry here was really worried about me, he was missing me badly Polly, pining even I would say."

To Samantha's astonishment, Terry did not disagree with anything she had said. In fact, he didn't say anything. Polly sat and raised her eye-brows to Samantha, inviting her to say something else to him. "It's none of my business Terry, but if you fancied a bit of company I could come with you, I mean, I don't know who these people are who you're going to see, but I could be some company for you if you fancied a passenger up there…only if you're-"

"That'd be lovely Samantha. But this is not what you think. These people who I'm visiting are not friends. They're not anything anymore, unfortunately, but they were the two most important people in my life at one time. My whole life was built around them. And then some sick bitch from my past came and took them away from me, excuse me."

Terry left the office to go to the latrines. Polly knew why.

"The two people he's talking about Samantha are his wife and son.

They were abducted by a very deranged woman who paid for an even sicker brain surgeon to, how shall I say it, alter their personalities. He'll tell you all about it on the way up there no doubt. You remember one day Samantha, you said to me that you thought that there was something eating away at Terry…well this is it. As I say, he'll tell you all about it soon enough. I'll be quite honest with you Samantha, he's never really been quite the same since. He's had some time of it. That's half the reason for his short-temperedness and his cutting remarks to everyone, bloody snapping and biting, but, I persevere with it because he's a bloody diamond Sam and I don't mind telling you. Underneath all that bravado stuff, he's a bloody good man, and of the rarest quality. He even looks out for me Samantha. It was he who advised me to get rid of my womanising husband and kick him into touch, which I did. I now have a new relationship with another man and I have never been happier in all my life, and it's all down to Terry."

"Perhaps I shouldn't go with him if it upsets him so much, I had no idea that it was something like this that was tearing at his heart, I knew something was."

"No, you go with him Samantha, it'll help to keep him sane. If he has you there with him it'll give him something else to think about instead of coming away from the place like he usually does all messed up. You go with him Samantha…he'll be really grateful for your company. I'll tell you something else, he was really worried when you were missing, I can tell you that, I mean really worried, frantic even. For whatever reason Samantha, I don't know. But you are something really special in his life, that's all I'm saying about that just now. He was lost without you Samantha, and that's the truth."

BELMARSH.

MAXIMUM SECURITY PRISON.

WOOLWICH SOUTH EAST LONDON.

Michael Saratov and Viktor Kulbertinov were in serious trouble. Their request for extradition had been rejected. They both knew that they would now face the full force of the British justice system. Money or influences in high-places would not be beneficial in this situation. They had both been separated from the moment they were brought here and so had no opportunity to come up with any kind of defence. It would have done them little good anyway because Scotland Yard had photographs and multiple eye-witness accounts of what was going on in Lithuania, and of the organised kidnappings here in Britain. Before they'd been arrested in the Warrington Hotel in central London, they had received the news of Claire Redgrave's death.
Whoever had disclosed their whereabouts to Scotland Yard was irrelevant now. There was no escaping this time. Saratov had come close back home but he had connections there who helped him out of the situation, for a price of course, but he had the evidence that could pose a threat to their marriages, so a deal was done. But here, he had absolutely nothing, no-one. Michael Saratov sat with his head in his hands on the small bed in the corner of his cell. The only visitors he'd received were a man and a woman from the NCA. (National Crime Agency.) and a gentleman from the Lithuanian Embassy. Saratov had thought that this man would be his ticket out of here but he was wrong. In fact, the man looked at him with disdain every time he asked him a question. Saratov had thought that he could have bought himself time by being released on bail until the time for the trial, but there was no way this was going to happen, as mister Segovia made abundantly clear. In their own mother-tongue he explained to Saratov that there was nothing anyone could do to save him and that his crimes were ineffaceable, giving Lithuania a bad name. And even if there was a way he could be momentarily released, he would do everything in his power to stop it. He also informed him that he was now a happier man because he knew that the pig in front of him would be locked up for a very long time.
"Perhaps now Lithuania could regain its' respect back now that the monster who tarnished its' good name was locked away."
He was being kept in solitary-confinement and had been since the day of his arrest. Three meals a day were brought to him. A small hatch-type opening was slid open each

time a meal was brought, the hatch only just large enough for the tray to slide through. Nothing was said to him at these exchanges.

His ten by ten cell was furnished with a single bed and a small bedside-table upon which a King James bible sat neatly on top. In a corner of the cell there was a small toilet bowl. The bed consisted of one hard mattress and a single pillow which smelled of the cheapest conditioner, almost like carbolic. His clothes were prison-issue underwear and socks, and a boiler-suit made from a cheap denim-type material which felt like sackcloth against his skin. He had heard about Belmarsh from David Weaver who had served a two-year sentence here, and how it was the hardest place in Britain to do time.

"In there Michael, there are no fucking privileges whatsoever, nothing. You speak out of turn in there and they'll kick the living daylights out of you, I kid you not.
I don't ever want to go back there."

He suddenly jumped up as the sound of the cell door being unlocked jolted him and brought him back to the present. One of the prison wardens entered the room followed by another two men wearing suits and collar and ties. One of the two well-dressed men was an interpreter the other was his appointed solicitor. The warden was only here to open and close the cell door or administer a rapid shot of electricity from a taser-gun into Saratov if required. He stood with his arms folded as he listened first to the interpreter and then the solicitor exchanging words with the prisoner. Warden Glover laughed out loud as the solicitor exclaimed to Saratov that it sickened him to the back teeth to have to defend him, and that he would be doing as little as possible to hinder the justice that was going to be delivered to him, and how his fellow solicitors had roared with laughter at the fact that he had drawn the short straw in who would defend the Lithuanian pig.

The interpreter glanced first at the solicitor, shocked at the statement, but then proceeded to tell the man in Lithuanian what `exactly` his lawyer had just said.

As soon as the interpreter had finished Saratov stuck his middle finger up to the man and muttered something again in his mother-tongue.

The solicitor stood up smiling at the Lithuanian and spoke out loud and very slowly, "I'll...see...you...in...two...weeks...Michael...have...fun...meantime."

The solicitor turned and looked at Saratov as he replied," A lot can happen in two weeks `meester` smarty pants."

At this point the warden laughed out loud again. "Not in this place Michael, not in here pal, see you at supper time kiddo."

The interpreter and the solicitor made their way down the hall and repeated the same things to Viktor Kulbertinov, also being held in solitary confinement.

It was a strange situation indeed for Michael Saratov. Over nine million Euros in three different bank accounts, and here he was stuck in a box-like bunker and not one penny of it accessible to him. Perhaps for a lesser crime the court may have had leniency on him, but for a case like this, where innocent girls had been snatched from the streets and then transported to a European country to become sex slaves, there would be no remorse. There would be no mercy. In all probability he would die here or wherever they sent him to serve his sentence. Life, as far as Michael Saratov was concerned, was well and truly over. For two years he'd been successfully transporting girls from four different European countries and making vast amounts of money. When Britain had first been suggested to him he'd had doubts and fears but the `whore-bitch` Angela Bates had convinced him that it would be easier than anywhere else in Europe to abduct teenage girls. "Most of them are illegitimate anyway. They're only here as a result of their mothers having a good Saturday night out. Most of the fuckers couldn't tell you who their fathers are anyway…they don't give a flying fuck about their kids." From what Saratov could make out the girls here in Britain were anything but neglected. He had to face facts, and the fact was there was nothing or no-one who could get him out of this mess. He'd made a lot of money over the years with his brothel, but now it was over. His only saving grace was the fact that Britain did not practice Capital punishment…perhaps it would have been better for him if they did.

KUANAS.

LITHUANIA.

Doctor Valarie Vercopte sat scrutinising the text message sent to her by Monica Carosova. The message informed her that her husband Viktor Kulbertinov was in prison in Britain along with Michael Saratov, and that by the looks of things, they were going to be there for a very long time...at least ten years. The kidnappers who abducted the girls for Saratov had also been imprisoned or killed. Saratov's fun and games had come to an end. Monica had also suggested a meeting that they could sit and discus what could be done now to help them, if indeed anything could be done. She informed Valarie that both men had been denied extradition and that they would have to stand trial in Britain, and therefore serve whatever sentence given to them in a British prison. Valarie had agreed to meet Monica and work out what they would do henceforth. From what Valarie could make of this it would seem that there was nothing or very little she could do to help her husband. Although the news was unfortunate about Viktor, it was never going to break her heart. She knew all about his visits to the brothel and how he'd had three or four hour sessions with teenagers so there would be no heartbreak or sleepless nights about the matter. She also guessed that Monica would have some kind of plan in her mind of carrying on the brothel perhaps in a different location than Saratov's mansion, and perhaps she wanted her to join in with this scheme.
She sent a text back to her `old friend` and agreed to meet her in a hotel in the city centre later that day.
Four hours later Monica Carosova and Valarie Vercopte had just finished a light lunch and were now enjoying their after-dinner coffees. Both women were dressed immaculately. Monica wore a multi-coloured blouse with white jeans and flat shoes, Valarie a red blouse with cream-coloured trousers and sandals.
They could have been fashion models.
Monica checked a message on her phone as she spoke to Valarie.
"Viktor is in just as much trouble as Michael Valarie. From what I hear Scotland Yard has proof that he was present at the brothel on numerous occasions, and in fact was a sleeping partner to Michael and I's business.
I honestly didn't know Valarie, about his involvement Michael never told me anything about it. I did know about him seeing the girls in there but I was told to keep my mouth shut and because I only have shares in the business I had no option but to remain tight-lipped about the whole matter...sorry Valarie."

"It doesn't matter Monica" said Valarie smiling smugly.

"Do you honestly think that I would visit the place sometimes three times a month and not hear about what he was up to? I bloody knew all along what he was up to. I have a lover as well that he doesn't know about, so, all's well that ends well, and anyway, as far as being unfaithful to each other is concerned, well, it hardly matters now. I could have a hundred lovers now and it wouldn't make any difference to him would it? To all intents and purposes, he is well and truly fucked, especially if you say he has to stand trial in Britain, and of course serve his sentence there. He won't be bothering me for a while that much is for sure."

"Exactly Valarie, and from the way you have just spoken about the matter, well it's just made my proposition that little bit easier to explain."

"Your proposition?" said Valerie, Smiling as though she were surprised.

"Valarie, you have a lovely big house there on the other side of Kaunas, almost as big as Michael's house. What do you say that you and I go into business just the two of us, it wouldn't take long to build up a stock of girls, and there wouldn't have to be as many of them as there were in Michael's house. We only need about eight girls and we could make an absolute fortune. Your house is nice and secluded in an area that is ideal for what we want in fact it's situated better than Michael's place. What do you say, me and you and only me and you, fifty-fifty with the profits, and you don't have to worry about stock, I'll get all the girls we need. We could even just start off with half a dozen Valarie. Those customers of Michael's will pay astronomical amounts of money to fuck with teenagers, hell you know that. Really, there's a fortune to be made.

I would do it in Michael's house but very soon the police will be investigating those premises, and anyway, he could and probably will lose the house altogether...he has no relatives to speak of. The house will be repossessed."

Valarie looked at her hopeful companion.

"In case you've forgotten Monica, you will quite possibly be named among the guilty parties involved in the brothel. Do you think for one minute that Michael Saratov is going to let you run loose and make money from girls while he's cooped up in some bloody British prison? Surely you're not that naive."

Monica's answer was anything but convincing.

"I don't think he'll disclose my name, really, we are good friends."

Valarie dabbed her mouth with a paper napkin and then proceeded to light a cigarette. Looking across the table at Monica, she said," I tell you what Monica. How about I wait to see what the outcome of their trials is. If it turns out that they receive their sentences and you haven't been named as a business partner or a collaborator then perhaps we can come up with a plan for our own business, but if you think that I am going to risk my home by sneaking kidnapped girls in there and then using them as prostitutes while all this is going on, then you're up a gum tree."

Monica nodded. "I can't fault that Valarie, and if it were my house I'd have the same attitude as you. But, after the trial and their sentencing we'll talk again ok? Are you in agreement with that?"

"Yes, why not Monica, but let me tell you something first, and that is to say it ever comes to fruition, there is no way any of the girls will be performing sick and depraved acts under my roof. It will be plain and simple sexual activities and nothing else ok? What I witnessed that day with that young English girl, I will never forget. They had the poor girls' rectum bleeding, poor little bugger was in agony. That, Monica, will not be happening here are we clear on that?"

"Yeah, I know Valarie, I know, but that was Michael charging extra money for stuff like that, can't say I was in agreement with it, but as I say, I was only a shareholder so I couldn't say too much. That was why I was so abrupt with you...I was protecting my financial interests, that's all, but no, it won't be happening again I assure you."

There was a short silence while Monica lit up *her* cigarette and then Valarie said "You know we'll both have to go over to London? Let me tell you something and please don't be offended. There is no way that I want to be seen anywhere near you just now ok? I will fly over there and you will fly over on a different flight than mine. You may think that you are safe Monica, but Scotland Yard could snatch you off the street at any given time. I for one do not want to be walking beside you should that happen, so, separate flights ok? Plus, you mustn't give Saratov the slightest hint of what we are contemplating. If he catches any note of suspicion in your behaviour he will squeal like the pig he is and you'll be off to prison before you can count to ten."

"Understood Valarie, but who says I'll be going over there to speak to *him*?"

Valarie sighed, almost as though she were exasperated at the woman's ignorance.

"You've just finished telling me that he has no relatives to speak of Monica, so, if he is allowed any visitors, who do you think he'll be asking to see? Who do you think he'll call if they allow him his phone calls? You'll see him alright, you just remember what I've just told you and don't let anything slip. If he asks you what you intend to do now, tell him you're going back to hairdressing and cosmetics, don't even mention girls to him ok?"

"I know Valarie, but I really don't think he'll contact me."

It was as though Monica had never said anything because Valarie continued.

"And remember, Scotland Yard would be curious anyway in who you are.

Why has he asked to see you? How much do you know? Are you part of his corrupt business? All these things Monica.

Don't think for one minute that just because they have Saratov in prison, that that's the end of the matter, remember there are girls back there in Britain who have been subjected to sexual torture, over at Michael's place. If they clap eyes on you, then you are in serious trouble missy. They will willingly testify against you and you'll end up in another prison somewhere over there never to be seen again...for a very long time, at least. So be very careful what you're doing when you're over there. It will indeed be a miracle if he doesn't request a visit from you, but, if he doesn't then it would seem that you are safe, for the time-being. I have no choice but to go over there and pretend to Viktor that I am devastated, a bloody hard act to perform, now that I am able to move my real lover in with me."

Monica looked across the table at Valarie Vercopte smiling broadly.

"You haven't changed *that* bloody much Valarie now that you are a doctor...you're still a slut at heart."

SCOTLAND YARD.

BROADWAY VICTORIA.

Terry and Samantha would have to wait for their week off. Polly had received a phone call from a prison governess stating that Angela Bates wished to have an interview with the two detectives claiming to have vital information about everyone involved in the kidnappings.
"Where are we going Terry? said Samantha fastening her seat-belt.
"We're going to Ashford Samantha, Bronzefield prison, to see this bitch Angela Bates. Apparently she has some interesting information for us.
She'll be trying to see if there's a way that she could have her sentence reduced, she's got no chance."
"Hm, so we're going to the monster mansion then?"
Terry smiled and nodded his head. "Yeah, this is where they put all the fruit-cakes. It's one of the highest security women's prison in the whole of the British Isles, and I mean high security...some bad bitches in here Samantha...even harder than you, I kid you not. Cut a man's cock off without thinking twice about it some of these women. If they have this Angela Bates here then she must be even more dangerous than we gave her credit for. Anyway, how did you know about its' nick-name? I've never mentioned it before."
"Think it was the locals around Ashford who gave it that name Terry, and I think I can see why by what you're telling me. There'll be some gruesome tales to be told about the inmates in here I would say, a gold mine for a crime writer."
"You're telling me. Anyone who comes here has not been caught shop-lifting I can tell you that, although it does serve as a local prison as well."
As they drove through the city heading out to their destination Samantha said something to him completely unexpected. It was a subject he thought she'd never bring up unless he had said something, but without warning, Samantha Reynolds' knocked the ball completely right out of the park.
"So Terry, what exactly happened to your wife and son? You said something about a deranged woman and a surgeon, what exactly happened?"
Before anything else was said, Samantha could plainly see she'd put Terry into a state of consternation. He seemed to flush and become unsettled, rattled even. His eyes blinked rapidly as he drove, the tell-tale sign of rubbing the back of his neck, something he done whenever he was flustered.
"I'm sorry Terry, I shouldn't have asked you that, I had no right to ask that, the subject is

obviously distressing to you. I wasn't trying to pry into your life, I just thought perhaps-"
"No, it doesn't matter Samantha, I have to talk about it some time, it's just that now is not the right time, I'll tell you in due course."
A little over half an hour later they arrived at Bronzefield where they were given passes at the gates by a stern-looking young lady who had scrutinised Terry's ID for more than thirty seconds before finally issuing him with a prison pass.
She reminded Terry of the Scottish singer Annie Lennox, at least the hair style and colour did...nothing else, and certainly not the personality.
The same young lady had only glanced at Samantha's ID for a couple of seconds.
The officer then informed them of where to report to and who to ask for.
Finally, before they were allowed to proceed she advised them not to lose their passes as additional ones would not be issued to them. As they drove on through the grounds of the infamous prison Terry glanced at Samantha.
"Not a bloody social word out of her, nothing. What the hell is wrong with wishing someone a pleasant day? Have a nice day, what the hell is wrong with that? But no, don't lose your passes, you will not be issued with another one Christ Samantha, do you think that working in a place like this robs you of your personality? If you don't like it here, then leave the bloody job...don't have to be a bloody misery-guts and talk to people like they're dogs...what a bloody miserable bitch."
"Well Terry, we can't expect her to be sitting there in a state of equanimity like she didn't have a care in the world. She'll have a lot of responsibility with that job. No doubt there have been numerous attempts of people trying to get in here to see partners or loved ones, you know, people trying to smuggle things in or out of the place. I dare say she'll have the same attitude to members of staff as well...it's not just us Terry. This place hasn't got the name of one of Britain's highest security prisons for nothing. Terry shook his head dismissing everything Samantha said. "It's no excuse, doesn't cost anything to be courteous Samantha, I mean we are officers of the law, it's not as though we're inmates...don't lose your passes Christ." Ten minutes later they were greeted by a Miss Geraldine Prowse, the prison governess. She escorted them to the cell of Angela Bates and was of a completely different temperament as to that of her security staff. The woman who was around thirty-five years of age and probably held the most stressful job in all of the prisons in Britain smiled cheerily at the two detectives. She was dressed in blue jeans and denim shirt and wore moccasin-type soft shoes. Her hair was several different shades of browns and was tied back with a colourful headband. She reminded Terry of a gypsy lady, or at least how a `gypsy lady` from a country song would be dressed. She walked with a swagger, her golden bracelets

`jingle-jangling` on her wrists as she manoeuvred majestically down the prison wing. She was escorted by a tall warden who looked far too thin for Terry's liking, his eyes almost sunk into their sockets and his skin the palest of greys. As she reached the door of the cell she turned to face the detectives, and again smiled as she pointed with her thumb to the door, "A nasty character by all accounts, kidnapping teenagers to make massive financial gains. I have no idea what she thinks she can achieve by having a debate with you, but, I put forward her request and you kindly accepted to have this meeting with her, so, enjoy your half hour with her. Perhaps she can give you more names of collaborators or addresses of recidivists who have been involved, but believe me, it won't do her one bit of good, she's going to be here for a long time. I'll have to be extra careful to keep some of the women in here out of her way, because they would tear her limb from limb. Quite a few mothers in here you see, and they won't take too kindly to monsters like this in here making money from kidnapping innocent little girls, especially what she was selling them on for."

Mercer smiled at the woman. "I don't envy your job miss Prowse, I can tell you that. It must test your nerves sometimes does it not?"

"I don't let anybody get to me in here Mister Mercer I can assure you. If they are foolish enough to step over the line, then they are punished severely for their actions…I don't tolerate any nonsense in here, and they all know it. This bitch in here has yet to discover that, but she will."

The male warden who accompanied Geraldine Prowse spoke for the first time as he opened the cell door with a massive key. "I'll be right outside if you need me." All the other units in Bronzefield were opened electronically, but the solitary confinement cells were still opened by hand, individually. The six foot plus skinny warden stepped aside as Miss Prowse entered the cell.

"On your feet Bates, you have visitors."

Terry and Samantha were quite taken-aback as Prowse stepped forward and slapped Angela Bates hard across the face.

"That was just to remind you who is boss in here, and if you give any of these detectives any grief, I will repeat that manoeuvre with a baseball bat.

She's all yours, John here will be right outside the cell if you need him, I'll see you both in my office when you're done."

The governess turned and left the two detectives to their `conversation`.

The finger prints of Geraldine Prowse's hand were plainly visible on the side of Angela Bates' face as she sat back down on her single bed. It had to be said that even without make-up Angela Bates was indeed a very attractive woman.

The warden had brought in two chairs for the detectives.

They both sat down in front of Bates. Terry began the conversation.
"So, Angela, what exactly is this information you have that is so vital?
You said you had vital information for us. As far as I can see, we have all the vital information we need, plus, we have you behind bars as well as Saratov and Kulbertinov, anyone else who's been involved are either locked up or, thanks to this ill-tempered lady here beside me, shot in the head, so, what is it you think you can do for us, and what do you hope to gain by ratting on someone because we all know you never do anything for nothing, there's always a price isn't there Angela, Quid-Pro-Quo, what's in it for me, well I'm afraid you're out of luck this time, because there is nothing you could say or do that could possibly pull you out of this shit-hole lady, you are one depraved individual and you will serve your deserved sentence...I would shoot you in the head if I had my way, honestly. You see, all you and your kind can see or want to see, is the financial profits that roll in from your handiwork. You don't see the stress and anxiety you cause people. The sleepless nights, the worry, the heartbreak, the hopelessness, you see nothing of that, and you couldn't care less could you? But here you are thinking you can worm your way out of this, well, no can do Angie baby...you're down lady."
Angela Bates gave it a few moments before she spoke, and then looking at Terry she said," You've forgotten about someone. And this someone is going to continue with the kidnappings. You may think that you have it all sorted out but I can assure you, there will be lots more girls going missing from the streets over here, and this time, there's no SAS soldiers or anyone who'll be able to locate them. If they are taken from Britain, then you can rest assured you will never see them again. This person has her own, how shall I say it, helpers, and these people will kill at the slightest signs of danger. And if"-
"Let me stop you there Angela" said Samantha. "If you're talking about Monica Carosova, then forget it. We already have surveillance looking out for her.
As soon as she steps foot on British soil she'll be apprehended.
We have all the airports in the country on standby. So if that is what your information is then you've wasted Terry and I's time, and your own."
Angela sat on the bed smiling now. "You really don't get it do you?
Do you honestly think she'd be stupid enough to land in a busy airport when she knows that half the country's police forces are searching for her? Give her *some* credit.
She could disguise herself in such a way that not even your best surveillance officers would recognise her. She knows people who can make her disappear, make her a completely different person, new identity, and on top of that, she isn't going to be running this brothel on her own. She has many others involved in her plans, people you don't even know about, but, you're not interested so, we'll just leave it at that, but don't come back here asking me for names or addresses when all these girls go missing

again and you two had the opportunity to prevent it from happening."

Mercer stood up. "Think we'll take our chances Angela. I think you're bluffing about Carosova having accomplices and partners and what not, but then that's what they say isn't it? When a rat is cornered and all that... it's desperation isn't it Angela, that's what this is all about, sorry, nothing doing, enjoy your break in here away from society, how's the jaw, that must have smarted when Geraldine whacked you, I hope to God she whacks you a lot more, especially when you're not waiting for it, like then. I would smack you myself but I wouldn't be able to control myself, I'd end up beating you to pulp. So, we'll be heading back now Angela, what a waste of time this was.

All you've succeeded in doing is to exacerbate your problem, and believe me, you *do* have a problem. You had better pray that Miss Prowse doesn't ever let the nice ladies in here mix with you or they'll be sweeping pieces of you up all over the prison. Seriously Angela, you're better in here in solitary, at least you're safe in here. Oh, and once your sentence has been passed I'm going to bring one or two of the girls you kidnapped in and let them have a chat with you, they'll be keen to let you know just exactly what they were subjected to when they were over in Lithuania...that'll be nice won't it Angela, see ya."

As Terry and Samantha reached the door Angela Bates said, smiling at both detectives, "Is that your final answer then is it?"

Mercer did not even reply, but knocked on the door for the warden to open up. Ten minutes later they were both in the governor's office having tea.

"She's only bluffing with you detective Mercer" said Geraldine Prowse.

"You done the right thing, just bloody ignore her. If I had a pound for every time some of the prisoners in here have tried to bribe either myself or one of the wardens trying to convince us that they have information, well, I could be sitting in the Bahamas or the south of France sipping champagne on a bloody cruise ship. She's desperate to change her situation, but, it `ain't` going to change. Her poisonous past has caught up with her, and now, she must learn to face the consequences of her deplorable actions. Some of my staff are taking bets on how long she'll get. The least of my troubles I must say, but it's fun for them. She could end up doing twelve years or more, wouldn't that be nice mister Mercer?" Samantha and Terry laughed with the prison governess who was so laid back it was unbelievable. She acted like she was in charge of the local tennis courts and not the highest security prison in the country. As Geraldine joined them at the office door Terry said, "She said to us there, is that your final answer? She had also instructed us not to return to her for names and addresses when the kidnappings begin again. She seems adamant that they will."

Geraldine Prowse held the door for the two detectives.

"I wouldn't worry about her idle threats mister Mercer as I say it's a desperate bid and quite a pathetic one I don't mind telling you. She'll just have to learn that she's not going anywhere, except the high court, and even that's just to find out how long her reservation in here will be. Go about your business, she's finished."

A few moments later they were once more at the gates of the prison and producing their passes to the stern-faced young lady who actually looked at the cards that she had issued and scrutinised them as though they were fakes.
Finally, after checking something on her computer screen she advised them again to be very careful with them and not to lose them "Otherwise-"
"We know miss, you've already informed us that we won't be able to obtain renewals, we *do* listen you know. Anyway, you have yourself a nice day and perhaps we'll see you some time in the near future."
The security guard looked at Terry as though he'd just challenged her to a fight, obviously offended at his attempt at humour. As she pressed the button inside her cubicle the gates began to slowly slide open. As Terry drove the car slowly past the door the warden warned them a final time not to lose their passes.
Terry smiled back at her, blowing her a kiss and repeating to her, "You have yourself a lovely day babes."
Samantha sat laughing with Terry and finally agreeing with him that she could at least attempt to be a little more civil to people, especially people who worked within the law. She laughed, this time mockingly as Terry proclaimed, "She's a fucking carpet-muncher without a shadow of a doubt Samantha, you can tell. They can't stand the sight of men, it's like we're only obstacles in their otherwise perfect world."
"Terry, just because she's ill-tempered, it doesn't automatically mean that she's a lesbian. As I say, she has a lot of responsibility, she can't spend all day laughing and joking with people...but yes, you're right Terry, she goes a bit far with seriousness of issuing passes I must admit."
"You see, that's something that confuses me Sam. They hate men, right I get that, and they prefer female company, that goes without saying, but, the first thing they do is, they get their hair cut like a fucking man, and they wear suits, you know jackets and trousers and heavy shoes, fuck, she's wearing brogues did you notice? Men's hair-cuts and trousers and everything but they hate men, how fucking weird is that?
I'm sorry Samantha but I just don't get it, they hate men and then they go out and fill their wardrobes with masculine clothing, what the fuck is that all about?"
"Terry, calm yourself down, it doesn't matter one wit to us if she's a lesbian or not, it's not important, now, getting back to the subject of Angela Bates, do you honestly think

she's bluffing?" Even though Terry had seemed totally convinced that she had been bluffing, the question sparked a jab of fear in his stomach. He turned briefly to look at Samantha. "Christ I hope she is. If it turns out that she wasn't then we are in for one hell of a time Sam...oh hell don't say that."
Samantha looked at him.
"What?"
"Nothing, it's just that, oh you know, I just get a gut feeling...she seemed so certain about it, like she knew for certain that it was going to happen, like it had already been planned out."
Sam watched as Terry's grip on the steering wheel tightened, his knuckles white. "Terry, listen, nothing has happened yet and probably never will, it's just us, you know after what we've been through, especially you over in Lithuania. You were actually part of the escape procedure, I was too busy getting myself all tied up and being taken prisoner to be troubled with all that."
"Was it that that made you shoot her in the head?"
"I snapped Terry. Yes, I suppose it was, being spoken to like that by a bloody slut no less, threatened with rape and then informing me what they were going to do to the young girl they brought in. I'm saying I snapped Terry but I was in full control, I can't deny it, and I have to admit, I don't regret it. As far as I could see I was doing everyone a favour, one less sicko to deal with, something like that. Why? Did it bother you Terry? What I done?"
"You've got to be joking Samantha, did it bother me, I would recommend you for a bloody award."
"If you hadn't arrived when you did Terry things were going to get really uncomfortable for me and that young girl. That's what made me want to kill her. There was no way I could let her walk out of there alive, not after her own callousness making threats about what she was going to have done to me, bloody punching my face indeed."
Terry sighed, laughing..."You are one nasty piece of work Samantha, gonna have to keep an eye on you."
"Perhaps you should Terry, because I feel no compunction for what I done.
And maybe Colin Green isn't so far off the mark with his attitude, because it seems to me that killing the bastards is the one and only sure-fire way of stopping their bloody games, oh Christ forget what I just said there Terry."

KAUNAS.

LITHUANIA.

Doctor Valarie Vercopte was talking on the phone to her worried husband.
He'd been allowed a single phone call and so who better than his wife to call. Kulbertinov thought he would be greeted by his wife who would be in a state of shock and despair. Instead he was having a conversation with a woman who didn't seem to have a care in the world.
"Valarie, I need you to get me the best solicitor we can find, I mean, the best, we can't really-."
"Wow, just hold your horses there Viktor, we?"
Valarie was well aware that the British authorities could, and probably would be listening in to the conversation. *We* need to get the best solicitor? Listen, I have found out about your sessions with these young girls you've been having behind my back. Do you think for one second, that I am going to spend good money on trying to save *your* arse after the way you have treated me? Let me tell you something. You always talk down to me and make out like I know nothing at all when we're out with your friends. You always did like putting me through the shredders didn't you? Well, I've got news for you, you are on your own mister clever-know-it-all Kulbertinov. Let's see how clever you are now. Get your nomology head on and get yourself out of this fix you and that perverted little fuck who thinks he owns the world. Let's see how clever you are because if you are unsuccessful then you stand to serve a long time in prison over there. How dare you ask me to help you after all you've done to me. Fuck you Viktor, you're on your own now and I hope they give you twenty years."
"Valarie, please, I'm begging you. Listen, if you want a divorce I'll give you one. I'll agree to anything you say. I'll pay you well if you just contact-."
"Sorry no can do, and anyway I have access to all our finances now, I don't need your permission to spend money, and trust me, I am going to spend a lot of money. My life has suddenly taken a turn for the better, thanks to you and that other pervert Saratov, I'm really going to live it up now I promise you that. I think I'll have me a string of lovers Viktor, you know real men, men who can give a woman a good time, as opposed to the weak good-for-nothing fuck-head that I've been married to who goes to bed with innocent little school-girls. Fuck you Viktor, I'm going to live life now to the full, just like you've been doing behind my back."
Viktor Kulbertinov knew it was hopeless. Even if his wife had agreed to find a lawyer, it

would be doubtful if he'd be allowed to use him or her in Britain.

Valarie listened for a reaction from her husband. After a few seconds he spoke to her for the last time.

"If I ever get out of here bitch, I will find you and I give you my solemn word, I will cut your throat from ear to ear and watch the life-blood drain out of you."

She responded to his threat. "I've known all along about your fetish for little girls and I have been having an affair with Jacob (Yacob) your best friend Viktor.

Didn't he tell you he's been fucking the living daylights out of me?

Couldn't you see me glowing with satisfaction? Oh, and his sperm tastes lovely as well. God he must have had some fun sitting there at business meetings with you knowing he was going to fuck me hard that night in a hotel, what a buzz that must have been for him, oh? Have to go Viktor, that's him here now, he's just came in. He's just came home actually, bye Viktor, have fun sweetheart."

The last thing Valarie wanted was the British authorities suspecting her of being part of what her husband had been involved with, and so if they'd been listening in, her apparent repulsion towards her husband's actions would surely put any such notions out of their heads. If there was any chance of Monica and her starting their own business-venture, then there'd have to be no suspicions whatsoever concerning her own involvement. Besides, it would be a while yet before anything like that could be started. They would wait for the outcome of the sentences imposed on Viktor and Saratov, and not forgetting of course, that Saratov could put the cat among the pigeons if he mentioned Monica's name. That being the case, she would have to start the business up by herself. All said and done, Monica was not the be-all or end-all of the venture. She was in no way a necessity.

CENTRAL CRIMINAL COURT.

OLD BAILEY.

LONDON.

Three months later.

The day of reckoning had come for Michael Saratov and Viktor Kulbertinov. It was a day they had both feared more than anything they had ever feared in their lives. They had no contact with one another in Belmarsh from the day they had been brought in. Each of the men had serious doubts as to what the other would say when trying to defend their actions. Perhaps the one thing that Viktor Kulbertinov had going for him was the fact that he'd had nothing at all to do with any of the kidnappings, apart from the financing. He was simply using a service offered to him by a friend, in his own country, and although illegal, had used the service on quite a few occasions. That said, he was still in serious trouble and would serve a severe sentence. And it was the severity of the sentence that worried him. He had heard quite a few times in his life people mocking the British justice system referring to it as a joke in fact. These people were nothing more than blind narcissists and would have been speaking of other people's experiences of the system and not their own. A police officer entered the holding cell informing him that he would be standing trial in court number one. This was the old court in the Old Bailey. He'd heard about infamous people who had stood trial in this courtroom. Ian Huntley for one, he was the man who had murdered two ten-year-old girls in Soham Cambridgeshire. The sixties infamous brothers, the Krays stood trial in here, as well as the Yorkshire ripper, Doctor Crippen, John Christie, to name but a few. Today though, the very small tightly-packed seats in court one would not be filled with curious and angered public.

Today they would stand trial in private, which to Viktor added to the seriousness of his crimes. There would be no jury, simply because there was no need for one. There needn't have been a trial...they were guilty and that was that. They were here not to defend themselves, but to find out what the British justice system seen fit to impose upon them. A barrister stepped into the room and raised both of his arms in a gesture for him to rise to his feet. The man did not speak one word of his language and it mattered nothing to either of them. He was here simply because the British justice system insisted that he was. The solicitor who'd visited him at Belmarsh had dismissed himself after only a couple of weeks informing him through the interpreter that he didn't stand a cat's chance in hell of receiving less than ten years and that "it was a complete and utter waste of time and money trying to defend a paedophile Lithuanian man who enjoyed fucking children for a hobby and only possessing the brains of a chimpanzee monkey." Two clerks of the court entered the cell and gestured him to follow them. The policeman who'd came in to inform him of what court he would stand trial in followed behind. He walked down a huge seemingly endless corridor until at last they entered the famous courtroom. Less than a dozen people sat around the judge's seat high above him. To his right the small figure of Michael Saratov stood with both of his hands in front of him, staring at the floor. Both men were still dressed in the prison issue uniforms. One of the clerks motioned them to sit down on the chairs behind them. Men and women in white wigs and black gowns sat in hushed conversation occasionally glancing at the guilty parties. Did they already know what their sentences were going to be? Were they here merely to gloat at the punishment about to be `bestowed` upon them? All the comments he'd heard about the British justice system were in no way humorous now. Kulbertinov glanced to his right and as he did he saw Michael quietly muttering to himself, or perhaps he was praying to his god and asking for forgiveness or mercy...or both. He did not even look in his direction, perhaps he was frightened to. All he could do was hope for the best.

Fifteen minutes later Viktor Kulbertinov was escorted out of the courtroom with the knowledge that he would spend ten years in a British prison with no option of parole. Michael Saratov was sentenced to fifteen years, also with no option for parole. The delivery of the sentences took less than ten minutes. Kulbertinov expected the judge to start pontificating about the laws in Britain and how they would not tolerate anyone breeching these laws and how important it was to impose strict sentences to those who chose to try and undermine the very values of the British people. None of that happened. The judge simply called out their names asking the two men in question to verify their identities. There was no opportunity to defend themselves or try to explain their actions, just the deliverance of the sentences.

Both men would serve the full sentences in Belmarsh. Even though Kulbertinov had expected a severe sentence, when the judge had informed him of what that sentence would be it sent a shockwave through his body almost as powerful as an electric jolt. His throat had completely dried-up, his mouth was as dry as desert sands. He was given a cup of tea in the holding cell and then escorted by two police officers out to the truck that would take him to the place where he would spend the next ten years of his life. Today, and in fact since the day he had been arrested, the Viktor Kulbertinov he'd known all his life had ceased to exist. From now on he was number 22547761 Belmarsh. As he was escorted into the awaiting vehicle he wondered if he would ever see

Lithuania again. A stab of anger punched at his stomach as he remembered what Valarie had told him.

His best friend Jacob.

Now, if what Valarie had said was true, Jacob was probably bathing beside her in the Jacuzzi sipping his beer and cuddling into the new life he would have with her. By the way she had spoken to him he wondered if she'd even arrange a party in honour of his absence. She had known all along about his visits to the brothel. She had just been saving up the evidence she would use to divorce him. Now she didn't even need that evidence. He had done it all for her. He sighed, frustrated with himself for not realizing that she was bound to find out about the teenage girls. Valarie visited the place sometimes three times a month checking on their hygiene, someone would have told her. She knew he done business transactions with Saratov and so seeing his car parked there would not have aroused any suspicions. Maybe even one of the girls had informed her. It didn't matter who or how. He was here, and he was here for a long time. If, at the end of his sentence he was able to return home he would kill Jacob Blint himself. The filthy German bastard had been seeing his wife all this time behind his back. He had lent the man twenty thousand euros to help him with financial difficulties he was having concerning his ex-wife, or so he'd said.

He'd probably used the money to impress Valarie.

He would pay the price for his betrayal. But that was a very long way off just now, ten years away in fact. All that remained now was adjusting to this new life or rather this new existence. It was going to be a long ten years.

How Michael Saratov would be feeling was anyone's guess. Fifteen years he would serve. Kulbertinov smiled to himself as the armoured vehicle pulled away and headed back to Belmarsh. He didn't think that Michael would be strong enough to take the sentence. He was already an old man although he'd never asked Michael his actual age. He guessed about mid to late sixties. There's no way he'd be able to do fifteen years. He'd either die through natural causes or he'd be found one morning swinging from a rope in his cell.

Saratov had got himself out of some sticky situations in the past over in Lithuania, but this time he was done for, they both were. There would be no bribing or threatening to inform someone's wife of their husband's infidelities.

This time he was down…and definitely out. If he had stayed in Lithuania it would have been practically impossible for the British authorities to bring him over here, but the fact that he'd been stupid enough to think that he could come over to Britain and kill a detective and then just head back home. He had the police commissioner in Kaunas under his thumb. He would turn a blind eye to lots of things that he was doing, but because he'd kidnapped British girls and had them taken over there, force them to take drugs, and then use them for his brothel, he had undoubtedly sealed his own fate. Viktor had even advised him to stay put where he was safe, but no, he thought, just as Valarie had said, that he was invincible, untouchable, and that he could get away with just about anything. For the next fifteen years he would pay the price for that very foolish notion.

KERRINGDALE

MENTAL HEALTH INSTITUTE.

WOLVERHAMPTON.

From the moment Terry Mercer had arrived here Samantha saw a change in him. Gone was the jovial partner full of friendly sarcasm and banter. Now, his expression was bland, distant. He had explained to her on the way here what exactly had happened to his wife and son. To say it was harrowing would be the understatement of the year. Samantha clearly understood now his blasphemies and his short-temperedness. How on earth could someone be evil enough to pay a surgeon to operate on a person's brain and deliberately inflict damage that would leave them practically in a state of vegetation. What kind of man could do this to two people he'd never met in his life, and one of them, a child?

That was exactly what had happened though. Terry went on to explain the outcome of the situation. He didn't even get the satisfaction of seeing them put on trial. The surgeon had poisoned the woman who died in hospital and he had taken his own life by jumping from a hotel window-ledge in Manchester.

Polly Shepard had informed her that Terry came here whenever he could just to see his wife and son, even though they hadn't a clue who he was.

The mother and son did not even know each other.

What a pitiful sight that would be, Samantha thought to herself, that a mother and son who would probably pass each other on numerous occasions throughout the days, but were incapable of acknowledging one another.

When Samantha had inquired of Terry *why* this woman had done this he simply replied, "Because I broke up with her when we were fifteen years old, that's why."

Samantha knew she was only scratching the surface of the enormity of what had actually happened, but even at this point she wasn't sure if she ever wanted to find out the full story. "Poor man." As they approached the front doors of the huge sandstone building Terry said. "Listen, you don't have to come in here. You could go to a local hotel or a bar and I'll come and pick you up when I'm finished in here." Samantha clinched his arm with both hands and snuggled her head into his shoulder. "I want to come in Terry, I'll be fine, and so will you. If it gets too much for me, I'll find the canteen and you can come and get me when you've done what you have to do...this must be bloody awful for you. I admire you Terry, I really do."

Fifteen minutes later Terry Mercer sat immediately across the table from the woman he had built his entire life around. Carol Mercer sat clutching a lemon-coloured tennis ball to her chest and mumbling the words he'd heard so very often…her only words. "I Cal…I Cal." Carol was slightly bloated now and at least three stones heavier than she'd been before she was kidnapped. He guessed it would be her mental health that was the cause of the bloating, that and the fact that she wouldn't be exorcising in the manner which she was used to. Her hair, although clean hung lank and shapeless compared to her past. Carol had always been meticulous about her hair, hell, every self-respecting woman was.

Terry reached into his jacket pocket and pulled out a tissue. He reached across the table and wiped his wife's mouth. Saliva had gathered at the corners. Although he knew fine well that the woman across the table had not a clue as to who he was, he spoke to her. "Hello Carol, it's me, it's Tel…are you ok?"

As always, Carol Mercer responded in her usual manner by thumping her fists on the table, tennis ball still clinched tightly. "I Cal…I Cal…"

Samantha looked away with a lump in her throat. This was even harder than she'd anticipated. Terry leaned across the table and took both of his wife's hands in his. Carol struggled to break loose and grab the tennis ball again. Terry handed it to her and then took her remaining hand in both of his.

Doctor Glover, a middle-aged gentleman with thinning grey hair sat beside Carol smiling at the scene. Looking now to Terry he said, "We have made some progress mister Mercer Carol can now practically feed herself. It can get a bit messy from time to time, but it's progress, isn't it Carol?"

"I Cal."

Terry felt the skin on Carol's hand and rubbed his thumbs on the back of them, something he used to do in a different life with her whenever she was stressed about something. Still smiling the doctor rose up to his feet and informed Terry to stand up. Doctor Glover now spoke to Carol again. "Stand up Carol, and give Terry a cuddle."

Carol stood up clapping her hands together, still with the tennis ball firmly gripped. "I Cal…I Cal."

The doctor motioned for Terry to come round to the other side of the table.

"Give her a cuddle mister Mercer, cuddle Carol. Carol? Give Terry a cuddle sweetheart…nice cuddle." For one brief moment she put down the tennis ball on the table and allowed Terry to give her a cuddle by holding her cheek out to him.

Samantha's heart broke in a thousand pieces as she witnessed Carol give her husband a cuddle in the manner of a small child, tapping him on the shoulder several times as if to assure *him* that everything would be fine. Carol then turned and cuddled the doctor in the very same manner before grabbing her tennis ball and sitting back down at the table thumping her fists once more.

Samantha had underestimated the inner strength of Terry Mercer. How on earth could the man withstand pain like this? Tears rolled down her face as Doctor Glover led the woman back out of the room to her own bedroom. This, without a shadow of a doubt had been the most harrowing fifteen minutes of her life. What it must feel like to Terry Mercer God alone knew. After the doctor had left the room with Carol Terry stood looking at pictures on the wall around the room. Some of the pictures had been drawn by patients. Samantha couldn't find any words to say to him. Instead she too looked around the walls at the pictures and paintings until the doctor returned. "Would you like to come and see your son now Mister Mercer?"

It was at that point that Samantha asked where the canteen was and excused herself informing Terry that she would wait there until he was ready to leave. She actually struggled to get the words out.

As Samantha walked down the corridor heading to the canteen, a male nurse was heading towards her pushing a young teenage boy in a wheel-chair.

The boy looked like he suffered from down-syndrome. His head was swollen and hung to one side. The nurse had tied coloured balloons on each side of the handles of the chair. The young boy mumbled incoherently as he was pushed. Just before Samantha entered the elevator she heard the nurse saying to the boy, "We're off to see your daddy Daniel, won't this be nice? You have to smile for daddy Daniel."

BROMLEY.

GREATER LONDON.

Mandy Spencer was at this moment in time a very proud mother. She had just received an e-mail from Greenwich University confirming that they looked forward to Sophie beginning her Sociology degree in the forth-coming term. This, not long before Sophie's sixteenth birthday was the best news she could have possibly hoped for. As well as Sophie being able to obtain her degree there was the added bonus of the fact that Greenwich was practically on their door-step. Mandy stood with her cup of coffee in her hand looking out of her living room window at the miserable rainy day. The rain hammered relentlessly on her windows being driven by a gale-forced wind. Her friend Carol Richardson was on her way round to celebrate the good news. Carol's daughter Kaylee had also been accepted and given a place. Mandy's son David had found full-time employment with a local builder and had settled really well into the job. His boss had offered to pay for the boy's driving lessons and so David had jumped at the opportunity. How very different her life was now compared to only a few months earlier.

Sophie was seeing a psychiatrist on a regular basis and seemed to be making progress. Thus far she had not gone in to any great details about what had happened to her in Lithuania. And why would she? It wasn't exactly the kind of subject you'd share with your mother, not in detail anyway. Sophie was different now though. She couldn't pin-point any particular change in her daughter but there was something...something different. Since she was brought back safely home she'd befriended a young girl by the name of Alison Green who had also been abducted and taken to Lithuania. On a regular basis Sophie rode the bus across to Mitcham to see her. Perhaps their ordeal had brought them closer together. Mandy knew about Alison's father Colin, and how he played a part in bringing the girls home. She'd also heard stories about how violent he could be when riled, but then who wouldn't be violent if someone had taken their child away from home. Sophie spoke very highly of him. Perhaps she saw him as some kind of surrogate father. It didn't matter. What *did* matter was Sophie's future, and thanks to the e-mail she'd just received, her future was as bright as any other girl of her age. Mandy was washing her cup in the kitchen when she heard the front door opening and Carol Richardson shouting out. "Hello, is anyone home?"
Mandy laughed out loud as the living-room door opened.
"Come in, you silly bugger, oh you're soaking wet."

The two women embraced each other, both of them genuinely happy for the other in their daughter's achievements, and relieved it had to be said.

Carol had been concerned about Kaylee's sudden interest in boys, or more accurately her enhanced interest. She was beginning to worry that it would interfere with her studies, but as luck would have it, the university had come just in time. Once she settled in there she would be too busy for boyfriends, or at least on a steady basis…she hoped.

Mandy said nothing as Kaylee threw herself down on the sofa, saying hi to her and connecting her headphones to her I phone.

Her skirt, yet again was ridiculously short.

Carol had always been strict with Kaylee in these matters, but lately Kaylee seemed to have a free hand in what she wore to school or elsewhere. Perhaps Carol had released her grip a little on the girl in a bid to keep their relationship friendly, and hassle-free. Mandy chased the thoughts from her head, it was none of her business.

She remembered one particular evening recently her son David had sat directly opposite Kaylee talking away to her. It took Mandy only a few minutes that evening to catch on to what was happening. In recent years David had hardly given Kaylee the time of day…but Kaylee was filling out. Kaylee was becoming a woman, and today she was proving that fact. Kaylee pulled out one of her ear-pieces. "Is Sophie home?"

"No, she's gone over to Alison Green's house, I think they were having a sleep over, she should be back some time this morning. The uni have sent her a text confirming her place there, but she hasn't texted me yet about it…I thought she would have."

Carol said, "You know what teens are like Mandy, they'll probably still be lying in bed. They'll have been up all night talking."

At that precise moment Colin Green pulled up outside of Mandy's house with Sophie riding shotgun. Alison Green was not in the car. For some unknown reason Mandy felt a little concerned as Sophie sat talking to Colin in the car. They seemed to be in quite a lengthy conversation about something. Mandy's concern slightly increased as she watched her daughter lean across the seat and kiss Colin Green on the cheek before climbing out of the car. Carrying her overnight bag she bounced into the house cheerfully and entered the living room greeting Carol and Kaylee first and then kissing her mother on the brow. "Hi mum, have you heard the good news?"

"Yes I just got the e-mail this-."

"Colin and Jillian are taking me on holiday with them, Alison and her sister Rebecca, Jillian and Colin and me, isn't that great? We're going up to Scotland for three weeks. Colin says he's going to learn me how to shoot. He hunts deer and things, it's going to be brilliant."

Mandy felt deflated. "Sophie, I thought you were referring to the good news of being

accepted into Greenwich university darling.
Did they send you a text message? They said they would."
"Oh yeah, I got that text message last night just after tea."
"Aren't you excited about it Sophie? Being accepted there? It's what you wanted wasn't it?"
"Mum, of course I'm glad I've got in but it's not the be-all and end-all of Sophie Spencer's life. I do have other things that interest me you know."
"Yeah we know" said Kaylee, "boys to be precise, that's what interests you Sophie."
Before Sophie left the living room, she turned and said to Kaylee, "You should lose some weight Kaylee, your legs are a bit too fat to be wearing mini-skirts honey, go on a diet otherwise you'll just look like a cheap piece of fuck-meat."
"Sophie! Language please, now you just apologise for that right now, there was no need whatsoever for a comment like that, what the hell has got into you?" Sophie merely sighed and headed off upstairs to her room.
Mandy and Carol looked at one another, both of them completely gobsmacked at Sophie's comment. Mandy knew there and then, she had problems. Yet again her happiness was short-lived. The first thing she'd have to do, was talk to Colin and Jillian Green. Whether or not it was coincidence that Sophie was talking this way would remain to be seen, but they had no right whatsoever inviting her on a holiday without at least asking her if she was alright with the idea. But here was Sophie, all excited about going away with them and this was the first time she'd heard anything about it. She would always be grateful to Colin Green for helping to bring back her daughter safe and sound but there were certain boundaries that should be respected concerning other people's children, especially holidays away from home...and learning her to shoot?

WOLVERHAMPTON.

A 4123.

For almost eight months Samantha had worked with Terry Mercer. Their opinions and methods were like chalk and cheese and yet here they were, still a partnership. What she had just witnessed in Kerringdale had changed her opinion of him in so many ways. Only a few miles out of Wolverhampton they hadn't really spoken to each other since they got into the car. It was by no means a difficult silence, only strange for two people who usually talked continuously.   `He must have moments in his life when all that comes back to him, and it must sting like nothing else on earth.` She fidgeted with the radio and then the glove compartment, and then she took out notes and attempted to read them. She checked her mobile phone for messages then she checked her pockets for nothing.
"What's wrong?" said Terry, aware that his colleague was uncomfortable. "It's...nothing I'm eh, I don't know what to say Terry. Christ I'm hurting for you so much, I had no idea of just how bad their conditions are…I'm, Christ I'm so sorry Terry."
"I told you not to come in Samantha. It's not easy, I mean for you. I'm used to seeing them in that condition. Yes, it still hurts me, it rips me apart sometimes, but there's nothing anyone can do. They don't feel what we do. They are not aware of their condition, it's us, we're the ones, the onlookers, we're the ones who hurt for them, especially me, when I remember how Carol used to be, and my little boy Daniel…but they don't know anything now. Some would say that I'm being cruel keeping them alive in that state and that I'm doing it just to preserve my own memories. It takes a good chunk of my salary to keep them there. Anyway, that's enough about that just now we have other issues to deal with. Polly wants to see us as soon as, are you ok with that? I mean we're supposed to be on a break. It must be serious Samantha when she's texting my private phone."
"I don't have any other plans Terry. I was going to ask if you fancied spending a few days with me somewhere, I mean, nothing silly.
I was just you know, I was just meaning that-"
"That'll be nice Samantha, and I know you're not being silly. We'll go and see what Polly wants and then I'll take you up on your offer, where were you thinking about going?"
"I don't know I hadn't specifically thought of anywhere in particular."
Terry smiled and glanced at her. "That'd be lovely Samantha, and by the way, thank you for accompanying me to see my eh…my wife and son, your company was appreciated, I

know it couldn't have been easy for you either. It's always a shock when people see them in that condition, especially the people who knew them, you know, before…before they were…set upon." The subject was becoming too intense for Samantha's liking and so she changed the topic immediately. "So Terry, what do think about this threat from Angela Bates, do you really think she's bluffing? She seemed so cock sure of herself that there'd be more kidnappings. Oh hell, don't say that's what Polly wants to see you about."

Mercer looked at his colleague. "See *us* about.

I don't think so Samantha, that bitch was bluffing, she had to be. It was just a last ditch effort to try and weasel her way out of a lengthy sentence, although, I can't think what else Polly would want to see us for if I'm being honest, but we'll see soon enough, we'll pull in here for something to eat and then head back down to see her." After a few seconds of silence he said, in hind sight, "Christ I hope not Samantha, I hope it's not about that."

"No I think you're right Terry, three months have elapsed since she said that, and so far nothing has happened."

"Well, we'll see soon enough Samantha, but God help us if it is that Polly wants to see us about, because if it is, then it's like starting over from the beginning. There'll be a whole new bunch of people involved who we've probably never heard of and a whole new bunch of parents distraught and heartbroken."

SCOTLAND YARD.

BROADWAY VICTORIA.

Although Polly Sheppard had been informed about what had happened in the old mansion in Buckinghamshire, she hadn't been informed of every single detail. Having said that, she knew Terry Mercer better than most people and she also knew he'd been keeping certain details to himself. At this moment in time she had no further concerns and the report, his report, had gone through to the VCD. (Violent Crimes Department.) She doubted very much if they would have anything to say about his assessment. Terry and Samantha sat directly in front of her in her office.
"What is it Polly"? Mercer sighed. It was inevitable that whatever it was, it was not good. "Don't say it's another kidnapping...please."
"No, it's not a kidnapping Terry. It's a murder, and a very brutal one I might add." "Are there any witnesses? Dare I ask?"
"Nope, only that a white Transit van was spotted in the close vicinity of the crime shortly before the murder took place."
"Excuse my abrupt attitude Polly, but why the fuck have you got us in here? Haven't you got someone working on this? We're supposed to be on our break, we've only had one day and-."
"The murder took place in Mitcham Terry. Do you know anyone in Mitcham who happens to own a white van? A white Transit van?" The question was rhetorical.
Terry looked at Samantha. There was one person they knew who owned one and Polly was well aware of who it was. Colin Green.
"Did anyone get identification of the number plates?"
"Not as far as I know Terry but its' early days, less than thirty-six hours ago.
I happen to know about Colin Green Terry, about all his past in the military and all that. Go and talk to him Terry. Now, I'm not saying it was him who committed this murder, but, when I give you the details of the victim."
"Which are?"
"A Polish gentleman by the name of Antek Kowalski, mid-fifties, bachelor, and registered paedophile. He's done time for interfering with young girls. Lives alone, unemployed for the last three months, that's when he was released from prison."
Mercer's head went down. Out came the cigarettes. He lit one up and stood on his feet. "I fucking warned him. I told him what would happen if he continued with this vigilante thing he's got in his head, stupid twat! If he's took that Spencer girl with him and done

this, I'll do time myself for the beating I'll give him, I warned him Samantha, you heard me threatening him with the consequences of his stupidity...stupid bloody man."
"Terry, calm yourself down." said Polly. "There's nothing to say it was definitely him who done this, I'm only saying, go and talk to him. Why I'm asking you to go and see him is for the plain and simple reason that if it should turn out to be him, well, we kind of owe him a favour for what he done for us in Lithuania. Of course, if that should be the case, then it would be his very last warning Terry, and that's to say we could get him off with it, if the evidence was not irrefutable." "Polly, that's illogical what you're proposing, letting him off, and illegal...but, you're the boss."

An hour and a half later Terry and Samantha sat in Colin Green's house awaiting his return. Jillian Green had made them cups of tea and was chatting merrily. She informed the detectives that she hadn't a clue as to where her husband was but that he'd texted her and said he'd be home within the hour. That was nearly an hour and a half ago. Terry and Samantha had been here now for nearly half an hour.
"I'm sure he won't be long now Terry, he said something about a couple of small jobs to do and then he was going to get the van washed out, something like that." Terry was tempted to ask her if her husband had left the house at any specific time of night in the last couple of days or so but decided against it.
It would sound like he was being accused of something, and God knows the woman had been through enough lately. Besides, he wanted to see Colin's reaction when asked certain questions as to his recent whereabouts. What Terry dreaded most was, if Colin *had* murdered this man, had he used Sophie Spencer as an accomplice?
If he had then the problem was considerably greater than it would have been.
In fact, it would be more than a problem, it would be a very tricky dilemma.
Even as Terry was contemplating the problem Colin Green pulled up outside of his house in his white Transit van. In the van with him was Sophie Spencer.
Jillian's daughter Alison came trundling down the stairs and ran outside to greet Sophie. The two girls embraced and then made their way back inside. Once in, they headed straight up the stairs and into Alison's room. Colin Green entered his house and cheerfully greeted his wife and the two detectives, placing his van keys on the credenza.
"How are you doing Terry? What brings you round here today pal?"
"Oh, just a catch up Colin, we were round this area anyway so we thought we'd nip in for a cuppa and a little chat, you don't mind Samantha and I talking to your wife when you're not in do you?"
Colin Green made no reply and only smiled. "As long as it's nothing serious Terry, Jillian and I have had enough of serious haven't we babes?"

"You can say that again." Replied Jillian, as she rose up from the chair to pour her husband a cup of tea.

As soon as she was out of the room, Samantha said quietly, we need to have a chat Colin, the three of us, and it's very bloody serious. So you just see us out to the car when we leave ok? Otherwise we can have the chat in here in front of Jillian if you prefer, it's entirely up to you."

"It's serious Samantha? What the hell is it? Does it concern me specifically? What the hell is it?" Have I done something wrong?"

Jillian Green re-entered the living room with fresh beverages for everyone.

"My daughter seems to have hit it off with Sophie, hasn't she Colin, the two are practically inseparable." She sighed and continued. "I expect their ordeal will have forged a bond between the pair. Maybe they're helping each other to evade the memories of what happened to them..." Jillian's voice trailed off.

It was indeed a raw subject for her to contemplate, the fact that the unspoken truth of what had happened to her daughter lay always just below the surface of her emotions. So raw in fact, that it almost felt like she had been there and suffered along with them. Through the filthy mire of these people's actions, her daughter's innocence had been cruelly ripped away from her and because of their evil acts, Alison had now been educated in the acts of sick-minded people...her innocence was gone. And that innocence had now been replaced with the most horrific nightmarish memories that could ever be imagined. She hadn't said anything to Colin, but she herself had had to have therapy to help her cope with the stress of it all. She would find herself almost sneaking up to Alison's bedroom door and peeking in the room just to convince herself that her daughter was safely tucked up in her bed at all hours of the morning, occasionally disturbing Colin and waking him up from peaceful sleep.

"Help yourselves to biscuits you pair, there's plenty, I'm just going up stairs to see if Alison and Sophie want anything to eat."

Terry stood up and informed Jillian that he was taking his tea outside to smoke a cigarette and then they would have to be on their way. "Nice to see you again Jillian, you take care and we'll be back soon to see you again, tell the girls we were asking for them."

And with that, Terry and Samantha stepped outside to the back yard to smoke their cigarettes. Colin Green followed them, closing the door behind him. Terry lit up his cigarette and offered the packet to Samantha.

"Where were you Colin a couple of nights ago, just out of curiosity, can you tell me?"

If Colin Green was guilty of anything it certainly wasn't showing on his face.

The man looked genuinely confused. "Lets' see, that'd be Tuesday, I was round at my

friends' house until half past nine and then I was home all night after that. You can ask my friend if you like, his name is Thomas Smith, he just lives round the corner, and I was laying some paving stones for him around his patio, what the hell is this about you pair, are you going to tell me? You obviously think that I'm guilty of something are you going to tell me what the hell I've supposed to have done?"
Samantha looked at Colin almost apologetically. "There's been a murder here in the town Colin, an old man, a registered paedophile. He'd been beaten severely and left on the street to die. The only connection we have is that someone saw a white Transit van around the scene of the crime just before the time of the murder, I say the time of the murder, it's only forensic guess work, we don't actually know the exact time, but as soon as the Transit van was mentioned, and after the way I heard you talking in High Wycombe well, you can't blame us for at least checking it out, we have a job to do Colin after all."
Colin stood nodding his head.
"Yeah, I heard about the murder, everybody is talking about it. I don't have a clue who would have done that. And I know what I was saying in that mansion but I had every right to talk that way, and I'm still glad I shot those bastards in the head, and if you two are honest with yourselves, so are you glad that I shot them. But I'm not going to attack an old defenceless man on the street of my home town now am I? Christ Terry give me a bit of respect would you, and you Samantha, hell I thought we were all friends here...you come to me first before anyone else? Christ Terry, thanks a lot pal. Lithuania is just a distant memory now is it?"
"Come on now!" said Samantha, "that's not fair Colin, you know we are all grateful for your help over there, don't hang that in front of us every time we ask you a question. Anyway, you were home all night after nine-thirty or there- abouts', is that correct?"
"Yes Samantha that is correct, you can even ask Jillian, she'll verify my story, you know that she doesn't tell lies...you'll believe her won't you?"
"Fuck you Colin" said Samantha as she and Terry made their way down the garden path and back out to the street.
Colin Green shouted after them, "I'll let you know if I hear anything you two, catch you soon." He was smiling broadly at the two detectives.
Mercer stopped in his tracks and spun round to stare at the ex-soldier.
"Terry? Ignore his sarcasm, just leave it, he's only being stupid winding us up, or trying to, just forget it Terry." Mercer drew on the last of his cigarette and threw the stub onto the ground.
"Come on Samantha, come with me, I'll wind him up alright."
Terry approached the man he'd classed as his friend and read him his rights.

He then proceeded to write down details of Colin Green's story.

"Now then Colin, I need to interview your wife and the Spencer girl, is she still here just now? Oh, and I'll need statements from Alison as well. They will all be interviewed individually. We'll start with Jillian's story and then Alison and Sophie's if she's here, you still haven't answered me Colin, is Sophie Spencer still here? Oh, and although your wife informed us that you have washed the van out we'll still bring forensics over here to check it out, you know, thoroughly. All this should only take a little more than an hour, and then we'll be out of your faces. So, lets' start with your wife shall we?"

Just at that moment, Sophie Spencer came out into the garden and asked Colin if he could give her a lift home.

Terry said, "Not just yet Sophie we need to ask everyone here some very important questions, yourself included. Tell you what why don't you go with Samantha here and wait upstairs until we call on you."

"What's this about inspector Mercer, I have to get home, my mother will-."

"This won't take very long Sophie and don't worry, we'll inform your mum where you are and we'll give you a lift back home to save Colin the trouble. So, you stay with Sophie Samantha until I've finished with Jillian and Alison."

Colin Green stood with one hand on the clothes pole shaking his head and looking to the ground.

"Something wrong Colin?" said Mercer as he pulled out a note-book from his jacket pocket. Colin Green did not even answer. Mercer made light of the questioning of Jillian Green stating that it was just an unfortunate procedure that had to be done.

"Yes, he came back from Tom's place that night Terry and then he was here all night after that, but you know what he's like, he's in and out of here like a rabbit in its' burrow, always on the bloody move." As Mercer was walking away from Jillian she said something that stirred his suspicious mind. "Oh, he did leave the house again Terry, now that I think about it, he took Sophie home that night.

He was away about an hour or so…said he had a cup of coffee with Sophie's mum, she's so relieved to have her back Terry, we all are, we've been very lucky and it was down to Colin and his friends and you that we did get them back. They've all wanted to thank him individually for bringing their girls home safely."

Mercer smiled at Jillian and agreed with her about her husband's endeavours.

The first thing he was going to do once he'd taken Sophie's story, was to go and talk with Mandy, Sophie's mum. What he dreaded most of all was if Sophie had played any part in the murder of the old man, and that was to say that Colin Green was in fact guilty. The man may have been telling the truth, but after a chat with Mandy Spencer he would be in a better position deciding whether or not to press Colin's story.

He changed the plan. He and Samantha would take Sophie home right now and ask Mandy some questions. They could question Sophie on the way over there.
Terry then informed Samantha of his plan and said his goodbyes to Jillian and Colin Green who was none too pleased with Mercer's questioning.

Samantha sat in the back of the car with Sophie Spencer making small talk and generally trying to make the girl feel at ease. She sensed that she was uptight about something. The situation with Sophie was delicate. She would have to tread very carefully when talking about Colin Green. The girl seemed to have a crush on Colin and it surprised her that Jillian had not picked up on this. Perhaps events from the last few weeks had fogged her vision somewhat. All that seemed to matter to Jillian was the fact that her daughter was back home safe and sound. So, when questioning Sophie, she'd have to be very careful. The last thing they needed was to exacerbate the problem further by making accusations about old men being murdered on the streets of Mitcham.
Samantha began the conversation. "So, Sophie, you and Alison seemed to have hit it off haven't you? She thinks the world of you doesn't she?"
"Yes she does, and I think the world of her."
Sophie then said something that completely shocked Samantha.
"Yeah, and we're free again. We take our liberty for granted don't you think Samantha? I mean, you've been kidnapped, you know what it's like, although I don't think you had men and women fucking the living daylights out of you every minute of the day and coming in your mouth with their foul-tasting sperm, and women sitting on your face while they rub their disgusting bits all over you. That's what Alison and I had to go through every fucking day for nearly five weeks. If it wasn't for Terry and Colin and those two other men, I dread to think what would be happening now. I think I would have fucking topped myself if I'd been caught trying to escape from that hell.
Have you ever had anal sex Samantha? When you're not expecting it, it can be the most painful thing ever. And the men who are raping you are all fucking laughing about it, can you believe that? They think it's some kind of joke, fucking three of them all taking turns at using yours truly here as nothing more than a shag-bag, a spunk-bucket...a slut, because to them, that's exactly what I was, and every other unfortunate girl in there. And then the fuckers have the audacity to leave you a fifty Euros tip...yeah, we take our liberty for granted...but so do they." Terry looked into the rear-view mirror. Samantha tried to hide her awkwardness and continued. "Alison's parents are brilliant don't you think Sophie?
They think the world of you as well."
"Yes, they are brilliant, especially Colin. I'm going on holiday with them soon, we're

going up to Scotland. Colin's going to learn me how to shoot and everything."
Samantha then thought about a different approach.
"That day in High Wycombe Sophie, what did you think of me when I shot that woman? Did it change your opinion of me, as a person I mean?"
"Why would it do that? The bitch was part of the gang that kidnapped me...and you forget, I didn't see you shooting her remember, I was too busy with Colin whipping the disgusting skin of that bastard outside. And before you ask, yes I was glad I witnessed Colin shooting those fuckers in the head after we'd wasted good energy dragging that piece of dog-shit down those steps. We should have made him suffer more before we allowed him to die, you should have heard the fucker screaming outside when I was whipping him, Colin learned me how to use the bull-whip, it's really cool and it fucking hurts them good, his back was bleeding like fuck. I fucking loved it, because each time I thought about the monsters in Lithuania interfering with me, it drove me to inflict as much pain onto him as was humanly possible...and then the fucker spoiled it, he passed out. It's no fun when they're unconscious."
Samantha was actually reeling from the shock of Sophie's language and attitude towards violence, and in particular, revenge. It obviously wasn't enough for her to be back home safe and well with her family, she was undoubtedly fuelled into revenge. Samantha remembered the condition of the man before Colin shot him in the head. There was not a single shred of skin left on his back, and here was a girl who was almost revelling in the fact that she'd inflicted most of the damage, proud almost at the fact that she'd learned how to use a bull-whip. And what the hell was she putting into Alison Green's head as well? Was she of the same opinion as Sophie here regarding revenge? The situation was turning for the worse it seemed with every passing second. It was as if Sophie describing in great detail what had happened to her over there was the perfect excuse for anything she would do in the future. And was Colin Green helping to fuel her anger? Was it he who was keeping the fires burning in Sophie's belly?
They arrived in Bromley to find Mandy Spencer frantic with worry.
"Sophie, why can't you text me to tell me where you are? You never tell me anything. I was so worried. Just let me know where the hell you are girl, don't you think we've been through enough lately? I hadn't a clue where you were. The last time I spoke to Jillian Green she said you hadn't arrived there yet. Hell Sophie, you know how worried I get, the least you could do would be to-."
"Mum, give it a rest would you. I can take care of myself, you don't have to worry about that. If any fucker gets in my way from now on, then it's them you should be worrying about not me, because I won't take any shit off anybody from now on...not anymore, and anyway, mister Mercer here said he was going to inform you that I'd be coming

home with him." She looked at Mercer who immediately apologised.
"I'm sorry Mandy, I forgot."
Mandy's voice was calm now and delicate. "Sophie, what's got into you darling? I've never heard you talking like this before about violence and aggression. What's made you feel like this? Are you being bullied? Because if you are I can-." "Mum nobody's bullying me I can assure you. And what do you mean what's made me like this? Is there something wrong with defending yourself? All I'm saying is you shouldn't worry about me the way you do. Colin's learned me how to defend myself against attack, he's showed me some things I can do to hurt them...I'm fine mum."
Sophie looked at Terry Mercer and Samantha Reynolds. Now, if everyone has finished with me I'd like to go to my room and listen to some music, would that be ok with everybody? Mum, should I send you a text message when I get there?" Mandy did not even reply, she just lit herself a cigarette and rose up from the chair to make herself and the two detectives a cup of coffee.
Sophie left the living room and headed upstairs to her bedroom.
Mandy came back into the living room. She sat down and sighed heavily.
Terry and Samantha looked at her sympathetically.
"I don't know what to do for the best you two, honestly. I'm at my wits end.
I ask her a simple question, I get my face bitten off. I ask her to keep in touch with me so as I know where the hell she is, and she deliberately ignores my request.
She's changing, and not for the better. Her brother asked her how she was feeling the other day and she tells him to go and fuck himself with a bread knife.
You've got no idea what it's like living with her just now.
I speak with her psychiatrist and she tells me that Sophie is making remarkable progress. When I tell her about her attitude to me and her brother she comes out with some shit like, oh, it's just a reflex to the ordeal she's just had. Something about the human-being's natural reaction is to only hurt the ones we love, well she's doing a bloody good job there for sure."
Mercer leaned forward on his chair and spoke almost in a whisper, as if Sophie could be listening at the door. "Have you spoken to Colin Green about this? She says he's been learning her how to defend herself. Maybe it's his influence that's making her talk like this."
Mandy looked at Terry and Samantha. "He's never even came in here for me to get a chance to talk with him. He drops Sophie off out there and then he drives off."
Samantha said, "Didn't he mention anything the other night, you know when he dropped Sophie off, he said he had a cup of coffee with you a couple of nights ago."
Mandy drew hard on her cigarette. "He's never been in here since the girls came back

from Lithuania. Who told you he was here?"

Mercer jumped in. "It doesn't matter Mandy I must have misheard Jillian Green. Does she go to the Green's house quite often then?"

"She's never away from there, and I'm going to tell you something in strict confidence ok? I actually think she is infatuated with him. Whether or not it has to do with him playing a part in setting them free or if it's because she's practically grew up without a father, I don't know, but she seems to spend as much time as she possibly can with him. I'm telling you this in the strictest confidence you understand. If she heard me telling you this she would never speak to me again. She's just received confirmation about being accepted into the university and she's neither here nor there about it. A few months ago she was boasting to me that she would make something of her life and that she'd achieve far more than working as a barmaid in a stinking pub. That was a dig at me by the way. Now, I don't think she cares two jots what the hell happens to her. I am going to arrange a meeting with him, this Colin, and I'm going to tell him a few things. Do you know, they've invited Sophie to go on holiday with them and they didn't even consult me. Sophie came in here and blasted it out that she was going to Scotland with the Greens and that Colin was going to learn her how to shoot and how to sharpen knives and put up bloody tents. All I want is for her to do well. She has an opportunity here at the uni to gain qualifications that could pave her way in life, but no, all she wants to do is learn how to live rough and shoot guns with soldier-blue there. I'm going to give him the sharp end of my tongue…bloody sixteen-year-old girl. What the hell is his wife thinking? She's bound to have noticed the amount of time he's spending with her Jesus Christ."

Samantha followed Mandy through to the kitchen. As Mandy made the coffee Samantha wrapped her arms around her and hugged her, tapping her on the shoulder. Mandy melted and broke down. The two women sat down at the kitchen table. Terry came through and made up the beverages. Now all three sat at the kitchen table. Terry began to speak. "I'm going to have a word with Colin Green Mandy. He seems to be ruffling quite a few feathers these days. He's not our favourite person just now either. The first thing I'll do is to inform him that we are not happy with the amount of time he's spending with a juvenile. What I can't do, is break up the friendship Sophie has with Alison his daughter, but I can tell him how much trouble he's causing by spending too much time with Sophie." Terry looked at Mandy who's' face was beginning to show the stress that he'd seen there just a few weeks earlier. He couldn't for the life of him inform Mandy of what he'd witnessed Sophie doing to a man's' back with a bullwhip. On top of all this, he now knew that Colin Green had been lying about having coffee with Mandy. So, as far as he was concerned, Colin Green could not produce an alibi for the night in question, the night the old Polish man was murdered. There was no doubt about it, this snowball was rolling down-hill fast, and it was gathering at an incredible rate. The next talk he would have with Colin Green would be very serious indeed. Although at this point they had no concrete evidence, the needle of guilt was pointing straight towards the ex-soldier. The first question he would ask him would be, why the hell was he intending to learn a young girl like Sophie Spencer how to shoot? What possible use would that be to any young woman who had her whole future in front of her? And how to sharpen knives? What the fuck was he thinking about…and did he intend to learn his own daughter these military skills? Or was this particular lesson in survival specifically for Sophie Spencer alone?

ST MARY'S ROYAL INFIRMARY.

STRATFORD.

Roxanne Styles had made a remarkable recovery, surprising the surgeon who'd been working on her for the past three weeks. Her broken teeth had been replaced or capped where possible by the hospital dentist as well which added to enhance her natural appearance. She still had bruising around her brow and her left cheek but she was now off the danger list. The swelling was down as well after her recent surgery. The surgeon had to repair both upper and lower jaw-bones, one of which had been broken in three different places. The swelling was down near her brain as well and it had been this that was worrying the doctors the most. Broken bones can be repaired or even replaced, but injury to the brain was a different story, however Roxanne was well on her way to a full recovery. She was now able to feed herself and with a certain amount of caution, walk around the ward. One of the nurses was even kind enough to escort her outside so that she could have a cigarette. When she'd been brought in here she'd lapsed into a comma lasting for almost four days, but despite that, she still remembered the faces of the thugs who'd put her in this condition.
They were two very big men indeed, well over six feet. Their heavy winter coats making them appear huge. She remembered the first blow she received from the man. It felt as though she'd walked right in front of a wrecking ball and took its' full force on her face. She remembered the loud crack she heard as she hit the floor, and then she couldn't remember anything after that. But their faces were still clear as a bell in her mind, she would recognise them anywhere. On the day the paramedics had come for her they had lifted her mobile phone from the floor. As soon as Roxanne had recovered consciousness the surgeon had gave it back to her. She sat on her bed now scrutinising the message that someone had sent her. Whoever it was had kept their number withdrawn. The message read; *Tell detectives Mercer and Reynolds to go and visit Angela Bates again. She has the names of the two men who did this to you. The same two men were also responsible for the beheading of Geoffrey Marsden.* Roxanne made a decision there and then. She would inform Mercer of the message and let him decide what to do. Whoever had sent this quite obviously knew the men and Angela Bates. She remembered on one of the nights at her flat seeing these strangers appear, and sure enough, they were very tall but they were no more than silhouettes in the darkness. She'd watched them enter the blonde's flat.

Half an hour later Terry Mercer arrived at the hospital with Samantha Reynolds. Terry was laden with arms full of gifts for Roxanne. He had brought her a couple of sleeves of her favourite cigarettes as well as get-well cards. The flowers had been taken from him by one of the nurses who said she would put them on display. He had boxes of soft chocolates and magazines, and above all, a smile that was as cheerful as a Christmas morning." Look at you little lady, sitting up here like a princess. I knew it, I just bloody knew it. They couldn't keep you down, didn't I tell you Samantha…hard as nails, you're my hero Roxanne, I'm so pleased to see you. How are you feeling sweetheart, are they looking after you?" Samantha smiled as Terry leaned over and cuddled Roxanne Styles, tentatively of course. She could see that the man was genuinely happy that she'd made this recovery. He picked up the boxes of cigarettes that had fallen from his arms and laid them on the small bed-side table next to Roxanne's bed. Samantha brought a couple of chairs over for them and sat them down.

"You can see for yourselves how they're looking after me Terry. I have never been looked after like this in my life, and as for that surgeon, he showed me photographs of me when they brought me in. The fucking Russian bastard walloped me right enough, and he was built like a brick shit-house. After the first time he hit me, I don't remember anything after that, all the fucking lights went out. Some kind bastard must have phoned for an ambulance because those two fuckers wouldn't. The nasty bastards left me for dead."

Samantha sat almost bursting into laughter with a hand over her mouth.

The profanations would continue in Roxanne's life as per usual. No change there then. Roxanne continued. "Here look at this, fuck knows who sent it, but they're saying that you two should go back and talk with this Angela Bates bitch. They're saying that she knows the names of the fuckers who done me in and something about a guy called Geoffrey being beheaded. It's supposed to be the same fuckers who done me in, you know, that beheaded this man, here you look at it."

Terry scrutinised the message on Roxanne's phone.

"Who's this Geoffrey guy, do you know him? I mean did you know him?"

Mercer looked at Roxanne nodding his head. "Yeah I knew him Roxanne.

He was a lovely guy, a nice old man. They killed him because he wouldn't tell them my address, just the same as they set about you for the same reason. But whoever is trying to get us to go and see Angela Bates is way behind the times. Both men who attacked you sweetheart were found dead in a flat a couple of doors along from you, so even if Angela knew their names it's not going to do her any bloody good."

"Who killed the bastards, was it you two?"

"No, it wasn't Roxanne, and that's just it, we don't know who killed them, but I can assure you they are as dead as door-posts."

"That's a shame" said Roxanne, "I would have loved to have met the bastards again and unleashed a mighty blow with my right foot straight into their fucking balls and repeat the exercise several times until my feet grew fucking tired...I would have fucking loved that."

Terry then said, "Samantha here has a nice surprise for you haven't you Samantha?"

"Yes I have Roxanne, someone, and we think it's the person who killed your attackers, must have went through your drawers in your flat, and retrieved some money you had hidden away. If those thugs hadn't been killed they would have probably stolen it. However, this money was posted to us at Scotland Yard and inside the envelope was a note stating that the enclosed money belonged to Roxanne Styles, wasn't that nice of them to do that Roxanne?" Roxanne smiled although it caused her quite a bit of discomfort. "Yes it was, what a nice gesture that was...killing those Russian bastards for me and saving my money."

"You'll find Roxanne if you look in the envelope, that whoever killed them went through their pockets and retrieved the princely sum of eight hundred pounds. They've put that in there for you as well." Samantha continued "As well as that, as a good will gesture and for your bravery, Terry and I have put a few quid in there as well."

In total when Roxanne counted the money, the figure had come to just under four thousand pounds. Roxanne thumbed through the notes with expertise counting in a whispered voice as she done so. "Thank you, you two, thank you so much, this is the nicest thing anyone has ever done for me."

Terry and Samantha were even more surprised when Roxanne stated, "This is brilliant, I'll be able to buy Mr Harper my surgeon a lovely present for helping me through this, and the little nurse who's been looking after me round the fucking clock. Can I give you two another cuddle?" Terry and Samantha leaned forward in turn to be cuddled by a very grateful Roxanne Styles. To brighten up Roxanne further Samantha said, "Oh, and by the way, Terry has seen to it that your rent has been taken care of for the rest of the year, he felt it was the least he could do, seeing as how you've been so brave. We thought we were going to lose you. So, you're all paid up Roxanne." The two detectives talked with Roxanne Styles for a further half hour or so. Terry, in particular was so relieved that the young mother had pulled through this. He'd thought just as the surgeon would have thought that Roxanne's addiction to heroin would hamper her chances of survival, possibly breaking down her body's defence system, through lack of nourishment, but everything had been taken care of and furthermore Roxanne had been put onto a programme to wean her off the dreaded drug. She herself admitted that her addiction had stolen so many things from her life and deprived her of so many opportunities.

Her main aim in life now, was to win back the authorities' confidence and be able to have her child back home with her.

It was going to be a long hard road, but a worthwhile journey.

Terry and Samantha left St Marys' feeling rather exuberated with the attitude of Roxanne Styles. As they headed to the car Samantha said, "You have a bit of a thing for Roxanne Terry don't you?"

He smiled as they walked, "Yes, I suppose I do Samantha, but not in the way that you are insinuating, I just like to see the underdog getting up and hitting back from time to time. I'm amazed at her recovery, she was in some bloody mess Sam, I have a thing for people rising up and believing in themselves...hell a thing Samantha, you make it sound like I fancy her...a thing, Christ."

MITCHAM.

Colin Green sat with Sophie Spencer in his transit van in the car park of the Cumberland care home. Sophie had taken to smoking cigarettes. She lit one up and offered Colin Green one. The only reason they were parked here was because Colin had some very important things to discuss with Sophie. Parked here, there would be little chance of them being disturbed, unless of course, they were being watched.
"Sophie, they're on to us." He said, lighting up his cigarette. "Plus, Terry Mercer has spoken to me about how much time I seem to be spending with you."
"What are you saying Colin? What the fuck has it got to do with him, or anybody else for that matter who we spend time with?"
"It's not that Sophie, I think he thinks that our relationship is eh...is sexual."
"What!!? What the fuck? Why would he think that? It's typical isn't it, fuck sakes, does the whole world revolve around fucking sex?
It seems to with men. Everything has to do with sex, it's just-."
"Anyway Sophie, we'll have to, I mean I'll have to spend less time with you.
I think Jillian is beginning to think the same as Terry Mercer and his partner, you know Samantha, they all seem to think that its' unhealthy, the amount of time we spend together, I'm just saying Sophie, that's where its' at just now, that's what they're all thinking."
"Listen Colin, if I'm-."
"Sophie, sorry for interrupting you. They know it was me who killed that old paedophile the other night. Oh they're not going to any great lengths to prove it, I can tell, but they sure as hell think it was me. They're worried in case you were involved."
"But I was involved Colin, I was with you remember?"
"Yes, but they don't know that Sophie." Colin sighed. "Look, I think we'd better call it a day just now Sophie, at least for a while."
Sophie looked away from Colin out of her window at nothing in particular as she drew on her cigarette. "I'm not changing my opinion on anything Colin.
My attitude will never change towards perverted men and women, not after everything I've been through, and your daughter by the way in case you've forgotten, I'm sorry for that Colin, I know you could never forget, sorry that slipped out. Alison will always be a friend of mine for the rest of my life now."
"Sophie, I know how you feel, and I feel much the same way, but if we are to continue with what we're doing we'll have to give it a rest for just now, Christ Sophie, we've killed four people up to now...we've been lucky. Terry warned me after I shot that

bastard in High Wycombe. He warned me to call it a day or he would arrest me. Even as it stands now, I think he knows it was me who killed the paedophile.
And he knows for certain that it was us who killed the two Lithuanians. By the way, that prostitute girl survived that beating. Listen, I won't forget what we plan to do Sophie, just…just leave it for now. After everything has calmed down a bit, and then maybe we can proceed, but if I'm not careful, they'll jail me as quick as look at me, and I can't have that, I can't and I won't leave my wife and daughters unprotected…never. Can you understand where I'm coming from Sophie?"
She nodded her head in agreement, accepting the situation he was in.
She didn't ever think she'd be able to pull any killings off herself, even though she despised all the sick bastards who took advantage of vulnerable women and children. She could never kill unaided, at least, she thought she couldn't.
Colin Green then proceeded to tell Sophie something he hoped would help her be patient. "You know, the best killers in the world are very clever people Sophie.
They are very rarely suspected. They live their lives as far as everyone around them are concerned, as normal. The finger of suspicion is very rarely pointed at them, and that's what we have to do Sophie. Now I hear that you've been a bit snappy with your mum and your brother lately, so what we have to do is make amends to that. I need you to be pleasant to them again, and before you say anything, I know you don't mean to be cutting with them but it's hurting your mum's feelings Sophie. And your brother David, you have to let them know how much you love them. Do that, and no-one will ever suspect you of anything. You don't tell your brother to fuck himself with a bread knife for goodness sakes. Terry told me the state that boy was in when you were abducted. You must win their confidence back. Give your mum a cuddle and your brother. Tell them how happy you are that you have them for your family. Let them know how much you love them. Tell your mum how much you're looking forward to starting university, and thank her for all her support. No-one will know just exactly what goes on in your mind. They won't suspect you are up to anything whenever you leave the house like they do now. They actually think that you and I are meeting up for sexual endeavours Sophie, and of course, if you are snapping at your mum and your brother every two minutes then that just fuels their suspicions. Are you catching my drift Sophie?"
She laughed at Colin's deliberate fumbled clumsy attempt to talk like a teenager. Everything he said made sense, and if she was honest with herself she had been treating her mum and brother a bit nasty lately. Now that Colin had pointed out why they were constantly keeping tabs on her she felt better, and loved, after all, no matter how annoying her mum was being she was only concerned for her safety. Her mum had had to be a mother *and* a father to her and her brother, and all said and done, she'd

done a bloody good job at the end of the day. She and her brother had never done without. She remembered prior to her abduction, that her mum was accepting the fact that she was a young woman now, and all the references to the short skirts was only for her own well-being. She was in fact, looking out for her...even then. Sophie nodded her head again. "Yes, I know Colin, and you're right, I have been a bit nasty, I'll have a talk with my mum when I get home today. Drop me off in the town centre, I'm going to buy her something nice by way of an apology, and I'll get my brother a pair of jeans, I know which ones he likes. Was he really in a state when I was missing Colin?"

"According to Terry Mercer, he was in more than a state Sophie, the boy was frantic...he loves you to bits Sophie. Show them how much you love *them*. David would defend you with his life, now you can't knock that. Meanwhile Sophie, I'll be keeping tabs on the streets finding out if there are any bastards talking about kidnappers, we just have to take the pan off the stove for a while...ok?"

"Thanks Colin, for the talk, and for pointing out to me how important my family are to me. But because of Lithuania there will always be a vengeful burning in my stomach. It's never going to happen to me again Colin."

"I know Sophie... we'll both see to that kiddo."

SCOTLAND YARD.

BROADWAY VICTORIA.

Terry Mercer sat in one of the canteens with Samantha Reynolds discussing where they would spend the next three days. Samantha didn't particularly want to leave the country and so when she mentioned a break up to York Terry was in full agreement. Samantha had always wanted to see the architecture in York and particularly York Minster. Polly Sheppard entered the room and brought her lunch over with her to join the pair. Before she had a chance to say anything Terry said, "I've had a word with Colin Green Polly."
"And?"
"He denies having anything to do with the murder. Of course, he's going to say that isn't he. He bloody knows how good he is at covering up his tracks, plus the fact we warned him of the consequences should he ever drop his guard. When I suggested to him that he was having an affair with Sophie Spencer he looked for a moment as though he was going to attack me. He stared into my face and said, "Please don't tell me you're accusing me of being a paedophile, because that's exactly what it would be if I were having sex with that girl, don't you ever repeat that question to me again, or you and I will part company forever." "Samantha couldn't resist. "So much Terry for the beating you were going to give him."
Terry looked briefly at Samantha and then continued with Polly.
"He's adamant he had nothing to do with it, the old mans' murder.
He told me not to bother mentioning that to him again. All he wanted to do was to get back on with his life now that he had his daughter safely back home. In other words Polly, he was telling me to leave him in peace. I think I will."
"That would seem to be a wise idea Terry." said Samantha, smiling at Polly.
Again, Terry ignored Samantha's sarcasm. "We went to visit Roxanne Styles at the hospital. She showed us a text message someone had sent her. The text said that she was to inform Samantha and I to go back and visit Angela Bates, and that she knew the names of the people who had attempted to kill her and who had beheaded old Treble-clef. But we know that those two were taken care of. Just thought I'd tell you Polly. Has there been any sighting of Monica Carosova do you know? She said according to Bates, that she was coming back over here to stock up on her girls. According to Bates, she and some other friends of hers' are going to start up another brothel somewhere else in Lithuania. I just wondered if you'd heard anything."

Polly answered with a mouthful of Lettice. "Not as far as I know Terry, and we've got surveillance on all the major airports. If she steps onto British soil again she'll be spotted right away."

Terry laughed out loud suddenly, making a few other people in the canteen look at him. "What? What the fuck is wrong with you lot? Is there a law against laughing now you nosey bastards? Get on with your fucking meals you nosey twats!"

"Terry, please, calm yourself, you and your bloody choleric personality, you gave them a fright that's all, and anyway what were you laughing at?"

"Nothing, it's just what Bates said. She asked us if we thought that the woman was stupid enough to enter Britain on one of the main airline airports. She seemed to think that she'd arrive in Britain at some little fishing port or harbour and that she'd be disguised, or at least looking nothing like any photographs we have of her."

Polly sat looking at the two and momentarily stopped chewing her food, as if she were contemplating the possibility of that happening.

"Spoil my lunch Terry why don't you. Christ I won't be able to get that thought out of my head now for the rest of the day. Oh dear God, Lord help us Terry if that should happen. I'll tell you what. I want you and Samantha to go back over there to Ashford, and have a word with that bitch again. Try and find out anything you can about that Lithuanian woman and anything else you can ok?"

"Can't it wait until we come back from our break Polly?" Polly had opened up her magazine on the table and was looking at it. Without looking up from the pages she replied, "No."

MITCHAM. 12:30pm.

Jillian Green was just finished washing the mid-day lunch dishes when the telephone rang. Colin was out at work and Alison was upstairs in her room listening to music with Sophie Spencer. She dried her hands and lifted the telephone from the small table in the hallway. "Hello, Jillian Green speaking."
"Hello Jillian, its Helen Morgan here. My daughter Kathleen was wondering if Rebecca is there. Kathleen's got tickets for the concert tell her, and she's just wondering if she's coming over. She says that Rebecca is not answering her mobile, we were just wondering if she is coming over today, she was supposed to stay over here last night but she hasn't showed up. Maybe something came up and she couldn't cancel, is she there Jillian?"
A stab of fear punched Jillian Green hard in the stomach.
She actually felt dizzy as she tried to answer the woman.
"She didn't show? She left here last night at about six o clock.
She said she was going to Kathleen's house in Stratford. She's left your phone number on the table here, and you say she didn't arrive?"
"Listen Jillian, perhaps she's had a change of plan.
Perhaps she's stayed at another pals' house, you know what they're like, Kathleen's terrible for changing plans at a moments' notice and not telling anyone. I'm sure she'll be in touch with you shortly, you'll see."
Jillian stood motionless half listening to Helens' reassurances.
A mothers' instinct tells them everything they need to know, and Jillian Greens' instinct was telling her that something was seriously wrong. For a kick off if Rebecca had changed her plans she would have undoubtedly informed her mother. She'd left here the previous evening intending to stay at Kathleen Morgan's house in Stratford. Jillian politely informed Helen Morgan that she would get Rebecca to call Kathleen as soon as she showed up, but it was more of a prayer than a statement. She placed the phone down on its' cradle and shouted upstairs for Alison to come down.
Alison Green came trundling down the stairs followed closely by Sophie Spencer. Sophie could see even before Jillian said anything that something was worrying the woman.
"Has your sister contacted you lately Alison? Has she said anything on her mobile to you? because I've just had Helen Morgan on the phone from Stratford.
She said that Rebecca didn't show up last night. She was supposed to stay over at Kathleen's house, has she said anything to you about changing her plans?"
Alison looked at her mum bemused. "No mum she hasn't. She said she'd see me today

when she got back. She was going to see if she could get me a ticket for the concert next week. She said she'd be home about lunch time today, what's wrong mum? Have you tried her mobile phone? Here, I'll try now."

Alison pressed the digit for her sisters' mobile and held it to her ear.

"No, her phone is switched off, she must be busy."

Jillian looked at her daughter. "Alison, you know we have a rule when you two are out and about, you know she never switches off her phone. Even if she doesn't answer it, it is never switched off."

"Mum, she might have run down her battery, she could be charging it."

"Alison, if you're charging your phone you can still receive an incoming call, hell you know that better than me. She would see that we were trying to contact her." "Listen mum, I think you're panicking a bit, I'm sure there's a perfectly simple explanation for her phone being switched off."

Alison and Sophie went back up the stairs.

Jillian Green was now on her mobile instructing her husband to come home immediately. In the forty minutes it took for Colin Green to return home Jillian had tried every single friend of Rebecca's to see if she had contacted them recently. Every single one of them said they hadn't heard from her in a while. Even as Colin entered the house Jillian burst out into tears and threw herself into her husband's arms.

"Oh my God Colin, they've got Rebecca now, I just know it, I can feel it in my bones, they've taken my girl from me, what the hell are we going to do?"

Colin had listened to all the details given to him by his wife and had to admit, that it didn't look good for Rebecca, of course, he couldn't tell Jillian that. He had to keep her as calm as he could for the sake of Alison. He was going to have to ask Polly Sheppard a few favours if his biggest fears materialised, and they were, that these bastards had taken his daughter deliberately. They had targeted her specifically because of his involvement in the rescuing of the girls in Lithuania. This would mean that whoever had done it was part of the original crew who'd taken the girls over there. Mercer had said something to him about the bitch Angela Bates and how she'd claimed to know the names of these other people who were going to continue the kidnappings.

First things first.

He would inform the police of his daughter's disappearance, but then he would get Mercer to issue him with a pass so as he could speak in person with Polly Sheppard. He calmed his wife down for as much as that was possible and informed her that he had to go and speak with Terry Mercer. As he made his way down the path Sophie Spencer came running out after him. "Colin, would you like me to come with you? You know as well as me that something is wrong. I haven't said as much to Alison or Jillian, but as soon as she told us about Rebecca not turning up last night at her friends' house I knew something had happened."

"No Sophie, you stay here kid, try and keep them calm."

He knew he'd hurt Sophie's feelings and so he said to her, "Listen, Sophie, if this has gone wrong, then I am undoubtedly going to need your assistance, so can I rely on your help if I need you?"

"I'm not even going to answer that Colin, you already know the answer to that question."

"Good girl, now you look after them in there until I get back, hell knows when that'll be though, I'll keep in touch Sophie, and remember, if by some miracle Rebecca comes home then you let me know immediately, will you do that for me?"

"Of course I will Colin." She looked at the man who had saved her from her ordeal.

"Colin I hope with all my heart that…you know…"

"Yes, I know Sophie, I'll talk to you soon." He started up the van and drove off to face whatever fate had planned out for him. The trouble with this situation was, that it wasn't like any other abduction. There would be no plea for a ransom payment, no bargain nor any quid-pro-quo situation. No, this would have been done for punishment, and specifically punishment to him. If it were these people, then they would know that he knew exactly what was going to happen to Rebecca. She hadn't been taken for her looks, pretty as she was, no, it wouldn't have mattered one jot if Rebecca had been ugly, they were taking her to put her through an even harsher experience than her sister had gone through, just to get to him. His only hope would be perhaps that somehow they could release one of the prisoners they had in exchange for his daughter, that was his only hope, and even if that was the case there was no way any of those three sadistic prisoners would be released. Polly Sheppard would never allow that to happen, and neither would Geraldine Prowse at Bronzefield Prison if they were trying to set Angela Bates free. He would inform Terry Mercer and Samantha Reynolds of the situation and hope to God that they could come up with some kind of plan of action, because right now he had never felt as vulnerable as this in his entire life.

It looked to all intents and purposes that they'd taken Rebecca to torture him. They hadn't been in touch and maybe that was part of the torture, to leave him and his wife worried sick every day of their lives, and waking up to each morning wondering what on earth had happened to their daughter, and was she still alive. He arrived at Scotland Yard. Terry had given him Polly Sheppard's number when they'd been in Lithuania in case he couldn't get hold of him or if something had gone terribly wrong.

He was told never to use the number unless it was extremely necessary.

This was extremely necessary.

He pressed the digits nervously on his mobile not really knowing what kind of reception he would get from Polly.

"Hello Polly Sheppard."

"Hi Polly, this em...this is Colin Green I'm outside the building, I was hoping to talk to Terry or Samantha but I've been informed that they're not here.

I was wondering if I could have a word with you, it is extremely important Miss Sheppard or I wouldn't bother you. I've had your number since Terry gave it to me in Lithuania. I need to speak –."

"Stay where you are Colin, I'm coming down to get you, it'll save you a lot of carry on filling paperwork in, because they won't let you in otherwise."

Five minutes later Colin was riding the elevator with the chief inspector.

"Colin, I'm not trying to make light of your situation, but don't you think you might be being a little pedantic? I mean it hasn't even been twenty-four hours that she's been missing. You may be worrying for nothing. Have you tried her friends' phone numbers?"

Colin did not even answer. She knew the answer to the question by the look of disdain on his face.

"There could be any number of explanations why your daughter hasn't returned home. Does she have boyfriends?"

"Miss Sheppard, with all due respect, I think I know my daughter.

If she had changed her plans in any way the first thing she would have done would have been to inform her friend and then us, Jillian and I, because she knows how much her mum worries about their well-being. She is a very responsible young woman miss Sheppard, that's how I know that something is wrong."

As Colin was talking to Polly, her mobile buzzed on her desk.

"Excuse me Colin."

Terry Mercer was sounding frantic.

"Polly, we need to get hold of Colin Green, I've just had a text message from those bastards about kidnappings. I think it's part of the crew that was involved with Lithuania, they're saying-."

"He's here Terry, he's right here. You get over here as soon as you can, I'll tell Colin to wait for you."

Polly switched off her phone and sighed heavily.

"That was Terry Colin, you've to wait here until he gets here. I'm sorry to say, it seems you were right. Terry said he's had a text message from people who were involved with the kidnappings."

"Oh Christ no." Colin mumbled through his hand which was over his mouth.

"Oh dear God, this is dire Miss Sheppard, this is bad."

"Colin, lets' wait and see exactly what they've said to Terry, they may want to negotiate with you. Terry said that Angela Bates girl had told him that the kidnappings wouldn't stop. He thought that she was just trying her hand at reducing her prison sentence, so much for that theory."

Colin Green was in a state of anxiety. "There's nothing, nothing I can do here."
"Negotiate?
Negotiate with what Miss Sheppard, I don't have anything they want.
No, it's like I thought, they've done this to punish me for what I done in Lithuania, oh my poor baby, my poor Rebecca."

Polly rose from her chair to make a fresh pot of coffee.

"We'll know better the situation Colin when Terry and Samantha arrive, it's horrible I know, but lets' wait and see what Terrys' saying." Just under half an hour later Terry Mercer sat down at the table with Samantha Reynolds, Polly Sheppard, and Colin Green. Colin immediately opened the conversation.

"What the hell are they saying Terry? Have they got her? Have they got Rebecca?"
Mercer cleared his throat. He hated moments like these.
"Yes, they've got her Colin."

He pulled out his mobile phone and showed Colin the message they sent him. "They're saying that you'd better stay at home tomorrow morning and wait for the postman. He or she are going to deliver a small package to your door and you do not want your wife to open this package because she'll be frantic enough and distressed beyond words without worsening her condition unnecessarily. Be a man and open it yourself. They also instructed him that after he'd scrutinised the contents of the package he was to phone them on the number provided. If he or anyone else for that matter attempted to phone them before he'd scrutinised the package, then Rebecca would die. It was as plain and simple as that. Colin handed the phone back to Mercer.

"What the hell can this package be? I've not to call them until I've scrutinised the package?"

Mercer shrugged his shoulders. Colin Green rose to his feet and paced back and forwards. Here was the man who had spent many years in military service, the last of those years in the elite S.A.S and yet here he was more scared than he had ever been in his life, because he didn't know what he was being scared of. Had they amputated something from Rebecca? Cut off a finger or something? Whatever it was, it was going to distress Jillian if she saw it?

`Be a man and open it yourself?"
Something very unpleasant, whatever the hell it was. And he was getting it in the post?
Mercer managed to get him to sit back down and drink his coffee. It

was going to be a very very long day and an even longer night for the Green family. Samantha spoke now to Terry. "Can I speak with you in private please Terry? I need to ask you something important."
Colin Green was offended.
"Hey, listen, I'm right here. Anything you have to say to him about me or my family, you can say it right here, and right now, don't have to fuck off like a coward and whisper to him what you think, I'm big enough to be able to withstand someone's opinion, so don't hold back Samantha, fucking spit it out." Immediately Colin Green raised his hands and apologised unreservedly for his outburst. "I'm sorry, I'm sorry, please carry on Samantha, I'm just em…I'm fucking worried sick they are going to kill my daughter. If that is what you think then please just say it, hell I know it's not you who's going to kill her…just say what you think, in fact it's imperative that you say what you think…so please…"
"I was just going to suggest to Terry Colin, that he and I go back and speak to Angela Bates again."
Samantha looked at Polly. "If she genuinely knows the names of these animals, then perhaps we could bribe her into telling us who they are, I mean she quite obviously doesn't mind grassing up her friends, she's already made that perfectly obvious." She let her words hang in the air and then said, "We could offer her, her complete freedom. We could pretend to abolish all of her charges and offer her her liberty in exchange for all the people involved. We would have to make it absolutely clear to her that it would need to be worth our while. We would want all the names involved. If she gives us the names and we are successful with the arrests, then she would walk free…all charges dropped, of course, we would have to make it look sincere. We would have to mean it. Then we would release this Bates but we would have surveillance on her at all times. After a few days, we would simply arrest her arse again, of course she would have to have proof that the names she gave us were genuine. What do you think Miss Sheppard, would you be prepared to chance it?"
"Polly looked at the three around the table, resting her eyes on Colin Green.
"If I were to permit this Samantha, then it would be a risk indeed.
These people whatever else they are, are not stupid.
They would suspect a trap or a trick and would do their utmost to make sure that Angela Bates remained at liberty. Surveillance can only do so much.
We haven't got unlimited resources to place here and there. There would be a strong chance, possibility even that she would escape the radar so to speak. If that should happen, then we'd be back to square one, and what then if the kidnappings continued? How would we explain ourselves when the chief of Police steps in here and asks me

how the hell one of Britain's most wanted marches out of supposedly the highest security prison in the country to her freedom?"
Colin Green spoke up. "If that should happen Miss Sheppard, I will personally go out of my way to hunt them down and execute them on the spot. You wouldn't even hear about it, they'd just be gone. I may as well confess to you that it was me who murdered the old Polish paedophile and although you all had a good idea it was me, there was not one piece of evidence you could pin to me. This old bastard had interfered with three-year-old girls by the way, well, not on my fucking watch. You had nothing you could stand me on trial for. If you help me get my daughter back, I swear you won't have a problem with these bastards, I give you my word on that Miss Sheppard."
Polly sighed again, this time with exasperation, as though there were a million bridges to cross before she could even start to think about such a manoeuvre, and she would be right. Rubbing her temples with her fingers she finally said,
"Look, Terry, go and see this Angela Bates and, well, kind of dangle the carrot, try and find out exactly what she knows, or rather, who she knows. Play her along for a while, she's bound to be suffering now being stuck in there and in solitary confinement, surely she'd do anything to get herself out of there. As well as that, these people are saying Colin that you have to contact them tomorrow after you have scrutinised the package. That leads me to believe that they are going to negotiate with you. It might be a shit deal you'll be offered but at least it would seem that at this point Rebecca is still alive. Don't ask me what the hell the package will be, and if I'm honest I'm frightened to think, but, at least it's a step forward, well, not forward, but a positive step, like I say it would seem that Rebecca is still alive, that gives us hope."
Mercer leaned over the table. "I'm not trying to burst the balloons here at the party, but when Samantha and I spoke to Bates, she *did* say to us when I refused to listen, that we needn't bother coming back to see her when the kidnappings began again, now I don't know how she is being treated in there, but I would imagine that she is not having a very pleasant time of it. I hope you're right Polly. I hope she is suffering, because the worse she's feeling the better our chances of getting these names from her. She seems adamant that there'd be more than this Monica Carosova involved. I think her words were, people we didn't even know about. She also said that these people were absolutely ruthless compared to Saratov. And one of them was a very important man."

HM PRISON, BRONZEFIELD.

ASHFORD. MIDDLESEX.

Geraldine Prowse ruled with a rod of iron in her prison. Although laid back in her mannerisms she was anything but laid back when it came to handing out punishments. Today she had decided to bring a certain Miss Angela Bates back to the land of the living. She'd been here now for a little over two months and in all that time she had never had to confront any of the other inmates. Solitary confinement was a godsend when you didn't want to meet up with angry women who had teenage daughters, and who had learned about Angela Bates and what she'd been up to, including making money from Europeans by selling British girls to them for astronomical amounts of money. They looked upon it as a form of slave-trading, and in this case, the worst case, sex-slave trading. Prowse would make sure that two of the inmates were left outside in the exercise yard after they'd had their cigarettes and 'recreation time.'
She would also make sure that there were three sturdy prison guards in the close vicinity, after all, she didn't want Bates to die.
This procedure, she would allow to happen from time to time until eventually Bates' spirit 'would be broken. She would visit Bates in the prison hospital and sit by her bedside while she healed and inform her constantly of just how much of a sub-human she really was and that it was a shame for the women in here to have to tolerate the presence of such a fucking scumbag who could sell her own young nationals to Eastern European businessmen. Four or five beatings over the course of a few months usually done the trick, however there were certain women in here who, it would seem were beyond breaking. These women were extremely dangerous, and Angela Bates was about to encounter two of them, hence the sturdy guards hidden close by armed with stun-guns and baseball bats. Geraldine sat at her desk awaiting the arrival of the prisoner.

Outside in the exorcise yard some of the inmates who had been having their cigarettes were being told to reassemble in an orderly fashion to re-enter the building. All but two that was, Barbara Stenning (Babs) and Elizabeth Hanley (Thin Lizzy) were told to remain in the yard and sweep up the loose cigarette ends. They were to start at one end of the yard and work their way to the other end having been informed that Miss Prowse would be along shortly to inspect their work, and God help them if they left any butt-ends lying on the ground.

There were two soft taps on the door of Geraldine Prowse's office. "Come in" she shouted knowing full well who was there. It was warden Pam Reeves. She'd been instructed to bring prisoner Bates to her office for an interview.

Angela Bates stepped into the office in front of the warden and stood straight with hands in front of her at Prowse's desk clad in her prison denims.

"Not so close scum, not so close, step back, there, stand there." said Reeves, a tall sturdy lump of a woman with a very unpleasant complexion. Her face seemed full of craters. To Angela Bates she looked like a typical `dyke.`

"That'll be all Pam just now thank you. Oh, you can go and make us a cup of tea if you wish, I'll be along just shortly after I have spoken with this."

"Yes mam" replied Reeves, who then grabbed Angela Bates from the back by the hair of her head and promptly booted her on the backside. "Fucking back." she said, "Keep off the governor's fucking desk, sow! See you soon Miss Prowse." Angela had a thought of her own. Maybe someday Pam Reeves would make the mistake of stepping into her cell…alone.

Reeves then left the office. Angela Bates stood motionless, and expressionless.

The governess began writing something down on a ledger on her desk and looked as though she'd forgotten that Angela Bates was standing there.

She continued writing for almost two minutes, and then said to her prisoner, without looking up from her writing, "Would you like to go outside for some fresh air? Scum-fuck? Would you like to have a cigarette outside?"

Bates, knowing full well what the governess was doing, replied, "Yes Please Governess Prowse."

"Ok then, I'll tell you what, seeing as how you haven't given any of my staff any grief since you've been here, I'll let you out for ten minutes to smoke a cigarette. And, because I'm not an inconsiderate cunt like you, I'll even let you have your cup of tea out there with you, now what do you say to that Miss Piggy, would that be suitable for your peroxide ass?"

"Please Miss that would be very kind indeed, thank you Miss Prowse."

"Ok then, go and see Pam, she'll be in the kitchen, and don't worry, all the rest of the rats are back in their lairs so you don't have to worry about being attacked. Tell Pam that I said you are to be allowed to take your beverage outside with you, but remember, ten fucking minutes, and not a second more, understand?"

"Yes Miss, and thank you again Miss Prowse."

"Well, move your fucking arse, you've got nine minutes left, shift your useless fucking arse out of here."

Three minutes later Angela Bates stood just outside the steel door which had been slammed behind her when she came outside to the yard. She wondered why they had closed the door it wasn't as if she could go anywhere. This was the first time since she'd been brought here that she'd be allowed to have a cigarette outside of the building. They let her smoke sometimes in the cell where she was but this was new, being allowed out in the open air. As she enjoyed her cup of tea and her smoke, two women appeared about fifty metres in front of her. One carried a bucket and shovel, the other, a hard brush. One of the women had short cropped ginger hair, the other was taller and very thin with a skin-head haircut. Both of them wore the traditional prison-issue boiler-suit. They weren't saying anything to each other, but both of them were staring right at her. As they approached their faces were stern and hard.

The tall one approached Bates.

"You're the fucking rat that wuz sellin the fucking kids aren't you, you fucker, `turnin em` into fucking whores, poor little fuckers `wuz` being fucking raped while you got fucking rich, aint that right bitch?"

Angela Bates looked straight into the face of her accuser.

"Yeah, that's right, I was, and what's it got to do with you?"

The woman's face took on a fierce look of maleficence.

She put down the bucket and exclaimed to her friend, "I'm gonna rip er fucking `ed` off Babs so I am." She lunged at Angela Bates head first and the two went sprawling onto the ground. The skinny woman had a hold of Bates' hair and began pounding her fist into her face. Bates found her throat and squeezed hard pushing her away and making her let go her hair. With her free hand Bates clenched a fist and began to pound the woman's face, making sure that she found the targets that would be most painful. First, the woman's nose exploded with a flush of blood that sprayed nearly two metres from where they fought. Then she pounded the lips of the skinny woman making sure that she caused as much painful damage to her teeth as she possibly could. Lizzy's friend actually heard a crack as two of her teeth went whizzing past her and onto the ground behind her. Finally, Angela Bates grabbed the crazed woman by both of her ears and rammed her right knee straight into her face. Thin Lizzy lay motionless.

Just at that point, the three wardens came outside with their stun guns and baseball bats ready to save the life of prisoner Bates.

They were shocked indeed to find that Thin Lizzy lay unconscious at Bates' feet. Staring at the other woman, Angela Bates picked up her cigarette from the ground and continued smoking it.

The whole incident had taken just over forty seconds.

One of the wardens raised his baseball bat and whacked Angela Bates across the back of her head sending her to the ground, the remains of her cigarette landing in a shower of orange sparks. One of the other wardens aimed the stun-gun at `Babs` and blasted her with a shot of electricity. "When you recover bitch you pick up the fucking cigarette butt from the ground, or else I'll zap your arse with another blast." Five minutes later Barbara Stenning picked up the cigarette end from the ground her eyes red and watering, and fixed onto the warden who'd just threatened her.

Both women were then immediately handcuffed and taken inside to Geraldine Prowse's office. Thin Lizzy was carried off to the prison hospital. Lizzy Hanley had been here for a total of nine years and six months. She'd had eleven fights in that time and not once had anyone managed to put her to the ground let alone knock her out completely, and on one of those occasions three inmates had teamed up against her.

One of those inmates walked around now with only half of a left ear.

Fifteen minutes later Angela Bates stood once again in front of Geraldine Prowse's desk, and yet again, Geraldine Prowse sat writing away on her ledger as if there was no-one else present in the room. Eventually she looked up and spoke to Bates. "So, little scum-fuck fancy peroxide blondie fucker, you think you're a hard nut is that it? You think you can come in here and rule the roost as it were? Well I've got news for *you* madam muck. You have just signed your own fucking death warrant do you know that? You don't know what you have done here bitch fuck. Don't think that just because you've put Lizzy's lights out today that that's the end of it, ho no, you've started something now that will only end when you die. Because of what you've done today, I'll have no alternative but to keep you in solitary confinement. It's either that or you fucking die, I kid you not. I don't mind telling you that Lizzy is an absolute fucking fruit-cake, she's a no hoper. Even now in her world of unconsciousness and oblivion, she'll be plotting your demise, honestly. Now you *are* going to be in solitary for a long time.

They tell me you've made a bit of a mess of Lizzy, well, little scrubber whore you have spilled the apples this time, say goodbye to the world because they won't be seeing you for some time, any time in fact...you're fucked madam, and you only have yourself to blame, you nasty cow."

Geraldine Prowse would never praise any of her inmates, never in a million years, but she secretly admired Angela Bates. She had sprung the attack on her with absolutely no warning whatsoever, and she'd handled it with ease. Thin Lizzy must have got the shock of her life when the little blonde bombshell had hit her with such ferocity. Up until today Lizzy was the bee's knees in and around the prison, certainly in her wing, but today, she had been humbled by a five foot six tornado. No doubt Lizzy would have had plans to have the blonde as her bitch and her play mate, but those plans would be scattered to the wind now. Now, she would do her utmost to kill Bates, and she would do it by any means necessary. Geraldine Prowse knew that she would have to keep

Bates out of the way of all the rest of the inmates. Lizzy would still rule the roost and have her `groupies` running errands for her, and they would be as much danger to Bates as Lizzy would be. As it stood now, Thin Lizzy would be in the prison hospital for a few days having her wounds seen to, and having dental plates made for the damage to her teeth, and nose-bone reset. One thing was for sure, there would be no-one in here now who would chance their arm against Bates on a one to one basis that much was for certain. "Now" said Prowse to the two women standing in front of her, "get to fuck out of here and back to your lairs out of my fucking face. Some friend you turned out to be Stenning, you stood and watched your bed partner get torn to pieces by the super cow here, what a cunt you are honestly. Well, don't think *you're* going to bed this fuck here because she's going back to the hole out of everybody's fucking way. You missed a trick there Babs, now fuck off, oh, and tell one of the wardens to give you a couple of whacks on the arse with her baseball bat, tell her I said so, it's for your treachery, standing there watching as your friend got bloody walloped, you should think shame on yourself. Some friend you turned out to be, you're a nasty fucker too Babs, a real bitch. Poor Lizzy lying there all fucked up and you just standing watching her take a beating, you nasty cow."

MITCHAM. 9:25am.

The following Morning.

Colin Green stood anxiously at his living room window waiting for the arrival of the postman. He could see him across the road making his way towards his house. He couldn't wait any longer. It could be another fifteen minutes before he got to his house. Terry Mercer and Samantha Reynolds were here as well at the request of Colin. Whatever was going to be in this package he wanted Mercer to see it first-hand.
"I won't be a minute" he mumbled to Mercer as he left the house to catch up with the postman.
Mercer watched as Colin spoke to the young man who was now searching through his bags. Then he handed Colin his mail and carried on with his rounds. Colin came into his house. "There's no package Terry." He said as he studied the three envelopes in his hands. One of the letters was from the Inland Revenue, one was just junk mail, and the last one was a jiffy envelope.
"It's not a package Terry."
He opened it up carefully with shaking hands. Inside the jiffy envelope was a disc.
A DVD disc. "This is it? This is the package they're on about?" And then, as he realized the possible horror he may well witness in the next few minutes as he would play the DVD, he asked his wife to go and make tea or coffee for everyone. Sophie Spencer entered the living room.
"Good, Sophie, go in the kitchen please and keep my wife there until I tell you to come back through, would you do that for me please?"
Sophie saw the DVD in Colin's hand and nodded her head. She understood why she was to keep Jillian out of here. Many customers of Saratov's had paid for their sessions with the girls to be filmed for their own private use at home. Samantha looked at Terry as Colin turned on his DVD player and switched on the TV. Perhaps someone would appear demanding this or that in exchange for the release of Rebecca Green.
Or maybe someone would demand an amount of money to be paid into a certain bank at a certain time. She'd seen them all, blackmail threats for ransom payment demands. What she hadn't ever seen was what she was about to see.
Colin placed the disc carefully into the machine and pressed play.
After a few seconds Rebecca Green's face appeared on the TV screen.
They could see straight away the girl was deeply distressed.
"Dad, I need you to listen to me carefully. These people who have abducted me are

going to give you an ultimatum, if you do as they say, they will release me without harm immediately. If you don't they are telling me that very unpleasant things will happen to me every day for the rest of my life."

Tears were rolling down the girl's face as she struggled to continue.

"Dad, there is a lady called Angela Bates, and she is in prison in Bronzefield, Ashford. If the authorities do not release her by the day after tomorrow, then they are going to begin hurting me very much. It must be done by the day after tomorrow or the deal is off and you will never see me again.

I'm so sorry daddy for this trouble I've caused. I'm frightened and they say they are going to make me cry every day. They also said that they are going to show you something on this DVD to make you understand that this threat is very real."

The picture went blank. All that could be seen were those little electronic dots. Just a haze, and then, the picture came to life again.

A man in a black mask, a hooded mask, approached the screen and spoke very quietly to the people in Colin Greens' living room.

"What you are about to see is nothing compared to what you will see in the future regarding your lovely daughter here Mister Green. We'll call this getting even with you for your heroics over in Lithuania. Don't worry, she's been slightly sedated for this little performance, so she'll recover...this time, but should you choose to ignore this warning, or if you can't cut a deal with the authorities then, like I say, and like she's just told you, very unpleasant things are going to happen to her every day of her life. Be assured that we will keep her alive so she will not be able to escape her daily ordeals, and believe me, they will be ordeals. So, enjoy your daughters' promiscuousness as she indulges in a bit of fun therapy. You have forty-eight hours to release Angela Bates...enjoy."

The date on the top of the screen was the same day when Rebecca had first spoken, so it was yesterday. The camera went on Rebecca as she sat on a beat-up old sofa, her head in her hands. She looked drowsy and confused. And then, to everyone's horror, two naked men appeared with their backs to the camera, and wearing the hooded masks that was worn by the other man. One of the men forced his erection into Rebecca's mouth while the other forced her legs open. He began to tear the clothes off the girl who was struggling the best she could against her attackers.

"Turn it off Colin, you don't need to see any more of this, turn it off man, Jesus Christ."

"I can't turn it off Terry." said Colin Green, barely able to speak. "That's my baby, that's my baby girl they have there. Look at what they're doing to her."

"Colin? Come on man, turn it off, we've seen enough." said Samantha, who then tried to put an arm around him to console him. Then he snapped.

"That's the trouble with you lot!!" he hissed, shaking Samantha from him. "Fucking turn it off, that's what you all do, you turn it off because you don't want to see what these bastards do. You never see the horror of what is happening to our kids. That's my daughter there, look at the bastards raping her. Look how pitiful she looks and helpless, and you don't want to see it, that's your trouble, you don't want to see the fucking truth!"

Sophie Spencer tried her level best to refrain Jillian Green from entering her living room, but when she heard her husband roaring at the detectives she blasted her way past Sophie and marched into the room. The look of horror on her face was indescribable as she witnessed her daughter's rape right there in her own living room. She screamed hysterically as she watched Rebecca struggling in vain to keep the monsters off her. By now Rebecca was naked apart from one of her legs still in her jeans. To make matters even worse, Alison came into the living room to see what was keeping Sophie and also witnessed the rape of her sister. Mercer dived to the TV and switched it off. Samantha took hold of Jillian and ushered her back into the kitchen. The scene was complete chaos. It took Terry and Samantha a full fifteen minutes to calm everyone down. The situation was a hopeless one. How on earth could you calm a man down while he watched his daughter being brutally raped? How could you tell him to take it easy? And then Colin Green's words came flooding back to him from months earlier, *"What if it were to happen again Terry? Would you still have the same opinion if it happened again? It would kill my wife Terry she couldn't take that again."*

Mercer's mind was racing. Colin had sworn to Polly Sheppard that if she helped him he would give his word that he would find these people and wipe them from the face of the earth, and that no-one would know anything about it. Now, he had to go back to Polly and ask her outright, if she would see to it that Angela Bates was released. This was indeed a tall order. Polly would have to go to the home secretary herself and speak, nay beg her for the release of this woman otherwise Colin Green's daughter would face torture for the rest of her life. Perhaps the one saving grace they had was that Polly was friends with the home secretary and were often out together socialising. Whether or not this would make a difference would remain to be seen. They would have to take the DVD disc with them as well to show Polly just how serious these people were. She would in turn no doubt take it to Emily Smith (The Home Secretary.)

And let her see for herself what exactly was at stake.

Forty minutes after Colin Green had placed the DVD disc into the recorder, he stood outside of his house in the back garden contemplating his plan of action. He would go and see Polly Sheppard again with Terry and Samantha and he would plead with her to do all she could to get his daughter back home safely. Failing that, he hadn't a clue in the world what he would do next. There *was* no plan B. How could there be? He was in the hands of the gods now, and so was the life of his eldest daughter. All hope rested on Polly Sheppard and her friend Emily Smith.

BRONZEFIELD

MAXIMUM SECURITY PRISON.

ASHFORD. MIDDLESEX.

Word had got around the prison about the beating given to Thin Lizzy by the blonde. Already there was a reward to any of the inmates who could get to the bitch who'd done this to her. Although feared, Lizzy was more than fair in distributing any of the `goodies` that managed to find their way into the prison. The last thing they wanted in here was for some new upstart coming in and taking over proceedings, and disrupting what was until now a perfectly good system. There was a ranking order, but even the ones at the bottom of the table still had their treats.
No-one was left out.
After all, none of the prisoners in Lizzy's wing were ever going to be released.
All of them were in for murder, some of them multi-killers, as was the case with Lizzy Hanley.
She, according to her lawyer addressing the court, had been pushed to her absolute limits, having been beaten continuously for more than twelve years by a drunken partner who would neither work nor even try to find employment. Instead, he made his living from selling drugs and all manner of illegal dealings with Merchandise, cigarettes and alcohol being his main deals along with heroin and or any other type of drug that could make him money. The final straw had come for Lizzy when the dead-beat bastard she lived with began to leather their kids with belts and ropes.
They had an eleven-year old girl at the time and an eight-year-old boy.
Both children had to make excuses to their teachers at school for the bruising on their legs and arms.
Lizzy had even tried to ask his mother to try and get him to see sense but when she informed her of her son's behaviour she was told not to be such a fucking dramatist and that kids needed to be disciplined these days or else they would grow up to be spoiled fucking bastards.
"And don't you ever come back here telling tales on John again or I will tell him what you are doing, now get away home and get my son's dinner on for him, and start being a fucking wife instead of griping and fucking moaning to me about how hard your life is, now fuck off!"
Elspeth Huntley had just signed her own death warrant.

Elizabeth Hanley had made a decision that very day that she would banish both bastards from the face of the earth, and do her children, and the world a very big favour.

One month later she put her plan to work.

She invited Elspeth over for dinner to celebrate John and hers' `anniversary`.

They had never married and so the anniversary thing was just an excuse to have them both here together. The useless cunt wouldn't have had a clue what date or year they had got together and so Lizzy could say any day and neither mother nor son would have known any difference, but, she had told him that it was thirteen years to the day since they first met.

Thirteen, unlucky for some. Lizzy herself, suffered from Triskaidekaphobia.

The scene was set, and so was the trap.

The children were at Lizzy's mothers' house and out of the way.

Lizzy had dressed up after having set the table for three places.

All fancy crockery adorned the table with Wedgewood she'd hired from a local pawn shop, because John had smashed theirs' in a drunken stupor.

She had cooked roast beef and potatoes with dumplings, (Elspeth's favourite) along with carrots and peas, and a lovely strawberry cheesecake for desert.

Lizzy was also still friendly with an ex-lover of hers' who could get his hands on any amount of Benzodiazepines as she wished.

"Just the eight please Paul, that'll do the trick."

"Are you gonna rape somebody Lizzy?" Her friend said, laughing.

"Not exactly Paul, not exactly, but I am going to fuck them."

And so, the plan was put into action.

Elspeth Hanley sat moaning about how the potatoes could have done with another five minutes and that the roast beef was slightly overdone but never the less she was to be commended for her efforts, after all, it wasn't really Lizzy's fault that she hadn't learned how to cook properly.

"You've done well Lizzy, and I have to say, I have tasted far worse than this if I'm being honest, a little bit worse than this."

What Elspeth hadn't tasted though, was the four crunched up Flunitrazepam tablets in her glass of red wine. The meal itself had been thoroughly enjoyable as far as Lizzy was concerned. It wouldn't take long for the date-rape drugs to kick in. She would have her revenge now. She poured more wine into their glasses. John Huntley's glass contained the same amount of tablets as his mothers'.

Paul had said that one tablet was more than enough in `his experience`.

"So, Elspeth" she begun "Couldn't you find anything decent to wear tonight you scabby

hag? You look like a fucking scarecrow if you don't mind me saying, of course, when I look at this fucker here I can see that it runs in the family.
He looks like he's just stepped out of a fucking salvation-army shop, and speaking of salvation, well there'll be none for you two fuckers tonight."
It had taken a little under fifteen minutes for the drugs to kick in, but they had kicked in now, well and truly. John Huntley sat almost paralysed as he attempted to get up and whack his woman a good one on the face for being so insolent to his mother, but he managed only to fall onto the floor.
"I'll just leave that lying on the floor just now rat hag until I've dealt with you, come on, into the bedroom with you, wicked witch of the north south east and west, your fucking time has come." She dragged Elspeth through to the bedroom by the hair and sat her on one of the chairs. Ten minutes later mother and son sat facing each other, naked and completely helpless. Twelve years of beatings and battering's had built up in Lizzy's head and snapped her mind completely. She took great pleasure in inserting the sharpened kitchen-knife blade into mother and her bastard offspring sitting in front of her who had caused her and her children so much misery. She also took great pleasure in explaining to them what exactly had been done to them. "Ironic isn't it bastard." she said to John. "The very fucking pills that you sell to people are your own downfall. Look at you sitting there helpless, the two of you, where's your big fucking mouths now? Have you nothing to say Elspeth? Fuck, it'll be the first time you evil fucking rat that you are, the potatoes were perfect you fucking whore!!"
Slowly and very deliberately, Elizabeth Hanley stuck the knife into her `partner` and its' mother, bringing to a close all the years of torture and suffering as she watched with complete satisfaction the lives of these overpowering bastards coming to an end. When the police had finally arrived, they found Lizzy in bed with her ex-boyfriend, who was completely out of his mind on something making love on the bed next to the two corpses, who had been positioned on two chairs facing the bed, as though watching proceedings. The post-mortem revealed that no less than one hundred and twenty stab wounds had been inflicted on each of the `victims`. Lizzy was classified criminally insane, and there was no mercy given to her despite her lawyer's attempts at pleading to the jury that the woman was pushed beyond human limits, making her commit murder this way. The coroner had stated that it would have taken at least an hour for each victim to die. Elizabeth Hanley was jailed for life, and that life should mean just that. No matter how much she had suffered, there was no excuse for the brutality of her crimes, verdict, criminally insane. Her two children were taken into care.

Geraldine Prowse had received a phone call from the home secretary informing her that she would receive a visit from detectives Mercer and Reynolds. She was advised to listen intently to what they had to say to her regarding a certain inmate. Angela Bates. She also informed her that she would come to the prison in person to speak with her and advise her of a very tricky situation that had arisen. As far as Geraldine could make out the detectives were coming to interview Bates again. No doubt they would fill her in regarding this so-called situation. Whatever it was, it was bloody serious for the home secretary to call her and then advise her that she was coming to see her in person. This Bates it would seem was at the heart of this `situation`. She had hardly put down the phone when it rang again. It was security informing her that Mercer and Reynolds had arrived unarranged and was she to let them past the gates?
Geraldine smiled to herself as she replied, "Yes let them in Hannah, for goodness sakes let them in."
Ten minutes later the prison governess sat with Terry and Samantha listening to the unfortunate predicament they were in. Geraldine could not understand why it was necessary to `bargain` with this woman. "There are certain methods Mister Mercer that can be used to obtain information as I'm sure you're aware. I can see no reason for offering her freedom. I could arrange to have every scrap of evidence or information extracted from her without taking these measures. Mercer was about to say something and she could see he was fearful of a refusal. She raised her hand to stop him even before he begun.
"Relax Mister Mercer, I'll let her out, *if* and I mean if, she gives you what you need. This is very dangerous what you are doing here, you do know that don't you?" She rose from her seat and picked up the printed e mail she'd received from the Home Secretary. "My prison is secure mister Mercer. No-one in all of its' history has ever escaped from here. I am proud of that fact. I allow things to happen in here for the sake of the inmates' well-being. They think I don't know how the odd eh…treat gets through security, but I know everything. But just imagine if this plan goes wrong, imagine how that would make me and my staff look, to let a known criminal walk out of here having to spin some cock and bull story. You had better get her back, I mean it, or I will spill the beans about everything that has gone on here. I feel it for mister Green I really do, especially after what has happened to his other daughter, but, until now we have prided ourselves in the fact that we never make deals with terrorists, no matter how much pain that may cause, but I have been advised to go ahead and give you permission to have your em…chat with this Bates and make this deal with her. She's actually caused a bit of a stir in here already, by giving supposedly the hardest inmate in here a bloody thrashing. When she arrives back in here she'll spend all her time in solitary confinement, and

that, for her own good. She is one dangerous bitch, so be warned, if your surveillance teams lose sight of her, you will never get her back. But, first of all you have to prove to me that the information she gives you is genuine.

If I am not convinced, then she goes nowhere, do you accept that you pair? Is that fair enough for you?"

Terry Mercer and Samantha Reynolds agreed wholeheartedly, after all, they weren't about to let this demon walk out of here without crucial information. They would find out now if she knew as much as she'd boasted. Whoever had Rebecca Green now had not been mentioned or indeed seen before, but they'd obviously been part of the whole thing from the very beginning. Five minutes later the two detectives were seated in the cell of Angela Bates. The deathly-thin warden had once again informed them that he would be right outside the door. Geraldine Prowse had decided not to accompany them this time for fear of lashing out at the prisoner who would now be feeling that she was in a position of importance once again. "I can't trust myself not to beat her to pulp before you have your information, so on you go and see what you can get out of her." Mercer had asked for a pot of tea and an ash tray.

He sat now at a small table in the centre of the cell beside Samantha Reynolds. "Come and get a cup of tea Angela" he said, and then from his jacket pocket, produced a packet of cigarettes. Before he or Samantha had a chance to say anything else Angela Bates said as she sat on her bed reading her bible, "I told you then, that last time you were here, I told you I could have prevented any further kidnappings didn't I? But you were not interested were you?

Well, you're too late now, they've started and there's nothing I can do to help you. They've started again haven't they Mister Mercer? That's why you're here, well it's too late. There'll be no deal now, and besides, I don't know all the people they'll have working with them now, there could be dozens of them for all we know. I did warn you, but you two were too busy downgrading me to listen." Mercer sighed as he poured three cups of tea from the giant tea-pot.

"You know *some* names though Angela, don't you?"

Bates did not reply.

"This opportunity I am about to offer you is unique to say the least Angela.

As I'm sure you'll be aware, no-one but no-one in your position gets out of here, unless it's the undertaker taking them away. We are here today Angela, to offer you a deal that will not be repeated in the course of British history. Give us the names of these people and you will walk out of here Scot free, I kid you not. If you don't believe me then I will send for governess Prowse, and she will gladly confirm what I say. We've even got a story ready for the press about how your name was wrongly used and that you were nothing less than a scape-goat for the real guilty parties. A full pardon will be printed in the national newspapers. It'll be official Angela, this is not a hoax, its' not a joke. I'm not going to pretend that I don't hate your guts and that I would take great pleasure in kicking your fucking face all around the parish, but I have been given orders. They want these kidnappings stopped Angela, and I'm afraid that if releasing you back into society is part of their plan, then so be it. The only thing is, you only have the time it takes Samantha and I to drink our tea to decide what you're going to do. If you give us the name or names of these bastards, then we check them out. If they are genuine, then within twenty-four hours you walk out of here with a chance to start a new life. I would give it some serious thought Angela, because a little bird tells me that you have knocked over the apple-cart in here so to speak, and that they have a tag on your ass. It's only a matter of time before you are history if you stay in here…so, what's it to be Angela, freedom or fear."

She slid off her bed and asked if she could have a cigarette. "Help yourself Angela. And I mean that literally as well, help yourself, whilst you can. If you refuse this opportunity, then there's nothing anyone can do for you from now on, that's it, you'll be here for a very long time, and I'll tell you something else, Geraldine Prowse down there is absolutely furious as to what is being proposed here. She doesn't want you going anywhere, but even she has to comply with what the Home secretary tells her. I'm not just saying this, but she plans in making your life here a complete hell I kid you not. Apparently you've beaten up one of the inmates' favourites. Even they have a price on your head, but, it's up to you Angela. Just for this short time, your future is in your own hands…but that time is fast running out." Mercer made a point by taking a sip of his tea as he mentioned the time.

At this point in time Angela Bates had some hard thinking to do.

Up until now there had been no-one from the organised gang making enquiries about how she was doing, even though she had been promised complete protection but had been instead completely ignored and now, left to rot it would seem. She had her suspicions about the proposition Mercer had given her but then in reality, she had no other options going for her. No-one cared quite obviously about her being stuck in here. She had been betrayed by the very people she had helped to make rich, and now they were out there living their lives and she was going to be stuck in here for a number of years, and that if she could avoid the inmates who had a tab on her arse. There wasn't really any thinking to do. The only trouble was, one of the names she was about to give them would send shock waves right through the country. They would not believe her, it was a simple as that, but if they wanted to get to the bottom of the kidnapping business, then they'd have to make enquiries…and once they done that, then the apple-

cart *would* well and truly be spilled. She sipped her tea as the two detectives sat waiting for her decision. Somehow she actually believed Mercer about her being released.
In all honesty she hadn't anything to lose so there was no gamble involved.
She had a name she could give them that could perhaps take away the burden of her releasing this person's identity. She would pass *that* responsibility on to someone else. As she stumped out her cigarette she said to Mercer, "I will give you a name of someone that you already have in custody, they will give you the name of the person who is at the top of the tree but I warn you now, be prepared to be shocked because you will not believe who this person is. I am not prepared to give you the name because of fear of the repercussions…but this other person can give you the name. He is the only other one in the whole syndicate who knows them."
Mercer leaned forward on his chair with his arms flat on the table.
"Are you telling me that Colin Briggs knows this person? Is it Colin Briggs who passed on the instructions to the others?" Angela Bates nodded her head.
"Colin Briggs had more to do with the kidnappings than you think.
He was the go-between concerning where and when the abductions would take place. It wasn't just hap-hazard you know, everything was done with extreme caution. And this Colin Briggs hates my guts by the way, we never struck it off. He asked me out on a date once and I refused, since then he had it in for me. If Polly Sheppard looked even closer into Briggs' files she'd have seen a name on his mobile phone. This name was a code name for the person you seek, it was all undercover and planned out meticulously. And you'll see why just shortly when he gives you the name."
"How do you know he will Angela? He might be too scared like you to give it if this person is as influential as you say."
Angela lit another cigarette. "Can I have a piece of paper please?" she said, blowing smoke up to the celling.
Samantha gave her a pen and a piece of paper from her note-book.
As Bates wrote she said, "Just for the record, I didn't *tell* you this name, I didn't say anything." She slid the piece of paper back over the table and smiled at the two detectives. Check that name out in the Bank of England and see what comes up, and I mean check. On face value he is a legitimate business-man living in London running his perfectly legitimate computer hard-ware company. If you're clever enough to find his real name then you will have reached the top of the tree concerning the kidnappings. All the transport provided for the abductions are down to him. The fast cars the fishing boats, the money put up front for Mister Michael Saratov to purchase his house in Lithuania, everything…all down to this man, and I can't wait until you find out who he is."

Mercer glanced at Samantha and then said to Bates, "Thomas Blythe? This is the man at the top you say?"

"The very top," Bates replied, "And remember, I didn't tell you that name. Briggs will though, if you bluff him and say that you've finally got to the bottom of it. Show him that name and tell him you can have his sentence reduced if he cooperates with you…he'll tell you. He's a fucking coward. Thinks he's a hard man detective but he's just shit, this…`Blythe` was using him to do all the dirty work, he just didn't see it. He got paid well for licking the right arses so he was happy. He's thick as well as I'm sure you don't need me to tell you, he'll give you the name alright, you can count on it…as indeed I am. Oh and don't think for one minute that this is the only little racket he runs, this Mister Blythe, oh no, I think you'll find he has lots of little pies he has his sticky little fingers in, including drug-smuggling, prostitution, money laundering to name but a few. And so now Mister Mercer and Miss Reynolds, I have done my bit.

I have disclosed information to you that could bring all this to an end, this kidnapping business. It remains to be seen if you keep to your side of the bargain.

Let me make one thing clear to you, I don't have anything to lose as you both well know, so whether or not you release me is entirely up to you. Personally, I can't see it. I don't think it will happen. I only gave you that name because no-one else who I was working with cares a jot about me. We'll see how they like it when they lose their liberty, because there'll be a few brought down when all this comes to a head, and it will, you'll see. I have given you the biggest name of all in organised crime in London. If you pull the right strings you will both be promoted, *and* Polly Sheppard of course, and when you pull the final string then, `down will come baby and cradle and all`. Now you two go and have a nice day."

Mercer headed back with Samantha Reynolds to Geraldine Prowse's office with the information given to them by Angela Bates.

"What do you think Terry? Do you think she's genuine? said Samantha, as they knocked on the door. Mercer sighed. "I think that Bates will be allowed to walk no matter if she's telling the truth or not. Those bastards who have Rebecca Green are genuine.

If Bates is not released then that girls' existence will be hellish, that much we *do* know. Look what they done to her on that bloody film, and that was just a warning they said."

Geraldine Prowse shouted for them to enter the office.

Mercer was about to unfold the information to her but was stopped by Geraldine's hand.

"Before you say anything, I've just had your superior on the phone and I have to release her straight away. She's just e-mailed me a statement for the press explaining that she was falsely arrested, Christ it makes me laugh. She's been falsely arrested and a written apology has been prepared."

She looked at the two detectives, bemused. "You've to go and get her. I have to supervise it, but you have to go and get her, it beggars belief."

Mercer and Reynolds could see that Geraldine Prowse was actually disturbed by the decision. She stood shaking her head, then, as though she'd just awoken from a hypnotists' trance she waved her hand to the door.

"Come on, let's get her majesty out of here and back out to society, Christ, we owe her an apology for goodness sakes, this is going to break Thin Lizzy's heart I can tell you that, she'd have had big plans for the blonde I kid you not."

Mercer looked at the governess confused. "Lizzy?"

"Oh it doesn't matter now. Lizzy will just have to wait until we get her back, and you better get her back, because if these kidnappings continue and this bitch has anything to do with it, then we're all fucking heading to the Job-centre so be warned…a written apology indeed, come on, let's get her out, can't have her suffering any more unnecessarily the poor lamb."

Thirty-five minutes later Angela Bates was saying her goodbye's to detectives Mercer and Reynolds. They had been instructed to offer her a lift into the city but she'd refused having ordered a taxi.

"Well, I must say Mister Mercer, I didn't think this was going to happen."

"No, either did I Miss Bates, it just shows you what can happen when you help the police with their enquiries, that's to say you've been telling us the truth."

Angela Bates smiled at the two detectives. "I think you know in your heart of hearts that I've told you the truth, and anyway, you'll soon find out once you've spoken to Briggs. And don't worry, if there are any more kidnappings taking place then you can be assured that I will have had nothing to do with them. If I hear anything, I'll let you know, but I won't be going anywhere near that lot. They left me for dead so to speak. Oh, and if you have surveillance put onto me, tell them to try and at least be conspicuous about it."

It was blatant sarcasm.

Samantha looked at Bates. "Whatever you do Angela, make sure you are not organising any more abductions, you are a very lucky girl indeed to be walking away from these prison gates, you do know that don't you?"

"Oh I know, and as I've just told you, I don't want anything else to do with these people. I have got money hidden away so I'll be comfortable for a while." Samantha was tempted to insult the blonde by exclaiming that they were well aware of how she got that money but decided against it, instead, the two detectives walked away towards the car park. All Samantha said to her over her shoulder as they walked was, "Stay clean Angela, whatever you do, stay clean." Bates replied smiling, "Oh I will, rest assured on that...bye."

As Terry and Samantha reached their car she said, "I wonder who this Thomas Blythe person is, Bates said we will get a shock when we find out who he is."
"One thing at a time Samantha. We've let her go, lets' hope these bastards keep their word and release Rebecca Green."
As he drove out of the car park towards the security gates he said "Yeah, and Bates she says that no-one is bothering about her being stuck in there, well someone is bothering, and they've gone to great lengths to get her out of there, she's kidding no-one if she expects us to believe that. However, lets` get over to Brixton holiday camp and see what Mister Briggs has to say for himself."

UNKNOWN LOCATION.

"Good news Rebecca." The tall masked man said as he entered the room.
"Now then sweetheart let me explain something to you. If we hadn't done what we done to you then they would not have released our friend from prison, and if that had happened well then we'd have been left with no option but to keep you with us, and by that I mean, you would have become a working girl. You'd have been sold to one of our associates and put to work in one of the brothels. But, all's well that ends well. They have released our friend from that nasty prison and so as soon as she arrives at her destination we'll be sending you home safely in a taxi. She is going to text us as soon as she arrives. Would you like something to eat in the meantime sweetheart?"
Rebecca felt repulsed even at the sound of this mans' voice.
He had stood laughing and making comment as two friends of his raped her.
How he could talk like this to her now like he was a life-long friend was beyond her.
"No thank you." She replied as politely as she could.
"Oh now come on Becca, it was just a bit of fun wasn't it, it's not as though we'd stolen your virginity was it. You're bound to have had boys you've been to bed with and then decided they weren't for you after all, and at the end of the day, the price for my boys' fun was your freedom, and you can't put a price on that now can you...was just a little bit of fuck fun wasn't it, now, would you like something to eat?"
Rebecca refused again.
The man left the room and locked the door behind him as he did.
She hoped above all hope that he wasn't pretending that she'd be set free. According to what he'd said, this person had been released from prison and in return she would be released. Ever since she was twelve years old her father had spoken to her about situations such as these. God forbid, he had said, but if you ever get attacked or kidnapped there are key things you can do to help yourself. For example, look for any distinguishing marks, tattoos or birth marks, hair colour, eye colour, any prominent features, big nose, big ears, big feet. Did they wear earrings, bracelets, wedding rings, anything that may help identify them at a later date. Rebecca had done all these things whilst being raped. One of her `rapists` had a ring on his right middle finger. It was a skull and crossbones. He also had a tattoo of a dragon on his right thigh, and it was incomplete. The outline had been put on but it hadn't been coloured yet.
The tattoo had been applied recently because the skin was still red around the edges. The other man had no such markings, but he did have an earring of a mermaid dangling on a small gold chain from his left ear. The mermaid was gold as well.

These things she would tell her father, *if* they were genuine that she was to be released. She looked over to the far end of the room where she was and saw the sofa, the grubby sofa, where she'd been raped.

In front of it the filming equipment still remained there, the tripod directly in front. She could still hear the laughter of the man who had just been in the room.

"Knock it into her boys, she fucking loves it. Look at her pretending to cringe, give her a good goosing lads, let her daddy see everything."

Rebecca had to fight back her tears. It was something she would never forget. God knows how Alison had coped having to face that several times a day.

She conceded that her little sister was far stronger than she was.

The door opened again and the tall man entered once more. "Lets' go Rebecca our friend has reached her destination safely, she's just texted us. Now then, I'm going to drive you a mile or two from here blindfolded because I just know you'll be itching to tell your dad all about us, and so, we have to hide our location, you understand don't you? Once we reach our destination you will wait until your taxi arrives and that's that, over and done with. I'm putting the blindfold on you so as I can take this hideous-looking fucking mask off that I've had to wear whenever I've been in your presence. So, lets' get you blindfolded and sent back to your daddy, he'll be over the moon don't you think? And I just know he will be a very relieved man indeed, because he'll know how this could have turned out. Perhaps this little fright will teach him a lesson. He got your sister back safely, he should have left it at that, but no, he's always got to be the hero. He'll think twice now before he dives in, killing a defenceless old man Now he's getting you back, surely he's learned his lesson. And I sincerely hope he has Rebecca, because we can abduct you again if needs be…that old man he killed was a good friend of ours and was excellent at getting young girls to step into our traps. If your father had failed to get our friend out of jail, then you would have been a very busy girl for the rest of your life, or your young working life anyway.

As soon as you became surplus-to-requirements you'd have been executed. Not to worry though, all's well that ends well Rebecca."

BRIXTON PRISON.

LAMBETH. SOUTH LONDON.

Mercer and Reynolds entered C wing where Colin Briggs now `resided`.
This prison was a far cry from previous ones they'd visited.
Even the wardens seemed relaxed and cheerful in here compared to Bronzefield, and as far as the security was concerned, well they were playing cards when they arrived. One of the two men at the gate-house simply leaned over and pressed a button allowing the electronic gates to slide open. No passes or ID here thank you very much. All said and done though, this was a prison of reform after all, there were no serial killers in here to worry about. As they walked down the hallway Mercer said jokingly to Samantha.
"These jeans you're wearing Samantha, they show your arse off nice, they do.
You should wear short jackets more often rather than those long bloody leather coats of yours. It's a shame to hide such class from society, if you've got it flaunt it, that's what they say isn't it?"
The warden who was accompanying them to Briggs' cell turned and smiled broadly as he walked in front of the detectives. A young man in his early thirties, he turned and smiled at Samantha as though waiting for her reply. She obliged by saying to the warden, "Oh don't worry about Mister Mercer, he doesn't get out much these days. He has a phenomenal stash of a certain type of DVD's at home I'm led to believe so he'll be an expert when it comes to the female anatomy I can assure you. Perhaps if he hadn't become a detective he'd have made himself a career being an accoucheur."
Now it was Mercers' turn to laugh as they continued down the huge hallway. Eventually they came to Briggs' cell. The young warden left them to their discussion with prisoner 2223156. Mercer entered the cell first.
"So Mister Briggs," He began. "You've landed yourself in the penthouse suite it would seem. How the fuck did you manage that after your treachery to your country, you horrible rat that you are. You must have friends in high places. Nice and easy you have it bud, huh bud? Are you a giver or a getter in here Colin? Wait, don't tell me, you're a giver. You'll give as much quality head as you fucking can won't you, because everybody knows that you haven't got the guts to stick up for yourself have you, you're a fucking crawler bud. Blow-job Briggs is what they call you in here did you know that? The warden just told us."
Samantha put in, "Oh, was that it Terry? I thought he said his nick-name was bend-over Briggs."

"Could have been Samantha, maybe I wasn't listening, but, talking about listening Colin, I would advise you to listen to us now, because you have been given a life-line here bud. Why, I don't fucking know, because I would just as soon hang you from the nearest tree, but, orders are orders. There were two chairs in the cell. Mercer sat on one and motioned for Samantha to sit on the other. "You sit where you are." He said to Briggs. "I'll cut to the chase bud. The cat is out of the bag. We know it all. And we know all the names too. Briggs who had said nothing up until this point looked up from the bed where he sat.

"It's true, it's all out bud, it's all done and dusted, fucking Thomas Blythe indeed. You would have thought he could have come up with a better name than that, wouldn't you bud?" All those false accounts, all that money, and him in the top job.

Even a huge salary like he gets is not enough for the greedy bastard, well he's been duped now Colin, and you have been involved with his escapades.

In case you're wondering what I'm going on about, this information we've received simply means that you have two options. One, you can officially give us his name, which will, I assure you help you considerably in your bid to leave here.

Or, you can take another seven years without remission if you decide to stay silent on the matter then you'll be transferred to, how shall I put it, a proper prison where of course there'll be none of the little perks you get in here. Far from it, you'll be disciplined and bullied on a daily basis and you don't need me to tell you how uncomfortable that would be for you. If there's one thing that those inmates hate, it's bent cops. They would make an example of you. You would be a priority.

However, the choice is yours bud, I know you're a hard bastard and all that but they would humiliate you beyond belief I'm quite sure. Now, all you need to do is give me that name. If the name you give me is the same as the one I have written down on this piece of paper, you'll be out of here in less than three days. If it doesn't, then we won't be seeing you for a long time. That's it Colin, those are your choices, now, what's it going to be bud? Tell me Thomas Blythe's real name and you'll be out of here in no time at all."

Samantha watched Briggs's face as he contemplated the situation.

He would know, or at least have a good idea that Terry was bluffing about knowing the name of his boss. He also knew that he wouldn't be bluffing about the extended prison sentence. He came to this conclusion. If they knew about the name Thomas Blythe, then it would only be a matter of time before they disclosed his real identity. All they would have to do would be to look at one of the banks' security footage and find out who was making these deposits for `Blythe`. He decided he would tell them who it was and take his chances. If they did not release him then he would die in prison because this person would have pulling power with the inmates wherever they put him. A price would be put on his head. If he didn't tell them, then Mercer would make sure that he was transferred to Belmarsh or somewhere like that and would undoubtedly find something to pin on him to increase his sentence, and as he'd said, no remission. Briggs rose to his feet. He stood almost six four and towered over Mercer as he asked him for a piece of paper. "I know you Terry." he said smiling. "And I would almost bet my bottom dollar that you are bluffing about knowing the true identity of Thomas Blythe. But I am going to give you the name anyway. I will warn you now, you had better have a concrete slab for a foundation to your allegations because if you haven't, you and Miss world here will be kicked out of the Met before you can say your names. Make sure you have hard fact evidence and that evidence is insurmountable or it'll be you who'll be having uncomfortable experiences I can assure you." Briggs wrote something on the piece of paper Samantha had handed him. "There, that's' who Thomas Blythe is, now, let me see you bring *him* down. Surprise surprise, he's your boss too. We both work for the same man, isn't that funny."

Terry Mercer looked at the name Briggs had given him and swallowed hard. Samantha read it too and quickly sat back down on her chair. The shock was etched into both the detectives' faces, because the name given to them was none other than John Carlton-Fletcher, the commissioner of the Metropolitan Police Force.

MITCHAM.

SOUTH LONDON.

Colin Green sat on the bench at the bottom of his garden smoking a cigarette.
His wife had gone for food shopping with Alison and her friend Sophie.
He had done all he could do to have his daughter released from her kidnappers. Terry Mercer had texted him informing him that Angela Bates had been released from prison.
He glanced at his mobile phone. No messages, nothing from the kidnappers.
Never before had a convicted prisoner been released as part of a deal for exchange of a hostage, but Polly Sheppard had managed to do just that, all he could do now was hope and pray. He sat gazing at the small apple trees he'd planted a few years earlier with the help of Alison and Rebecca. He could see them still, crouched over with their small spades and their pink wellies busy patting the soil around the base of the plants, two little girls helping their daddy to `make a fruit tree`.
His mind suddenly flashed to the horrendous footage on the DVD forcing him to relive the horrors of the film and the helplessness of his daughter's situation.
He had to rise from the bench and jolt himself into some kind of movement to erase the nightmare from his mind.
Another glance. No messages.
He found himself in the shed pottering about with this and that to try and keep his mind occupied. Once again he smiled at the memories of his girls growing up. Over in the far side of the shed, the two little bicycles Alison and Rebecca had learned upon. They would jokingly mock him from time to time for him keeping them reminding him that they were young women now and not little girls.
"The wicked Witch is dead now dad, there aren't any evil witches in the woods. We live in the real world now, and we'll never be able to ride those bikes in the shed again, you have to accept it, the world of make-believe is gone forever, throw the bikes away dad."
Colin lit up another cigarette and sat down on the upside-down wheel-barrow in the corner of his shed. Yes, its' true girls, the world of make-believe has passed on, but as far as the wicked witch was concerned, he wasn't so sure.
He smiled having just heard himself speaking out loud, to no-one *but* himself.
He looked at his mobile phone again. No messages.
Now, he was back out in the garden with an old wicker basket picking up the rotten apples that had long ago fallen from the trees.
Another glance, no messages.

As he picked up the apples he began to ask himself some horrible questions. What if they were bluffing? What if they had no intentions of letting Rebecca go? What if it was just a ploy to get that Bates woman out of prison? What was he going to do then to get Rebecca back? Where would he start looking? He threw down his finished cigarette end onto the compost heap but then immediately lit up another. Jillian had been lecturing him about his heavy smoking, although lately, because of circumstances she hadn't bothered, in fact she'd taken to smoking an odd one or two herself. Colin carried the apples over to the compost heap. He then made himself a cup of tea and took it back outside with him.

Another glance at his phone. Another disappointment.

It had been about six hours since Terry had informed him about Bates' release. Perhaps it was foolish to think that these evil people would do something like keep their word. They had got what they wanted, Bates was out of jail and so now the ball was at their feet. If they wished, they could take the piss out of the Met by withholding Rebecca. That would certainly put the cat among the pigeons. Polly Sheppard would find herself in a very precarious situation indeed. She could lose her job. It was a mess, a complete and utter piss-take by the kidnappers. His phone buzzed in his pocket. He pulled it out so quickly that he dropped it onto the garden path. He snatched it up only to find that Jillian was texting him and asking if he'd had any word from the kidnappers. He cursed, not his wife, but the bastards who had been so cruel as to play a trick like this. He sat back down on the small garden wall and took a sip of his tea, and an extra-large draw of his cigarette. He sat defeated, with his legs apart and his head bowed between his knees wondering what on earth he could do to save his daughter from these monsters. As he exhaled he heard himself exclaiming, "Oh dear Christ help me." Perhaps Jesus *had* been listening to him because just at that moment his phone buzzed again. This time he gently pulled it out of his pocket fully expecting to be disappointed again. It was Rebecca.

"I'm in a taxi dad on my way home, I should be there in about fifteen minutes. Thank you for everything you've done dad, I love you so much."

Colin Green threw the phone down and began to laugh out loud.

They had kept their word.

He laughed and laughed and paced about the garden for a couple of minutes and then he fell onto his knees and began to break his heart. In his time in the SAS he'd done two tours of Afghanistan and almost lost his life on more than a couple of occasions. He'd seen friends of his blown up by roadside bombs. Others shot by snipers.

He'd 'visited friends who he'd served with and who now had only one leg or one arm, or no legs or no arms, but nothing had put him under such pressure as this what had happened to his two daughters. He sat now or rather on his hunkers with his right hand on the wall, and he done something he'd never done in all of his time in the forces. He looked up towards the sky and thanked his Lord God for delivering his daughter safely back to him. Two minutes later he was being observed by curious neighbours as he paced back and forwards on the road outside of the front of his house. After what seemed an eternity a taxi cab rounded the corner at the bottom of his street and headed towards him. As the taxi pulled up one of the back doors flew open and an excited young woman by the name of Rebecca Green ran to her father and threw her arms around him. Father and daughter stood embracing and crying into each-others' shoulders, both of them holding on to each other and never ever wanting to let go.

SCOTLAND YARD.

BROADWAY VICTORIA.

"How the hell do we go about this"? said Mercer staring down at the name on the piece of paper in front of him. "Jesus Christ, the Metropolitan Commissioner? The shit is going to hit the fan this time Polly."
Polly Sheppard nodded in agreement. "I know Terry, I know it will, but he can't get out of it. We have proof of his comings and goings with the Lithuanians. We've had a team check out all his recent movements. There are no less than five bank accounts he has under false names, Christ Thomas Blythe, what the hell was he thinking of using a stupid bloody name like that? Having said that, he would be running out of names to use because we've discovered another three names he's been using for accounts. John Charles, Andrew Milton, James Richardson. He must have been running out of ideas when he settled for Thomas Blythe. Two of these names have money in Swiss bank accounts, and when I say money, I mean money. Two and a half million in one account Mister Richardson has. Mister Milton has three quarters of a million in another Swiss account. And Mister Charles has a total of one point two million pounds with a bank here in the capitol. All of these names legitimate businessmen as far as the banks are concerned. But here's the real diamond, you remember three years ago half a dozen girls went missing in and around Glasgow? Guess who was doing business with the Bank of Scotland up there at that time? You got it, Thomas Blythe. Four hundred thousand pounds was deposited into Mister Blythe's account within five weeks of the girls' disappearances'. According to the investigations `Mister Blythe` then went on holiday to Mexico for three weeks, at the same time as our boss Mister John Carlton-Fletcher did, what a coincidence huh? There is no record of where Carlton-Fletcher stayed when he was there…of course."
Mercer grinned at his superior.
"The fly bastard stayed on a Yacht didn't he?"
Polly nodded.
"Yes he did Terry. There were photographs found on his files. In one of the photos he's standing posing in front of the boat with the name clearly visible behind him. The Carrie-Anne. The yacht is owned, or was owned by a Lithuanian businessman who goes by the name of Viktor Kulbertinov, and it gets better Terry, sitting on the rail of that same yacht were a number of women clad in bikinis, one of whom is none other than Monica Carosova."

Mercer's smile slowly turned into a grin.

"There is no way Polly this fucker can get out of this, not with all this evidence. He is well and truly fucked."

Again Polly nodded. "It would seem that way Terry, but we have to be very careful indeed. Everything has to be one hundred per cent concrete.

Every accusation we bring before him has to be water-tight.

The evidence must be irrefutable because he'll have the best lawyer that money can buy you can count on that. The advantage we have just now is the fact that he has no idea whatsoever that he is being investigated. So, we have an unlimited time, within reason, to gather everything we can for the case against him. If we get this right, then he'll do more time than Saratov or Kulbertinov, simply because of his rank, and his responsibility not only to the Met but to the British public. In short Terry, he won't be seeing any daylight for quite a few years. That, of course is if everything goes to plan, that's why we have to make sure everything is solid."

Polly rose from her seat and said over her shoulder, "Anyway, it's out of our hands Terry. This is being dealt with by the serious fraud squad now.

He's in deep water now Terry, and God help anyone who's been in it with him, especially if they're connected with the Met. Anyone who has worked for or with him will be thoroughly investigated. If one of his secretaries has been on holiday with him or accepted a cash bonus, anything, then they're in trouble. They and their families will be thoroughly scrutinised. This could quite easily be a pebble in the pond type of effect here Terry...lots and lots of ripples. Who knows who'll be pulled under when this ship goes down, and these fraud guys, they know exactly what they're doing. They'll wait until the time is right to strike, and they better, because if they get it wrong then we could all be joining the Job-centre-plus queue...with no references."

Samantha Reynolds entered the office having knocked on the door.

"How's Colin doing Samantha?" said Polly. "He'll be a very relived man to have his daughter back."

Samantha smiled and nodded her head, but said nothing.

"What", said Terry. "What's wrong Samantha, I know something is. What's he saying now?"

Samantha sat down next to Terry.

Polly brought a cup of coffee over for her.

"Colin, he's em...he's searching all over for tattoo parlours. Rebecca said that one of the men who raped her had a tattoo of a dragon on his thigh. The outline was on but it hadn't been coloured. Colin is searching diligently for information around the parlours to try and find the tattooist who applied it. I tried to tell him that he could have had it done anywhere but that's not stopping him. He told me not to tell you two what he was doing."

Polly sat down with a fresh cup of coffee, and nodded her head as she sipped her beverage. "That's right Samantha, and you didn't tell us that did you?"

Polly raised her eyebrows at the detective.

"No, no I didn't tell you, I kept my word."

Terry lit up a cigarette. "God help the fucker if he finds him, and I'll tell you something Polly, I'm not doing anything to try and stop him either. He'll deal with this the proper way, like any other father would, and I don't blame him one little bit. I'm turning a blind eye to this Polly, and anyway, if he does find him then he'll extract other names from him of who else is involved with these bloody kidnappings...he could be an asset to us. In fact, I may even try and look for this tattooist myself and help him."

Samantha spoke again.

"According to Rebecca, she said it was quite a large tattoo so if it was someone around this area then they would surely remember applying it, especially if it is still to be coloured. There would be an appointment made surely because it'll be quite a lengthy process I would imagine."

Mercer turned to Samantha. "Get on that Samantha, try and find out as many tattooists as you possibly can and chalk down the names, we'll bloody help him if we can."

Whether or not Terry was trying to play Samantha Reynolds up or not would never be known because she turned to Polly and began to talk about how Rebecca had been coping with her kidnapping. She continued speaking to Polly as though Terry hadn't said a word.

"So I said I would go back over there from time to time to visit them and keep tabs on how they were all coping."

Polly smiled back at her detective as she watched Terry waiting for Samantha to reply to him.

"Right Terry" she said, finishing her coffee, "we need to be heading over to your place. Surveillance have contacted us with news of suspicious looking characters lurking in Holburn. They want to know if you recognise any of the two vehicles they've filmed roaming around the area."

"Well we can go there just as soon as you've finished searching for the tattooists. Maybe you can do it on your lap top as we head over to Holburn sweetheart."

Samantha washed her cup and picked up her hand bag from the floor and then headed to the door.

"Maybe." she said as she left the office.

Once again Polly Sheppard was smiling broadly.

"They do say that Terry don't they Terry? The more you live with someone the more you become like them. I remember you answering a certain senior detective when he gave you something to do in much the same way as Samantha has responded to your request. You can't deny it Terry, she knows you inside and out. There's a connection there as well Terry in case you didn't know. That girl thinks the world of you do you know that?

Terry headed for the door. As he reached it he stopped and turned and then said to his boss, "I wish Polly."

Terry would be half way down the corridor when Polly said to her office door,

"You'll see, you silly man. The girl is in love with you."

CANTERBURY.

Valarie Vercopte sat in the small café with Monica Carosova discussing what their next plan of action would be. Carosova had been in Britain for almost three weeks but Valarie Vercopte had only arrived here hours earlier. She had boarded a flight in Poland under an assumed name and flown across to France. As soon as she'd landed in Paris she arranged for an associate of hers' to drive her to Port Deauville where she paid a fishing-boat skipper the princely sum of one thousand Euros to take her across to England. There was no way she could chance landing in any airport in Britain and so the round-about journey was necessary…and relatively safe. Monica had picked her up at Margate and they had driven here to Canterbury to have their discussion. Monica herself had taken a similar route when she had come over here. There were always little fishing vessels who were only too pleased to boost their takings on their working voyage. The money paid to them would be put up against the boats' expenses and so boost their wages when they returned home. Kulbertinov had referred to the boats as `sea-taxis`. Monica sat smiling at her companion across the table as they enjoyed their coffees. Although Valarie had been over in Lithuania she seemed to be in tune with everything that had been happening over here in England. Monica was pleasantly impressed when Valarie said, "I take it you have a good reason for releasing the girls you had in captivity. Four of them you've released I hear?"
"Yes well, I've been waiting on an answer from you whether or not you are interested in our little venture. It would have been too risky holding the girls over in Lithuania especially when there's nothing up and running yet and then if you decide not to go ahead with it I'd be stuck with them and it would be very dangerous holding four British girls in those circumstances. I need to know for sure what you intend to do Valarie."
"Before I answer that Monica, I think you done the right thing there. Whether or not I decide to invest in this project is irrelevant just now. At this moment in time it is far too dangerous to do anything. We need to wait until this all calms down a bit. Have you heard anything from Scotland Yard? I mean have they asked to speak to you about anything? I can't believe for one minute that that little bastard Saratov has not connected you with all of this. He stands to spend the rest of his life in prison and yet he hasn't even asked to have any contact with you. Scotland Yard must know that you have had something to do with the running of the brothel in Lithuania. Why have they not approached you for questioning?"
Monica sighed. "I know, I know Valarie, and that's one of the reasons I've released the girls. I'm just as wary as you are about everything. I don't want to be taking any chances

either."

"So why did you arrange to have the girls kidnapped in the first place then, nothing has changed regarding our circumstances. You kidnapped them and had nowhere to keep them…a bit foolish if you don't mind me saying, especially with everything that's going on over here just now there's surveillance teams everywhere."

"And just how do you know that Valarie, you've just bloody landed here. So you have people looking out over here. Do you have them looking out after me?
Are they following my movements? Are they scrutinising my movements, because if they are I can tell you right now-."

"Relax Monica. I wouldn't do that to you, I'm not going to spy on your comings and goings, please don't think that for a minute. I'm just saying, I think it's better for all that we leave things just now until everything cools down a bit. I think we should give it a couple of months before we try and venture out on our little project."

"So you *are* interested?"

"Of course I'm interested, but I'm determined to do it properly. I have some news for you. I have or I am just about to purchase a little property on the outskirts of Kaunas. I intend to open a massage parlour… perfectly legitimate.
The property contains two upper levels and it will be from there that we will conduct our little business venture. I don't want my house involved in anything like this, plus it's less suspicious-looking if it's done this way, whereas if the authorities see vehicles coming and going to and from my house then I think we're just asking for trouble."

Monica nodded her head just as the waitress approached them with the second cups of coffee she'd ordered. The girl who served them would be no more than sixteen. Valarie smiled at the girl and thanked her. Monica glanced at her friend. "They're everywhere," she smiled, "There's money everywhere. Imagine the trade she would bring in. Nice little filly like that." As the girl returned to the kitchen Valarie turned in her chair to look at her and then smiled at Monica as if to agree with what she'd just said.

"We'll just take our time Monica. First, I will purchase the building, it doesn't need much renovations. A few weeks, and then it'll be ready for business.
But, Monica, we have to be patient. Do you have transportation ready for when we do start? Have you people we can trust? All these things we have to have put in place before we even begin to think about going ahead.
And you just said it yourself you made a mistake by kidnapping those girls and then having to release them. Everything we do will have to be planned out meticulously. If we mess up in the slightest then we'll be joining Saratov and Viktor before we know it."

"I have three people I can trust, sorry, we can trust. I will pay them for the kidnappings as and when they execute them. I have another two men who will accompany the girls on the boat to get them over there. I take it you could arrange transportation for them once in Europe, you know, to take them to their destination?"

"Of course I can."

"Well then Valarie, I shall wait to hear from you.

Once you're ready to set your plan into action you just let me know and I will proceed to collect the merchandise, it won't take long. How long do you plan to stay here in Britain if you don't mind me asking, I take it you're not here to visit Viktor."

"No, I'm not. If Viktor had his way he'd have me killed in no time at all. I explained to him how I'd been having an affair with one of his colleagues and how I planned to move my lover in with me as soon as possible, and he just went-."

"Hold it there Valarie, this lover of yours, he's not going to be interfering with anything we do is he? He's not going to be running the show or anything like that. I don't want to be answering to any Tom Dick or Harry you happen to be screwing with, this is me and you Valarie, and no-one else, or else the deal is off."

Valarie sat shaking her head.

"He won't even know anything about it. It's got nothing to do with him. It's not like you think Monica. Hell, he won't even be in my shop never mind knowing about anything that we are doing. I've just spent too many years of my life with a man who wanted to control every move in my life, I'm not about to start all over again having another one wanting to know every minute of the day where I'll be, I thought you knew me better than that Monica. Our business is our business. I will want to meet these people you tell me you can trust, I'll want to meet them before we proceed with anything, and if I'm not happy with something, then you can respect my opinion won't you?"

"Of course Valarie, I planned to introduce you all anyway. I wouldn't expect you to trust people you have never met before…there's far too much at stake for that."

Valarie then bent down and retrieved her hand bag from the floor which she had placed at her feet. She reached inside and produced a mobile phone.

"Here, don't say I'm not good to you. Only use this phone to contact me, nothing else ok? I have one the same and I will use it for no other reason than to make contact with you. It's just a cheap piece of shit but it will do for the purposes that we want. Communication Monica, between you and I and no-one else. I am spending the night in London tonight but I'll be heading back over home tomorrow morning. I shall purchase the building I would say within a week or two, I'll keep you informed. In the meantime, there'll be no harm done if you can set yourself some kind of targets out, you know, desirable girls fit for purpose, we'll only need a few, no more than eight I would say. They should make us a nice little wage packet Monica.

You make sure you pick us some nice little beauties…money-spinners Monica."

"You leave that to me Valarie. You just set up the building, I'll do the rest." Twenty-five minutes later Monica Carosova sat at the window of the Old Mill café in Canterbury and watched the taxi take Valarie Vercopte off to London. If everything went to plan, then they would be making good money in no time at all. It was still the easiest thing in the world to do, to pick up girls from the streets of Britain. Even after all the warnings the British government had been televising about the dangers of walking around unaccompanied, these young girls thought they were safe, and that it couldn't possibly happen to them.

BROMLEY.

South East London.

Mandy Spencer was quite taken aback when Sophie had asked her to have a little chat with her. She also wanted David to be present which was also a shock to Mandy as she'd done nothing but snap at her brother since she returned from her ordeal in Lithuania. Mandy carried her cup of tea through into the living room and sat down on one of the easy chairs. She did not have an inkling about what to expect from Sophie. The girl had changed, there was no mistaking that, and no wonder, any girl would, having been through what she'd just endured. David sat on the sofa with his can of high-energy drink and his guitar magazine waiting to hear what his sister had to say to him. It wouldn't be pleasant whatever it was, judging by previous conversations between them. He'd all but given up on being nice to her, although he did try his best to remain civil to her…whenever he could. It was getting harder and harder as time passed though. Sophie entered the living room and sat down on the sofa opposite her mother.
"This won't take very long." she said as she placed her cup `on the coaster` on the coffee table. "First thing I want to do mum is to apologise to you for the way I have been. My behaviour has been less than acceptable I have to admit.
I cannot imagine the suffering you endured while I was being kept in captivity. The fact that you wouldn't even know where I was would be unbearable. I have been too busy thinking about myself lately and haven't given a thought as to how you and David were feeling. I just want you to know mum that I am as proud as any daughter could be to have you as my mum, and you David for a brother." A pin could have been heard falling on the carpet.
"I love you both with all of my heart."
David looked up from his magazine to his mother and then to Sophie, as though he was waiting for a sarcastic punch-line to follow.
Sophie continued.
"I don't know what I would have done without your support, the both of you.
I can't imagine my life without you. What I went through in Lithuania was horrendous, there is no denying that, but the thought of having you two here worrying about me and probably praying for my safe return gave me strength I never thought I had. I just hope that the two of you can forgive me for my discourteous behaviour in recent times and allow us all to make a new start. As far as going to uni is concerned mum, I am really looking forward to it, honestly. I'm excited about gaining qualifications that could

lead me to better things in life. I know how much you hoped I would be accepted mum, so I'm telling you now, you have nothing at all to worry about. I know that that is what you were wanting for me and that you only had my interests in mind.

You have nothing to worry about, because I want to make something of myself and I know to do that I must have the qualifications to do it. That means hard work, studying and concentrating on the things that matter and not on the things that have been tearing me apart lately. I meant what I said mum, to do what you have done is nothing less than a miracle. To be left with two children and no-one to support you in a strange town must be one of the hardest things anyone could do in their life. You brought us up mum and we wanted for nothing David and I, and I'm sure he'll agree with me when I say, that you are the best mum anyone could ever wish to have.

I can't express just how much I love both of you. I've never been very good at that kind of stuff. You are all I have in the world, but also, you are all I want in the world. I don't need anything else as long as I have you two."

As Sophie rose from the chair and headed back to the kitchen, she looked over her shoulder and said, "I just wanted you both to know that. I love you both and I'm sorry for the way I have been with you. Thank you for standing by me and not giving up on me, even when I was thinking about giving up on myself."

Before she entered the kitchen she said to Mandy Spencer, "Whatever I achieve mum at uni, nothing could compare with what you achieved, and that's a fact. You don't get a certificate for that kind of achievement mum, but you should get a crown. Against all the odds you succeeded in raising your kids on your own.

If I can achieve half of that at whatever I study, then I shall be a proud young woman indeed...thank you mum."

David Spencer rose from the sofa and put down his magazine, entered the kitchen and threw his arms around his sister. No words were exchanged.

There were no words necessary. Just a couple of taps on each-other's shoulders was enough to let them both know that they appreciated each-others' company and that they were happy to be siblings.

Mandy Spencer sat completely shell-shocked.

Ten minutes earlier she'd been going through in her mind where exactly it was that she had gone wrong in Sophie's life, and at what point had she lost her daughters' respect. In the space of something like five minutes Sophie had not only put her mind at rest, but had also assured her that her love for her mother was unconditional and eternal. She hadn't done anything wrong. Her daughter had just told her that. In fact, her daughter was the first person in her life to even sit up and take notice of her achievement. Mandy knew that her friend Carol respected her, having come through very similar herself, but no-one had ever actually said to her, "Well done for what you have achieved."

No-one until two minutes ago when her own little girl, the girl she cherished so much since the day she was born, that little girl had just said, "Well done mum."

It wasn't even her place to say that, but she did.

And as all the worry and frustrations flowed from Mandy's eyes onto her handkerchief she thought back to that horrible day when she found out for sure that her husband had been having an affair and that he planned to leave her to live with his new love. That alone had frightened Mandy more than anything had in her entire life. The very thought of having to bring these two children up on her own and not knowing a single person in the area where she lived at that time. To bring them up with a broken heart and a broken spirit, in a broken home. And now, all these years later, the daughter she thought she was losing expressed to her in her own words that she realised just how hard it must have been for her.

"If I can achieve half of what you have achieved mum, I'll be a very proud young woman indeed."

Mandy Spencer surmised that whenever anyone won the lottery then how she felt now must come very close as to how those jackpot winners feel.

SCOTLAND YARD.

BROADWAY VICTORIA.

"Well that's it Terry." said Polly Sheppard, as Terry Mercer and Samantha Reynolds entered her office. "They've lost her. Angela Bates is now officially off the map. That didn't take them long did it? I must remember to ask if these surveillance teams have had any training at all before they're put out onto jobs. According to their report Bates entered a hotel in Dagenham twenty-four hours earlier and hadn't exited the place. Two of the team went in to make enquiries about her and it turns out she'd disappeared. We've lost her Terry, she's bloody free now alright. Christ Emily Smith will go ballistic. I promised her that we'd keep Bates under close scrutiny and that we'd be able to re-arrest her at any given moment in time. It was on my reassurance that she allowed her to be released. On top of that Geraldine Prowse will be pulling the hair out of her head as soon as she hears about this. She won't be laid back for much longer now Terry, those incompetent baboons have seen to that. She was so looking forward to Bates returning to the monster mansion. Four of them, and all they had to do was follow her around and clock any acquaintances she rendezvoused with, that's all, it's not a hard task Terry. Four of them, two vehicles…Emily will have me executed for this. I can just see the headlines now Chief Inspector resigns due to complete incompetence. And what may I ask Terry are you smiling about, this is serious. We have just released a very dangerous individual back into society, there's little to laugh about for crying out loud, how the hell do I explain this to Emily Smith? Let alone the chief of police."

As Terry headed straight for the coffee machine Samantha sat down opposite Polly. "Mam, she's been in touch with us, Angela Bates. Well, she's been in touch with Terry. She's given us some names. We have the names of three men who are in cahoots with Monica Carosova. Terry will explain everything."

"There's nothing to explain is there Samantha, you've said it all. Always love stealing my thunder don't you Sam."

Mercer sat down with his coffee. "Yeah, she's been in touch Polly. She's been so sickened by the way her so called associates have treated her that she's decided to try and work out a deal with us which would all but guarantee us to capture all concerned with the kidnappings. She said she could get us names and addresses of all the people involved with Saratov Kulbertinov, and Carosova. Most of them she said live in this country." Polly raised her eyebrows to Terry in a gesture for him to continue. She knew there was more to come.

Terry sipped his coffee. "She wants to be left alone. That's the deal. She'll give us everyone she can if we guarantee her that she'll have her liberty, that's it.

She said she ditched the surveillance team deliberately so that we might know that she could do so any time she wished. She said she walked right past one of the vehicles outside the hotel as they ate their burgers. The other two officers were at that moment in time in the hotel itself. She also emphasised that the officers in question were in no way to blame as she is one of the best in the business at creating elusion, after all, why would the officers in the car be paying any specific attention to an old lady with a grey tweed coat carrying a Tesco polythene bag and pulling a shopping trolley behind her, limping slightly, she'd be of no importance to them."

Terry looked up at Polly. He'd been quoting from Bates' text message.

He continued when Polly hadn't said anything. "She said it hadn't taken her long to find out the names of the people who were associating with Carosova.

Did you know Polly, that there have been four more girls kidnapped recently, only this time, for some unknown reason, they were released. Bates is as confused about that as I am. But she said there would be a very good reason, and that because they had been released we weren't to assume that that would be the end of the abductions."

Again Terry waited for Polly to say something.

"She's wanting to help us Polly. Yes, there's a price for her help, but she is willing to deliver them all to us for the price of her liberty...what do you think?"

Polly very slowly inhaled a deep breath as she sat with one hand in her chin and the other tapping on the desktop, and then exhaled exasperatingly as she contemplated the situation. "I don't really see how we have much of a choice Terry, do you? She's escaped the surveillance team with little effort. She already *has* her liberty. I'll put this to Emily Smith but I'll put it to her in such a way as to give the impression that I have...eh...collaborated with Bates. At least then if she thinks I have made a bad decision then it's just a matter of bad judgment on my part, rather as a team of surveillance officers losing her off the radar right in front of their eyes. Emily may curse my stupidity but it would end there, rather as having a full enquiry as to how the baboons managed to lose their subject in broad daylight. On top of that Terry, if this Bates trusts you then it's quite possible that she'd be prepared to meet with you at some point. If that should happen, then if we chose, we could put in a proper surveillance team who could then re-arrest her after you'd left, you know, a team who have actually done surveillance as part of their job, who have had experience in people trying to limp past them with shopping trolleys in an attempt to escape their attentions."

Terry smiled at Polly's immaculate sarcasm, as did Samantha. At least her mood had brightened slightly. All was not lost, if this Bates was serious about giving them the names then they would make considerable progress, and who knows, perhaps even bring an end to these abductions altogether. Polly nodded her head. "Yes, tell her we'll leave her be, if she gives us the names and addresses.

And tell her she'll even be rewarded if she can find us this Carosova. She'll be in no hurry to land back in this country if she's in touch with all events, especially when she finds out that her friend Mister John Carlton Fletcher has been arrested. He's going to get the shock of his life Terry in a couple of days when the fraud squad land at his house in the early hours and kick his door in. I spoke to one of them this morning. They've got everything they need to prosecute. Maybe *he'll* spill the beans on this Carosova. Anyway, in the meantime tell our friend Angela Bates that she has a deal...and try to be convincing Terry, like we mean it."

QUEEN ELIZABETH CONFERENCE CENTRE.

CENTRAL LONDON.

Two and a half thousand people sat in the conference hall awaiting the start of the Awards and Recognition Ceremony of the Metropolitan Police. This annual event rewarded officers of all categories including young recruits who have excelled in their fields. It was an honour indeed to be recognised by the Metropolitan Police chiefs and all but guaranteed the recipients a secure future in the police force. Medals and certificates sat on specially prepared tables up on the stage. A dozen seats were placed side by side just behind the tables all with name-tags placed on their backs with the identities of the dignitaries who'd be seated upon them.
Nervous eager young recruits sat on the front row of the congregation awaiting instructions from the stewards of when they'd be called up on stage to receive their awards and the procedure they'd follow once called upon.
Following the presentations, they'd all be wined and dined by some of the best caterers in the city.
It would be the proudest moment in their young lives, a day to remember.
Among the dignitaries to be seated upon the stage were representatives from Surrey Police, Devon and Cornwall, Hampshire constabulary, City of London Police, and the Police Federation of England. Anyone who was anyone in the major police forces in England were here this evening.
Less than a mile from the conference centre chief inspector Rosemary Harrington of the fraud squad sat with her two colleagues in their B.M.W just killing time until they decided to head to the centre and spoil the party completely.
Rose, a thirty-eight-year old veteran could think of nothing better than to expose a villain to their unsuspecting audience. It had only happened once in the course of her career when she'd exposed a man of the cloth for being a misogynist.
That had felt good, but this tonight was far bigger and better than that.
Mister Carlton-Fletcher would be brought down a peg or two in front of all and sundry. They had all the proof they needed to convict him of authorising the kidnapping and selling of young British girls. Rose, a brunette in her younger days touched her `slightly-dyed` hair with her fingers and asked her colleagues inspectors John Murphy and David Banes if her hair looked alright.
She was dressed in black dress trousers and wore a crimson blouse underneath her dark blue quilted winter jacket. "I've got to look my best boys, she joked, "after all, it's not

every day we have the privilege of telling our boss he's under arrest for authorising and funding kidnappings now is it? And in font of all the representatives of all the police forces in the country, you couldn't wish for a more humiliating experience if you tried."
John Murphy, a devout colleague of Rosemary Harrington in his forty-second year, smiled at his superior nodding his head in agreement.
"Yes Mam, and it serves the bastard right." John Murphy had worked with Rosemary since she was promoted three years earlier and bore no grudges to the woman for receiving the promotion even though he'd had his heart set on the post. He respected her and accepted her as his superior and had nothing but praise for the woman. Three months off his forty-second birthday he'd all but given in on the idea that he'd be promoted to any higher post in his career.
As for young Banes, he had his whole career in front of him and could probably look forward to many promotions in the future. As it stood now, he was nothing more than a dogs' body. He would be sent to the shop for cigarettes or pies or soft drinks, and he would drive them around as and when required. A twenty-six- year old recruit, he had shaved his hair off and only the dark outline could be seen on his scalp giving him a look of a thug in Rosemary's opinion. John Murphy on the other hand was slightly jealous of the lad in the fact that David's hair was absent through David's choice, whereas *his* hair had gone through natural processes...namely age. And if Murphy was being honest with himself he would admit that he'd let some weight accumulate over his body. He could certainly do with losing a few pounds. Standing at the height of five feet ten inches he guessed he'd be perhaps half a stone overweight. Rosemary Harrington stepped out of the B.M.W and proceeded to light up a cigarette. As she smoked she scrutinised her phone for messages. According to what she'd been told the presentations were due to begin at eight thirty. What she wanted to do, if they got their timing right, was to walk into the conference hall right in the middle of Carlton-Fletchers' speech. He was always invited to give a speech after the awards were completed. What better situation could she ask for than to walk in unannounced and then walk right up onto the stage and declare that he was under arrest.
A couple of thousand people would witness the procedure and she would revel in the moment. Murphy and Banes as well would be there in case there was a struggle although she doubted that very much. The man would be totally dumbstruck. No doubt he would proclaim that there had obviously been some huge mistake made and that the situation would soon be resolved.
Murphy climbed out of the car and joined his superior.
"Are you nervous mam?"
"About what exactly John?"

"Well, you know, doing this, arresting the commissioner of the Metropolitan Police Force, In front of all and sundry mam. We'll be able to hear a pin drop when you arrest him."

"Not in the slightest John. This man is a criminal, and a very callous one.

It wasn't so long ago that inspector Samantha Reynolds was kidnapped and her life put in jeopardy. Countless young girls snatched away from their loved ones to be used as whores. Innocent little girls John, and this bastard Carlton-Fletcher was funding it all. He was actually dictating where and when the abductions were to take place. Remember, we found those lists of girls' names and addresses in his files on his laptop.

Nervous? You're fucking kidding me, I'm looking forward to this more than you could ever imagine. This evil bastard is going down, and he's going down for a very long time. I'm just waiting for a text message from a friend of mine who happens to be at the conference hall. She's there to pick up an award.

Constable Rachel Cook will let me know the minute he begins his speech.

It'll only take us ten minutes or so to get there, and then we can bring him down in every sense of the word. As soon as he is arrested I'll inform Charlie to arrive with the van to take him away because he's not travelling with us in the B.M.W that's for sure. I've also arranged for a couple of press men I know to come and take photographs of him being escorted into the van. It'll be all over the papers in the morning. On top of that, as soon as he's arrested there's a team going round to his house to see what else they can find regarding his kidnapping arranging.

In a word John, fucked. He is totally and utterly fucked. And may the bastard rot in jail for what he's done. Judas Isacariot has got nothing on this bastard."

Fifteen minutes later Rosemary Harrington arrived at the Queen Elizabeth Conference Centre with her colleagues. No fewer than four different security men attempted to halt them on their way to the main hall, but one flash of her badge put an end to any attempt at stopping them. In truth, wild horses couldn't have stopped Rosemary Harrington from doing her duty tonight. As they approached the main hall doors, she turned and asked her colleagues if they were ready. Both Murphy and Banes nodded their heads. As they entered the hall Carlton-Fletchers' voice came booming out at them from the PA speakers which were placed all around the conference hall.

He was at this moment in time commending all the officers of the Metropolitan Police Force for all of their hard work and dedication they'd shown to the British public, and that they should all take a bow for their efforts.

"Be proud of yourselves for being part of the best Police Force in Europe.

We have come a long way since John Peel formed the first Metropolitan Police Force in

1829. Many things have changed since those days.

The type of crimes we have to deal with in this day and age demands that we are at the top of our game. There are some very clever recidivists out there who will stop at nothing to defeat us. In some cases, it takes us a little time to capture these people, but in the end very few of them escape justice, and thanks to people like yourselves the streets of London and indeed all the streets of this country are as safe as can be. I say again to you all, take a bow and be proud." Almost everyone in the hall rose to their feet and applauded Carlton-Fletchers' speech. Rosemary Harrington was on a high. It was that old saying; the `higher you fly, the further down you're going to fall`.

Even young David Banes was smiling as they walked down the aisle towards the stage. All the dignitaries on the stage had also risen from their chairs and stood now applauding the Commissioner of the Metropolitan Police Force. The man in question looked to his left as the rapturous applause continued. Harrington doubted if he would even know who she was. He was going to know in a minute who she was. She was his worst nightmare, that's' who she was, and she actually had butterflies at the thought of the task in hand. Stepping up to the microphone she raised her hands to the audience. It took about a minute for the applause to die down until there was almost complete silence as the bewildered crowd wondered what on earth she was about to say. Some of the audience knew who she was and so were puzzled as to why she was here. As she addressed them she could hear Carlton-Fletcher asking her colleagues what on earth was going on.

"Mister Carlton-Fletcher here is asking my colleagues what on earth is going on. And he may well ask, because that is a very good question. Well, I'll get straight to the point and put him out of his misery. I'm afraid I have some grave news for you all and especially for Mister Carlton-Fletcher. I am here with my colleagues to arrest him for his involvement in the kidnappings of teenage girls. You all know about these abductions and how much misery and stress this has caused these girls and their families." She turned and pointed to Carlton-Fletcher shaking her head, and then turned back to the audience. "This man here, who is supposed to be our leader and lead by example, is responsible for most if not all of the abductions. Over a period of around seven years, it could be more, he has made vast amounts of money, selling these kidnapped girls to Europeans who then use the girls as prostitutes in brothels. He stands here and has the audacity to praise the work that the Metropolitan Police do knowing full well that he, and his collaborators are making fools of us all, and knowing that because of his status there would be very little chance of his actions being investigated.

Well, he was wrong.

Mister John Carlton-Fletcher, I am arresting you for arranging the kidnappings of

numerous teenage girls, anything you say may be used in a court of law-".
There was horrendous shouting and jeering from the audience as well as the dignitaries on stage.
Carlton-Fletchers' face was crimson with anger and embarrassment.
Harrington ignored the ruckus and proceeded to handcuff the guilty party.
"You, my friend have just made the biggest mistake in your entire life, you have no idea the trouble you are in now. This is the end of your career make no mistake about that!"
With his hands behind his back, Rosemary Harrington marched the Metropolitan Police Commissioner down the steps and off the stage.
"You, my friend have just made your last speech to the public I'm afraid."
She replied "The next speech that you make will be in a court of law, and I would advise you now to rehearse it well, because it will have to be, phenomenally good." Together with officers Murphy and Banes she marched him along the aisle along the side of the hall in front of very confused and by now, angry people.
Three police officers waited outside by the van driven here to take him away.
Officer Charles Hasty, Rosemary's friend and colleague climbed out of the drivers' seat when he saw them coming and proceeded to open the back doors of the van.
She smiled broadly as he said to her, "Get the rat in here Rosy, I wouldn't put the bastard in a kennel, fucking twat, come on, get in there you fucking prick!"
"You are all making a very serious mistake" protested Carlton-Fletcher.
"You will all face the consequences of your stupidity. You will all be disciplined for this!"
Charles Hasty promptly replied to the head of the Metropolitan Police Force, "Yeah Yeah, just get your arse in there and shut your fucking mouth you nasty bastard!"
Charlie then used the heel of his right boot to catapult Carlton-Fletcher into the back of his van, and then slammed the doors closed.

SCOTLAND YARD.

BROADWAY VICTORIA.

When Terry Mercer and Samantha Reynolds entered Polly Sheppard's office she was busy arranging plants around the room, and administering water to them as she done so. "Come in you two I have some news for you. Rosemary Harrington arrested Mister Carlton-Fletcher last night at the awards ceremony.
What a bloody shock he would get. That would be the last thing he'd expect to happen to him."
Mercer nodded in agreement, and smiled.
"Yeah well, when you've got away with something like that for so long I expect you'd feel almost undetectable. Greed Polly, that's what gets them in the end." Polly looked up from her hunkers as she finished watering a plant and asked Samantha why her colleague was looking so smug with himself today.
As Terry poured the coffees Samantha replied "Oh he's received a letter from Angela Bates, I think they've arranged a date or something. You could tell Miss Sheppard, that they had the hots for each other from day one, it stuck out a mile. Bloody drooling at the mouth every time we went to her flat, but, she's put him out of his misery this time by agreeing to go out with him, at least that's what I think, I could be wrong."
Terry sat a mug of coffee in front of Samantha and pulled out a letter from his back pocket and then placed it on Polly's desk.
"There...read that. That was lying in my hall last night when I got home. As you can see, it wasn't posted, huh, so much for surveillance." Polly sat down and began to read the letter.

Detective Mercer, following our last discussion and all that bull-shit you expected me to believe about me receiving a full pardon, I have come to a decision. As you can see, your surveillance teams are of no use whatsoever, at least at trying to keep tabs on me, and so it would seem that I already have my liberty. That said, I intend to move away from this area completely and start again. Before I leave I am going to do you one last favour. This favour I am about to do for you is in no way complementary to you or any of your staff but rather an act of vengeance against the people who let me down so badly. So, as a final farewell gesture I have decided in aiding you to put an end to all these kidnappings. Later this evening you are going to arrest John Carlton-Fletcher who as you know has been profiting from these abductions, and as you also probably know has been funding the kidnappers. It would seem that you now have most of the main guilty parties imprisoned. All but two that is, and it is these two who I am going to give you on a plate, so to speak. At 8;30 tomorrow evening from the harbour of Clacton-On-Sea there'll be a little fishing boat that sails by the name of Sally-Anne. She and all of her crew will set off at high tide to do their little fishing trip.

On board that same little boat there'll be two stowaways who go by the names of Monica Carosova and Valarie Vercopte. I don't suppose we'll ever meet again Mister Mercer and so you can take this as a good will gesture. If you can arrest these two before they leave British waters then I think we can safely say that it will bring an end to this unfortunate course of events. Perhaps as a good will gesture to me you could in the unlikely event of your surveillance team spotting me somewhere, turn a blind eye, after all, I could have kept this information to myself. Take care Mister Mercer, and I wish you well for the future...kind of. Angela.

"What do you think Polly?" said Mercer who was looking deadly serious now.

"Do you think she's sending me on a wild goose chase?"

Polly looked at the two detectives. "There's no harm in checking it out is there, and she's right, if we can get these two then that would be them all captured, unless of course there are yet more people involved in this, there doesn't seem to be. Yes, I would check it out Terry. My God these people have crossed the wrong girl here have they not? She's sending them down the river isn't she? Pardon the pun. They must have pissed her off big time for her to do this."

Samantha said to Polly, "You can see though that it's basically a love-letter to Terry here, wouldn't you agree Miss Sheppard?"

"Oh hell yes, it sticks out a mile there Samantha, you're right, any damn fool can see that there is love between the two of them...without a shadow of a doubt, hell, she even wishes him well. They're a pair of love-birds Samantha, and all said and done, she is rather an attractive trollop in a funny kind of way, I could see the attraction. Watch out for him Sam."

Mercer as usual completely ignored their banter.

"We'll make sure Sam that we're down at the docks tomorrow night to bid the Sally-Anne a fond farewell, after we have relieved her of her stowaways, and by the way you pair, other than the blonde being sick in the head she's as attractive as any woman I can see around here, maybe even more attractive, so don't try and rip the piss out of me about fancying her, hell any read-blooded man would take the opportunity to bed her, and I am no exception."

Nothing was said by the two women while they digested Terry's words, and then, as he was rinsing his mug he turned smiling and said, "See? We can all play at that game ladies. Having said that, she is a rather beautiful woman, she could knock the spots off many a woman as far as looks are concerned. Polly instinctively rubbed her face where a couple of pimples had developed just under her right eye.

KAUNAS.

LITHUANIA.

Jacob (Yacob) Blint was an accountant. He was also an opportunist. Here he was in the home of a very good friend of his. Viktor Kulbertinov had been more than kind to him in the past three or four years since he began working for him. Viktor had lent him money on more than one occasion and had never asked for a penny back. He'd invited him back here to have dinner with himself and his adorable wife Valarie on numerous occasions. It was unfortunate indeed that Viktor had landed himself in deep trouble and was now serving a lengthy prison sentence for participating in sexual acts with kidnapped youths from Great Britain. The fact that Viktor had been made to serve out the sentence in Britain played right into Jacob's hands. He would be away from his home and more importantly, his wife, for ten years or more from what he'd been told and so Jacob had taken full advantage when Valarie had invited him to move in with her on a permanent basis. The fact that he'd been `bedding` Valarie for the past four months made his decision all the easier. This, he knew would break his ex-boss's heart but there was absolutely nothing he could do to help Viktor, other than `take good care of his wife for him`. He sat now on the luxurious sofa in the lounge sipping away at a bottle of one of Viktor's best wines as he arranged on the phone to meet up with a call girl in the city centre later that evening. Valarie would not be home until the following evening and so he had taken full advantage of the bank account she had kindly given him access to. Life, for Jacob Blint had never been so good.
He had made some handsome profits in the past with his con-man style of working, using bribery as his main weapon but nothing ever as profitable as this. He was set here for quite some time to come he surmised, with access to Valarie's credit cards and Viktor's bank accounts. He was in a very comfortable position.
He had just paid two thousand Euros for the services of a young Lithuanian girl who had promised him the night of his life. Two thousand Euros that Viktor would have no need of at this moment in time. It wasn't as though he and Valarie were not enjoying fun together, it was just that Jacob had never been in a position like this before, where he could pay for a high-class hooker's company, and so his attitude was, why waste a perfectly good opportunity like this, after all, it would do no-one any harm, and in fact, it would do him a power of good, or at least, his ego. Standing at the grand height of five feet six he wasn't the most confident man in the world. He sat back on the sofa and toasted himself for achieving this remarkable situation he'd `played` himself into. Also,

because he was Viktor's accountant he knew exactly how much money he had hidden. What Valarie didn't know was, that her husband had a number of overseas accounts, and he knew exactly where they were, and under what name. He sipped from his wine-glass again. Life was indeed looking good for Jacob Blint. It wouldn't matter one jot to him if Valarie threw him out tomorrow because he had access to considerable amounts of money. He would leave that be for now though. That money was safe enough and would provide for him if or when rainy days arrived. He had never suffered from atelophobia, but this nest-egg would ensure him a safe and comfortable future. It is amazing what financial security can do to boost self-confidence. For the first time in his life Jacob Blint was in a truly unbelievably comfortable position. Nothing could go wrong. And the beauty of these overseas accounts was, that no-one else in the world knew of their existence, other than Viktor of course, but he would withdraw the necessary amounts of money long before *he* was due to leave prison...and he would disappear from the face of the earth so that Viktor could not trace him. Until such times, he would enjoy the comforts of Viktor's lovely home and his lovely generous wife. As he sat sipping his wine and contemplating the course of events that would take place later that night in the hotel room he'd booked, the doorbell rang. Valarie was accustomed to having many visitors coming here to see her at all hours of the day. This was the third time that her clients had come to see her. He sighed impatiently as he rose from the sofa to answer the door, muttering to himself. *"She should tell people when she's not going to be home."* He opened the door to find two gentlemen he'd never set eyes on before. Two giant men, both of them standing well over six feet. Jacob smiled at the gentlemen. "Can I help you?"

Viktor had befriended a couple of `cons` in Belmarsh prison who just happened to know of a way to sneak messages out. This overjoyed Viktor to say the least and he promised the men a very good payday when finally he'd be released.

The two inmates had nothing to lose and so they sent out the messages to be passed on as requested to two individuals who went by the names of Charles Deacon and Arthur Ward. These men had been very good friends of Claire Redgrave's. If there were any awkward situations, violent situations, to be dealt with Claire would call upon these men to deal with it. Viktor had remembered the men's names when Claire had introduced them months earlier. They too were promised substantial amounts of money if they dealt with Valarie and Jacob. They were informed that there was a safe in the house in Kaunas and were given the combination to the safe. Each of them were to take twenty thousand Euros for doing the job. They were then to close the safe and delete the existing combination. Whether or not the men could be trusted to do this would remain to be seen, but Viktor's need to eliminate the `unfaithful` pair overrun

any doubts he may have had concerning their honesty, he wanted them dead.
There was over eighty thousand Euros in the safe, cash, or at least, there was, Valarie could well have made a huge dent in that amount. According to what Claire had said, she would trust these men with her life. As with the inmates who passed the message on to their friends who would in turn pass the message on to Charles Deacon and Arthur Ward, Viktor had nothing to lose. If the job was done correctly, and honestly, he would receive confirmation in a few days that his wife and her lover had sadly passed on to the sweet by and by. The two men ignored Jacob's question and made their way past him into the house, closing the door. Both men dressed immaculately in suits and collar and ties could have been friendly salesmen. But they were far from that.

"Who are you? You can't just march in here like this, Valarie is not home, and I will be informing her of your complete-."

"Shut your mouth thief!" The taller of the two men shouted.

"We are here to see you and to ask you some questions about your affair with Mrs Kulbertinov. You are a nasty piece of shit are you not Jacob?
You shag your boss's wife behind his back, you steal money from him, and what's this? Bloody wine from Mister Kulbertinov's cellar no doubt. Now sit your arse down and don't you move a muscle until we tell you to. We are here to ask you questions and find out just how much you have stolen from your ex-employer, and you dare tell any lies and we'll make our visit a long, slow agonising affair. Both men sat down, one of them placing a Smith and Wesson pistol on the arm of the chair, complete with silencer. It was plain to see. These men were here to execute him. If only Valarie had kept her mouth shut about the affair Viktor would have been none the wiser, but no, she had to blab to him and rub it in his face that she was having an affair and not just with anyone, but with *him*.

Obviously Viktor had got the information out of the prison somehow and now these two lowlifes had been sent to deal with him, and Valarie if he wasn't mistaken. There was no way out of this, other than buying himself as much time as he possibly could, although for what purpose he did not know. There would be no chance of an escape. He thought he would begin by trying to give these two thugs a reason why he had behaved in such a way.

"Gentlemen, I have one or two things to say to you that may change your-."

"Just forget it Jacob. It's too late pal. Nothing you can say is going to change our opinion of you. You are a cheating no good son-of-a-bitch and that's the end of it as far as we are concerned. Even before Viktor had been sentenced you were banging his cheap-cow wife doctor pox weren't you. That, to me Jacob, is the biggest insult you could give anyone, especially as the man had been looking after you. Lending you money, more

than once we've been informed, treating you to dinner, paying for your expenses wherever you went, all these things. And how do you repay him?
You bang his wife behind his back, and now you help yourself to the best of his wines. You'll be spending his money no doubt. You are Jacob, a very undesirable human being and need to be taught a valuable lesson. Now, before we set about seeing to that, we have been informed that Viktor's slut wife arrives back home this evening. Now we know that you were informed that she'd be back home tomorrow night, but we happen to know different. Perhaps she doesn't trust you, and she'd have good cause wouldn't she Jacob, you nasty piece of shit that you are…fucking weasel. So, you will inform her if she texts you that everything is well, won't you Jacob."
Jacob Blint did not answer. He didn't have to.
The other man stood up. The one who'd placed the pistol on the arm of the chair. "I'm just going for a wonder around the house Jacob, to familiarise myself with my surroundings, you stay here with Charles, I shan't be long."
What Arthur Ward was really doing was searching for the safe. He'd been given instructions as to where it was hidden, and sure enough, when he pressed the small button on the wall hidden behind a painting in the master bedroom he heard a mechanical clicking noise at the other end of the room. He pushed his hand in the middle of the wall and lo and behold, the wall swivelled exposing a large metal door with a small wheel-like handle in the centre. He read from a piece of paper in his hand a number of digits he'd been given. He pressed the digits on the small keypad underneath the handle. Again, there were clicking noises and this time, the large metal door swung slowly open towards him. Arthur Ward smiled as he saw the bundles of cash stacked neatly inside the safe. The information they'd been given was all true. This would be the easiest twenty grand himself and Charlie had ever made in their lives. He made his way back down stairs and entered the living room once again where he found Charles binding Jacob to the kitchen chair he'd brought through.
"I need to make myself something to eat Arthur I'm fucking starving, and so we can't have weasel Jacob wandering around the place like he fucking owns it." Arthur Ward smiled at his companion. Deacon looked at him.
"What? What did you find?"
Ward sat back down on the chair.
"I found the safe, exactly where those two fucks told us it would be. It's there Charlie, it's all fucking there. Twenty grand each, and lots more if we want it.
He must have half a million in there I'm not kidding, come and see for yourself." Ward was excited about finding the safe and the money. Although this fact made Charles Deacon happy, he was more in charge of his emotions, more down to earth…more

realistic about the situation. He looked at his companion. "Arthur? You go back in there and you take out forty grand, and forty grand only. After you have done that you close that door and you scramble the existing code numbers on the safe. We were promised twenty grand each, and that's what we'll take, not a penny more or a penny less. There are more than enough people in this world who are untrustworthy don't you think? We are not two of them. Don't you think Mister Kulbertinov has had the piss taken out of him more than enough? Whoever comes into this house between now and the time that Mister Kulbertinov is released from prison, well, they won't be helping themselves to however much is left in that safe. At least he'll have that to come home to, and anyway, Kulbertinov could put someone on our tails and fucking whack us, I'm not risking that, God knows everything else has been taken away from him."

Ward sighed heavily. "Yeah, you're right Charlie. I'll go and take out our share and then scramble the code on the keypad. Or I could put in a new code and write it down. Maybe those two fucks back in London could give it to him."

"Just do like he told us to do Arthur. He knows what he's doing, he'll have no trouble getting into his own safe I'm sure. If there was going to be difficulty he'd have told us different wouldn't he?" Ward left the room to retrieve the money and scramble the code, as requested by Kulbertinov.

Charles Deacon, with his grade-one haircut and designer stubble proceeded to untie Jacob again. "Change of plan."

He pointed to Jacob and instructed him to make coffee.

"Move your arse Jacob and do something for other people for a change, come on, make three coffees and be quick about it. Your fucking fancy days are over pal. Leeching from your boss, shagging his wife, stealing his money, drinking his wine, and you an accountant as well, a corrupt one by all accounts, pardon the pun."

Deacon laughed at his own joke.

Jacob Blint said nothing as Deacon poured on insult after insult.

As Jacob stood by the percolator he wondered if there would be a chance that he'd be sent or taken to the master bedroom. In there he had a Magnum 3-57 hidden in a shoe-box on top of one of the wardrobes. If he could somehow get to that room, he could put all this to an end. He hadn't killed anyone in his life-time, but today he thought he could willingly make an exception.

But there'd be no chance of that happening any time soon. There was nothing he could do to save himself, and by the looks of things, as soon as Valarie arrived she would face the same fate as himself. This was the last thing he'd expected to happen, but then again, Viktor Kulbertinov was a very influential man. A very powerful man as well. Even so, the fact that the man had been convicted and imprisoned in Britain gave him the peace of mind to think that he'd be safe from anything he could do.

How wrong he was.

Viktor would be sitting laughing in his cell with the knowledge that very soon his unfaithful wife and his untrustworthy accountant `friend` would soon be executed. He'd obviously managed to get word out to these gorillas to deal with the situation. They'd be paid handsomely no doubt when the job was done. As far as Jacob could make out, they were prolonging his agony by waiting for the return of Valarie. There would be some kind of mental torture involved no doubt before they'd finally be executed for their sins. Five minutes later Jacob sat on one of the single chairs in the lounge whilst his captors sat on one of the giant sofas. As Charles Deacon sat his cup down on the coffee table he said to Jacob, "What exactly makes you the kind of man you are Jacob. Is it in your blood to be a fucking thief and a low-life? I mean Viktor gave you everything you needed and more did he not? You were well off working for him. You never had a financial problem or anything. The man had your back, and yet…"

Jacob sipped his coffee and whispered as an answer. "Opportunity, I suppose."

"Opportunity? The man gave you everything you asked for, why would you be looking for opportunities? You know what, I'm glad I'm going to kill you.

People like you make me sick to the back teeth do you know that?

The man was setting you up for life. He was your friend, and he thought that you were *his* friend, but he got that wrong didn't he Jacob. All you do is look out for yourself and fuck anybody else, that's your policy isn't it wide boy. You are a very foolish man Jacob. You could look the man in the face and ask him for favour after favour whilst all the time you were banging his fucking wife, and don't worry, you're going to see her die first before we shoot you in the fucking head…greedy bastard. She is even more guilty than you, fucking bitch. We've been told about how she's been boasting to Viktor about the affair she's been having with you, but there'll be no more affairs after today Jacob, you've had your last bang at *that* cheap slut, I hope you enjoyed it wise man."

Arthur Ward then informed his colleague that he was going upstairs for a shower. It was agreed that they would then get Jacob to send out for food. Ward, who was similarly built to Deacon and had the same haircut, slipped off his jacket and folded it over one of the chairs. Deacon looked at him. "Did you take out the money?"

"Yeah, and I've scrambled the code on the safe, even we can't get back into it now, that's it sealed until someone puts in the emergency code."

"Good." said Deacon. "Well done Arthur, I know how tempting that must have been for you. Get your shower, and then we'll get this pig here to send out for dinner for us, no wait, come and get your coffee and then you can get your shower." Deacon looked at his watch. "That bitch will be here in less than three hours." Once again he looked at

Jacob Blint. "And then the fun begins."

Fifteen minutes later Arthur Ward stood in the luxury shower cubicle enjoying the cascades of soothing warm water wash away the rigours of a long journey that had begun the day before. It was worth it though, twenty thousand Euros which would work out at roughly fifteen grand English currency was the incentive for the arduous journey, and of course, the task in hand, which was to relieve the world of a certain German gentleman named Jacob Blint, and a whore who went by the name of Valarie Vercopte. Not the hardest task in the world, and by what he'd been told these two more than deserved what was coming to them. As he showered, someone entered the bathroom, he could see their silhouette through the frosted glass.

"I hope you've tied up Mister Blint good and tight Charlie before you came up here, I wouldn't want to be running around Lithuania hunting for the bastard. Fucking bad enough having to come here in the first place to get him."

No answer.

"I'm saying Charlie, have you tied the fucker up?"

No answer.

Arthur Ward switched off the water. "Can you hear me now, I'm saying, I hope you've got that German fucker secured, little thieving bastard."

Silence, only the final drops of water from the shower-head could be heard splashing upon the tiles.

Ward could now see the silhouette standing still right in front of the shower compartment. He could see that it wasn't Charles Deacon.

"Hey, what the fuck is wrong with you, have you turned into a cock-watcher? And say something you're starting to make me nervous, what the fuck's wrong with you?"

Just before he opened the door a female voice called out to him.

"Mister Ward, your friend Charles will not be coming up. In fact, he'll not be doing anything, ever again, his time has run out, and so has yours. Come out now, don't make me shoot you through the glass, come out and be a man and take it in the head like a hero, come on, step out of the shower."

Ward was completely helpless. If what this woman had said was true, then he'd be dead in less than thirty seconds. His only hope, as far as he could make out, was to keep her attention for as long as he could by having a conversation with her, and then burst through the door and pin her to the floor before she could shoot him. It wasn't much of a plan, but it was all he had. He stood naked and vulnerable.

"Who are you? And what do you want?"

"I am a friend of Mister Kulbertinov's wife Valarie, that's who I am. And you are a lowlife recidivist from the East end of London over here with your scum friend trying your best to make a quick buck by killing Jacob Blint, who happens to be a *very* good friend of Mister Kulbertinov's wife as well."

Ward's voice was pleading and soft. "Listen, I'm not interested in the money, if you let me go, you'll never see me again, and I can vouch-"

Ward dived at the door head first and landed at the feet of Monica Carosova, grabbing her by the ankle and knocking her completely off balance and landing her against the tiled wall with a thump. But the gun was still firmly in her hand. "Nice try, but your efforts were in vain. You are going to die today lowlife."

Valarie Vercopte entered the bathroom followed by Jacob Blint. Blint stood at the doorway behind Valarie.

"What's going on Monica?" said Vercopte aiming Blint's gun at Ward's head.

"He almost caught me out, but not quite." Monica rose to her feet.

Valarie paid no attention to what her friend had just said but instead looked directly at Arthur Ward.

"Get up on your feet, and stand against the wall, put your hands against the wall. Do it now, move now." Arthur Ward knew he was done for.

His only hope in gaining control of the situation had failed miserably.

Valarie continued.

"Turn your back to the wall. Turn around and face me, come on, nobody's going to laugh at your miniature penis, come on turn around."

Ward done as he was told, there wasn't much else he could do.

At that point Jacob Blint entered the bathroom. Blint stood now smiling at Ward.

"How terribly fortunate for me that Mister Kulbertinov's whore wife returned home even earlier than *you* anticipated. How quickly the tables can turn Mister Ward."

Blint's last word came out as `Vard`.

There was silence as Valarie stepped forward toward Blint. She handed him the gun and said, "Ok Jacob, you can have the honour of finishing Mister Ward's life, after all, he came here to end yours. Shoot him in the head and don't be all day doing it, I have affairs to see to."

Valarie stepped back and watched Blint.

His reaction did not surprise her.

"I...I don't know...em...I...can't we just send him back?"

Valarie's next words shocked Jacob beyond belief.

"I knew it. I knew you were a coward. You're quite happy spending my money and living it up but when push comes to shove, you're a fucking coward.

And you *have* been spending money haven't you Jacob? You've already spent four thousand Euros today haven't you, on `another` whore. Do you think for a minute I would let you spend my money without having you observed or monitored? You are nothing but a little lily-livered fucking pathetic loser.

Monica, do the honours please...in the head, make it quick."

Before Jacob had the chance to say anything else Monica Carosova raised the hand gun and shot him in the centre of his brow. His body fell in a heap at the feet of Arthur Ward, who then pleaded again with Valarie.

"Please, I beg you, I'm sorry for everything, I really am, I promise you here and now, you will never see me again, I have learned my lesson. I shall never-" Monica's aim was perfect as the bullet entered Ward's temple thumping his head against the tiled wall before he fell dead onto the floor.

Monica and Valarie stepped forward looking down onto the two corpses.

"Well that's that then." said Valarie as she stooped down to inspect the bodies.

"You would think so wouldn't you." said Terry Mercer, as he and Samantha Reynolds stood at the doorway of the luxury bathroom.

"Just lay the guns down gently on the floor ladies, nice and easy. Don't be making any sudden moves, there's been enough killing in here for one day, wouldn't you agree Valarie? Mind you, from what Samantha and I have heard about those two from London and the German here Mister Blint, your actions could hardly be described as flagrant." The shock on Valarie Vercopte's face was plain to see. She stared in disbelief at the two detectives standing before her.

"How did you know that-?"

"It doesn't matter Valarie, how we knew or how we got here, the fact remains that we *are* here, and now Samantha and I have a problem. Two problems in fact, and those two problems are you and Monica here. The problems are, that we can't get you back out of this country. We can't take you back to London where you should both stand trial. So...what do we do? We could shoot you now and then we'd know for sure that the kidnappings in Britain would cease."

Before Mercer said anything else Valarie said "Can we go down stairs and talk about this? What you've seen today is not as callous as it looks. Monica and I are not cold-blooded killers. Can we at least go down stairs and be civilised as we talk instead of standing here in my bathroom."

Blood was oozing from the wounds in both men's heads and was swirling slowly around Valarie and Monica's feet on the white tiled floor.

"Ok" said Mercer, let's go and talk down stairs. Let's see if we can work out a deal here shall we?"

Mercer's words gave the two women fresh hope that they'd be spared, but Monica knew that this was the end of any British girls being kidnapped for immoral purposes. This was going to be the end of everything, and that's if Mercer kept his word. She knew that it would be the easiest thing in the world for the two detectives to just shoot them both here and now and then quietly slip away back to London...but there was at least hope.

It would be a good deal indeed if Mercer and detective Reynolds let them off with their lives. But this had gone on for far too long anyway. They had been lucky on more than a few occasions not to be apprehended, but now they were at the end of the line.

Brick wall. There was nowhere to run.

As they descended the stairs Valarie's frame of mind could hardly be described as sanguine, but there was at least hope. This detective Mercer seemed to be a decent kind of man who looked at situations from more than one perspective.

In just a few moments time she would find out just how decent he really was.

There were three corpses lying around the house at this moment in time.

If this discussion went wrong, two more wouldn't be much of a problem for them.

As they were all seated in the lounge Valarie said with not just a little disgust, "That's a fifty-year-old bottle of wine there and that little leech has been guzzling it like cola."

Mercer smiled at the woman. "I don't think that Mister Blint drinking your expensive wine is at the top of your list of troubles Valarie, however, seeing as how he's opened the bottle I wouldn't mind sampling a glass if you have no objections, Samantha and I are quite partial to a glass of white wine."

"Do you mind if we have one as well?" replied Valarie.

After a few minutes Valarie said, "How would this do for a deal? If you spare Monica and I, then I give you my word that we shall never participate in anything like this ever again, the kidnappings I mean. As well as that, if we hear anything at all about people arranging anything, then we will contact you with plenty of warning. We'll give you names and times of arrivals, everything we can, I promise you, we both do, don't we Monica?" Monica agreed, nodding her head vigorously.

Mercer sipped his wine and screwed his face up. "Hell Valarie, this wine tastes like piss, god, it really does taste like it is fifty years old."

He sat scrutinising the two guilty parties as if he were deciding whether or not to believe what had just been said. "It's not really much of an offer is it Valarie, I mean you could land back to Britain in a few weeks and start the whole thing all over again couldn't you. You could-"

"Pardon me for interrupting Mister Mercer, but please hear me out."

She took a deep breath. "As you know, my husband Viktor is locked away in a prison somewhere in Britain and from what I've been told, he shan't be released for another ten years. As things stand just now, I have all the money I shall ever need, and more. I intend to open a beauty salon for my friend Monica here and get her started with her own business. We have no need to kidnap teenagers. We have no need to keep company with people who do, but I can find out lots of valuable information for you with regards to those who plan to, I give you my word."

"Can you guarantee Valarie? Can you guarantee you can get me names and give us warnings?"

Valarie Vercopte smiled as she sipped her wine and looked at the two detectives who held her destiny in their hands and then proceeded to play her ace. "Yes I can Mister Mercer, and just to prove how sincere I really am, I am going to give you an opportunity to return home absolute heroes, both of you."

"Really"? said Samantha, placing her Glock pistol on the coffee table.

"And just how might you do that? If you don't mind me asking?"

As Valarie drained her wine glass, she leaned over the table, smiling at the two detectives. "I know where they are keeping four English girls here in Kaunas, now, do we have a deal Mister Mercer?"

Mercer lifted the wine glass as if to take another sip but then replaced it back onto the table. He didn't respond to Valarie's information, instead he said to her, "Your little obsequious friend here has taken care of Mister Ward and Mister Blint, so what on earth have you done with Mister Deacon, we don't see any blood stains."

Valarie lit up a cigarette. "He's outside in the garage in a compost container, I have good quality furnishings in here, I didn't want his blood staining my carpets and furniture."

Mercer stood up placing his hands in his trouser pockets. Looking first at Monica and then to Valarie he said, "And you can take us to this place where these people are holding the English girls?" Valarie drew on her cigarette. "I can take you there, but you'll have to be careful. You won't be able to just go in and release them. They'll probably have at least a couple of people guarding them, probably night and day. They are worth an awful lot of money to certain people, but yes. I can take you there."

Samantha Reynolds said, "Do you know these people personally? Have you had dealings with them before?"

Valarie nodded her head. "Yes, they are friends of Michael Saratov. They were also friends of Mister Carlton-Fletcher as well."

Mercer spoke again to Valarie. "Is it far from here this place where the girls are being held?"

Stubbing out her cigarette in the crystal-glass ash-tray she replied, "It's about a fifteen-minute drive from here. It's just a small cottage."

Samantha spoke again, looking directly at Valarie. "So you wouldn't look out of place if you decided to pay them a visit? You've been to this place before then?"

"Yes, I've visited there with Monica here and with Michael Saratov."

Samantha continued. "So, what if Terry and I came in with you, say as potential buyers, I take it these girls would be for sale?"

"Are you kidding me?" said Valarie incredulously, "His face was all over the papers here when those girls were rescued from Michael's place. In fact, and I don't mind telling you now that he's in Jail, but Mister Carlton-Fletcher was planning to kill you Mister Mercer. You had become, how do you say in English, a thorn in his side, a nuisance. There was going to be a contract put out on you...on both of you as a matter of fact."

Mercer sighed as he looked at his colleague. "It's at a time like this w
hen we could do with Colin Green Samantha, he would sort it all out for us."

Mercer turned to face Valarie again. "What about the authorities, is it worth our while informing them?"

Valarie raised her eye-brows and shrugged her shoulders. "Perhaps, but I must warn you, there is some corruption within. It would be a gamble as to who you spoke to, and if you happened to speak to the wrong person...well, I don't have to tell you what would happen."

Monica Carosova spoke up now. She was desperate to maintain her freedom and so had hatched up a plan in her head. "I have an idea. How much money do you have in the safe Valarie, I mean, I'm not trying to be personal but if you can produce a substantial amount to show that gang then we could trick them.
We could lay a trap."

Valarie turned to look at her friend. "Didn't you just hear what I said Monica? They know his face, they would know something was up as soon-"

"Yes, they know *his* face, but they don't know her. If she was willing to go along with this, she could pose as a buyer. Give her a briefcase full of money and she can come with me, they'll be convinced, they'll fall for it, especially when they see the money."

Mercer interrupted. "That's a brilliant half plan Monica, but this is how it will work out. You'll call them to come here and you'll inform them that you have a trustworthy client here with you who is in possession of lots of money and this client is keen to do business with them. You will entice them *here* and Samantha and I will see to the rest, how's that for a plan. And of course Valarie, your money will not be at risk. If you can do that for us, then we will call that a deal, we will walk away with the girls and take them back to Britain and you two will never again step foot on British soil, unless it's only for a brief visit, because if we hear that you have-"

"Please, Mister Mercer. We have a deal, I give you my word, we both do. But I must ask

you, what if four or five of them come here, what are you going to do then?"
Mercer smiled. "Tell them to bring the girls here. The sale will take place here. Now, unless they're travelling in a bloody mini bus, or they come in a convoy, then I don't think there'll be any more than two coming in here. If there are more than two, then you and Monica will just have to get busy digging a very big hole. That'll be your problem ladies, after all Samantha and I are trusting you.
You could end up collaborating with them and turn against us, in which case, Sam and I would have a big problem, and you would have three SAS men hounding you from here to kingdom come until they found you and then buried you alive.
That's what they do to double-crossers, so be warned if that is part of your plan. They'll take you to a field and dig a grave for you, or rather, they'd make you dig your own graves. They would then place you in a casket. Then they would lower the coffin, which would have a hard Perspex lid so that you could see the first shovelfuls of dirt hitting the lid from six feet above you. Slowly but surely the sounds would fade. You wouldn't be able to see anything anymore, and the sounds of the earth hitting the coffin lid would get fainter and fainter as they filled the grave until you'd be left with nothing but darkness...and the thought of having about an hour and a half's worth of oxygen left in the box until you would start to suffocate. So, are we all clear on the double-crossing consequences ladies?"
Valarie lit up another cigarette, her hands shaking slightly.
The thought of what Mercer had just said unnerved her, more than a little.
And she knew he wasn't telling any lies about how they'd be hounded...and buried.
"No-one will double-cross you Mister Mercer, I can assure you, besides, Monica and I are not *that* close to these people. But trustworthy enough for them to believe us when we tell them we have a buyer, and besides, they'll be keen to get rid of these girls as soon as they can. When we tell them we have fifty thousand in cash here they'll be over here before I can put the phone down...so to speak."
"Yes," said Mercer, "So to speak. Now then, what are you going to do with those two up there?"
"They can go in the compost bin, it's big enough to hold them.
I don't know how we will dispose of the others if you kill them, but like you say, it's our problem not yours."
Samantha was standing looking out of the window.
She turned smiling, "If that happens Valarie, you and Monica will just have to burn some garden rubbish won't you, there's no-one out here to bother you is there, it's not like you have nosey neighbours is it...it's not a big problem really. But if you do this and get those girls here, we will keep our word, and considering what you've been up to I

think you've got a bloody good deal, don't you?"
Valarie and Monica nodded and answered in unison. "Yes."
"Ok then" said Mercer, let's get the German and the thug out to the compost heap then, and then you can call your friends with the good news about having this sexy leather-clad piece of ass here with loads of money to dispose of."
Only the ghost of a smile appeared on Valarie's face.
"But before that, could someone please make me a cup of coffee because this bloody wine tastes like nothing I could describe…fifty-year-old wine, Christ I don't know what you connoisseurs are tasting when you buy this shit, it's like fucking vinegar to me."
As Valarie sipped from her re-filled wine-glass she said, looking up at Mercer, "Yes, to you it does Mister Mercer."

Terry Mercer had been tipped off one final time by Angela Bates.
"One final favour," She had said. Her phone call had informed him about Kulbertinov's wife returning to Lithuania with her friend Monica, and why they were going there. How she had found out all this information he did not know and neither did he care, why they had changed their plans at such short notice so long as it was all true. She informed him about Blint having an affair with Valarie (Vercopte) Kulbertinov and how two men had been hired to kill her and her lover. She also informed them that the women had changed their plans about how they would travel to Lithuania. Mercer saw this as an opportunity to kill two birds with one stone. He gave the information to Polly Sheppard who had then arranged flights for himself and Samantha. Being in Lithuania this time would be dangerous, even more dangerous than the first time. There were no SAS men this time to cover them or advise them. Polly even offered Samantha the option of not going with Terry. The fact that the two men hired by Kulbertinov to kill his wife and lover were involved in all the kidnappings here in Britain made her mind up for her. She wasn't about to let the opportunity to dispose of these thugs pass her by, and besides, this was not like their first visit. This time they had addresses and names to work with. They could actually plan their moves. They would have a certain amount of control. But she also knew and was informed by Polly yet again, that it would be extremely dangerous. Mercer was more than a little pleased when Samantha had decided to come with him. They sat now in this luxurious lounge of Valarie `Kulbertinov's` home.
They were waiting for her phone to ring.
Monica had called these `friends` of theirs and explained that she had a potential buyer who was prepared to purchase the girls they had with them for a substantial price.

Monica had also informed them that the woman was trustworthy and genuine. "Call me back" she had said, "When you've thought about it, but she'll only be here for a couple of hours. If you want to make some money quickly then I'd advise you to bring the girls here to Valarie's house as soon as you can. Call me back if you are interested."

It had to be said Monica Carosova had done a good job convincing these people, having said that, it was in her best interest to be convincing. Her freedom was at stake. Her life was at stake.

Quite obviously their trust in her was misplaced, but that was of no concern to Samantha and him. All that mattered was to get those girls out of this country and back home safely. Terry and Samantha had decided that they would keep their word to Valarie and Monica if everything went to plan. They also agreed secretly that if any of these two women showed their faces again in Britain, anywhere in Britain, they would be immediately arrested and charged for kidnapping and conspiring to kidnap. Obviously, they wouldn't say anything about that to them at this moment in time. They would give them the confidence to think that they were free to enter the country any time they wished, which they were, it was only that Terry and Samantha withheld the details of the consequences should they choose to. These two women in front of them now were responsible for dozens of girls disappearing from their homes. They had made money from the sales of these girls, or at least Monica had, most of them just kids really and thought nothing of it, having little or no concern for the girls or for the girls' parents. They were ruthless, particularly Monica, who wasn't as financially secure as her friend. None of these details meant anything to the two detectives as they sat now waiting for the telephone to ring. The situation they were in now was in fact a bonus to them. They had come here to kill Ward and Deacon but as it had turned out, that job had been done for them. They knew little about this German, Blint, he had not even been in the equation, and had nothing to do with any of the girls kidnapped. But now, here they were on the verge of being able to rescue some more young girls. It would all depend upon how desperate these people were for money. If they were amateur, then there'd be little chance of them turning down the opportunity. If they were professional, then they'd perhaps be suspicious of the offer, especially at such short notice. Half an hour had elapsed since Monica had called them.

Then the phone rang.

After a short conversation in their mother tongue, Monica informed the two British detectives that they were on their way over.

However, there was now a problem which had been unpredicted, or unforeseen.

Either Ward or Deacon had scrambled the combination on the safe and so Valarie could not gain access to it, or retrieve any cash. Luckily she had a couple of thousand Euros on her person and so the plan was, to place books or papers inside a small briefcase and then place a thin layer of money on the top, hopefully convincing the would-be buyers that the case was full.

"If that fails." said Mercer, loading his hand-gun, "We'll just have to shoot them, because if they bring those girls here with them then they are coming home with us, make no mistake about that."

They would have to be shot at some point he knew, because they would want to see the cash, there was no doubt about that…all of it, whatever the price would be. All Mercer wanted was to have them off guard, and hope that they didn't bring silly numbers with them. If there were more than four they would have a problem. When Terry had mentioned this to Samantha Valarie spoke up again. "How much do you trust us Mister Mercer, because Monica and I can at least half your problem. As you have seen for yourselves, Monica is not afraid to use a gun. If you give us back our firearms we can assist should a problem arise, and I'm sure at some point a problem *will* arise. As soon as they get suspicious then it could get tricky but that would depend upon how many bodies they bring. Now, before you say anything I assure you that Monica and I's freedom is worth more than these thieves' lives. I take it your superior knows that you are here and why you are here. If anything happens to either of you, all hell would break loose, and then we *would* have the bloody SAS onto us, and I for one do not fancy living like that, having to look over my shoulder everywhere I go. So, will you give Monica her gun back? Believe me, I do not want to be buried alive Mister Mercer."

Mercer sat and scrutinised Valarie Vercopte.

After a few seconds he said, "I'll tell you what we'll do Valarie."

He pointed to a fruit bowl that was placed on a cabinet.

"I'll place Monica's gun in there and should Samantha feel that there's going to be trouble, She'll ask Monica to pour you all some drinks. We'll place some bottles of spirits on the cabinet now, and some glasses. That will be the signal. I shall be in the kitchen of course, now, just one final time Valarie, if you and Monica's plan is to double-cross us, I would advise you to think twice before-"

"There will be no double-crossing. I gave you my word."

Mercer smiled, "Yeah well, up until now Valarie, your word doesn't exactly stand up well does it? Prove me wrong, and I assure *you* that it will be very beneficial to you both…I give you *my* word." Samantha had been to the bathroom. Upon returning she said, "Everything's ok now, look what I have found…." She held up a leather bag and proceeded to empty its' contents onto the floor in front of her. It was the money the thugs had taken from the safe.

Five minutes later, everything had been put into place. They had stacked paper-back books into a small valise and then layered the top with thin bundles of Euro notes. For all intents and purposes it looked like a case full of money. They all knew that it wasn't that important. If there were less than four people here with the girls, then it certainly wouldn't be a problem. A vehicle could be heard coming up the drive. It was a van. An old British bashed-up Transit by the looks of it. It came to a halt just outside of the front door of the house. Two men got out and stretched their arms as though they'd been travelling for a thousand miles. Mercer could tell by the way they placed their hands inside their jacket pockets that they were both armed. They were checking their guns. Both men clad in heavy leather jackets and jeans walked towards the front door. Mercer could tell immediately that they were amateurs. He doubted very much that these guys had had anything to do with the kidnapping of the girls. Someone else had done that for them, and then left them in charge.

Having said that, they could still be dangerous.

Monkeys with guns could be dangerous.

"You ok Samantha?" he asked.

"I'm fine Terry." Samantha answered in a calm controlled voice.

"You'd better disappear for now, we'll handle this."

Mercer entered the kitchen and pushed the door almost closed.

Valarie walked to the front door and opened it to invite the two men inside.

Both men had shaved heads and had what looked like five-o-clock shadow on their faces, giving, to the untrained eye, a menacing look, but to Terry Mercer they looked like what the Americans referred to as, `doosh-bags.` However this was going to turn out, it wouldn't take long, as long as the girls were in the van.

The two men sat down on one of the sofas opposite Samantha and Monica. Samantha sat nursing the briefcase on her lap. Valarie began speaking to them in their mother tongue. Samantha then interrupted them. "English please, if you don't mind."

Valarie then explained that the gentlemen couldn't speak English and so she would have to translate for them.

Samantha then rose to her feet, keeping the briefcase close to her chest.

"Before you translate anything Valarie, I want to see the merchandise.

I'm not parting with fifty thousand Euros for a bunch of scrubbers, tell them that."

Before she did, she said to Samantha that she could speak openly and say anything she wanted, the men really couldn't speak nor understand a word of English.

"Tell them what I said anyway Valarie, we have to act realistically, I've got to look genuine."

Monica rose to her feet as the men stood up and walked to the door gesturing to

Samantha to follow them. Even though she knew they couldn't understand her she shouted to them, "Are you fucking kidding me on? Bring the fucking girls in here. Do you think I'm going outside to look into a shit-heap of a van? Bring the fucking girls inside!" The men looked startled and panicked after Samantha's outburst. They could see that she was upset about something. Valarie explained to them why she was annoyed and that she felt insulted that they expected her to go outside and peer into the back of a van. The two men nodded their heads, eager to please, giving some kind of an apology and then holding up their hands gesturing her to sit still and signalling that they would go and get the girls and bring them indoors. As Valarie went outside with the men Monica said, "Well done inspector, you are very convincing. They knew what you meant."

Mercer's voice came through from the kitchen. "Everything ok Samantha?"

"So far so good Terry, they've gone out to get the girls."

Mercer spoke again. "Monica? When Samantha tells you to get the drinks, then you retrieve your gun ok? But don't use it just keep it there until Samantha or I give you the signal."

Valarie returned to the lounge followed by four young girls who looked to Samantha to be no more than fourteen or fifteen years of age. All of them dressed in jeans and jackets that were either too large or too small for them and all of them tearful and miserable. Samantha instinctively wanted to get up and comfort them by informing them that everything was ok and that they were going home very soon. But they would have to wait just a little while longer. If everything went to plan they *would* be on their way home soon. She only hoped that they wouldn't have to witness any shooting.

Samantha rose from the sofa and told the girls to sit down which didn't please Valarie for fear of the girls' clothes dirtying her furniture, such was the state of the denims they were all wearing. There must have been grit and dust lying on the floor of the van.

The girls sat down unsure of what was happening. They looked to each other nervously. Perhaps they thought they were going to be sold individually.

Samantha looked at the two men and said, knowing that Valarie would translate to them. "Have you been keeping them in a sewer? These girls are filthy, and you have them dressed in rags. Do you honestly expect me to pay top-dollar prices for wretches like these? What kind of people are you? Are you rats?

Who would keep young women in a state like this, you are obviously fucking amateurs. I'm not interested in buying them in a state like this, who's your boss?"

Who is responsible for treating them like this!?" Valarie had been translating as Samantha had ranted on to the men. Mercer stood behind the kitchen door smiling to himself, impressed with Samantha's performance.

Samantha then spoke again. "Monica, pour us a drink please, I need something to calm myself down." Still looking at the two men she said, "You are fucking buffoons, both of you…idiots!"

Again Valarie translated to them. They didn't look too pleased with Samantha's comments but they knew she had a point about how the girls were dressed.

One of the men looked at Samantha and said, "Boss coming, he coming soon."

"Oh, is he now, and suddenly you speak English. When…when is he coming because I'm not waiting all day for him to arrive, I have places to be, he better not be long."

Samantha stepped over to the girls and one by one gently lifted their chins up as though to study their faces. She looked at the man who had spoken to her.

"Tell your boss, thirty thousand for all four and not a penny more, and tell him to get his arse here pretty quickly or that offer will be withdrawn, text him that!"

Again Valarie translated.

The man pulled out his phone and raised it to his ear. After a few moments he said, "Boss be here in five minutes, no more ten."

"No more ten? What the hell is that supposed to mean? Does he mean no more than ten minutes, is that what he means?"

Valarie nodded.

Monica stepped over to Valarie and the two men offering them a glass of vodka and coke each. Then she handed Samantha a glass. Her gun was in place.

All that remained to do now, was wait until this boss arrived whoever the hell that was. Monica and Valarie had no idea of who it could be, and would he be alone?

If he brought more men with him, then there *would* be a problem. As it was, the situation was dodgy enough without it being exacerbated. All they could do was wait.

Samantha stepped over to the girls again, lifting their chins and gently turning their heads from side to side. Then she told them to stand up.

As they stood she walked slowly along them turning them gently around and making out that she was studying their figures. She looked at the two men again.

"Put them back in the van."

Valarie told them what Samantha had said.

They ushered the girls back outside and put them back into the van, closing the double doors behind them. As they returned to the house a black BMW pulled up in the car park.

As Samantha looked outside she almost let out a sigh of relief, whoever this was, he had come alone. He looked about forty years of age, well dressed in a grey suit and overcoat to match. He looked authoritative. He marched confidently into the house and pulled a pair of brown leather driving gloves from his hands.

His actions reminded Samantha of actors' she'd seen on TV playing the part of a leader of the Schutzsaffel, as though he were about to ask a number of questions.
Valarie gestured for him to take a seat. She had never met him before, but she knew who he was, as did Monica. Now there would be a very big problem, and not just for Terry Mercer and Samantha Reynolds. Sitting on Valarie's Vercopte's sofa was none other than Oleg Smertsov, the chief of Police for Kaunas.

Samantha knew instinctively by the expressions on Valarie and Monica's faces that all was not well. Whoever this man was, he'd put the fear of God into them. Valarie nervously offered him a drink which he accepted. As Valarie handed him his brandy he said to Samantha, "So you're looking to buy some girls? Has my men showed you what we have on offer?"
Samantha replied, "Yes they have, and I must inform you, I'm not impressed with their present condition, they look malnourished, and they're dirty, their clothes as well, if you can call them clothes. I expect a discount for this."
"Do you now. And where may I ask do you intend to run your business from, not here in Lithuania I'm guessing."
Samantha tried to remain as cool as she could. "That, my friend is of no concern to you, but no, it will not be in Lithuania. How much are you asking for them?
I need to know, I am not here on holiday, I have business to see to."
Oleg Smertsov stood up and placed his brandy glass onto the coffee table and took off his coat, placing it on the arm of the sofa.
He then sat back down reaching inside his jacket pocket and pulled out his wallet.
"You've seen the girls, you tell me what you think they're worth. I know how much I could get for them in the right market."
Samantha lit up a cigarette and said, "Valarie informs me that you're asking for fifty thousand Euros. I will go no higher than thirty-five, and that is my top offer, and considering their condition I don't think that that is a bad offer."
Smertsov sat back on the sofa like he was relaxing resting the brandy glass on his right knee and holding it there. He had placed his wallet on the table. "I find it very strange young lady that you are allegedly about to part with thirty-five thousand Euros, and yet you have not even asked who I am.
Do you know who I am?"
Samantha looked the man straight in the face.
"I care not one jot who the hell you are and if you are not interested in my offer then there is no point in us introducing ourselves is there. Now, do you want my money or not, as I say, I have business to attend to."

He sighed and pulled out a card from his wallet and then gestured for Valarie to come over to him.

"I shall overlook the fact that you are being very discourteous to me in my own country, and you here a visitor." He handed Valarie the ID card. "Show my friend here who I am, perhaps then she might speak with me in a more civilised manner...or show a little decorum."

Valarie placed the card back down on the table as she went to pour herself another vodka. As she did, she said to Samantha. "He is Oleg Smertsov, the chief of police for Lithuania."

Mercer cringed in the kitchen as Samantha replied, "Is that supposed to frighten me? You are obviously as corrupted as the rest of your staff here in Kaunas.
Are you trying to intimidate me? Is that what you're trying to do? I don't care if you're Keizer Wilhelm, do you want my business or not? Do you think I would come into this country and not do my homework? I know what goes on here, I have done deals with Mister Saratov, I have purchased before, now, for the last time, do we have a deal...Mister Smertsov, do we have a deal or not? Monica, get me a drink please."

Smertsov's men watched Monica eagle-eyed as she headed to the cabinet.
She looked over to the men. Would you two like another drink?" They seemed to relax and nodded their heads. There was only the sound of Monica clinking the bottles and glasses as she made the drinks. Nothing was being said. Samantha sighed and then said, "Well? Do we have a deal Mister Smertsov?" Monica returned to the two men handing them their glasses and watching to see which hand they accepted their drink with. They were both right-handed. She returned to the cabinet and then turned with the gun in her hand, pointing it directly at Smertsov. "I'm sorry Samantha, but I can't stand this tension any more, don't you move a muscle Mister Smertsov, please, I don't want to shoot you." Mercer came through from the kitchen holding his magnum 3-57 in his right hand. Samantha then stood up and retrieved her pistol from her hand bag.

"You just keep those glasses in your hands gentlemen." She said as she approached Smertsov. "Stand up." The chief of police stood up slowly, smiling as though he knew this was going to happen all along.

"My dear girl, you have no idea how much trouble you have landed yourself in. How do you think you'll be able to leave this country? You think you can come here and play out the hero don't you? Ah, Mister Mercer, the hero from London. Are you here to gain some more publicity, are you going to save some more girls from their ordeals? You have no idea what you have stepped into here. I deliberately let you into my country. You have both been monitored from the minute you stepped foot onto the aeroplane at Heath Row."

Mercer did not reply as he held his gun at the man and watched Samantha skilfully retrieve the pistol and the mobile phone from Smertsov's jacket pockets.

"Sit down!" said Samantha. "Valarie, do you have masking tape in your house?"

"Yes."

"Well go and get it and then and bind this mouthy piece of shit up so as we can relax. Start with his mouth."

Monica was holding her gun to the other two men who were now frantic.

"Just relax gentlemen, and keep those glasses in your hands. No-one is going to get hurt providing you do as you're told, and do not pretend to me that you don't understand. You understand *some* English, don't you?"

Valarie returned with a giant roll of masking tape.

"Sorry I was so long, I had to go to the shed to get it." She then proceeded to bind Oleg Smertsov's hands and feet, and finally, as requested, his mouth.

"Do the same to them" said Samantha, pointing to the van driver and his accomplice.

"Nice and tight Valarie," said Mercer.

All three men were now secured. They could all relax.

"There now, that wasn't so hard to do was it ladies." said Mercer.

Valarie looked anxious. She was pouring herself a drink and consuming it before she'd completed pouring. Three times she swallowed before finally pouring a full glass of vodka and coke. "I'm not so sure about this." She said, pointing to the Kaunas chief of police. "You are soon going to be leaving here, I have to live here, and I won't be living for very long if this man has anything to do with it. I had no idea that he was part of this kidnapping thing, Viktor never mentioned anything nor did Saratov. I'm in big trouble here now, very deep trouble, I could lose everything, including my life, you have no idea."

Samantha told her to relax.

Mercer said to her, "Listen, you can put a bullet in his head and start a fire outside, no-one would know, burn his bloody car as well. Do the same with those two as well, who's going to be coming out here? I'll bet no-one even knows that *he's* here." He pointed to Smertsov. "He won't want anyone knowing what the hell he's up to."

"Even so," Said Valarie, "If he is killed there will be serious consequences, Monica and I would die without a doubt."

Suddenly, someone rang the doorbell.

Mercer asked Valarie if she was expecting visitors.

She shook her head. Mercer nodded for her to answer the door. Samantha was right behind her. Valarie opened the door where a young lady she'd never seen before greeted her with a smile. The young lady stood with a skin-head haircut and a green

camouflage jacket with torn pale blue denim jeans and baseball boots.
She spoke to Valarie in Lithuanian. "I am here to see a Mister Terry Mercer, is he here?"
Terry heard his name and cautiously stepped up to the door.
"Ah, Mister Mercer, we meet again, I told you we would."
Samantha looked at Terry, smiling as she did.
"Who the hell is this Terry?"
Mercer smiled back at the girl. "Come in come in Lena, what a lovely surprise. What brings you here today?" he said, as though he'd lived here all of his life. "Your boss Mister Mercer, she called us she and Mister Green. He's here too, he's come to help you. We've come to make sure you ok. Antoni here too, you remember him?"
"Yes," said Mercer. "It would be hard to forget someone as big as him, where is he?"
"He's coming, and with Mister Green, he's here too."
Moments later Colin Green was standing in Valarie Vercopte's living room explaining why he'd arrived with his Polish friends. Terry then explained to *him* who these people were. Antoni Dabrowski knelt down in front of Oleg Smertsov but spoke to Valarie and Monica. "We heard what you said, we were listening outside. You won't get into any trouble, because we have information about what Mister Smertsov has been doing. We know who you are don't we Mister Smertsov. We have photographs of him raping some of the girls over here, and we have proof that he has been selling girls on to lots of other Europeans for to work in brothels."
He looked round to Smertsov. "It's up to you whether or not to believe me Mister Smertsov, but if you make the wrong decision you will go to prison for a very long time. Now, if you have any brains at all in your head, you will not only leave these two in peace, you will help them dispose of the bodies outside. If you ever come here or if you send anyone over here to arrest them I promise you here and now, your wife and two daughters will be dead before your men arrive back with them. Now, what's it to be, because when I relieve you of this masking tape you will answer me, yes or no. Yes, you believe everything I'm telling you, or no, you think it's all bullshit, it's up to you." As Antoni tore off the masking tape he proceeded to inform Smertsov of his home address and the names of his wife and two daughters, where his daughters went to school and worked, and where his wife worked and how long she had worked there. He then went on to inform Smertsov that his wife has a birth mark just above her right buttock and a mole just under her left arm near her left breast. Also that she'd engaged in an affair after she found out about him having sex with minors, and that the only reason she was staying with him was for the security of their two daughters. "And finally, Mister Smertsov, if that is not enough to convince you, then we also have proof that you had two members of your staff put to death because they'd found out about your

involvement with the sales of young English girls. So, take your time and give us your answer…give us your decision. Providing you leave these two women alone we will let you carry on in your post and no-one need know of anything you've been doing. If not, then I'm afraid…well, *I'm* not afraid, but you will be. Oh, and should you agree to what I have suggested, you will make arrangements for flights back to Britain for those poor girls outside in the van, and you will compensate each one of them with five thousand pounds. I'm quite sure you can manage that seeing as how you have a bank account here in Kaunas with over three quarters of a million Euros, and another one in Switzerland containing just under two million Euros."

Antoni Dabrowsky stood up and turned to face the other two men who were tied up.

"Tell the girls to come in here." He said to Colin Green.

Moments later the four petrified girls entered the house once again.

They were asked to sit down on the sofa. Antoni turned to them as he pointed to the two men. "Now then girls, do not be frightened, just answer me the truth.

Did any of these two men rape you when they held you captive, just answer by nodding your heads or shaking them."

Two of the four girls nodded and began to cry.

Antoni motioned for the two men to get up on their feet.

"Unbind their feet Mister Mercer."

He turned to the girls again. "Does any of you wish to see their executions? You're welcome to, if not the ladies will take you upstairs."

"Antoni" said Mercer, there's no need to-."

"Oh but there is Mister Mercer, there is need of it."

He pointed again to Smertsov. "If this piece of shit here thinks we are joking or how you say, bluffing, then he'll continue with what he's doing."

Valarie ushered the girls upstairs with Monica.

Their feet now free, Antoni ushered the two men outside.

"Against the wall!" He ordered them.

"Look at me, face me! This is for raping young innocent girls and thinking you can do just whatever you please."

Smertsov was forced to watch as Antoni raised the pistol and shot both men in the head. Oleg Smertsov began to be sick. Antoni Dabrowski picked him up by the scruff of the neck. "You see this? This is nothing compared to what you and your family will get. I will not hesitate to execute your daughters and wife in front of you if you as much as look at a young girl again, do you believe me?"

Smertsov nodded his head. "Yes…please, I understand."

Antoni stood looking down upon the broken man.

"This day Mister Smertsov, you will never forget. Let it be a lesson to you that you and your kind will not be tolerated any more. You think because you sit in a seat of authority that you can manipulate people into doing whatever you want.
Well, no more."
Lena Kowalski stepped over and rammed her right knee into Smertsov's face sending him sprawling face-first into the dirt. She too picked him up by the collar. "You ever fuck about again, with any young geerls, then I will hear about it, and I will be standing by your bedside with the very sharp knife, and I will be cut off your balls and feed them to your dog…you piece of sheet!!"

SCOTLAND YARD.

BROADWAY VICTORIA. 48 hours later.

Mister John Carlton-Fletcher the chief of The Metropolitan Police Department had been standing trial at the Old Baily while Terry and Samantha had been in Lithuania. He was sentenced to fifteen years' imprisonment and it had been overwhelmingly decided that he'd serve out the full sentence with no remission.
Polly Sheppard sat with Terry and Samantha overjoyed in the fact that not only had they achieved their goal in Kaunas (Although that job had been done for them.) but had brought home four very grateful young girls back with them and had saved them from a life of complete and utter misery.
Polly had admitted that she was worried about Terry and Samantha having no protection whatsoever over there and so had contacted Colin Green and arranged a flight to Lithuania for him. He in turn had immediately contacted his friends in Poland who were more than willing to assist him in helping locate the detectives and to cover them. These friends of Colin's had also taken the opportunity to do some research on Oleg Smertsov who had served at one time in the Lithuanian army. They had information regarding him being involved with the sale of young girls.
Kacper Kaminski had friends in the Polish Criminal Investigations Department.
They knew even before they reached Valarie Vercopte's house what he'd been up to. They had all the information they needed to put him away for a long time, however, their main concern was to help detectives Mercer and Reynolds to get the kidnapped girls out of the country and back home to Britain. They had heard about the kidnappings.
"He's one in a million" Said Mercer addressing his superior, referring to Colin Green, "Although it has to be said that you don't hold much faith in Samantha and I. We were coping fine. We were handling everything well weren't we Samantha?"
Samantha felt exhilarated at the thought of the girls being back home safely and was in a humorous mood. "Yes we were Terry, but that said, I was glad when Colin arrived with his Polish friends, especially the girl called Lena. Very soon Polly the Royal Mail is going to be inundated with love letters between Terry and her. You should have seen his face when Lena arrived." Polly smiled as Samantha leaned across the table to show her a photograph she'd taken of Terry embracing Lena when she arrived. Terry had also embraced Antoni but Samantha had only taken this one photograph. She was teasing Terry again with reference to the Polish girl. But Terry was ready.

"Oh no." he answered. "My heart belongs to Angela Bates and fine well you know it, I'm not a two-timer."

For all their light-hearted banter, they were all very relieved that the situation had been resolved, at least for the time being.

They sat now discussing affairs concerning Valarie Vercopte and Monica Carosova. All said and done, Valarie had had very little to do with the kidnapping of the girls, in fact it was the news of her husband's unfaithfulness that had made her start the affair with Mister Blint. She hadn't chosen Blint not because of his looks but rather because he was close friends with Viktor Kulbertinov and of course his personal accountant. It was through Blint that she'd learned about her husband's overseas accounts. She had sneaked into Blint's files and found out everything she needed to know and now had access to millions of Euros. It had been a fruitful affair. Having said that she was still guilty, or at least partly so for the deaths of two British subjects, albeit they were villains, and Terry and Samantha had been sent there to eliminate them.

Polly sighed heavily as she came to her decision about the two women.

"I'll call surveillance off them Terry. If they come over here and keep their noses clean then we'll leave them be, after all Valarie could have chosen to say nothing about the four girls you brought home, so for that reason... as far as this Monica is concerned, I think she just used the situation with Saratov to her own advantage, after all, she's not the sharpest tool in the box by any means, but she's a looker. She used her bi-sexual tendencies to enhance her life-style by introducing the girls into the world of prostitution. This kept her sweet with Saratov who would no doubt reward her handsomely for her services. She doesn't seem to be dangerous-."

"Hey." Said Mercer, "She killed two men in succession with no remorse, shot them both in the head, and probably three, Samantha and I didn't see the execution of the first guy, he had already been taken care of by the time we got there. Don't say that she's not dangerous."

"Well Terry, I'll ask you now, do you think she'll kill again? In Britain I mean."

"No, if I'm honest I don't think she will, not unless she's threatened, but no, I don't think so."

"So, do you think I'm doing the right thing by leaving them alone, and after all, they both promised that they'd give you information if they found out anything about would-be kidnappers didn't they?"

Terry just nodded his head in agreement with Polly as he rose up from the desk.

"I won't be long." He said as he exited the office.

"Where's he off to Samantha, he usually just opens the window in here and smokes his head off."

Samantha knew where he was going, or rather, what he was going to do.

"He's gone to use a private telephone to speak to the girls' parents, the ones we brought home with us. He promised them on the aeroplane that he'd come and visit them and that he would have a discussion with their parents. The discussion will be about the amounts of money that will be put into each of the girls' bank-accounts. All four of them stand to inherit five thousand pounds for their troubles, and that was all down to Antoni Dabrowski, one of Colin Green's Polish friends. He still goes to the other girls' houses. He keeps in touch with them all. Working with him Polly has been an experience, a nice experience. A lot of people in here don't like him and consider him abusive and abrupt, but I'll tell you something, and this is strictly between us, he is one of the most considerate people I have ever met in my life. He loves people Polly, he loves life. I watched him when we visited his wife and son.

The pain he hides from the world. How that must tare at his heartstrings, and yet he carries on, he does the job. The job is his life, it's his escape.

The sarcasm he inflicts is all part of his cover.

Only yesterday when we arrived at Heath Row he accuses me of being androgynous because I put my leather coat back on.

"You think you're a fucking man sometimes don't you Sam." I think were his exact words. He doesn't mean anything by it, it's not really aimed at being sarcastic, I think he was trying to humour the girls, probably because they wouldn't know what the word meant. Whether or not they did, they all laughed anyway.

And there he was, making them laugh after everything they'd been through, that's the kind of man he is. Even though the laughter was at my expense, it doesn't matter to me, I was just happy he could have them laughing, and I do admit, sometimes when I wear jeans with the coat I suppose I do look a bit masculine."

Polly scrutinised the young woman in front of her and grinned, "Not with an ass like that you don't girly, you're all woman it's just him.

So, you wouldn't be disappointed if I asked you to work with him for a while longer Samantha?"

"If I'm honest Polly I was rather hoping that that was what he wanted."

"Well, Samantha, your prayers were answered because he asked me if I had any plans of moving you, and when he does *that*, then you can rest assured that you're in his good books, in fact, he's never asked me before about wanting someone to work with him, and that's the truth. You have obviously grown innocuous to his insults and his rantings. Congratulations Samantha, you are the first detective to actually crack his code. You see right through him don't you. He thinks he's calling the shots when he works with you when in fact you are manipulating him to your advantage, am I right?"

The two women smiled as Samantha put her pointing finger up to her lips.
"Sshh." As Samantha rose from her chair Polly said, "Just do me one favour."
"What's that?"
"If you get involved with him, don't break his heart again Samantha, I ask that of you, you've seen the results of what he's been through and there's more, much more than even you have seen. But like you say, he does his job. Did you know that he's writing to the authorities a letter of recommendation on behalf of Roxanne Styles, so she can get her baby back? She's clean now and has moved her older daughter in with her. Did you know that?"
"No, I didn't, but it doesn't surprise me one little bit."
As Samantha reached the door, she turned and said, "Don't even know how he feels about me...like that I mean."
Just before she closed the door to leave the room, Polly smiled and answered, "I do... look after him Samantha."
"The chance would be a fine thing Polly, but I hope you're right, I've waited all my life for a man like Terry Mercer. Huh, never thought I'd ever hear myself saying that."

LEXINGTON SQUARE.

BROMLEY.6am.

Sophie Spencer awoke from yet another nightmare. *Her* nightmares were different from the average person's bad dream, because she had lived hers' in the real world. Forced into a life of drugs and sex she had lived what others may have referred to as *"Their worst nightmare."* Forced into sexual activity with men and women she had never met in her life and who didn't even speak the same language, and being used several times a day as someone's sexual plaything. She knew she wasn't unique, all the other girls who had been kidnapped had been treated the same way as she had but they seemed to be recovering better than she was. Waking up with the bedsheets soaking wet was nothing new to her. She had lied continuously to her psychiatrist informing her that she was coping well and was now looking ahead to forge a career with the qualifications she'd achieve at university.

`Looking to the future` was what was keeping her mind occupied, and as far as she could make out, she was fooling the doctor into thinking that all was well with her. Sure, she was glad to be home safe with her mum and her brother, she wasn't lying about that. The relationship she had with them was healthy and at this stage in her life, essential to her recovery, if there was to be one.

The fact that she had now started a course in Sociology at university seemed to convince the psychiatrist into thinking that all was well.

But it wasn't.

All *wasn't* well at all.

Never a day went by without her thinking about her ordeal. A flash-back to one of the `animals` who used her was what had awoken her suddenly this morning, and it was one of the worst instances.

Being held by the hair of the head whilst a small chubby sweating `man` ejaculated into her mouth. Sophie barely reached the bathroom before emptying the contents of her stomach into the toilet. The recollection was vivid, so very real, almost like it was reoccurring. On a couple of occasions in the recent past her mum had asked her if she was using protection after hearing Sophie vomiting. Sophie had put her mind at rest by telling her that she was, when in fact, the very thought of a boy touching her repulsed her beyond belief. And not just boys, but girls as well, in fact the thought of any human touch made her nauseous, apart from a cuddle from her brother or her mum, that was different though, that didn't sicken her. She'd laughed the incidents off with her mum informing her that she'd been eating too much chocolate after Chinese take-away food the night before.

"Don't you worry mum, I'm not having a baby yet." She'd laughed.

Every single day she was troubled in her mind.

Depression was there always although her psychiatrist had proscribed her with Mirtazapine which did help her, but there was always a deep dark feeling of consternation. There was only so much medication could do.

But Sophie had a plan, and this course she was on was the perfect excuse she needed to camouflage her intentions...to get back at overpowering people.

There was a small establishment on the outskirts of Bromley which housed abused women. This place was a safe-haven for those who had been battered and bullied by the `men` they'd lived with, and women in some cases. It was simply called Safe Haven. Sophie had visited the place several times to talk to some of the girls in there. She heard their stories about what they had endured, and how long they had suffered their torment, even talking to them in the `safe house` she could feel their fear.

Some of them glanced nervously at the entrance as though expecting the door to be kicked open and their dreaded `partners returning to take them back `home` to resume their nightmares. She understood exactly how they felt. The difference between these girls and women and her, was the fact that she wasn't scared like they were. Sophie had always had this take-no-shit-from-anybody kind of attitude and would never hesitate to defend herself from school bullies, or anyone else for that matter. She supposed she was like this due to being brought up without a father. Her brother David as well, a quiet lad until someone pushed their luck or put him into a situation where there was only one option. To her recollection, he'd never lost a single fight.

After she had showered Sophie made her way down stairs to make tea.

Today she was going to visit the institute to continue her interviews with the women there. She was now on first name terms with two or three of them.

What Sophie was intending was to get close enough to them that they might inform her of their names, and slip out the addresses of where these pigs lived, and then she'd make damn sure that they would never again beat them up.

She knew within herself that she had psychological problems and what she was planning out was in no way *"The right thing to do."* However, if no-one done anything about these animals who were making these women's lives a living hell, then nothing would change. And if nothing changed then there was no hope for these people. Was it to be that women would just have to face facts that men sometimes got violent? Like it was just a fact of life?

"Not on my fucking watch mister."

Even when she'd been trapped in Lithuania, Colin Green and Terry Mercer were the only ones who seemed to give a fuck about her and the other girls. The repulsion concerning the boys touching her did not apply to Terry Mercer and Colin Green. Another psychological mystery she'd have to unravel.

But here were these poor women, in their own country, living in complete fear. Oh, the law would take the bastards to court and place some kind of injunction on them forbidding them to go anywhere near the women...sometimes. Did they think that would stop them? If they had it in their heads to beat up `their` woman, then that's what the fuckers would do, and then what?

Two months in jail? And then back out to kick the bitches into oblivion again.

What was needed was a firm message to be put out there, that women were no longer going to take this shit from these fucking weak halfwits.

If one or two of them were `dealt` with, in the appropriate manner, then maybe the others would take heed and realise that they'd be in for a bad time if they continued to inflict injury to their partners. It would be rather difficult for a man to intimidate a woman if he'd had his front teeth knocked down his throat with a crow-bar, or if he was rendered helpless and tied to a busy street lamppost, naked, exposing his miniature penis to the world on a Saturday morning, and a sign pinned onto him reading.

They done this to me because I'm a wife-beater. One of the girls in the institute said that she loved her partner so much and after all, each time he beat her, he would treat her to something really special, like a nice piece of jewellery or take her out for dinner, or buy her some new clothes. He said he would seek help about it. The girl couldn't see where the problem lay. The fact that it was *him* who decided when she'd get new clothes, and it was *him* who bought her a piece of jewellery, *Him...him...*he fucking decided everything, and the gifts only came *after* the beatings. In other words, if she hadn't received a beating then she could forget about any gifts or treats.

But Sophie knew the problem. This girl had been beaten into submission and this kind of life over so many years, or at the very least, so often, that she took this to be normal. As soon as Sophie had learned that there were no children involved in this relationship she had made her decision about nice mister jewellery man.

She had some old earrings at home that would look nice placed down the throat of this kind-hearted fucker. There were others as well who said they always forgave their partners because most of the time they were really nice men.

But then there were some who were just plain shit-scared of the fuckers.

These ones would go out with their `friends` for a night on the town and then return home and accuse their women of fucking with other men behind their backs. There was no convincing them. That was the excuse they needed, even though they had made it up in their own heads, to beat the shit out of them and learn them a lesson for being a cheap no-good-deceitful fucking tramp. Sophie Spencer had plans for *them* though. They were going to be in for the shock of their lives...very soon.

Perhaps Sophie had been clever enough to fool her psychiatrist, but she hadn't fooled her mum. Mandy Spencer had been concerned for some time regarding Sophie's behaviour. She had approached Mrs Kirkpatrick, Sophie's psychiatrist and asked about her daughter's progress. She was informed that Sophie was doing even better than was expected especially after such a short time, and the fact that she had now settled in at university would only accelerate her full recovery. "So you don't think I have anything to worry about Mrs Kirkpatrick?"
Mrs Kirkpatrick stood almost six feet tall and that was her wearing flat brown shoes. A woman in her early fifties Mandy guessed was dressed like something in between Mary Poppins and an elderly school teacher that she couldn't for the life of her remember what her name was. She stood with a long grey wool cardigan and a hideous multi-coloured floral dress which clashed not only with the rest of her attire, but with the entire room. Absolutely nothing matched anything. Even her horn-rimmed glasses were bright blue. Her appearance gave Mandy the impression that it was *she* who *needed* to see a psychiatrist.
"Certainly not Mrs Spencer, Sophie has her moments, don't get me wrong, but then, look what she's been through."
"Has her moments? What do you mean by that exactly?"
"Well, you know, sometimes when I'm asking her to go over something that happened, she sometimes...well, you know, she has a temper, she gets rather...I shouldn't be telling you these things, even though you're her mum, she's still entitled to patient confidentiality. Trust me Mrs Spencer, Sophie is fine."
Even after the interview with the psychiatrist Mandy made a point of having a meeting with Terry Mercer. Why she did not know, other than the fact that it was he who had helped bring the girls home from Lithuania. If there was anything to find out concerning Sophie, then Terry Mercer would succeed in finding it out. Sophie had respect for him, as she did for Colin Green, and although Colin would have a slightly better chance of getting to the bottom of Sophie's behaviour, Mandy didn't trust the man a hundred percent. Terry Mercer she did.

One week later Terry sat with Samantha in Mandy's house discussing her beloved daughter. "Don't get me wrong Terry, I can't say that my daughter is behaving in a bad way, there's nothing abnormal that she's doing, it's just that, she's different. I can't explain it really, there's just something…it's strange. Sometimes it's like she's a different girl completely…almost like she's trying to hide some secret from me and her brother. Do you know, since she returned from Lithuania she hasn't said one nasty thing to her brother…or me, I mean, well, it seemed like it was a healthier atmosphere when she cursed at us, or moaned about something, hell she used to call me the laziest mother on earth if I asked her to feed the cat for goodness sakes. Oh, she did at the start, when she first returned. She was always casting insults to me or David, but then one day, she sat me and her brother down and apologised to the both of us for her discourteous behaviour, and since then, well she's been nice…too nice in fact."

Terry leaned forward on the chair he was seated upon, resting his arms on his knees with hands clasped together. He smiled at Mandy, and sighed sounding like he felt really sorry for the woman. "Mandy, I understand how you are feeling, and why you are uncomfortable with Sophie's behaviour. No-one but no-one will know your daughter better than you, but what we have to remember is that Sophie has had one hell of an experience, that is why she has these consultations with her psychiatrists.

Have you said anything to her psychiatrist about your concerns with her?"

Mandy looked at Terry as though he'd just asked her what two and two was.

"Of course I have, I spoke to her first before I came to you.

She tells me that I have nothing to worry about and that Sophie is making remarkable progress, and I can tell by the way she looks at me that she thinks that it's *me* who has the problem, but I'm telling you, there is something different with that girl, and I don't know what it is. I'm frightened about something and I don't know what that something is, does that make sense to you?"

Samantha Reynolds nodded her head. "It makes perfect sense Mandy, and Terry and I don't think for one minute that you have a problem. So, can I just ask for your permission to…well, not exactly tail her, but rather, keep an eye out on her, just to see if she's going somewhere or doing something that she's not telling you about, would that be ok with you Mandy?"

"Of course it's alright, just don't let Sophie spot you…eh…spying on her, as she would put it."

As Samantha had been talking to Mandy Terry was remembering the night they gave Sophie a lift home and the language she was using. She'd asked Samantha if she'd ever had anal sex and had asked the question with the same ease as though she'd asked her if she liked apples. As Terry sat listening to Mandy's dilemma he came to the conclusion that whatever was causing Mandy concern almost certainly had to do with Sophie's

experiences in Lithuania. He didn't for one second consider informing Mandy that Sophie had, at least been present at the murder scene of the old pensioner who had been `executed` recently. Or had whipped the skin off a man's back whilst he begged for mercy, or how she had spat the words out after Colin had shot the same man dead, *"I should have made the bastard suffer longer before you shot him."*
They would have to tread carefully how they spoke to Mrs Spencer.
Perhaps he could approach Sophie and ask to have an interview with her.
Colin Green had given his word to him that he'd stop encouraging her to learn the skills of Karate and other Martial arts. And he had kept his word.
Sophie was now at university and so her visits to his house were few and far between. Most of the corresponding with Alison was done on twitter or face-book, and even that was becoming less frequent.
He didn't have concrete proof, but it was taken as accepted that Colin Green and Sophie Spencer were guilty of the murders of the two men who had beaten Roxanne Styles nearly to death. Yes, he would *have* to chat with Sophie.
And he'd have to have Colin Green with him at the time, so that he could explain to them that everything that had happened in the past would stay there, but that there was to be no more vigilante executions. He had warned Colin before about his acts of revenge and because of his help in Lithuania he had turned a blind eye on events, but this time, this time it was finished and from now on he'd be treated like any other citizen.
Any crime from now on would be punished accordingly.
As the two detectives climbed back into their car Samantha asked him if he thought Sophie was up to something, like, away from Colin Green, something on her own. Terry didn't answer verbally but nodded his head. He sat looking ahead of him at nothing in particular holding his seatbelt in his right hand but not yet fastening it. He sighed and said "Maybe it's nothing. It could be that Mandy is overreacting, I mean she knows there's something up with the girl, hell we could have told her that Sam, but I think now that she's at uni she'll be distracted from all that shit Colin Green was putting in her head...fuck learning her how to use a gun Christ what was he thinking."
Finally, he fastened the safety belt.
"They killed that old paedophile Sam, Sophie was there at least...at least, if she's had anything to do-."
He stopped half way through his sentence as he remembered the look of hatred on the teens face standing there with a bullwhip in her hands covered in blood. "Oh hell Samantha, I shudder to think what she could be up to. And if she *is* up to anything it'll be all down to those bastards who kidnapped her and the bastards who abused her

whilst she was in captivity. Maybe she won't be distracted by university work, it's maybe too late, let's hope we're not, but first things first. We are having a little chat first with Colin Green and then with both of them together. And this Sam, will definitely be his last warning, and as for Sophie, well, we'll keep an eye out on her for a few days at least. Let's see what she's getting up to in the course of an average day. As for Colin, well that's twice he's came to the rescue for us, you know, in Lithuania. It's hard to be angry with someone who continuously comes to your aid."

BROMLEY.

"What the hell is she doing in a joke shop Sam?" Terry said to his colleague, as they sat in their BMW about sixty metres off the store he was referring to.
"You know what teenagers are like Terry these days. Maybe someone is having a party and its' fancy-dress, she's maybe buying something to wear at the party." Terry exhaled cigarette smoke out of the window, annoyed that Samantha had answered his rhetorical question so matter-of-factly, as if he couldn't have worked that out for himself. Adding to his annoyance she continued to *correct* him.
"Anyway, it's not a joke shop as you put it Terry, it's a costume parlour, they come here for all-."
"Hey, I fucking know what it is, I'm just saying, what the *fuck* is she doing here that's all. You've always got to be putting me down haven't you, you're not happy unless you're keeping me right...I know it's a bloody costume shop...hell." Samantha smiled to herself and completely ignored his temper rant. She knew he was concerned about Sophie. He was worried in case she was going to land herself into trouble. And so was she.
"Do you want to follow her Terry when she comes out?"
"No, we'll head off Sam, I think she's heading to the bus stop. She must be going back to the university. We'll just check on her from time to time. She's not going to see Colin Green, that's the main thing, so she's not planning to kill any fucker it would seem. Come on, let's get some dinner, I'm starving. I started the day anti-jentacular." He looked at Samantha as though she wouldn't understand what his last word meant. He smiled at her when she answered him.
"I always make a point of having breakfast Terry, no matter how late I'm running." It was that shit and sugar again, one-minute poison, the next, sweet talk and compliments. It was just an occupational hazard that she would have to cope with, and if she was honest, she quite enjoyed pulling his strings now and again, and watching him go off on one of his `tantrums`. Again she smiled to herself at the thought that she could stop and start him like clockwork. How she longed to be able to pull his strings and wind him up in their own home. Another occupational hazard...to be in love with the person you're working with.

Sophie exited the shop and walked the short distance to the bus stop along the street. Her next journey would only take five minutes. She was heading to the shelter where the abused women were housed.
She had just purchased something that would come in very handy for the `job` she had

planned. Today she was going to have tea with one of the girls she had befriended. The one who'd had gifts bestowed upon her after her many beatings. The girls' name was Claire, but today, as they had their tea or coffee she would get her to give her his name, and where he worked, if he did. The fact that Claire had informed her that her boyfriend didn't approve of her working, led her to believe that he *did*. It also confirmed to her that this `man` whoever he was, was extremely jealous and this would be the reason he did not want her working, solely because that would mean that she was socialising and of course, independent. That would be his main thing. He was the bread-winner and so that gave him his upper-hand attitude. He would dictate how much money she could spend, and on what. By the sounds of things, she wasn't able to just go and buy something for herself, without `confronting` him about it...but that was going to change if she could get Claire to give her his name. Her experiences in Lithuania had given her a different mind-set on human beings now, in particular men. It was as though she'd been awoken from some kind of dream and that now she saw clearly what men thought of women in general...at least the majority of them. She pondered to herself as she waited for the bus just how many women, even in their own country, were living in complete fear. She'd heard stories about how some victims had called the police after a beating and when they'd arrived they'd practically turned their backs on the situation calling it a "Domestic affair.
And that they wanted very little to do with an argument between a man and his wife. A word of warning to the boyfriend or husband about keeping their hands down was about all the visit amounted to. *"Well fuck you!"* She had hissed to herself, almost speaking the words out loud. There was no doubt about it, Lithuania had changed her opinion on a lot of things. If these women were too scared to do anything about the monsters they lived with, then she would do something about them on their behalf. Whether or not they decided to go back with the monsters would be their decision at the end of the day, but if they did, they would discover that the bastards had changed their attitude towards them...big time. Half an hour later Sophie sat at a table in one of the bedrooms of the shelter with her `friend` Claire. As they spoke Claire said something that didn't really surprise her. "If you don't mind me saying Sophie, I think your skirt is a little on the short side. Alan's always telling me about wearing skirts at a respectable length.
He said that women only invite trouble onto themselves when they expose themselves blatantly.
`So his name is Alan`.
He said they only have themselves to blame when they're attacked.
He said I shouldn't wear anything higher than my knee, and even then I should be

aware of attracting attention."

Sophie thought back to her time in Lithuania and how Monica the beautiful monster had complained about how long her skirts were and that she should wear them really short, and that it would help her make more money.

"Show yourself off girl and let them see what they're getting for their money."

"Is that right Claire, is that what he tells you. And what do you think?

How do you feel about wearing short skirts? Do you think that women deserve to be raped because they're wearing a short skirt? Do you think they should be beaten for it? And bullied? We need to have a good chat you and I Claire."

Claire suddenly looked uncomfortable. She took a sip of her tea and looked out of the window.

Sophie picked up on her discomfort.

"What's wrong Claire, have I said something to offend you?"

Claire responded first by just shaking her head but then said, "I used to like wearing short skirts, well, around the house anyway. They were very comfortable whilst I was doing house-work. But Alan came home from work early one day and he was aghast. I may as well have been in bed with another man, such was his disgust. In fact, he more or less accused me of having a lover and warned me that if he caught me wearing it again he would kick me out into the streets where I belonged." A tear was forming in the corner of Claire's right eye.

She quickly wiped it away.

Sophie then spoke sympathetically to her.

"Did he punish you that day for wearing it?"

She looked to Sophie as though she would only be a few years older than herself. Her short brown hair hung lank and lifeless though anyone could see that she was beautiful. She had a lovely full face with high cheek bones and reminded Sophie of a very famous model who went by the name of Kate Moss.

Claire had that same sultry sexy look going on, just like the beautiful Kate Moss.

Both women had been born with faces that would let them get their own way.

Claire lit up a cigarette and nodded her head as she did.

"Yes, he gave me a savage beating. He punched my ribs and kicked me in the stomach. Then he dragged me outside by the hair of the head and made me burn the skirt and then made me promise that I never again would wear anything that would offend him as long as I lived with *him*."

Sophie cursed under her breath. Now she *had* to find out her address and where this bastard lived. She spoke quietly to Claire again.

"Margaret informs me that your, em...man beat you really bad this time, and that you

had to spend three days in the hospital, is that right Claire?"
Margaret was one of the women who ran the place, herself a victim of a heavy-handed twat like the one Claire lived with. At fifty-two years of age Margaret's days for being beaten up were over, but she was determined to help as many women as she possibly could and save them from a similar fate that she'd had.
Claire nodded her head. "Yes. He really lost it this time."
"Do you mind telling me what sparked it off Claire?"
"I didn't realise that wearing denim shorts came under his same category as trash. He called me a whore and a slut and that I was just trying to catch the neighbour's attention while I hung out the washing showing off my flesh by wearing the skimpiest thing I could find. I said something to defend my wearing them…and he just lost it. He started reigning punch after punch into my face this time.
Normally".
"Huh, normally."
"he would hurt me in the ribs or the back where it was harder for anyone to spot the bruising, but this time he just completely lost all control and began punching everywhere and anywhere. I was just losing consciousness when he finally burned out. That's the last thing I remember. I could hardly see anything because my vision was impaired with all the blood, but, breathless, I remember him saying through gritted teeth, just before I passed out, "Let that be a lesson to you, you fucking cheap whore!" The next thing I knew I awoke in the hospital bed with a nurse standing over me smiling and asking if I'd like a cup of tea. I've been in here since the hospital released me. That was six weeks ago."
"Have the police been to visit him since this em, incident took place Claire?"
"The doctor at the hospital reported him, but according to the police, he hasn't been seen at the house since that day."
Now, Sophie had an opportunity. "Do you know where he works Claire?"
The girl shook her head. "He never would tell me that. He just said he worked in the construction business. I know where he drinks though, or, at least he used to.
He may have stopped going there in fear of the police arresting him."
"Where is that sweetheart? said Sophie, again, with the sympathetic tone.
"Is it local?"
Claire drew hard on her cigarette. "Yeah, he drinks in The Swan and Mitre.
They do lovely meals in there. He loves to eat there. It's very popular with locals and the staff there are always friendly and helpful. He's taken me there a couple of times in the last four years or so."
Sophie thought to herself, that although he'd only taken her there twice in four years

she was telling her that the staff were always nice and helpful, perhaps she just had to take Alan's word for it.

"Four *years* Claire, is that how long you've lived with him?"

"No, I've lived with him for nearly six years, but he's taken me there twice. The first time was when we had our first date, and then again about two years ago. His mother came to visit him and so he took us out for a bar lunch. His mum's dead now, she died last year sometime. She was a really nice woman." Sophie was completely gob-smacked. *Her* ordeal in Eastern Europe had been horrendous, but here in Britain there were women living under unbelievable circumstances. And here were these bastards wandering around making out to everyone no doubt that they thought the world of their girlfriends or wives and that they were enamoured even, when all the time, when they got home they would unleash hell onto their `partners` using fictitiously-created accusations, their actions incorrigible.

How these women managed to live with these mercurial animals was beyond her. How could they live like that? "Oh Hi honey is my tea ready? Are you telling me you've had all fucking day to make my tea and it's still going to take another half an hour, take that you cheap cow that you are! Oh this steak pie is lovely my angel, well done, it's delicious sweetheart, you fucking nasty whore you!"

Sophie had a starting point.

That's what she came here for today, and it was a lot easier than she'd thought it would be.

But now it was as though Claire had caught on to her, just as she was about to ask her his full name.

For a second or two Claire stared at her with an apoplectic glare, as though she might rise up and strike her. Sophie continued asking questions to her though in an attempt to show the girl that she meant well but all of Claire's answers now were succinct and spoken sharply. Sophie continued. "I can tell Claire, that you still have feelings for this man, am I right? In fact, you think the world of him don't you?"

"Yes."

"And would you take him back if he approached you?"

"Maybe..."

"Be honest with me Claire, do you feel safe living in here. Do you feel less stressed when he's not around?"

Now Claire's face was positively stern. Her demeanour changed instantly.

"Listen, we've spoken for long enough today. Already I can see what you're doing, and I have been foolish enough to tell you things that I should never have told you, and by the way, your skirt *is* too short, you look like a slut, and you come here from uni making out that you're everybody's friend. Well I know what you're doing. You're getting all these stories from the women in here and listening to what we've all been through, and it's just so that you'll get higher marks in your sociology exams. You don't give a fuck about anybody in here, you're a fucking phony, so don't try and pretend that you care because you don't. You haven't got a clue what it's like to live like this but you come over, or at least attempt to, that you know everything there is to know. You're a little jumped-up mummies-girl with your little fucking silver spoon in your mouth. You're just a fucking kid, and listen to you asking questions here like you were a shrink. Get yourself back out there and start to live in the real world, then you can come back and ask people questions about their private lives, I'm done talking to you. And don't bother coming back either, at least to speak to me, cos I'm just not interested."

Sophie could barely contain her temper.

"I'm a phony Claire? *I'm* a phony? You suffer beatings from this fucking clown you live with, and yet you put on this demeanour to the world that you're as happy as can be, too frightened to stick up for yourself. Living petrified of a fucking bully who pulls your strings and dictates to you how you'll live. I'm the phony? Don't fucking kid yourself lady, and as far as the silver spoon thing goes, I was brought up by my mother because my bastard father deserted her and left her with two fucking kids to bring up in a place where she knew no-one. I was kidnapped a few months ago and taken into Lithuania where I was raped several times a day for more days than I care to remember. Phony? You don't know the meaning of the fucking word. I came here to see if I could do something to try and help you all, but it's plain to see that you don't want any help. Do you know what I think? I think you're all fucking kinky, and you enjoy these beatings, well, good fucking luck to the lot of you, cos you're all beyond help. You need to see a psychiatrist, the whole lot of you. There, that's my opinion. That's how I see things. Good luck with your beloved partners, and who knows, maybe someday Claire he'll take you out again and give you some money to spend, wouldn't that be good? And then he can order you a cab home and kick your teeth down your throat just before you make his supper. I may be younger than you Claire, but don't you think for one minute that I haven't faced hardship. The only difference between you and me though Claire is, I'll fucking get up and hit back. I won't lie down like you fuckers.

And if they were too strong, then I'd come back with a fucking crow bar.

And if that didn't do the trick, I'd come back with a shotgun, but get one thing straight, the one thing I would never do, is lie down.

Good luck to you!"

And with that, Sophie rose from the chair and headed for the door.

Claire then said, and quite genuinely, "I'm sorry Sophie."
As Sophie exited the room she replied, "Yeah, sure you are."
Before she closed the door Sophie heard Claire's voice once more.
"His name is Alan Flint."
She walked down the hall to sign the register that she had signed when she came in. Margaret Hall addressed her as she signed out.
"Will we be seeing you again soon Sophie?"
As she reached the main exit she replied over her shoulder, "I doubt that very much misses Hall, have a nice day dear, and thank you for all your help and kindness."
Margaret Hall sighed and said, "Sophie? Have you got a minute?
Sophie turned and walked back to the desk.
"Take a seat love." She said, almost despondently to Sophie's way of thinking.
"No, in second thoughts, come on let's go and get a cup of tea dear."
Margaret led the teenager down the small corridor to the staff canteen.
Canteen was a slight exaggeration. It was a kitchen that you'd find in any two-up two-down anywhere in Britain, after all, the establishment had been just that in recent times. It was a converted house, although in here there were four bedrooms and they had been converted into eight smaller rooms with a single bed and not much room for anything else, other than a bedside cabinet. But to the women who lived here it was a fortress where they could have a nights' sleep without the fear of being abruptly awoken to receive a thrashing by a drunken husband. Margaret poured them both a cup of tea from the giant teapot that sat on the worktop. Sophie could see that the woman still held her looks. She was an attractive lady, there was no doubt about that, but you could see the strain of life's `mishaps` by the premature lines on her experienced face. Although her hair was greying she still held an air of beauty. She stood at about five foot seven and still held the figure of a far younger woman. She wore rings on several fingers but none on the third finger of her left hand. The clothes she wore would have suited a woman in her thirties but did not look out of place on Margaret. They sat down at a table near the window. As Sophie sat down she was left wondering if what Claire had said to her was true, because she spotted Margaret glancing at her skirt. It was only for a brief moment but it was enough to capture Sophie's attention. "What?" She said to Margaret Hall. "Do *you* think my skirt is too short as well?"
Calmly, Margaret answered the teen, sensing her aggression.
"My child, I care less if you sat here in your knickers, I do not pass judgement on people concerning their attire. In case you're wondering, I was merely admiring your legs. You have a very good figure young lady of which I am rather envious it must be said. And

don't tell me that I'm the first to inform you of *that*. Anyway, I asked you in here because I could hear that things did not go well with you and Claire today, am I right?" Sophie smiled at the friendly woman.

"Well, it started off really well but then I think I said some things that upset her. Perhaps I touched on some nerves that are still a bit raw to her. Anyway, it wasn't *that* bad because she apologised to me as I left…it wasn't a row or anything, maybe I was getting a few things off my chest if I'm honest. I'll come back and see her again soon if that's alright with you. I just told her I wouldn't be back." Margaret sipped her tea.

"Claire has just experienced an horrendous beating. As you probably know by now this was not the first time her `boyfriend` has laid into her. He went over the top this time though."

"For wearing a pair of denim shorts I believe" Said Sophie, smiling sarcastically. Margaret nodded. "I know Sophie it beggars belief doesn't it. And while we're on the subject of nasty experiences, I received a phone call from someone, and I don't want you losing your temper when I tell you who called me, they were just making sure that you are."

"It was Mrs Kirkpatrick wasn't it, my psychiatrist" Sophie said looking straight into her eyes.

"Yes it was Sophie. But she only called me to make sure I was aware of *your* experiences. I informed her that I was. Your councillor at the university informed me of your ordeal, and I must say Sophie, I admire you enormously for how you are dealing with it. And here you are, trying your best to help other people. I know you're not here just to collect information for your resume'. And although you are not unique, you are certainly a rare breed Sophie. There are very few people especially your age who are willing to help others in the way that you are. Just being able to talk to someone helps the women in here tremendously, even if you are far younger than they are." As Sophie sipped her tea she thought that Mrs Hall wouldn't think so highly of her if she knew what she had in store for some of these men who had beaten their wives or partners. She'd already learned the location of where one of the bastards drank, and that was a start. Vigilantes would not be made so welcome she surmised, but it wasn't about being a vigilante, it was about hitting back and trying to get these bastards to experience what life could be like if someone bullied *them,* and made *their* lives a complete hell. Margaret continued. "You must understand Sophie, these young ladies in here are very frightened and Claire in particular is no exception. In fact, I'm surprised that she has taken to you in such a short time. It took us quite some time to get the truth out of her, you know, for her to admit that this was a regular occurrence in her life, these beatings. Some of the other girls as well, they've opened up to you sharing their stories with you,

I say stories, I mean nightmares. As you will have gathered there are some who are still petrified of their partners, you know, in case they come in here and snatch them away. So, you really are quite honoured indeed that they confide in you.

I think you have a remarkable talent Sophie and might suggest to you that you could seek a future in psychology, you certainly have the credentials to pursue this."

Sophie rose to her feet purposefully pulling her skirt down a little.

Misses Hall merely smiled.

"Well, in the meantime Sophie I hope we can be blessed with another visit from you soon, after all, Claire is only one of the women who have suffered, there are eight living in here and I'm quite sure many more of them would be glad of a little chat with you, I think they find it therapeutic."

Sophie smiled at the kindly woman and thanked her for her invitation.

"I'll make an appointment if I decide to return Misses Hall, and once again thank you for your words of encouragement."

As Sophie stepped out into the cool air she felt exhilarated.

She had obtained the desired information. Alan Flint, and he usually drank in The Swan and Mitre. It wouldn't take her long to find him now, because even if he *had* stopped drinking there, there were bound to be acquaintances of his that could give her details of where he could be found. As she walked she began to wonder if Terry Mercer and his partner Samantha Reynolds felt as good as this when they got a lead. There was a lot to be said about this detective business, and at this moment in time she felt that she was getting quite good at it.

She'd gained the confidence of Misses Hall and some of the victims in her safe-house. She would head back to university now and actually do some studying.

She smiled within herself as she made her way to the bus-stop. Studying was fine, and very helpful, but you couldn't beat experiencing the practical.

As Sophie sat listening to music on the bus her phone buzzed. A text message.

Hi Sophie, its Lisa Jenson, you know, we met in Lithuania. Just wondering how you are. Was thinking maybe you and I could go for a coffee for a little catch-up, what do you think? Sophie remembered Lisa. She was a really pretty girl, and she'd been through the mill so to speak as much as herself, in fact, Lisa had been given a *really* hard time, she was one of Monica's favourites, and so was always in demand with lots of `customers`…and with Monica, in Monica's room…alone.

Yes, it would be nice to have a chat with her. It was nice of Lisa to even ask her for a coffee. Apart from Alison Green and her sister Rebecca none of the others had even bothered staying in touch. Maybe they didn't want to. Maybe seeing her or any of the other girls would just remind them of the nightmare times…it was understandable.

Sophie replied to Lisa offering to meet her in a café in Bromley the following morning if she had nothing else planned. Lisa texted her back and agreed to be in the café at the suggested time.

As Sophie rode the bus listening once more to her music, she smiled in the knowledge that at least one of the other girls had remembered her.

"Yeah, it will be nice to see Lisa again."

It was 10-15am and Lisa was a quarter-of-an-hour late. Sophie sat at the window absent-mindedly watching traffic pass to-and-fro along the busy high-street, and people going about their everyday business…just like *she* used to do. Had Lisa decided not to come, and if she had she could at least have informed her, even if it was a lame excuse. Sophie's phone buzzed with another text message. *Hi Sophie, please don't give up on me, my mum's driving and she's terrible. It takes her ages to get anywhere. Anyway, with a little luck I'll see you in ten minutes. Please don't leave, I really am looking forward to having a chat with you. See you soon… I hope. lol.x.*

Almost twenty minutes later Lisa Jenson entered the café with a woman who was undoubtedly her mother. Sophie could see the strong resemblances between the two. Lisa's mum was very pretty as well. She was slim like Lisa, blonde hair like Lisa, and natural blonde hair, very rare in this day and age, and both of them with the bluest eyes she had ever seen. Lisa's mum had jeans on with white trainers and a loosely-fitting blouse, cream-coloured.

To Sophie's surprise, Lisa was wearing a mini skirt that really was mini, shorter than the ones she wore herself. This obviously did not bother her mum.

After Lisa had said hi, it was her mum who spoke.

"I'm so sorry we're late, it's all my fault. I'm a very nervous driver.

Since Lisa's father and I have split up I have to drive myself everywhere, it's been years since I drove on a regular basis. I'm getting used to it though, although you wouldn't think that by Lisa's comments, she's always complaining about my driving.

Listen I'm not staying I just came in here to apologise for Lisa being late."

For some unknown reason Sophie found herself saying, "Would you not like to have a coffee with us misses Jenson, it'll help to calm you down before you go back out to drive."

"Oh, I'm so sorry Sophie, it's Carol, Carol Jenson, and it's very nice to meet you." Carol turned to her daughter. "Would you mind sweetheart if I had a quick coffee with you and Sophie, I won't stay long, I'll be out of your way in a few minutes." Lisa reached out and gave her mum a hug. "Don't be silly mum, of course you're welcome to have a

coffee with us. She's always like this Sophie, she's always on edge, nervous. Stop it mum, relax will you." Lisa smiled at Sophie and said, "She knows I love her to bits."
Five minutes later they were all seated round the table with their cappuccinos.
As they sat talking it wasn't long before the subject of kidnappings and Lithuania came up, the subject being raised by Lisa.
Carol Jenson lowered her voice as she spoke to Sophie.
"Those experiences could not have been easy for you, and I just want you to know that I am so proud of you both the way you're carrying on with your lives.
I admire you pair enormously for your attitude."
Carol looked away out of the window as though she was too emotional to continue. She bent down and retrieved a handkerchief from her handbag pretending to wipe her nose. Already in this short space of time Sophie understood why Carol had said nothing about the length of Lisa's skirts, or rather the lack of length. Lisa would be able to do anything she wished. The woman was petrified about losing her again.
She would agree to almost anything Lisa said, just to make sure that her daughter was happy. There would be no friction between Lisa and Carol Jenson, that was for sure. In a nutshell Lisa had a free hand.
Sophie leaned over the table and spoke to the loving mother.
"It wasn't easy em, Carol. They made us do quite terrible things as I'm sure Lisa has told you, and I -."
"Please" carol pleaded, "Please, don't tell me anymore Sophie, I don't want to hear the details...God you're just children, how could they...I'm sorry Sophie, I'm sorry Lisa I'll have to be going now, you're just bloody kids...I...I'll see you later Lisa, let me know where you are at all times remember. Let me know when you're coming home and what bus you'll be on. I'll be waiting for you at the bus stop.
It was nice to meet you Sophie and I'm sorry for...I just can't talk about that, I'm sorry."
And with that Carol Jenson was gone.
"Sorry about that Sophie, she's always like that whenever I try to tell her what happened, she just locks it out, she refuses to listen. I suppose it's because she can't come to terms with her daughter being barely sixteen and having had to perform sexual acts to all and sundry.
She knows what we done Sophie, or rather what we were forced to do, but she just lets it lie at the back of her head somewhere out of reach, that way she can live her life as normal...she means well Sophie."
"I know she does, she's lovely Lisa, you're very lucky to have a mum like her, but then again, so am I, my mum is very special as well, and my brother if I'm honest. We're both lucky, me and you Lisa, wouldn't you agree?"

"Yes I would, we are very lucky Sophie…now. Having come through what we did and be able to make it back home to loving mothers who try too hard constantly to erase the damage inflicted upon us, yes I do think we're lucky…we're very lucky indeed."
Sophie looked at her friend across the table. "I think Lisa, that we all take our liberties for granted, you know, our freedom. Hell, what our poor mothers' must have gone through while we were being held prisoners…must have been almost as bad as the ordeal we went through."
Lisa smiled back at Sophie.
"Yeah…almost."

STRATFORD.

COUNCIL BUILDINGS.

It was a big day for Roxanne Styles. An important day. One of the most important days of her life actually. She was here to answer questions to a panel of people from the welfare department and the health board. The first to decide if she was able-minded enough to look after her baby daughter Rosemary and the second, to see, or rather, to prove that she was living in an environment clean enough for the well-being of the child. Two members from the health board were here to support Roxanne and to verify that she had in fact, `kicked the heroin habit` that for so long had destroyed her life. Terry Mercer was here with Samantha Reynolds for no other reason than to support and offer a character-reference. By now they had befriended Roxanne's teenage daughter Hollie who now sat next to them at the back of the small room chewing gum and nodding occasionally as though she was having a conversation with herself and agreeing to whatever she was thinking. Hollie was as pretty as her mum and had the same dirty-blonde hair. She smiled nervously at Samantha as the meeting commenced. As usual there were people for and against Roxanne and her ability to lead a `normal` every-day life. Roxanne sat at the front of the room dressed in a black knee-length skirt with a pale blue blouse and black one inch heels with black tights. She nursed her matching jacket over her lap with her handbag.
Mister Graham Tindel, a tall gentleman in a light grey suit about sixty-years old stood up, his thin hair matching his attire. He addressed the panel and then the sixteen people seated in front of him. He cleared his throat and then addressed Roxanne. "Miss Styles" he began, looking at the file spread out before him on the huge cedar-wood table. "It seems that you have led a rather…eh…promiscuous life if you don't mind me saying. You have had a history of court appearances involving prostitution, and violence, especially in the past few years. You say in your defence that you were forced into prostitution to feed your child and your heroin habit, but according to your records you were involved in prostitution long before you became an addict. Adding to that, residents in the Hensingham apartments have complained to the council on numerous occasions in recent times about your violent conduct whenever you are confronted with a situation. Violence is all you know according to some of them. Also they have complained about `visitors` arriving at your house at all times of the night and day." Terry Mercer was furious.
"Also noises, namely sexual noises coming from your home, and of course, baby crying

through all of this as though it was being ignored and neglected.
Of course we know now that *that* turned out to be the case.
This was one of the many reasons that your baby was taken away from you, as well as your heroin addiction and your failure to keep a clean home.
In a nutshell Miss Styles, you live in a house of ill-repute for want of better words. You are using a council property to make money from prostitution and no doubt drug sales. For this reason alone, you should be punished, at least financially.
He paused for a moment to let the information settle into the minds of the people in the panel. "How on earth do you plan to convince myself and the good people of this panel that you are in fact capable of living a normal life both for your baby and yourself, and not to mention your teenage daughter, whom you have encouraged and encroached into a similar life-style. She is also violent.
Hollie Styles continued chewing her gum and occasionally nodding as though she was thinking that this meeting was going exactly as she'd though it would.
"I fail to see how you can convince anyone in this room that you have overturned all these...eh...habits in a ten-month period of time."
A woman from the medical board who was seated near Terry Mercer stood up to say something to the man who was literally destroying any chance of Roxanne being successful in her bid to have her child back home.
Before the woman even managed a single word, he raised his hand stopping her in her tracks.
"Misses Smith", he said impatiently, "Miss Styles and your good self, and anyone else for that matter who wishes to defend her, will have an opportunity to have their say just as soon as I'm finished, so please be seated. Now, to carry on if I may, if it were up to myself whether or not you should be allowed to have the child back home with you Miss Styles, then I'd be recommending a refusal for the simple reason that I do not think that you are capable of looking after a child. I'm still not convinced that you can even look after *yourself*. Can you guarantee the people sitting in this room that you would no longer practice prostitution? And can you guarantee them that you will never take heroin again? And that you'll keep a clean house? That you will refrain from using foul language and violence in any confrontation? Because if you can't guarantee us that you can live a normal life, then I'm afraid that this meeting is a complete waste of time. I think that your child is in too much danger to allow you full custody."
Mister Graham Tindel sat down folding documents and placing them on the giant table in front of him. Mercer could see the smugness on the man's face as he sipped from a bottle of water. He looked like one of those lawyers you see on TV after they've delivered an extraordinarily good defence. The fact that he'd used information from

Roxanne's past and not of the present would have left him overwhelmingly defeated in any court of law. Anyway, Terry Mercer knew lots of influential people and knew who would be taking the chair today. So he'd done some `homework` on Mister Tindel. There were numerous people in the room chomping at the bit to stand up and defend Roxanne Styles, but alas, none of them were necessary. Terry stood up and introduced himself and Samantha Reynolds to the council board as he handed Sam his bottle of water.

"Ladies and gentlemen, we have sat and listened to a very accurate and brutal description of Roxanne Styles and how she's lived her life in the past."

He looked around the room and then fixed his vision on Graham Tindel.

"In the past MisterTindel. Things that Roxanne done then was the reason her baby was taken away from her, and rightly so. However, you haven't mentioned once anything that Roxanne has achieved in the past few months and how she has turned her life around. She has, whether or not you grant her custody of her baby today, turned her life completely around. She no longer is addicted to heroin and no longer participates in illegal sexual activities, and I for one feel that you have been grossly unfair in your assessment of Miss Styles. You have gone out of your way to downgrade the woman in front of her daughter and her friends, of which Samantha and I here are closest. You seem to hold a personal grudge or dislike to prostitutes Mister Tindel, which I must confess confuses me somewhat, you being a regular user of their services."

Suddenly there were gasps from not only the sixteen people seated beside him, but from the council board themselves.

Tindel's face immediately turned to crimson.

"I don't know where you're getting these accusations from Mr Mercer but-."

"Hold it there Mister Tindel, you'll get your chance when I'm finished ok?

Am I not right in saying that your wife Gladys Tindel threatened to take you to court when she found out that you were frequenting certain premises for your sexual gratification using your expenses money to fund this? And that she at this moment in time is filing for divorce, correct me if I'm wrong Mister Tindel, and may I add, that if you hadn't been so brutal in your assessment of Miss Styles, none of this would have been brought to the panel's attention. And if I might say to yourself, and everyone in this room, Roxanne included, I feel that you are too dangerous to be left in charge of the public's funds when it comes to distribution of that said money, and of course, what that money is spent on. Roxanne has proved herself in front of all these health-workers who have helped and nurtured her through all the hard work she has done. You my friend need to prove yourself, firstly to Gladys, although I think that *that's* a bit late, and then to the good people of this panel who incidentally placed their trust in you.

As far as Roxanne is concerned, she, in my book is more than deserving to a second chance in society...I'm not so sure about you though Graham, and you being a justice-of-the-peace as well, goodness me man, you should think shame on yourself. Roxanne openly admitted that she had problems and dealt with them the only way she knew how, because she didn't have the luxury of the public's purse to come to *her* rescue." Terry Mercer sat down beside Samantha Reynolds who was more than impressed with his speech. She sat now wondering how on earth he had obtained so much information about Tindel in such a short time. Hollie Styles leaned over Samantha who was sent into a state of hysterical laughter as Hollie momentarily stopped chewing her gum long enough to whisper to Terry, "Hey, you're fucking brilliant hey, you should be a fucking lawyer honestly, fuck."

BROMLEY.

"Are you saying you killed them Sophie?" Lisa Jenson was addressing her friend. Sophie nodded her head and reminded Lisa to keep her voice down. There were only a few others in the café and they seemed to be a safe distance away from the pair but there was no harm in being careful.
Sophie whispered. "Yes I did, I stabbed the bastard in the stomach several times, and shot him but you should have seen the state these bastards left that poor woman in, honestly Lisa, I thought she was dead, and so did Colin. I spewed my guts up after it. You remember Colin? He was the one who helped us all escape …that place."
Lisa smiled at her friend as she sipped her second cappuccino.
"What? Are you shocked Lisa? Did you not think I was capable of such actions?"
"No, I'm not shocked that you could kill someone, it's just the brutality of how you done it that surprises me. Did no-one find out? Sorry, that was a stupid question."
Sophie leaned over the table and continued to whisper.
"I've done it again since then. Colin Green found out about this old pervert who'd been interfering with little children, and I mean babies. I didn't actually kill him but I kicked his teeth down his throat…it was Colin who finished him off. Everybody was talking about it round here, and as far the public are concerned, no-one has been prosecuted for the murder. Nobody had any sympathy for the sick bastard when they found out what he'd been up to."
There was silence between the two girls as they each sipped their coffees.
Finally Lisa said, "I'm impressed Sophie, I'm really impressed. Can I say something to you in trust, I mean can I trust you not to let this go any further?"
Sophie looked to her friend incredulously. "Trust Lisa, have you not been listening to what I've been saying…Christ trust?"
"Of course, sorry. No, it's just this thing I've got going on in my head."
For a brief moment Lisa looked almost as uncomfortable as her mother had.
"I can't get those experiences out of my head. I tell everybody, everybody that matters, that I'm fine, but I can't forget it Sophie. I wake up at nights and go down stairs when mums' sleeping, and I stand there at the kitchen window with a carving knife in my hand with gritted teeth and tears streaming down my face and all I want to do is get hold of even just one of the bastards who violated me, does that sound mental, do you think I'm mental Sophie for thinking like that?"
Sophie leaned across the table and took Lisa's hands in hers.
She didn't answer verbally but just sat shaking her head…and smiling.

Almost in tears, Lisa confessed to Sophie. "I can't stand the sight of any boys near me Sophie. I mean, I like boys, I'm not...you know, I'm not a lesbian, but I can't stand the thought of any boy touching me just now...I actually cringe at the thought of any connection between myself and them, I just...I just don't want them near me. I am going crazy am I not?"

It was clear to Sophie that she and Lisa had lots in common, albeit through their experiences in Europe, but for the first time in a long time Sophie felt a real connection. And it was with this girl here in front of her.

"No, you are most definitely not going mental Lisa, and I am so glad we're having this conversation. For a kick-off, I feel exactly the same way as you do about boys just now and I don't mind telling you that I am relieved to hear someone else has the same problems as me. I thought I was going mental Lisa, and that's the truth. Shall we get out of here and go for a wander round the shops?"

"That sounds like a brilliant idea Sophie."

As the two girls walked along Bromley high street they received several wolf-whistles from young men in general, passing in cars and from building workers high up on scaffolding. Never once did it occur to them that it was their short skirts that was attracting attention to them. It was indeed a male-chauvinist world they lived in.

HENSINGHAM APARTMENTS.

STRATFORD.

Terry and Samantha could hardly believe their eyes when they'd entered Roxanne's flat. Samantha had never actually entered the flat before but Terry had and was completely gob-smacked at the transformation. Roxanne's support group had helped her with obtaining furniture. They had carpeted all the rooms in the flat and had tiles laid on the kitchen floor. The bathroom had been tiled as well as a brand new shower unit which overhung the bath-tub itself. In Roxanne's living room, which had been papered with lovely floral patterned paper, there was a polished credenza which supported photographs of herself and her daughter Hollie, both of them holding their babies in bright colourful frames. A brand new forty-six-inch TV sat proudly on a stand in the corner of the room. Gone was the old beat-up sideboard with handles missing from various drawers. Gone was the grubby carpet stained with nicotine and cigarette ash. Gone was the discarded clothes and in their place, a clothes horse held all of Roxanne's washing. It was unbelievable the differences that had been made. Roxanne had been granted custody of her baby Rosemary but under supervision and probation. Each day a health worker would come and report back to her superiors that Roxanne was more than capable of being a good mother. Her daughter Hollie had now moved in with her and had her own room for her and her baby. The situation was only temporary and as soon as they could find Hollie a suitable home, the Bromley council would move her. Roxanne came to the door with Terry and Samantha as they left. Terry was smiling broadly at the lady he had witnessed surviving the result of one of the most savage beatings he had ever seen. "This is all down to you Terry, you and Samantha here, none of this would have happened if it hadn't been for you two, especially you at the hearing Terry, I can't thank you enough for all the help and support you've given me." Roxanne stood in a lemon-coloured dress which came down to below her knees and flat red slippers. She leaned over and hugged the detective and then hugged his colleague with equal sincerity. Hollie appeared at the door where she proceeded to take hold of both Samantha's hands in her own. "You're very pretty." She said to the detective, and then looked at Terry Mercer and repeated to him. "She's very pretty, and you two would make a nice fucking couple honestly, you should live together really, you're a nice fucking couple really, you really are, any fucker can see that."
"Language Hollie" Her mother said smiling at the only two people in the world who had given her any time. As Terry and Samantha left the threshold he turned and said to

Samantha, "We'll come back and visit you from time to time, make sure everything's going ok for you. Hollie, you look after your mum please and those lovely two babies in there."

Hollie stood chewing her gum and nodding her head as she waved them goodbye.

"Yeah, you're a really nice couple…fucking lovely, really."

BROMLEY.

The two teenagers had spent all morning and half of the afternoon together visiting clothes shops and cafes, sharing the experiences they'd had in Lithuania. Sophie had also confessed to Lisa about the use of the bull-whip and how she was disappointed when Colin had killed the man by shooting him before she could inflict more pain onto him. And how she did not regret any of her actions, in fact, the whip-skills could come in very handy in the near future. She was now walking her friend to the bus-stop.

Lisa had arranged this after her mother had texted her several times wanting to know exactly where she was, and was she still with Sophie. As they walked Sophie said, "I'm so glad we had this little day out together Lisa. It's good for me to know that someone else feels the same way about certain things as I do, you know, with the boys thing and all that. But what was it Lisa that made you call me?

Were you going through all the girls who were with us or what?"

Lisa shook her head.

"No Sophie, it wasn't that. I've eh…I've found out something that might be of interest to you."

"Really? And what might that be?"

"Remember when we were talking together in Lithuania? We were all sharing our experiences with each other how we were abducted."

"Yes? What's that got to do with anything now?"

"Well, as you know, I live just outside Bromley, and they abducted me the very same way as they kidnapped you. You remember telling me about the guy who was pretending to be a street-sweeper? And how he grabbed you from behind and bundled you into the van? Well, I know who he is, and where he lives." Sophie felt faint. Her legs felt suddenly weak. She began to sweat, her mouth became dry as paper, she couldn't swallow. She quickly opened the tin of fizzy drink she held in her hands and took a large mouthful. Eventually, she replied to Lisa "When did you find this out?"

"A few weeks ago, I've been watching him."

"And you're only telling me now? We've been together all day Lisa, for fuck sakes…oh Christ. And you're sure about this, I mean, this isn't some fucker looking for glory for being part of the kidnappers is it, you're certain about this?"

"One hundred and ten per-cent certain Sophie. I just wanted to know what frame of mind you were in, because I want to pay this bastard back for what he's done, but I…I haven't got the nerve to do it on my own, that's why I contacted you. Don't get me wrong, I still want to be your friend and I hope that you still want to be my friend, no matter what we do, it's just that I don't have the guts to do anything on my own. Will you help me Sophie, will you help me get even with him? You know when I told you, when I'm waking up from the nightmares and standing at the sink with the carving knife in my hand? Well, it's his face that I see, and I really want to hurt him badly Sophie, because as far as I'm concerned, he was the start of all the hellish things that followed, he started it all, all the nightmare times."

Just as Sophie answered her friend, Lisa's bus approached and pulled in to the lay-by.

"Can you come back here tomorrow Lisa?"

"Yes, at the same time? And the same café?"

Sophie nodded.

"And Lisa? Not another word to anyone, ok? Not a word. I'll see you tomorrow sweetheart."

As Lisa boarded the bus, she called back to Sophie, "Will you help me?"

Sophie nodded her head. "Definitely, see you tomorrow."

As the bus pulled away the two girls waved to each other.

To all and sundry it looked like any other young teenage girlfriends waving to each other. No-one in the world could possibly know what had been done to their lives, or to their ways of life, to their ways of thinking, and their attitudes now, and most importantly, no-one out there could possibly know what had been done to their minds. Young as they were, they had been violated and sexually degraded beyond belief. They had been used and exposed to all manner of depravity that no woman should ever be subjected to in their life-times, never mind a teenage adolescent. Sophie thought about all the counselling she'd received and was still receiving, but nothing was taking away this savage thirst for revenge. This, what was in her mind now had nothing to do with Colin Green or Terry Mercer or anybody else in the world. This only concerned Sophie Spencer and Lisa Jenson, and the bastards who had turned their lives upside down and then some. All these councillors and psychiatrists and everybody else who were trying to help her, couldn't begin to understand how she felt. They, recommended this and that, and "Try not to think about all that bad stuff and carry on with your lives."

And that was where Sophie had the problem. Just carry on with your life, what, as though nothing has happened? Is that what they called success? Is that what they call a full recovery? While those beasts over in Europe or anywhere else for that matter just continued with their lives like they'd done nothing wrong?

Lisa couldn't manage it on her own? Well, she had no fear there then, because she would help Lisa get even with this low-life, whoever the fuck he was, and after all, if Lisa was right, and she seemed certain she was, then this prick had ruined *her* life as well as Lisa's. She was right, it all started with him. All the rapes, the drugs, the swallowing sperm, the evil sick women sitting on their faces, all the fucking cocaine-snorting, it all started with that bastard, and his actions on that cold rainy morning when she was late for school.

But the beauty of this situation, because it was beautiful, was the fact that this creep would probably not even recognise any of the two of them, "Even if we were standing right beside him."

She thought to herself as she walked.

Revenge is a dish best served cold they say?

Well, this need for revenge had never gone cold...and now it was boiling.

MITCHAM.

"You said you had some news for us Colin. News that concerns Sophie Spencer, well, we're all ears." Terry and Samantha sat in Colin's living room. Colin's wife and daughters were out shopping.

"Yes, I eh...I've done something that I'm not particularly proud of, but I'm doing it, or rather I've done it for Sophie's own good. I don't want her to get into any trouble." Colin Green held a small red memory-stick in his hand.

"What have you done Colin?" Samantha said, warily. "Don't tell us you've -."

"No, it's nothing that will cause her any harm, it's just a trick I learned when I was in the forces...I've eh...I've bugged her phone."

Terry was not what anyone would call, a technical man by any means, but when Colin led him through to the kitchen and opened up his lap-top and then inserted the memory-stick it didn't surprise him in the least when, suddenly, on the screen all of Sophie's text messages appeared.

All the messages from the past four days when Colin had taken the opportunity to `mess` about with her phone for a few minutes while she was busy talking to Alison in her room. He looked at the two detectives with a look of self-loathing. "It's for her own good. I just feel that Sophie has something going on within herself that she's not telling anyone, me included. What's interesting me at the moment is this." He scrolled forward to the last few texts that Sophie had received. "Here, look. This girl here called Lisa. It's one of the girls we rescued from Lithuania. Her name is Lisa Jenson. She lives alone with her mum just outside of Bromley. Her mum's recently divorced. What's interesting me is, Sophie has not mentioned this girl before, since they've came back home. Not once. Suddenly they're arranging meetings in cafes in Bromley, and a friendship seems to be developing between the pair. Now I'm not saying that there's anything wrong with that, in fact, it's perfectly normal as far as I'm concerned, but it's this last message that made me sit up and take notice. Look, it may mean nothing, or it could be something. They might just be talking."

"What are we supposed to be looking at Colin?" Samantha said, standing with her arms folded looking over the lap-top. "Two teenage girls, probably exchanging experiences they've had over in Europe...there's nothing wrong with-."

"Yes, but look." As Colin Green scrolled down the screen to the very last message sent by Sophie Spencer, there in plain black and white print was the message that had raised the alarm bells in his mind.

"Don't you worry Lisa I'll help you sort this bastard out. He's destroyed my life as well as *yours sweetheart. The authorities seem reluctant to find the bastard but we've found him ourselves. Now he's going to pay for everything he's done to us and our families. And remember Lisa, not a word to anyone else about this. Rest assured Lisa, you have found your soul-mate. Revenge is sweet indeed. Remember to delete this message after you've read it x*

Mercer stood and puffed out his cheeks as he exhaled. "Jesus, Colin. When did she send that message.?"

Samantha seen something in Terry's eyes that she hadn't seen before.

His expression was changing.

Colin glanced at the screen and clicked something with his mouse.

"Eighteen minutes past eleven last-night."

"Here goes" Samantha thought to herself.

Terry was in a state of high-dudgeon.

"Yeah well, it seems that she's planning something with this Lisa girl. Revenge. Of course, she was doing just fine wasn't she until you started getting her interested in fucking fighting and learning how to use guns and fucking martial-arts and all that shit. Now, she's going to take on the world with all her new combat skills that she's learned from you, I hope you're fucking happy how things have turned out. You had your girl home safe and sound but you had to keep putting the boot in so to speak until they took your older daughter as well, and look at the state *that* put you in, you were fucking lucky with that outcome pal."

"Terry leave it just now." said Samantha trying to bring some kind of order to the situation.

"Leave it? That's what he should have done Sam, but no, he's got to be the fucking hard man, the big man, fucking learning a young girl how to use a fucking bull-whip what the fuck is wrong with you, are you fucking sane? I'm telling you something now my friend, you'd better hope she doesn't pull this off before I can get to her because if she does this, if she and this other girl kills this bastard then I will make damn sure that you go down with her because as far as I am concerned, it's you who has put all this revenge shit into her head...you fucking prick! Your military days are over. This is the real world now you live in where people go to work and make a living to provide for their families and loved ones, not a fucking scene out of a wild-west movie where you tie some fucker up and whip the skin off his back and then laugh and boast about the fact that you learned a sixteen-year-old girl how to do that. Fucking wanting to learn her how to shoot and build fucking tents and use knives for fuck sakes, you need help yourself, you silly fucker, honestly, get a fucking grip of yourself man!"

Terry Mercer stepped over to the sink and rinsed out his cup, placing it on the unit.

"You'd better hope she's not successful in this thing she's planning because I meant what I said, and after everything we've been through together, I really wouldn't want to send you away, but believe me, I will, without hesitation I will!"

Terry left the house by the back door.

As Samantha followed him she turned and ordered Colin to keep them in touch at all times concerning Sophie's messages. "What she sends and what she receives.

Do it Colin, for your own good, you can see what he's like just now, don't, whatever you do, antagonise him any further."

As Samantha left the house Colin Green let out a massive sigh.

He was going to be in serious trouble if he couldn't get hold of Sophie and have a talk with her. He'd been all but forbidden to do so by Terry and Samantha after their last discussion. He'd been warned not to go near the girl and leave her alone to try and build back her life into some kind of normality, and she wouldn't be able to do that as long as he kept putting shit ideas into her head. The problem Colin had now was something he'd left undisclosed when talking to the two detectives, and it was a very serious problem for all concerned, a precarious situation in fact. He'd given Sophie Spencer a hand gun...and she knew how to use it.

BICKLEY.

Sophie Spencer and Lisa Jenson had taken the bus from Bromley out to Bickley.
It was a short distance but it was pouring down with rain, and so, the bus.
As they walked down Hawthorne Road Lisa asked her friend if she had anything specific in mind for the dog they were about to track down.
"We'll play it by ear Lisa. I want to see where this fucker lives first. I take it he still stays with his parents I mean he's around the same age as ourselves is he?"
Lisa nodded, but did not verbally respond.
"What's wrong Lisa, are you having second thoughts about this? I can do this on my own you know, I don't have any fear about dealing with him, in fact, since Lithuania, I don't have any fear of anything now. The worst that could happen to any girl *did* happen didn't it, so there's nothing more to be frightened of is there…apart from death, and I'm certainly not afraid of that, in fact, I prayed for it on two or three occasions over in Europe."
Lisa held down her umbrella as the girls ducked under some low-hanging branches that were bridging the pavement upon which they walked.
"Certainly not Sophie, in fact, I have butterflies in my stomach at the thought of having revenge, and the fact that, as you say, he won't even know who we are. When he manhandled me he tried his best to keep me from seeing his facial features, but I saw him, his hood slipped down. As those animals in the van wrestled me to the floor, I saw his face. Then they slammed the back door of the van shut, and they injected me with something. I've seen him Sophie, you know, going about, like before we were kidnapped. I'm sure I've seen him hanging out in cafes and shit."
Sophie pulled out a pack of cigarettes from her jacket pocket and offered one to her friend. Lisa just shook her head. Sophie stopped to light her cigarette up. "Is it much further Lisa?"
"No, it's just at the bottom of this road. He lives in Hawthorne Close, it's just down here, a hundred metres or so."
Sophie looked around the area as she walked. "Well, his parents must have money if they live around here that's for sure. And if that's the case Lisa, then why would he do something like that, you know, kidnapping girls to get money, I take it those bastards would pay him for what he helped them to do."
Lisa smiled at Sophie, but said nothing initially.
"What? What are you smiling at?"
"You, my friend, are going to love me when I tell you what I'm about to inform you."

Sophie took a long drag of her cigarette and exhaled up into the air. "Well? *Are* you going to tell me or am I just to guess what it is?"

Lisa sighed. Not a sarcastic sigh but rather a sigh of excitement, like she couldn't wait to tell her. She said, "His father has all but washed his hands with him, he'll have little to do with him. Apparently he stole money from his dad, a lot of money. His father kicked him out of the house. He comes here to his house, well, what used to be his house every Friday evening between six and seven. His father is never home between those times and so I guess his mother gives him a meal and some cash to tide him over. He stays for no longer than forty minutes and then he's gone. He doesn't come here at any other time than that day and time I told you. Friday, between six and seven, that's it. He would kidnap us to get some money to no doubt feed his habit, he's an addict Sophie, a heroin addict, am I not a nice girl for telling you that Sophie?"

Sophie Spencer stopped in her tracks and looked at Lisa.

"Oh you fucking beauty that you are. Only you could do it Lisa, only you could make the cake taste even sweeter, you absolute fucking honey that you are, come here." Sophie kissed her friend on the cheek and embraced her.

She then held Lisa at arms-length and said, "I loved you long before you told me that Lisa Jensen."

For a brief moment the two girls looked into each-others' eyes.

If there was anything other than friendship going on in the girls' minds, neither of them said anything.

They continued walking.

Everywhere Sophie looked there were trees. Every garden in the area had trees of some description, and or panelled fencing or brick walls. Seclusion...perfect for what she had in mind. Sophie wasn't revelling in the fact that this guy was a heroin addict, in fact she had a friend who was an addict and she was one of the nicest people she knew. It was that no matter what people say most of society take a dim view on heroin addicts and see them as nothing less than pathetic losers. This boy's own father had turned his back on him for stealing from him. He didn't try to help his son by the sounds of things, no, he just turned his back on him for hurting his pride..."no son of mine." To Sophie, the fact that he was an addict just made it easier for her as far as the law was concerned, because if he were to suddenly disappear from society there wouldn't exactly be a search-party out looking for him. There'd be no big concern, the fact that a junky had gone missing. And there was no doubt about that, a junky *would* go missing...and very soon, and for a very long time.

SAFE HAVEN.

BROMLEY.

Terry and Samantha approached the premises of the shelter for abused women. They had been to Sophie's house where they were informed by her mum that she could be here at the shelter. Sophie had been doing university work here for a few weeks. They'd been informed that Sophie was not at university today and so here at the shelter was their best bet to find her. If she wasn't there, she'd probably be with her friend Lisa Jensen, Mandy Spencer had said.
"She seems happier now than ever, I mean there's nothing wrong with the Green girl, but since she's started hanging out with this Lisa she seems to have taken a new lease of life, going around the house humming and singing, and above all, being courteous to me and her brother continuously, she's a different girl Terry.
She grabbed her brother in a head-lock the other day in a mock fight. She quite surprised me, god she spun David round and had him on the floor at her feet in a flash, you know like some form of Judo or something. Then she said to him as he lay on the floor laughing, "You used to look out for me David at school, now I will look out for you, nobody round here will fuck about with my bro." "I think David was as surprised as I was."
Samantha said to Terry as they approached the entrance of the shelter.
"It would seem that Sophie has had lessons of some description, you know, self-defence and-."
"Self-defence my arse Samantha, that twat will have been learning her all kinds of martial-arts, it's more than just basic self-defence she's learned from Colin Green. It's like I told him at his house, he's got her all trained up with all these fighting skills of his. Now, with all this revenge shit going on in her head she'll be itching to use them on her victims. What the fuck was he thinking Sam, to learn a girl how to use a bull-whip. And the fact that she used it on that bastard in High-Wycombe with such gusto…Christ we might have a problem here kid."
Terry held the door for Samantha to step in before him. "Kid? What the hell is that, you're the bloody kid mister.
No wonder they call you Terry tantrum back at the yard.
"What? Who the fuck calls me that, tell me!"
"Come on." She replied, smiling to herself as they entered. She was pulling his strings again.

Misses Margaret Hall greeted the two detectives as they approached the reception desk. Terry produced his ID and asked if Sophie was here, or indeed had been here today.

"Not today" said the kindly woman, smiling.

"Sophie has been coming here to talk to some of the women to learn about their problems and ordeals and experiences. It's for her sociology work at the university. One or two of the women in here have quite taken to her, she's a very nice girl is Sophie, and wise beyond her years without a doubt."

Terry smiled and agreed with misses Hall. "But she hasn't been here today though?"

"She's not been here since over a week ago. She and Claire, oh Claire is one of our residents, had something of an argument and Sophie up and walked out stating that she wouldn't be back. Oh but she thanked me for my encouragement and advice. I tried to calm her down that day and went on to suggest that she might seek out a career in psychology, the girl has remarkable skills in sociology you know. Within days of her interviewing the women she had a few of them opening up to her about their violent experiences, and if you've ever dealt with any women who have been abused then you'll know just how difficult it is to get them to talk...but Sophie done it, and a lot faster than some professionals could and that's no lie. She's a remarkable girl detective Mercer. Please don't tell me she's in some kind of trouble."

Again Terry made light of the situation. "No, nothing like that misses Hall, we just need to have a little chat with her about something, it's just routine."

Samantha said, "What did Sophie and this Claire fall out about, do you know?"

"Well no, not really. Sophie just said that she told the girl some home-truths, something like that. It was something about sticking up for themselves, I don't really know. You could ask Claire herself, I'm sure she'd be willing to speak to you, would you like to do that?"

"That would be super misses Hall." Replied Samantha.

"Ok I'll just go to her room and ask if she will talk to you, mind you, don't hold your breath if you're expecting her to go into great detail about their conversations. Wait here and I'll just go and ask her."

Ten minutes later Samantha and Terry were in the kitchen-come-canteen having a coffee with the young woman named Claire. Misses Hall was right. She was very defensive concerning her conversations with Sophie Spencer. Every question they asked her was answered succinctly. But eventually Samantha had her speaking about the day in question. Terry had to admit to himself, she was far better equipped at extracting snippets of information from people than he was. If he'd been here himself he'd have had no luck whatsoever, but here was this young woman now explaining everything about her falling out with Sophie.

"It was my own fault really. I got off on the wrong foot that day by mentioning to her that I felt her skirt was far too short to be wearing in public. All she was trying to do was to convince me to hit back, and that if I didn't, then the beatings would just continue. Make a stand for yourself she'd said and stand up to him. I kind of went off the tracks then by accusing her of being a spoiled little brat or something and then she all but exploded. Telling me that I need to see a psychiatrist and that I must be kinky and enjoy being beaten up to pulp."

Again Samantha stepped in before Terry could. "Did she ask you at any time the name of your partner or husband. Did she talk about him at all, I mean, where you live or where he works, was she curious as to find out where she could find him?"

Claire nodded her head. "Yeah, she seemed very interested in finding out where he worked. He's not been home according to the police since the last time he...he em...beat on me. So she asked me where he worked, and I honestly couldn't tell her. All I know is that he tells me he works in the construction industry, that's all I could tell her." Claire rose from her chair. "I'm going outside for a cigarette now, there's nothing more I can tell you. But if you see her tell her I'm sorry for my outburst and that I'd be only too pleased to have another chat with her."

Samantha smiled. "We will, oh, did you tell Sophie his name Claire by any chance?"

"Yes, I told her. His name is Alan Flint. Remember to tell her I'm sorry."

HAWTHORNE CLOSE.

BROMLEY.

"Well, that's it there Sophie, that's where he lives." The two teenagers stood at the junction of Hawthorne Road and Hawthorne Close. "His name is Gareth Tate. Like I say, once a week he comes here. He gets off the bus back there where we got off and he walks down here to see his mother."
Sophie lit up another cigarette. "How come you know all this Lisa? Have you been following him around?"
"Not around exactly, I just followed him one day when I clocked him in the town. Even then I was certain it was the same guy who was masquerading as the bin man. I walked right past him on the bus. I sat four or five seats behind him.
I paid to go further but when I saw him getting off here I just got off at the same stop. I began to walk in the opposite direction he was walking until I was sure he wasn't suspicious and then about-turned and began to walk a distance behind him. We were walking down Hawthorne Road here and then he turned into the close. I thought I'd lost him but when I got to where we're standing now I saw that door over there closing. Just to make sure I had the right house, the following week I got the bus at the same time. Sure enough he boarded it and got off at the same stop. I happened to remember that it was the same time as the week before. This time I hung around along the street there so as I could see the house. I was just about to walk away when he came out of the house and began to walk towards the bus stop at the top of the road there. As luck would have it, there's a girl I know who lives at the far end of Hawthorne Close and so when I sat beside her on the bus, well, I thought it would take any suspicions he had, in case he'd clocked that I was following him. It worked because he never flinched. Any time he saw me after that, if he was watching me, well, he'd just think I was meeting Heather, that's her name Heather Lockley, she lives just along there. I came here about six times in all, making sure that it was him...and it is. It was Heather who told me about his heroin addiction and all that shit to do with him and his dad falling out." Sophie smiled at her friend. "You're a smart cookie Lisa it has to be said, you done well. Do you know anything else about the twat? any of his haunts or his friends?"
"Couldn't say about friends, but he goes to Bibas night club. Every Saturday night. I wouldn't know any of his regular pubs, but he's at the night club every Saturday night...without fail."
"Ok Lisa, we've got enough information, let's head back to the bus stop."

"Don't you want a closer look at the house?"

"No need, I can already see there's an abundance of bushes and trees in his garden to spring a trap, however we deal with him Lisa, it'll have to be done here, I mean right here because neither of us drive and so we can't exactly force him from here to somewhere else without rendering him unconscious, and so that's out of the question, and anyway, where would we take him? *Oh hi mum, this is Gareth, I'm just taking him upstairs to beat the shit out of him for kidnapping me, and then I'll throw his corpse out of my bedroom window to save me carrying the fucker back down again.*"

Both girls laughed as they made their way back to the bus stop.

As they walked Lisa said, I had it worked out differently to what you're thinking Sophie. I thought maybe we could dope him in the night club. Spike the bastards' drink or something."

"Again Lisa, where would we take him? Supposing we did do that, where the hell could we take him, no, that's out of the question."

"Can I have a cigarette please Sophie."

Sophie handed Lisa the packet. "Come on, what are you smiling at now missy." Lisa took a draw of the cigarette. "It's not out of the question Sophie, definitely not. You know my mum and dad have split up right? Well, my dad has a large workshop about two hundred yards from my house. He used it for storing things. Old furniture or odds and ends, gas bottles for his welding and shit like that. Well *now*, it's sitting completely empty. When we get back we can go and see it. You can see what you think. My mum is on about selling it to someone but she hasn't got round to it yet, what do you say Sophie, you think it's worth a look? If you don't agree then we can just think of something else, no harm done, but I was thinking we could keep the bastard there for as long as we liked...torture the fucker for what he done to us. What do you say?"

MITCHAM.

Sophie walked across Mitcham common towards the A 239.
Today, she had another little project she was working on. This one, she would pursue on her own. It was better that she worked alone on this one. The less people who knew about this the better her chances of pulling it off. She was walking across the common to reach the local police station which was situated just off the main road.
She had passed it many times when travelling in Colin Green's Transit van, but today she would enter the station, and for a very important reason. Sophie entered the station where she was greeted by a very pleasant young female officer who asked her how she could be of assistance.
Sophie paid particular attention to the officer's attire because this was the reason she was here.
"Hello." She responded politely, "I wonder if you could help me.
My name is Sophie Spencer and just now I am doing a project about the history of the Metropolitan Police. I have been able to obtain most of the information I require on the internet but I'm having difficulty in finding out about emblems, badges and so on, and how they have changed over the years. I was wondering if you had anything that perhaps I could look at, and maybe allow me to take a couple of photographs of them so as I can be more precise when I write out my resume."
The blonde officer who looked about thirtyish to Sophie wore a white blouse which had black shoulder straps and a black cravat tied neatly around her neck. She smiled at Sophie and asked her to take a seat in the small waiting room while she spoke to a superior. Sophie took a seat and waited for the young police-officer to return. When she did, she was accompanied by a man perhaps in his early forties with short neat jet black hair which looked to be gelled heavily.
His shirt was neatly rolled up to his elbows. She could see by the three stripes on his left sleeve that he was the sergeant.
"Well now young lady, officer Crosby informs me that you wish to learn about the emblems of the police force, and the badges, is that correct?"
"Yes sir, it's for my project at university. I'm doing a study of the history of the Metropolitan Police forces in England. I was wondering if you would let me see some badges from the past and up to the present day."
The very tall sergeant stood smiling at her. He seemed pleased in the fact that a girl her age was taking an interest in such a subject. He was smiling like it was his own daughter who was showing an interest. Or perhaps it could have been her legs, he'd glanced at

them once or twice.

"And do you know who the founder of the Metropolitan Police force was?"
He leaned forward with his hands on his hips and half bent down turning his head to one side as though he were hard-of-hearing. "Can you tell me that?"
He was talking to her like she was six-years-old, which suited Sophie perfectly.
She would conveniently play along. Smiling at the sergeant, she replied to him, "Yes sir, it was Sir Robert Peel."
He now stood upright again and rolled on the balls of his feet.
Sophie half expected him to hand her a coloured lollipop.
"Indeed it was miss, indeed it was. Well, I'm quite sure that officer Crosby here can show you one or two from our display case in the corridor."
Again, he spoke to her like she was a small child.
"And if you're good, she may even take it down from the wall and open it up so that you might examine them closely. It's been a pleasure talking to you miss, good luck with your project."
"Thank you so much sir, that's very nice of you."
The sergeant's face seemed to light up even more. He looked at officer Crosby and said, nodding his head in the direction of the corridor, "Show her Melony, show her what we have." And with that, he was gone, disappearing down the hallway back to his office.
Sophie was shown seven different badges from years past up until the present day. Melony Crosby had taken them out of their display case and handed each one to her so that she had a good look at them all individually. She was then quite taken a-back when officer Crosby offered her a cup of coffee. Sophie accepted. Melony poked her head through a hatch in the wall and said to the other girl who had been in reception when she entered the building, "I'll just be ten minutes Linda, ok? Do you want a coffee?"
Sophie heard the other woman decline the offer. "Oh, while I'm making this, would you knock on the door opposite this one and ask sergeant Anderson if he'd like one Sophie please."
"Of course." replied Sophie, over the moon about how this was turning out.
She crossed the corridor and gently knocked on the sergeant's door.
"Enter." Came the reply from within, making her want to burst out laughing.
She kept a straight face with difficulty as she said, "Excuse me sir, but officer Crosby wishes to know if you'd like a cup of coffee sir."
As soon as sergeant Anderson saw it was her, he bounced up from his chair and accompanied her back into the other room. He accepted Melony's offer of the coffee and soon was seated opposite Sophie and smiling at the display case on the desk before them. He began to explain the very small changes in the emblems and badges and the

reasons for the changes. Sophie tried to shut him up by explaining that officer Crosby had explained all this to her but it made no difference…he continued. In fact, he began to sound like he was ranting or pontificating about the history of the police force.
But then, a bonus for Sophie. He rose from his chair and returned to his office.
A few moments later he returned and closed the door behind him.
Sitting back down he placed upon the table a shiny silver badge with his majesty's crest upon it. Smiling yet again, he first looked at Melony Crosby and then to his left and his right, as though there may be other people in here, and handed the badge to Sophie placing his pointing finger to his mouth, and again, like she was six, he said, "Sshh, you're not supposed to get these, but I'm pretty sure you won't be going around impersonating a police officer now will you."
Sophie laughed almost child-like, and purposefully. "Of course not sir. Is this? Are you giving this to me sir?" He nodded his head vigorously, smiling.
"Yes, you'll look after it won't you."
Sophie could play this game all day.
She'd caught him two or three times glancing at her legs and wondered if it was this that was making him warm to her. Whether it was or not, she had obtained something far beyond her expectations, and was genuinely grateful. She stood up and threw her arms around the sergeant's neck.
"Oh now now miss, we mustn't, I'm not supposed to-."
"Oh thank you sir, thank you so much. You have no idea how much this means to me. Oh my God, I can't believe this."
"That one went out of circulation in nineteen ninety-nine. They changed the badge for the new millennium you see…but it's still, you know, it's original Sophie, it's a real police badge."
"Sir, you don't know what this means to me. I'm going to put this in a frame and hang it on my wall at home. May I take some photographs of the other badges please sir?"
"By all means miss. Perhaps you can write something along the lines of what life was like at the time of these badges being in use. Some of them go back as far as the nineteenth hundreds."
Sophie stood and embraced Melony Crosby and sergeant Anderson again thanking them both yet again for all their help and kindness. She even offered to wash out the cups they'd been drinking from which, yet again seemed to jolt sergeant Anderson into being even more helpful. "Wait here miss, I shan't be long. He returned moments later with a small polythene bag. Here you are, you can place these with your badge."
To Sophie's utter delight inside the bag were two shoulder straps. There were no numbers on them, but she would soon see to that. As Sophie left Mitcham police

station she felt exhilarated yet again, and well she might, because now, she held in her possession, an official police badge, albeit out of date, but no-one was going to be looking that close at it, and official police shoulder straps which would attach nicely onto the items she'd purchased at the costume parlour a few days earlier.
All that remained to do now was visit the Crown and Mitre back in Bromley.

B251.

PICKHURST LANE.

WEST WICKHAM.

There was a time, fairly recently in fact that Carol Jensen would have been pleased to see officers of the law arriving at her house in the hope that they may have news as to the whereabouts of her missing daughter. Today however, as detectives Mercer and Reynolds pulled up outside of her house she immediately fell into a state of consternation. Lisa had said she was nipping to the shops for something and that she'd be back within the hour. Even before the detectives opened her gate Carol was texting her daughter to ask if she was alright, and to please reply immediately. `It's very important Lisa`. Carol opened her front door before Samantha or Terry had a chance to ring her doorbell.
"Good afternoon misses Jensen" said Samantha Reynolds, "we were wondering if we could have a little chat with Lisa."
"Why? Why do you need to have a chat with Lisa? She hasn't done anything wrong has she?"
"No no no, Misses Jensen, this is just routine. We're going round all the girls who were abducted, you know, it's just to find out how they are coping. There's nothing at all to be concerned about. Just ten minutes, and we'll be on our way."
Carol remembered how Terry Mercer had played a vital role in the rescue of the girls in Lithuania. As far as she was concerned, they'd still be stuck there if it hadn't been for the man in front of her.
She would be eternally grateful for his endeavours.
"I'm afraid she's not home just now but she said she wouldn't be long. She's gone into Bromley for something for one of her friends I believe. I offered to take her in the car but she insisted that she took the bus…she says I'm always fussing too much about her. I em…I can't help it, not since…you know. Please, you're both welcome to come in and wait for her, she said she wouldn't be long."
Mercer looked at his watch. "Will she be back home within the next half hour misses Jensen do you think?"
"I'm sure of it." She replied as she stepped aside to let the detectives into the hallway. "I'm waiting for her to reply to my text message in fact. I feel a lot better than I did a couple of minutes ago. When I saw you pulling up I em, you know, it's not very often

police officers arrive at your door with *good* news now is it." Mercer smiled at the nervous woman. "Well, be that as it may Misses Jensen there is nothing to concern you today I can assure you of that."

"Please, it's Carol, I always feel when people address me as misses that there are serious issues at hand. Please, take a seat. Would you like a cup of tea while you wait for Lisa." Carol picked up her phone from the coffee table and looked at the screen. She then smiled to the detectives. "You're in luck, she's on her way home on the bus. She'll be here in less than ten minutes she says."

Carol seemed relieved, even of the fact that her daughter was returning home safely from a visit to the shops. Anxiety is a horrible thing.

It was plain to see that this woman was absolutely besotted with her daughter. And now, after everything that had happened, she'd be on edge every time the girl left the house without her, and rightly so. There were some nasty people out there who cared nothing about devotion or love or heartache and misery. We, as society never speak of them much really. Sure we're subconscious of their existence, but they are of little concern to us until, *one day your child is making their way innocently to school and then snatched up by this breed of low-lives who intend to sell them off to the highest bidder.* Then, they become real. Then we are only too aware of their existence. Terry Mercer completely understood Carol's protectiveness towards her daughter. He and Samantha were here in effect to do the same for Lisa, to protect her, to stop her from falling into danger. Whatever she and Sophie Spencer were planning, it undoubtedly involved violence, and perhaps even worse than that. And if that was the case, then the law would work in a somewhat similar manner as to that of the kidnappers, not caring about backgrounds or good behaviour in the past, or how much they loved their parents. If you committed murder, then you were going to jail for a very long time indeed. Good intentions or revenge or self-protectiveness, it didn't matter.

If you were guilty you were guilty. That was the law.

"We'd love a cup of coffee Carol, if that's no trouble." Said Samantha, who noticed just how much on edge this poor woman was, a very flighty state of apprehension, constantly. "Terry here gets quite grumpy from time to time, it's the caffeine Carol, I'm in his bad books when he gets like that, you know, when he can't get his fix of the stuff. I just give him his coffee and he's fine again. It's like when a child cries for something and then as soon as they get what they want, they're fine again."

Carol only smiled at Samantha as she informed her of her colleagues behavioural patterns sensing the humour between them. Mercer sat smiling as he scrutinised his mobile phone.

As they sat drinking their coffee Samantha said, "Does Lisa have lots of friends around here Carol?"

Carol sat on her easy-chair with her hands clasped between her legs.

She wore pale blue jeans and a dark blue denim shirt and white trainers.

Sam could see where Lisa got her good looks from. Even without make-up Carol Jensen was a very attractive woman.

"She hasn't got what you could say, loads of friends, but she has a few.

Funny you should say that, because just recently she's started meeting up with a girl from Bromley, Sophie Spencer. Now I'm not saying that Lisa was ever a shy girl in any way, but since she's started hanging around with Sophie, well, she's changed a hell of a lot. And I mean changed in a good way. I met Sophie recently when I took Lisa through to see her, they were both, you know, Sophie was abducted too, do you know the girl?"

"Yes we do Carol, and you're right, she is a very nice girl. Perhaps they are good for each other. I expect they formed a friendship whilst they were…"

"Yes, it would certainly seem that way. Anyway, Lisa seems to have more patience for me these days. She was always moaning to me about me being far too protective, but now she seems more tolerant of my protectiveness, she says these things in jest now. Sophie told her in the café that day that she was a very lucky young lady to have a mum like me."

"And so she is." said Terry, a little too quickly as far as Samantha was concerned. He realized this, and leaned forward reaching for his coffee but as he did he accidently knocked the table with his knee and spilled a little of the coffee not just from his own cup but from Samantha and Carol's as well.

"Fuck, I'm, oh Christ and fuck I'm so sorry Carol. Go and get a cloth and I'll clean this up, I'm so sorry."

"It's alright" smiled Carol, accidents will happen mister Mercer, relax."

Samantha stepped in again, she just had to. "You'll have to excuse Terry Carol, he always falls to pieces every time he's confronted with an attractive woman, he can't help himself. It's as though he's just reached puberty again. Look, look at him blushing now. He'll probably think about beautiful women before he goes to sleep at nights thinking about what he will say to them, but then when he's confronted by one, as you can see, when the moment of truth arrives he falls flat on his face, he can't help it. He's fine until a beautiful woman shows up, and then he goes all to hell…completely falls to pieces, I'm so sorry Carol, I'll get him to clean it up."

"Yeah, that's right Carol, I fall to pieces whenever I'm confronted with beautiful women, which is why I'm always fine around you Samantha, no fear of me cracking up in front of you, is there."

Terry knew exactly what Samantha was doing. She was getting Carol Jensen to relax and bring her out of her anxiety. The atmosphere by the time Lisa returned would be happy and relaxed, perfect for being able to ask her some very serious questions.

"Honestly Carol" continued Samantha, "I've been in houses where he's dipped his digestive biscuit into his coffee and it's fell in. He sits there and tries to fish it out with a spoon whilst I'm left to ask the host some questions, it's very embarrassing indeed. It's like working with a chimpanzee honestly. Did you hear what he said there Carol?

Go and get a cloth. It's his fault but he's still giving out the orders…go and get a cloth indeed. Oh, and the profanations, he's terrible."

Carol Jenson was now in a state of hysterics and actually holding her stomach as she laughed heartily.

MITCHAM.

Colin Green sat in his kitchen awaiting the arrival of Terry and Samantha.
He'd contacted them through text messaging because it seemed that Terry was refusing even to speak with him. For whatever reason, he wasn't answering his phone.
He'd sent the same message to Samantha's phone. He had found out something that was of the utmost importance. By writing that, surely Terry would have to come and see what it was.
Colin's daughters Rebecca and Alison were making last-minute adjustments to their hair and make-up as they came into the kitchen to say goodbye to their father. They were off to see a pop concert and were spending the night with friends.
As the girls came to give him a kiss he said, "Who else is going to this concert? Is Sophie going?"
Alison turned to him and casually replied. "No dad, Sophie doesn't want to come, she hasn't much time for us now since she's started hanging around with Lisa Jensen…we're not good enough now…who cares, we'll see her when we see her. Bye dad, love you, and don't be worrying about Rebecca and I, we'll keep in touch with you and mum, so…no bloody texting us every five minutes ok? We won't hear our phones when the concert starts. If there's a problem, we will contact you and mum immediately…is that fair enough?"
Colin Green kissed both of his daughters on the cheek and told them to enjoy themselves, and of course, to be very careful.
Jillian Green kissed her daughters on the front step as they made their way out to the taxi which was now waiting for them at their gate.
She stood waving to them with mixed emotions. She came through into the kitchen to make herself and her husband a cup of tea.
"This is their first time away from the house Colin since Rebecca's return from…" Jillian had no need to say anything else. It was perfectly understandable she would feel this way. Colin could see that she was practically in tears.
She was hellish emotional these days, and again, he understood why.
To try and help his wife cheer up he rose from the table to come and wrap his arms around her as she prepared the cups.
"They'll be fine Jillian. They both know and understand how we feel about them going out. They know how much we'll be worrying sweetheart, but we have two very sensible girls there my darling, and two intelligent ones as well. You heard what Alison said there, the slightest sign of a problem and they'll be in touch with us straight away, so,

we can't ask any more than that from them angel can we, we have to let them be who they are, and considering what they've both been through I think it's a major achievement what they're doing, because I was frightened that the very opposite would happen, that they would both become recluses and not want to leave the house. Look at them there, they're behaving like neither of them has endured anything at all...they're normal teenage girls Jillian, and that, my darling is an achievement for us. We should be proud of ourselves with what we've achieved with them."
Jillian placed the cups of tea onto the table and sat down next to her husband.
"I know you're right Colin, it's just me. Everything that has happened in the last few months, God I don't know how the hell we got through it."
Colin put his arm around his wife's shoulder again.
"But we did sweetheart, we bloody did, and we would again if we had to.
It's just who we are Jillian. We love each other and we love our kids, that's all there is about it. Just because I don't say much does not mean that I am not grateful for all you do. I could not have gone through this without your support, I know that much. When Terry and Samantha said I was going on a suicide mission when I told them about me going to Lithuania, you were the only one who had faith in me, and because you knew the risks I was taking, well, that gave me the will and the determination I needed to proceed, because if I'd failed, then, hurt as we would have been, I know you would know that I tried my very best."
Jillian leaned over and kissed her husband on the cheek.
"But you didn't fail Colin, did you. You brought her back home just like you said you would. I know Jim was a big help and that other S.A.S guy, but you done it Colin."
Colin and Jillian Green kissed passionately at their kitchen table.
He was just about to suggest that the two of them take their cups of tea upstairs with them when Terry Mercer's enormous fist pounded on their back door, making the couple almost hit the ceiling with fright.
In the next instant Jillian burst out laughing at her husband's ferocious statement. Knowing fine well who was at the door even before he'd answered it, he shouted, "Jesus fucking Christ does he think we're hibernating!"
As Colin made his way to the door Jillian looked up to the God she'd prayed to every minute of her husband and daughter's absence and whispered, *"My Lord, if you made anything better than that man there, then you kept it to yourself...thank you for Colin Green."*

Jillian sat down at the table with her husband and the two detectives. Seeing how Mercer had ignored his phone calls Colin Green addressed detective Reynolds. "I've found out a name for you, and it's this name that I think Sophie and Lisa are gunning for, and rightly so some would say."

"Some?" said Terry Mercer.

Colin ignored Mercer's sarcasm. He continued speaking to Samantha.

"You pulled this guy in months ago. Somebody reported him for being part of the syndicate. For whatever reason or reasons, he was released. Sophie told me that the man who had wrestled her into the van was masquerading as a council worker, a street-sweeper to be precise.

Lisa Jensen was abducted the very same way as you both know. I have reason to believe that the name I'm about to give you is the same guy who wrestled the girls into the van. If it is, then you can bet your bottom dollar that it's him that the girls are plotting their revenge upon."

Again, Terry stepped in with sledge-hammer sarcasm.

"*You* have reason to believe?"

Colin Green sighed and tried to hold back his temper.

"Ok Mercer, if that's the way you want to play, then fuck you. I'm not giving you the name now, and if those two girls land themselves in trouble then just remember this moment in time, when you pushed me too far. I'm trying to do you a favour and all I'm getting is childish fucking sarcasm from you. Listen to me, yes I made a mistake with Sophie by learning her a few things, but the more I learn her, the less chance there is of anything like this ever happening to her again. You approach her now the wrong way and she'll put you on your arse before you know what's happened. I have taught my own daughters the very same things. And these skills I have learned them will make your job a lot easier. I'm sick to death of you poking at me with accusations and curses and talking down to me like I was shit. Don't you forget who helped to orchestrate that rescue in Lithuania. If I had listened to *you* pairs' advice, my daughter would still be on the other side of Europe being fucking raped on a daily basis by all those sick bastards. But oh no, your advice was to sit here and just hope for the best, that was *your* fucking answer to everything wasn't it, just sit still and hope for the best. Well, fuck you Mercer you can find out the name for yourself, and I'll tell you something else. I have given Sophie Spencer a Glock hand-gun so you'd better get your finger out and find out who the fuck it is that she's planning on clipping. I don't care if you arrest me for doing it, go ahead and put me in jail, but I know who those girls look upon when it comes to people who actually care about them, people who genuinely doesn't ever want that to happen to them again. So, you'll have to pull out all the stops now and go over all those files of who you had in for questioning over that period of time.

His name is on those files somewhere, so good luck, because you're getting fuck all

from me…bud!"
Colin lifted his cigarettes from the work-top and made for the back door.
"If you're not arresting me today for supplying a minor with a firearm then by the time I come back in here I expect you to be gone, I'm fucking finished with you Mercer and your hard man fucking sarcasm…huh, my fucking daughters could put you on your arse before you even finished your cursing. Get out there and do your fucking job instead of people like me doing it for you. Go and find out the name before they get him." Colin Green stepped outside of his back door and slammed the door behind him.
Terry Mercer and Samantha Reynolds sat dumbstruck at Colin's outburst.
Truth be known Terry wasn't completely shocked, and all said and done, he'd deserved that. He had been a bit rough with Colin lately. He would go now and apologise to him for his behaviour. As he made to go to the back door Jillian Green said, "Don't, whatever you do, don't approach him now. He'll hurt you. When he's like this he cares nothing of consequences, so please, do as he says and leave… unless you are arresting him…just leave."
Terry and Samantha left by the front door and made their way to the car. Samantha initially climbed in but then said to her colleague "Wait here Terry, wait in the car I won't be long."
"Samantha, don't, you heard what she said."
"He's hardly going to attack me Terry is he, wait here." Samantha made her way round to the back of the house. Colin was on his hunkers smoking his cigarette with one hand on the clothes pole at the top of his garden. He said nothing as Samantha approached him. She was down on her hunkers now as well.
"Can I have one of those please Colin?" she said pointing to his cigarette packet. She picked it up and extracted a cigarette, taking the lighter offered to her.
"He means well Colin. I know sometimes he's a bit of a twat and I'll be the first to admit that. He's fucking hard work if you want the truth and there have been times when I myself felt like shooting him in the head, I kid you not…fucking twat he is sometimes. But I'll tell you something, he cares Colin. He genuinely cares about people. You should have seen his face when he was told he was invited to go to Lithuania, really, you'd think he'd won the lottery. He's cared Colin since the first day he picked up the file about all the missing girls. He didn't sleep, he admitted that to me. He felt so strongly about it that it was as though it was all his fault that the girls had been abducted. That's the kind of man he is. He was going to come outside there to apologise to you but your wife stopped him…said it was for his own good, and I believed her."
Samantha stood up onto her feet. Nothing was said as they both smoked, but then, just as Colin finished his cigarette he said to her, "The boy you're looking for is Gareth Tate.

He's seventeen years old and he lives in Hawthorne Close in Bromley. I don't know the exact number. Get him and hold him for questioning. You'd better get hold of Sophie as well and that Lisa girl. Maybe you can stop this. I want you to know something, if it were up to me, I wouldn't be stopping them...not after what's happened to my daughters, I wouldn't be stopping them, I'd be encouraging them."

Samantha stubbed out her cigarette. "Thank you Colin, from the bottom of my heart, thank you." As she began to walk out of the garden she said, "If it were up to me Colin, I'd be encouraging them as well, so now you know. Thank you."

SAFE HAVEN.

BROMLEY.

Sophie stepped off the bus to make the short walk to Safe Haven. It was time she made up with Claire and put that last little incident behind them. Claire was a very likeable girl and Sophie felt that she was forming a long-term friendship with her. Today Claire would not get the chance to make any comments about the length of her skirt because she was wearing jeans and so there'd be no chance of *that* subject being brought up but as soon as Sophie entered the premises she knew something had happened, by the look on Margaret Hall's face. Something bad. "Good morning Sophie, I'm afraid we've had a bit of bad news honey, would you like to come through to the canteen and I'll explain. The police have just left didn't you see them as you came in?"
"No, I em, I didn't notice them, what on earth has happened? You haven't been broken into have you?"
"No." Margaret sighed wearily, "We haven't Sophie, come in to the kitchen sweetheart."
Margaret smiled and spoke to a young woman who was busy washing up some dishes at the sink.
"Just leave them Rosemary, I'll get them darling after I've had a word with Sophie here." The woman smiled again and left Margaret and Sophie alone.
Margaret poured two cups of tea and sat down at the table with the teen.
"I take it you are here to see Claire Sophie?" Again she sighed heavily.
"She's a silly girl. I warned her, at least I tried to warn her, but she left here to go back home. She said he deserved another chance."
"What the hell has happened Margaret?"
"She received a text message from this Alan Flint, you know, her partner, huh, well, after texting each other for five minutes or so they decided to phone.
I heard her talking to him. I was standing outside of her room listening.
I don't make a habit of doing this but when I realised who she was talking to I kind of eves-dropped. Whatever he was saying to her it was working because I heard her referring to him as sweetheart and darling. I also heard her saying to be fair to her that she couldn't keep on living like this and hiding bruises and bumps."
Margaret sipped her tea shaking her head. "I've heard it all before Sophie, how they'll change and how they have learned their lesson and that it will never happen again."
Another sigh. "Well, after she was finished on the phone she came to see me to inform

me that she was signing out. At first she tried to hide the fact that she was going back to him. It was then that I informed her of the fact that I'd overheard some of her conversation. A row broke out between her and I. She accused me of sticking my nose into other people's business and that I was just a sad old woman who liked nothing better than to gossip about other people's affairs. That was it. She stormed off to her room to pack her things and told me she was getting to fuck out of this shit-hole, I think were her exact words. All I said to her as she passed me at reception was that I hoped everything worked out for her. I also told her not to hesitate to return here if she thought for a second that she was going to be in trouble."

"What did she say to that?"

"In a temper she said, Oh, don't you worry, this'll be the last fucking place I'd come to for help. Anyway, away she went to restart her life with this Alan Flint. That was three days ago. To cut a long story short, Claire Rennie is lying in hospital in a comma. Her injuries are horrendous. She has four broken ribs and a broken arm as well as serious head injuries. She has a fractured jaw as well. The police were here only ten minutes ago asking me bloody stupid questions about how Claire was in here. Half an hour they asked me questions. Huh, they even asked me if she'd seen her partner here, in here, can you believe that? As if I would allow the bastard in here. Anyway, they're saying that at this moment in time they have no witnesses and so they can't go accusing people of something unless they have the evidence to prove it. They would have to wait until Claire recovers consciousness before they could proceed with their enquiries, honestly it beggars belief. We all bloody know who done it but they say they need evidence before they can go and charge him. They also say that this Flint bastard is nowhere to be found. He's out there somewhere Sophie, why can't they at least make an effort to find him and question him of his whereabouts on the night in question...but no."

Sophie could see tears forming in Margaret Hall's eyes.

"I try to protect them Sophie, I try my best to discourage them from going back to these monsters, but they...they hardly ever listen to me. She's lying there in hospital, again, and this time she's fighting for her life. I told her when she came in here the first time, I told her never to go back, that we'd have a court order put on him but still the stupid girl goes back. Now look what's happened."

Sophie could tell that no matter what she said to Margaret Hall the woman would blame herself for this happening to Claire. She was one of those rare people who actually cared about her fellow human beings, especially the beaten women.

It wasn't as though she had anything against men in general, it was just that ninety-nine per cent of the victims in here had been unfortunate enough to have picked the bad ones. To try and change the subject Margaret said to her, "How are you getting on with your university work Sophie? Are you enjoying your time there? Sophie lied to Margaret Hall that she was thoroughly enjoying the courses she was on and that she was learning all the time. Sociology was a wonderful subject. In fact, she was doing just enough to convince the people who mattered that she was exhilarated with the studies and that there were endless possibilities for employment if she was successful in her subject. She'd had a meeting with her psychiatrist earlier this morning and did not mention the fact that she couldn't stand to have any male people around her, and that she was awakening regularly with images of the men and women who had degraded her, and how they all laughed and pointed to her in her nightmares. Or that she regularly woke up in a sweat because she thought that the rats had found their way into her bedroom and that they were scurrying about the floor as she tried to sleep. If she had told her these things she'd have her on drugs that would make her so drowsy that she'd hardly be able to function. Fuck that. Sophie passed her sympathies on to Margaret and said she'd come back soon to see her. She gave Margaret her mobile number and asked her to let her know if or when Claire regained consciousness. "I will sweetheart, and I'm sorry you had to hear that today pet. Now don't you let any of this stuff interfere with your studies. Maybe soon you can come back and continue your conversations with the girls in here, one or two of them have been asking where you are." Sophie said she would and then left Safe Haven…with a heavy heart.

BROMLEY POLICE STATION.

Terry and Samantha were conversing with the desk sergeant requesting her to find out the address of a certain young man who went by the name of Gareth Tate. As luck would have it sergeant Alice Thomson didn't even have to scan her computer because even as they spoke two constables entered the station. They were escorting two shop-lifters into the premises and planned to take them to one of the interview rooms. The names of the shop-lifters turned out to be Christine Hope and Gareth Tate. Both of them were registered heroin addicts.

As the two accused stood at the desk confirming their names, Terry and Samantha almost burst out laughing with elation, this was unbelievable.

Just as the two constables were explaining to their sergeant why they were being brought in Terry interrupted them.

"Excuse me my good friends, we'll take mister Tate with us.

He and I have lots to discuss. Detective Reynolds and I will take it from here with this young gentleman. You can have all the fun Christine with these two young officers here in the interview room. You can take the rap for young Gareth here as well, because he's coming with us."

The girl looked no more than fourteen or fifteen years of age.

She scowled at Mercer dressed in scruffy unwashed denims and even scruffier trainers that had long since seen better days. Her hair was cut short and was the brightest ginger he had ever seen. "Fuck you." She replied to detective Terrence Mercer as he and his fellow detective marched Gareth away from the desk.

"I fear not sweetheart." He replied over his shoulder to the disgruntled youth. Gareth Tate was dressed similarly to his female companion, although someone had been taking better care of *his* denims.

He looked much older than his seventeen years. The unshaven face and unkempt light brown hair together with the pot-holes and crevices that acne had so cruelly inflicted upon him gave him the appearance of an older boy. As they walked Tate said, "What the fuck is this about? Why do you need to speak with me?

I know you are detectives. I haven't done anything wrong."

"You haven't done anything wrong mister Tate?" said Mercer.

"So those two officers back there at the desk were just making that up about you and your girlfriend shop-lifting then? You have been wrongly arrested then?"

"I don't mean that, I mean I haven't done anything wrong that merits two detectives questioning me, that's what I meant. Detectives only speak to you when it's serious

shit, and stuff like that. I haven't done anything…not like that…shit."
They continued down the corridor until they came to one of the interview rooms.
"This'll do Gareth, in here bud, in you go, take a seat, we're going to be here for a while, I can tell already. Oh, have you had your hit today, or whatever you call it these days, your fix, have you had your shit today?"
Tate made a feeble attempt at proclaiming himself as a non-drug-user.
"I'm not a fucking junky, and you have no right to imply that I am, that's all fucking wrong pal, and-."
Mercer grabbed the youth by the hand and pulled up his sleeve.
The boys' wrist was stick-thin, and covered with needle-punctures.
Nothing more was said. He pulled back the boys' sleeve and then proceeded to take off his jacket and fold it over the chair. The young man looked worried, or at least flustered, agitated. Samantha took off her jacket and hung it up on one of the three pegs on the wall. By doing this the two detectives were giving the youth the impression that they were indeed going to be here for a while.
That also informed Tate that the time spent in here was going to be somewhat uncomfortable. They could hold him here for as long as eight hours before they were obliged either to release him or charge him with something. At this moment in time Tate was scratching his head metaphorically speaking wondering what on earth they were planning to do with him. Apart from the shop-lifting he couldn't think of anything serious enough for him to be questioned by detectives.
Mercer sat down opposite the boy. Samantha sat next to Mercer.
"You're not a drug-user huh? Well I can see by the mess on your arms that you certainly do not suffer from belonephobia, that's for sure."
Samantha leaned over the table and almost whispered "That word means fear of needles Gareth, he's a bastard sometimes isn't he?
I myself Gareth suffer from pocrescophobia."
Mercer now smiled first at Samantha, and then to Tate. "That means fear of gaining weight Gareth, I'm not the only bastard here, am I?"
Mercer sat straight up on his chair. "Anyway Gareth, why did you deny being a drug user, Christ you're registered for goodness sakes. But that's not why you are here today, oh no. It's a much more serious matter."
Suddenly Mercer's face was deadly serious.
"You are here today kiddo for your own good. You are being protected.
There's a mark on your scalp, and you'd better hope we find the person who is gunning for you before it's time for us to release you. If we don't, then you'll march out of here and from that moment in time your days are numbered I kid you not sunshine so I

would advise you to answer the questions we are about to ask you with complete honesty. If you do that then perhaps we can save your arse. If not…"

There was silence in the room while Mercer's words hung in the air.

Gareth Tate was aware of the fact that there was nothing jovial about the detectives' words any more. But he couldn't for the life of him think of anyone who would want him dead. Although, according to this detective, it was a fact. Mercer suddenly rose up from his chair. "Right, I'll just go and get the coffee detective Reynolds, would you like one Gareth ? At first the youth thought he was joking with him again but Mercer stood waiting for an answer.

"Come on we haven't got all day do you want one or not.?"

"Yes please…eh sir…milk and sugar…sir."

"Ok, I shan't be long detective Reynolds, milk and sugar for the lying drug addict."

Mercer left the room closing the door behind him.

Samantha Reynolds was looking at some documents she'd placed on the table. There was silence now and the youth didn't know whether or not to start any kind of conversation. Eventually he plucked up the courage to speak.

"Excuse me miss, can you tell me what this is all about please?"

Samantha raised her head and smiled at the teenager. "Weren't you listening? Detective Mercer informed you of what this is about. We have brought you in here because someone is desperate to kill you, and as far as I can tell your murder would be revenge because that's what was said to their accomplice. What you can do to increase your chances of survival is to tell us, revenge for what?

What have you done to somebody Gareth that would make them want to kill you? It must be something bad or horrific. Anyway detective Mercer will explain to you again the importance of your honesty, and by the way he wasn't joking about your fix. If you need methadone or whatever the hell you get we can arrange for a pharmacist to come and administer the dose because we're not having you making complaints about being treated unfairly whilst you were in here, so, tell us now before we start the interview."

"I'm ok miss, I'll be ok until later tonight, I've had eh…"

"Yes, you've had a fix today am I right? That would be why you were caught shop-lifting, you'd be all relaxed and drowsy, you and your little friend through there. She's a bit young for you is she not Gareth, is she legal? I mean, is she old enough for you to stick your little shrivelled drugged-up fucked-up penis into her?"

"She's nearly nineteen miss."

"Fuck off, never, she's never nineteen. That's what she's telling you. She's never nineteen."

She is miss, you can check her birth certificate, it's on her record."

"Well, she won't be looking younger than her years if she persists in taking that heroin shit that's for sure. Look at you, you're seventeen and yet you look about twenty fucking seven and that's no lie, look at all the mess on your face, fucking spots and holes and red raw boil things weeping all over the place, dirty needles Gareth?"
"Acne miss, something I cannot control. I've had it since I was twelve, it's out of my control."
"Yes, just like your heroin habit, the only difference being, you had a choice whether or not to be a silly cunt and inject that shit into your body or not. You made the wrong choice, and inadvertently because of that choice that's why you are in here today and not in university making something of yourself, instead, you're in here making a cunt of yourself and at risk of being shot in your acne-infested face."
If Tate had thought for one minute that because he was left alone with the female detective, that he could play on the weaker-sex ploy. He found out now that he was seriously mistaken. She was verbally tearing lumps out of him and down-grading him beyond belief. There would be no sympathy here.
A few moments later Terry Mercer returned with the beverages.
"Hey, detective Reynolds, you know the little ginger bint who Gareth here is shagging? Well, guess what age she is, what age do you think she is?"
Samantha Reynolds smiled at her superior. "Oh, I'd say she'll be about nineteen sir, something like that, eighteen or nineteen. What age is she sir?" she said, smiling.
Mercer placed the tray on the table and mumbled, "She's a hundred and forty-one that's what age she is now can we get on with our interview."
Samantha leaned forward over the table to retrieve her cup of coffee.
As she did she spoke to Mercer. "I have explained to mister Tate here how important it is to tell us what he's done to make someone want to kill him."
As mercer sipped his cup he looked at the boy straight in the face.
"I have asked you to be honest Gareth so I think it's only fair that I am honest with you." He took a breath and said "We know that you were brought in here a few months ago, and we know why you were brought in. In case you have forgotten I'll remind you. Someone at some point identified you as an accomplice to a kidnapping."
Tate shuffled on his seat. "Ah, now I get it, is that all this is about. I thought I'd been all through that, and by the way, whoever that was never had any proof whatsoever that it was me. That's why I was released. Fucking hell, I thought it was something serious you had me in here for. For a minute there I thought-."
Mercer raised his hand to stop the youth talking. "Well, I'm glad mister Tate that you feel better now, and that you think that this is not serious but let me ask you something. What was it specifically you were being accused of, can you remember?

What were you supposed to be doing exactly to be accused? And let me tell you something else, you were there, whether or not you were guilty. You see, those girls who were kidnapped were taken out of the country over into Eastern Europe, and they were subjected to the most horrendous experiences you could ever imagine. Sexual experiences. And here's the bugger, not just once but several times a day, every day. Can you imagine being stuck in a room and you had all these strangers coming in Gareth, just to shag your arse, four, maybe five times a day, like I say, every day. Or for two or three men to have their way with you while your arse bled and then they decide to ejaculate into your mouth and make you swallow the sperm, and then laugh at you when you vomited it back out, choking with the experience, can you imagine that? Well, Gareth, some very brave soldiers went over there and rescued the girls from this living hell they had endured and brought them back safely to this country. Now, as you can imagine, some of these poor creatures have been mentally scarred for life. They don't want to be anywhere near boys now. They have been raped hundreds of times, some of them losing their virginity to these fuck heads over there. Anyway, as I was saying, they were all brought back home safely, at least physically safe...not so sure about mentally safe bud.

Now then mister Gareth Tate, I know full well that when you were brought in here you had a fancy lawyer who was able to worm you out of the equation, however, some of these girls have excellent memories Gareth, and God forbid, if any of those girls got a good look at whoever had abducted them, well, I for one would not like to be in their shoes. What I'm saying Gareth is, it won't matter one monkey's fuck to them how good your solicitor is or was, they are past all that.

If they know who it was, then they are coming for them, because whoever helped abduct them well, in their eyes, they are the ones who started all those horrible experiences. It's down to them. Now, I'll ask you this one last time, and be careful how you answer me, because once you are out of this door there is nothing more we can do to save you. Do you know anyone who would want to seek revenge on your arse? Nobody is going to say anything now about the kidnappings, that's all done and dusted, so have no fear of that, but whatever you do, if you value your life kid tell us now if you had anything to do with those kidnappings. Tell us now, and I promise you here and now it goes no further than Samantha and me, I give you my word, we both do."

Mercer continued to lie to the youth. "I'll tell you something else kid, they won't stop at you, they'll kill your mother and father as well. It's not girls coming for you kid, it's their fathers, and so you can imagine the fury they're feeling after what's been done to their daughters. I'm pleading with you kid, tell us now so that we can protect you from their wrath. You surely wouldn't want anything to happen to your mother and father. Do you have any brothers or sisters? Because you know what they'll do to them, before they kill them…just tell us Gareth, this is serious son, I mean really serious."

The youth took a sip of his coffee, and looked first to Samantha and then to Terry Mercer. "I was accused of grabbing a girl and bundling her into a van. I was supposed to be disguised as a street-sweeper. I never even-."

"Hold it there Gareth, we know all that kid, we know all about it.

What we need you to tell us is, were you guilty? Was it you who bundled the girl into the van. Now I know how hard it is to be addicted to something and how desperate things can get when you need money."

Mercer looked into the boys' face. "Somebody approached you and offered you money didn't they? They offered you money to do it and you were desperate for drugs, it was something like that wasn't it Gareth. Somebody offered you money to do it, am I right?"

Just for a few moments it looked like the youth was about to confess, but then he just sat there and started to smile. "Nice try sir, but I was released on the grounds of insufficient evidence. I don't know what you're talking about just as I didn't know then when I was brought in for questioning. So, if there is nothing else you wish to discuss then I suggest that you charge me for the shop-lifting and then release me. If there is anything else you wish to discuss with me then I insist that I have my solicitor in here with me, and by the way sir, you make a lovely cup of coffee." Samantha Reynolds switched off the recorder and sat back on her chair. Terry smiled in the boys' face again. "You've obviously not been listening to me kid. You can sit there and smile until your hearts' content, but you are in serious trouble boy, make no mistake about that.

Now, we have it recorded, this interview, you know, after they find your body, it's there for all to hear that we pleaded with you to try and help you out of this very serious situation you are in. No blame can be placed on Samantha and I that we didn't give you fair warning of the very real danger you are in.

We've tried kid, but like I said, the people who are coming for you are not interested in the law. They don't want to see you put in jail, oh no, they want you buried pal. Dead and buried. Then, and only then will they be satisfied that justice has been done.

So, mister Gareth Tate, after you have finished your coffee, we will escort you back to the desk where you will be charged for the shop-lifting and then most likely you'll be released. And from that moment on kid the clock will be ticking down the minutes left in your pointless sad little span of time you have had on this earth. I would wish you all the best for the future, but that would be hypocrisy on my part because I already know that you don't have a future.

All you have now my friend is borrowed time.

Please remember my words here and now when they have you where they want you and they will, because I could go and bring them in and threaten them with the consequences of taking the law into their own hands, but it won't change a thing. It's exactly like you said yourself mister Tate, insufficient evidence. If we don't have the evidence, then they walk. And then they'll come for you. Look over your shoulder boy wherever you go, and like I said, remember these words I've said here today. The last day you had a chance to stop all this, and to eliminate the certainty of your death. You will suffer kid. They won't make it quick. They'll torture you, perhaps for days on end until they feel the time is right to send your soul to wherever it is destined to go.

Now, you have yourself a nice day Gareth, and say your goodbyes' to your little ginger girlfriend through there.

If I were you, I would inform her not to be anywhere near you from now on, after all, she hasn't done anything wrong other than to pick up a few stolen items to feed her habit, and to make the mistake of making your acquaintance."

Mercer sighed and smiled sympathetically to the youth. "I'm sorry for you kid, really because I can see that you think that this is just all a big joke.

You are smiling at the only two people on God's good earth who could have at least mitigated your problem, and believe me Gareth, you do have a problem.

But, it's your decision kid, it's your life…well, what is left of it, get to fuck out of here and report to Sergeant Thomson at the desk, on you go."

EDGELEY ROAD.

CLAPHAM.

SW LONDON.

Alan Flint had had a very long tiresome day. As is the case with every construction foreman the stresses of the day can sometimes be immense.
Deliveries not arriving on time, building progress delayed, carpenters not turning up, or arriving more than two hours late. Plumbers complaining about joiners laying down floors before copper pipes had been installed, plasterers moaning about not having received last months' bonuses for work completed, and lets' not forget labourers complaining about inadequate heating in the canteen.
He climbed laboriously out of his BMW and made his way to his house.
The house where he'd grown up with his father and mother and two sisters, and the house that was once more, his home. His mother had died last year and left their home to him. His two sisters had both married into money and had no need whatsoever of the house. They hadn't even asked him for a token payment.
In her will his mother had suggested that the property be sold and the proceeds divided equally but his sisters had told him to do whatever he wanted with it.
One of them lived in Utah in the united states, the other lived on the outskirts of Aberdeen. At their mothers' funeral they'd all had a chat about her estate and everything had been more or less finalised there and then.
That family reunion had been the first time in more than twelve years that the siblings had actually sat down to a meal together.
He couldn't visualise the occasion happening again any time soon.
He entered the hallway and closed the door behind him, kicking off his heavy steel-capped boots. He was greeted by lovely comforting warm air as he made his way down the hall to his living room, glad that he had persuaded his mother three years earlier to have the new central-heating system installed. The house felt homely to him, just as it had all those years ago. Even if for some reason the premises hadn't landed in his hands he would have always remembered it. He had had a happy childhood and grew up aware of how lucky he was and that there were other kids in his class at school who were not as fortunate as he was. He and his sisters were always taken on good holidays every summer and were never disappointed with anything their parents bought them for birthdays or Christmases. In one of the four bedrooms in the house there were

boxes and boxes of holiday photographs bundled together and dated from all of the holidays and special events throughout their childhoods. When he found time he'd have to get them all and take them to the tip, or start a fire outside in the back yard and burn them. To his mother the photographs were precious, but to him they were merely taking up valuable space. In that same room his mothers' wardrobes still stood untouched. Her clothes still hung up on their hangers. He would have to take them to the charity shop when he found the time. There were in fact lots of things to do in here, but they would have to wait. He was at his work six days a week and on each of those days he didn't make it back home until after seven, as was the case tonight. He walked into his kitchen and retrieved a bottle of beer from his fridge and then hunted in the freezer-drawer for something to eat.

"Fuck it, I'll order out." He mumbled, as he returned to his living room.

He switched on his TV and sat down to enjoy his beverage. He would have his beer as he listened to the evening news and then have his shower and then order his meal. By the time his meal would arrive and by the time he'd consumed it, it would be time to go to bed, and then the whole bloody process would begin again, starting from six o clock in the morning. The delayed deliveries, the lack of building progress, the joiners late for work again, the unpaid plasterers, the moaning fucking labourers, and the chiefs tearing lumps out of him because they were way behind schedule and at risk of being financially penalised.

He found himself drifting off with the comfort of the central-heating, and that glad-I'm-home feeling that you only get when you've had a long arduous day.

Suddenly his TV went off. Then the lights.

"What the fuck?" Now in complete darkness, other than the dim light shining through his living room window from the street lamp outside, he cursed some other inadequate bastard for severing a fucking cable doing unnecessary road-works. He had a torch in his car which he'd have to retrieve because he'd have to check his meters just in case it was a fault in his own electrics. His hallway was in complete darkness as he made his way down to the front door. He groped around until he found his boots. There was no way he could put them back on without untying the laces. "Oh you fucking stinking bastard!" He cursed as he fumbled with the boot-laces. Eventually he had to open the door to let in the light from outside, and of course by doing that he was letting all the cold air into the house. "Absolute useless fucking bastards that you are!" He groaned referring to the road-works men. "You're as useless as those fucking baboons that I have to deal with every day, useless twats!" At last, he was able to slip on his work-boots again and make his way to the car. He salvaged the torch from somewhere in the boot. It was lying at the bottom underneath theodolite stands and spirit-levels and boxes of tools and rolls and rolls of construction plans and boxes of rubber gloves. He locked the car and just before he entered his house he switched on the torch. Nothing. Off and on he switched it several times. Nothing.

"John, I'm going to sever your fucking pelvis with a still saw I swear, you useless vagrant that you are!"

Alan Flint was referring to the night watchman who occasionally borrowed his torch whenever he'd mislaid his own.

He was also guilty of taking out the batteries and not replacing them, or forgetting to replace them. The vagrant title he'd given John Stokes was because he lived in a bed and breakfast since he and his wife had parted company.

He re-entered the house closing the door behind him and made his way down to the kitchen. He knew where there were spare batteries. He fumbled his way to the specific drawer where the batteries were and managed to find them.

He placed two triple A's into his torch and switched it on.

Many years ago his father had built a basement-cellar when the house was being renovated and where access to all the services could be reached easily.

The key for the basement hung on the wall outside of the door.

He was almost certain that the fault, whatever it was, had nothing to do with his power-box. But he would check it anyway. If it had been careless work-men, then the lights would come back on themselves eventually, they would repair the cable. If he had looked closer outside, he would have noticed that all his neighbours still had their electrics on. He placed the single large key into the door and turned it. As he descended the stone steps he remembered his sisters when they were about ten years old being scared to come down here because they'd been told, by him, that it was haunted, and that an old man who had lived in the house many years ago would come out of the walls and kill any children who dared to `trespass.` Sophie Spencer did not come from out of the wall, but she did come from underneath the stair-well, armed with Alan Flints' very own nail-bar which had been conveniently lying on a work-bench down here. As Alan approached the power box he immediately saw the problem. Every single one of the power switches had been put up. They had all been deliberately switched off. "What the fuck"?

What the fuck happened to be the last words he uttered before he was rendered unconscious by the power of the swipe Sophie Spencer administered to the back of his head with Alan Flint's favourite nail bar.

LEXINGTON SQUARE.

BROMLEY.

"I'm afraid I have no idea Terry why she'd be refusing to answer her phone. She hasn't said anything to David or I about being annoyed at anyone."
Mandy Spencer seemed genuinely confused about her daughters' behaviour.
"I'm sure if she was annoyed at you Terry for something she'd have said something, you know what she's like."
And that, if Terry was being honest was the problem. He *did* know what she was like. But Mandy didn't. He had no idea of how she used to be prior to Lithuania, but he certainly knew what she was like now. Terry sat beside Samantha on one of the sofas. Directly opposite them sat Mandy and her son David.
"Well" started Terry, I'm afraid if she doesn't respond to-."
"Oh, here she's back now." Interrupted Mandy, as she rose from the sofa.
A taxi had pulled up just outside her door. Sophie Spencer climbed out of the vehicle and made her way to her front door. She entered the house shouting out even before she'd entered the living room. "Hi mum, hi David, what's for supper, I'm starving. Is that Terry's car mum, is Terry here?"
Sophie entered the living room. "Hiya. What a nice surprise Terry and Samantha, it's been a while since we've had a chat."
"Hello Sophie, yes it has been a while." said Terry. "But it wouldn't have been so long if you'd answered your phone young lady. Samantha and I need to have a long chat with you, a private one, and an uninterrupted one.
Now, I know it's getting a bit late tonight but we must talk, and so tomorrow morning I want you to come into town and meet us-."
Once again Terry was interrupted, this time by Sophie.
"Terry, I know what this is about, I do, but if you'll just wait for a few minutes while I make myself a sandwich then I will explain everything, and I mean everything. Anyway, I want my mum and my brother to hear what I have to say. Now, can you give me ten minutes whilst I have shower? Mum, would you make me a cheese and ham sandwich please, I know it's your night off but just a sandwich and I won't bother you again tonight. I'll bring you your breakfast in bed tomorrow morning."
Even Terry smiled at the girl's humour, and if he hadn't known better he would have believed that there wasn't much wrong with Sophie. But he did know better. It would be interesting to hear what she had to say.

"No problem Sophie." said Terry. "as long as your mum doesn't mind us being here at this time of night." It was coming up to 10:30.

"It's fine Terry." Said Mandy. "we're not exactly early-bedders' in this household, we're always up watching something, usually bloody rock music programs eh David."

Terry felt genuinely sorry for the woman in front of him.

He had witnessed her desperation when her beloved daughter had been taken away from her. His biggest fear now, was that Sophie was going to do something that would put her liberty at risk, and that if she went through with this, then he would be coming back here to take Sophie away again, and this time she wouldn't be coming back home, and he would be the cause of Mandy Spencer's heartache...this time. They would no longer be friends.

He spoke now to Mandy. "Listen, me and Samantha are going outside for a cigarette, anyway we'll have to inform our superior of our whereabouts. Can we take our cups of tea out with us?"

"Of course, would you like some cheese and toast or something while we're waiting on Sophie, it's no bother."

"Thanks, we're fine Mandy, thank you for the offer." Replied Samantha as the two detectives made their way out to the car. They had no need whatsoever to contact Polly Sheppard. It was just so that he could have this conversation with his colleague. They had both scrutinised the message that Colin Green had sent them regarding Sophie and her friend Lisa. The last message Sophie had sent her friend read; *Ok Lisa, that's it settled then. We'll do it in two days' time.*

Terry lit his cigarette and exhaled smoke up into the night air. He leaned back on the car resting his back. As he did, he said to Sam. "I wonder what cock and bull story she's going to come out with. She can't tell us that her phone is not working because we both know that it is. She's been communicating with Lisa Jensen constantly, and by the way Samantha, we're heading back over there to her house first thing in the morning. She's just as keen on doing this thing as Sophie is. They're definitely collaborating with this revenge shit." Samantha was leaning on the car with one hand on the roof while she smoked her cigarette with the other.

"She wants her brother and her mum to hear what she has to say. She's saying that she knows what this is all about. Do you think that Colin Green has informed her of what's happening? Even though he's bugged her phone. He's maybe feeling guilty for what he's done to her."

"That's a good point Sam. We know he thinks the world of her, you know, not in a silly way, but like she's another daughter, he certainly treats her like his own." Five minutes later they were all seated in the living room. Sophie had gone up-stairs again and had brought down a carrier bag which she'd placed at her feet. No-one asked her what it was or why she'd brought it down.

She lit up a cigarette. "Ok mum, David, be prepared to be shocked with what I have to tell you, but please let me finish before you pass any comment. Terry is here mum for a very serious matter. He is here because he found out somehow that I planned to kill someone."

"What? You planned to kill Sophie?"

"Mum, please. How he found out I do not know, but he did. I have been planning something with Lisa Jensen mum. You see, she found out who it was that bundled us into the van on the days we were abducted. We had a plan of revenge that we were going to carry out."

"Sophie, tell Terry who it is and he'll arrest him, won't you Terry, you'll put the bugger in jail."

Sophie continued. "Mum, it's not as plain and simple as that, is it Terry. You see mum, this man was indeed taken in for questioning not long after it happened. There was insufficient evidence to convict him and so he was released. Unless you have absolute concrete evidence then there's nothing anyone can do. That was why Lisa and I were going to kill him ourselves. We would administer our own punishment upon him. That is why Terry and Samantha are here mum, and that is why I have deliberately been ignoring his texts and calls. However, Lisa and I have come to our senses. If we went ahead and killed him then we would spend the best years of our lives in prison and the people who done this to us would inadvertently win. That is not going to happen. Terry, you can check this up if you like but I have changed my psychiatrist. I was getting nowhere with misses Kirkpatrick. She just wasn't getting where I was coming from. I have been lying to you mum about how much I am enjoying university. I have hardly been attending, and when I do attend, my mind is not where it should be. I had become obsessed with taking revenge on the bastard who had helped to kidnap me. Lisa Jensen was of the same frame of mind." Sophie handed the carrier bag to Terry. "Here, this is for you Terry, I think you know what's in there. Take it away, I have no need of it any more. Don't ask me where I got it and then I won't have to tell you any lies, just take it away with you tonight. I'm sorry mum, but that's what's been going on in your daughters' mind...but it's all ok now mum, I assure you. I'm all sorted out now, and so is Lisa."

For the first time in the conversation Sophie's brother spoke.

"Do I know this guy Sophie?"

"David, don't even go there." replied Sophie. "I know you mean well, but don't even think about it, don't you think I've put mum and you through enough? Anyway, I don't think you know him David, and besides, it wouldn't be much fun taking revenge on him now. He's a junkie. He's addicted to heroin. He's been kicked out of his house for stealing a large sum of money from his father. His father has turned his back on him. That poor unfortunate bastard is suffering enough. It won't be long before he lands himself in serious trouble and then he'll end up in prison for a long time, and thankfully, me and Lisa will have had nothing at all to do with it." Sophie rose to her feet and approached Terry. "I'm really grateful Terry for what you and Samantha are doing and have done, but you have nothing to fear, and neither does the junkie, at least, not from me. It's at this point where I put my life plans into gear. I'm determined to get all my qualifications and start to work on a career for myself and start to repay my mum here for everything she's done for me over the years. Yes, it was a horrible experience over in Lithuania, but it's over, it's done, and I'm home and safe and have the rest of my life to look forward to. From the bottom of my heart Terry, I thank you, you and Samantha, for caring enough to protect me from myself. I shudder to think what would have happened to me if I hadn't come to my senses. Now, I'm off to bed, I have an early start in the morning. What is it they say when you're starting over? Tomorrow is the first day of the rest of your life." Sophie kissed her mum and said goodnight to her brother and to Terry and Samantha. "As promised mum, I shall bring you breakfast in bed in the morning. Once again Terry Samantha, thank you for everything, especially going over to Lithuania to help rescue me. I couldn't let you down after doing all that."

Terry had to say this. He really didn't want to, but he had to. He wanted to see her response. "Just before you go to bed Sophie. You said to Lisa last night, that's it then Lisa, we'll do it in two days' time. What is it you're going to do in two days' time if you don't mind me asking?"

As quick as lightning Sophie replied, "Lisa and I are going to be joining the gym, we have to get ourselves in shape. You must have spoken to Lisa for you to know that Terry, or has she shown' you her phone?"

Terry avoided answering Sophie's question by saying, "Joining a gym? Look at you woman, you're as fit as a flea, there's not an ounce of fat on you, you're like a bloody model, isn't she Sam?"

"Hell yes, I am quite envious of your figure Sophie, you young girls, you worry about nothing, but I know where you're coming from. It doesn't do any harm to stay healthy and fit Sophie, tell him to shut his bloody mouth. You might want to get him a membership when you're there, look at the belly on him. He pretends to you Mandy that he doesn't really eat much, I kid you not, he eats like a bloody grizzly bear just before hibernation, bloody stuffing his face every two minutes. Anyway, we'll have to be heading off now, thank you Sophie for putting our minds at rest now that we know you've had a change of heart. We were genuinely worried for you sweetheart. What's the name of your new psychiatrist?"

"Emily Crawford, and she's a lot better than misses Kirkpatrick that's for sure. I've only had one meeting with her and that was just an introduction really, but I can tell when people are good at what they do, just like you two, you just know instinctively when people are genuine don't you, anyway, I'm off to bed, goodnight all." Sophie left the room and headed off to her bedroom.

"Well, that must have been quite a shock to you Mandy." said Samantha as she rose to her feet. "It's all fine now though, you heard what she said. No-one could have blamed her Mandy for feeling that way. And the fact that she now knows who it was, I admire her. That's a strong girl you've raised there Mandy, you should be proud of yourself for having raised a daughter to be as strong-willed as she is. And you too David. But please, listen to what your sister said there, don't you be going out there hunting for him, your mum's had enough worries to deal with lately. I take my hat off to you though for looking out for her."

Mandy stood up and said, "What's in the bag Terry?"

"Nothing at all Mandy for you to concern yourself with I promise you, don't worry about a thing."

The two detectives left the house and walked down the path to their car. "Christ he's given her a bloody Smith and Wesson 45 calibre pistol. She'd have taken some buggers' head clean off if she'd used this."

"What do you think Terry?" said Samantha as she climbed into the vehicle.

"Well, we have to give her the benefit of the doubt just now Sam. She hasn't done anything to break the law, at least as things stand. But we're still going over to have a chat with Lisa in the morning. If Sophie texts her tonight, she'll be wanting to know why she let us see her phone. If Lisa tells her she hasn't let us see it, then she'll be wondering how on earth we found out about her message concerning the two days thing, that'll get her thinking. At least we know that Colin Green hasn't told her what he's done."

As Terry climbed into the drivers' side of the car, he happened to look up at Sophie's bedroom window. Her dark silhouette looked sinister against the light as she stared down at him, not waving, but just standing with her arms wide and up in the air. Then she drew the curtains.

SCOTLAND YARD.

BROADWAY VICTORIA.

The following morning Terry and Samantha had spoken to Polly Sheppard to ask for her permission to put surveillance on to Sophie Spencer, just for this morning, or until she made her way to Greenwich university. They had already been to see Sophie's doctor and inquired if she had changed her psychiatrist. It turned out that Sophie had been telling the truth, she had indeed terminated her counselling with misses Kirkpatrick and had a whole new schedule in place with miss Emily Crawford. Sophie's doctor thought that it was because misses Kirkpatrick was on the elderly side that she and Sophie didn't exactly hit it off, and the fact that Emily Crawford was considerably younger would make it easier for her to connect. "Only time will tell." said the doctor, walking away from the detectives and giving out the very clear message to them that they'd taken up enough of his valuable time.

By the time they arrived back at Scotland Yard they'd been informed that Sophie Spencer had entered the university premises at 10:15am. She had taken a bus out from Bromley.

Sophie had known that she'd be followed and had played along. She'd spotted them as soon as she'd boarded the bus. She knew that Terry would do this, that he wouldn't trust anything she said to him. She could tell last night that he wasn't really buying what she was telling them, but she also knew that she was getting a message to him right in front of her mum and brother by explaining to Mandy that, unless you have absolute concrete evidence then there is no way you can charge anyone. Her equanimous posture would have led him to believe that she was being at least, partly truthful. Terry and Samantha were going to be disappointed later today as well when she would buy her new phone. She'd called Lisa last night on her land line and asked her if she'd had a visit from Mercer. Lisa said she hadn't and so that meant that somehow they'd managed to bug one of their phones, maybe both. She told Lisa to buy another phone or change back to an old one if she had one in the house. Also, what they had planned would have to be put on hold for a while, it was too dangerous to attempt anything just now. She also informed Lisa that she'd probably have surveillance on her but not to worry and just go about her business as normal. Sophie then arranged to meet with Lisa at around five o clock this afternoon. She climbed the steps along with dozens of fellow students all heading to one of the lecture halls. She stopped half way up the stairs to see if surveillance was still there. She had spotted them upon her arrival. They were just pulling away. She about-turned and began to descend the stairs again heading for the canteen, where she would have a cup of coffee and then continue with her plans for the day. Ten minutes later Sophie sat in the canteen with her beverage.

She called Margaret Hall at Safe Haven to see if there had been any change in Claire Rennie's condition. There was some good news. Claire was now out of intensive care. She'd regained consciousness from her coma. Her condition now was stable. At least that was one bit of good news. Whether or not the experience was enough for Claire to finally see sense, well, that remained to be seen.

Suddenly, she cringed. A young student sat down at her table uninvited.

"Hi, I'm Connor, I've seen you going about here. You don't seem to have many friends. Anyway, I was wondering if you'd like to go out for a drink with me some time soon, I was thinking maybe-."

"Just leave!"

"Hey, you don't have to be like that, I'm only asking if-."

"Just fucking leave please." She snapped through gritted teeth. "For your own good, take a hike, I won't be telling you again. I don't want to go out with you ok? Not now, not ever, now just leave the table please, and next time, wait until someone asks you to join them instead of just planting yourself down uninvited. If you come near me again I will hurt you very badly, now leave."

The bewildered student left Sophie's table quite shell-shocked, and gutted, because he'd actually felt sorry for her not having any friends. This one-minute encounter he'd just had with her told him exactly why she had no friends…she didn't want any.

EDGELEY ROAD.

CLAPHAM.

SW LONDON.

Alan Flint had lost all trace of time. He was numb from head to toe. He was also extremely cold. In the basement where he'd been secured to an old wooden chair he had awoken from a state of unconsciousness to find the room completely empty. At least he was sure it was empty. Someone had struck him on the back of his head with something and when he had come round he found himself in this present condition, bound extremely tightly to the arms of the chair. To make matters even worse, the room was in complete darkness. Whoever had done this to him hadn't bothered to turn the lights back on and because it was a basement there were no windows and so he had no idea of what time of the day it was. He didn't know how long he'd been unconscious therefore he couldn't tell if it was still night or if it was the next day. His pulse thumped like a jack-hammer in his head. He'd also discovered upon regaining consciousness that he had urinated himself. His feet were frozen and he had no feelings whatsoever in them or his legs for that matter.

His brain was working overtime trying to figure out why this had been done to him. He surmised that it hadn't been burglars, they wouldn't have tied him up like this. They would have killed him or just left him lying unconscious. He was, for the first time in his entire life completely and utterly helpless. His mouth had been secured with masking-tape, although whoever had done this needn't have bothered because his father had long-ago sound-proofed the room when he'd been learning the drums at the age of thirteen and so he could scream his head off and no-one would hear him. In a situation like this, the human mind goes into overdrive. It tries it's best to make sense out of the situation.

It also weighs up the possibilities, the what-if's and the if-not's.

What if he was just going to be left here? He was so tightly secured there was no way on earth he could free himself from the chair. He had tried to rock the chair over but the chair had been secured to the floor by means of two lengths of six-by-four pieces of CLS timber which had been drilled into the concrete floor. They had used four-inch masonry screws for the job. Some of the excess screws lay around his feet all around the chair. Even his drill that had been used for the job lay close by. That was as far as he could see though. Other than that, complete darkness. He was trying to fight it, but panic was setting in now at the thought of what would happen if he was left here in a completely sound-proofed basement. Suddenly he heard the door at the top of the steps being opened, and then closed. Whoever had opened the door had done it with the hall light off because no light came into the basement.

He was still in darkness. He smelled food, onions or something similar.

The light came on. At first he almost cried out with the pain as the sudden light attacked his eyes. As his vision adjusted to the light he focused on a female form standing just to his left at his work-bench.

A policewoman? Was this a policewoman?

She stood with what looked like a brown paper bag over her head.

But the uniform, It was a policewoman.

She pulled up another chair and placed it a few feet in front of him but as she sat down her back was to him. She took off the paper bag and then opened up a cardboard food carton and took something out of it and began to eat.

Still with her back to him.

"Mm, cheese and onion pasties, my favourite. I expect you'll be a bit peckish by now."

So this was the person who had done this to him, but why?

And more to the point, what else was she going to do to him? If only she would take the masking tape from his mouth, then at least he could find out why she had done this to him. She drank from a bottle of something and then continued to eat, still with her back to him. After a few minutes she threw one of the pasties down over her shoulder onto the floor in front of him. She had replaced the brown paper bag back over her head. The eyes were cut out of it as was the mouth-piece. She spun the chair round so that she was now facing him, and lit up a cigarette. If this was a police-woman then she certainly wasn't working officially.

"You, are a very clever bastard are you not?

I wonder how long you've been getting away with this?

No wonder my colleagues can't find you."

She took a long drag of her cigarette.

"You work for Condor Construction and have done for more than eight years, am I right?" Alan Flint nodded his head, vigorously, keen for the communication to continue.

"Oh, by the way, Claire has come out of her coma, that's good news isn't it?"

Now he was scared. Now he knew.

"We called the hospital this morning and they told us that perhaps in a couple of weeks or so she'll be fit and well enough to answer some questions. According to our records, this isn't the first time that you've laid into her, is that correct?"

Alan Flint groaned under the masking tape.

"Just nod your head...or shake it, depending on your answer.
Now, have you beaten the girl before and had her in hospital yes or no, it's a simple question. Nod or shake."
Flint nodded his head. There was no point shaking it, they would have it on file. She rose up from her chair and walked over to the work-bench, picking up the very same nail-bar that had rendered him unconscious. He knew what was coming next. At least he thought he did. Standing in front of him with the nail-bar in her right hand and her cigarette in her left, and with the paper bag over her head the scene in front of him was nothing less than a nightmare.
"As I was saying, you are a very clever bastard are you not, but alas, not too clever for constable Reed here, no sir. The reason why my colleagues can't find sight nor sound of you is perfectly simple isn't it mister Carter. Mister James Carter. Nothing like Alan Flint is it. As far as Claire is concerned, that's your name Alan Flint, but when I made independent enquiries, well, I found out from the guys who used to drink with you in your local in Bromley, until you stopped going that is, that, low and behold, that's not your name at all. When I made further inquiries at your place of work, they tell me that the only foreman on their site is not Alan Flint, but James Carter. I should be a detective don't you think? I mean my superiors couldn't find that out about you, but I did, and do you know how I done it? Do you? I'll tell you. I put on the shortest skirt I could find and I visited your local and I asked questions about you saying that you worked in the construction industry. They were queuing up to fuck me I kid you not. One by one they disclosed all the information I needed as they all feasted their eyes on my thighs. Wearing that same short skirt, I avoided the security at the entrance of the building site you're supposed to be supervising and I told some guy there that I was looking for my uncle James. They kindly told me your address.
Wasn't that fucking nice of them! You were back in mummies' house.
You see James? Wearing short skirts can get you more than your brains bashed out of your head, it can actually pay you dividends when worn' at the appropriate times. I told them I was going back home to Weymouth that night and I was desperate to see you before I returned.
One of them even escorted me back off the site as he lusted after my legs.
They were so helpful.
And so...here we are James. What are we to do with you?
I don't want to inform my superiors of my discovery in case they think I'm trying to prove that they are incompetent, which they are by the way, which is why you and I are going to sort out our differences in private. I mean Claire cannot speak for herself just now because her mouth and her arms are full of tubes and shit helping to nourish her

and save her the need to be carried to the bathroom. She also has wires holding her jaw-bones together and so it would be difficult indeed for her to say anything in her defence. I don't know how short her skirt was this time, or her shorts, or if she just happened to breathe in the wrong direction to start you off on one of your turns, but I'm sure we'll think of some kind of compromise James to sort out this unfortunate situation, and to learn you once and for all that women are not going to tolerate being pushed around and beaten by bully scum-fucks like you."

She leaned forward pushing the lapel of her jacket collar almost in his face.

"You see this badge? I live for this badge, and someday I will prove to those useless colleagues of mine that I am a far better police officer than they will ever be. I shall be detective Rosemary Reed and God help any of those bastards if they've given me a hard time."

She stood back and then sat back down onto the chair, this time facing him.

"Now then, listen closely to what I say to you. I know you are cold and hungry and thirsty no doubt and although you are an utter bastard, I shall let you have something to eat, after all, at least you allowed Claire to eat, but only at home of course. You certainly didn't take her out much did you?

Now, I am going to remove the tape from your mouth.

If you at any time attempt to speak to me, I shall blast your face with this fucking incapacitant spray and I shall hammer your mouth with this truncheon, and I will make sure you lose teeth. I shall sit here and watch you eat, and then I shall let you have a drink of water. That'll be the end of today's luxuries, and they are luxuries, considering the condition of Claire. So, not a fucking word ok?

Or you know what will happen to you, officer Reed keeps her word.

Ok? We're all clear on the no talking policy?"

She then proceeded to rip the tape from his mouth. There were used rubber gloves staggered all over the work-bench. She picked up a pair that were smeared with oil or some other substance that was black and picked up the discarded pasty. She then rammed the food over his mouth and pushed with her hand more or less rubbing the food over his face rather than feeding him with it.

"Come on come on, I haven't got all day, eat it up!"

Carter managed a couple of mouthfuls.

"Now then, time to wash it down. You open your mouth and I will throw the water over your face. You try and take in as much water as you can into your mouth because I'm only doing it once."

Frightened to speak, he watched her fill a bucket that was in the corner of the room from the tap his father had installed. He couldn't think when the last time that tap

would be used. His mother certainly wouldn't have used it. She approached him laden with a bucket of cold water. "Are you ready? One, two."
She swung the bucket back and unleashed the water full-force on his face making him choke with the sudden shock of the blast. He coughed and spluttered for a few moments. The `police-woman` lit up another cigarette and sat back down on her chair. She placed her pointing finger over her lips as a reminder of the danger and pain he'd be in if he attempted to speak to her. She then sat back down and retrieved some more of the mess that had been the pasty and offered it to him from her gloved hand. He leaned forward and ate from her hand, like a pet dog, what was left of the `treat`. Lifting an oil rag that was lying on the work-bench, she proceeded to wipe his mouth dry, and then she applied a fresh strip of waterproof masking tape.

"There now James. That's you fed and watered for the day, I'm too kind for my own good, don't you think?

I just bet you that Claire would love to be able to eat a nice cheese and onion pasty like that. Now then, I know your clothes are soaking wet and everything with all the mess you've made, so, before I go, I'm going to get you some clean things from upstairs. I'm also going to let you stand up and stretch your legs, you know, just to keep your circulation going, but, like I say, the treat is more than you deserve. I'll just go and get you some things." As she walked away from him, she called over her shoulder as though she were addressing a friend, "I really am spoiling you James, you're a very lucky man."

Fear would not be the word to describe how James Carter felt at this moment in time. Dread would be closer, but still not accurate.

Who was this woman, and how on earth had she known about Claire?

Why the remarks about the short skirts and shorts?' She must have had a conversation with her at some point. His face now burned after the cold water shock and there was a piece of carrot or something stuck up his left nostril.

The situation was dire. From down here he could hear voices from above.

Had she brought someone here with her? No, it was the television he could hear. She'd turned on the TV probably to let his neighbours think that he was home, and that everything was normal. Whoever she was she was clever and by the sounds of things, she had worked out a plan of some sort. The fact that she'd gone to get him clean underwear and trousers gave him just a glimmer of hope that she was going to keep him alive, at least for the time being. If she was going to do that, then it would seem that she planned to torture him. Torture him for what he'd done to Claire? The `policewoman` returned with clothes for him. "Here, I've brought you clean things to wear, you don't deserve it though do you, you nasty piece of shit. Now if you try anything when I stand you up, anything at all, I will slice off your penis, I promise you, and just leave you to bleed to death. She untied his legs and then unwrapped the masking tape. Careful when you stand up, you'll be numb. If you fall, I'm not helping you up. Now, don't worry when you see the Stanley-knife, I'm only going to cut these stinking jeans off your body. You've pissed yourself in case you don't know. Come on, up, up you get."

James Carter *did* fall as he attempted to get to his feet.

"Thought as much, this'll take a bit of time for your blood to circulate, you'll probably get pins and needles before you get your feelings back in those scabby legs of yours. No fear of you wearing shorts is there, God, what a state."

She pulled the jeans from his legs as he lay helpless on the floor.

Oh they're stinking with the piss, wait and I'll get something to dry them with."

She gathered up some more oil-stained rags and dusters from the work-top and proceeded to rub his legs dry, with the filthy pieces of cloths.

"Christ your penis is miniscule, I couldn't cut that off could I, fuck I'd be all day trying to find it, how on earth do you manage to wank off with that piece of skin, fuck, where is it?"

Eventually, she was able to get him back onto his feet.

"Now, she sighed, I've had a brilliant idea. I've brought you down some of your mothers' clothes to put on, they are more sensible for the purpose. If, while I'm away you piss yourself again, or indeed mess yourself then this pinafore will be better than trousers. You'll be able to keep your legs dry, or drier anyway.

James Carter made a feeble attempt to grab the policewoman by the neck, but he hardly had any feelings in his hands.

In no time at all she had him back on the chair.

"You're lucky I'm not whacking you in the nuts with the crow-bar for that you silly man. Here, I've brought you down a pair of your mums' knickers. It's the old lady type that keep your back warm, they go right up to the middle of your back.

Might as well put this blouse on as well and one of her nice flowery cardigans.

I've even brought you a pair of her tights, they'll help to keep your warty fucking stick-thin legs warm. You see how good I am to you? I tell you, you're a spoiled fucking bastard mister Carter." Five minutes later James Carter sat bound and tied up in his mothers' clothes. Humiliation.

"Now then, just let me take a couple of photographs James. It's not often you see grown' men of your age dressing up as their mummies is it. I wonder what your workmates are going to think of this when I leave the prints of these in your canteen. Maybe they think you're a cross-dresser anyway James, in which case there'll be no shock there. Anyway, here's what's going to happen. I'm just about to head off now. In two days from now I am going to inform the local authorities of your predicament. I was going to do it tomorrow but because of your foolishness we'll make it two days. I'll leave a key for them to get in outside your front door, and then you can resume your sad pathetic life, just as soon as you get out of hospital."

Carter's eyes were once again full of fear.

She stepped back over to the work-top and picked up a mash-hammer.

"Now, this is for Claire. This is for all the bad things you ever done to her. If I ever hear that you have weaselled your way back into her life, I will come back here and I will castrate you. Do you believe me?"

James Carter nodded his head. He believed her alright.

"Ok, close your eyes and grit your teeth, because I promise you right now, this, my friend is going to hurt like fuck." She hoisted the ten-pound hammer above her head and began to smash his knuckles with the instrument.

Several times on both hands she brought it down, crunching his bones.

By the time she was finished, his hands were just two thick bloody stumps at the ends of his arms. James Carter screamed under the masking tape making guttural noises from his throat. The pain was indescribable. Once the `police woman` got her breath back, in a calm and serene voice she said, "Now you remember my promise frock boy, constable Rosemary Reed keeps her promises. You'd better pray we never meet again and you'd better pray that Claire makes a full recovery or I'll be back here with a pair of secateurs."

And with that, the `policewoman` threw the heavy-hammer onto the floor, and made her way back up the steps.

This time she left the light on, and the central heating.

Just before he passed out with the pain he heard the door being closed, and then the room fell into darkness as he once again, drifted into complete oblivion.

HAWTHORNE CLOSE.

BROMLEY. 7pm.

Marjory Tate had sent her son a text message informing him that she and his father would be out of the house for a few hours. She had to attend a show that she didn't particularly want to see but had no choice if she wanted a peaceful life. She also informed her son that there was a key in the green-house underneath the first plant-pot on the left as you go in. She told him to help himself to the casserole she'd left in the oven and to take whatever else he needed from the cupboards. There had also been some money left for him underneath his pillow in his bedroom. *"Make sure you're out of the house son by 9:30 just to be on the safe side. And don't leave any mess. If he thinks for one minute you've been in the house he'll make my life hell. Talk to you soon Gareth.x*

Gareth Tate was making his way down to Hawthorne Close having just disembarked the bus with his `girlfriend` Christine Hope. Today had been a good day for the pair having successfully shop-lifted several items which they had sold on and had boosted their funds considerably. Both had court-cases coming up regarding shop-lifting attempts that had not exactly gone to plan.

He was hoping he would hear from a woman called Clair Redgrave again.

She had paid him four hundred quid just for dressing up as a council-worker and bundling a couple of girls into a van. He didn't even have to put the girls into the van, there were already guys in the van who done it. All he'd had to do was grab them and approach the vehicle. It was the easiest four-hundred quid he'd ever made. Claire said she'd be in touch again soon, but he hadn't heard from her in over two months now. Her name and number was on his phone and happened to be just under his mothers'. That's what had made him think of her. "It's five past seven Christine, we'll have time to get a shower and a nice meal in here before that bastard gets' back with my mum, they've gone to some shitty show somewhere. She said we've got until 9:30 before the twat gets' back. We can have a decent fuck as well, in a nice soft fucking bed too. I'm going to fuck you in his fucking bed as well, the bastard. I'll learn him for kicking me out of my home just because I stole some fucking money, I mean what the fuck is five-grand to him? You'd think I'd stolen the crown jewels or something. I think my mums' fucking sick of him anyway. Might not be long until she tosses *him* out onto the street and I hope she does. See how he likes it. If she does that babe our troubles are over, we'll live in complete luxury. He's nothing but a domineering bastard that's all he is."

Christine Hope was only half listening to what Tate was saying.
She couldn't care fucking less if his father had thrown him out.
All that concerned her at this moment in time was that there'd be countless opportunities in this house. There was bound to be valuables lying about that she could sneak into her bag without this cunt finding out. Also, there was food on the go and doubtless a drinks-cabinet. She was an opportunist and would be a fool to miss an opportunity like this to further boost her finances. So when Tate had invited her along, she jumped at the chance. All said and done, she knew without a shadow of a doubt that Gareth Tate would sell her down the river at the drop of a hat. What Gareth Tate didn't know was, she would do exactly the same to him. All this meant to her tonight was a hot meal and a funds booster. He was nothing but an immature fucking idiot who thought that he had a say in the world, like he was important. In truth, he was a narcissist. Only important to himself. No other fucker paid him any attention, especially when he boasted about his father being minted. One of the boys that she fucked with behind his back had told him straight out, "Yeah, your fucking father is minted, but you're not, fucking clot-head. You're just the same as the rest of us, a fucking junkie."
She nestled her head into his chest as they made their way down to the house. She done this not to be affectionate but to shield her face from the bitter wind that blew onto them. Christine revelled in the heat as they entered the house. "The cunt was right." It was very luxurious. Before long they were both sitting at the kitchen table consuming the piping-hot casserole his mother had left for him, along with a nice bottle of red wine with a label she could never dream of pronouncing. All she knew was that it tasted delicious. It didn't take him long.
Off he went again on one of his boastful rants. "I'll tell you something babe, someday this will be mine. My mum will kick his arse out of here and then we can move in, and then when she pops her clogs, this'll all be mine. It would be in your best interest to stick with me kid. I am your meal-ticket out of that shit-hole where we live just now." The fact that this fuck-head was only a few years older than her angered her further having to tolerate his childishness. Kid indeed.
Christine looked at him disdainfully. "That shit-hole where you were begging me to put you up in when your father threw your arse out onto the street, is that the shit-hole you're referring to Gareth?"
"Listen babe, I didn't mean it to sound like that. I am grateful for you putting me up honey, I'm just saying, that this here can be ours someday, that's all, and you must admit, it's fucking lovely. Anywhere else would be a shit-hole compared to here, not just your place honey, here, have some more wine."
She noticed that the song had changed from "all mine someday" to "all ours someday."

It was another pathetic attempt at winning her affections. But, good business is where you find it, and so she decided to play along with his game. She would ask him to show her all around the house and she'd fake him just how very impressed she was with everything and that she couldn't wait until his mother threw his father out so that they could live here together and inherit it someday as their own. He poured more wine into her glass and smiled into her face thinking that he had this bitch exactly where he wanted her, practically eating out of his hand.

She smiled back into *his* face, thinking, that of all the wankers she'd had the misfortune of fucking with, this here in front of her was, by far and a way, the most useless wanking boasting bastard she'd ever set eyes upon. Pity, that's what it was. She'd pitied him when he'd come crawling for a place to live.

All said and done, he wasn't a bad looking guy, apart from his acne, it was just that he had an unbelievable need to boast. She began the game. "Before we have a nice fuck on your dads' bed you get your shower darling, and I'll familiarise myself with the house, after all, if you are right, then we'll both be very happy living in here. I can just see me and your mum making your dinner together and everything, oh it's going to be brilliant isn't it Gareth."

"You fucking stupid bitch, as if my mum would make friends with you, you stupid cow, fuck."

"Yes it will babe, and I can't wait either."

He then told her to wander around the house and take a look at everything that would someday be theirs. "Don't fucking touch anything though, don't nick anything or that twat will know I've been here. I'm just going to get my shower you can get yours' when I'm done. And then we'll have a nice shag, what do you say to that?"

"Suits me babe."

The house was quite big Christine thought to herself as she explored each of the rooms. She could hear the shower being turned on along the hallway.

"Clean up you stinking fucking weasel that you are, you're fucking rotten."

She then entered Gareth's mothers' bedroom. "This is what we're looking for. Lets' see what we have in here worth taking."

Suddenly, she looked to her left. Had he come out of the shower?

She thought she saw...a shape flash past the bedroom door.

She went to the door and looked all down the hallway and listened.

Only the sound of the shower coming from the bathroom, and the wanker *in* the shower giving some kind of piss-poor rendition of a rock song.

"Fuck, I'm hallucinating now, I could have sworn..."

She returned to the bedroom and proceeded to open the small chest of drawers in

front of her. "It's like Aladdin's fucking cave."
As quickly as she could, she took out some jewellery and stuffed it down her jeans. There'd be time enough to check what she'd got when she got home.
She would put this stuff into her hand-bag before the skunk exited the shower.
She was just opening the other chest of drawers when the gloved hand grabbed her from behind and squeezed the cloth tightly around her nose and mouth.
She passed out almost instantly.
Gareth Tate had finished his shower and was making his way to what used to be his bedroom. "Christine? Christine where are you babe? I hope you've not got into my mum's bed without having a shower, she'll fucking smell you.
Your jeans have got a kind of sour smell babes. Maybe we can give them a quick wash before we leave and I'll put the fuckers in the tumble-drier, fuck."
He looked into his parents' bedroom.
"Christine? Where the fuck *are* you, we haven't got time to play games, and you haven't fucking stolen anything have you? Because if you have-."
There were horizontal wooden beams that ran across the ceiling at the top of the stairs. Before Gareth Tate knew what had happened the rope noose had been wrapped around his neck and tightened with unbelievable ferocity.
There was nothing he could do as this figure in black swung the rope over one of the beams. He was kicked in the stomach winding him which rendered him completely helpless. He then felt himself being physically lifted by the neck and hoisted high in the air. The noose tightened even more. It felt like his head was swelling and would burst. His hearing had gone. He couldn't even raise his hands up to try and loosen the noose. And now he was swinging violently to and fro eight feet from the floor with his hands dangling by his sides and his feet desperately kicking out to try and find non-existent purchase.
Slowly but surely his vision dimmed and his breath went from his lungs.
Gareth Tate drifted off just like Terry Mercer had told him, to wherever his soul was destined to go. All that could be heard now in the house, was the gentle creaking of the rope as it swung slowly backwards and forwards from the hard-wood rafters. And again, just like Terry Mercer had said, Gareth Tate's short and pointless life had run its' course.

Forty minutes later no less than six neighbours of misses Tate's came running to the aid of Christine Hope as her high-pitched screams reverberated around Hawthorne Close.

LEXINGTON SQUARE.

BROMLEY. 7am.

It was with a heavy heart that Terry Mercer and Samantha Reynolds made their way up to Mandy Spencer's front door. Their visit today was not a social one. A man had been found dead in his home at Edgeley Road in Clapham. He had multiple injuries to his hands and a single bullet-wound in his brow. Sophie Spencer's prints and DNA were all around the basement of the apartment. It was with extreme reluctance that Terry Mercer rang the door-bell.
"I don't think anyone's up Terry" said Samantha as she peered into the living room window.
"Well" Terry sighed, "We'll just have to keep ringing the bell until someone *does* get up Sam, because we're not leaving here without her, not this time."
Eventually, a bedraggled David Spencer answered the door. Rubbing his eyes, he looked confusingly at the two detectives. "Hi Terry, what's wrong? Is something wrong?"
Samantha spoke now, unsure whether or not Terry could actually get the words out without his voice breaking. "We're eh, we're here for Sophie David, is she here?"
"Yeah, I think so. She's in her bed I think, what's wrong?"
For the first time in all the visits they had made to this house, Terry and Samantha entered the premises uninvited. Samantha continued. "Could you go and get her please David, we need to ask her some questions, and I'm afraid she'll have to come with us this time."
Mandy Spencer came running down the stairs. "Hi Terry, Samantha, what can we do for you? Why on earth are you here at this time of the morning? Sophie is still in bed."
Terry smiled at the woman he thought the world of. "I'm afraid we'll have to take Sophie with us today Mandy, we can't tell you any more at this stage. Could you go and get her for me please."
Terry would have loved at this point to be able to say to Mandy that she had nothing to worry about, but that would be just blatantly lying. There was plenty to worry about.
Sophie must have awoken hearing all the voices because she came down stairs dressed in a blouse and jeans with trainers and carrying her denim jacket over her arm.
"I'm ready to go Terry. Mum, I just want you to know that I love you with all of my heart." Sophie kissed her mum on the check and cuddled her brother.
David looked on at his sister. "Sophie? What the hell is going on?"
"I love you too David." And with that, Sophie Spencer made her way past the detectives

and down the path to the pavement awaiting the two people who had done so much for her. As Terry and Samantha approached she said to them, "There'll be no need to hand-cuff me, I don't intend to try and escape. Terry couldn't for the life of him find any words to say to her.

Samantha opened the back door of the car and placed her hand on Sophie's head as the teenager climbed into the back seats.

A very confused and frightened Mandy Spencer stood now at her gate in dressing-gown and slippers wondering why on earth her daughter was being taken away at this time of the morning. She knew, whatever the reason, it must be serious.

She didn't wave as the car drove off, but just looked on in bewilderment, and with tears streaming down her face, she whispered to no-one, "Oh Sophie, what have you done my baby?"

SCOTLAND YARD.

BROADWAY VICTORIA.

There were no fewer than five people in the room with Sophie Spencer as she sat with her carton of coffee awaiting the interrogation to begin. Terry asked the two detectives who had answered the emergency call and discovered the body to give them five minutes with Sophie.
They consented, knowing that Terry and Samantha had known the girl for some time. Polly Sheppard stood at the window contemplating everything that had happened to this poor girl, and what *would* happen to her, unless she could come up with nothing shorter than a miracle. The evidence it seemed was irrefutable. Sophie sat at the table tapping her fingers on her coffee carton. No-one at this stage was saying anything to her. "I take it this is about the bastard at Edgeley Road is it?"
Terry pulled a chair up and sat opposite Sophie. "Yes it is. Would you like to tell us why you done it Sophie? As far as we know, this Carter man has had nothing at all to do with Lithuania or any kidnappings."
Sophie took a sip of her beverage and began to explain. "You know that I'm doing sociology at university don't you. Well, I have visited Safe Haven, the home for battered and abused women. I have befriended a few of the women in there.
One of them I believe you've spoken to. Her name is Claire Rennie, and even as we speak, she is fighting for her life having received, and not for the first time I hasten to add, a severe beating from your mister Carter, who incidentally has been using a false name. Claire knew him as Alan Flint. The police couldn't find him to interview him simply because he doesn't exist. I found him though.
You should have seen his face when I informed him that his game was up.
That bastard has given the girl a life of hell. He beats her if she wears a short skirt for goodness sakes, or a pair of shorts. She's not allowed to go out without him. She's not allowed to work. He doesn't want her socialising in any way or form.
He wants to have complete control over her. What kind of a life is that for any girl, and now, to top it all he's beaten her to within an inch of her life. He'll think twice now before he bullies any more women. And before you say anything else, I do not regret smashing his hands to pulp. I have also sent photographs of him sitting in his mummy's clothes. We'll see how he likes it when his workmen find the photos I've left in his office."
"How he *likes* it Sophie? I hardly think it matters to him now, do you?"

Sophie shrugged her shoulders.

"Well, I don't know how long he'll be in hospital, but don't think for one minute I'll be taking him any flowers or apologising to him, you haven't seen the mess of Claire Rennie, have you?"

At this point Samantha pulled up a chair beside her colleague.

"You don't know how long he'll be in hospital Sophie?"

"No I don't, and I don't care. I just hope all his workmates are having a good laugh at him now, that's if he still has a job to go to, he's been off for a few days now, and more of course, depending upon how long it'll take to heal his hands."

Terry was raging inside at the girls' lack of concern. He spoke now looking straight into Sophie's face. "Might take a little time as you say Sophie, but I don't think his swollen hands will be the surgeon's immediate concern.

They'll be more concerned with the fucking bullet wedged in his fucking brain, that's their biggest problem, or had you forgotten about that?"

"What?"

"Oh, had you forgotten the fact that you shot the man at point-blank range. Slip your mind Sophie did it? Were you concentrating on his hands so much that you forgot about shooting him?"

Sophie looked at Terry Mercer. "I'm telling you now Terry, I did not shoot anyone, I gave you the gun back remember? That wouldn't have been revenge if I shot him. I don't know who else has been there but I swear to you, I did not shoot that man Terry, I swear I didn't."

Terry rose to his feet. "Well, you can swear all you want Sophie, but as far as forensics are concerned, the only DNA samples they have are yours and James Carter's, and seeing how he was all bound up on the chair that only leaves one person who could have shot him. Do you see the problem you have? And while we're on the subject of honesty Sophie, Samantha and I made some inquiries, and guess what, you never made any appointment to join any gym did you? That was another lie. In fact, everything you've said to me and Sam these last few weeks has been nothing but bullshit. You need to wake up. You're in deep water now young lady, and there's no-one can save you from this little escapade. You've been talking about taking revenge for weeks now, you and that Jensen girl. I think you've planned all this out Sophie. You went to Edgeley Road with every intention of killing that man, and you done it. All this, when he gets out of hospital shit! You know fine well what you've done, and now you're going to pay the price for your actions...I'm sorry Sophie, you're fucked lady, you are well and truly fucked." He calmed himself down and sat back down at the table.

He let out an exasperated sigh. "Sophie...oh Sophie" he said, shaking his head.

We can't save you this time. Those two detectives out there are going to come in here, and they will tear you apart. This is what's known as an open and shut case sweetheart. All, I repeat all the evidence points to you. I mean, I'd like to believe that someone was watching your movements and then when you'd left, they entered the house and finished the job off, I'd love to believe that, but again, the evidence. Your DNA and only your DNA can be found in there Sophie. What do you think the jury and the judge are going to conclude from that? Huh?"

At that moment the door burst open and the two detectives began to try and take over. "Come on Terry, you've had long enough, it's time for us to do our jobs come on, this is our case, you know the score bud."

Before he could stop himself, Terry grabbed the detective by the throat and pinned the man up against the wall. Through gritted teeth he said, "You get your fucking stinking crawling arse out of here until I fucking tell you to come back, you fucking rat that you are, get to fuck out of here!!" Both Samantha and Polly grabbed Terry and pulled him off the shell-shocked detective.

"That's it, I'm reporting him Polly. You won't punish him, and so I'll take it higher than you. You're fucking history Mercer!"

Polly Sheppard took over at this point.

"The lot of you, my office, now!

I've had enough of this back-biting shit. Get down to my office and wait for me there. If you decide to come to blows before I get there, then consider yourselves suspended without pay, now get out of my sight!" Polly slammed the door behind them as they left. She then turned to Sophie. She sat down at the table where moments before Terry had sat. "Would you like a cigarette Sophie?"

"Yes please Miss Sheppard."

There was a time when Sophie would have cried out and would have been shocked at the sudden burst of violence, but the way her life had been changed in recent months had put paid to that. She sat unmoved by the confrontation.

Polly handed her the packet which belonged to Terry. Sophie lit up a cigarette and took a large draw.

"He's worried sick about you Sophie, do you know that? He thinks the world of you and your family. Why on earth did you do it? What possible good can come from it? Does it make you feel better now that he's no longer with us? If he's beat up this friend of yours then there are certain channels to go down, within the law Sophie."

"Miss Sheppard, I know what it looks like, but I swear to you, I did not shoot that man. Yes, I bashed his hands to bits, but you haven't seen the mess of that girl. I've been told that her jaw has been broken in two places. She has broken ribs, broken bloody arms, you name it. Certain channels you say Miss Sheppard? Well, the police couldn't even find him. I found him myself, and that's just it Miss Sheppard, there's so much of this going on that the police officers don't have the time to do any research like I done. And so these monsters are getting away with it constantly. They have their partners so petrified that some of them don't even report the incidents because they'll get another beating as soon as the police leave, and that's to say they arrive, sometimes they don't."

Now it was Sophie's turn to sigh. "Miss Sheppard, I am prepared to take a lie-detector test. I did not kill that man. I know what I've been saying about revenge and all that, but I did not shoot that man."

Polly stood up and looked at the teenager who had been to Hell and back.

"Well Sophie, be that as it may, the evidence says otherwise, no matter how you do in the lie-detector test. It's the evidence. Perhaps the forensic team can come up with something to support your story but I have to be honest girl, it's not looking good for you right now is it? I mean, how long were you in there?

Did you just go in and, I mean, how did you manage to get him tied up to the chair? He wouldn't just sit still for you while you bound him, so how the hell did you do it, you're just a skinny teenager."

Sophie looked down to the floor as she answered the chief inspector.

"I made two visits to the house. I left him tied up for a full day. Then I went back to…to punish him, you know psychologically…to make him suffer, like he made Claire-."

"Wait a minute, you were there on more than one occasion?"

"Yes, Miss Sheppard, I've just told you, I was there twice. The second time was when I bashed his hands. I dressed him up in his mothers' clothes to humiliate him, and then…and then I bashed him with the hammer, but I sure as hell didn't shoot him. I swear on my mothers' life, and my brothers', I did not kill him Miss Sheppard."

As far as Polly was concerned, there was a glimmer of hope for the girl, but that was to say she'd been telling the truth. "Well, if you've made more than one visit, then the forensic team will find that out. And you still haven't told me how you got him into the chair, would you like to elaborate?"

Sophie stumped out her cigarette in the biscuit-tin Terry had been using as an ashtray.

"I broke into his house on the first night. I entered the house by the back door. Someone I know showed me how to pick a lock. It was easy. I broke in and looked around for his electric power-box. There was a key hanging up on a wall outside of this door at the bottom of his hallway. I used the key to open the door to the basement, and then I hung the key back up. Once I was in the basement I used my wire to lock the door from inside the basement. I then found his power switches and waited for him to come in. I could hear him wandering about in his kitchen and then I could only just make out the volume of his television. When I was ready, I put all the power switches up knocking every electrical appliance out. I knew he would have to come and check them, so I waited underneath the stairwell in the basement. I had picked up a nail bar that was lying on his work bench, and that was how I rendered him helpless. As he approached the power box, I whacked him on the back of his head and he fell to the ground. Your forensic team will surely discover the bump on the back of his head, there's bound to be one. I tied him to an old chair and strapped his arms and legs with masking tape. That was on his bench as well. Just to make sure he couldn't escape, I drilled the chair to two pieces of timber and fixed the chair solidly to the concrete floor. That was it. That's how I got him. Can I have another cigarette please Miss Sheppard?"

"Help yourself, take one and light it up. I'm going to leave you in here for a while, I'll be back as soon as I can. Do you have enough coffee?"

"Could I have another one please Miss Sheppard?"

"Yes, I'll inform the policeman outside the door to go and get you one. The door will have to be locked Sophie you understand."

Polly lifted Terry's cigarettes and lighter and headed for the door.

"If you need the bathroom just inform the officer and they will escort you."

Polly Sheppard left the room and headed down the corridor to her office where she found Terry and Samantha in full argument with the other two detectives. When they saw Polly arrive they immediately calmed themselves down. Detectives Henderson and Grimshaw looked at her disdainfully as she promptly informed them that they were, as from five minutes ago, off the case.

"You take it as high as you like Henderson, and report me to whoever you feel fit, and we'll see who comes off best. Now, disappear while you still have jobs, or you'll be taking me to a tribunal, now, off you go."

She pointed to Terry Mercer and Samantha and then her office door.

"You two, get your arses in there, now!"

Terry and Samantha sat facing Polly at her desk.

For a few moments nothing was said.

To all intents and purposes, the two detectives looked like a pair of scorned school-kids. Terry in particular was waiting for a lecture on how to conduct his behaviour. It didn't happen. Finally, Polly spoke. "I don't know what the hell has happened at that house in Clapham, but I'm telling you now Terry, that girl down there did not shoot Mister Carter. She's sat there and explained to me in great detail how she got into the house and what she done once she was in. She sneaked in and waited for him, this Carter, and when he was home, she waited until he settled down and then she knocked out his

power. When he came to check his power-box, she whacked him on the back of his head. That's how she got him tied up to the chair."
Samantha and Terry had sat listening intently.
"*Somebody* has been watching her. She made two visits to the house.
This was psychological punishment she said, for what this man had done to her friend. As far as Sophie was concerned she was merely making him suffer for his deeds. It was pay-back, to make him feel humiliated."
There was a faint smile on Polly's face as she said, "She dressed him up in his mother's clothes. It was humiliation. She said, as you heard, that she'd printed copies of the photographs she'd taken and hung them up in his office at his work so that his workmen could see them. She wouldn't go to all that trouble if she intended to kill him, now would she?" Before Terry or Samantha could answer their superior there was a knock on the door.
Polly shouted them in.
Detective John Henderson entered the office without looking at Terry or Samantha. He had a printed e mail in his hand. He approached Polly's desk and threw the e mail down in front of her.
"Another murder." He said, as he turned to leave. "Just get your superman here to deal with it, he'll have it solved before dinner time, because he's the best isn't he, there's nobody better than muck-mouth Mercer is there."
Terry swiftly responded. "John, on your way back down there do you think you could get me and Sam a coffee please, oh and tell Grimshaw that the toilets on the second floor need cleaned. On you go now, Samantha and I have business to discuss with Polly, there's a good lad."
"Someday Mercer, I'm going to tear your fucking face off, you wait and see, your fucking time is coming."
"And that'll be two sugars for me and Sam please John, good man."
Detective Henderson slammed the door as he exited the office.
Polly scrutinised the e mail. "It's your boy Terry, the Tait boy. He's been hanged. It's murder. It's been done in his mother's house. Hawthorne Close, Bromley.
Get hold of the forensics, see what they can tell you.
Lets' hope Sophie's DNA is not all over *that* house as well. They've got his girlfriend down stairs.
Maybe you can find out from her what the hell has been happening there.
He's been involved with drugs hasn't he? Maybe his murder is drug-related, see what you can find out, and for Christ's sake Terry, stop winding those buggers up.
He'll end up attacking you if you push him, after all, it was their case Terry, they were

appointed to that case, but anyway, on you go, see what you can find out. I'm going back to talk to Sophie. Jesus, it's a hell of a day at sea. Somethings not right Terry. This is very strange indeed."

INTERVIEW ROOM.

No 2.

Mister Gareth Tait senior sat at a table in the small interview room tapping the table as he awaited to be interviewed. Terry Mercer entered the room on his own. Samantha had gone down to interview room number three to speak with Christine Hope.
Mister Tait was a tall well-built gentleman who reminded Terry of a rugby union player. Already Terry could see that he was irritated.
"At last. I've been in here for almost an hour.
I was spoken to by one of your detectives, but that was half an hour ago, I mean what the hell is going on here? My son has been murdered and nobody seems to give a fuck about it. Gareth is dead and nobody cares!"
Terry sat down opposite the distraught father. "We do indeed care Mister Tait, and we want to try and find the person or persons who done this to your son." The giant man sat shaking his head. "No you don't, you don't care if his murderer is ever found. My son was a junkie. I happen to know that he's been caught shop-lifting on numerous occasions, you'll be sick of the sight of him. Mercer smiled inwardly at the thought of shop-lifters being brought to Scotland Yard.
This'll just be what you lot were hoping for. He'll be a weight off your shoulders, he won't be causing you any more trouble now will he. You'll all be glad about this. Well he was my son, and I had plans for him. I had a future worked out for him. He was going to be set up with an apprenticeship.
I had it all set up for him...and then he had to go and get involved with bloody drugs. And that little evil bitch you have down the corridor there, she was the main cause of his downfall...little fucking bitch, nothing but a two-penny whore, that's all she is. She was in my house with Gareth. The police caught her with half of my wife's jewellery down her bloody jeans. She's had something to do with this. I wouldn't be surprised if she's been collaborating with whoever done this. Little innocent fucking butter-wouldn't-melt-in-her-mouth scum bitch. You'd better find out what the hell she's had planned here I'm telling you now. She *must* have had something to do with it.
It was a robbery, and my Gareth knew nothing about it, the poor bugger. That bitch has had it planned out though, and she's played on Gareth's good nature. The boy would do anyone a good turn before he done them a bad one...it's that fucking slut down there, that's who done it, and my Gareth is dead because of her."
Terry had seen this a thousand times, parents falling to pieces after the death of their

sons or daughters. He'd been told about Gareth senior refusing to let his son stay under the same roof as himself, and how junior had ruined the family name dragging it through the gutter-world of heroin. The man could not find it in his heart to forgive his son for the shame he'd caused himself and his mother. To top it all Gareth junior had stolen five thousand pounds out of one of his father's accounts. If there had been any chance of a reconciliation between father and son, then juniors' actions with the fraudulent money-exchange had put paid to that and extinguished any chance of that spark coming to light. And from that moment on Mister Gareth Tait had turned his back on his son completely, forbidding him to even come anywhere near the house.

The bitterness coming out of him now was perfectly normal in a situation like this. It wasn't about the `slut` down the hall, or her being part of his murder, it was sheer disappointment, and frustration, because he'd had so much hope and faith in his son at one time, and pride.

That's what all this was about. Regret, that and the fact that his only son had turned his back on what his father had set out for him. What most parents seem to forget though is, that some kids don't want the same things as their parents want for them. They want to make their way in the world their own way. Whether or not that turns out to be the correct decision, whether it be right or wrong for them, it's what they want. Independence. And so when a parent can't see that, or fail to accept it, then you get a situation like the one here with Mister Gareth Tait, who can't for the life of him understand why his son turned his back on everything offered to him.

INTERVIEW ROOM.

No 3.

Christine Hope had witnessed violence many times in her five years living rough on the streets. She herself had suffered beatings from jealous girl-friends who had found out that she'd spent the night with their boyfriends. She had also administered beatings to individuals who'd attempted to steal her `stash`. But nothing she'd witnessed could have prepared her for the sight of Gareth Tait hanging naked from the rafters at the top of his stairs. She would never forget his bulging eyes and his tongue protruding hideously out of his mouth. There was also a pool of urine lying on the floor underneath him and on some of the stairs. She had been making her way down the hallway having just recovered consciousness when mister and misses Tait entered their house.
She had only just discovered Gareth's body when his parents came rushing up the stairs. All she could remember was screaming her head off at the shock of the sight before her. Misses Tait had fainted almost immediately.
Then, within a few seconds neighbours and friends of the Tait's came rushing into the house. In no time at all the police arrived and were hand-cuffing her and escorting her to one of their vans.
When they stripped her in here, they discovered the stolen jewellery which did not help her case in any way.
"This is not looking very positive for you Christine now is it?"
said Samantha Reynolds as she scrutinised the teen in front of her.
"You need to be more specific in your details. Tell me again, right from the start. From the moment you stepped off the bus with Gareth."
Christine sipped her coffee. "Look, I've already told you what happened, why do you keep-."
"Listen here young lady. You, are in very serious trouble here. Now, when I am finished questioning you in here, someone else will come and ask you to go through it all again, and let me tell you something, it had better be identical to what you tell me. So, you get used to it lady. Now, start again, from the minute you stepped off the bus with Gareth."
The teenager took a deep breath and exhaled. She then proceeded to explain to Samantha the course of events. She was truthful in detail admitting that she saw the visit to Gareth's parents' house as an opportunity to boost her finances, hence the jewellery. She was also truthful as she unfolded the events that took place once she was in the house. She told the detective that, as she was stealing she thought she saw a

shape gliding past the bedroom door. It was just a flash, a glimpse of a shape. She couldn't even be certain that she saw anything or anyone.

She explained that she'd went to the doorway and looked down the hallway. There was no-one there. Gareth was still in the shower.

"The next thing I knew was, someone grabbed me by the head and pulled me back forcing something like a handkerchief over my nose and mouth, a strong hand. Like a man's hand…but I could smell perfume, and that's all I can remember. You know the rest. When I woke up, eh…I discovered Gareth hanging from the ceiling. I was still feeling a bit groggy…everything was a blur.

Then Gareth's parents came rushing up the stairs, and she, misses Tait, she eh…she fainted.

There was a lot of shouting from mister Tait, and then neighbours were in the house, everything was pandemonium. Then the police came. And now I'm here. That's all I know, I swear, that's it."

All kinds of scenarios were forming in Samantha's head at this moment in time.

As with Edgeley Road in Clapham they would have to wait and see what the forensics would come up with. She handed the girl her cigarettes which had been confiscated on her arrival and arranged for more coffee for her.

"You just sit tight Christine, I'm just going to talk to a couple of colleagues.

And I hope for your sake lady, that you've told me the absolute truth, because if you haven't, you're in for a very uncomfortable ride missy I can tell you that.

Oh, and just before I go, do you happen to know a girl by the name of Sophie Spencer? Answer me honestly, because if you lie, we'll find out."

The tear-stained youth looked up to Samantha and told her that she'd never heard of the girl in her entire life. Even by the expression on Christine's face Samantha knew the girl was telling her the truth.

Fifteen minutes later Samantha and Terry were back in Polly's office.

"I've asked the pathologist to check this James Carter's head for an injury Sophie said she'd inflicted. I'm waiting to hear from him any time now. He said he'd call me right back. If Sophie *is* telling the truth, then who could this be who's done this? It would seem that there's someone trying to get Sophie into trouble."

"Fuck Polly, she's already done that hasn't she, she's already landed herself in trouble, taking the law into her own hands like that, and who's this James Carter anyway? Why has she involved herself with this Claire woman's problems?

If she wants to live with this lady-basher, then that's her prerogative.

Sophie shouldn't interfere with things that don't concern her. Even if she hasn't killed this guy, she's still in deep trouble Polly for smashing his hands to bloody pulp, Jesus

Christ what the hell has gotten in to her?" Terry sat back in his chair looking at Samantha as Polly answered her telephone.

He was asking Samantha how her interview had gone with Christine Hope. Polly interrupted them.

"Well, that was the pathologist. It seems that Sophie was telling me the truth. Mister Carter does indeed have a massive lump on the back of his head caused by a heavy blunt instrument of some sort. Sophie told me she used a nail bar to knock him unconscious. I'm going back down there to talk with her, you and Sam go back and talk with Christine Hope, and let me know if the forensic team at Hawthorne Close finds' any prints in there that shouldn't be there, namely Sophie Spencer's prints."

Five minutes later Terry and Samantha entered interview room number three. Immediately Terry could see that the girl in front of him was suffering from shock. She also looked like she could use a fix. He sat down opposite the teenager. Christine had been staring down at the floor. She looked up when Terry sat down. "You're the smart-arse who told me to have fun with the two officers that day when Gareth and I were picked up for shop-lifting aren't you."

Terry smiled at the youth as he handed her a cigarette. He'd seen Christine's empty packet lying on the floor.

"Yes, yes indeed Christine, I'm the smart-arse, I'm always the smart-arse according to everyone around here, so I can't disagree with you on that one.

We got off on the wrong note that day didn't we."

He handed her a light for her cigarette. "Anyway, today, I'm here to help you Christine. As you've probably guessed you're going to be in here for quite some time so I have taken the liberty of arranging a pharmacist to come here and administer your drugs to help you through this uncomfortable time.

In the meantime, is there anything else we can get you. Are you hungry?"

The girl just shook her head." "No, I'm fine thank you. I could do with another coffee though, if that would be ok."

Samantha spoke into her mobile phone and smiled at the teen. "Your coffee will be here soon Christine."

Terry studied the girl's face. He already felt sorry for her. He'd felt sorry for her even when he'd met her for the first time in the police station.

Society were ruthless when it came to sympathy. Very few are curious enough to wonder *why* someone is a drug-addict. What has happened in their lives to make them this way? Every one of us has a story to tell, and in most cases, somewhere along the line we have all suffered a hardship of some description, and because we've got through it, then we expect that everyone else should if they are determined enough and strong enough. But some of us aren't. Some of us look for comfort or relief from this constant shitty life that we lead. Anything, anything at all that can take us away from reality, to give us a break from the dead-end fucking nightmare of unemployment and poverty, and complete and utter fucking misery that we wake up to, every single day of the week. The young lady sitting opposite him now represented all of that. There would be a good reason why she didn't live at home at this time of her young life. Sometimes it was rape by a step-father, or violence, or negligence, there was always a good reason, and perhaps someday when he had more time he would find out Christine's story, and why her life had turned out this way. Even as he looked at her now, he wanted to reach out and give the girl a reassuring cuddle, a loving hug, a caring hug, just to let her know that not everybody in the world was out to hurt her. She was hard. And she was hard-hearted. In the world where Christine Hope lived, she had to be, because the other world, the world where you and I live, they wanted nothing at all to do with her.

"Thank you for doing that for me sir, you know, the pharmacist and all that, I appreciate it, I'm starting to get a little uncomfortable. I need something to help me."

"You're quite welcome Christine." replied Mercer, lighting up his own cigarette.

Christine Hope had to go through the whole story again from the time she'd stepped foot off the bus and arrived at Gareth's house. He looked at Samantha's report and the details taken from the girl. Everything that she told him matched what she'd said to Samantha. Terry leaned forward with his arms on the table folded.

"This is not very nice for you Christine is it. You could do without this in your life I'm betting...a horrible experience indeed, and a tragic one.

Had you known Gareth for long?"

"A few months. His father had kicked him out of his house, something like that.

It was when he discovered that Gareth was taking drugs, I don't know the full story. Anyway, the situation worsened when Gareth stole money out of his father's account. Five grand I think it was, anyway, he didn't have the money for long. Those fucking hyenas got to him and had him stripped of all his finances in no time at all. I felt sorry for him and so I took him in.

Samantha spoke now. "You took him in? So you're no longer homeless?"

"No, I have a flat now, a shit-hole Gareth called it...but it's better than the streets, well, warmer." She took another draw from her cigarette. "If you want to know the truth, he was extremely annoying at times."

"I know exactly how that feels Christine." said Samantha, smiling at the girl.

"Anyway carry on."

"There's nothing more to say really, I persevered with him because I knew he was up shit creek if I threw him back out onto the streets. He wasn't cut out to be living that that. Some people can cope with it, but he wouldn't have been able to…he was a mummy's boy, and I don't mean that in a bad way…Gareth wasn't what you could say, street-wise…huh, far from it. But he had this swagger about him, like a confidence. He kept telling me that he was going to work things out and that it was in my best interest to stick with him. All said and done, he just used me, and I used him. His mother would get money to him now and again, and he shared it with me it has to be said. He was kind that way."

As Christine continued to explain to the two detectives her relationship with Gareth, there was a knock on the door.

A junior detective entered. She would be no more than twenty-five Terry guessed. "Yes? Can we help you?"

The young lady approached the table in the centre of the room.

"I have to find a Detective Terry Mercer, are you him sir?"

Terry smiled at the girl's nervousness. He waved his arm around the table.

"Two females here Miss. Unless any of these two are called Terrence then I think you can guess which one I am." He looked at Christine. "Is your middle name Terrence Christine? No? Well then I guess that just leaves me then, I must be him. What's the message?"

The petite brunette stood with jeans and leather jacket and Cat boots.

She would be barely five feet six inches tall. "I'm afraid I cannot tell you in here sir, I have to tell you this in private."

Terry stood up and yet again tried to make light of the situation.

"Look, if this is about me standing you up last week when I promised to take you out to a nice hotel, I have already explained my reasons, and anyway, I sent you flowers did I not? We can't mix our love-lives with business, we've already been through all this."

The young woman's expression did not change one little bit.

Samantha leaned over the table and said to Christine, "This is him dreaming again Christine, wishful thinking honey. He does it from time to time.

One of these times he might actually be successful, but as far as this young lady is concerned, he doesn't stand a cat's chance in hell."

Even under the present circumstances Christine couldn't help but burst out laughing at Samantha's comments.

Mercer sighed at the young detective knowing that his attempt at humour had well and truly gone for a burton. "Come on, let's find somewhere secluded where you can reveal your precious secrets to me. What is it with you lot and your leather jackets, come on, bloody messages and Cat boots, Christ."

Half an hour later Terry and Samantha were on their way to Clapham. The message given to him from the junior detective was from the forensic team. They had found a part of a footprint on the floor of the basement. One that definitely did not belong to mister Carter. The message had been sent by the chief forensic officer Andrea Bortelli. Andrea did not trust mobile phones as far as privacy was concerned. She'd sent the information to him through junior detective Joan Vincent who had been accompanying detective John Henderson. She'd withheld this information from Henderson knowing that Terry Mercer had an interest in the girl Sophie Spencer, who's prints were found all over the basement. Andrea had taken Joan aside and told her who to pass this information on to, and also not to inform this Henderson of the message. "Tell no-one but Terry Mercer ok? No-one, and you make sure you are alone with him when you tell him." The young detective was only too pleased to carry out the task. Terry Mercer was not the only one who despised this John Henderson. He and his side-kick Grimshaw were always making derogatory remarks to her. If she wanted to progress further in the C.I.D. then she'd just have to grin and bear it. It wasn't much fun, unless someone could help her get moved away from them.

Terry and Samantha arrived at Edgeley Road where they were greeted by Andrea Bortelli. She was standing by the roadside smoking a cigarette. She smiled at the approaching detectives. "So you got my message alright?" Terry smiled back at the woman who had comforted him the best she could after he'd witnessed the scene in old Treble's apartment. "You know I don't trust phones Terry, so I sent young Joan over to tell you. She's going to be a good one Terry you can tell you know. It doesn't take long to find out which ones are a cut above the average." Mercer motioned towards Samantha. "Don't know what happened here Andrea, Sam must have slipped through the net...they're even referring to her as a detective, can you believe that?"

Andrea smiled at Samantha, and not sarcastically this time. "Yes I can believe that Terry, I have heard some good things about Samantha, and how she has managed to tame you and train you into behaving humanely. You are to be congratulated Samantha in your achievements. Most of the detectives I know, give him a wide space. Your persistence and perseverance are to be admired."

"Come on, let's see this fucking print you've found, bloody yacking there like a couple of old ladies, and this had better not be Henderson's big fucking size twelve footprint you've found or you'll be getting a belt on the ear, bringing me all the way over here." As they put on their suits Samantha said to Andrea, "He's grumpy because Joan did not show him any interest when he tried to come on to her, well, in his way of it, I say come on to her, it was more a kind of fifteen-year-old schoolboy kind of attempt...she didn't buy it, probably owing to the fact that he's old enough to be her papa."

Andrea laughed as she finished her cigarette. "Yes, she's a little honey Terry is she not, our Joan. Oh, and by the way, she's asked me to ask you if you could have a word with Polly Sheppard and get her moved. She doesn't like working with this Henderson she's been put on with, she says that nothing but filth comes out of his mouth constantly." Mercer stopped in his tracks and turned, grinning at Andrea. "I'll see what I can do. You see? There's hope for me and Joan yet Samantha." Samantha smiled back at him and looked to Andrea as she replied, "Which Joan are we talking about here sweetheart, Joan Vincent, or the French martyr, mind you, you're more in the French girl's age-group."

Andrea burst into laughter again. "I love you already Samantha, that's shut the bugger up."

Less than three minutes later Terry and Samantha were being shown the partial footprint. In fact, it was almost half of a footprint, enough for the forensic team to be able to determine what type of footwear it was.

Andrea informed the two detectives that it was a particularly favoured training shoe very popular with the younger generation. "Lots of young men wear these, and because they are made by this brand, then they are quite expensive, usually around the hundred and fifty-pound bracket." All the previous humour had all but disappeared from all three. Terry spoke to Andrea. "So you're telling me that a young man has been in here as well as Sophie Spencer and this Carter bloke?" "No I am not. I'm telling you that someone wearing this training-shoe was in here, that's what I'm telling you. Girls can wear men's shoes Terry."

Samantha stepped in at this point. "Do you know the actual size of the trainer Andrea?" "Indeed we do. The trainer is size seven, and by what my colleagues are telling me, the shoe was filled. By that I mean that whoever was wearing it, *is* actually a size seven." "Well that knocks' out any chance of a female wearing it doesn't it?" said Mercer. "Don't know many girls with that size of feet do you Andrea? Maybe Samantha does, she spends lots of time with females in her spare time. She's a member of an all-girls tennis club. The guys at the yard call it the carpet-club."

Andrea sighed and rolled her eyes. "How the hell do you cope with his constant sarcasm Samantha. Anyway, I think you'll be interested in what you find across the road there Terry. Go and speak with mister and misses Williamson, they live in number eighty-seven. They have some interesting footage on their security-cameras. There, that's me doing your job for you Terry...again. Go and speak to them and have a look at the footage, and don't say I'm not good to you. I'll have to be going now. If you have any more questions my colleagues will answer them for you, take care, and I'll see you both soon. Keep him on the straight and narrow Samantha." Andrea took off her forensic suit to reveal a pair of skin-tight jeans. She filled them to perfection as she bent over to tie her laces.

"God almighty Andrea, I'll have to get him out of here pronto, he's going to be drooling all over the bloody floor for goodness sakes. You really are cruel Miss Bortelli. Come on Terry, I'll pick your eyes up off the floor and then we'll go and see mister and Misses Williamson. Do you need to go to the bathroom for five minutes? I can wait outside."

As Andrea left the basement she could be heard laughing all the way down the hallway. "Have a nice day you pair." She shouted, as she exited the house.

A few minutes later Terry and Samantha were looking at the footage of mister and misses Williamson's security camera. "That's him looking for the torch." said Terry, as they watched James Carter rummaging in his boot.

Sure enough, the man on the film closed the boot of his car carrying a torch.

He stood at his step looking down at the torch as he must have been trying to switch it on. Nothing was happening. He went back into his house and closed the door behind him. After that, there was nothing, only the odd vehicles passing by here and there. There was no more activity outside of the house.

The elderly couple said they'd looked back to the beginning of the evening to see if there was any sign of anyone breaking into the premises. There was nothing, only mister Carter pulling up in his car and entering his house. Again, nothing, until he came back out to search for his torch.

Without saying anything to the pensioners Terry and Samantha both knew that at this point Sophie Spencer was already in the house. She must have entered by the back door. When Carter had entered his home he hadn't closed the curtains and so his house lit up as he'd turned on the lights. From here, you could almost see into his living room. Lace curtains had prevented that. After a few minutes, his living room went into darkness. A few minutes more, and there he was searching for the torch. Terry fast-forwarded the footage for a few moments. Nothing was happening on the screen.

But then, just as they were about to switch off Samantha said, "There, roll it back a bit Terry, there!" On the screen, and just out of view from the camera, the front wheel of a motor-cycle. Half of the wheel was just in the right-hand corner of the screen. Whoever was riding the motorbike had headed away from the Carter house rather than towards it. Mercer turned to Mister Ronald Williamson.

"Do you know anyone around here who owns a motorbike mister Williamson?" Ronald Williamson looked at his wife and then shook his head. "No, we don't. Oh, there's a man down the road there who has one, he works for the post office, but he lives almost half a mile from here, he wouldn't park his bike here would he?"

"No...no he wouldn't mister Williamson. And you're sure no-one else around here owns one?"

"Not to my knowledge, we're all elderly residents around here sir. This whole row is populated by pensioners. Across the road there are younger families, but not this side. Misses Carter lived in that house you're looking at, she was elderly...that's her son, this mister Carter."

Samantha inserted a memory stick into mister Williamson's device. The apparatus was digital. Once loaded, the detectives thanked the elderly couple for their assistance and returned to the scene of the crime. They spoke with one of the forensics who informed them that mister Carter had been shot at close range by a Glock 20/ 10mm Automatic. It is the most powerful hand-gun in Glock's pistol-range. The officer went on to explain that whoever had done it had stood no more than six feet away from the victim, and needn't have bothered. "They could have shot him from the other side of the room and it would still have done as much damage as it did." The officer who was wearing his mask and who's voice sounded muffled continued, "They were making damn sure he was going to die."

SCOTLAND YARD.

BROADWAY VICTORIA.

Polly had received a phone call from down stairs. There was someone asking to speak with her in person and that it was of the utmost importance. The officer on the phone went on to inform her that this person had information regarding Sophie Spencer. Polly had informed the officer to frisk this person and escort them up to her office. Across the desk from her now, Margaret Hall sat with a large envelope on her lap. "As soon as I heard what has happened with Sophie I set out to see what I could do to help her. Now I know miss Sheppard that you have a job to do, and I also know that there are circumstances in which crimes of passion are committed, and this is one of those crimes. You can ask any of the girls or women who live in Bromley's Safe Haven, and they'll all tell you what kind of a girl Sophie is. You have no idea how much good that girl has done. She's sat and listened to them as they revealed to her what had happened to them. As I'm sure you already know, there is one girl Claire Rennie. She and Sophie became friends. I think Sophie felt particularly sorry for her. This…this bloody Alan Flint or whatever the hell his name is, well, he put Claire into hospital with a severe beating, I'm sure Sophie will have told you all this. And-."
"Yes she has misses Hall, and I appreciate you coming here and giving me your opinion on Sophie, but the fact remains that a man has been murdered. Sophie's prints are all over the apartment. She's telling me that she didn't kill this man. But, I'm afraid, the evidence is telling me that she did. Now, what myself and my colleagues have to do, is search diligently in that apartment to try and find some form of evidence that would back up Sophie's claim. So far we have nothing.
Now, I appreciate you trying to help her misses Hall, but I'm afraid that it's out of your hands, and mine if I'm honest. If we can't find anything to back up Sophie's story, then she will face the full force of the law. If nothing else, she'll be found guilty of murder on circumstantial evidence. Now, I am as you can imagine, a very busy woman, so, the officer outside the door will escort you back down, and thank you for trying to help Sophie. I'll tell her you were here."
Margaret Hall slid some photographs from out of the envelope she nursed. "Before I leave, please, look at these Miss Sheppard. These are x-rays of Claire Rennie's injuries. The young man who sneaked these copies for me risked his job to try and help me. Please look at them."
Polly accepted the prints from the kindly woman and looked at the x-rays.

Along with them, there were three photographs taken as Claire lay unconscious on the trolley in the theatre in the hospital where she was admitted. As Polly looked at the horror of the photographs Margaret Hall said, "She didn't make it I'm afraid Miss Sheppard. They'd managed to get her out of the coma but she died with internal bleeding. Her lungs had flooded. Poor Claire died yesterday afternoon. Don't tell Sophie that please. She'll be feeling bad enough as it is. You'll find something I'm sure Miss Sheppard you'll find something that will clear Sophie from murder.

But remember this, what you're looking at now was why Sophie done what she done to that man, and I have no sympathy for him whatsoever, no matter who killed him. Claire was a beautiful wee girl and we all loved her." She pointed to the photographs in Polly's hands.

"And she didn't deserve to die like this."

Polly asked Margaret if she could keep the photographs for a while.

Margaret consented. "Misses Hall, let me make one thing clear here, we will try our utmost to find any evidence that would clear Sophie, believe me.

She has made an impression on more people than you care to think. And I hope from the bottom of my heart that she is not prosecuted for murder…but until we find something that backs up her claim to innocence, well, to put it bluntly misses Hall, she is the prime suspect."

MITCHAM.

Colin Green was outside his house polishing his car when Terry and Samantha pulled up a few yards in front of him. Without stopping what he was doing he greeted Samantha as the detectives approached him. Pleasantly he said to her, "What can I do for you today miss Reynolds? I take it this is not a social visit." "Well, yes it is Colin in a manner of speaking, although we have come to ask you a couple of official questions as well."
"Official? Am I in trouble again? Have I done something wrong?
Like, breathe in the wrong direction?"
"Come on Colin, that's not fair. We just need to ask you a couple of things. You're aware of Sophie Spencer's predicament I take it?"
Colin stopped polishing and looked at Samantha. "Predicament?
No, what's happened? Is she alright?"
"Can we talk inside please Colin?"
"You can. He can wait out here." Colin pointed to Terry who was standing by the wall with his hands in his pockets looking at the ground.
"You can come in, but he can wait in your car, I've had it up to here with his fucking shit."
Samantha sighed and said, "I'm afraid I can't do that Colin. Either you let us both in or I go back to HQ and return with a warrant, please don't make me do that. You two will just have to bury your differences and act like grown' men, instead of a pair of school-boys. Now, are you going to let us both in Colin or do I have to do it by the book, either way, we'll be having a conversation."
He threw the duster onto the bonnet of the car and made his way up the garden path towards his back door. As he walked in front he asked Samantha again what was wrong with Sophie. As they entered the kitchen Rebecca Green was busy making cheese and toast. "Hi Terry, would you like some cheese and toast, I'm making some for Alison and mum."
Before Terry had a chance to reply Colin said, "No he doesn't want any cheese and toast Rebecca, he's getting fuck all that's what he's getting, and don't be making him any tea or coffee either, he's much too busy to be drinking tea."
As they walked through the living room heading upstairs Jillian greeted Terry and Samantha although not in the same pleasant manner to which they had become accustomed. It was a short sharp, "Hello Terry Hello Samantha." And then she continued dusting her ornaments. As they all reached the top of the stairs they were greeted by Alison who took the time to remove her headphones and say hiya to the two

detectives who answered her equally as cheerful. At least the girls weren't against him. They entered Colin's bedroom and he motioned for the detectives to have a seat. He sat on the double bed. This room was obviously the handy-work of Jillian. It was absolutely beautiful. Samantha even felt guilty for sitting on the stool in front of Jillian's dressing table.

"Well? What predicament are you going on about? What's Sophie got herself into?" Although Terry knew he wasn't being spoken to, it was he who informed Colin of the situation. He cleared his throat. "There's eh…there's been a murder Colin, over in Clapham. The guy has been bound to a chair in his basement. He's been beat up a bit, and then shot in the head at nigh-on point blank range."

He let the information hang in the air for a few moments.

"Sophie's DNA is all over the place. She's admitted to bashing this guy's hands with a hammer, but she's denying murdering him. The trouble is, there's only Sophie's DNA in the basement along with the victims'. There's no other samples. It's not looking good for her just now. We have her in custody.

It's bad Colin…it's bad."

Colin Green sat on his bed and clasped his hands together with his fingers under his chin as though he were about to say a prayer. He took in a very deep breath and exhaled through his nose. For the first time he looked at Terry Mercer.

"You're sure there's no other prints in there?"

Terry didn't answer. He didn't have to.

Colin got up from the bed and stood at the top of the stairs. "Rebecca? Rebecca, make us all coffee, make three cups of coffee please."

A voice came back up the stairs to him.

"Dad, I thought you said-."

"Never fucking mind what I said, make some coffee now, and none of your fucking back-chat, just do as you're told!"

Jillian was up the stairs like a shot from a gun. "Colin, what the hell is wrong with you!? You've made her cry for goodness sakes. You told her you didn't want coffee, what the hell? You get down there and you apologise to her. And why the hell are you all up here? You can talk down stairs, bloody sitting up here in my bedroom, come on, down stairs the lot of you. Christ Colin."

As they reached the bottom of the stairs Colin attempted to apologise to his daughter, but the girl just brushed past him bursting out into tears again. "Just leave me alone." Even as Rebecca reached the top of the stairs her father called up after her. "I'm so sorry sweetheart…I didn't mean to hurt your feelings…I'm sorry darling."

Samantha and Terry felt it was better for everyone if they stood outside in the garden.

There they waited for Colin. Eventually he came outside with cups of coffee for the detectives. If Terry and Samantha thought that the situation for Sophie was bad just now, then in about two minutes it was going to go from bad to absolutely abysmal. They all lit up cigarettes. "The thing is Colin, that gun you gave her, well she gave it back to me and Samantha. She said something like shooting this guy wouldn't have felt like revenge if she'd done that. And she's adamant that she didn't shoot *this* man…but then…her DNA."

Colin sat down on a ledge. "What have you done with the gun?"

"We've got it in the car. We didn't say anything to anyone else about it.

Polly Sheppard doesn't know you gave her a gun."

Colin looked up at Terry.

"Can I have it back please?"

"Sure, I'll just go and get it for you."

As Terry walked away from Samantha and Colin she said, "He's hurting Colin.

He's bloody suffering here I can tell you that, and I know you will be too.

It sticks out a mile Colin how much you think of that girl, I mean, you treat her like your own daughter."

Colin just nodded in agreement as he smoked his cigarette. "And I know Samantha before you remind me. I shouldn't have given her a gun.

The idea behind that was to make sure that she'd never be kidnapped again, that she'd have some kind of protection in the house should the occasion ever arise again. I didn't mean for her to go out looking for trouble, and certainly not to take the law into her own hands. I admit it, it was a mistake on my part but I can't change anything now. I regret it."

A few moments later Terry returned with the carrier bag Sophie had handed him. He handed the bag to Colin who looked inside it. "What's this?"

"What?" replied Terry.

"This isn't the gun I gave to Sophie. This is a Smith and Wesson. I gave her a Glock 20, 10 mm. This isn't the gun I gave to her."

Terry Mercer fell to his knees and with his hands on his face he cried, "Oh my dear sweet Christ."

SCOTLAN YARD.

BROADWAY VICTORIA.

Terry and Samantha entered the interview room where Sophie Spencer was being detained. "Lies lies lies Sophie, isn't it? You can't help yourself can you.
You are a compulsive liar, and you're so good at it that you can even convince yourself that you're telling the truth."
"I don't know what you mean Terry." replied a confused Sophie.
"Oh you don't know what I mean? Well, let me remind you. Here you are Terry I shan't be needing this, me and Lisa have come to our senses. Oh I'm so sorry mum for putting you through all this, but I've got the rest of my life to get on with. It's time to put my life-plan into action. Thank you so much Terry and Samantha for everything you've done for me, but there's no need to worry any more. Does that ring any fucking bells in your lying little head, does it!?"
Sophie sat with her head down unable to look Terry in the face. In a somewhat whispered voice she said, "I know I lied about the gun. Lisa got a Smith and Wesson pistol on the internet. I kept the gun Colin gave me.
But I have no intentions of using it. I kept it because it was security should anyone break into my mum's house. I would have protection. I didn't want to think about the possibility of what being kidnapped again would mean. I swear to you, I have never used it, not even to practice shooting."
Terry stood above the girl over the table looking down at her. Then he turned.
With his back to her he said, "And can you tell me what type of gun Colin gave you?"
"I don't know exactly what size or what do you call it, calibre? All I know is that it is a Glock something or other, that's all I know."
"Is it now, is that all you know. Well, I'll enlighten you my lying little madam.
It is a Glock 20/10 millimetre, that's what it is. It is the most powerful pistol in the Glock range. And do you know what else I know Sophie? Shall I tell you? It was a Glock 20/10 millimetre that killed mister Carter, that's what else I know.
Now, taking into account that, your DNA is the only other alien DNA in that basement and the fact that Sophie Spencer happens to be in possession of a Glock 20/10 millimetre, what do you think the outcome of this investigation is going to be, huh? What do you think your chances are of ever returning home again? Is there anything you can say that would convince a jury or a judge that you did not kill mister James Carter, because I'll tell you Sophie, I can't think of anything. And don't think bursting

out crying is going to make the jury feel sorry for you, oh no, not after the damage you done to the man before you shot him. Now you can sit there and swear all day to me and Samantha that you didn't commit that murder, but it's not going to make one little bit of difference to the outcome of your trial."

Samantha sat quietly scrutinising the troubled teenager sitting across the table. Even with all this evidence against her. Her prints and her admission that she'd bashed the man's hands with a hammer, and the fact that she was in possession of a Glock pistol. All this, and still she wasn't a hundred percent certain that Sophie shot the man.

But she also knew that this gut-feeling she had would not help Sophie's case in any way. Terry was right. There was not a judge in the world who would not convict her of murder, or at least manslaughter. Sophie Spencer was going to jail. It was as simple as that.

All three sat now in silence. As far as Terry was concerned it was over, even before Sophie went on trial. On the grounds of the damning evidence, the trial would not be delayed. He guessed around six weeks, tops.

He leaned over the table.

"I want you to do me a favour Sophie. I need you to tell me now where you keep the gun. Where have you got it hidden? Tell me the truth, because if you don't they will barge into your mum's house and they will turn it upside down I kid you not. Now, you don't want that to happen to your mum, surely. Tell me where it is so that the forensic team can inspect it. You say you have never fired it?

Well Sophie, these people are very clever indeed, and they can tell me if the gun was fired this time last year. So, if you say you haven't fired it, then there is a glimmer of hope for you, but it's only a glimmer, and that, of course depends upon whether you're telling us the truth."

Sophie looked at Terry and then Samantha.

"It's hidden in a red shoe box underneath my bed. Colin told me to keep it somewhere it would be easy to reach."

"Did he now, and did he give you any ammunition for this fucking cannon did he?"

"Yes, the cartridges are in the box as well. I haven't opened the package they're in. They're sealed in polythene, in a small box."

Samantha looked at Terry. Another glimmer of hope.

"Ok Sophie, I'm just going to make a phone call to my forensic officers.

Now, this is your last chance to change anything you've just told us. After I make this phone call, the forensic team will arrive at your mum's house with a warrant to search the premises. You're sure the gun is where you say it is?

And you're sure you haven't fired it even one time, not even to practice?"

"Yes, I'm certain. I've told you the truth Terry."

"Yeah well, if you don't mind Sophie, I'll take that with a pinch of salt until I get verification from the forensic team. Would you like to get us all some coffee please Samantha?"

Samantha was tempted to hit him back with a sarcastic comment, but this was neither the time nor the place. "Sure." She replied politely.

Ten minutes later Samantha Terry and Sophie sat at the table in the centre of the interview room. "Well, I've made the call Sophie, I only hope that you've been telling us the truth this time. Even as we speak a couple of officers are on their way over to your mum's house. In less than an hour they'll be able to tell me if you have. And if you haven't then I can safely say that this will be the last conversation we'll be having for a very long time."

Once again as Terry sat with the teenager and his colleague there was a knock on the door. "Ah, miss Vincent, how nice to see you again.

Another private message?"

This time Joan Vincent was dressed in black trousers with a white blouse and one-inch heeled dress boots. "Yes sir. It's from miss Bortelli, may we speak in private sir?"

"Yes miss Vincent, we can speak in private if it means that much to you. How are you and mister Henderson getting along these days?"

With a wide grin Joan Vincent replied, "I don't know how he's getting on sir, I've been moved. I'm working with another detective now. Thank you sir, I really appreciate your help."

As Terry left the room with the junior detective he turned and smiled at Samantha who smiled jokingly back at him. He said to her just before he closed the door, "Joan of Arc indeed Samantha."

Less than five minutes later Terry re-entered the room. "Let's go Samantha. I'm afraid we'll have to be leaving you again Sophie. I hope with all my heart that we'll be having further conversations, but all that depends on what those two officers find at your mum's house." Before she left, Samantha turned and handed Sophie a packet of cigarettes. "See you soon Sophie." And with that, she and Terry Mercer exited the interview room.

They were on their way to Bromley. Hawthorne Close. Andrea Bortelli informed Terry that she'd be waiting for them there. This time Andrea was standing outside of the house drinking from a polystyrene carton that had a famous coffee brand stamped upon it.

"It's always nice to see a happy couple you know. You can tell when two people are deeply in love, because they're always arguing the toss with each other night and day. What's he moaning about today Samantha?"

As Samantha locked the car door she replied, "oh, that I'm the slowest driver in all of the boroughs' of London. There's nobody drives slower than me.

He feels ashamed sitting next to me, and that any journey further than six miles requires him to bring provisions, as in, having to spend the night somewhere." Andrea only smiled as she turned from where she stood. "Follow me you pair, I have some interesting evidence for you. More than interesting, exhilarating would be closer to the truth. I expect a bar lunch out of this Terry, because it could quite easily have been overlooked."

Neither Terry or Samantha said anything as Bortelli led them to the back of the house. They reached the back of the premises where Andrea stopped and pointed to the ground. She continued. "There were so many people here on the night of Gareth's murder, neighbours and friends and all. More than eight people all running around the grounds of the house, you know, in the garden and all around the house. But then, as I was having a cigarette the following day, I happened to spot something."

Terry looked at the head forensic. "You found another footprint didn't you Andrea, tell me you found another footprint, and I'll buy your whole team a bar lunch."

"Better than that Terry. Not only did I find another footprint, but it happens to be the exact replica of the one at Edgeley Road in Clapham. We were wrong about the training shoe."

"What? It wasn't a size seven?"

"Oh it's a size seven alright, but we were wrong about it being a trainer.

It's a trainer-boot. There's a difference. As you know, with some brands they recommend that if you're wearing boots, to buy a size larger than your usual size, it's for comfort, so that your feet can breathe. Now, come with me. Oh, I take it you spotted the motor-cycle wheel on Mister Williamson's security camera?"

"Of course," Mercer replied, smiling at Samantha.

"Well then, you go across there Terry, to number eighty-three and ask nicely to see mister and Misses Priestley's footage. Mind out though, they have a particularly nasty Doberman bitch that patrols the back garden.

It's best if you get the Priestley's attention first by standing at their front window from the safety of the pavement, otherwise Terry, Misty will tear your bum and balls to pieces and ruin those twenty-quid jeans you're wearing.

But, before you do, let me show you something. She led them back round to where she discovered the footprints.

"On the night of Gareth's murder it was dry, and quite windy.
But it had been raining all that day so the ground was sodden.
Whoever murdered Gareth came in through the kitchen window here.
You see this? On the roughcast? Mud sticks Terry.
You can't see it with the naked eye now, but our fancy forensic cameras can.
It works like night-vision apparatus. We were right about the brand of trainer.
The boots have the very same tread, so you can excuse our minor error.
Anyway, let's get you pair over to mister and Misses Priestley's house, because this is the bit where you will have your orgasm Terry, I kid you not.
Thank goodness for security cameras, that's all I can say.
Now, according to my team, Gareth was murdered around seven-thirty, eight o clock.
What you should do is pay attention to the time on the camera footage of the key moment."

"And what, may I ask is the key moment?"

"Oh you'll see Terry, trust me, you'll see, and then it's bar-lunches for six of us my friend, and you heard him Samantha."

"Indeed I did, but hey, bar-lunches for six people is nothing to Terry, is it babe. He's used to parting with barrow loads of cash to his snitches. Bloody bottles of whiskey and boxes of cigarettes by the hundreds, and paying people's rent for them for a whole year if they happen to be pretty enough, hell no Andrea, you have nothing to fear of him keeping his word buying half a dozen bar-lunches I can assure you."

The camera on the garage roof belonging to the Priestley's looked directly onto their front door and drive. However, in the background the Tait premises could plainly be seen. They watched Gareth and his girlfriend entering the house at seven-fifteen. What Andrea had been referring to was what happened next. Right in front of the Priestley's house, but directly across the road, a motorcycle pulled up. Unmistakably a female form slipped off the bike. A tight black bikers' suit that could have been leather casually walked down towards the Tait house. She disappeared around the back of the house. At two minutes past eight, the female biker re-appeared further up the street from behind another house and boarded the motorbike taking off into the night. Never at any point, were they able to see a face. Even as she'd made her way to the Tait house, the crash-helmet had remained on her head.

As the two detectives returned to the Tait household, Samantha said, "Well Terry, it looks as though Sophie has been telling the truth after all.
There's been somebody else there at Clapham as well, it would seem, and by the looks of it, it's the same person, whoever she is."

As they walked Terry said, "I can't for the life of me think of anyone who would have a grudge on her, to frame her for murder, and of course Samantha, we know a female motor-cyclist was here, we still have no concrete proof that they were at Clapham as well. Sophie is far from out of the woods yet."

When they arrived back at the house, Andrea was standing with a huge grin on her face. "Do you ever get one of those days Terry when everything just turns out perfect?"

"No."

"You know, when you need a break, and it doesn't look like you're going to get one, and then, bang. There it is, right in front of your face. Those days are few and far between we can all vouch, but I'm glad to say mister Mercer, that today is indeed, one of those days. I've just had a phone call from my team over in Clapham, some more footage for you and Samantha to look at. Somebody three doors down from the Williamsons' has security cameras as well, and guess what's on their footage? When you say bar-lunch Terry, I hope you're not expecting us all to sit down to scampi and chips. I was thinking more in the way of a good T-bone with all the trimmings and an elaborate desert to follow, with a couple of bottles from the Heitz Cellar 2014 Linda Falls vineyard, Cabernet Sauvignon perhaps?"

Terry looked at Samantha.

"About a hundred and sixty-quid a bottle sweetheart."

Andrea smiled, impressed with Samantha's knowledge concerning really good clarets.

"And do you happen to know where it is made Miss Reynolds?" said Andrea, smiling again at the shell-shocked Terrence Mercer.

"It's made in the Napa Valley, California, and I have to say, if you're a fan of the red wines you certainly would not be disappointed, although Terry here tried one in Lithuania and informed the woman who poured it for him that it tasted like something you'd put on your chips. He's not a fan shall we say Andrea and I'm sure I'm on the right track by saying that you'd be hard-pushed indeed, even for him, to part with that kind of money for a bottle of wine. Terry would be thinking more along the lines of those bottles you find on the shelves at Tesco or one of the other leading super-markets, you know, the two-ninety-nine bracket. The ones that taste like something you'd use to clean the insides of your toilet." Andrea stood with her hands on her hips studying the odd-couple in front of her. One minute they were tearing lumps out of each other verbally, the next, they were complimenting each other whole-heartedly. "I can see you pair getting married, honestly. I'll see you over in Clapham."

"Come on." Snapped Terry, "And I'm driving. Huh, I have no choice if I want to get there before tomorrow." As they walked to the car Terry said, "That wasn't the wine I had in Lithuania was it? You were talking about there."

"No, it wasn't Terry, the wine you had in Lithuania was French. It was a Vosne-

Romanee…that costs about a thousand pounds a bottle." As they walked on Mercer mumbled something about people with money not having the slightest idea about how good wine should taste… a thousand pounds indeed, for a bottle of vinegar. "Huh, kidding themselves on that they're experts and turning their heads away as they screw their faces up at the horrible taste in their mouths."

EDGELEY ROAD.

CLAPHAM.

She's not very tall is she?" said Samantha as they scrutinised the footage on the Hudson security camera. Once again, the motorcycle had pulled up on the opposite side of the road from her intended target. There was a public path that ran in between the terraced houses, probably for residents to be able to obtain access to their wheelie-bins. The woman dismounted the bike and crossed the road, again without removing her crash-helmet, and disappeared between the houses.
"Never seen her again." Said Tom Hudson, an eighty-one-year-old widower.
"She got back onto the bike and pulled away and she's never been back, don't know who the hell she is, and anyway it was her that heard it, I didn't hear a bloody thing." The elderly gentleman pointed to an ageing black Labrador lying underneath his cabinet. Terry stifled a grin as he clocked Tom's hearing aids, one on each ear. They were the old-fashioned type. The ones that looked like you had a wooden clothes-peg wedged behind each ear. Even as they spoke now, the TV was playing at an extremely high volume. And, once again Samantha down-loaded all the footage onto a memory stick. Terry attempted to thank the man for allowing them to see the footage.
"Well mister Hudson, we'll have to-."
"What?"
"I said, we'll have-."
"Wait, I can't hear what you're saying, you'll have to speak up."
"It's ok mister Hudson we're just-."
"It's no good son, you'll have to talk louder, it's the bloody batteries, and they cost a fortune, bloody things. I shouldn't have to pay for them at my age. What!?"
Rather as continue attempting to communicate Terry and Samantha just about-turned and left the living room. As they reached the sanctuary of the front path, they both breathed a sigh of relief. "No wonder he didn't hear the motorbike pulling up, hell that tele must be at its' highest volume, poor bugger. I'm surprised the bloody dog even heard it with all that din."
"We have that to look forward to Terry, in our dotage, of course, you'll be there a decade before me, but none-the-less, it's coming to us all. Anyway, our biker's arrival and departure co-insides with the time of James Carter's murder Terry, that's the main thing. Whoever she is, it's looking a lot like she's committed a double murder."
Mercer agreed with his colleague. "But, Samantha, there is still no proof that she's been

in here. They can't find a bloody thing. A half of a footprint. There's no DNA samples to be found of our mystery woman. She's done this before whoever the hell she is. This is not the first time she's killed. Not a bloody trace. And, we still haven't heard from the forensic officers we've sent to Sophie's house.

If that gun has been fired recently Samantha, then she's going to jail for a very long time. All of her bad experiences over in Lithuania will stand for nothing now. Not having taken a bloody mash-hammer and done that to the poor bugger.

No matter how you look at it, it's nothing less than callous Sam, in fact it's brutal, and that's the way the jury will see it as well, there'll be no remorse for her." After a short discussion with Andrea Bortelli Terry and Samantha headed back into the city. "A good nights' sleep Samantha, that's what I need. Early to bed early to rise."

Half an hour later Terry dropped Samantha off at her apartment and then made his way back over to Holburn. He would indeed have himself an early night. As he entered his home he picked up the days' mail from the hallway floor and made his way into the kitchen, throwing the letters wearily onto the table. He put the kettle on to make himself a coffee. As he waited for it to boil he began to open his mail one item at a time. There was nothing of any importance or interest in the bundle until he came upon a rather elaborate envelope.

One that perhaps a lover would send to their sweetheart. It had fancy trimmed edges and of a pale pink colour. It was also scented. He opened up the letter and began to read. At first he thought it was Samantha who was perhaps playing a joke but he soon learned that it was no joke. He made his coffee and sat down to read the contents of the letter.

Dear inspector Mercer. I know I said that you wouldn't be hearing from me again, but then things can change very quickly, as we both know. Circumstances can change really quickly. Anyway, down to business. I understand that a young lady you have in your custody is in serious trouble. Namely Miss Sophie Spencer. It would seem that the evidence is stacked against her concerning the murder of a mister James Carter. Let me start from the beginning. I knew about the girl for some time. She was one of Monica's favourites over in Lithuania, her and the Jenson girl. So, it was with some interest I watched her, you know, to see how she was going to cope after her ordeal. It seems that she and the Jenson girl were going to take revenge on one or two people, and of course starting with Gareth Tait. Gareth was a dog's body for Claire Redgrave. She would get people like Gareth to assist in some of the kidnappings. It was he who bundled Sophie over to the van on the day of her abduction, dressed as a council-worker. He also played a part in the abduction of Lisa Jenson. So, this being the case, I sensed that the girls would land themselves in serious trouble, if they ever found out his identity, which they obviously did, and so I took matters into my own hands. I began to follow Sophie, and it wasn't long before she decided to take revenge for someone who'd been given a hard time. I believe her friend's name was Claire Rennie. The man who was murdered in Edgeley Road Clapham had been beating this Claire. She had been put into hospital with the severity of the beatings she'd received. I followed Sophie for a few weeks, taking a great deal of interest in her movements, and after all, I was part of the syndicate that had destroyed her life, and so I felt obligated to help her out. I left enough traces for you and your forensic friends to know at least that Sophie did not kill the man. She had indeed inflicted some serious wounds to his hands, but it was me who shot him in the head, and not Sophie. I left enough evidence to make everyone think, at least initially, that she was the murderer. This was to help Sophie. Even now, although she knows in herself that she didn't kill him she's thinking that she will be sentenced for murder. What I have done mister Mercer, hopefully, is that she has finally learned a lesson in not to be taking the law into her own hands. I also murdered Gareth Tait as well. I let you see me on my motorcycle, particularly at Hawthorne Close. This was to let you know for sure that someone had an interest in Sophie Spencer. Now, inside the basement in Clapham, your forensic team were working day and night picking up all the evidence they could concerning Sophie. What they overlooked mister Mercer, probably owing to the fact that mister James Carter had a bullet stuck in his brain, was the fact that, although Sophie would confess to you that she bashed the man's hands with a hammer, which she undoubtedly did, but, there are no prints on the mash-hammer lying on the floor in that basement. I saw to that. What I done was, after I shot him, was to obtain another hammer similar to the one Sophie used, and I proceeded to put my prints onto the shaft, and then I smeared some of the blood onto that hammer. So, in a nut-shell mister Mercer, if Sophie has not signed a confession to the fact that she did indeed inflict those wounds onto him, she can now deny even doing that to him, and that she'd visited mister Carter to have a discussion about Claire. Now then mister Mercer, you must be thinking that all this is perhaps bullshit but I assure you, you will find all the evidence you need to support my story. You have no idea of my whereabouts and further-more it is of no interest to you where I am. I have committed these murders to repay some of the damage I caused to that poor little girl and her friends. I suppose you could say I done it to help clear my own conscience and perhaps there is an element of truth in that. But most of all, I done it to help Sophie get on with her life. The person who bundled her and her friend into the van that day, is dead. The person who inflicted the terrible beatings to the young woman she'd befriended, is dead. The old man who had trapped her into a world of sex and drugs, is in jail. Tell her now mister Mercer, that she and the big bad world are even. And now to sum up. In the shed at the back of the house in

Edgeley Road, you will find a bundle of hessian sacks. Tell your forensics to lift the sacks and there they will find the Glock pistol that killed mister Carter. My prints are all over it. They will also find the afore-mentioned mash-hammer, complete with my fingerprints all over the shaft. Underneath misses Tait's chest of drawers in Hawthorne Close, you will find the gloves I wore on the night I murdered Gareth, along with the small bottle of chloroform I used to knock out the young lady who accompanied him. So, that's us done mister Mercer. It is of course entirely up to you if you inform your superiors of this letter. Or you could keep it as our own little secret as a reminder of how some people can change...for the better. Tell Sophie and her friend that I wish them both all the luck in the world, and as I wish you mister Mercer, the very same. Oh, and don't worry, by the time you read this, I'll be out of the country. This time mister Mercer, it really is goodbye. Take care, and God bless. Angela Bates.x

Terry Mercer sat dumbstruck. Was all this information true? If it was, then Sophie Spencer would be back home in less than a couple of days. He sipped his coffee and went over the letter again, word for word. If Angela Bates was telling him the truth, then Sophie's troubles were over, at least as far as going to jail was concerned. But these days he found it hard to believe anyone, apart from Samantha and Andrea. Fellow detectives selling their souls for cash, dealing in kidnappings. The chief of police being involved with human-trafficking. What the hell was the world coming to?
And now, to top it all, a perpetrator of the kidnappers committing a double-murder to help a teenager she'd had kidnapped. It didn't make sense, but then, hardly anything that was happening in the world was making any sense these days. He lit another cigarette and read the letter for the third time. Whatever the outcome, he would keep this letter under wraps. No-one was going to know about this until he'd seen for himself if the evidence was where Angela claimed it to be. There'd be no early night for him now, that was for sure. Twenty minutes later he was heading over to Bromley.
His first port of call would be Hawthorne Close.
A combination of exhilaration and apprehension surged through his veins as he drove through the night. All manner of thoughts were sweeping through his head. Right back from the beginning of the kidnappings, Colin Greens' seemingly suicidal trip to Lithuania. Old Treble-clef's gesture, taking he and Samantha over there as his chosen guests. Driving the people-carrier from Kaunas over to Poland with the girls in the back, half of them scared beyond belief, just as he was himself. Treble's beheaded corpse in Pinkerton, everything was racing through his head now. His own colleague Samantha Reynolds, shooting Claire Redgrave in the head in front of a petrified teenage girl. He turned on the radio to try and take his mind off everything. He didn't know how he

would feel or react if he arrived here in Bromley to find that Angela Bates had been toying with him and sending him on a wild goose-chase. He would find out within the next half-hour. Mister and Misses Tait were now living with friends until the forensic officers were finished. Even after they were, he doubted very much that they'd be able to live there, not after that. They'd never be able to climb the stairs again without remembering how they found their son. They would sell the house.

After what felt like an eternity, he finally pulled up at Hawthorne Close.

He switched off the engine and walked the short distance over to the house. There was one officer guarding the premises. Mercer approached the man who was suspicious of Terry until he showed the policeman his ID. "Good evening sir." Said the now nervous officer having identified mister Terrance Mercer.

"I certainly hope so." replied Terry, ducking underneath the police-tape which had been wrapped around practically all the vicinity of the house.

Markers lay all around the floor of the house instructing him where he could walk and where he couldn't. A urine stain at the top of the stairs had some kind of chalk drawn around it. He looked up to the beams where Gareth had met his fate and imagined the Tait couple finding their son, probably still swinging from the rafters.

"You could have done it more humanely Angela."

A few seconds later he entered misses Tait's bedroom. There, at the far side of the room was the chest of drawers Angela Bates had referred to.

He got down on his knees and ran his hand underneath the piece of furniture.

"Bastard!!" There was nothing there. In sheer temper he pulled the chest of drawers out from its' position. Nothing at all lying on the floor, other than a lip-stick holder.

"You fucking cruel bitch, I'll hunt the ends of the earth for you, you fucking scrubber bastard that you are!" He stepped away from the chest of drawers and broke the code by sitting down on the double bed. He sat with his arms resting on his thighs and his hands clasped together, just looking at the floor, and shaking his head. Why on earth would she do this to him? Nobody was bothering her. She was living free compared to her companions who were either dead, or serving long sentences for their endeavours. Why would she be so cruel as to play a dirty trick like this. After a few minutes when he'd got himself together again and accepted the situation, he rose up to leave the room, and indeed, the house, but as he reached the bedroom door, he stopped and turned back to replace the chest of drawers. Before he did, one last hope. He pushed the piece of furniture gently onto its' back on the floor. There, in a sealed polythene bag, cello-taped to the under-side of the chest of drawers was the gloves and the small bottle of Chloroform along with the cloth she'd used to render the teenage girl unconscious. Angela Bates had not been lying after all. Terry Mercer just sat there on his knees, staring at the crucial evidence. With his hands on his thighs he looked up to the ceiling. "Thank you Angela, thank you so much…you were telling the truth."

To proceed correctly he couldn't remove the evidence. He would have to make sure that someone else found it. What he decided to do was to take several photographs of the polythene bag and its' contents, as proof that he was the first to find it, if that should ever become necessary. He carefully replaced the chest of drawers into its' original position and left the room. As he left the house the policeman guarding the premises asked him nervously having heard him scream out a swear-word which reverberated in the still night, if everything was alright. Mercer only replied to the man with, "You're doing a fine job officer."

As he drove it crossed his mind to inform Samantha of the course of events.

He felt a stab of guilt keeping this from her, but she'd be the first to know as soon as he had executed his plan, and after all, he still had Clapham to go to.

He had to admit he was more hopeful this time of finding the evidence that would clear Sophie Spencer of murder. What if he hadn't turned the chest of drawers over? What if he'd left there in a temper and gave up? Sophie would be in deep water. As it was, the evidence was there, backing up everything Angela had said in her letter. Now, when he got to Clapham, the evidence he was about to recover would undoubtedly clear Sophie from murder once and for all.

Having stopped at a motorway café for a snack and a coffee, he arrived at Edgeley Road in Clapham. There were two police officers on duty here guarding the Carter premises. A male and a female. Once again he had to produce his ID.

The first thing he'd have to do was get them away from here for the length of time it would take him to search the shed at the bottom of the garden, and so he instructed them to go and get him cigarettes.

The male officer said, "Sir, it doesn't take two of us to go and get cigarettes does it? She can go and I'll stay here with you, that sounds more sensible does it not…doesn't take two of us."

Mercer looked at the smarmy constable with a look of disdain.

"Listen to me smart arse! I have two fists, but it'll only take one of them to dislodge several of your fucking buck-teeth and wipe that fucking grin off your face. And who may I ask is She? Who the fuck do you think you are? You refer to your fellow-officer by her name in future do you hear me? Otherwise I'll kick you so hard in your fucking balls that they'll knock your eyes right out of their sockets, do I make myself clear, cleverdick? Now, you get in that fucking car and go and get me my cigarettes and no more of your shit…she indeed. You're a skinny fucking crawling rat, that's what you are, fucking fancy boy. Now here, take this money and go and do as you're told.

What's your name miss?"

"Emily sir, Emily Stevenson." The officer replied, smiling.

"Well, Miss Emily Stevenson, you go in the house and make us a nice cup of tea while fucking kipper-face here goes and gets' my cigarettes, how does that sound. Does that sound more sensible?"

It was all the young lady was worth not to burst out laughing at her partner's reprimand, because detective Mercer had hit the nail right on the head.

Constable Jones was indeed a skinny crawling smart-ass who thought he knew better than everyone else. He knew better now.

The embarrassed officer accepted the money and asked Mercer what brand of cigarettes he was to get, and then trundled despondently down the path to the patrol car.

"Don't let them talk down to you officer Stevenson. He's only the same rank as yourself. Don't let them intimidate you. Anyway, it won't be too long until you'll be giving him his orders because he has as much chance of promotion as the Pope does of being the Brothel-master."

This time Emily Stevenson did burst out laughing.

"Ok Emily, you go and make the tea and I'll just check something out at the bottom of the garden. Two sugars for me please Emily, and milk if there is any...should have got goat-boy there to get us some."

Emily was now almost in hysterics because she knew that the goat-boy reference was because of the tuft of ginger hair at the base of Jones' chin. She had only met detective Mercer for a few minutes but already she admired him immensely.

She had never met anyone so fast with sarcastic insults. This man could cut you to ribbons in seconds with his tongue. Emily disappeared into the house to make the beverages. Mercer made his way to the bottom of the garden. Angela Bates was indeed a very clever girl. She'd left all the evidence in the house for the forensics to find. Why would they bother to walk thirty-odd yards down the garden when all the evidence was in the basement? There was a rusted padlock on the shed door but it was not fastened. He opened the door of the shed. It creaked loudly like in the horror films, the hinges groaning as he pushed the door fully open.

Sure enough, there in the corner of the shed were the hessian sacks Angela had told him about. He gently pulled back the sacks. There they were.

The Glock pistol, the blood-stained hammer, even the nail bar Sophie had said she'd used to knock out James Carter. Again, he took photographs with his phone and then replaced the sacks.

And again, he'd have to make sure someone else other than he or Samantha found them. That wouldn't be hard to do. In the distance he heard Emily's voice calling out to him. "Tea's ready detective Mercer." Mercer smiled at this situation. Bates had made things a lot easier now. With all the evidence to back up Sophie's statement he could all but guarantee her release. As he headed back to the house for his tea he reflected on how he'd spoken to the male officer who'd gone for his cigarettes. They had to be taught how to respect each other. He remembered how his superior Sam Hargrieves had educated him in how to address other officers. He slapped his face hard in the canteen in front of all the other officers in there and told him to stop being such a petted bitch. "Coming Emily."

HAWTHORNE CLOSE. 9am.

Samantha had received a pleasant surprise at eight o clock this morning when Terry Mercer had pulled up in front of her apartment. He said it was to save her the bother of driving into the city in this horrible drizzle. It was indeed a stinker of a day although you wouldn't have thought so by the smile on Terry's face. He was cheerful and jovial as opposed to the usual grump and moan he usually was on days like these. He'd even came into her apartment and accepted her offer of some coffee and toast while she got ready for work. Not a single complaint about anything this morning. If only…if only he could be like this all the time, but it would no doubt be short-lived, this spritely attitude. "Perhaps he's won a tenner on a scratch-card." There had to be something. As the day progressed and his mood changed, she would eventually find out what it was that humoured him. Andrea was sitting in her car when they pulled up outside of the Tait's house. She climbed out of her car when she saw them arrive.
Standing with some documents under her right arm, she greeted them with her usual humour. "Let me see your left hand please Samantha. Oh, no fancy vivid yet? Never mind Samantha, he's maybe waiting for the right time."
Terry looked to Samantha. "What the hell does that mean, fancy vivid, what's that?" Samantha laughed out loud. "The words refer to the particular colours of a diamond Terry, that's what it means. In other words no engagement-."
"I know the rest now Samantha, I guessed that with the diamond reference. Anyway Andrea, what's the result from Lexington Square. I'm almost frightened to ask."
Making her way into the house she said over her shoulder, "Well you shouldn't be Terry, the girl's been telling the truth. The gun has not been fired, and there is not a single cartridge missing from the box of ammunition that was found with it.
Of course, we know now that Sophie didn't kill mister Carter, the hard part is going to be finding the person who did." Again, Samantha was surprised at Terry's casual answer. "Oh, I'm sure something will turn up Andrea. We'll find something that'll give the killer away, we always do." Even Andrea looked surprised by his comments. She continued. "The motorcycle in the security footage is a Honda CBR 1100 XX. I am informed by one of my colleagues that it is, to use his exact words, a fucking flying machine, this Honda Super Blackbird CBR 1100 XX. Whoever the girl is in the footage she believes in getting from A to B rather quickly. I made some enquiries and there are over three hundred of these bikes in and around the boroughs of London. I tried to zoom in on the machine on the footage but guess what, she didn't even have any number plates on the vehicle, isn't that a bugger Terry."

Yet again, Terry seemed dis-interested.

The number-plate absence would normally have sent him off on one of his rants, but no…nothing. Samantha was indeed confused. Terry pulled out his cigarettes and offered one to the two women.

"Oh, I nearly forgot Andrea. I need a small favour from you today."

"A small favour? Is there such a thing in the Terry Mercer needing a favour note-book?"

"Yeah, you know the junior detective you asked me to help, Joan Vincent?
Well, I want her to get some experience in the forensic field.
Now, I'll keep her out of your way. I want her to look around outside of the house over at Edgeley Road in Clapham. Now, you and I know that there's nothing there to find but I want her to feel confident. Confidence leads to success.
The girl has been hampered by that useless twat Henderson and has no self-confidence whatsoever. Anyway, just tell her to look around the garden and round the grounds of the house, hell, tell her to look in the bloody shed, yeah, that's it, tell her to search the shed in case something or other has been discarded by the murderer. That should make her feel that at least she's doing something worthwhile. Will you do that for me please Andrea? After all, it was you who said she was going to be a good one, well, give her a break and let her feel part of a team, it would do her the power of good."

Andrea smiled at him suspiciously. "You'll never bed her Terry, if that's what you're playing at, and anyway, your future wife is standing right beside you, how do you think this makes her feel, letting young Joan sniff around the place, this could cause friction."

Samantha jumped in. "He breaks my heart every day Andrea, you have no idea how much he hurts me. All those nasty comments about me driving too slow, and how I look like a thug when I wear my leather jackets or coats, the list is endless, but no-one helps me. Nobody looks after me when I'm being constantly bullied and harassed every day by this male chauvinist pig of a man who is now showing sexual interest in another woman. He just uses me Andrea, he vents out all his anger and frustrations on me, and just like you say, shows no sign whatsoever of discussing a fancy vivid with me, it breaks my bloody heart."

As Andrea walked away laughing, she replied, "Ok Terry, send her over to Clapham, but I don't want her in the house, you make that clear to her.
There's still lots of work to do in there, and she's not ready for intense forensics yet. But I'll do it Terry, just for you, although I can't see how cleaning out a shed is going to boost her moral, especially on a day like today."

Terry smiled at his colleague and friend. "She'll be fine Andrea, and thank you."

As Samantha walked back to the car with Terry she smiled at him.

"Why are you doing this Terry, you know, for Joan. How the hell is cleaning out the shed going to improve her confidence? because in effect, that's all she'll be doing."

Terry didn't even reply to Samantha's comments about Joan Vincent. All he said was, "Come on, I'm driving. I'm going to treat you to a proper breakfast today Samantha. You won't get far on tea and toast my angel. And before you say anything else, I don't mind driving you around really. In fact, I feel rather proud having you sitting here beside me. You know, some people actually think we're a couple, and that makes me feel honoured...what a lovely thought."

As they drove, Samantha was thinking to herself that any minute now her alarm clock was going to go off.

SCOTLAND YARD.

BROADWAY VICTORIA.

"Well Christine, I have some good news for you. Some, it's not all good news.
We are releasing you today. You are free to go home, however, you will be notified shortly of when you are to attend court for the theft of jewellery taken from Gareth's mum's house, and of course to give evidence when the court-case comes up concerning Gareth's murder. The fact that the jewellery has been returned may help you. As they say in the movies Christine, don't leave town. I hope you realise just how lucky you've been because this could have turned out much worse than it has."
Polly Sheppard sat opposite a very relieved Christine Hope. "We can't hold you here and we can't send you to prison simply because we don't have enough evidence to convict you of murder. Your prints were not on the rope that hung Gareth Tait, and besides, you being only about seven and a half stones, it is highly unlikely that you'd be able to hoist Gareth up from the ground by pulling the rope thrown over a beam from the floor, he being more than eleven stones."
Polly sighed heavily, as though her next statement grieved her. "You are guilty though, of stealing jewellery, and therefore you will be convicted of theft. You may well receive a custodial sentence Christine for this, as this is not your first time in court for stealing, in fact, you've been up in front of the magistrates on numerous occasions and so I think it's fair to say that you should prepare yourself. Now, as you can understand, mister Gareth Tait senior is blaming you for the death of his son and is adamant that you at least had something to do with it, and so, we have had to place a restricting order on him to keep him away from you and your flat.
I would advise you Christine, to stay away from Hawthorne Close although I can't for the life of me think of any reason why you'd want to go back there."
The young girl had sat quietly listening to everything Polly had said to her.
Polly could see the relief in the young lady's face as she informed her of the situation. She'd also done some research on the teen and discovered that she'd had a hellish up-bringing, born into a world of violence and drug-abuse. In fact, she was horrified to read from Christine's birth certificate, that she was born in Holloway Prison. Polly looked at her watch. "Now then Christine, I have taken the liberty of ordering you a taxi that will take you from here to your home. I have booked the taxi for two o clock this afternoon. Before that, you can have your lunch here and perhaps you'd like a shower to freshen up and put some make-up on. Again, I have taken the liberty of purchasing some

cosmetics for you. Now, would you mind if I had my lunch with you in here. When I'm in here I get peace and quiet Christine."

The teenager smiled softly and humbly at the chief inspector, perhaps only half-believing what was being said. "Of course mam, that'd be lovely...I mean, if you want to have your dinner with me."

"Ok Christine, it's just after twelve now, we'll have lunch and then I'll leave you to get ready for your taxi. Now I don't have to tell you that what I have done is against the rules, you know, buying you some make-up, so, not a word to anyone ok? Even outside of here, you don't ever mention that, or I will be in serious trouble."

The confused teen smiled at chief inspector Polly Sheppard. "I won't say a thing mam, I promise you. And thank you, thank you very much."

Anyone looking at the two women now would think that they were mother and daughter. The longer the conversation continued, the more at ease Christine was. Half an hour later, they were sitting across from each other enjoying their meals, Polly reading her magazine and Christine reading hers'. Half an hour more, and Polly was instructing Christine of the events to follow, and how she'd be escorted from this interview room by an officer down to the exit point where her taxi would be waiting.

"Now then Christine, I shall have to ask you to excuse me, I can't hide in here all day unfortunately. I wish you all the best for the future. Whatever you do sweetheart, you keep on that program you're on and get yourself off that bloody horrible drug, do you hear me? There's no future in it. If you don't, it will destroy your life. Oh, an officer will come in here shortly with a parcel for you. You don't let them see what's in the parcel, it's just a little gift from me to you, and again, you don't say anything outside of here. Take care Christine, and even if you get a custodial sentence, remember, it's never too late to change." Much to Christine's surprise, Polly gave her a good luck hug.

"You take care Christine." Those last four words that Polly had just spoken was the only time in Christine Hope's existence that anyone had ever said to her.

Polly exited the room and headed back to her office. Less than two minutes later, an officer entered the interview room with a rather large parcel, just as Polly had told her they would. The female officer smiled as she laid the parcel on the table. "I'm to inform you miss that you can use the shower-rooms down the hall here if you wish. At two o clock I am to escort you down stairs where a taxi will be waiting. Here, I'll show you where the shower rooms are." After showing Christine where to go the officer left her. Christine opened the brown paper sack. Two brand new pairs of high-quality jeans two stylish winter jumpers with scarves and gloves to match, and a pair of fashionable winter boots. Inside one of the boots, there was a small card. Inside the card there was two hundred pounds in twenty-pound notes. All the note said was;

Remember Christine, not a word to anyone. Even as Christine was inspecting her new clothes another officer entered the room. A young-looking detective approached her and handed a slim-lined two-foot squared parcel. "I've been instructed by Miss Sheppard to give you this." He laid the parcel on the table and left, closing the door behind him, and not locking it. Again, Christine removed the brown paper and discovered a collection, of top-of-the-range cosmetics set. Lip sticks of all colours and nail-varnish, mascara, face creams, everything a woman could possibly need. Christine sat the cosmetics tray down beside her new clothes and boots. Why on earth would she do that? She thought to herself. "This must have cost an absolute fortune."
She whispered to herself. Everything before her was of the highest quality.
Plus, she had put two-hundred pounds in the card to help her out. Encouragement as well, as though she was willing her to beat the heroin habit. For the first time in her life Christine had come into contact with someone who was on *her* side. She would try. This time she would try. Up until now she'd been taking advantage of the methadone given to her by the pharmacists and then stealing things to buy crack. But now, she would try her level best to use the program in a more positive manner…it had felt good being spoken to like a `normal` human being. She could get used to that.

INTERVIEW ROOM

NO 2.

Sophie Spencer was not as lucky as Christine Hope had been. She hadn't seen Terry or Samantha since the day before. No-one had been in to speak to her or let her know what was happening. Only an officer coming in with meals and drinks, and they didn't stay long. Today, something was different. Two detectives were now standing inside her room whispering to one another. From time to time one of them casually pointed over to her. Both men left, closing and locking the door behind them. Nothing had been said to her. On three different occasions this had happened throughout the course of the morning. If she'd had apprehensions before, now, she was down-right frightened. Something was going on today, something specifically concerning her. Where was Terry? Why had he not been in to see her today? And at least shout at her. But Terry or Samantha were nowhere to be seen. And then, quite suddenly, the door opened and the two detectives who'd been talking at her door all day, entered the room. One of them carried a set of hand cuffs. Sophie was sitting on her bed. She swallowed hard, her throat as dry as sand-paper.

"Miss Spencer, the taller of the two detectives said, "come and sit here at the table please, we have some information for you." Sophie stood up, her legs feeling like jelly, and sat down at the table. The other detective pulled out what looked like some sort of recording device and sat it on the table. The taller man spoke again. "Miss Sophie Spencer, you are being arrested on suspicion of the murder of Mister James Carter. You are to be remanded in custody in her majesty's prison Bronzefield, Middlesex until such time as your hearing. You will be tried for murder in The Old Baily on a date yet to be arranged. You are not obliged to say anything but if you do" …

Sophie could hear the man's words fading away like a record fade-out. She sat in complete shock at the news just given to her. She struggled to speak as the detective asked her if she had anything to say. All that came out from her lips were the words, "I hurt him, I know I hurt him, but I didn't kill him, I didn't shoot him, no. Where's Terry? Where's detective Mercer? Where's detective Reynolds? I didn't kill anyone I swear I didn't."

The two mercy-less detectives merely continued, unmoved by Sophie's pleas of innocence. "Get your things together miss, a vehicle is on its' way to transfer you from here to Bronzefield, it'll be here in less than half an hour. We'll come back shortly to escort you into that vehicle. Once in Bronzefield, you'll be allocated a solicitor if you do not have the means to obtain one. Everything will be made clear to you by the prison governess. We'll come back in fifteen minutes, and we'll expect you to be ready." The two detectives left the room and closed the door once again, and once again, they locked it. Sophie Spencer's world, was yet again falling apart. She'd been warned by Terry Mercer on numerous occasions not to be taking the law into her own hands. She had ignored his warnings and now...and now she was going to face the consequences. But someone else had murdered Carter. Someone had obviously been watching her. And they'd followed her and entered the house to shoot this man and make it look like she was the guilty party. Surely Terry would have heard by now from the forensic officers who'd visited her mum's house. They would have found the gun and the ammunition, and they would know that the weapon had not been fired. Where on earth was Terry? Sophie had been handed a clear polythene sack to place her things in. As she packed the few belongings she had with her, tears rolled down her face. She began to cry even more as she remembered Terry's last words to her.

"If you haven't been telling me the truth Sophie, then I can safely say that this will be the last conversation we'll be having for a very long time." What if this person had sneaked into her house and somehow got access to her gun, taken the gun away somewhere and fired it? If that was what had happened then she wouldn't be seeing Terry, as he'd said, for a very long time. She wouldn't be seeing anyone for a long time. And now, the fact that neither he nor Samantha had showed face, made her think that that was exactly what had happened. She sat and sipped the remains of the coffee that had been brought for her more than an hour ago. Even the cold coffee would seem like a luxury compared to what was in front of her. All she knew about Bronzefield was that it was a purposely-built prison for women only. She lit a cigarette and finished her cold beverage. She jumped with fright as the door opened and the same two detectives entered the room.

"I'm sorry miss but you'll have to extinguish the cigarette, the transport is here to take you to Bronzefield. I'll have to confiscate them as well. You're not allowed to have anything like that on your person when you travel in the security van."

The tall thin man lifted the cigarettes and lighter from the table and placed them into a small polythene bag. "I'll have to take your jewellery as well miss. Any rings or bracelets, bangles etcetera, earrings as well miss." A few minutes later, she was hand-cuffed and taken from the interview room down the hall to the elevator.

In less than fifteen minutes, from sitting on the small bed in the interview room, she was now sitting in the back of the security van, hand-cuffed and completely helpless. Some of the things Terry had said to her when he was angry, came back to her now. *"And don't think bursting out crying is going to help you. You won't fool anyone. You're guilty Sophie, and now you are going to face the consequences of your actions. Lies lies lies Sophie, isn't it. You are a compulsive liar."*

Sophie sat miserably going over everything she'd done, and everything she hadn't done. She'd read stories in newspapers about people who had been put in jail for crimes they had not committed. As things stood now, she was going to be just another statistic of injustice. Yes, she deserved to be punished for inflicting such injuries on James Carter, but to be imprisoned for his murder, that was wrong.

As the vehicle pulled away from Scotland Yard, she began to think back to her ordeal over in Lithuania. Those guilty parties were walking the streets of wherever they lived free as birds, like nothing had happened. Perhaps someone else had opened up a place and started another brothel using innocent kidnapped girls like herself and Lisa and Alison and all the others. She took a deep breath and sat back on the seat, looking despondently at the hand-cuffs attached to her wrists. Whatever lay ahead, she would deal with it. She would just have to, because there was no-one coming this time to save her. This time she was on her own. She only hoped her mum and David were not too disappointed in her. Little did Sophie know that her mum had arranged a surprise birthday party and had invited all the girls she'd been kidnapped with to a special birthday get-together. In four days' time Sophie Spencer would be sixteen years of age...but she wouldn't be spending it with her friends. In less than forty minutes the security van came to a halt. She couldn't see anything because there were no windows. Then she heard a beep, and the back doors of the van opened up. One of the guards offered her his hand to assist her to climb out. So this was it, this was Bronzefield. Where the van had pulled up there was a neat silver-coloured cheerful sign reading Bronzefield HMP. Below the sign there was a flower bed which was bare but would probably be filled with colourful flowers in the spring and summer months.

The entrance itself reminded Sophie of a hospital she'd visited with her mum when she was a child. She was escorted through the double-doors and led to a reception desk where a bright cheerful-looking young lady typed busily on a lap-top. The two guards who had brought her here had made this journey many times and were very familiar with the procedures. They motioned for Sophie to sit down on one of the comfortable chairs in the reception area. Even at this point being in the actual prison, the hand-cuffs were still not removed. The two guards picked up magazines from the small table in the centre of the room, and began to read. They knew that this could take up to half an hour. Sophie just sat looking at the floor. Whatever else anyone could say about Sophie Spencer, the girl could adapt very quickly to any circumstances. Already in her mind, the hurt from being ignored by Terry Mercer and Samantha Reynolds was turning into, not hatred, but bitterness. They could at least have let her know what had happened at her house concerning the gun, obviously something had, and it would seem that it was not satisfactory to them whatever they discovered, hence, she being brought here. But, just like in Kaunas, she would have to stand up for herself. No doubt there were dangerous women in here, although she supposed that she'd be taken into the YOI (Young Offenders Institute.) wing. That would remain to be seen. At this moment in time Sophie was very highly strung and jumped with fright as the door beside her suddenly burst open. The two guards jumped to their feet as none other than Governess Geraldine Prowse entered the room. This was not part of the usual procedure. Sophie stood up. She said nothing as the governess and the guards exchanged words. "She was supposed to have been brought in here yesterday, what the hell is going on with you people, do you think this is a holiday hotel where you can just arrive any time you please? This is the second time this month that this has happened, there had better not be a third time or we'll have to be looking for another security company, do I make myself clear?"

"Perfectly, miss Prowse, but you see, there was-."

"Ah yes, but you see, there's always a but you see isn't there, there's always an excuse as to why you cannot run efficiently, isn't there. It's always somebody else's fault. Give me the documents and get yourselves away, I'm quite sure some other people will be waiting for your appearance somewhere…waiting being the operative word, on you go. Sign at the desk there, Pamela will show you where to write your names."

The last comment was nothing less than a blatant insult to the two security guards. Geraldine Prowse, dressed in pale blue slacks and a white blouse and brown moccasin soft-shoes turned to Sophie. With her auburn hair held back with a colourful band she could have been a doctor. She was also younger than Sophie would have thought a prison governess would be. She held the door open for Sophie to go through.

"Come on you, lets' get you sorted out."

As they left reception they were quickly walking down a long corridor of meshed doorways along a squeaky-clean polished floor. The governess was now walking in front of Sophie, who still had the hand-cuffs on. "They say you're a little sharp-shooter huh? Handy with a gun…and a crow-bar I'm led to believe. Well, there'll be none of that in here I can assure you. You will learn the rules in here and you will learn them quickly."

They walked at a brisk pace. The governess continued. "Have you eaten?"

Sophie replied in a soft dry voice. "I'm not hungry."

The governess stopped in her tracks and shouted right into Sophie's face.

"I didn't fucking ask you that, I asked you have you eaten, didn't I! I don't give a flying fuck if you're hungry or not, now, have you eaten?"

"No miss, not since this morning."

"Fine, thank you, that wasn't very hard was it?"

"No mam."

They continued walking along the narrow rows of meshed cells, through a door and then another long row of cells until finally, the governess opened a door and they were standing outside of her office. "Come in here just now, stand there where the two white foot-prints are, we'll get you sorted out shortly."

Geraldine sat down at her desk and began to write in a ledger. She said nothing as she wrote. After about a minute, she looked up briefly to Sophie and continued writing.

"You're a size six are you not?"

"Yes mam." Replied Sophie, impressed with the governess's accuracy.

"And you're a size six shoes?"

"Yes mam." Nothing more was said as the governess continued writing.

Suddenly, a quick knock on the door and a stern-looking well-built woman entered the office. Her thinning grey hair was jelled into her head, making her look like she had hardly any hair at all. The grey hair matched her uniform of jacket and skirt. She wore heavy brown lace-up shoes on her feet.

She only looked to see where Sophie's feet were on the floor but said nothing to her. The governess said to the woman. "This is her. Two-gun-Tess here. She is to be remanded in custody until her court case comes up. She'll be staying with us until that time arrives. Make sure she's kitted out with our latest Paris collection of clothes and footwear."

The large woman said, looking disdainfully at Sophie, "It'll be hard to get anything to fit that. Look at it, it's like a fucking skint rat, I've seen more meat on a hen's lip. How the hell did she muster up the strength to whack some fucker with a crow bar, the crow bar would be heavier than her, fuck it just shows you mam."

In her mind Sophie said, "*It would be hard to get anything to fit you, you fucking fat frustrated bastard that you are. And look at your feet, size four by the looks of it, and supporting four fucking tons, fuck it just shows you mam.*"

"Take her away Elizabeth, and make sure she does not come into contact with any of the other inmates at this moment in time. Get her washed and dressed and then take her to her cell. Get her something to eat. She says she's not hungry but get her something to eat. She'll eat in her own cell, I'm not having a little murderer mixing with the guests in here, although we do have a problem with over-crowding. Anyway, get her away Elizabeth. Make her feel at home, after all, after her trial, this *will* probably be her home." The prison warden smiled with a sinister look in her eyes. "And then we'll have some fun."

Half an hour later, Sophie sat alone in the cell allocated to her with a cheese burger and

French-fries and a mug of tea. By now, the shock had lost its' sting partially and she was actually enjoying the food. The cell was small, but comfortable it had to be said. There was a single bed and a small writing desk-come table in one corner of the room. In another corner was a toilet bowl and wash-hand basin. There was a small toughened-glass window which overlooked an open field. Every now and again the shock of what had happened today bit at her viciously but it didn't take long to calm herself down again. Dreadful circumstances was nothing new in Sophie Spencer's life these days. Still, she couldn't understand why Terry or Samantha had not been to visit her when she was in Scotland Yard. Even if they had found something negative in her bedroom concerning the gun surely it should have been them that should have come and explained what was happening. But, for whatever reason, she was here, and that was all there was to it. Late afternoon turned into early-evening, and then early evening turned into night. She was not permitted a television but had been granted a small radio. The radio would have to be switched off at ten pm, that was lights out time. However, at around nine pm governess Prowse arrived at her cell. She came in to Sophie's cell with another mug of tea for the teen and carrying one for herself. She sat down on the only chair as Sophie sat on her single bed. She handed Sophie the mug of tea.

"How are you feeling?" She said, smiling at the teenager. "It's a bit of a shock to the system coming into places like these, especially at your age. It's a whole new ball game. Everything you've ever known has just flown out of the window. Some of them that come in here really struggle with their new circumstances. Also, the wardens in here are quite stern, they have to be Sophie. But they're fair, I have to say that. If you come and go with them, then they'll be easy to get along with. They have to give you that nasty rough impression when you arrive, but then once they get to know you, they'll be fine. Anyway, I just came in to see if you were alright. Are you alright Sophie? I mean, under the present circumstances that might seem like a foolish question, but, you know, are you alright?"

"I'm fine mam." said Sophie, quietly.

"Good." said the governess. "Here, I brought you these. You can put them on when it's time for lights out." The governess handed her a small set of earphones. "That'll give you some comfort through the night, and you know Sophie? You never know what tomorrow will bring, goodnight." The governess rose to her feet and left the cell carrying her mug of tea.

BRONZEFIELD. 6am.

Sophie was abruptly awoken by the hefty Elizabeth. "Come on, up you get, you're not lying in your bed all day like you usually do. In here you have to learn rules, and you have to obey them, or else you'll get clattered it's as simple as that. Come on, get dressed and get out into the hallway, it's time for your porridge, pardon the pun." said the stern woman laughing, as she stood with her arms folded at the doorway.

"Come on, get dressed, you've not got anything I haven't seen before, move your skinny arse into gear, or you'll be getting nothing for breakfast. By the looks of you an egg-cup full of porridge will fill you up anyway, you must be the skinniest runt I have ever seen, and I've seen a few in here, I can tell you. Thin Lizzie's got nothing on you. Do you need the toilet?"

"Yes mam."

"Right, you've got five minutes to sort yourself out and then I'll be back in here kicking your arse if you're not ready." Sophie used the toilet and had a quick wash and was dressed. She had also made her bed. Elizabeth returned more than ten minutes later, and smiled as she looked at Sophie's bed. But she said nothing about it. "Right, lets' go, or that lot down there will have eaten the lot, move." They walked down a long corridor and through a set of swing doors. They were now in the canteen. There were about fifty girls ranging between the ages of sixteen to twenty-years-old. Sophie was led along one of the huge dining tables and told to sit down right at the very end. To her surprise Elizabeth walked up to the counter and returned with a bowl of breakfast-cereal and a cup of tea.

"You eat that, and then I'll be back to take you to the governess's office, I think you're in trouble already little miss nothing! And what are you lot gawking at, get on with your breakfasts or you'll be joining her...bunch of bitches!" Elizabeth left the dining hall but there were still another two wardens patrolling the room, wandering around slowly with their hands behind their backs. A mail and a female officer. None of them said a thing to her, or to any of the other inmates for that matter. Sophie got the impression that if you spoke out of turn you'd soon know about it. The young girl sitting next to Sophie whispered when she thought it was safe. "You're going to get fucked hard in here bitch I can tell you that for nothing. There's going to be a fight to see which one gets you for their bitch. Have you ever licked a pussy before? Because you're going to fucking learn how to in here."

When Sophie thought the coast was clear she responded, without even looking at her, "I could kill you with this spoon, do you know that? If you as much as breathe near me

again, I'll prove it."
The girl was shocked at Sophie's response, and just continued eating her toast. She didn't say another word. Even before everyone else was finished Elizabeth returned to the dining hall and marched up to Sophie, standing directly behind her chair.
"Come on skinny Jenny, get your arse up off there and back to your cell, and wait until the governess is ready for your scrawny butt!"
"Excuse me mam, but what do I do with this?" said Sophie, purposefully lifting the spoon from the bowl and looking directly at the girl who'd given her the threats.
"Do you really want me to tell you what to do with it? What do you think you stupid girl, you take it over there to the counter, there's nobody going to be running hand and foot after your skinny arse, and hurry up about it, I've got better things to do than escort you all over the parish, move yourself runt."
Ten minutes later, Sophie was once again left in her cell. She'd distinctly heard governess Prowse telling Elizabeth not to let her mix with the other inmates, and yet, she'd just had breakfast with about fifty of them, and left alone practically.
It was nothing but confusion for Sophie. And now she was wondering what the governess was wanting to see her about. Perhaps this was the point where she'd be introduced to a solicitor. She would find out soon enough no doubt. As far as the law was concerned she'd still be classed as a child surely, and if that was the case, then her punishment would be different as to that of an adult. Again, that would remain to be seen. She sat down on her bed and plugged in her earphones to the radio to listen to some music. She wasn't used to getting up at six o clock in the morning, and even in Scotland Yard, they'd let her sleep until someone needed to ask her something. But Scotland Yard was not a prison. Prowse was right, there'd be none of that in here. However, after about ten minutes listening to the radio, she fell asleep. Much to her surprise, she woke up and it was after ten o clock. Had they let her sleep? What surprised her more was the fact that Elizabeth sat on the chair in the cell opposite her bed. Smiling at Sophie she said, "Come on, lets' get you a cup of tea and a cigarette, I expect you'll be needing one by now. Come on, we're going outside to the exorcise yard. There's someone on their way to see you, they'll be here in about ten minutes."
The transformation in Elizabeth was unbelievable. How could she change from the monster she'd been, to this. Sophie stood outside alone in the yard holding a lovely cup of coffee and smoking a cigarette having been given back the packet that was confiscated from her by the detectives in Scotland Yard. Confusion and mystery. Sophie's mind was in turmoil trying to work out why they had suddenly started being nice to her. This wasn't going to last. It was probably some kind of treatment that tricked you into thinking that this was how it was going to be. But she knew different.

The girl at the breakfast table informed her that she was going to be fucked hard, and taught how to eat pussy. They were a bit late to do that unfortunately, thanks to a certain Monica Carosova. And who could this visitor be? Would it be someone from the young-offenders institute? A solicitor perhaps? Either way, no matter who it was, they weren't fooling her. The bottom line was, she was in here, and by the looks of things, she was in here for a very long time. Perhaps this person, whoever he or she is has an influential position, someone who reports on the conditions in prisons perhaps. Yeah, that must be it. They were being nice to her to influence this person who was on their way to see her. Outside in the yard, a brisk chill wind blew onto Sophie's face but the cold did not make her feel uncomfortable, rather, it gave her a sense of freedom, and after all, this would probably be the closest she would get to that. She watched some crows flying overhead and croaking as they flew past. Freedom. She stood thinking about the morning all this had started. That wet miserable morning she had made the fatal mistake of sleeping in and being late for school, and then her mind flashed back to her lashing a man's back with a bull-whip. Was that really her? Did she do that? Smashing a man's hands to pulp with a mash-hammer? What the hell had happened to her? Kicking an old man time after time in the ribs in an alley-way? And then laughing with Colin Green as she done it? *I deserve to be in here. I deserve everything that's' coming to me, and more. How could I do these things to people? Revenge? I really do need a psychiatrist. I am a danger to society. I've just threatened a girl with her life if she as much as breathed near me. What has happened to my life? My poor mum, who has struggled on her own bringing up David and I, sacrificing everything just so that we could have things. So that we could be the same as all the other kids...and she achieved it, only this is how I repay her. I have turned into a monster worse even than the people who used me in Lithuania. More worry for her now, and heartache, knowing that I'll spend years in an institute. It would have happened before now if they'd found out about all the things I'd done. Yes, I deserve to be here. I am dangerous...and I can't control my temper.*

"Sophie?" Elizabeth called to her from the door a few feet behind her.
"Your visitor is here, come on in. Bring your coffee with you."
Sophie put out the cigarette in the wall-mounted ash tray and headed towards the prison warden, who was standing holding the door for her, and smiling pleasantly.
"Come on, through here child, let's not keep them waiting."
Sophie walked zombie-like completely confused at the course of events today. They reached governess Prowse's office. Elizabeth knocked three times on the door and stepped inside. "She's here mam, Sophie's here."
Sophie was ushered by Elizabeth to step into the office. There, at the far side of the

room, sat Terry Mercer and Samantha Reynolds. Was she supposed to be pleased to see them? Was she supposed to be elated with their arrival? because she was neither of those. Terry and Samantha sat smiling at the teen as she stood on the two white footprints on the floor. Terry spoke first.

"How are you Sophie? We got here as soon as we could."

Sophie completely ignored Terry's greeting and turned to ask governess Prowse if she could go back to her cell now. Terry began to approach. "Sophie we're here to help you. We're-."

"Governess Prowse, could you please inform the foul-mouthed detective and his sidekick to go and fuck themselves please and not to waste any more of your time. I'd much rather be in my cell than talk to this piece of shit. In fact, I'd much rather spend time with this fat fucker behind me than talk to either of them." There was silence in the room for a brief moment, but only a moment. Governess Prowse spoke now, and sternly. "As you wish Madam. Take her away Elizabeth, and lock her in her cell as she so wishes. This afternoon, you get her assigned to the laundry rooms with some of the others. Let her get acquainted with some of the other girls in here. Perhaps detective Mercer can make another appointment in six months-time and then perhaps Sophie will be in a more pleasant frame of mind to receive visitors. Visitors who have driven here from London especially to try and help her, but, she's not in the mood to receive any help just now, so off you go madam, lets' see how many times you get away with calling Elizabeth a fat fucker. Take her away, oh, and no more meals for her today. And take away her radio and headphones, just leave the bible in her cell, that might do her some good if she reads that."

As Sophie was led by the arm, she turned and said to Terry Mercer. "See ya, bastard." In a matter of seconds, the situation worsened. Elizabeth must have man-handled Sophie a bit too roughly for her liking and a scuffle broke out in the corridor outside of the governess's office. By the time governess Prowse reached them, Sophie had the warden pinned down to the floor reigning punch after punch into the warden's face and head. Terry and Samantha helped along with Geraldine Prowse to pull the teenager from the warden. Another two wardens appeared and took Sophie off to her cell as she kicked and screamed all the way down the corridor. Another took Elizabeth to the first aid room. The two detectives and the prison governess re-entered the office.

"I told you this wouldn't work Mister Mercer, I knew it, and now look what's happened. She's in trouble now detective. She has assaulted one of my staff, now it's my business and my decision as to what happens to her."

Terry's idea was to give Sophie a small taste of prison life in the hope that she'd be so shocked and frightened at what she seen in here, that it would once and for all knock out any more nonsense about taking the law into her own hands. He'd told Samantha everything that had happened concerning Angela Bates and showed her the letter. He also explained that that was why he'd sent the junior detective to search the shed in Edgeley Road, knowing that she'd find the evidence. But his plan had not worked. Now, he would somehow have to sweet-talk governess Prowse not to keep Sophie here, but she was in no mood to let the teen go after this incident. Assault on a member of staff, her staff, was taken very seriously, and the punishments were severe. Before Terry could even begin to address the situation with Sophie, Geraldine Prowse looked at him. "And what about your other plan mister Mercer, that went tits up as well didn't it, because the little peroxide blonde roams our streets as free as a bird doesn't she? Who was it that re-assured me that she'd be re-arrested and back in here in no time? Even when that little tramp was in here, she caused major damage, and permanent damage I might add to thin Lizzie's nose and teeth. In a nutshell mister Mercer, your plans are not very good are they? They rarely succeed. I'm telling you now, that girl down there in her cell is a hard nut. Has she seen a psychiatrist? because she needs one. She is violent, and she is dangerous. Now, you expect me to just let her march out of here and into your car to continue her life happily-ever-after, is that what you expect? Maybe she can team up with this …this fucking Angela Bates, and together wreak havoc on the rest of society. No no no mister Mercer, it's not as easy as that I'm afraid. She has committed a serious offence in here today. I will have to make out a full report of the incident and trust me when I tell you, that there will be consequences. Now, I am going down to her cell now to punch her hard in the stomach and then I shall return here to decide what to do with her. Hell, your superior doesn't even know you have her in here, what the hell do you think *she's* going to say when she hears about this? No, your plans are shit mister Mercer. Go and wait for me in the canteen until I come and get you."

Terry was about to say something else but Samantha tugged his sleeve. Reluctantly, he made his way down to the canteen as instructed.

"There's no point pushing her just now Terry, we have to wait until she's calmed down a bit. The last thing we need to do is aggravate her. Don't worry, she's not going to punch Sophie in the stomach, she's only going to give her a lecture and threaten her."

Terry and Samantha had sat in the canteen for nearly an hour before Geraldine Prowse returned. She sat down at the table opposite the detectives. "I want you to listen to me very closely Mister Mercer, and take heed of what I tell you. I run this prison as I've told you before, very efficiently, and the last thing I need is little troublemakers like Sophie Spencer coming in here disrupting everything. I have given it some thought and have decided to let you take her away with you on the condition that you get mental health

therapy for her, because she most definitely needs it."
Mercer did not inform the governess that she was already seeing a psychiatrist.
"Of course I will governess Prowse, you have my word."
"Your word? Well, lets' hope that your word is more reliable than your half-baked plans. Don't ever come back here asking me for any more favours either, because it won't be happening. Now, make sure you keep your word because if I ever see that little brat's face again then I guarantee you, she will regret the day she was born. And you have my word on that. Now, get her out of here and out of my sight. Think yourself very lucky mister Mercer that I am not keeping her because I have every right to. No-one would challenge me after her behaviour in here today as I'm sure you're aware."
"I understand miss Prowse. And I know the authority you have and I'm extremely grateful for your leniency, thank you Miss Prowse."
The governess stood up and said, "You might find that you'll have to force her to go with you because she does not want to speak with you I can assure you of that. Neither of you. Would you like me to give you a set of hand-cuffs, because you're going to have to man-handle her out of here."
Samantha said, "We'll try and persuade her first Miss Prowse."
Geraldine Prowse laughed. "I never thought I'd live to hear that, that someone would have to be forced out of here, Bronzefield must grow on them. Warden Henley will be through here directly to show you to her cell.
Goodbye Mister Mercer, Miss Reynolds, and remember what I said, no more favours."
Once again Terry thanked the governess for her kindness.

THE BLACK HORSE INN.

Near Maidstone. M20.

It had taken Samantha almost half an hour to persuade Sophie to come along with them. There was something different about the girl, and not just her attitude. She'd kept telling Samantha that she deserved to be in prison and that she was not running away from any crimes she'd committed any more. All the way up the M20 she hadn't spoken a word to Terry when he'd tried to open a conversation with her. She would only answer Samantha's questions. And this continuing acceptance of punishment that she felt she should endure. Samantha was puzzled by this sudden compunction from Sophie. Up until now, the girl had fought tooth and nail to defend her actions, but now, it seemed that there lay a deep regret within her. Perhaps this could be a good thing, if they could get her to accept the help that was now available to her. A way out. An exemption from all crimes committed. But at this moment in time, Sophie was not interested. Terry pulled in to the beautiful Inn situated just off the M20.

Terry was no stranger to the place. He used to come here regularly with his wife Carol. That seemed like a thousand years ago. There were many beautiful walking trails around here as well, in this picturesque little setting, which Carol and he had taken advantage of. And, of course, Carol being the enthusiastic historian, informed him that it was less than five miles from here to the famous Leeds Castle. He knew how Henry the Eighth would have dealt with his dilemma.

As they walked towards the entrance, Samantha and Sophie walked a few yards behind him. He couldn't make out what was being said, but at least it was a conversation of some kind. The girl was communicating with Samantha if nothing else. There was no way just now that he could inform Sophie that she'd been imprisoned at his request. She was in no mood to try and understand why he had done it, and that it was in the long run, supposed to be beneficial to her, that she would see the horrors of being locked away and frighten her into thinking that she'd never want to return there.

But, judging by the way Sophie was talking now, it had had the opposite effect. Perhaps the girl did feel regret for her crimes now, and that was a good thing, but as far as prison was concerned, she was not daunted in any way. He genuinely felt that she wouldn't have flinched if he and Samantha had left Bronzefield without her, in fact, she'd asked them to do exactly that. He stood now at the entrance of The Black Horse Inn, holding the door for his female companions.

"Huh." Sophie grunted as she stepped past him.

Samantha smiled at him as she walked past, giving him that look of, "Don't panic, I've got everything under control."

Knowing full well that any invitation to eat would be rebuked by the teen, Terry just headed off to the bar and ordered cheese-burgers and French-Fries for everyone. He hadn't yet met a teen who did not eat French-Fries. He also ordered side salads for himself and Samantha, at least to try and add a bit of dignity to the meal. He also informed Samantha that she'd be driving for the rest of the day because there was no way he was visiting The Black Horse Inn and not having a delicious pint of Kentish Cask ale, and besides, the beverage would genuinely be medicinal. He was pleased to note that very little had changed since his last visit here. He always felt comforted with those beautiful wooden beams that ran right throughout the building. He had no idea how old it was, but it was always homely to him with its' open fires, rather than some electrical fan blowing too rapidly in most cases, hot air that usually smelled of whatever they were cooking in their kitchens. And that was another thing he liked about The Black Horse Inn, they grew their own vegetables as well, and so everything was always fresh. He took the drinks from the bar and headed to where Samantha had found seating, having been informed by one of the waitresses that she'd bring their meals over to their table. In the very short time it had taken him to order the drinks, a miracle had been performed by Samantha Reynolds. He had taken the liberty of buying a vodka and coke for Sophie, knowing that the girl was partial to the drink, as well as the glass of coke to have with her meal. Samantha was handed a glass of grapefruit juice. To his absolute astonishment, Sophie smiled at him and said, "Thank you Terry."

After their meal, they went for a short stroll around the grounds and surrounding area of the Inn.

As they walked Terry explained to Sophie everything that had happened, including the confession-letter from Angela Bates. He also explained that Bates had set everything up to look like she had also whacked James Carter's hands as well. A detective had found evidence in the shed at the back of the house in Edgeley Road. Sophie stopped and looked at the two detectives. Samantha smiled at the girl. "It's true Sophie, she said she'd done it to try and make up to you all the damage she'd caused you and your family. She can't take it back what she's done but she felt that killing the person who bundled you into the van and killing the man who inflicted so much damage to your friend would take away your need for revenge. And on that note Sophie, I'm afraid I have some bad news for you.

Claire didn't make it. She died from internal bleeding.

The surgeons done everything they could, but alas, the poor girl died.

The man who done it, is dead. That was why Angela Bates shot him in the head."

Terry and Samantha could see the devastation in the teenager's face. She turned away from them and took a few steps to stand on her own. They watched as she lit up a cigarette. Everything that had happened to Sophie Spencer and her friends, and everything that Sophie Spencer had done all came tumbling down inside her head now like a mental avalanche. The shame she felt for her behaviour, the bitterness she felt towards her kidnappers, the friendship she'd been building with Claire Rennie, the murders she'd committed in the name of revenge, the hurt and worry she'd caused her mum and brother, everything. The girl fell down to her knees and began to break her heart. The cigarette fell from her hand onto the path. Tears flooded through her fingers as she sobbed bitterly. The teenager was mentally exhausted.

Terry Mercer got down on his knees and held the girl in his arms.

He knew all about mental exhaustion. He just cradled her in his arms and held her tight whispering that it was all over now, and that he was taking her back home today to her mum and her brother. Samantha was now down on her hunkers as well placing an arm over Sophie's shoulder. "Everything's going to be fine now Sophie, you'll see, you just let it all out my angel, all the bad stuff is finished, we promise you that." Samantha could also see the tears in Terry's eyes as he held on to the girl like she was his own daughter, and in many ways, she was, at least, it felt like she was.

LEXINGTON SQUARE. BROMLEY.

Three months later.

Everything had worked out well for Sophie and Lisa. Sophie was cleared of murder and indeed from causing grievous bodily harm. She'd been given a fresh chance, a clean sheet. The opportunity to begin a new life, a chance to put everything behind her and to concentrate on all good things that lay before her. She stood now in her back garden with all the girls who'd suffered with her over in Lithuania, celebrating her belated sixteenth birthday. As they stood having their drinks and smoking their cigarettes she wondered how *they* were feeling about starting afresh. No-one here particularly wanted to speak about events that had taken place in Eastern Europe, but the experiences were etched in their faces. They would never be forgotten. How could they be? And even though Sophie felt better now there would always be that nagging urge inside her to punish anyone who was involved in devastating her and her family.
Of contributing to `The Nightmare Times,` and stealing away her innocence in such a devastating manner. Her sessions with her new psychiatrist were going extremely well and she felt she was making considerable progress. But there was always that little part in a far corner of her mind, that voice, calling to her in her sleep to take revenge, and to inflict punishment to the people who had come so close to destroying her life. As she stood watching her guests, smiling with them and enjoying the moment, Colin Green approached her with his two daughters Alison and Rebecca. They all stood and happily chatted together, and then, as fate would have it, Lisa shouted Alison and Rebecca over to her. Colin stood and now spoke to Sophie in a different manner. "Are you ok kid?"
"I'm fine Colin. You don't have to say anything. I know, I know we were lucky to get off with everything we done, and I know that I have to put all this bad stuff behind me, just as your own daughters have to. But there's something inside me that won't let go, you know, that urge to get even. There are still people going around over there in Lithuania, living perfectly normal lives...people who raped me and your daughters, and I kind of find that part of it very difficult to deal with. Oh, I can control it...now, but that doesn't mean that revenge is not in my mind from time to time. I know Colin, those murders we committed were wrong, no matter how evil those people were, but there's a part of me that revels in the fact that they were dealt with. That poor girl Roxanne, what a bloody mess her face was." Sophie took in a deep breath. "I'm fucking glad we killed those Russians or whatever nationality they were. I didn't regret it Colin. I don't regret it. But I have to try and put it all behind me now.

Thanks to Terry Mercer and Samantha Reynolds, I have been given a second chance. If they hadn't intervened with what I was planning, I'd probably be spending a big part of my life in Bronzefield, or some other high-security prison.

I suppose I'm just letting you know Colin, that I am, and always will be grateful to you for all your help, but this is where I part with violence. I have to, or I will be taken away from my family and friends for the rest of my life.

Those people in Lithuania? They're going about their lives like nothing happened, well, that's exactly what I have to do, although it's easier said than done.

But I must try. Look at them all, My mum and my brother, your daughters, Lisa, Chloe, everyone, all so happy that we are here and we survived, thanks to you and your SAS friends, and Terry Mercer. We all owe it to you, for putting your own lives at risk, to put all this away and to cherish all the remaining times we have left, to love life, and to live for every breath, to live for every day."

As she walked away from Colin, she said smiling, over her shoulder, "I don't think I'll ever moan about the hair-ruining weather again." She picked up her pet cat Tigger and kissed him on his head. "I've got more important things to think about now."

KAUNAS. LITHUANIA.

Angela Bates rang the doorbell at the residence of Valarie Vercopte. She didn't wait long. Valarie opened the door almost immediately, and invited her into the house and made her welcome, unsure of the reason why she'd be visiting her. Monica Carosova did not have any such doubts but screeched with joy at the sight of her old friend from London. Valarie had only met Angela on a few occasions and knew that it was she who helped ship the girls over here from Britain. But that was all she knew about her.

The three women spent a couple of hours chatting merrily about past times, especially Monica and Angela. Valarie had had nothing to do with any of the kidnappings but had inherited thousands of euros because of her husband's involvement. She had emptied Viktor's overseas accounts and was now thinking of emigrating to another country with Monica. The pair had become lovers and were now living together as a couple.

"Well, I'll have to be going soon." said Angela, as she finished off her glass of wine.

"I only came to say goodbye to you Monica, and to wish you all the best for the future. And I do, I wish you both all the very best, but I would strongly advise you not to continue with your plans. My contacts in London inform me that you intend to continue in running a brothel. This is not a wise move my friends, particularly if you intend using British girls. The British authorities are watching eagle-eyed for kidnappers and so I would cast your plans to the wind if I were you. If you don't want to join your husband Valarie, I would forget it."

Valarie sighed and looked to Monica. Shall I tell her sweetheart?"

Monica replied to her lover. "I think you should."

Valarie looked at Angela. "I wish it were that simple Angela, really. We want nothing more to do with any kidnappings, but we eh...we receive visits from Oleg Smertsov, and he insists that we keep bringing the girls over here. He is the chief of police over here and he runs a-."

"I know exactly what he runs Valarie. I know exactly what he intends to do, that is why I am over here. Don't you worry about him." Angela looked at her watch.

"I plan on paying him a visit after I leave here. I am going to fuck up his life well and truly right in front of his wife, who, by the way is perfectly aware of his involvement with young girls. What I am about to tell him will finish off his marriage once and for all. He claims to love his wife, although that is bullshit.

His love for his daughters however is another matter, and it's that that will put a stop to all his shit. He's already been warned by some Polish people to leave you two alone. He obviously didn't believe their threats. He'll believe mine I can assure you...especially

when the welfare of one of his two daughters is at stake. Trust me, after I have visited him you will never set eyes on him again. Valarie smiled. "And you plan to sort him out on your own? Do you know how powerful this man is? I mean, I admire your bravery and your good intentions, but he could have you shot before you get out of Kaunas. Anyway, He's probably got twenty-four- seven surveillance on his daughters, especially after those Polish people threatened him, they frightened him that's for sure."
"But obviously not enough Valarie. I'll frighten him more than they did.
Anyway, I'll have to be off and set about business with mister pervert."
Valarie rose from her chair and stepped over to one of her cabinets.
She retrieved a cheque-book from one of the compartments and wrote upon one of the leafs. She tore out the piece of paper and handed it to Angela.
"Here, this is for at least trying to solve Monica and I's problem with Oleg, I wish you luck Angela and hope that your confidence in the matter is well-founded.
But I fear for you, I really do. I hope you live to spend that because it will be well-deserved if you do."
Angela looked at the cheque in her hand for ten thousand euros. "Thank you Valarie, thank you very much. And I will live to spend it. But, I must be on my way, and remember what I said about those British girls, I don't want to have to come and visit you Monica years from now in some prison over there, because that's what will happen to you if you don't stop. Angela made her way out to her hired car and climbed in. Once in the car, she rolled down the window and said to the women, good luck with everything you do."
"You be very careful miss Bates." said Valarie with her hand in Monica's.
"He's very dangerous."
Angela smiled back at the concerned couple. "Ah, but so am I ladies, even as we speak I have one of his daughters bound and gagged stuck down a disused manhole, take care you two, and good luck to you both." And with that, Angela Bates drove away.

A little under half an hour later she pulled up outside of Oleg Smertsov's mansion. It was situated ironically less than a mile from the hotel where Terry Mercer and Samantha Reynolds had stayed when they were here as guests of Geoffrey Marsden. A tall thin elderly gentleman looked up from his gardening when he saw Angela pulling up close to the front door. This, it would seem was a forbidden manoeuvre judging by the way he looked at her. He shouted something out to her in his native tongue but Angela continued to approach the house. The old gardener busied himself once more unwilling to play any further part in proceedings. She rang the doorbell. No-one answered. She rang it again, and stood back on the top step of the ten that led up to the door. Still no response. Then a car came up the drive behind her. A Rolls Royce. Even the chauffer gave her a stern look as he pulled up the vehicle beside Angela's. Still staring at her, he climbed out of the driver's seat and opened the back door of the Rolls to assist a very angry-looking Oleg Smertsov out. He began to shout out in his own language. Angela was not in the slightest unnerved by the outburst and held up her right hand immediately. "English please, I don't speak Lithuanian. We need to have a little chat, and I would strongly advise you sir, to speak to me in a civil manner, I'm not your fucking dog, ok? Did you understand that alright?"

Smertsov said something to his chauffer who climbed back into the Rolls Royce and headed around to the back of the house, still staring at her as he drove slowly past. "What do you want? This had better be important.

Do you know who I am?"

"Yes I do. Said Angela. Do you know who I am?"

Smertsov glared at her. "I am not in the slightest bit interested in who you are, now, why are you here?"

"Ok" said Angela, smiling at the disgruntled man. "We got off on a bad note there. Here's what we should do. You should invite me in to your house and speak to me like I was one of your very best friends as you make me a nice cup of tea, and then we'll sit and chat about finances, and how I can save you an awful lot of worry and trouble."

"I will tell you exactly what I'm going to do with you, shall I? If you are not off of my drive in a minute, I am going to shoot you in the head, and have Simon bury you in the garden, under the compost heap, that's what I'm going to do. Are you a friend of those Polish bastards are you? Coming here talking to me like this. You get yourself away while you can still breathe, you piece of trash, now, get out of my way and into your car or you will suffer the consequences, this is your last chance."

Angela pulled out her cigarettes from her coat pocket and proceeded to light one up. "And this is *your* last chance to put the kettle on, or you will never see Janina again, I'm fucking freezing out here, and right now, although Janina is well wrapped up, she'll be feeling rather uncomfortable. So, shall we go inside and talk like human beings. My name is Angela. I'm only telling you this so that you can convince your wife that we are friends. Oh, you are going to receive a phone call or a text message from Darius, Janina's eh…body guard. I would imagine he'll have a lump on the back of his head the size of a hens' egg, but it's not really his fault. I was already in the back seat of his car when he set off to pick her up from work. Anyway, what do you say we finish this conversation off indoors Oleg, you wouldn't happen to have any nice biscuits would you? I'm really partial to a nice digestive with my tea." Angela stood on the top step gesturing to a very angry, and very worried and confused Oleg Smertsov. "Come on, in we go, it'll be dark soon, and you'll have to have a torch to find Janina, she'll be crying her eyes out by now I'd imagine. Oh, as you will understand, if anything should happen to me, you know, like being set upon by one of your thugs in here, or indeed if you should attempt to attack me, or shoot me, then I guarantee you right here and now that Janina will die very slowly. So, I'm counting on your best behaviour in here ok? No trying to threaten me or anything, or else I'll tell your wife that I'm here because you got me pregnant, and you try and convince her I'm lying, because she well knows your track record in the infidelity game doesn't she…poor woman."

Smertsov grudgingly allowed Angela into his luxurious house, where they were greeted by a chamber-maid who informed her employer that he was wanted on the telephone. Angela smiled at him. "Told you."

Smertsov led her to a lounge. "You wait in here until I come back."

"Oh, don't you worry Oleg, I'm not going anywhere until you've been to the bank, go and take your phone call, and remember, it's not really Darius's fault…I'm a bit sneaky. Oh, and Darius also suffers from periorbital haematoma, he did try to defend Janina. Don't worry though Oleg, it just means black eye."

Smertsov was enraged at the thought of this half-pint peroxide blonde whore who had suddenly appeared from nowhere and dictated the odds to him, telling him what to do and what not to do in his own house. He swore to himself as he headed off to answer the phone, that if he got Janina back alive, he would set out to find this bitch and he would take her to some secluded spot and then pour petrol all over her and laugh in her face as he lit the match. He was only out of the lounge for a few moments. When he returned, he had a very different approach as to how he conversed with the blonde.

"Ok, it would seem to me that you have me, how do you say in English, over a barrel. I take it this kidnapping has something to do with money?"

"Correct first time Oleg, god you're a frog are you not, I mean up close.
We'll make this as quick as possible seeing as how I'm prone to Cacophobia.
I want half a million pounds, half a million, and I mean pounds, not euros."
She looked at her watch. I want it here in a valise, oh, that's a suitcase by the way, in one hour. How you get it here in that time I am not in the slightest bit interested, but it had better be here, or your daughter dies. Once I am on the plane you will then receive a phone call from a friend of mine who will inform you of your daughter's whereabouts, just in case you were going to have me arrested at the airport. So…that's it Oleg. That's where we're at. Is your daughter worth half a million pounds?
And do you think your maid could get me that cup of tea please, Christ you're not very sociable over here in Lithuania are you. It's the first thing we do over in England, we make our guests a cup of tea as we chin-wag."

Fury was not the word to describe how Oleg Smertsov was feeling now.
Blistering rage surged through his veins as he picked up a telephone and began to speak to someone in his native-tongue.
"Well?" said Angela, sitting down on one of the leather sofas. "Do we have a deal or not?"
Smertsov sat down opposite Angela with a sinister smile on his face. "You seem very self-assured, eh…Angela, but you really don't know who you are dealing with here. Oh I know you know my name and my position here in Kaunas, but you don't know what you are doing here. I have many friends in London, of whom you know nothing about, dangerous people, and particularly dangerous to you. Yes, we have a deal, and yes, the money will be brought here within the hour. You will board the plane with your ill-gotten-gains, but don't think for one minute that that will be the end of matters."
Suddenly, there was a knock on the door and the chamber maid entered the room pushing a trolley upon which there was a giant stainless-steel teapot and china cups and saucers. It was as though Smertsov hadn't said anything.
"Ah, at last, my tea. Will I do the honours Oleg, or will you pour, oh and she's brought biscuits as well."
Smertsov sat with that same sinister smile as his maid poured her employer and his `guest` their cups of tea before leaving the room and closing the door behind her. As Angela picked up a teaspoon and put two spoonful's of sugar into her cup she said, referring to the maid, "You'll have her on minimum wage no doubt Oleg, cheap labour is she?"
He ignored Angela's sarcasm. "As I was saying, you fail to realize just how dangerous these friends of mine really are, and if-."
"No, just hold it there mister bastard! It is *you* that doesn't realize the reality of the situation. Do you think for one minute that I haven't done my homework on you? I know all about your murdering friends in London, and by the way, your illegal friends who have no right to be in my country. Don't you think I know they'll be looking for me when I get home? But here's something for you to think about. You haven't got your daughter back yet. What if my friend decides not to contact you when I'm on the plane? What if I let your daughter die in a very horrible place by the way, cold and frozen, deserted because of her father's stupidity, what then? Do you think I care what happens to me? Shoot me now and see if I'm bluffing about Janina. No, you sit there and you treat me like the guest I'm supposed to be, and you better pray that I keep my word. Dangerous people? You don't know the meaning of the words. Your friends are mindless killers, granted, but take their guns away, and they haven't got the brains they were born with. How many people do you know could come into your house here and

have you over a barrel without brandishing a weapon in your face? I am sitting here drinking tea out of your best china waiting for a suitcase full of money and I don't even have a weapon of any description on my person. How many people do you know could do that to you? Now, open that packet of biscuits and be nice to me…for Janina's sake. And how well do you know your own men over here? The man who will give you directions as to where your daughter is, works for you, but he will speak to you through a device that will obscure his voice. Now I know you have many men under your belt over here, but they can all be bought for a price mister Smertsov, I can assure you. So, no more down talking ok? You can do all that when I'm on the plane home. You might find that Janina has some serious questions to ask you when she sees you again…*if* she sees you again. That, is entirely in your hands Oleg…oh these biscuits are lovely, can I have another? One thing I don't suffer from is pocrescophobia."

Smertsov lit up a cigar and retrieved an ash tray from a table in the far corner of the lounge. He sat down with a grunt. "What will you do with the money, if you don't mind me asking, eh, Angela. Half a million pounds is a lot of money?"

Angela, who was proceeding to eat another biscuit replied matter-of-factly,

Oh the money is not for me mister Smertsov. It's a gift from you to a certain young lady and her friends who were prisoners of Michael Saratov. They were all violated by you no doubt whilst they were here, and two of them under-age. You should think shame on yourself. It's a gift from you to them to compensate for everything you and your friends put them through. In case you didn't know it was me who was partly responsible for their kidnappings. Saratov paid me well for my services, but you see, I have seen the error of my ways, and I have changed. And by the way, I would advise you to do the same. I happen to know, and I'm not supposed to tell you this, but I happen to know, that if you make one more threat to Valarie Vercopte or Monica Carosova, your daughters are going to be raped and then stabbed to death in front of you and your wife. They will then kill your wife and damage you so badly that you'll be left alive but only able to be spoon-fed. Apparently they'd warned you before about this, but they have found out that you have been badgering those two ladies. It's time to stop Oleg. Count your blessings and throw the towel in, because the people who are making these promises *are* dangerous, trust me, and I think you already know that."

KAUNAS INTERNATIONAL AIRPORT.

2 Hours Later.

Dovidas Balkus watched the blonde in front of him with great interest. He'd been informed by Oleg Smertsov to follow her when they got to London. A friend of Oleg's in the airport was instructed not to search Dovidas but to let him board the plane without any problem. For doing this Oleg's friend would be gifted a thousand euros. The plane bound for London was filling rapidly as Dovidas found his seat, which was only three seats behind the blonde. The small suitcase she was now placing in the shelf above her head contained half a million pounds. After he had dealt with the peroxide thief, he was to retrieve the suitcase and return home on the first available flight. He was also told that if somehow the blonde escaped him, he was to stay there in London until he'd completed the task given to him.

For the sake of the safety of his daughter Janina, his airport-security friend was also instructed to let the blonde board the plane without being searched. He could, and would deal with her in his own way. Dovidas Balkus was one of his most loyal employees and could be trusted to carry out any tasks given to him. Killing came as a second nature to him. He had little or no emotions, and so, killing the blonde in front of him would certainly not cause him to lose any sleep. He watched the woman in fascination as she occasionally glanced up at the briefcase. Perhaps she thought she was smarter than mister Smertsov, coming here and kidnapping his daughter to use as ransom. His boss had also informed him, that, if the situation and location was suitable, and if he were attracted to her physically, then he should feel free to rape her before he killed her. How he was to kill her was entirely up to him, just as long as he could make her suffer and of course, inform her of who was doing this to her. The blonde in front of him looked behind her, and then all up and down the aisle, and then once again up to her briefcase. Dovidas smiled to himself thinking, *"Oh yes, you'll be very nervous just now, and you have every right to be, oh? You're looking around again. Which one of us aboard the plane is marking you?...You silly girl."*

The plane was taking off now and she was more at ease. Was she under the illusion that she was safe once the plane took off? No doubt as the journey progressed and the stewardess came along she'd be indulging in a little drink or two to celebrate her achievements. She was taking off her jacket now and making herself comfortable. Thus far, she had not attempted to use a phone to send a message. Although all phones were supposed to be switched off she would surely keep her part of the deal to mister

Smertsov, after all, she had the money. Or perhaps she'd made the call from the airport. The blonde girl turned round again, her eyes searching the passengers' faces, and stopping when she saw him. She smiled politely at him and Dovidas returned the compliment. He heard her saying to the man seated beside her, "I'm always nervous when the plane takes off." The man just smiled at her not having a clue as to what she said. After ten minutes or so, just as Dovidas was beginning to drift off, she done something that put a stab of apprehension into his heart. She smiled at him again as she reached up to the shelf and took down the briefcase.

What on earth was she doing? She could cause herself a lot of trouble if she done what he thought she was going to do…and she did. She opened the briefcase. And then she began to take out some documents. As far as he could see, there wasn't any money in the briefcase, only business documents. She put on a pair of spectacles and gave the papers her full attention, leaving the briefcase open at her feet. There was definitely no money in there.

About twenty miles behind them, back in Kaunas International Airport, Angela Bates was boarding the plane bound for Germany. In her conversation with Smertsov she had kept referring to *Home. When I get home.* This was for him to presume that she was talking about London. But that was one place she could never go back to, or at least, not safely, and certainly not for a few years yet. But she could post parcels there from Germany, and give those girls back there a little nest-egg for their futures'. She would send the parcels to Terry Mercer at Holburn, with a letter. And this *would* be the last correspondence between them. Whoever Smertsov had put on that flight to London, well, they'd be frightened to report back when they found out that she wasn't on the plane. Still, he'd got his daughter back safely, that was something, surely.

THE Z HOTEL. VICTORIA.

CENTRAL LONDON. One week later.

Terry Mercer had booked a small conference room in the hotel with the help of Samantha Reynolds, and the permission of Polly Sheppard. Terry and Samantha had visited each and every one of the homes of the kidnapped girls.
He and Samantha had informed them that it was of the utmost importance that they accepted the invitation to the Z Hotel Victoria for a last get-together.
There would be a dinner that would be followed by a short speech by Polly Sheppard, and that this speech would change their lives in so many ways.
Sophie Spencer Lisa Jensen Kirsty Crawford, Chloe Prowse, and Alison and Rebecca Green all sat staggered around the table accompanied by their parents and guardians, as was the case with Chloe Prowse, who was accompanied by her sister Susan. As far as the girls were concerned, everything that could have been said, had been said and so they were left wondering what this meeting could possibly be about. Terry Mercer sat with Samantha and Polly at the foot of the table. They had all enjoyed a beautiful four-course meal and were now sipping wine and conversing with each other. For some of these parents it was the first time they had actually met each other. They were all chatting merrily when Terry rose to his feet and tapped his wine glass with his spoon.
"Ladies and gentlemen, this will only take a few minutes I promise you. I am not going to bore you with any long-drawn speech." As Terry was talking, one or two of the guests looked at Polly Sheppard as she reached down to the floor and picked up a small leather valise, taking out some documents and neatly laying them on the table. "I have been a detective for more than fifteen years now, and it is practically non-existent that kidnappings like these, end on a bright note, but I would like to think that this is one of those extremely rare occasions where it does. I can't kid myself on that I fully understand what all of you went through in those last few months, but I do understand the pain you all suffered. First and foremost, these poor unfortunate young ladies sitting round this table have suffered something so terrible that words cannot describe what their experiences must have been like, and in another country, unable to communicate properly with their tormentors. However, they made it, and they are seated around this table re-united with their loved ones. I can only say, or rather, promise, that myself and Samantha here, and miss Sheppard, along with all our colleagues, will do everything we can to avoid this happening again.
It shouldn't have happened this time, but, as I'm sure you'll all agree, we can't be

everywhere and so there will always be opportunities. Opportunities for low-life's to take advantage of situations that are presented to them. I look around this table and I am genuinely overjoyed at the sight of all you parents' sitting here with your daughters, oh, and sons." Terry pointed to David Spencer.

"Over the last few months I have got to know one or two of you very well, which makes this occasion all the more joyful. I'd like to thank Colin Green in-particular for being patient with me and for looking after me when I was in Lithuania with him. He and his colleagues looked out for me from the moment I arrived there. I'd also like to thank miss Polly Sheppard, my boss, also for persevering with my, eh...with my ways shall we say, and for risking her own position sometimes to help Samantha and I when we were struggling in our investigations. This young lady here beside me, miss Samantha Reynolds deserves most of the credit for the way she applied herself to this case, she herself being abducted and held prisoner at one point. She has been a tower of strength to me and not just as a colleague, but, dare I say it, a friend, inadvertently giving me advice and encouragement throughout the course of time, and putting up with my, sometimes inappropriate language." Terry looked around the table at the faces he had seen devastated and desperate, heart-broken and defeated. He saw them now, all smiling at him with genuine warmth.

"Anyway, today ladies and gentlemen, I am pleased to inform you all that my superior miss Polly Sheppard has got some, how shall I say this, amazing news for you, I give you miss Polly Sheppard." Polly stood up and waited for the rapturous applause to end, which took almost a full minute.

"Thank you Terry, and I mean for everything. I'm sure you are all aware by now that it was he who helped Colin and his friends to escort the girls from their place of imprisonment, and to get them safely over the border into Poland. Again, a special thank you to Colin's Polish friends who played a vital part in their rescue, but, ladies and gentlemen, that is not the reason why we are here." Polly took a sip from her wine glass and continued. "About three days ago, Terry here received a parcel at his home. The parcel had been sent to him from Germany. In the parcel there was a note. The person, or the people who sent this package made it very clear that the contents of the parcel should be divided equally among the six girls seated around this table. The girls and their families.

Whoever it was said that it was a small consolation for the hell that they had all been put through. Now, there are certain rules about money that comes into Britain from other countries, but thanks mainly to Samantha's knowhow we managed to find a way to bypass these rules. Ladies and gentlemen, there was a substantial amount of money in that package, which, in the meantime has been deposited safely in a bank until such times as you are ready to accept your share." Polly smiled at Terry and Samantha. "I know Samantha, I can see him chomping at the bit. He can't wait for me to tell you. Ladies and gentlemen, it is with great pleasure I can inform you that in that parcel, there was half a million pounds. That is the amount to be shared equally between you. You will all receive eighty-thousand pounds plus. I hope from the bottom of my heart that this amount of money can at least help to heal some of the emotional scars you all bear, and that it can help to ease some of the pain that was so cruelly inflicted upon you." There were gasps of astonishment from the families around the table. Polly continued. "These documents I have here are to be signed by at least one of each of the parents. In about ten days' time, you'll all be able to have full access to your money, and as I say, I hope that this will take away some of the stress that you all suffered. There now, that's the speech over with, enjoy the rest of your afternoon ladies and gentlemen. You can sign these papers when you're ready, there's no hurry."

As Polly sat chatting with the girls and their parents, Terry and Samantha excused themselves to go outside for a cigarette. As the two detectives enjoyed their smoke they were joined by Sophie Spencer and Colin Green who both had the same idea.

"I'm stuck for words Terry." Said Colin Green, lighting up. "Is this for real?"

"It sure is Colin, it's for real alright."

"Do you know who sent the package Terry?"

"Not a clue bud," Terry lied. "But hey, what does it matter who it was? They obviously think that you deserve it, whoever it was. And they are right, you do all deserve it. I'm just glad that I was the bearer of good news for a change, because we've all been through the mill with this, none more so than you Sophie and all the girls in there. I'm really pleased for you kid, you and your mum and your brother."

Colin's wife came outside and instructed him to get back inside because Polly wanted him for something. Colin finished his cigarette and headed back indoors. As Samantha finished hers' Sophie said, "Do you mind if I have a little talk with Terry please Samantha.?"

"Of course Sophie, I'm just going back inside anyway honey, see you in a minute." Terry looked at the teen. "Listen Sophie, before you say anything. I'm sorry for letting you down. I made a bad decision and it back-fired on me. I thought that-."

"Terry, it doesn't matter. I know. I know you had my best interest at heart. I'm not mad at you, I'm mad at myself for being so stupid. I nearly ruined my life, and if it hadn't been for you and Samantha, I probably would have. I'll be forever grateful for what you done for me and those girls in there, and how you done your best for my mum right through all of this.

I know I'm only young, but if there is anything I can ever do for you and Samantha, I

want you to know, that I'll be first in line to help you, and you know I mean that."
Terry pulled the teen into his arms and kissed her on the head. "I know you do sweetheart. I know you do. Now, you get back in there and celebrate with your mum and your brother, I take it you'll be giving something to David?"
Sophie nodded her head vigorously, I know what kind of guitar he's been saving for, now he can have as many as he wants." Sophie turned and re-entered the party. Terry stood shuffling nervously on his feet. Not because of the events today, but for something that he'd been thinking about for some time.
He'd been losing sleep over this, and so, there was only one way to sort this out, once and for all. If everything went to plan, he would catch Colin Green off guard, and that would be that. They would be even, but only if things went to plan. He had to wait another ten minutes out here in the cold before Samantha re-appeared. "There you are, for fuck sakes."
"What? What are you moaning about now?"
"Listen, I'm no bloody good at this. I haven't...I don't know how...it's just, oh fuck, I've-"
"Come on Terry, spit it out will you? What have I done to offend you, I've obviously done something wrong, now what is it?"
Terry put his hand inside his jacket pocket and pulled out a small box.
He opened it up and got down on one knee and said to Samantha Reynolds exposing a beautiful diamond ring and began mumbling, "It's a fancy vivid.
Do you fancy getting engaged to me? I mean, I know I'm a bit older than you but I think I could make you happy I think...I think I could...I can try to..."
Samantha laughed at his awkward grammar and declared to him.
"Terry, I would crazy to do that don't you think? But I'd be crazy not to, come here you silly man." Terry placed the ring on her finger and the couple kissed passionately outside of the Z Hotel.
Polly Sheppard appeared at the door. "Have you asked her yet Terry?"
Samantha turned and looked at Polly. "You knew? You knew about this Polly?" "Of course I knew about it. You didn't think he'd be capable of purchasing an engagement ring that fitted you, did you? Come on, let's join the party, and now we have reasons of our own to celebrate, congratulations you pair, but what a bloody time you take Terry to do things. He's loved you for months now Samantha, he was just very frightened that you'd say no."
"Was I fuck!"
"Terry, you told me when you came back from Lithuania that you had never seen a woman as beautiful as Samantha Reynolds, and that you'd cut your right arm off just to be able to lie beside her. Did you, or did you not say that?"

"All I said was, she looked nice, that's all, fuck Polly, you've always got to blow things out of fucking proportion haven't you. You never-."

"Terry, answer me honestly, did you say that to Polly or not?"

"Yes."

Fifteen minutes later Colin Green was indeed caught off guard when Terry asked him to be his best man. Sophie Spencer was overjoyed at the thought of her and her mum Mandy being asked to be Samantha's bridesmaids.

As the news was spread around the table of Terry and Samantha's engagement, everyone joined in with the celebrations. Just as Terry was heading back outside for another cigarette he was approached by a young lady receptionist who informed him that he was wanted on the telephone. He was led to a small room where he would have privacy. He picked up the phone. "Hello?"

"Hello mister Mercer. You know who this is?"

"Yes."

" I Just wanted to let you know that a certain mister Oleg Smertsov has been found dead in his car. He was found with a single bullet hole in his temple. I can't for the life of me think of who could have done such a thing, but, there you go. Strange things happen. Did you get the parcel?"

"Yes I did. And thank you. I'm here in the Z hotel with them now celebrating."

"I know where you are Mister Mercer, how do you think I managed to contact you on the telephone, are you sure you're a detective?"

Terry cursed inwardly at his own foolishness.

"Anyway, this is goodbye mister Mercer. Although I shan't be returning to Britain for a while, I'll keep my eyes and ears open if I should hear about any kidnappings being planned. Monica and Valarie send their best wishes."

"Thank you Angela, and I mean that. God I never thought I'd hear myself saying that to you."

"Strange world...eh, Terry? Anyway good luck to you in all that you do. Oh, and if you should get the chance tell miss Prowse at Bronzefield that I'm sorry but I'll shan't be re-visiting her after all. I know it'll probably break her heart, oh, and could she, in turn tell Thin Lizzy, no hard feelings."

"Yes I will, Terry laughed "if I get the chance. Anyway, if you don't mind me asking, how on earth did you know I was here?" After a short silence, she replied, "I know everything I need to know. And just for the record? I wish you and Samantha all the very best for the future, I'm sure you'll both be very happy together." Then the line went dead. Terry replaced the telephone onto its' cradle. He'd been engaged for forty-one minutes. "How the hell...?"

THE END.

WILLIAM HURST.

Printed in Great Britain
by Amazon